THE ABYSS BEYOND DREAMS

By Peter F. Hamilton

The Greg Mandel series
Mindstar Rising
A Quantum Murder
The Nano Flower

The Night's Dawn trilogy
The Reality Dysfunction
The Neutronium Alchemist
The Naked God

The Commonwealth saga
Pandora's Star
Judas Unchained

Chronicle of the Fallers
The Abyss Beyond Dreams

The Void trilogy
The Dreaming Void
The Temporal Void
The Evolutionary Void

Short story collections
A Second Chance at Eden
Manhattan in Reverse

Fallen Dragon
Misspent Youth
The Confederation Handbook
(a vital guide to the Night's Dawn trilogy)
Great North Road

Peter F. Hamilton

THE ABYSS BEYOND DREAMS

CHRONICLE OF THE FALLERS

MACMILLAN

First published 2014 by Macmillan,
an imprint of Pan Macmillan, a division of Macmillan Publishers Limited
Pan Macmillan, 20 New Wharf Road, London N1 9RR
Basingstoke and Oxford
Associated companies throughout the world
www.panmacmillan.com

ISBN 978-0-230-76946-5 HB
ISBN 978-1-4472-3592-7 TPB

9 8 7 6 5 4 3 2 1

A CIP catalogue record for this book is available from the British Library.

Typeset by Palimpsest Book Production Ltd, Falkirk, Stirlingshire
Map artwork by ML Design
Printed and bound by CPI Group (UK) Ltd, Croydon, CR0 4YY

For my agent, Antony Harwood.

After twenty years, it's probably
about time I said thank you.

In a unique project aimed at enhancing the reader's experience, composer Steve Buick has produced an album of musical atmospheres inspired by Peter F. Hamilton's new novel *The Abyss Beyond Dreams*. There are three long pieces which embody the feel of the story using layers of ambient and often eerie soundscapes. Peter actually wrote part of the novel to the first track Steve completed. The album is available on iTunes and the Amazon MP3 store under the same title.

More information can be found at www.stevebuick.com

Commonwealth Timeline

1,000,000 BC (approx.)

　　Raiel armada invades the Void. Never returns.

AD

1200　　Prime species' home star system and renegade Prime colony star (Dyson pair) quarantined behind force fields by the Anomine.

1900　　Starflyer crash-lands on Far Away, 400 light years from Earth.

2037　　First attempted human rejuvenation, Jeff Baker.

2050　　Nigel Sheldon and Ozzie Isaacs open a wormhole to surface of Mars.

2057　　Wormhole opened to Proxima Centuri. Start of interstellar colonization.

2100　　Eight new worlds settled. Official formation of Intersolar Commonwealth Council, the 'Parliament of Worlds'.

2100 onward　　Massive expansion of human settlements across H-congruous planets. Rise of the Big15 industrial worlds.

2102　　Huxley's Haven founded, genetic conformist constitution.

2150　　Prime star disappears from Earth's sky – unnoticed.

2163   *High Angel* discovered orbiting Icalanise.

2222   Paula Myo born on Huxley's Haven.

2270   Prime star pair identified as Dyson Emission Spectrum twins.

2380   Dudley Bose observes Dyson Alpha vanish.

2381   Starship *Second Chance* flies to Dyson Alpha.

2381–2383   Starflyer War.

2384   First colony fleet (Brandt Dynasty) leaves to found human colony outside Commonwealth.

2545 onward   Use of large starships to establish Commonwealth 'External' worlds.

2550   Commonwealth Navy Exploration fleet founded to explore the galaxy beyond the External worlds.

2560   Commonwealth Navy ship *Endeavour* circumnavigates galaxy, captained by Wilson Kime, discovery of the Void.

2603   Navy discovers seventh *High Angel*-type ship.

2620   Raiel confirm their status as ancient galactic race who lost a war against the Void.

2833   Completion of ANA (Advanced Neural Activity) first stage on Earth. Grand Family members begin memory download into ANA.

2867   Sheldon Dynasty gigalife project partially successful, first human body biononic supplements for regeneration and general iatrics.

2872   Start of Higher human culture, biononic enrichment allowing a society of slow-paced long life, rejection of commercial economics and old political ideologies.

2913   Earth begins absorption of 'mature' humans into ANA, the inward migration begins.

2984   Formation of radical Highers who wish to convert the human race to Higher culture.

3000   Sheldon Dynasty colony fleet (thirty starships) leaves Commonwealth, believed to possess long-range trans-galactic flight capability.

3001   Ozzie produces uniform neural entanglement effect, known as the gaiafield.

3040   Commonwealth invited to join Centurion Station, the Void observation project supervised by Raiel, a joint enterprise between alien species.

3120   ANA officially becomes Earth's government, total planetary population fifty million (activated bodies) and falling.

3126   Brandt Dynasty trans-galactic colony fleet launched.

3150   External world Ellezelin settled.

3255   Kerry, a radical Higher Angel, arrives on Anagaska, Inigo's conception.

This Era (time uncertain)   Edeard born in the Void.

3320   Inigo begins duty tour at Centurion star system, his first dream.

3324   Inigo settles on Ellezelin, founds Living Dream movement, begins construction of Makkathran2.

List of Characters

Commonwealth

Nigel Sheldon *inventor of wormhole technology*

Paula Myo *Senior investigator, Serious Crime Bureau*

Starship *Vermillion*

Cornelius Brandt *captain*

Laura Brandt *Molecular physicist*

Ibu *Gravatonics professor*

Joey Stein *hyperspace theorist*

Ayanna *quantum field physicist*

Rojas *shuttle pilot*

Bienvenido

Slvasta *lieutenant Cham Regiment, revolutionary leader*

Ingmar *trooper, Cham Regiment, Slvasta's friend*

Quanda *forester's daughter*

Bethaneve *tax officer, revolutionary leader*

Javier *meat-stall worker, revolutionary leader*

Coulan *bureaucrat, revolutionary leader*

Arnice *Major, Joint Regimental Council*

Lanicia *society debutant*

Gelasis *Colonel, Joint Regimental Council*

Bryan-Anthony *leader, Wellfield union*

Philious *Captain*

Aothori *First officer*

Trevene *chief of Captain's Police*

Gravin *professor, Faller Research Institute*

Kysandra *owner of Blair Farm*

Sarara *Kysandra's mother*

Ma Ulvon *underworld boss*

Akstan *Ma Ulvon's son*

Julias *Ma Ulvon's son*

Russell *Ma Ulvon's son*

Madeline *madam, Hevlin hotel*

Proval *a Faller*

Demitri *ANAdroid*

Marek *ANAdroid*

Valeri *ANAdroid*

Fergus *ANAdroid*

Yannrith *ex-sergeant Cham regiment*

Andricea *ex-Cham regiment*

Tovakar *ex-Cham regiment*

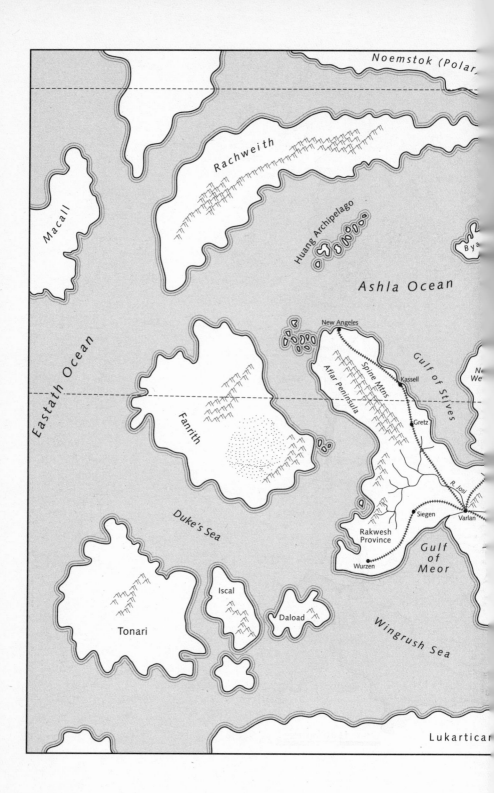

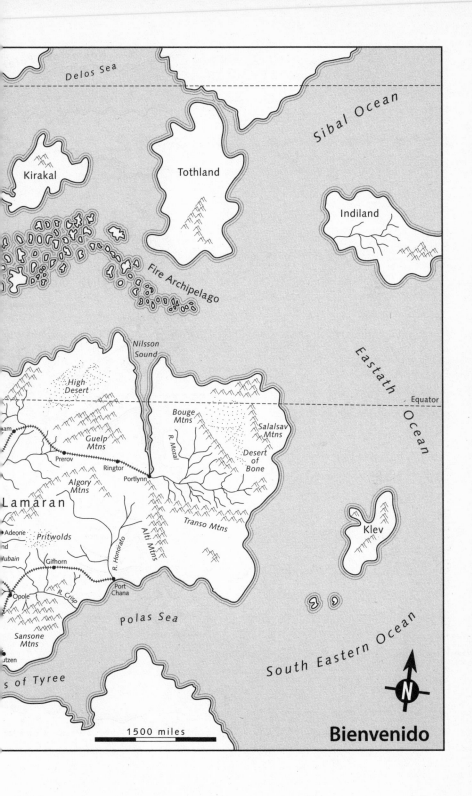

BOOK ONE

Twenty-Seven Hours and Forty-Two Minutes

Laura Brandt knew all about coming out of a suspension chamber. It was similar to finishing the old-style rejuvenation procedure she'd undergone back in the day before biononic inserts and Advancer genes being sequenced into human DNA and practically eradicating the ageing process. There would be that slow comfortable rise to consciousness, the body warming at a steady rate, nutrient feeds and narcotic buffering taking the edge off any lingering discomfort and disorientation. So, by the time you were properly awake and ready to open your eyes, it was like emerging from a really decent night's sleep, ready to face the day with enthusiasm and anticipation. A full breakfast with pancakes, some crisp bacon, maple syrup and chilled orange juice (no ice, thanks) would add that extra little touch of panache to make returning to full awareness a welcome experience. And when it happened this time, there she would be at the end of a voyage to a star cluster outside the Milky Way, ready to begin a fresh life with others from the Brandt dynasty, founding a whole new civilization – one that was going to be so very different from the jaded old Commonwealth they'd left behind.

Then there was the emergency extraction procedure, which ship's crew called the tank yank.

Someone slapping the red button on the outside of her suspension chamber. Potent revival drugs rammed into a body that was still chilly. Haematology umbilicals withdrawing from her neck and thighs. Shocked muscles spasming. Bladder sending out frantic pressure signals into her brain, and the emergency extraction had already automatically retracted the catheter – oh, great design, guys. But that wasn't as bad as the skull-splitting headache and the top of her diaphragm contracting as her nauseous stomach heaved.

Laura opened her eyes to a blur of horrible coloured light at the same time as her mouth opened and she vomited. Stomach muscles clenched, bringing her torso up off the padding. Her head hit the chamber's lid, which hadn't finished hinging open.

'Hell's teeth.' Red pain stars joined the confusing blur of shapes. She twisted over to throw up again.

'Easy there,' a voice told her.

Hands gripped her shoulders, supporting her as she retched. A plastic bowl was held up, which caught most of the revolting liquid.

'Any more?'

'What?' Laura groaned.

'Are you going to puke again?'

Laura just snarled at him, too miserable even to know the answer. Every part of her body was forcefully telling her how wretched it felt.

'Take some deep breaths,' the voice told her.

'Oh for . . .'

It was an effort just to breathe at all with the way her body was shuddering, never mind going for some kind of yoga-master inhalations. Stupid voice –

'You're doing great. The revive drugs will kick in any minute now.'

Laura swallowed – disgusting acid taste burning her throat – but it was fractionally easier to breathe. She hadn't felt this bad for centuries. It wasn't a good thought, but at least it was a coherent one. *Why aren't my biononics helping?* The tiny molecular machines enriching every cell should be aiding her body to stabilize. She tried to squint the lights into focus, knowing some of them would be her exovision icons. It was all just too much effort.

4

'Tank yank's a bitch, huh?'

Laura finally recognized the voice. Andy Granfore, one of the *Vermillion*'s medical staff – decent enough man; they'd met at a few pre-flight parties. She shuddered down a long breath. 'What's happened? Why have you brought me out like this?'

'Captain wants you out and up. And we don't have much time. Sorry.'

Laura's eyes managed to focus on Andy's face, seeing the familiar bulbous nose, dark bags under pale brown eyes, and greying hair that was all stick-out tufts. Such an old, worn face was unusual in the Commonwealth, where everyone used cosmetic gene-sequencing to look flawless. Laura always thought that humanity these days was like a race of youthful supermodels – which wasn't necessarily an improvement. Anything less than perfection was either a fashion statement or a genuine individualistic *screw you* to conformity.

'Is *Vermillion* damaged?'

'No.' He gave her an anxious grin. 'Not exactly. Just lost.'

'Lost?' It was possibly an even more worrying answer. How could you get lost flying to a star cluster that measured twenty thousand lightyears in diameter? It wasn't as if you could lose sight of something of that magnitude. 'That's ridiculous.'

'The captain will explain. Let's get you to the bridge.'

Laura silently asked her u-shadow for a general status review. The ubiquitous semi-sentient utility routine running in her macrocellular clusters responded immediately by unfolding a basic array of mental icons, slender lines of blue fairy light that superimposed themselves within her wobbly vision. She frowned. If she was reading their efficiency modes correctly, her biononics had suffered some kind of serious glitch. The only reason she could imagine for that level of decay was simple ageing. Her heart gave a jump as she wondered how long she'd been in suspension. She checked the digits of her time display. Which was even more puzzling.

'Two thousand two hundred and thirty-one days?'

'What?' Andy asked.

'We've been underway for two thousand two hundred and thirty-one days? Where the hell are we?' Travelling for that long at ultradrive speeds would have taken them almost three million lightyears from Earth, a long, *long* way outside the Milky Way.

His old face amplified how disconcerted he was. 'It might have been that long. We're not too sure about relativistic time compression in here.'

'Whaa—'

'Just . . . Let's get you to the bridge, okay? The captain will give you a proper briefing. I'm not the best person to explain this. Trust me.'

'Okay.'

He helped her swing her legs off the padding. Dizziness hit her hard as she stood up, and she almost crumpled. Andy was ready for it and held her tight for a long moment while she steadied herself.

The suspension bay looked intact to her: a long cave of metal ribs containing a thousand large sarcophagi-like suspension chambers. Lots of reassuring green monitor lights shining on every unit, as far as she could make out. She gave a satisfied nod. 'All right. Let me freshen up and we'll go. Have the bathrooms been switched on?' For some reason she was having trouble interfacing directly with the ship's network.

'No time,' Andy said. 'The transport pod is this way.'

Laura managed to coordinate her facial muscles enough to give him a piqued expression before she allowed herself to be guided along the decking to the end of the bay. A set of malmetal quad-doors peeled open. The pod on the other side was a simple circular room with a bench seat running round it.

'Here,' Andy said after she slumped down, almost exhausted by the short walk – well, shuffle. He handed her a packet of clothes and some spore wipes.

She gave the wipes a derisory glance. 'Seriously?'

'Best I can offer.'

So while he used the pod's manual control panel to tap in their destination, she cleaned up her face and hands, then stripped off her sleeveless medical gown. Body-modesty was something most people grew out of when they were in their second century and resequenced like Greek godlings, and she didn't care about Andy anyway; he was medical.

She saw in dismay that her skin colour was all off. Her second major biononic re-form on her ninetieth birthday had included some sequencing to emphasize her mother's northern Mediterranean heritage, darkening her epidermis to an almost African black. It was a shading she'd maintained for the entire three hundred and twenty-six years since. Now, though, she just looked like a porcelain doll about to shatter from age. Suspension had tainted her skin to an awful dark grey with a multitude of tiny water-immersion wrinkles – except it was paper dry. *Must remember to moisturize*, she told herself. Her hair was a very dark ginger, courtesy of a rather silly admiration for Grissy Gold, the gulam blues singer who'd revelled in an amazing decade of trans-Commonwealth success – two hundred and thirty-two years ago. That wasn't too bad, she decided, pulling at badly tangled strands of it, but it was going to take litres of conditioner to put the gloss back in. Then she peered at the buffed metal wall of the travel pod, which was hardly the best mirror . . . Her normally thin face was horribly puffy, almost hiding her cheekbones, and her emerald green eyes were all hangover – bloodshot, with bags just as bad as Andy's. 'Bollocks,' she groaned.

As she started pulling on the dreary ship's one-piece suit she saw how flabby her flesh had become after such a long suspension, especially round the thighs. *Oh, not again!* She deliberately didn't look at her bum. It was going to take months of exercise to get back in shape, and Laura no longer cheated by using biononics to sculpt bodyform like most; she believed in earning her fitness, a primitive body-pride that came from those five years hiding away from the world at a Naturalist faction ashram in the Austrian Alps after a particularly painful relationship crash.

With the drugs finally banishing the worst of the tank yank, she sealed up the suit and rotated her shoulders as if she was prepping for a big gym session. 'This had better be good,' she grunted as the pod slowed. It had taken barely five minutes to travel along the *Vermillion*'s axial spine, past the twenty other suspension bays that made up the giant starship's mid-section. And still her u-shadow couldn't connect to *Vermillion*'s network.

The pod's quad-door opened to reveal *Vermillion*'s bridge – a somewhat symbolic claim for a chamber in the age of homogenized network architecture. It was more like a pleasant franchise coffee lounge, with long settees arranged in a conversation circle and giant high-res hologram panes on the walls.

About fifteen people were in there, most of them huddled in small groups on the settees, having intense exchanges. Everybody looked badly stressed. Laura saw several who had clearly just been tank yanked like her, and recognized them straight away; also like her, they were all from the starship's science team.

That was when she became aware of a very peculiar sensation right inside her head. It was like the emotional context of a conversation within the gaiafield – except her gaiamotes were inactive. She'd never really embraced the whole gaiafield concept, which had been developed to give the Commonwealth the capability of direct mind-to-mind communication through an alien adaptation of quantum entanglement theory. Some people loved the potential for intimate thought sharing it brought, claiming it was the ultimate evolution of intellect, permitting everyone else's viewpoint to be appreciated. That way, the argument went, conflict would be banished. Laura thought that was a bunch of crap. To her it was the creepy extreme of voyeurism. Unhealthy, to put it mildly. She had gaiamotes because it was occasionally a useful communication tool, and even more sporadically helpful for acquiring large quantities of information. But for day-to-day use, forget it. She stuck with the good old-fashioned and reliable unisphere links.

'How's that happening?' she grunted, frowning. Her u-shadow confirmed that her gaiamotes were inactive. Nobody could connect directly to her neural strata. And yet . . .

Torak, the *Vermillion*'s chief xenobiology officer, gave her a lopsided grin. 'If you think that's weird, how about this?' A tall plastic mug of tea floated through the air towards him, trailing wisps of steam. Torak stared at it in concentration, holding out his hand. The mug sailed into his palm, and he closed his fingers round it with a smug grin.

Laura gave the bridge ceiling a puzzled look, her ever-practical mind immediately reviewing the parameters of ingrav field projector systems. Theoretically it would be possible to manipulate the ship's gravity field to move objects around like that, but it would be a ridiculous amount of effort and machinery for a simple conjuring trick. 'What kind of gravity manipulation was that?'

'It's not.' Torak's lips hadn't moved. Yet the voice was clear in her head, along with enough emotional overspill to confirm it was him 'speaking'.

'How did you . . .?'

'I can show you what we've learned, if you'll let me,' Torak said.

She gave him an apprehensive nod. Then something like a memory was bubbling up into her mind like a cold fizzy liquid, a memory that wasn't hers. So similar to a gaiafield emission, but at the same time definitely not. She had no control over it, no way of regulating the images and voices. That scared her.

Then the knowledge was rippling out inside her brain, settling down, becoming instinct.

'Telepathy?' she squeaked as she *knew*. And at the same time, she could sense her thoughts broadcasting the astonished question across the bridge. Several of the crew flinched at the strength of it impinging on their own thoughts.

'In the purest sense,' Torak responded. 'And telekinesis, too.' He let go of the tea mug, which hung in mid-air.

Laura stared at it in a kind of numb fascination. In her head, new insights showed her how to perform the fantasy ability. She shaped her thoughts *just so*, reaching for the mug. Somehow feeling it; the weight impinged on her consciousness.

Torak released his hold on it, and the mug wobbled about, dropping ten centimetres. Laura reinforced her mental grip on the physical object, and it continued to hang in mid-air. She gave a twitchy laugh before carefully lowering it to the floor. 'That is some serious bollocks,' she murmured.

'We have ESP, too,' Torak said. 'You might want to close your thoughts up. They're kind of . . . available.'

Laura gave him a startled glance, then blushed as she hurriedly tried to apply the knowledge of how to shield her thoughts – intimate, painfully private thoughts – from the scrutiny of everyone on the bridge. 'All right; enough. Will someone please tell me what the hell is going on? How are we doing this? What's happened?'

Captain Cornelius Brandt stood up. He wasn't a particularly tall man, and worry made him appear stooped. Laura could tell just how worn down and anxious he was; despite his efforts to keep his thoughts opaque and calm, alarm was leaking out of him like ethereal pheromones. 'We believe we're in the Void,' he said.

'That's impossible,' Laura said automatically. The Void was the core of the galaxy. Up until 2560, when the *Endeavour*, a ship from the Commonwealth Navy Exploration fleet, completed the first circumnavigation of the galaxy, astronomers had assumed it was the same kind of supermassive black hole that most galaxies had at their centre. It was massive. And it did have an event horizon, just like an ordinary black hole. But this one was different. It wasn't natural.

As the *Endeavour* soon learned, the Raiel – an alien race more technologically advanced than the Commonwealth – had been guarding the boundary for over a million years. In fact, they'd declared war on the Void. From the moment their first crude starships encountered it, they'd carefully observed the event horizon undergoing unnatural expansion phases. Incredibly for anything that large on a cosmological scale, it appeared to be an artefact. Purpose unknown. But, given the severity and unpredictability of its expansion phases, it would eventually inflate out to consume the entire galaxy long before any natural black hole would have done.

So the Raiel invaded. Thousands upon thousands of the greatest warships ever built tore open the Void's boundary and streaked inside.

None returned. The entire armada had no apparent effect on the Void or its atypical, inexorable expansion. That was a million years ago. They'd been guarding the boundary ever since.

Wilson Kime, who captained the *Endeavour*, was politely but firmly ordered to turn back and fly outside the Wall stars which formed a thick band around the Void. After that, the Raiel invited the Commonwealth to join the multi-species science mission that kept a constant watch on the Void. It was a mission which had lasted since the Raiel armada invaded, and in those million years had added precisely nothing to the knowledge of what lurked on the other side of the event horizon boundary.

'Improbable,' Cornelius corrected. 'Not impossible.'

'Well, how did we get inside? I thought our course took us around the Wall stars.'

'Closest approach to the Wall was three thousand lightyears,' Cornelius said. 'That's when we fell inside. Or jumped. Or got snatched. We're still not sure how. Presumably some kind of teleport connection opened up inside hyperspace. It would take a phenomenally advanced technology to create that; but then, as we've all suddenly been granted superhuman powers, quantum hyperfield theory is the least of our problems.'

Laura gave him an incredulous stare. 'But why?'

'Not sure. The only clue we have is Tiger Brandt. Just before we were brought in, she said she experienced some kind of mental contact, like a dream reaching through the gaiafield, but a lot fainter. Something sensed us or her. Then, next we know . . . we were inside.'

'Tiger Brandt?' Laura asked. She knew all about Tiger, who was married to Rahka Brandt, the captain of the *Ventura*. 'Wait – you mean the *Ventura* is in here with us?'

'All seven ships were pulled in,' Cornelius said gloomily.

Laura looked at the tea mug again, ignoring all her tank yank discomforts. 'And this is the inside of the Void?' she asked incredulously.

'Yes. As far as we understand, it's some kind of micro-universe with a very different quantum structure to spacetime outside. Thought can interact with reality at some fundamental level, which is why we've suddenly acquired all these mental powers.'

'By the action of watching, the observer affects the reality of that which is watched,' she whispered.

Cornelius raised an eyebrow. 'Neatly understated.'

'So how do we get out?'

'Good question.' Cornelius indicated one of the large holographic images behind him. It showed her space with very few stars and a number of exotic and beautifully delicate nebulas. 'We can't see an end to it. The inside of the Void seems to be some kind of multidimensional Möbius strip. In here, the boundary doesn't exist.'

'So, where are we going?'

Cornelius's mind emitted a sensation of desperation and despair that made Laura shiver again. 'The Skylord is taking us to what it claims is an H-congruous planet. Sensors are confirming that status now.'

'The what?'

Cornelius gestured. 'Skylord.'

With a stiff back, Laura turned round. The high-res image behind her was taken from a sensor mounted on the forward section of the starship, where the ultradrive unit and force-field generators were clustered. The bottom fifth of the image showed the curving carbotanium hull with its thick layer of grubby grey thermal foam. At the top of the hologram was a small blue-white crescent, similar to any of the H-congruous worlds in the Commonwealth – though its night side lacked any city lights. And between the hull and the planet was the strangest nebula Laura could have imagined. As she stared, she saw it had some kind of solid core, a long ovoid shape. It wasn't truly solid, she realized, but actually comprised of sheets of some crystalline substance warped into an extraordinary Calabi-Yau manifold geometry. The shimmering surfaces were alive with weird multicoloured patterns that flowed like liquid – or maybe it was the structure itself that was unstable. She couldn't tell, for flowing around it was some kind of haze, also moving in strange confluences. 'Serious bollocks,' she grunted.

'It's a kind of spaceborne life,' Cornelius said. 'Three of them rendezvoused with us not long after we were pulled into the Void. They're sentient. You can use your telepathy to converse with them, though it's like talking to a savant. Their thought processes aren't quite like ours. But they can fly through this space. Or at least manipulate it somehow. They offered to lead us to worlds inside the Void where we could live. *Ventura*, *Vanguard*, *Violet* and *Valley* followed two Skylords. *Vermillion* is following this one, along with *Viscount* and *Verdant*. We decided that splitting the starships gives us a better chance of finding a viable H-congruous planet.'

'With respect,' Laura said, 'why are we following any of them to a planet at all? Surely we should be doing everything we can to find the way out? All of us are on board for one reason: to found a new civilization outside this galaxy. Granted, the inside of the Void is utterly fascinating, and the Raiel would give their right bollock to be here, but you cannot make that decision for us.'

Cornelius's expression was weary. 'We're trying to find an H-congruous planet, because the alternative is death. Have you noticed your biononic function?'

'Yes. It's very poor.'

'Same for any chunk of technology on board. What passes for spacetime in here is corroding our systems a percentage point at a time. The first thing to fail was the ultradrive, presumably because it's the most sophisticated system on board. But for the last year there have been fluctuations in the direct-mass converters, which were growing more severe. I couldn't risk leaving them on line. We're using fusion reactors to power the ingrav drive units now.'

'What?' she asked in shock. 'You mean we've been travelling slower than light all this time?'

'Point nine lightspeed since we arrived, nearly six years ago now,' Cornelius confirmed bitterly. 'Thankfully the suspension chambers have remained functional, or we would have had a real disaster on our hands.'

Laura's first reaction was, *Why didn't you get me out of suspension back then? I could have helped.* But that was probably what everyone on board would think. And from what she understood of their situation, the captain had done pretty well under the circumstances. Besides, her specialist field of molecular physics probably wouldn't be that helpful in analysing a different space-time structure.

She was drawn to the bright crescent ahead. 'Is it H-congruous?'

'We think so, yes.'

'Is that why you tank yanked me? To help with a survey?'

'No. We're six million kilometres out and decelerating hard. We'll reach orbit in another two days. Heaven alone knows how we'll cope with landing, but we'll tackle that when it happens. No, you're here because our sensors found something at the planet's Lagrange One point.' Cornelius closed his eyes, and the image shifted, focusing on the Lagrange point one and a half million kilometres above the planet's sunlit hemisphere, where the star's gravitational pull was perfectly countered by the planet's gravity. The area was filled with a fuzzy blob that either the sensors or Laura's eyes couldn't quite focus on. It seemed to be speckled, as if it was made up from thousands of tiny motes.

'What is that?' she asked.

'We're calling it the Forest,' Cornelius said. 'It's a cluster of objects that are about eleven kilometres long, with a surface distortion similar to our Skylord friend.'

'More of them?'

'Not quite; the shape is wrong. These things are slim with bulbous ends. And there's something else. The whole Lagrange point is emitting a different quantum signature to the rest of the Void.'

'Another quantum environment?' she asked sceptically.

'So it would seem.'

'How is that possible?' Laura's shoulders slumped as she suddenly realized why she'd been tank yanked – her and the other science staff sitting in the bridge. 'You want us to go and find out what it is, don't you?'

Cornelius nodded. 'I cannot justify stopping the *Vermillion* in a possibly hostile environment to conduct a scientific examination. My priority has to be getting us down intact on an H-congruous world. So you'll command a small science team. Take a shuttle over to the Forest and run whatever tests you can. It might help us, or it might not. But, frankly, anything which can add to our knowledge base has to be considered useful at this stage.'

'Yeah,' she said in resignation. 'I can see that.'

'Take Shuttle Fourteen,' he said.

Laura could sense that the shuttle had some kind of significance to him. It was the sensation of expectation running through his thoughts which signalled it, but her brain still wasn't up to working out why. She told her u-shadow to pull the file from her storage lacuna. Data on the shuttle played through her mind, and she still didn't get it . . . 'Why that one?'

'It has wings,' Cornelius said softly. 'If you have a major systems glitch, you can still aerobrake and glide down to the surface.'

Then she got it. 'Oh, right; the shuttle doesn't need its ingrav units to land.'

'No. The shuttle doesn't.'

Laura's blood seemed to be chilling back down to suspension levels again. The *Vermillion*, over a kilometre long, and not remotely aerodynamic, was utterly dependent on regrav to slow to zero velocity relative to the planet and ingrav to drift down to a light-as-a-feather landing. Of course there were multiple redundancies built in, and no moving parts, making failure just about inconceivable. In the normal universe.

'Once we've confirmed H-congruous status, I'll be launching all twenty-three shuttles from orbit,' Cornelius said. 'As will the *Viscount* and *Verdant.*'

Laura told her u-shadow to recentre the bridge display on the planet. It still couldn't interface with the starship's net. 'Uh, sir, how did you load your orders into the command core?'

'Gaiafield. The confluence nest is one system that hasn't been affected by the Void.'

And the confluence nest which generated the local gaiafield was hardwired into the ship's network, Laura realized. Funny what worked and what didn't in the Void.

*

Laura thought the *Vermillion*'s excursion-prep facility looked identical to the bridge; the only difference was the blue-grey carpet, which was noticeably lighter – a difference due to six years of coffee stains, she assumed. Amazingly for a project to build trans-galactic colony ships there must have been some kind of budgetary issue, either with time or design aesthetics. When it came to compartments in the *Vermillion*'s command section, someone just pressed the duplicate button.

Including Laura, there were five people in Shuttle Fourteen's crew. As a gathering, they resembled a bunch of sheepish friends getting together the morning after a particularly wild party, with everyone looking like crap, staring doubtfully into their mugs of herbal tea and nibbling plain biscuits.

Laura sat next to Ibu – a professor of gravatonics who was nearly twice her size, with most of his bulk made of muscle. Suspension hadn't done him any favours. Flesh sagged, making it look as if he'd deflated somehow, and his normally bronzed skin was a paler grey than Laura's. He regarded his body's condition mournfully. 'Biononics failure has got to be the worst part of this,' he confided. 'It's going to take an age to get back in shape.'

'I wonder how the Void continuum can tell the difference between natural organelles and biononics,' Laura said. 'They're both fundamentally the same.'

'Biononics are not sequenced into our DNA,' Ayanna, the quantum field physicist mused. 'Not natural. Somehow it must be able to distinguish between them.'

'Discriminate, more like,' Joey Stein, their hyperspace theorist, said. His inflated cheeks were constantly twitching, which Laura suspected came from complications with the tank yank. 'Our microcellular clusters are all functioning away merrily. Yet they're not a natural part of the human genome.'

16

'They're part of us now,' Ayanna said. She was combing out her long chestnut hair, wincing as she tugged at various tangles.

'The Void responds to thoughts,' Laura said. 'Has anyone simply thought that the biononics work?'

'That's not thinking, that's praying,' Ibu said.

Rojas, the shuttle pilot, sat down next to Joey. Captain Cornelius had brought him out of suspension a month ago to help plan the *Vermillion*'s landing. With his healthy Nordic-white skin and firm jaw showing five o'clock stubble, Laura thought he was the only one of them that didn't look like a third-rate zombie right now.

'Thinking systems into functionality has been tried,' Rojas said sympathetically. 'The awake crew have spent years attempting to mentally affect onboard equipment. Complete waste of time: the Void doesn't work like that. Turns out, you can't wish our machinery to activate.'

'The Void has an agenda?' Ayanna asked incredulously. 'You're talking as if it was alive, or at least aware.'

'Who knows?' Rojas said dismissively. He nodded at one of the big wall panels, which was showing an image of the Forest. 'This is our assignment, so let's focus on that, please.'

Ibu shook his head bullishly. 'All right, then. What do we know?'

'The Forest is a slightly ovoid cluster of individual objects we're calling distortion trees, measuring approximately seventeen thousand kilometres down its axis, with a maximum diameter of fifteen thousand. Given the average tree size of nine kilometres and the distribution we've mapped, we're estimating between twenty-five to thirty thousand of them in total.'

'Are they all identical?' Laura asked.

'So far, yes,' Rojas said. 'We'll be able to perform more detailed analysis on our approach.'

Another pane started, showing the elongated shape of a distortion tree. All Laura could think of was a streamlined icicle with a bulbous base, its profile a moiré shimmer. Despite the curious shifting surface pattern, it seemed smooth.

'They're like crystal rocket ships,' Ayanna said in a reverential tone.

'Hold that thought,' Ibu said. 'Does anyone know what the Raiel warships looked like?'

Joey gave him a sharp glance. 'You think this is their old invasion fleet?'

'Just asking. The Raiel arkships we've encountered are some kind of artificial organism.'

'Their arkships are bigger than these distortion trees,' Laura said. 'A lot bigger.'

'We've no records of any Commonwealth starship encountering a Raiel warship,' Rojas said. 'Wilson Kime reported that the *Endeavour* was approached by a ship smaller than an arkship, but with the same layout. It looked like an asteroid which had sprouted domed cities.' He pointed to the shimmering spire. 'Nothing like that.'

'What's their albedo?' Ayanna asked.

Rojas grinned. 'One point two. They're radiating more light than the local star shines on them. Just like the Skylords.'

'This can't be coincidence,' Joey said. 'That would be ridiculous. They're related; they have to be. Same technology, or parents. Whatever. But their origin is shared.'

'I agree,' Laura said. 'The Skylords can manipulate the local continuum to enable them to fly. These are changing the quantum structure around themselves. The basic mechanism has to be the same.'

'Those are the conclusions of the captain's review board,' Rojas said. 'What we need to find out is how and why.'

Joey attempted a laugh, but his twitching cheek muscles made it difficult. He drooled from the corner of his mouth. 'Why are they changing the quantum signature? How do we find that out?'

'Ask them,' Ibu said. 'If they're sentient like the Skylords.'

'Good luck with that,' Rojas grunted. 'Our mission target is to understand the new quantum composition of the continuum inside the Forest. If we can define it, we might be able to derive its purpose.'

'Quantum measurement is fairly standard,' Laura said, then caught herself. 'Assuming our instruments work.'

'Ayanna, that's your field,' Rojas said. 'I'll need a list of equipment you want. If there's anything we're not carrying, we'll see if the ship's fabrication systems can manufacture it. Don't be too ambitious; the extruders are suffering along with all the other systems.'

Ayanna gave him a sly smile. 'I'll try and remember that.'

'Laura,' Rojas said, 'you're tasked with determining how the disturbance is created. Other than their size, which varies by a few hundred metres, the distortion trees seem uniform, so we're assuming the ability is integral to their structure.'

'Got it,' she said. 'Do I get to take samples?'

'If the Forest zone isn't instantly lethal to us. If the shuttle can manoeuvre and rendezvous. If the trees themselves aren't sentient, or self aware. If they don't have defences. If our spacesuits work. If their structure can be sampled. Then, possibly, yes. We'd prefer an in situ analysis, obviously. Commonwealth encounter regulations do still apply. Please remember that, everybody.'

Laura pressed her lips together in bemusement. 'Okay, then. I'll draw up my wish list of gadgets.'

Rojas stood up. 'We launch in four hours. As well as your equipment, you might want to transfer some of your personal packs onto Fourteen. Once the mission's over, I can't guarantee we'll land anywhere close to the *Vermillion*.'

After Rojas left the excursion-prep facility, Laura turned to Ibu. 'Was that a guarantee he will land us on the planet?' she asked, trying to make it light hearted.

The huge gravatonics professor rubbed a shaking hand along his temple. 'You think we'll make it all the way to the planet? I wish I had your optimism. I'm going to check that my memory secure store is current.'

'I'm more confident about Fourteen getting down than I am about *Vermillion*,' Laura said. 'Actually, I'm surprised Cornelius didn't assign more specialists to our mission. Fourteen can hold – what, sixty people?'

'If it works,' Joey said. 'I think he's balancing the risk about right. If we make it to the Forest, we might just contribute something that'll help us find a way out of the Void. If we don't . . . Well, face it, the likes of us aren't going to be missed on a pioneering world where the only machines that work belong to the twentieth century.'

'Twentieth century?' Ibu challenged. 'Another raving optimist.'

'I grew up on a farm,' Ayanna protested. 'We worked the land.' She pulled a face. 'Well, I helped Dad program the agribots.'

'I'll get my list together, then I might just go check on my secure store,' Laura declared. 'Not that any of us will ever be getting a re-life clone in the Void. Looks like we're back to having one mortal life again.'

*

Time was short, and there were a lot of preparations to be made, all of which were more problematic than they should have been, thanks to glitches in the *Vermillion*'s network and command core. But Laura found a few spare minutes to go back to the suspension bay. Her sarcophagus was still open, the mechanisms inside cold and inert. She'd half expected engineeringbots to be swarming all over it, but nothing disturbed the tranquillity of the long compartment. There was a simple personal locker at the foot of the suspension chamber. Thankfully it opened when her u-shadow gave it the code. It didn't hold much – one bag of decent clothes, another of sentimental items. That was the one she unzipped.

Inside, there was the hand-made wooden jewel box Andrze had bought her on their honeymoon on Tanyata, its colourful paint faded now after three centuries. The rust-red scarf with aboriginal art print she'd picked up in Kuranda. Her flute with its wondrously mellow sound, made in Venice Beach – and she couldn't even remember who she'd been with when she acquired that. The phenomenally expensive (and practically black-market) chip of silver crystal from the ma-hon tree in New York's Central Park. A bag of sentiments, then, a little museum of self more important than any secure store holding memories her brain no longer had room for. Strange how these physical items gave her a more comforting sense of identity than her own augmented, backed-up, reprofiled neurones. She picked up a ridiculously thick, and impractical, six-hundred-year-old Swiss army knife, with something like twenty different tools and blades. A gift from Althea, she recalled, the artist who made a virtue of rejecting all the technological boons which the Commonwealth provided for its citizens.

Althea, who would have sneered at the very concept of a flight to another galaxy – if Laura had ever gained the courage to tell her she was going. Laura grinned at how her old friend would greet the news that they were trapped in the artificial weirdness of the Void. 'Hubris!' she'd no doubt shout gleefully. And now the penknife was probably the most functional possession Laura owned. Althea's smugness would turn supernova at that knowledge.

Laura put the ancient penknife in her shipsuit's breast pocket. The weight of it was a comfort, something whose simplicity wouldn't let her down. It belonged in the Void.

*

Shuttle Fourteen had a basic delta planform, with smooth rounded wing-tips giving it a slightly organic appearance – an unusual halfway machine between an old-fashioned aircraft and the flattened ovoid shape of the Commonwealth's standard regrav capsules. As well as ferrying passengers down to a planet, it was designated a mid-range preliminary exploration vehicle, able to hop around the planets of a solar system, launching detailed observations, delivering researchers and scientific equipment. Examining a space-based artefact was well within its capabilities.

Inside, Laura could easily believe she'd just stepped back five centuries to the aircraft era. The forward cabin wasn't quite cramped; there were ten large acceleration couches, in two rows, which seemed to fill a lot of it. Up at the front, the pilot's couch was solo; overhung by the big curving windscreen. There was a nominal horseshoe console of glossy dark plastic, which usually displayed a few basic craft functions. As with everything in the modern Commonwealth, Shuttle Fourteen was controlled by a cognitive array with the human pilot as a (mainly psychological) safety fallback.

Today Rojas had pulled every emergency manual control out of the console, cluttering it in a bewildering assortment of clunky switches and ergonomic toggles. Flight trajectory graphics slithered about inside the windscreen like holographic fish. Smaller panes that had popped up out of the console glowed with complex system-status symbols.

Laura eyed them suspiciously as she strapped herself into her seat. The colourful 3D glyphs were ominously similar to those she used to see on wall posters at primary school when she dropped her first batch of children off in the morning – and that was three hundred and fifty years ago. *Haven't they come up with anything more advanced since then?*

Rojas was sitting comfortably in the pilot's couch, studying the ever-changing holograms and flicking switches like a twentieth-century astronaut, his voice a low-level murmur saturated with confidence as he talked to the array.

'Looks like our glorious leader has the right stuff,' Ibu said quietly as he settled into the couch next to Laura. 'It makes you feel grand to be alive, doesn't it, putting your life in his hands?'

She grinned back at him. Ibu had the kind of phlegmatic outlook on life she approved of. He was a good choice for the team. She still hadn't made her mind up about Joey. If anything, the spasms afflicting his facial muscles had increased. It was pure prejudice on her part, she knew, but it did make him look as if he had some kind of bad neurological problem rather than just some damage from the tank yank, which he kept assuring them was inconsequential. Aside from that, the emotions which did escape from his guarded mind indicated disapproval of the mission. His heart wasn't in it.

As for Ayanna, she acted like a consummate professional, interested only in the science. The problem with their newfound mental abilities was that everyone could sense the sheer terror leaking from her mind.

'Two minutes,' Rojas announced.

Five metres in front of the shuttle's stubby nose, red warning lights began to flash around the docking bay's inner doors as they slid shut. Laura made a face and pulled on her padded cap, then used the backup straps to stop herself floating out of the couch, clicking them together in the way she just about remembered from her childhood. Nobody was relying on the couches' plyplastic cushioning to hold them.

With the straps pressing into her shoulders, she tried to steady her breathing. Apart from the two mandatory emergency training sessions before the colony fleet left Commonwealth space, she hadn't spent any real time in zero gee for decades. Some people loved it for the freedom of movement. Every time she was weightless, she'd needed her biononics to help suppress the nausea. Andy Granfore had given her some drugs he promised would help, but she didn't hold out much hope. Besides, she was still so full of tank yank suppressors, her biochemistry would probably register as alien if she was given any decent kind of scan.

'Fusion chambers active and stable,' Rojas announced. 'Onboard systems ninety-four per cent functionality. Umbilical links closing.'

A large purple star flared in one of the console displays. 'You're looking good, Fourteen,' Cornelius Brandt's voice boomed from the cabin's speakers.

'Bollocks to this,' Laura muttered. It was just a shuttle launch, for crap's sake. All these reassurances were really starting to crank her tension up.

'I just wanted to emphasize that your mission is important, but not worth taking any dangerous risks for,' the starship's captain continued. 'Once we're established on the surface, we'll be able to turn every resource into finding a way out of the Void, and there are a lot of very smart people in suspension. Any information you can provide will be valuable, even if it is negative.'

'Copy that, *Vermillion*,' Rojas said. 'And thank you. Fifteen seconds to launch. Umbilical disconnect confirmed. Five greens on clamp release. Regrav units on line. Initiating lift.'

The red docking bay lights turned purple, signalling vacuum, and the outer doors slid back, to reveal a midnight-black universe outside. The shuttle wobbled slightly as it rose from its docking cradle. Rojas eased it out through the airlock.

Despite herself, Laura craned forward for a better view through the windscreen. The weird space she'd only seen on *Vermillion*'s holograms unveiled for real as Fourteen emerged from the bay. Somehow, Void space managed to appear darker than ordinary space. It was the contrast, Laura reasoned. On the Commonwealth worlds there were always so many stars visible at night, from the faintest wisps of the Milky Way up to the sharp specks of white giants. They were all around and forever. Here there were so few stars visible, probably no more than a couple of thousand. But the nebulas made up for their absence. There must have been hundreds, from the great smears of luminous plasma dust sprawling over lightyears to fainter smudges glowing in the unknown depths.

Gravity fell away over a long moment as they glided clear of the *Vermillion*. Fourteen began a slow roll, and Laura saw the massive cliff of foam-coated metal slide past as if they were falling parallel to it. It wasn't an elegant structure, more like heavy-duty industrial modules bolted together and sprayed in the ubiquitous foam, which had bleached and pocked from its long vacuum exposure. Things poked out of the coating on spindly poles: sensors, comlinks, molecular force screen nozzles . . . Bright orange-neon lines glowed in deep fissures that were the seams between modules, the thermal-dump radiators energetically beaming the starship's excess heat out into the vacuum. Regrav and ingrav propulsion units were clusters of stumpy cylinders as big as the shuttle, made out of dark glass shot through with green scintillations. *Vermillion*'s rear third was all segmented cargo tubes, like a geometrical intestine. They contained everything you needed to establish a technologically advanced human civilization on a virgin world.

All useless here, Laura thought bleakly.

24

Rojas applied power to Fourteen's main regrav drive units, and the shuttle started accelerating away from the *Vermillion*. Laura's sense of balance shifted rapidly as the gravity built to one third standard. To her perception, the shuttle was now standing on its tail, putting her flat on her back in the couch while the floor had now become the wall. Rojas was above her, his couch creaking as it absorbed the new weight loading.

'Are you all right?' a smooth mental voice asked her.

Laura didn't need to be told this was the Skylord. The mentality she could sense behind the thought was massive and intimidatingly serene.

'Er, yes, thank you,' she replied, instinctively tightening her own thoughts so her emotional leakage was minimal. Judging by the stiff postures all around her, the others were taking part in identical telepathic conversations.

'You are leaving,' the Skylord said with a tinge of concern. 'Is my guidance no longer acceptable? We are so near a world where you will flourish and become fulfilled.'

Rojas held up a hand, stalling anyone else's reply, and opened up his own telepathic voice. 'We thank you for your guidance, and anticipate joining our friends on the world you have brought us to very soon.'

'I am glad for you. But why do you delay?'

'We wish to explore the nature of this world and everything close to it. It is the way we reach our fulfilment.'

'I understand. Your current trajectory will take you close to our parturition region.'

'Do you mean this clump of objects?' Rojas sent a mental picture of the Forest.

'Yes.'

'Is this where Skylords come from?'

'Not this parturition region. We came from another.'

'What are the objects in the parturition region? Eggs?'

'The parturition region creates us.'

'How?'

'It does.'

'Do you object to us going there?'

'No.'

'The region is different to the rest of the Void. Why?'

'It is a parturition region.'

'Are they important to you?'

'We come from a parturition region. We do not return. We guide those who have reached fulfilment to the Heart of the Void.'

'Where is that?'

'It is at the end of your fulfilment.' The Skylord's presence withdrew from the cabin.

Rojas shook his head and sighed. His thoughts were showing a degree of frustration. 'Thus ends every conversation with the Skylords,' he concluded. 'Enigmatic shits.'

'That's a fantastic discovery,' Joey said. 'The distortion trees birth them or conjure them into existence, or something. This is where they come from. Our mission is half complete and we've only been going two minutes.'

'If you believe it,' Rojas said. 'They're slippery little swines.' He flicked a switch to open a channel back to *Vermillion* and began reporting the conversation.

*

Three hours seventeen minutes accelerating at point seven gees, then Shuttle Fourteen flipped over and decelerated at the same rate. Six and a half hours after launching from *Vermillion*, Rojas performed their final velocity match manoeuvres and the delta-shaped shuttle was left hanging in space, two and a half thousand kilometres out from the Forest.

Laura stared at it through the shuttle's windscreen – a huge patch of silver speckles that gleamed brightly, blocking off half of space. Her eyes fooled her into thinking each speck was drifting about, while in fact it was just the bizarre patterns of their surfaces that flickered and shimmered. Sensors zoomed in, giving them a decent image of the distortion trees on the edge of the Forest.

'They don't have that fog around them that the Skylords do,'

Joey slurred. His facial twitches were growing progressively worse. Now that they were in freefall, drool was slipping out of his open lips to drift round the cabin. Laura didn't like the way his problems were developing. Shuttle Fourteen had a medical capsule, but it wasn't as sophisticated as any of the ones on *Vermillion*. Not, she admitted to herself, that she'd like any medical capsule to run a procedure on her right now. Fourteen's systems glitches were steadily increasing.

In tandem with Joey's affliction? she wondered.

'Other than that, there's not a lot of difference,' Ayanna said. 'These are smaller.'

'Narrower,' Rojas said. 'And they are rotating very slowly around their long axis. Nine-hour cyclic period.'

'A thermal roll?' Laura asked.

'Looks like it. That's the easiest way to keep a stable temperature in space.'

'So something's making them roll,' Laura said.

'Nothing visible. It's not a reaction-control system.'

'Magnetic?' Joey asked.

'I'm not picking up any significant magnetic field,' Rojas said. 'They're almost inert.'

'What about the anomalous quantum signature?' Laura asked.

Ayanna studied several of the displays, a frown growing. 'It is very strange. The temporal component of spacetime is different in there.'

'Temporal?' Ibu queried.

'I think time is progressing at a reduced flow rate inside. It's not unreasonable; our wormholes can manipulate internal time flow in a similar fashion. We can even halt temporal flow altogether inside exotic matter cages if they're formatted correctly.'

'You mean things happen slower in there?' Rojas asked.

'Only relative to outside the Forest.'

'So are the trees made out of exotic matter?' Joey asked.

'I've no idea. But negative energy is the only way we know of manipulating spacetime, so there's got to be something like it in there somewhere.'

'We have to go in and take physical samples,' Laura said.

'So you keep saying,' Ayanna replied drily.

'Let's see if we can, first,' Rojas said. His hands moved nimbly over various switches on the pilot's console. Two thirds of the way along the shuttle's lower fuselage, a malmetal hatch flowed open. Four Mk24 GSDs (General Science Drones) emerged from their silo and began flying towards the Forest, looking like black footballs studded with hexagonal diamonds.

'Functionality is good,' Rojas said. Each Mk24 was displaying a visual image on a console pane. 'I'll send them in one at a time.'

'There isn't a clear barrier,' Ayanna said. 'The effect simply increases as you approach the outermost layer of trees.'

'You mean I'll get an increasingly delayed telemetry response?'

'Could be,' Ayanna replied. Uncertainty tainted her thoughts.

'The first should reach the trees in forty minutes,' Rojas said.

Laura kept looking at the view through the windscreen; she found it easier than constantly reinterpreting the images from the Mk24s. They weren't getting much more than the full-spectrum visual feed. Hard science data was sparse. The solar wind was normal, as was the cosmic radiation environment.

'I wonder if this is what schizophrenia feels like,' Ibu said after twenty minutes. 'I wanted a new and exciting life; that's why I joined the colony project.'

'But not this exciting,' Laura suggested.

'No fucking way. But I have to admit, the Void is intriguing. From a purely academic point of view, you understand.'

'I'll take that over boredom.'

The big man cocked his head to look at her with interest. 'You were going to another galaxy because you were bored?'

'I've had six marriage partnerships, and a lot more fun partners. I've had twelve children, not all of them in a tank; I've actually been pregnant twice, which wasn't as bad as I was expecting. I've lived on the External and Inner worlds and sampled every lifestyle that wasn't patently stupid. I thought becoming a scientist on the cutting edge of research would be infinitely thrilling. It wasn't. Damn, unless you're in it, you have no idea of how much petty politics there is in academia. So it was either a real fresh start, or download myself into ANA and join all the incorporeal minds bickering eternity away. And I just didn't believe that was a decent solution.'

'Interesting. What faction would you have joined?'

'Brandts traditionally join the moderate Advancers. That sounded more of the same. So here I am.'

Ibu gestured at the vast silver stipple beyond the windscreen. 'And is this not the infinite thrill you were searching for? You must be very content at what fate has dealt us.'

'Hmm. More like infinitely worrying.'

'Maybe, but we are in the middle of the galaxy's greatest enigma. Unless we solve it, we will never return to the real universe. You can't beat that for motivation.'

'The more I see and understand,' Laura said, 'the more it seems to me we're lab rats running around a particularly bizarre maze. What kind of power has the ability to pull us in here, then apparently ignore us?'

'You think we're being watched?'

'I don't know. I suspect this place isn't quite as passive as the captain believes. What would be the point of it doing nothing?'

'What's the point of it at all?'

She shrugged, which didn't work well in freefall.

'*Vermillion* has decelerated into low orbit,' Rojas announced. 'They're launching environment analysis probes into the planet's atmosphere.'

'It's an oxygen nitrogen atmosphere,' Ayanna said disparagingly. 'And spectography showed the kind of photosynthetic vegetation we've found everywhere we've been in the galaxy. Unless there are some hellish pathogens running round loose down there, Cornelius will give the order to land.'

'He doooesn't,' Joey began. The erratic spasms afflicting his face and neck mangled the words, so everyone had to listen hard now whenever he spoke. 'Ever ned t-t-to lanid.'

'How's that?' Laura asked.

'Because of the Skathl . . .' A burst of anguish flowered in Joey's mind as his traitor muscles distorted his words beyond recognition. 'Thusss Skahh.' He shut his mouth forcefully. Began again. 'Moih woold . . .' His head bowed in defeat. 'Because of the Skylords,' his telepathic voice said clearly. 'They brought us here for whatever this ridiculous fulfilment kick of theirs is. If they wanted to kill us, the very least they had to do was just leave us drifting in space while all our systems glitched and crashed. But they found us and guided us here, specifically here to this star which has an H-congruous type planet. On top of that, this whole place is artificial. Like Laura said, we're here for a reason. Death isn't it.'

'Makes sense,' Laura said. 'On the plus side, it probably means the *Vermillion* and the others will be able to land intact.'

Ibu grunted in agreement. 'And probably won't be able to fly again.'

'Fulfilment,' Rojas said, as if hearing the word for the first time. 'You're making it sound like a sacrifice to a god.'

'Best theory yet,' Ayanna said. 'The Void is the most powerful entity we've yet encountered. God's not a bad description.'

'Now you're into infinite regression,' Ibu said cheerfully. 'If this is a god, what does that say of whoever created it?'

'I'm not sure this qualifies as an entity,' Laura said. 'I'm sticking with my theory that the Void's a more advanced version of ANA. Just a big-ass computer, running a real-life simulation that we're trapped in.'

'Nothing so far disproves that,' Ayanna said sympathetically. 'But that still means there's a reason for it existing, and there'll be a controlling sentience.'

'My vote's for a work of art,' Joey told them. 'If you can create this, you're a long, *long* way past us on the evolutionary scale. Why not do it for fun?'

'Because it's dangerous and going to kill the galaxy,' Rojas said.

'If you're a god, that might be fun.'

'Let's hope we don't meet Her then,' Ibu said sardonically.

Laura looked at the Forest again. 'Well, I don't think she's likely to be in there.'

'We might not get to find out,' Rojas said. 'The first Mk24's telemetry feed is going weird on us.'

'Weird, how?' Ibu asked.

Rojas was studying several displays. 'The datastream is slowing down. I don't mean there's less information; it's dopplering – the bit rate separation is increasing.'

'Temporal flow reduction,' Ayanna said in satisfaction. 'The quantum sensor data was right.'

'Where's the drone?' Laura asked.

'A hundred and fifty kilometres from the nearest distortion tree,' Rojas said. 'Approach rate, one kilometre a second. I'm reducing that now; I need more time to initiate manoeuvres.'

'How's it responding?' Joey asked. There was a lot of curiosity behind the question.

'Sluggish,' Rojas admitted. 'Oh: interesting. The second Mk24's data is speeding up.'

'The effect is fluctuating?' Ayanna asked. 'Now that is odd.'

'Okay, and now the second Mk24's telemetry is dopplering back down,' Rojas said.

'Maybe it's a variable threshold,' Laura suggested. The lack of instant information was exasperating; this mission was like operating in the Stone Age. Once again, she instinctively asked her u-shadow to connect to the shuttle's network. Startlingly, the interface worked. A whole flock of icons popped up in her exovision. Secondary thought routines operating in her macrocellular clusters began to tabulate an analysis on an autonomic level. The raw torrent of information suddenly shifted to being precise and edifying.

Joey and Ayanna immediately turned to look at her, and she realized she'd let out a mental flash of comfort. 'What's the antonym of glitch?' she asked. 'I've just got a full-up connection to Fourteen's network.'

'Resurrection?' Ibu suggested.

Small icons in Laura's exovision told her the rest of the team were taking advantage of the shuttle's return to normality as the glitches faded. But she was concentrating primarily on the quantum environment which the first Mk24 was gliding through. The temporal components were certainly different. There were other abnormalities as well.

'Do you understand this?' she asked Ayanna.

'Not really.'

Laura closed her eyes as the Mk24 passed within seventeen kilometres of a distortion tree on the fringe of the Forest. The image it relayed of the tree was excellent. Its long bulbous structure was made up from the wrinkled folds of some crystalline substance; they were arranged in a much less convoluted fashion than a Skylord. Pale multicoloured shadows rippled vigorously inside, as if there was something deeper within the tree that was prowling about. The image flickered.

The Mk24's datastream was dopplering down fast. Even with buffering, it was degrading badly. Laura shifted her focus to the second Mk24, which was five minutes behind it, approaching the outer tier of trees. The image was much better.

With that front and centre in her consciousness, she ran a review through the rest of the data construct that Shuttle Fourteen was assembling.

'Are you catching this?' she asked abruptly. Secondary routines pulled another datastream into principal interpretation. It wasn't from the Mk24 drones. The shuttle's main radar was showing a kilometre-wide circular formation of small objects. They were already seventeen thousand kilometres away from the blunt apex of the Forest, and receding at one point eight kilometres a second. Each object was globular and measured about three metres in diameter. Visual imaging was showing nothing; their surfaces were dull. She flicked the shuttle's thermal imaging to tracking them, which registered an interestingly high infra-red emission.

'Thirty-five degrees?' Ibu muttered in surprise. 'What are they?'

'Whatever they are, radar shows eleven of them,' Laura said. 'They're holding that circular formation, too, with minimal separation drift. Zero acceleration. Something flung them out like that.'

'Heading straight for the planet,' Rojas said. His mind flared a peak of alarm. 'I'm calling *Vermillion*, warning them something's approaching.'

'Baby Skylords?' Joey asked. 'This is the parturition zone, after all.'

'Reasonable guess,' Ibu said. 'I wonder what their lifecycle is. Grow up on the planet then jump back to space when they're mature?'

'They're inert,' Laura told them. 'No gravitational or spacetime distortion registering at all. They're not Skylords.'

'Skylord eggs?' Ayanna said.

'The Skylords said they didn't come from here,' Ibu said. 'They're not exactly clear speakers, but I don't think they could even grasp the concept of lying.'

'*Vermillion* will send a shuttle out to rendezvous,' Rojas said. 'If they can afford to.'

'We can always study them in situ if not,' Joey said. 'This is where they came from, after all.'

The third Mk24 flew past the outer layer of trees and lost contact less than a minute later. The fourth lasted for seventy-two seconds before the datastream dopplered down to zero.

'Just so we're straight,' Rojas said. 'Slow time isn't fatal, right, Ayanna?'

'It's only slow inside the Forest relative to the Void continuum outside,' she replied with growing annoyance.

'So now we just need to know if that quantum signature affects living tissue,' Ibu said.

'Okay,' Rojas said. 'I'll launch a Laika drone.'

Laura knew that, on an intellectual level, she ought to be having some kind of conflicted sentiment, maybe with a small sense of moral disapproval thrown in. But, frankly, after so many centuries of witnessing genuine death (as opposed to bodyloss) in both animals and humans, it didn't bother her any more. Besides, it was hard to work up much sentiment about a gerbil.

The little rodent was nestled in the centre of the Laika drone, which had almost identical sensors to the Mk24, with the addition of a tiny life-support globe at its core. They all observed through the sensor datastream as the Laika drone glided past the outer distortion trees. Through its waning telemetry link, they saw the gerbil twitching its nose, heart rate unchanged, breathing regularly, trying to suck water from the nozzle by its head. Muscles and nerves were all performing normally. The link dwindled to nothing.

'The Forest interior doesn't kill you,' Ibu said. 'Doesn't even affect life.'

Joey grunted – a nasty twisted sound more like a hoot. 'Not for the first minute.'

'The data has dopplered down beyond detection because of the temporal environment,' Ayanna said. 'We lost it, that's all. The Laika didn't fail. That gerbil is still alive in there.'

'That's your official recommendation?' Rojas asked.

'Yes. I believe it's safe for us to go inside. The only thing I don't know is the rate which time progresses in there. If we're inside for a day, it may be a month that passes outside. It may be more. It may be less.'

'Thank you. Joey?'

'We've come this far.'

'Laura?'

'I *need* to have samples of those trees. Whatever mechanism they're using is way outside anything we've encountered before. And I desperately want to know what their energy source is. You don't change temporal flow without a phenomenal amount of power. That's got to come from somewhere, and we're not seeing the neutrino activity to indicate direct mass energy conversion, or even fusion. It can't be solar. So, where . . . ?'

'Where does the energy come from for our telekinesis?' Ibu asked immediately. 'I don't think you're using the right references here, Laura. The Void continuum is different.'

'You mean the trees are *thinking* time to be slow?'

'Thinking. Wishing. Who knows?'

'All right, settle down,' Rojas said. He stared at Ibu. 'I take it you're happy to go inside?'

'Not happy, but I don't object. Laura's right: we need to get a good look at whatever processes are going on in those trees.'

Rojas exhaled loudly. 'All right, then, I'll tell the *Vermillion* we're going inside. I'm assuming once we're in there, we'll lose our link with them. I don't want them to launch a rescue mission just because we can't talk for a few days.'

Ibu opened a private link to Laura's u-shadow. 'Why do I get the notion a rescue mission isn't going to be featuring heavily on the captain's agenda?'

*

Rojas kept the manual controls active as he piloted Shuttle Fourteen forwards, heading for a large gap between distortion trees. Laura preferred to watch the approach through the windscreen rather than access the shuttle's sensor suite. However, her exovision display did provide a secondary interpretation, detailing their exact progress.

Acceleration was a tenth of a gee, enough to keep them in their couches. Laura used the time to quickly munch down some chocolate wafers. Even the small amount of gravity allowed her stomach to digest food without complaining.

'Somehow I feel we should be making preparations,' Ibu said.

'What kind?' Laura asked.

'I'm not sure. Putting on some kind of protective suit? Carrying a personal oxygen tank? Inoculation?'

'I've got a force-field skeleton web on under my shipsuit,' Ayanna said. 'Does that count?'

'That only helps if it doesn't glitch.'

'I thought you were the optimist.'

Laura rapped a knuckle on the cabin's padded bulkhead. The beige cushioning was arranged in squares; nearly half of them were the doors to small lockers. 'There are emergency pressure suits stowed in every cabin. You'll be fine.' She broke the seal on a carton of orange juice and started sucking at the straw.

Ibu glanced at the wall of trees that stretched across Voidspace outside the shuttle's windscreen. 'You called us rats in a lab maze. More like bacteria under a microscope. Our feelings are irrelevant. The only thing that's going to keep us alive in here is competence and logic.' He smiled round the cabin. 'Thankfully we've got both.

Can you imagine what this mission would be like if we only had a bunch of fifty-year-olds for company? A rollercoaster of panic and tears the whole way.'

'Link to *Vermillion* is dopplering,' Rojas said.

Laura checked her exovision displays. Fourteen was now thirty kilometres from a distortion tree, and closing. Rojas cut their acceleration to zero. Everyone fell silent as they glided past the slimmer end of the tree, which was oriented planetwards. Its shadow enveloped them. Rojas flipped the shuttle, and accelerated at half a gee to kill their velocity relative to the Forest, leaving them stationary inside. Laura's u-shadow noted the time. She was intrigued what the difference would be when they emerged out into 'ordinary' Voidspace again.

'I am showing a slight blueshift from several baseline stars,' Ayanna said. 'We're inside the altered temporal flow.'

'And still alive,' Ibu said.

'The link to *Vermillion* has gone,' Rojas said.

'I wasn't expecting that,' Ayanna said. 'I thought we might still receive them, but at a higher frequency.'

Rojas pulled a face. 'Nothing, sorry.'

'What about the Mk24s we sent in ahead of us?' Laura asked. 'Shouldn't we be picking them up again now we're in the same timeframe?'

'Nothing yet,' Rojas said. 'I'll run another scan.'

'Nothing from the Laika,' Ayanna reported.

'The Mk24s aren't showing up on the radar, either,' Ibu said.

'That's not right,' Laura said. 'Fourteen's radar is good enough to pick up a grain of sand from two hundred kilometres away. Even if the Mk24s' power glitched completely, they should register.'

'They must be behind another tree,' Joey said.

'All of them?' Laura said sceptically. 'After their link antennae failed and they went inert? Bollocks to that.'

'So how do you explain it?'

She glanced at the huge crystalline fissures of the nearest distortion tree. 'Something pulled them in.'

'We didn't detect any anomalous gravatonic activity,' Ayanna said. 'I don't know what else could divert their trajectory.'

'Telekinesis,' Rojas said. 'If those trees are alive by any standard, they'll have a big old brain buried somewhere inside.'

They all fell silent again. Laura gave the tree outside a mildly concerned glance. 'If it's alive, it's not talking to us.'

'This is where you're in charge,' Rojas told her. 'What do you want to do next?'

'Get closer to one. Run some density scans, see if we can get an image of its internal structure, then apply some sampler modules above the more interesting sections.'

'Close enough and we can use our ESP on it,' Joey said.

'Whatever gives us a clearer idea of what is going on inside the trees,' Laura told him without irony.

Shuttle Fourteen approached to three kilometres of a distortion tree; Rojas locked its position halfway along the crystalline behemoth, using tiny puffs of cold gas from the shuttle's reaction-control nozzles. A flock of AISD (Advanced Interlinked Sensor Drone) Mk16bs burped out from a fuselage silo. Two hundred and twenty of the glittering fist-sized drones swirled into a wide bracelet that surrounded the distortion tree. With their formation locked, and datastreams unified, they slowly slid along the tree's nine-kilometre length, deep scanning it.

Laura tried not to show too much disappointment with the image that built up in her exovision. The intricate curves and jags of the creased crystalline structure were mapped with millimetre precision, revealing the exact topology of fissures that extended for over a kilometre below the meandering ridge peaks. But the sensor flock couldn't resolve anything beneath the surface.

'Like a mountain range scale fingerprint,' Ibu described it.

Laura closed her eyes, immersing herself in the sensor imagery. 'The quantum distortion is strongest along the ridges,' she said. 'But that's not telling me where the generating mechanism is.'

'There's definitely some kind of negative energy effect going on in there,' Ayanna said. 'The trees are the source of the temporal flow change, all right. That illumination within the crystal must be this continuum's variant on Cherenkov radiation.'

Under Rojas's guidance, the drone flock split into two and slipped down into the gaps on either side of a crystalline ridge, sinking out of the sunlight to be illuminated by the eerie ever-shifting phosphorescence.

'We can keep in contact with the flock but not the Mk24s,' Ibu said. 'Curiouser and curiouser.'

'They're closer,' Rojas pointed out.

'If the Mk24s are just drifting around in the Forest, one of them would be out from the radar shadow of the trees by now.'

'Okay, so what do you think happened to them?'

'I don't know,' he said solemnly.

'Definitely some carbon in the tree mass,' Laura said, reading the fresh batch of data from the flock.

'It's a diamond?' Joey asked in delight.

'No, sorry. There are traces of other elements in there as well, nothing too elaborate. But this is interesting: valency bonds seem stronger than we're used to, and matter density is certainly higher than normal. I don't suppose there's much vacuum ablation. But I still can't get a reading more than a few millimetres deep.'

'So that means you have to go out there and chip a few bits off, right?' Ibu said.

Laura reviewed the density results again. 'I think the filaments on the sampler modules should be able to cope.'

'Damn, I was hoping to hit it with a hammer,' Ibu said with a grin. 'Can you imagine it? A single tap, and this one tiny little crack starts to multiply . . .'

'The Commonwealth First Contact Agency would fine you to death,' Laura told him.

'Let's just allow the flock a little more time,' Rojas said.

'I'm reading some interesting fluctuations in the quantum signature inside the fissure,' Ayanna said. 'I'd like the flock to complete a full scan down the whole length of the tree, find out where it's strongest.'

'That'll help me,' Laura admitted. 'But we are going out there, aren't we?'

Rojas sighed. 'We'll run some functionality tests on our equipment while we wait for the flock to finish this run.'

*

The shuttle's service compartment was sandwiched between the forward cabin and the main passenger cabin. It contained the boarding airlock, a small galley and washrooms, along with a hatch which led down to the payload bay running the length of the fuselage beneath the passenger cabin.

Laura floated after Rojas, keeping a respectable distance between her head and his feet. Even though her biononics were slowly recovering, she still wasn't terribly proficient in freefall. The risk of getting kicked in the face was always on her mind.

She allowed herself to float down the hatch, occasionally using one of the handholds that bristled from every bulkhead. The first quarter of the payload bay was a narrow corridor with walls of equipment lockers. That opened out into a larger metallic cavern, where the thick tubes of the drone silos formed twin rows. Laura grabbed the handholds and hauled herself along its length, trying not to bang her elbows into anything. At the far end of the silo compartment was an airlock hatch into the EVA hangar. Two spherical exopods were secure in their cradles – two-person spacecraft with a cluster of electromuscle tentacles on the front; retracted, the tentacles were coiled in a fashion that somehow managed to look faintly obscene. Spacesuits were stored in small cabinets, together with three sets of personal-manoeuvring harnesses. A long array of tools and science sensors were clipped to the bulkhead, opposite a row of inert zero-gee engineeringbots half the size of a human. At the far end was an airlock chamber big enough for an exopod.

'I'll power up one of the exopods,' Rojas said, 'if you'd like to check the suits.'

'Sure,' Laura told him. The suit was simple enough, a slippery one-piece of silver grey fabric lined with elecromuscle threads. It expanded like a loose sack so the wearer could pull it on, then the elecromuscle would contract, making it cling to the body like a second skin. Pores and capillaries harvested sweat, while a thermal-conductor web dissipated the excess heat a body generated, keeping temperature constant and comfortable. The helmet was a classic transparent globe, with a multitude of filter functions and sensors built in. The suit collar adhered to it easily. Oxygen regeneration was handled by a small package at the top of the spine. Usually, a force-field skeleton was worn on top, but Laura didn't trust them right now. She checked some of the other lockers, relieved to find thick protective outer suits that would be almost as effective at shielding the wearer from micro particle impacts. Exactly the kind of thing Ibu had talked about putting on. *I should take one back up to him.*

Her u-shadow reported Ayanna opening a direct connection. 'We're getting some interesting results from the Mk16bs,' she said.

'I'll take a look,' Laura replied. Her u-shadow opened the feed from the flock, and she stopped bundling the protective oversuit back into the cabinet as she saw what her exovision was presenting.

The flock had almost completed their exploratory flight along the deep ridge. Right at the narrow tip of the distortion tree, where the twisting ridges began to merge, the scan had revealed some irregular lumps. Lumps that had a surface temperature of thirty-five degrees Celsius. The flock shifted sensor focus, concentrating on the anomaly.

In Laura's exovision they were dark spheres, tumours that had swollen up out of the elegant glowing crystal of the main structure. The visual sensors showed over fifty of them, ranging in size from pebbles to globes nearly three metres across. Their skin was wrinkled, a dark grey that might have been at the extreme edge of green.

'Avocados,' she murmured. 'Ripe avocados.' For that was what they resembled.

Despite the best efforts of the drone flock to magnify the site, the point where the crystal ended and the globe began was uncertain; they merged together as if the globes were somehow rooted into the ridge, emphasizing the whole tumour concept.

'Skylord eggs,' Joey said.

'We need to go and take a sample,' Rojas said.

'We do,' Laura said, reviewing the rest of the results from the flock. 'But our primary mission is to assess the Forest's quantum abnormality. Take a look at the negative energy effect down at the bottom of the ridge; those are very complex patterns. That has to be where the whole time-flow manipulation is generated.'

'Okay, I'll prioritize that,' Rojas said.

'Great.' Laura flashed him a smile of thanks across the EVA hangar.

'Let me know what functionality the sample modules have got, and check the deep sensors as well, please.'

'Sure.'

'Ibu, come down and grab yourself a suit,' Rojas said. 'You can take the right-hand seat.'

'On my way,' Ibu replied.

'What?' Laura snapped. She'd simply assumed she'd be the one in the right-hand seat of the exopod.

'Ibu has a thousand hours' zero-gee work logged in the last twenty years,' Rojas explained patiently. 'You have a couple of mandatory one-hour safety drills, and the report said you didn't handle them well.'

'But it's my field,' Laura shot back, knowing she was responding peevishly.

From the side of the exopod, Rojas gave her a sympathetic glance. 'Whatever molecular structure makes up this thing is your field. Hammering sensors onto it and getting results for you is down to us.'

Laura gave a curt nod. 'Yes, of course. I'll check the systems I want you to deploy.'

'Thank you.'

A minute later, Ibu came gliding down the length of the silo compartment. Laura pressed her teeth together; despite his size, he was as graceful as an angelfish. *Ah, bollocks, Rojas is right to take him.*

'Sorry,' Ibu said as he came level with her. 'Just think of me as your additional pair of hands.'

Laura's face coloured slightly. She wondered just how effective her mental shield was. 'I'd like a quintet of deep scan packages on these areas.' Her u-shadow sent him the file. 'And when I've refined their results, I'll show you where to apply the sampler modules.'

Ibu's eyes closed as he examined the locations she'd selected. 'Going for the exotic matter, huh?'

'If we're going to understand the process here, I need to see what manipulates energy flow. It's clearly molecular based.'

'Like our biononics?'

She grimaced. 'Get me the samples and I'll let you know.'

*

Laura was back in the forward cabin when the exopod left the shuttle's small hangar. Ayanna was sitting in front of her in the pilot's couch, officially running the mission. Joey was strapped into a couch near the rear of the compartment. Laura was starting to get seriously concerned about the hyperspace theorist. The muscle twitches in his cheeks had now grown to such an extent that they'd effectively paralysed his face into a straining mask, leaving his lips twisted up into a wretched sneer. She'd seen his shoulders begin to shudder with increasing frequency. If he hadn't been strapped in, he'd be bouncing about the cabin. And it was telling that he kept his hands behind the couch in front, out of view from her and Ayanna. When she sneaked a look with her ESP, she could see his hands jerking about; his feet were afflicted too. Maybe she should suggest he try Fourteen's medical module – except she knew what his response would be.

The silver-white sphere of the exopod slid past the windscreen. Laura resisted the impulse to wave.

'How are your systems?' Ayanna asked.

'Mostly working,' Rojas replied, his voice coming through the cabin's speakers. 'Stand by for ion drive burn.'

Cold blue light emerged from four of the slim rectangular nozzles in the exopod's fuselage, and the little craft drifted away from Fourteen at a gentle rate.

'Burn vector good,' Rojas said. 'Rendezvous with tree in seven minutes – mark.'

Laura sighed and shook her head at all the gung-ho theatrics. *Boys and their toys.*

'They don't get out to play often,' Ayanna said quietly. They grinned at each other. Then Laura groaned as her link to Fourteen's network went down.

Ayanna started flicking switches on the console; one hand typed fast on a keyboard. Laura envied that skill; she was sure her fingers weren't so dextrous.

'Getting some power dropouts,' Ayanna murmured. 'Rojas, what's your status?'

'Good, Fourteen.'

'They're not dopplering,' Ayanna said.

The cabin lights flickered. Laura glanced suspiciously up at the strips. 'Great, that's all we need. Real power failures.' She shut up as her u-shadow reported it had re-established a link to Fourteen's network.

'You might want to make sure all the mission data is backed up,' Ayanna said.

'Good idea.' Laura ordered her u-shadow to open a new file in one of her storage lacunas and began downloading copies of all the drone logs.

While they were downloading, Ayanna altered Fourteen's attitude, so they could see the exopod through the windscreen. Her thoughts were cheerful at demonstrating how she could fly Fourteen just as well as Rojas. The off-white sphere itself was soon lost against the flickering phosphorescence within the tree's folds, but the navigation strobes kept up a regular pulse that remained visible against the massive alien object.

'Positioning burn complete,' Rojas eventually reported. 'Holding station two hundred metres from artefact's surface.'

When Laura checked through the windscreen, she saw the

strobes flash about a quarter of the way along the tree from the slim end. 'Ibu, I'd like to ride your optics, please.'

'Sure,' his voice came back.

Laura shut her eyes and settled back in the couch. Ibu's vision expanded out of a green and blue eye symbol in the middle of her exovision, and she looked round the restricted interior of the exopod. Rojas was next to Ibu, held in what resembled a standing position in front of the exopod's small port by a web of broad straps. The cabin walls were mostly display panels, lights and handholds.

Ibu slipped a helmet down over his head. Rojas was doing the same thing. Then several of the lights surrounding the pair of them turned from red to purple.

'Vacuum confirmed,' Ibu said. 'Opening pod airlock.' He disconnected the webbing straps that were holding him in place, and twisted round. A third of the cabin's rear wall had dilated. Ibu carefully crawled out into Voidspace. Just outside the airlock lip was a rack with a free-manoeuvre harness. He wriggled his way into it, and the clamps closed round his shoulders and thighs. 'Testing harness.'

Little spurts of cold gas coughed out of the nozzles on the harness extremities, like puffs of white dust. 'Function good. Heading over.'

He drifted slowly round the bulk of the exopod. The tree rose round the curving grey-white globe like planetdawn on a gas giant's moon. This close it was massive. Just seeing it through human eyes made Laura shiver. Something that big, quite possibly alive, and thoroughly alien, was somewhat intimidating. Curiously, it disturbed her more than the Void itself.

'I don't think the trees are part of the Void,' she murmured. 'I think they were pulled in, just like us.'

'What makes you say that?' Ayanna asked.

'If they were part of it, they wouldn't be trying to change Voidspace. They're prisoners, like we are. That's bad.'

'How so?'

'Their control over mass and energy is clearly more advanced than ours, and they're still here.'

'If they are from outside,' Ayanna said hastily.

With her eyelids still closed, and her vision still coming directly from riding Ibu's eyes, Laura smiled. 'They are.'

Ibu was gliding slowly along the top of the ridge which the drone flock had scanned. The data feed from his suit was undergoing micro-second dropouts, making the vision flicker every few seconds.

'Going inside,' he said.

The little jets of gas puffed again. Then the crystalline wall was sliding past his helmet. He held his course level, staying a constant fifteen metres away from the side of the vast fold that opened into the tree. His entire silver-white oversuit shone with the weird radiance that slithered through the crystalline structure. Laura was aware her heart rate was increasing, and she wondered if it was some kind of telepathic feedback from Ibu.

'You're approaching the zone I designated,' she told him, reading the inertial coordinates from an exovision icon.

'Yeah. Noticed that.'

Laura grinned. 'I also have some eggs I'd like to show your grandmother how to use.'

'I'm sure she'd welcome it.'

Ibu halted close to the bottom of the ride. Fifty metres away, the crystal curved sharply to form the base of a narrow valley. The other wall of the ridge was only seventy metres behind him. 'Beginning phase one,' he announced.

Laura's relayed vision wobbled as he reached down and removed a deep-scan package from his fat utility belt. It was a simple green circle the size of his gauntleted hand.

She gripped the cushioned edge of the couch as Ibu triggered his harness and slowly glided forwards. She could see his arms stretched out ahead. The actual surface of the crystal was hard to make out in the odd shifting light glowing within.

His fingertips touched, and he rebounded slightly. Then the gas jets were puffing, holding him in place.

Laura let out a breath she didn't know she was holding.

'It's practically frictionless,' Ibu reported. 'My suit's stkpads aren't holding.'

'That'll be the increased valancy,' Laura told him. 'That crystal is going to have fewer surface irregularities than ordinary matter.'

'Okay. Applying the package now. See if that attaches.'

Laura wasn't sure what kind of adhesive was on the deep-scan package, but when Ibu pressed it to the surface and applied a short burst from the harness jets to push it down, the glue seemed to work.

'Tactile contact confirmed,' Ibu said. 'Telemetry good. Moving to second location.'

'Well done,' Ayanna told him.

'We have a problem,' Joey's telepathic voice claimed.

Laura blinked her eyes open, banishing Ibu's visual feed to a small ancillary icon in her exovision. She looked round the forward cabin, but everything seemed to be okay. 'What's wrong?'

Joey's eyes stared at her from his twisted-up immobile face. 'I've been using the shuttle's optronic sensors to try and find *Vermillion*. I can't. It's vanished.'

'What?' Ayanna snapped, and there was no shielding strong enough to guard against the flash of alarm in her thoughts.

'I can't find it,' Joey said. 'Look, there's something seriously wrong about losing contact with the drones and *Vermillion* just because of dopplering. It doesn't matter how much the link frequency shifts, we should still be able to pick up the signal.'

Ayanna's expression was edgy. 'Yeah. I know.'

'Okay. So. It bothered me – a lot. I started reviewing visual data. The *Vermillion* is thirteen hundred metres long, for fuck's sake. You should be able to see it with the naked eye from this distance. The kind of optronics Fourteen is carrying are capable of reading the damn serial number. We know the orbital track, we know where to focus the search. I've run the basic scan five times now. There's nothing orbiting that world. Not *Vermillion*. Not *Viscount* and not *Verdant*. None of them is in orbit any more.'

'That can't—' Laura started. 'Oh, bollocks. They couldn't all crash.' She gave Ayanna a desperate look. 'Could they?'

'They were in a thousand-kilometre orbit,' Ayanna said. 'We confirmed that before we entered the Forest's temporal shift zone.

I cannot imagine what kind of power could pull them out of orbit.'

'The same power that slows time in here,' Laura said. 'Joey, we are slower in here. Any chance they're all on the other side of the planet and they're just taking a long time to track round into visual range?'

His misshapen face showed no emotion, but his thoughts dripped scorn. 'Oh, yeah. Really never thought of that. Come on! Their spacing was equidistant round the orbital track. One of them is always in view. Most of the time, two of them are.'

'Those spheres we tracked heading down to the planet,' Ayanna said. 'Perhaps they're weapons.'

'And we didn't see the explosions?' Laura asked. 'No. Something else has happened.'

'If they were pulled down from orbit, they'd create the devil's own crater,' Ayanna concluded. 'Right now there'll be megatons of rock vapour spewing up into the atmosphere. The planet's entire climate system will be wrecked. Joey, any sign of that?'

The hyperspace theorist managed to blink. 'No. But I'll run a decent scan. Maybe they didn't crash, maybe the ingrav held out long enough.'

'Do it,' Ayanna said curtly.

'Do we tell . . .?' Laura waved a hand at the titanic alien artefact glowing beyond the windscreen. The exopod's strobes were still flashing regularly.

'No,' Ayanna said quickly. 'Let them get back here before we hit them with this. I don't want anything to distract them out there.'

'Okay.' A slow shiver ran down Laura's spine. It seemed to generate its own chill. 'Even if the ships were pulled out of orbit, that doesn't explain what happened to all the drones.'

Ayanna gave a quick nod. 'I know.'

Laura watched Ibu fit the remainder of the deep-scan packages. They started to reveal the amazing molecular substructure within the tree's crystal edifice: millions of distinct layers interwoven in the most incredibly complex patterns. Each band possessed a different energy level, many of which dipped into negative functions.

'This is some seriously impressive bollocks,' Laura said faintly. Her secondary routines were trying to map the pathways which the packages were exposing, but her macrocellular clusters simply didn't have the processing capacity to hack it. Even with Fourteen's array working on the problem, it would take weeks. 'And we're only seeing a tiny fraction. The whole thing is a giant solid state circuit that manipulates negative energy – and that's just the part I do understand. It must be generating its own valency differences, too, which is practically in the realm of perpetual motion.'

'So there has to be a control mechanism somewhere,' Ayanna said. 'Perhaps a section that runs its routines?'

'Somewhere. Yes. But we're dealing with cubic kilometres here.'

'Logically it would be at the centre of the bulbous section at the other end.'

'Sure. Logically. Ibu, Rojas, are you sensing any kind of thoughts coming from the tree? They wouldn't necessarily be as fast or even similar to ours.'

'Sorry, Laura,' Ibu said. 'Nothing. My ESP can barely get a look inside the crystal, not that I understand half of what I can perceive, anyway.'

'Okay. I'm sending you a file with the coordinates I want for the sampler modules.'

'Laura,' Rojas asked, 'this is one very complex molecular structure we're seeing in the crystal. Is sampling appropriate, do you think?

'Appropriate?' she spluttered. 'This is the most incredible molecular mechanism I've ever seen!'

Ibu chuckled. 'What he means is, if we start sticking sampler filaments in there, is it going to be like shoving a pin in a balloon?'

Laura took a breath to calm down. 'I'm going to take ten grams out at the most, and none of that is coming out of the negative energy channels. Sampling isn't going to damage anything, okay? It's safe.'

Ayanna turned round in the pilot's couch and raised a very sceptical eyebrow.

'Safe,' Laura reiterated, refusing to back down.

'All right,' Ibu said. 'Applying the first module now.'

The first thing they learned was how difficult it was for the filaments to slide through the crystal surface with its enhanced atomic cohesion. 'This might take a while,' Laura admitted as she monitored the painfully slow progress the filament tips were making.

Ibu applied the last of the sample modules. 'I'm going to take a look at the eggs,' he said.

Laura expanded the optical ride he was providing, and observed him slide along the bottom of the illuminated valley. As he progressed, the harness emitted occasional puffs of vapour which glittered in the eerie light. The fold grew smaller and narrower, merging with several others as it curved about.

'Ibu, is the light dimming?' Laura asked. The image she was riding had been suffering an increasing number of those annoying judders as he moved along the fold, and now she was struggling to make out the fluctuating slivers of phosphorescence inside the crystal. It was as if he'd moved into shadow, which was impossible.

'No,' he replied. 'Why? Are the sample modules screwing with the tree?'

She pressed down on a smile. 'No.'

'Signal bandwidth is reducing significantly,' Ayanna warned. 'Ibu, you're moving into some serious interference. Is there anything different inside the crystal?'

'No. But I can see the globes now. It's like . . . hell. I can't—'

Even though her eyelids were closed, Laura wanted to squint. She could just make out the dark globes that were melded with the crystal. Riding Ibu's optics was a portal into a world of shadow upon shadow.

'What's happening?' Rojas asked urgently.

'Nothing,' Ibu said. 'I just can't use my ESP on these things, is all. It's like they're shielded, the way we learned to protect our thoughts. But they're really wonderful. I know it.'

49

'You mean they're alive?' Laura asked in alarm.

'I'm not sure.'

'His heart rate's really building,' Ayanna warned.

Laura saw him gliding up close. The image fuzzed, then stabilized. It was very hard to see anything now, just shades of dark grey. The lighter outline of Ibu's arm slid across the image, reaching towards one of the globes.

'Going to – make out – holding ste—'

The image vanished completely. For a second there was just some basic telemetry, then that too ended.

'Rojas?' Ayanna said. 'Do you have visual on Ibu?'

'Just. He's close to the globes. I think—'

Ibu's link came back up. It was weak, Laura's u-shadow reported. Voice circuit only.

'. . . fucking thing . . . doesn't . . . can't . . . hell . . . really, really can't . . .'

'What's happening?' Ayanna demanded. 'Ibu?'

'Stuck. It's stuck . . . all round . . . every finger . . .'

'What?' Laura asked. 'Ibu, your visual is down. We can't see anything. What has stuck?'

'. . . Laura, its . . . molecul . . . my hand . . . fucking hand . . . can't move it . . .'

'Crap,' Laura grunted. 'Ibu, is your hand stuck? Is that what's happened?'

'. . . yes . . . yes . . . yes, fucker's got me – Solid but . . . Shit, shit, nothing . . . cutting . . . free it . . .'

Ayanna gave Laura a worried look. 'What's going to happen if he cuts into that thing?'

'I don't bloody know!'

'Ibu, be careful,' Ayanna said.

'. . . gotta be fuc—' Ibu snarled.

'Just get your hand clear,' Laura told him. An auxiliary display showed her the exopod was moving.

'Rojas, what are you doing?' Ayanna asked.

'The man needs some help,' Rojas replied calmly.

'Can you give us a visual feed?' Laura asked. She unfastened the couch's straps and airswam until she was right up against the windscreen. The exopod's strobes were still flashing reassuringly against the pale waves of light slithering through the tree's crystal.

'Exopod's signal's reducing,' Ayanna warned.

'Ibu, can you hear me?' Laura asked.

'. . . isn't . . .' Ibu's distorted voice said.

Ayanna started typing on one of the console keyboards. 'Lost his signal.'

'I see him,' Rojas said. 'Looks like a hand and a knee are touching the globe surface. Definitely sticking to it.'

'Just get him off the damn thing!' Ayanna said. 'What kind of cutters have you got on the exopod?'

'Don't worry; the powerblade can cut through monobonded carbon fibre. This isn't going to be any problem.'

'Can you get close enough to use it?' Laura asked.

'It's detachable . . . if I need to . . . easily done . . .'

'No, no, no,' Laura exclaimed as her u-shadow showed her the exopod's signal strength reducing sharply. She hit the windscreen angrily, and had to hurriedly grab a couch as the blow sent her flailing backwards through the air.

'. . . that's really awesome . . .' Rojas's voice had taken on a reverential tone. '. . . going to go out . . . with him . . .'

Ayanna's body stiffened. 'Rojas? Rojas, don't leave the exopod. Do you copy?'

'. . . closer . . .'

'Retain line of sight! Rojas? Rojas, do you copy?'

Laura pushed herself right up to the windscreen again and stared frantically at the tip of the distortion tree. 'I can't see the strobes! Bollocks, the idiot's gone down into the fold.' The communication icon in her exovision showed her the exopod's signal fading to zero. It ended.

'What's really awesome?' Joey's mental voice asked. 'What was he talking about? Did he mean Ibu was cutting himself free?'

Laura gave Ayanna a guilty look, then glanced back at Joey. 'I don't know. Yes. Yes, that must be what he meant. We—' The cabin lights flickered, then dimmed before coming back up to full strength.

'These dropouts are killing our systems,' Ayanna snapped. 'The processors are rebooting each time, then they get hit by another surge before they've completed. It's not helping.'

'Order the Mk16bs back to the tip of the tree,' Laura said. 'We need to see what's happening out there.'

'Right,' Ayanna gave a little nod, as if she was dazed. 'Yes. Good.'

Laura gripped the rim of the console with one hand, and flicked several switches. A hologram projector slid out of the cabin ceiling above her couch. It started to show a composite picture from the drone flock. They were moving now, converging on the tip of the tree.

'Lost seven of them. Fifteen more showing functionality reduction,' Ayanna said.

'No kidding,' Laura muttered. She couldn't stop thinking about Rojas. *Really wonderful.* What did he mean? Had he seen something?

'How long?' Joey asked.

'Twenty minutes,' Ayanna said. 'The flock is mapping the other end of the tree.'

Laura wanted to shout loud and hard – why hadn't they left some drones close to the exopod? Surely that was procedure? But then, this level of communication failure was inconceivable in the Commonwealth. It was wrong-footing everyone. Blaming Ayanna wouldn't solve anything.

For every few hundred metres the flock slid along the tree, they would lose another. Sometimes two or three would fail within seconds of each other. There was no pattern.

'There won't be one left by the time they reach the exopod,' Ayanna grumbled.

Laura ignored her. Shuttle Fourteen was also suffering an increased number of glitches. The network was having trouble maintaining its integrity, so many subsystems were dropping out. She watched in dismay as several primary flight systems went off line – forward reaction-control thrusters, one of the fusion tubes, three of the regrav drives, main passenger cabin and environmental systems.

'Dammit,' Laura grunted when the passenger cabin systems went down. 'We can't afford to lose environmental.'

'There's enough oxygen on board for three of us,' Joey said.

'To do what?' Laura snapped. 'And there's going to be five flying down to that planet.'

'Calm down,' Ayanna said. 'Worst-case scenario: we can wear pressure suits.'

'If they work,' Laura said, hating herself for letting her anxiety show. But . . . The prospect of asphyxiation was firing her imagination into overdrive. Seeing herself in a pressure suit with every red light flashing, clawing feebly at the windscreen just as Fourteen approached the planet, so near . . .

'Flock's approaching the exopod,' Ayanna said in a level voice.

Laura tried to clear her mind and focus on the hologram which was showing the imagery from the flock. There were only eighty-seven of the little drones left now. They had rearranged themselves back into their ring formation, gliding over the tapering end of the distortion tree. The folds meandered in sharp curves, merging and becoming shallower as they neared the tip. Long moiré phantoms slithered about erratically inside the crystal, though even their intensity was reducing. Large sections would remain dark for some time between visitations.

'There!' Ayanna said. The exopod was floating twenty metres from the side of a narrow curving valley just over a hundred metres from the tip. Dark globes were sprouting from the crystal all around it.

Laura couldn't see Ibu anywhere. She ordered the image to rotate, checking the other clefts in the crystal around the tip. They were all covered in the dark globes, ranging from acorn size up to the full three metres in diameter. Ibu wasn't in any of them, either.

'The flock is relaying a signal from the exopod,' Ayanna reported, 'but I'm not getting any reply from Rojas.'

'What about their suit transponders?' Laura asked.

Ayanna pursed her lips and shook her head.

'Focus on the exopod, please,' Joey said.

Ayanna's hands flicked several toggles, and the image jumped up through magnification factors until it was centred on the exopod.

'Hatch is open,' Joey said. 'Can you get some drones closer?'

Ayanna started steering a couple of the Mk16bs over to the exopod.

'As close as I can get,' she announced eventually.

The hologram was showing the pod in high resolution. It hung above the forward cabin's couches like a chunk of collective guilt. They could all look in through the open hatchway and see the coloured graphics flashing across the display panels inside. Web straps floated lazily, their buckles weaving about through the empty space as if they were chrome snake heads.

'He's not in there,' Laura whispered. It felt as if her space sickness was returning; certainly she was light headed. Her skin was chilling down rapidly.

'Where the fuck is he?' Joey asked.

'The flock would see the suits if they were anywhere within fifty kilometres,' Ayanna said.

'You know where they are,' Laura said, forcing herself to say it. 'Inside.'

'Inside what?' Joey said. 'Inside the tree or inside the globes? Are they like an airlock?'

'We haven't picked up any cavity inside the crystal structure,' Ayanna said.

'Scan the globes,' Laura told Ayanna. 'I don't care if you have to smash the drones into those bastards and crack them open. We've got to find them.'

'Right,' Ayanna nodded abruptly, and set about redirecting the flock.

The wrinkled surface of the globe was some kind of carbon, but the interior was impervious to any scan. Ayanna had eight drones poised in a bracelet formation around one of them, but their sensor radiation hit the surface and got no further.

Laura took control of a drone and sent it racing at the globe. The rest of the flock showed them a perfectly clear image of it striking – and rebounding, spinning away erratically.

Refusing to give up, Laura took control of another, over-rode the tiny ion drive's safety limiters, and accelerated it from five hundred metres' distance. It was travelling at four metres per second when it struck. The impact killed half its systems, but the globe didn't even have a scratch.

'Zero effect,' Ayanna said levelly; there was an implication of censure in the tone.

Laura flew a third probe two kilometres out from the tree, then accelerated it in. This one reached twenty-eight metres per second when it hit a globe. Its casing shattered and the fragments went tumbling off into space. The globe was unscathed by the impact.

'What the hell are they made of?' she demanded. 'They must open somehow, like a clam shell. Ibu and Rojas must have been taken inside.'

'Laura, there is no inside,' Ayanna said.

'Bollocks to this! The drone flock sensors aren't good enough. They're inside! Where the hell else can they be?'

'I don't know.'

'I'm suiting up. I'm going to take the other exopod over there, and I'm going to cut—'

'No,' Ayanna didn't speak loudly, but it was definite, and her thoughts made it very clear she meant it. 'You're not taking the exopod anywhere. Not until we know what happened to them and have some kind of recovery plan.'

'You heard Rojas,' Laura said heatedly. 'The exopods have powerblades that can cut the globes open.'

'Then why didn't he do that? Laura, just stop and think. Please! We're in Voidspace, which is weird enough; the tree is an alien mechanism operating at a molecular and quantum level we cannot comprehend, and two of our people have vanished and we don't know how or where. Charging over there all angry isn't going to resolve anything, and it certainly won't help Ibu and Rojas. We need information, a *lot* more information.'

'She's right,' Joey said. 'Rojas is smart and experienced, and he knows exploration mission protocol better than we do. And now he's just as gone as Ibu.'

Laura knew they were right, but . . . 'Ah, bollocks,' she said. Admitting she was wrong, behaving like some hothead young first life, was painful. She hadn't acted on wild impulse for centuries. 'I'm not thinking straight. Sorry. Must be the tank yank.'

'No,' Joey said. 'The Void is getting to all of us. It's not natural.'

'We're going to get them back,' Ayanna said earnestly. 'We just have to figure out how.'

'I don't think this is entirely a physical problem,' Joey said. 'Remember, Ibu said they were amazing. Where did that come from? He'd just finished telling us he couldn't use his ESP to see inside the globes. What else, what new piece of information, could make him say that? He's as smart and as rational as the rest of us. He's not going to blurt that out without a reason. Same goes for Rojas.'

'That's really awesome,' Laura said, pensively. 'That's what Rojas said. And you're right; it's a complete disconnect from everything that was happening. A colleague stuck to an alien arte- fact – all he'd be thinking about was what to do, what procedure to follow.'

'Something got inside their heads,' Ayanna said. And once more the terror was leaking out of her own mind. 'It pulled them in.'

'Bee to pollen,' Joey said. 'Shark to blood.'

'The distortion tree is sentient,' Laura said. There was no reason to doubt the notion of mental compulsion; she could remember when narcomemes emerged into the gaiafield back in 3025. The first ones were simple product placements, amplifying the pleasure effect of various beers and aerosols. Modifying the memories available in the gaiafield to produce enhanced enjoy- ment was a trend that lasted for several years, almost wrecking the fledgling gaiafield concept entirely, until counter-routine filters were developed for the confluence nests. Having experienced those, Laura could well believe in more forceful variants of telep- athy working in the Void.

'Yes,' Joey agreed.

As one, they looked through the windscreen at the massive bulk of glowing crystal.

'So how do we get it to let them go?' Laura asked.

'First, we need to work out why it wants them,' Joey said.

'But we don't even know what it is. What other drones have we got? There must be some kind of sensor we can use.'

'The sample modules would be best,' she said cautiously. 'They were giving a good picture of the interior where Ibu placed them.'

'But they have to be applied by hand,' Joey retorted. 'It has to be a drone.'

'Half of them are designed for planetary exploration,' Ayanna said. 'Surface landers, atmospheric researchers. There's not much more we can send out there.'

Laura thought for a moment. 'Do any of the surface landers have drills? Something that cuts through rock to lift core samples?'

'Yes. The Viking Mk353. It was designed for regolith coring down to a hundred metres.'

'Send it.'

Half of Fourteen's backup power systems failed while the Viking Mk353 flew over to the distortion tree. Ayanna and Laura turned off all the systems in the main passenger cabin to cut power consumption. Six of the fans in the forward cabin's environmental systems also packed up. That was more worrying. The air was still breathable, but the gentle rush of air coming from the vents was severely reduced.

Laura went down to the payload bay's equipment lockers and returned with two portable atmosphere filters. The thick metre-long cylinders were completely independent, with a grille on each end. One end sucked in air, which was scrubbed and filtered and blown out of the other end. She strapped them onto a couple of couches. She tested them, and switched them off again.

She did her best not to stare at Joey when she was sorting out the portable filters. He was still strapped onto his couch. But the shakes on his hands were moving down his arms, causing both limbs to twitch.

'Keep going,' his mental voice told her. 'I can manage.'

'You sure?'

'Yes. I'm keeping busy. The shuttle's external sensors are still working – some of them, anyway. I'm still trying to see if I can spot the ships down on the surface. There's certainly no evidence of a crash so far.'

'That's good.' She caught the unease in his thought. By now she had enough experience to know it was powered by something more than just his physical deterioration. 'What is it?'

He shook his head – a sharp juddering motion. 'There's something wrong.'

'Wrong?'

'Yes. I'm looking and looking at the planet, and I know there's something wrong with what I'm seeing, but I don't know what.'

'What kind of thing?' she asked cautiously.

A spasm rippled over his twisted-up features. 'I don't know. I'm looking right at it. I know I am. But I can't see it.'

'Can I help? Do you want me to review the images with you?'

'No. Thanks. I'll find it.'

'Okay.' There was a lot she wanted to say about how his illness might be affecting his thoughts. Instead, she gave him a sympathetic smile and pushed off to glide down the aisle.

'How's the Viking's signal?' she asked, when she rejoined Ayanna up at the front of the cabin.

'Not bad.'

A display screen on the console was showing the Viking approaching the tip of the tree. The exopod's strobes were flashing away in the centre of the picture.

Laura watched the lander approach the shallow fold where Ibu and Rojas had vanished. Ayanna was remote flying it competently, bringing it to rest a hundred metres from the exopod.

'I was thinking,' Ayanna said. 'If they are inside those globes somehow, we don't know which ones. So I'm going to start drilling one of the small ones, something they couldn't possibly be held in.'

'Sure,' Laura said. 'Good idea.' She hadn't been thinking quite along those lines. Some part of her was expecting to use the drill to free their missing team members – even if exactly how eluded her.

The Viking descended to hover less than a metre above a globe that measured a metre ten in diameter. The little onboard array held it in place with small bursts from its ion thrusters and deployed the drill.

'We're going to have trouble countering the torque,' Laura said. 'There's not much fuel on board. The Viking wasn't designed for space operations, just getting through the atmosphere intact and landing.'

'I know,' Ayanna said.

The ion thrusters flared and the Viking began to rotate around its axis. The drill spun up. Powerful landing thrusters flared briefly, pushing the Viking hard towards the globe. The picture shook as the drill touched the upper surface of the globe. Then it turned to smears as the Viking began to spin. Thrusters fired again, trying to compensate. Now the image was of juddering smears.

'What the—' Ayanna exclaimed.

The Viking was suddenly shooting off, away from the tree, tumbling end over end.

Laura stared at the hologram which was showing the combined imagery from the Mk16b drones. 'Oh my, will you look at that?' The Viking's drill must have succeeded in penetrating the small globe. It was squirting out a pale white liquid, a thin fountain that was over three metres high before it started to break apart into a shower of globules that kept on going, oscillating wildly as they sprayed out into the vacuum.

'Did the Viking get any?' Laura demanded as Ayanna tried to regain control of the tumbling lander, slowing the gyrations and stabilizing the trajectory.

'What?'

'The samplers in the drill head? Did any of that stuff touch them before the pressure blew it off?'

'I think so. Hang on.'

The pale fountain was slowing, shrinking. Within seconds it was just a tiny runnel of syrupy fluid trickling out of the puncture hole. A thin fog swirled gently around it as it began to vacuum boil.

'If all the globes are full of liquid, then Ibu and Rojas can't be inside them,' Joey said.

Laura glared at the globe and its bubbling wound. 'Then where the hell are they?'

'Same place as the *Vermillion* and the Mk24s.'

'You're not helping.'

'I've got the Viking stable,' Ayanna said. 'The drill samplers did get something.'

They both turned to watch the display screen on the console bring up the preliminary spectral analysis.

'Hydrocarbons,' Laura read the raw data, the routines in her macrocellular clusters running analysis. 'Water. Sugars. What's that? Looks like a protein structure.'

'The fluid's organic,' Ayanna said in shock. 'The globes are alive.'

The cabin lighting went off, to be replaced by the low blue-tinged glow of the emergency lighting. Somewhere in the shuttle a fire alarm was shrieking.

*

It had taken a power screwdriver from the equipment locker to prise the panel off the passenger cabin bulkhead. By the time they did that, the composite panel was blackening and starting to blister. There were no flames inside, but the power cell was glowing. Spraying it with extinguisher gel wasn't the answer.

Laura yanked one of the emergency suits out of its overhead wallet and jammed her arm into the sleeve. The glove had just enough insulation. With Ayanna cutting through the power cell's surrounding cables and mountings, she tugged it out and lumbered her way down to the payload bay. The whole suit went into the airlock, wrapped around the now-sizzling power cell. She slapped the emergency evacuation button. And the smouldering mess went flying off into space when the outer hatch peeled open.

'Got another one,' Ayanna was calling from the passenger cabin above the multiple alarm sirens.

Laura started opening lockers, hunting for some decent tools.

Her hand was blistered where the power cell's runaway heat had soaked through the suit glove's insulation. She hauled herself back to the passenger cabin, lugging a utility belt.

In the end they had to remove four of the shorted-out power cells and physically inspect the rest. There were seventeen in the shuttle.

'Just brilliant,' a shaking Ayanna said when they checked behind the last panel. 'There have been so many Void glitches they finally induced a genuine problem.'

Laura's u-shadow managed to link to the power cells' management processor. 'Power surge broke the cut-offs here, but they fused in safe mode. We need to replace the main circuits if we want to enable the systems it supplies.'

Ayanna gave the passenger cabin a disgusted look. The blueish emergency lighting was somehow cooling, and the panels floated about chaotically, along with fragments and broken cabling they'd cut free. One of the portable atmosphere filters they'd brought in to deal with the fumes was creating a steady breeze, which stirred all the fragments. They were constantly flicking them away from their eyes. 'We don't have time to deal with this crap,' she said. 'It's only the backups which have failed, not the main fusion tubes. And there are still a whole load of power cells left. It was just the ones in here that absorbed the surge.'

Laura followed her gaze round the shambolic cabin. There was still a tang of ozone and burnt plastic in the air. It had taken them over three hours to deal with all the power cells and their associated ancillary systems, which had to be disconnected as well. There wasn't much to show for all that work, and they hadn't even begun repairs. 'You're right,' she admitted.

Joey was in the service compartment, staring at a panel they'd opened on the ceiling to expose an environment system unit which had suffered in the power surge, shutting down to protect itself. His arms and legs were now twitching constantly, preventing him from doing any precise work. But Laura watched in fascination as wires and electronic modules moved obediently as he manipulated them with telekinesis. Even screws unwound themselves under his control and hovered in a neat three-dimensional stack to one side.

'Cool,' she said.

'Thank you.' His mental tone was one of relief. 'I do have a use after all.'

'You've had a use right from the start.'

'Yeah, right.'

'Come on, you're not some first-life sympathy junkie. All anybody does in this age is think. We don't measure people by their physical ability any more.'

Joey emitted a low grunt of disparagement. 'That might just be about to change once we reach the surface. No bots down there; it'll be back to physical labour for us.'

She arched an eyebrow coyly. 'A Brandt doing manual work? We're doomed, then.'

He let out a guttural laugh and focused on the complex innards of the unit he'd exposed.

Laura airswam into the forward cabin and took a look at all the display screens and holograph projections. The drone flock was still surrounding the tip of the tree, though it was down to sixty-three operational units now. There was no sign of Ibu or Rojas, no signal from their suits. The exopod remained in place, holding station where Rojas had left it. And her burnt hand hurt like hell.

'Ouch! Bollocks.' Laura pushed stray fronds of hair back inside her padded helmet with her good hand. Like a child, she'd imagined that everything would have come right while she was away giving her attention to the shuttle's screwed-up power systems.

'Take a rest,' Ayanna said. 'You're exhausted.'

'So are you.'

'Grouchy, too.'

'I'm . . . Ah, crap.'

'It's okay. I'll wake you in a few hours. I need sleep, too; you're right.'

'We have to do something.'

'The shuttle's falling apart. We're too strung-out to think

62

objectively. Nothing out here makes any sense. We don't have enough data. You want me to go on?'

'No.'

'Get something to eat. Spray some painkiller on that hand. Go to sleep. Trust me, I won't let you have long.'

'Right.' Laura nodded in defeat. She drifted to the rear of the cabin where they'd stowed thermal bags of food. 'You know what worries me more?'

'More than Ibu and Rojas? You're kidding.'

'I guess they're a part of the worry.'

'Go on.'

'Where everyone goes.' She opened a medic kit on the bulkhead above the thermal bags. 'I get that the tree snatched Ibu and Rojas, or zapped them, or teleported them back outside the Void or something. But the *Vermillion*, too? Everybody vanishes apart from us. Why? What's different about us three?'

'Ask a Skylord. They'll tell you it's because we're not fulfilled.'

'Screw the Skylords. There's got to be some reason.'

'Eat. Sleep. Once we've all recovered from the tank yank, we'll have some functioning neurons and know what to do.'

'Sure.' Laura sprayed some salve on her red-raw hand, wincing at all the little blisters, then peeled the wrapper off a taco – meals in freefall were always tacos or something similar; bread produced crumbs that messed with the filters and jammed in bad places. 'How long are we going to give them?'

'We'll find them. Don't worry.'

'You said it. The shuttle's screwed. If we're going to help them, we need the *Vermillion*. Crap, I hope they got down okay.'

'Once we're outside the Forest, we'll make contact again.'

'Joey couldn't spot them on the surface.'

'Okay, either you go to sleep, or I grab an aerosol from that medic kit and put you under.'

'All right. All right.' Laura settled on a couch and fastened the straps – not too tight. It was pointless because she knew she couldn't sleep. Her hand throbbed. She chewed on the taco again, tasting nothing. She was about to start asking what Ayanna thought about using the Viking drill on the tree itself, when she fell asleep.

*

Something shook Laura roughly. For a confused moment she thought she was being tank yanked again; the whole thing was like a fading dream that was just too real.

'Wake up,' Ayanna was saying, her face centimetres away. Behind the face, thoughts shone with delight and relief – a lot of relief. 'Wake up. They're back. They're coming back.'

'What?' Laura asked sluggishly. 'Who?'

'Rojas and Ibu. The exopod is coming back.'

'Huh?' She tried to sit up. The couch straps dug in, and she fumbled round to release them. 'How?'

'I don't know,' Ayanna said, her expression half fearful. 'We've lost most of the Mk16bs now. I noticed it was moving a minute ago.'

'Hell's teeth. What did they say?'

'There's no contact. All I know is the exopod's coming, and it's not the greatest bit of flying I've ever seen.'

Laura felt a little burst of alarm. 'No contact? Is the signal down again?'

'No. The exopod is transmitting. They're just not saying anything. Hell, that's no surprise. Our systems have taken a real beating from the Void.'

Laura tried to get her breathing under control. She looked round the forward cabin. There were a lot of red symbols shining on the console. Five of the blue emergency lighting strips were dark. And she was sure it was several degrees colder. 'What's their ETA?' As she said it, she noticed her exovision time display. Ten hours! She'd been asleep for ten hours. 'Why didn't you wake me?'

Ayanna gave her a sheepish glance. 'I fell asleep myself. Only woke up an hour ago.'

Laura winced as she finished releasing the last strap with her burnt hand. The skin was still red, but the salve had turned the blisters hard. For one silly moment she wondered if the Void had glitched the spray's chemical structure, rendering the salve useless – or worse.

Several screens on the console were running feeds from Shuttle Fourteen's external cameras. They all showed her the exopod gliding sedately towards them.

She anchored herself on the front couch and stared through the windscreen. Sure enough, the exopod was close enough to show as a small speck against the glowing crystal, its strobes still flashing away faithfully. 'It's them,' she said in amazement.

'I told you,' Ayanna said happily. 'They're back.'

'Where the hell were they?'

'They had to be inside the distortion tree,' Joey said.

'Right.' Laura hadn't taken her eyes off the exopod. Her u-shadow had a narrow link to the shuttle's faltering network, which was monitoring the exopod's signal. Only the basic telemetry was coming in. 'Have any of the Mk24s reappeared?'

'No,' Ayanna said.

'I just don't get any of this. Why—?'

'Just ask them,' Joey said. For a moment he managed to force his mouth into a smile.

The three of them went back through the service compartment. Joey lagged behind, his spasming limbs making it difficult for him to manoeuvre as easily as the others. Laura resisted the urge to offer him any help. He was way too proud for that.

Once they were in the EVA hangar her u-shadow lost the link to Fourteen's network. She grabbed the handholds in front of a backup console on the bulkhead and activated its manual functions. Two screens slid out, showing her that the exopod was a lot closer.

'I'm opening the outer door,' she said.

'Wait,' Joey's mental voice urged her as he wriggled his way through the hatch. 'We don't actually know what's inside the exopod.'

'You've got to be kidding,' Laura said. 'What do you think's inside? A Prime motile?' Even as she said it, her secondary routines pulled an image file from her storage lacuna, showing her the eggs of a Prime. They were nothing like the globes on the distortion tree. *Bollocks, I'm getting paranoid*, she thought.

'I don't know. And that's the thing, isn't it? Why haven't they ordered the airlock door to open?'

'With the state of our communications? Come on!' she appealed to Ayanna.

'I'd be happier knowing,' Ayanna said awkwardly.

'And how are we going to do that?'

'Wait until it's on the docking cradle, but don't open the airlock,' Joey said. 'The umbilical will plug in and we'll have a decent link.'

'Well?' Laura asked Ayanna.

'Seems reasonable.'

Laura turned back to the console, and keyed in the cradle recovery sequence. She felt a tiny vibration run through Fourteen's structure. On the screen, long electromuscle arms were pushing the exopod's cradle out from the rear of the shuttle.

'What the hell is that?' Joey's mental voice was twinned with a great deal of concern.

Laura peered at the screen showing the approaching exopod. Its cluster of electromuscle tentacles were curled protectively round one of the dark globes from the distortion tree. 'They can't be serious,' she exclaimed. 'How did they detach it?'

'Are you going to let them in carrying that thing?' Joey asked.

Ayanna shot Laura a glance, her thoughts emanating all kinds of uncertainty. 'They wouldn't bring anything harmful into the shuttle. They know the protocols.'

'If it's them,' Joey said. 'If they haven't been brainwashed. We don't know what we're dealing with!'

'What do you think?' Ayanna asked.

'I think Joey may have a point,' Laura said reluctantly. Her delight at seeing the exopod return was dwindling fast. Carrying the alien globe back to Fourteen was unusual, at the very least. 'Let them dock on the cradle, but keep the airlock closed until we establish just what's going on.'

'Right,' Ayanna said. 'Good call.'

It took several minutes for the pilot to manoeuvre the exopod over the cradle. Laura made no comment about that. Rojas had certainly seemed more competent when the little craft was flying out to the distortion tree.

'Are they eggs?' Joey asked as they watched the exopod wobble about unsteadily.

'We know they contain organic matter,' Laura said slowly, wishing she'd thought more about the problem before. 'And we've seen a batch flying down to the planet. Logically they're eggs or seeds, or some kind of biological agent.'

'Agent?'

'They come from the trees, which are completely different objects. Shape, nature, material – none of it's the same. So . . . I'd say the trees manufacture the globes molecule by molecule. And on this scale, that probably means it's a bioforming system. These trees arrive at a planet in a new star system and start converting it to the kind of environment their creators live in.'

'That works for me,' Ayanna said.

'So what are the Skylords?' Joey asked.

'Oh, bollocks to you, Joey,' Laura snapped at him. 'They're the tugboats? I don't know!'

'Sorry.'

'Let's just keep it calm, shall we?' Ayanna said.

Laura made an effort to damp her temper down. The screen was showing her the cradle arms reaching out and clamping onto the base of the exopod. One of them carried the data umbilical.

Laura keyed in a series of instructions. The console's second screen played the feed from the exopod's internal camera. Laura let out a small gasp of relief. Behind her, Ayanna made an almost identical sound.

The camera was set near the top of the exopod's cabin. It looked down on Rojas and Ibu suspended in the webs. Both of them were in their suits – without helmets.

'Welcome back, guys,' she said inanely.

They both looked up at the camera. Ibu grinned weakly. It looked to be a big effort on his part.

'Good to hear your voice,' he said croakily.

'This is Ayanna. What happened? Where have you been?'

'We've been inside.'

'Inside what?' Laura said. 'The tree is solid.'

'No, it's not,' Ibu said. 'There's all kinds of chambers in there.'

'Where? The drone sensors showed us a solid structure. How did you get in? You were stuck to that globe when the links went down.'

'There are entrances along the bottom of the folds. The crystal just morphs like our malmetal and plyplastic.'

'Can you let us in now, please?' Rojas said. His voice croaked like Ibu's. It was as if both of them had caught laryngitis.

'Ask him about the globe,' Joey's mental voice urged.

'Rojas,' Ayanna said, 'why have you brought one of the globes back?'

Rojas looked away from the camera, studying the displays on the bulkhead in front of him. 'Analysis.'

'What?'

'Analysis.'

'Hang on. Wait,' Laura said. 'What have you been doing inside the tree? How did you get in and out? Why were you in there so long? You've been out of contact the whole time. You know that's against every protocol ever written.'

'Sorry about that,' Ibu said. 'It's fascinating in there. You'll have to come in, Laura.'

'What's happened to your voice?' Ayanna asked. 'Have you been exposed to the alien environment?'

'No.'

'Then what—'

'Nothing; we're fine. The exopod's systems are glitching. That's the problem.'

'What's in the tree?' Laura asked, trying to keep her concern from creeping into her voice.

'Nothing. We think the cavities are conduits of some kind. We'll go over the recordings when we're back inside.'

'What was wonderful?' Joey asked. 'Ibu said the globes were wonderful, Rojas said they were awesome. 'Why?'

'Ibu,' Ayanna said, 'what was awesome about the globe you got stuck on?'

'What?'

'We need to come in,' Rojas said.

'You said it was wonderful. What did you mean?'

'This whole place is wonderful, that's all.'

'Please open the EVA hangar door,' Rojas said. 'We need to get the exopod inside.'

'Rojas, I can't let you bring that globe into Fourteen,' Ayanna said. 'Please release it.'

'We need to examine it,' Rojas said. He still wasn't looking up at the camera any more. His fingers were moving fast across the keypads in front of him.

'Yes, we will, but after we've established it's safe. You know the protocol.'

'Open the door.'

'Jettison the globe,' Laura said firmly. 'It won't go anywhere. We can run tests on it out there.'

A set of graphics on the console turned from amber to blue. The EVA hangar lights flickered. Laura could feel a slight vibration through the handholds.

'Son of a bitch!' Ayanna exclaimed. 'He's overridden the airlock. It's opening.'

'Bollocks,' Laura grunted.

They all turned to face the airlock's inner door, just past the remaining exopod. Caution lights were shining purple.

'What do we do?' Laura asked.

'Are there any weapons on board?' Joey asked.

Ayanna gave him a startled glance. 'Crap. There's probably something in the emergency landing pack.'

'It won't come to that,' Laura said, but it was more like a mantra than anything she believed. Nobody in this era needed weapons; biononics could be configured into quite aggressive energy functions if anyone was seriously threatened.

69

'You wouldn't want to mess with some of the engineering tools,' Joey said.

'Are they real?' Laura asked, mostly to herself. The screen showed her that the docking cradle had finished pulling the exopod inside the EVA hangar airlock. 'Is that Ibu and Rojas?'

'What the hell else can they be?' Ayanna asked. 'Oh, fuck, what is happening?' Her mental shielding was cracking open, flooding the EVA hangar with raw fright.

Laura found herself in the centre of swirling shadows. They were growing fangs and teeth, turning from phantom grey spectres to solid black figures. Thousands of people shrieking somewhere far away were growing closer. She raised her hands in reflex to ward them off, worried that perhaps Ayanna's telekinesis would give substance to her imagination. 'Ayanna! For fuck's sake get a grip.'

'I don't want them in the shuttle,' Ayanna wailed.

'Nobody does! We can't stop the bastards, now. We'll just have to manage them when they do get in.'

Ayanna looked just as panicked as before, but the outpouring of emotion reduced slightly.

Joey spun round to face the other way. 'Can we lock the hatch to the silo compartment?'

'If we can lock it, Rojas can sure as shit unlock it,' Laura said.

'Then we break it,' Joey said. 'Use telekinesis, wreck the circuits behind the bulkhead.'

Laura glanced at the hatchway herself. It was incredibly tempting. The lights above the exopod airlock turned from purple to green. The malmetal door started to peel open.

'Oh bollocks,' Laura muttered. The hatchway to the silo compartment was barely four metres away. She was sure she could get through in a couple of seconds if she powerdived for it – assuming she aimed right, no guarantee of that given her free-fall skill level. Her ESP started to pry around the bulkhead, reducing it to a translucent blue sheet in her mind. It was threaded with dozens of cable conduits. *Which ones control the hatch?*

The docking cradle trundled into the EVA hangar and placed the exopod on its lockdown clamps. All Laura could do was stare at the alien globe the electromuscle tentacles were clutching. Her ESP revealed nothing; it was a blank zone inside her perceptive field. And yet . . . She smiled, knowing now that there was no reason to worry. Whatever it contained was absorbing Ayanna's malicious phantoms. A temperate sense of relief filled the EVA hangar. And her heart was racing away inside her chest.

'Fight it!' Joey's mental voice told her, a jarring discord to the tranquillity Laura was feeling.

'Oh no!' Laura groaned. 'No no no!' Her own dread at the realization of what was happening was enough to damp down the emotional balm the alien globe was giving off. She saw Ayanna had started to move towards the globe, and grabbed her arm. 'Stop! Ayanna, for crap's sake! It's like a narcomeme.'

Ayanna's head twisted back to stare at Laura, and now she really looked frightened.

'Let's get out of here,' Joey said.

Laura swung round on the handholds, and prepared to push off against the bulkhead. She heard the exopod's hatch open. There was a brief hiss of pressure equalization. And even though she knew it was stupid, she paused to glance at what was coming out.

Ibu slid out smoothly, catching hold of a handhold on the EVA hangar's wall. 'What's happening?' he asked, and his voice was still weird, as if there was fluid in his throat.

'You tell me,' she barked. 'What is that thing?'

'Who knows? We brought it here to study.' He was bending his knees, swinging round slightly so his feet were pressed against the exopod's hull.

Ready to pounce, Laura thought.

Rojas glided easily out of the hatch.

'Get out of here!' Joey's mental voice shouted. He began scrambling along the bulkhead, hauling himself towards the hatch into the silo compartment. Shaking arms made him miss the second handhold.

Ibu kicked off, flashing along the middle of the EVA hangar like a human missile. Rojas followed.

Laura screamed and jumped for the hatch. Her foot caught Joey's shoulder and the collision flicked her sideways. She spun and slapped at the bulkhead, righting her trajectory. Ayanna was right beside her.

Rojas caught Joey's ankle. The squeal that came through Joey's spasming throat was like a pig grunting. Then Rojas was clambering along the hyperspace theorist as if the two were caught in some weird dance move. It quickly turned into a furious wrestling match as they squirmed against each other.

Again, Laura hesitated. Her hand grasped the hatch rim. Ibu was close, reaching forwards. And Ayanna was level with her. 'Go!' Laura yelped. Ayanna wriggled through the hatchway with the agility of an eel.

Joey's cries of dread were echoing round the hangar. Ibu's hand clamped round Laura's shin. She squealed, first at the shock, then the yell grew wilder as she realized just how tight and painful his grip was. Stronger than any normal human. 'What the—'

His other hand clamped round her right ankle. She tried to pull herself through the hatch into the silo compartment, but she couldn't move. Now Ibu began to pull her the other way. She felt her arms starting to straighten out as his unnatural strength overpowered her, tugging her back. Various ancient unarmed combat routines began to unfold from her storage lacuna, slipping into the macrocellular clusters. But Laura didn't wait; she instinctively lashed out with her free foot, catching Ibu on the side of his head.

It had all the impact of hitting him with a feather.

He snapped her ankle. She heard the bone break with a terrible *crack*, and her leg went numb for a glorious instant. Then the incredible pain fired into her brain. Secondary routines damped down the impulse, reducing it to a manageable level. But Ibu slowly and deliberately rotated her foot. The fractured bone made a fearsome grating sound. Her macrocellular clusters cut the nerve impulses altogether.

Laura felt sick. But manic strength allowed her to cling on to the hatchway. Through watering eyes she looked back at Ibu, whose face was impassive. He was simply waiting for her to let go, so he could—

What?

Laura couldn't understand any of this. Rojas had now subdued a frantic Joey, putting him in some kind of submission lock.

Ibu bent her ankle again. Laura knew she only had seconds before she lost her grip and was drawn back. Then Ayanna was back in the hatch, her telekinesis jabbing at Ibu's face.

Now he grimaced, his own attention diverted, a counter telekinesis parrying her attack. But he didn't let go of Laura.

Hanging on grimly to the hatch rim, Laura directed her telekinesis to her breast pocket. The Swiss army knife wriggled free, and she flicked the longest blade out. It rotated in mid-air to point at Ibu. Laura shoved it forwards with all the power she had.

The blade sliced down Ibu's cheek and stabbed into the gap between his suit's helmet ring and his neck. He froze. Ayanna gasped.

Laura's ESP perceived the blade penetrate a good six or seven centimetres into his flesh just behind the clavicle bone. A dark blue liquid began to pour out along the side of his neck. For one confused moment, she thought her knife had cut through some kind of coolant tube in the suit. Then she finally acknowledged it was blood – or whatever the Ibu-copy used for circulatory fluid.

With a yell, she twisted the blade, pouring all her savagery and determination into the thought.

The Ibu-copy snarled as the knife turned, scraping against his clavicle. Laura jerked her ruined foot free of his grasp and tugged herself up through the hatch, with Ayanna helping heave her along. The pair of them tumbled into the silo compartment. Laura banged into one of the metal silo tubes, rebounded, and grabbed at the first handhold she could see, steadying herself. 'Move!' she bawled. And reached for another handhold.

Ayanna raced along the other side of the compartment, heading for the equipment lockers.

The Ibu-copy squirmed through the hatch, his collar still spitting out blue globules.

Laura was barely thinking. Survival instinct had cut in. She just had to get away. At the back of her gibbering mind was the notion of her and Ayanna barricading themselves inside the forward cabin. Nothing else mattered apart from getting some kind of secure reassuringly physical barrier between herself and the alien *things*.

She swept past the lockers and dived up the ladder to the service compartment, slapping the rungs as she went, adding speed and stability to her flight. For once she performed the manoeuvre with a decent amount of agility. Ayanna was right behind her.

A hysterical scream tore through the shuttle.

Laura turned in fright, and shock locked every muscle. Ayanna was halfway along the ladder. The Ibu-copy had caught up with her. One hand gripped her thigh, allowing him to bite her calf. Not some angry streetfight snapping of jaws. He had sunk his teeth in, penetrating the shipsuit fabric, and closed his jaw around the calf muscle. As Laura watched, his head wrenched back so he tore out a chunk of Ayanna's flesh. He began chewing it.

Ayanna wailed in helpless dread. Blood was pumping fast out of her ragged wound, scarlet globules forming a sickly galaxy around her leg. The Ibu-thing lowered his head again and took another bite.

Laura threw up.

The Rojas-copy arrived at the ladder. He swarmed over Ayanna, opening his jaw wide. His strength tugged her arm away from the ladder, and forced her fingers into his mouth.

Ayanna's screaming was deafening, blotting out the sound of her knuckles breaking as they were bitten through. Her mental voice was an incoherent yell of pain and utter horror. It was like an assault on Laura's senses, battering her as violently as any physical blow. Yet still the survival instinct was strong enough to goad her into action. She grabbed her way along the service compartment floor and into the forward cabin, her own piteous wailing like a soprano whistle, tears wrecking her vision. Her hand thumped down on the hatch button. The malmetal closed.

ESP showed her a dozen conduits and power lines around the hatch. Her telekinesis reached out and clawed at every one of them, shredding the insulation and the conductors, ripping them apart. The lights went out. Alarms sounded as short circuits blew safety cutoffs. The background whining of several fans faded to silence. Red lights flared on the console.

Laura pushed herself away from the hatch. Ayanna's screams had stopped before it was closed. Something hit the other side of the hatch. Another strike. Another and another. Then silence.

She curled up into a foetal ball and began sobbing.

*

It was a feeling that took a long time to register. Not a compulsion, but a sensation akin to recognizing a smell.

Laura blinked in confusion. It was her gaiamotes gently apprising her that someone was wanting to talk to her. Joey – that was the mental scent.

Very cautiously, Laura opened up the gaiamotes' sensitivity.

'Laura?'

'Joey?'

'Yes.'

'I don't know if it's really you. They . . . Oh, bollocks. This can't be happening. They ate her, Joey. They ate her! And I left her behind.' The shame was so overwhelming, she wanted to body-loss – re-life herself free of all this. *Vermillion* would break out of the Void somehow, and everyone left behind would be re-lifed using memories in the starship's secure store. Her life would go on without any memory of Shuttle Fourteen or the Forest. No knowledge of what Ayanna had endured.

'It's me, I swear it.' The surge of emotion that slipped through the gaiafield connection from him was profound, and utterly sincere.

Laura started crying again. 'Oh, Joey, Joey. What are they?'

'I don't know. Some kind of copies.'

'Where are you? What happened?'

'I'm still in the EVA hangar – look.'

When she closed her eyes and accepted his vision through the gaiafield, she saw the EVA hangar from an off-kilter angle. She/Joey was looking at it from the airlock end. The emergency blue lighting was on, and there was no sign of the alien human-copies.

'They fastened me in place. But I did it, Laura. What I said – the same thing you did. While they were busy with Ayanna, I closed the hatch with telekinesis, then screwed up the power cables, shorted everything out. They can't get to me.'

'Can you move?'

A wash of stoic regret came through the connection. 'No. My telekinesis isn't strong enough to break the bond. It's some kind of tough polymer wrapped round my wrists and ankles.'

'Can you manipulate a tool? Cut through it?'

'Laura, please. I'm not sure I'm that accurate. You have to get back here.'

An involuntary tremor ran the length of her body. She let out a pitiful squeak of fear. 'No. No, I can't.'

'They will come for you. You know that. They will find tools. They will cut through the hatch.'

Just the thought of it made tears well up again. Without gravity, the liquid simply swelled up on her eyeballs, distorting her vision. 'I left her, Joey,' she confessed. 'I just left her with them. I didn't even try to help, I was too scared. How awful am I? She was all alone with them. And she died like *that*. She died alone, Joey, with those things eating her. Nothing could be worse than that. Nothing! Maybe I deserve them coming for me.'

'Stop it. They're strong – much stronger than us. You couldn't have done anything. It would have happened to you, too.'

'Have they . . . ? Did they . . . ? To you?'

'No. I'm intact. I just can't move, that's all. Laura, you have to get down here. You won't have much time.'

'I can't get through the hatch; I screwed it up pretty good. But even if I could get it open again, I wouldn't ever get past them.'

'I've been thinking about that. Don't even try to fight your way past them. You have to EVA.'

'What?'

'There are emergency suits in the forward cabin. Put one on and break the windscreen. I control the exopod airlock; my telekinesis can reach the control panel. I've already opened the outer hatch ready for you. I wouldn't have suggested this otherwise. Check the network if you don't believe me.'

It took a long time for Laura to make herself move. Her macrocellular clusters were still blocking the terrible pain from her ruined ankle. Exovision icons were flashing up constant warnings about tissue damage and internal bleeding, which she'd ignored along with everything else as she dropped into a dangerous denial state. She hauled herself along the couches to the curving console under the windscreen. There were several system schematics up and running. They confirmed it: the EVA hangar airlock's outer door was open.

'I see,' Laura said.

'Then come and collect me,' Joey said. 'We'll fly the second exopod down to the planet and find *Vermillion*.'

Laura gave the windscreen a long look. The remaining hologram graphics blinking inside the glass were mostly warning symbols. 'Joey, how the hell am I going to break the windscreen? It can withstand aerobrake entry into an atmosphere, and the shuttle is rated for gas giant work. The damn thing is tough – probably tougher than the rest of the fuselage.'

'Yeah, but any chain is only as strong as the weakest link, remember? Take a look at how it's fastened to the main structure.'

Laura took a breath and sent her ESP into the fuselage itself, examining the layers and material, the seal all around the superstrengthened glass. Her mind's eye revealed the coloured shadows that were stacked against each other like strata in rock – the same as a crude hologram display, she thought. There didn't seem to be many weak points. Her perception ranged wider, probing the rest of the forward cabin. 'I'm not coming through the windscreen,' she told him. 'There's an emergency rescue panel in the roof.' She pushed off the console, and reached out for the rectangle above the second couch. When she squeezed a small recessed handle, it allowed her to pull it away. The metre-wide circle it exposed was covered in warnings about having equal pressure before triggering. 'There's a lot of safety locks,' she reported.

'Bureaucrats should never be allowed anywhere near aerospace design teams.'

'True.'

'Now put your suit on.'

'Joey, this is a bit—'

Something started buzzing intermittently against the hatch to the service compartment. Softly at first, the way a bee knocks against glass. But then the frequency began to rise and became continuous.

'A bit what?'

'Nothing.'

She tugged one of the emergency pressure suits from its overhead wallet. There was a moment of hesitation as she bent her knee, ready to push her foot into the baggy clump of silver-white fabric. Her ankle had swollen dramatically. The small gap between the hem of the shipsuit trouser leg and her shoe exposed skin that was a nasty purple red. She was pretty sure she wouldn't be able to get the shoe off. The sight of it made her nauseous again – not that there was anything left to throw up. For a moment her nerve block seemed to fail, that or she imagined the pain. It practically overwhelmed her.

Nothing, she told herself with miserable fury. *You're feeling nothing compared to Ayanna.* She forced her numb leg into the spacesuit, then pushed her arms into the sleeves. Her u-shadow managed an interface with the spacesuit processor, and the fabric contracted around her.

The intense buzzing from the hatch rose towards ultrasonic. A blue-white point appeared along the edge of the hatch, shining like an arc spot.

Laura grabbed the helmet and jabbed it onto the thick metal collar. It sealed immediately, and dry air hissed in, cutting off most of the buzzing sound. Molten droplets were spraying out from the hatch. They glowed like embers as they swarmed along the central aisle. She pulled down the quick-release lever on the overhead rescue panel. Alarms sounded, and the rim of the hatch turned scarlet. Two safety latches clicked out from the lever, warning her of a one-atmosphere pressure difference. She flicked them back with her thumb, and the alarm grew even louder.

With one hand wrapped round a couch strap to hold her in the cabin, Laura twisted the lever round ninety degrees. The hatch immediately blew out amid a fast, violent blast of air. It pummelled her hard, shunting her around so her knees slammed into the cabin ceiling. More pain poured into her brain as she was spun round by the howling stream of air, to be quickly damped down by the nerve blocks.

It took only seconds to evacuate the forward cabin's atmosphere. Laura found herself flailing about on the end of the strap, engulfed by a muffled silence. The distortion tree had vanished from view. The rest of the Forest was a smear of motion as the shuttle lurched from the impetus of the abrupt gas vent. All she could hear was her own ragged breathing.

She checked the service compartment hatch. The blue-white light had dimmed to a patch of glowing crimson metal. A tiny jet of white vapour was shooting out from a hole in the centre of it.

'Was that it?' Joey asked. 'I felt Fourteen jolt round. Was that the cabin air blowing?'

'Yeah.'

'You need to get down here. They'll realize they need the exopod to escape alive.'

'Ah, bollocks. Okay, I'm coming.'

She unwound her arm from the strap and pushed herself through the hatch. The Forest whirled around her. Shuttle Fourteen was performing a lazy nose-over-tail flip every two hundred seconds, with some yaw thrown in just to make the sight even more disorientating.

Stkpads on her wrists and soles adhered to the shuttle's fuselage, allowing her to crawl along. With the nerve blocks effectively paralysing the lower half of her right leg, she could only use her left foot. Even so, it was easier than she'd expected. It probably helped that she didn't look round at the Forest trees tracing their glowing arcs across Voidspace. Her eyes were focused hard on the grey thermal shielding that was the outer layer of the fuselage. She made her way down the side of the forward cabin until she was clinging to the belly, then began the long haul to the tail.

Peel a wrist stkpad off with a roll – ignore the fact that you're now only attached by two stkpads and if they fail the shuttle's tumble will fling you off into Voidspace – and extend the free arm as far as you comfortably can, then press down again. Apply a slight vertical pressure to make sure the stkpad is bonding correctly, then twist the sole's stkpad free. Bring the leg up as if you're going into a crouch, press down. Check.

Repeat, and repeat, and repeat—

'I know what it is,' Joey told her through the gaiafield.

'What?'

'I told you I was seeing something wrong with the planet. I know what it is.'

Laura brought her head up to check she was crawling in the right direction. Fourteen's tail was about twelve metres away now, and she was veering off line slightly. She pushed her arm wide to compensate and pressed the stkpad down. 'Go on, then. At this point, I seriously doubt that knowing will make anything worse.'

'You sure about that?'

'Bollocks, Joey! What is it?'

'I'm telling you because you need to know.'

The crawl was becoming harder. Her body was feeling the strain. She could hear her heart pounding away; she didn't need the exovision medical graphics to know that, nor see she needed more oxygen. *How can zero gee be so exhausting?* 'Joey, either tell me or shut the fuck up.'

'All right. The planet is spinning the wrong way.'

'What?'

'It's reversed. When we were in *Vermillion*, the continents were turning east to west. Now we're in the Forest, they're going west to east. That's what I saw, the continents going the wrong way round. Which is why it took a while to figure out – it's almost too big to grasp.'

'I don't understand.'

'We're seeing the planet going backwards. There's only one thing that could cause an effect like that. Now do you get it?'

The shuttle's tail was about seven metres away. Laura had to pause to give her over-exerted muscles a rest. 'No,' she whinged. 'Joey – just, what is it?'

'Time,' he said, accompanied by a wash of wonder and dismay. 'Ayanna said the trees were distorting time, and she was right, but they're not slowing it down inside the Forest, they're reversing it.'

'Reversing?'

'The Forest is travelling back in time, Laura. That's why we can see the planet spinning backwards. *Vermillion* didn't vanish; we're travelling back to a time before it arrived.'

Laura let out a distraught groan. She didn't need *this*, not on top of everything else. She rolled her stkpad and moved her arm, resuming the punishing crawl. 'Time travel is impossible. You know this. Causality. Paradox. Entropy. They can't be beaten, Joey.'

'They can't be beaten in ordinary spacetime,' he said. 'But we're in Voidspace.'

'And Voidspace exists within spacetime,' she said. 'The fundamentals are unchanged.'

'The planet's spin is reversed,' he told her stubbornly. 'We're travelling back in time.'

'Whatever.'

'You need to know, Laura. Once you leave the Forest, all you have to do is wait for the *Vermillion* to show up and warn them about the globes.'

'Which isn't going to happen,' she retorted almost angrily. 'Because I didn't show up, I didn't meet me and I didn't stop us from coming here. Did I?' She reached the flat trailing edge of the delta wings and started to clamber up around them. The blunt end of the fuselage swung into view. Clamshell doors had hinged up and to one side, exposing the wide circular airlock which made up the end of the EVA hangar. Its outer door was open. It made her let out a small whimper of relief; Joey had been telling the truth about that at least. She was starting to worry the tank yank malady was affecting his brain.

'Joey, I'm at the airlock.'

'Great. Find something to hang on to. You'll need to be really secure.'

'What?' she asked in bewilderment.

'I've overridden the safeties. I'm going to open the inner door, blow the hangar's atmosphere out. It'll be quite a blast, so you need to be secure. I don't want you blowing away, okay?'

'Joey, what the fuck . . .'

'You'll see. And you'll make it out of the Forest, too. The second exopod's intact.'

'What's happened?' she sobbed. 'Why are you doing this?'

'I can't come with you. Please, Laura, find something to fasten yourself to.'

'What have they done to you, Joey?' she asked in dread. 'Why are you doing this?'

'Are you secure?'

She couldn't argue; she was too exhausted. Besides, the fatalism he was releasing into the gaiafield told her there was no point. She looked round the inside of the big airlock. There were a dozen handholds and several empty equipment racks. She crawled over to one of them and hinged its titanium latches around her. 'Secure.'

The inner doors began to peel apart. Gas rushed out of the expanding hole, thin white vapour streaking past her. Shuttle Fourteen began to move, propelled along a weirdly erratic course, the escaping plume of atmosphere exaggerating its original tumble. Laura saw the glowing distortion trees whirl round and round as she was shoved against the rack's latches. The distant planet crescent whipped by once.

There seemed to be an incredible amount of atmosphere in the

EVA hangar. It even kept roaring out in a vast hurricane when the airlock doors were fully open. Streams of vapour played across her spacesuit – it was like being caught in a powerful water jet. She could actually hear the noise.

Then it was over. A cloud of twinkling ice crystals swarmed around the end of the whirling shuttle, expanding fast. Laura freed herself from the rack and started to crawl inside where the blue emergency lighting cast everything in sharp relief.

'That worked, then,' Joey said.

Laura could feel his emotions through the gaiafield link, satisfaction and fatalism combined. Also fright. He was allowing that to show for the first time. Pain was starting to colour his thoughts now, a dull ache spreading out from his empty lungs. She scuttled past the airlock's inner door and saw him. Every limb locked rigid in shock. 'Joey! Oh, Joey, no. No, no, no.'

He was stuck to the alien globe. One leg, an arm and a third of his torso had sunk into it. The side of his head was up against the wrinkled black surface, an ear already absorbed.

Laura used the handholds now, gliding over to him.

'Don't touch me,' he warned.

'Why didn't you say? Oh, bollocks, Joey, *why*?'

Explosive decompression had ruptured capillaries under his skin, turning his flesh scarlet. Blood oozed through his pores and wept out from around his eyeballs. His mouth was open, also emitting a spray of fine scarlet droplets with every heartbeat. 'I was bodylossed the moment the fake Rojas grabbed me. This way you get to live. And they don't get to copy me. Worthwhile.'

'Joey.'

'Say hi to my re-life clone. Tell me how noble I am.'

'Joey—'

The gaiafield connection faded out. Laura stared at Joey's awful ruined face as the blood droplets started to vacuum boil. It was only when the swelling scarlet mist started to smear her helmet that she suddenly moved again.

She hauled her way over to the second exopod and slipped in through the open hatch. The webbing floated about in a tangle, which she sorted out, clicking the buckles together to hold her in place. Power-up was a simple sequence. The hatch closed; air squirted in.

Piloting wasn't exactly her talent set, but there were some basic files in her storage lacuna. They ran as secondary routines in her macrocellular clusters, and she managed to steer the little craft out through the open airlock, only scraping the sides twice as she went.

The shuttle twisted about, its spin rate increased massively by the loss of the EVA hangar atmosphere. She stabilized the exopod and carefully brought it back as close as she could to the floundering delta shape. The biggest engines she had were three high-density ion rockets in the base of the spherical fuselage, capable of producing a fifth of a gee.

Laura fired the rockets at full thrust. Three plumes of high-energy plasma stabbed down onto Shuttle Fourteen's fuselage, striking at the port wing root just behind the forward cabin. They punctured the grey thermal shielding and roasted the composite and metal stress structure beneath. Systems vaporized. Tanks ruptured. The pressure hull fractured, blowing out the passenger cabin's atmosphere.

The exopod was two hundred metres away from the shuttle when Laura switched the ion rockets off. She fired the manoeuvring thrusters, turning the little craft so she could see the shuttle through the wide circular port. It was tumbling even faster now, surrounded by a cloud of scintillating debris. The port wing was badly buckled, with a dark ruptured crater still venting spurts of gas. One of the clamshell doors had broken off. When the tail swung into view, even the EVA hangar's emergency lights were out. But the centre of the shuttle was still intact; the alien things could still be alive in there.

She flew the exopod back to Fourteen, nudging it as close as she dared. Radar tracked the tumble, showing her the tail swinging around towards her. She fired the ion rockets again, sending the ice-blue spears of plasma slamming into the EVA hangar. They must have scored a direct hit on the other exopod's fuel tanks. An explosion blew the rear quarter of the shuttle apart. Jagged fragments came whirling past the port, along with a vivid plume of vapour that was alive with snapping static discharges.

When she manoeuvred the exopod to view the results, Fourteen had broken in two. The port wing had ripped free, and the main cabin section was split open along the length of the remaining fuselage. She stared numbly at the wreckage for several minutes as it drifted away. There was no satisfaction, no sense of winning. She'd done what was necessary to survive. That was all. Behind the dwindling shuttle, the vast distortion trees maintained their radiant constellation, unknowing or uncaring about the demise of their creatures.

The exopod's sensors locked on to the planet one and a half million kilometres away. Laura loaded that into the network, which incorporated it into the existing navigation data and began to plot a vector for her. The first burn, lasting three minutes, took her out of the Forest.

As she passed through the edge of the distortion trees, a time symbol flicked up into her exovision. It had been twenty-seven hours forty-two minutes since Shuttle Fourteen had actually entered the Forest and its altered temporal environment.

Laura shook her head ruefully. She still didn't believe poor Joey's theory of time travel.

The second burn lasted seventeen minutes and consumed sixty-eight per cent of her fuel. There would have to be regular corrective burns, but flight time to the planet was calculated at ninety-two hours.

She took off her helmet and smelt the tiny cabin's air. It was a lot fresher than the recycled atmosphere the suit had been feeding her. Her first priority had to be her ankle. Half her exovision was filled with medical displays, most of which were red or amber.

The suit released its grip on her, and she wriggled out with a distinct lack of elegance. It was cramped in the little craft, and the straps didn't help. Elbows, knees, head, feet – they all bumped into some part of the walls or port or consoles.

When she finally rid herself of the suit, it was an effort not to wince at the sight of her ankle. Released from the suit's grip, the flesh was swelling badly. She did have to cut the shoe free and slice the trouser leg open. The Swiss army knife would have been really useful for that, she acknowledged grimly. Fortunately, the medical kit had an old-style scalpel blade. What it lacked was a decent selection of medicines and treatment packs. Not that she would have trusted the packs in the Void anyway. It really was a basic emergency pack, intended to triage wounds until the exopod returned to the main ship where there would be a hospital and doctors who knew how to program biononics properly.

So she had to make do with anti-inflammatories and a large dose of coagulants to stop any further internal bleeding. Thankfully, her nerve blocks were still functional. She didn't like to think what the pain levels would be like otherwise. And she had no idea what to do once she had landed. The bone needed setting properly, and the fluid draining.

There were files in her storage lacuna that showed how to deal with such an injury using only primitive equipment. It was like a text left over from the twenty-first century. Laura had no idea if she could self-operate even with one hundred per cent pain blocks.

Once the medicines were administered, she ordered the exopod's sensors to scan for the *Vermillion*'s beacon. Even if – *and you're being ridiculous here*, she told herself – she had somehow travelled back in time, the *Vermillion* would be approaching the planet. Captain Cornelius would be preparing to launch a science mission to the Forest. And somewhere deeper in the giant starship, medical staff would be tank yanking her and Ayanna, and Joey, and Ibu, and Rojas.

The exopod completed three scans and reported no beacon signal of any type or at any strength. Not in space. Not coming from the planet, either.

'Bollocks! Bollocks, bollocks.' Where the hell were they? Three starships that size couldn't simply vanish.

Unless they haven't arrived yet, a traitorous part of her mind whispered. So she did what she should have done as soon as she left the Forest and switched on the exopod's own beacon. It made her feel better, even though it didn't exactly help her situation.

She ran a quick inventory. There was enough food for two weeks. That's if you counted dehydrated packets as food. They'd all have to be rehydrated. Water wasn't a problem. The exopod carried ten litres – and a recycle filter system. Laura wrinkled her nose up at that, but there wasn't much choice. *Only eighty-nine hours left.*

A day later, she wasn't sure she would make it. Her ankle was the size of a football, the skin dark purple, and a fever was taking hold. She was shivering with cold as her flesh burnt. More worryingly, there were odd moments when she was losing lucidity. Lapses of time when she thought she was talking to Ayanna. Twice she woke up shouting at Joey not to open the airlock.

Every time it happened, she cursed herself for being so weak. She was afraid to take any more drugs for fear of making the delirium worse. She knew she had to drink more, but couldn't bring herself to suck on the tube. Her mind started to drift, constructing terrible scenarios of the world she was heading for. That the surface would be nothing but mounds of the dark alien globes. That the exopod would sink into them. That they'd penetrate the hull from every direction, and contract around her. She'd be stuck to six different globes at once, and they'd each start tugging at her, trying to be the one that consumed her –

'Where are you?' she shouted as the sensors reported there was still no beacon signal from *Vermillion.*

By the end of the second day she had withdrawn into a perfect storm of misery and self-loathing. There was so much she could have done to help Ayanna. If she wasn't such a coward. If she had a shred of human decency. Joey too could have been saved if she hadn't been so totally self-absorbed.

Maybe Joey had the right of it, she wondered. Accept bodyloss and get re-lifed when the *Vermillion* escaped the Void. She just wished she could believe that would happen.

She had to take some drugs ten hours out from the planet. Even in her wretched state, she acknowledged the next trajectory correction burn had to be performed correctly. If the exopod was going to aerobrake, it had to hit the outer atmosphere at a precise angle. There was little margin for error.

It was a fifty-two-second burn, aligning the exopod to graze the top of the atmosphere. Too long, and she would shoot past the planet, to be lost in Voidspace. Too short, and the exopod would hit the atmosphere at a steep angle, overloading the thermal protective coating.

There were so many factors involved, so much that could go wrong. No Commonwealth citizen was used to this level of uncertainty any more; technology simply worked. Aerobrake entry was the ultimate safety fallback, a capability provided almost as an afterthought. Nobody ever expected an exopod actually to do this. And as for using parachutes to land – she had to pull that file out of her lacunas, all the while praying that the explanation of the chute system too was some kind of Void-derived glitch. Her life was going to depend on a bit of fabric and strings? *Seriously?*

Fear began to supplant Laura's misery. *Perhaps bodyloss isn't such a good idea after all?*

The burn lasted its pre-programed time, and cut off. Sensors measured her new vector and reported she was on track for a correct aerobrake insertion.

'Wow, something went right.'

She forced herself to eat on the final approach phase. She hydrated a tube of pasta. As always, it tasted of nothing, a gooey paste with spaghetti chunks blocking the nozzle every time she squeezed. She drank water to wash it down, mildly grateful she couldn't taste that, either.

An hour out from the atmosphere, she fastened herself back in the webbing. There was no way she was going to risk any weight being placed on her ankle. By now, the skin colour around the broken tibia and fibula bones had darkened considerably, although she managed to convince herself that the swelling had gone down slightly.

The exopod hit the atmosphere. It was only the sensors which told her that to start with, showing the increased density of ions outside. Then the exopod started to tremble. That soon evolved into a pronounced shaking. A ruby glow crept in through the pod, overwhelming the bright white radiance of the clouds far below.

Laura's hands tightened on the straps holding her upright as gravity began to reassert itself. A rumble began to penetrate the hull insulation as the exopod tore its way down at hypersonic speed. Her weight increased, straining the straps. The exopod reached four gees, and Laura's nerve blocks began to fail. Her ankle was a throbbing mass of red-hot pressure. She cried out – a sound that was lost amid the tormented howl of air being shredded by the little craft's deceleration.

Incandescent sparks were starting to zip past the port as unprotected systems vaporized off the hull. Sensor coverage was non-existent now. Not that she could have concentrated on anything they showed her. The exopod was shaking so much she couldn't focus.

Gradually the shaking began to ease off. The shriek of obliterated air faded away and the red glow of the thermal coating died out. Bright sunlight shone into the cabin. It was a glorious sapphire blue outside. Sky!

The exopod slowed to subsonic speed fifteen hundred metres above the ground. Laura let out a relieved groan, which was immediately knocked out of her as the drogue chutes deployed, jerking the exopod viciously. Savage pain jabbed up her leg, and she screamed. Then the main chutes deployed. The exopod began to drift gently towards the planet's surface.

It's actually working? Fuck me!

Breathing heavily, Laura peered out through the port, eager to see the type of ground she was going to land on. It was a uniform ochre, undulating away to the horizon.

'A desert!' she shouted in fury. 'After all this, a fucking desert? You've got to be fucking kidding me.' She started crying, big tears rolling down her cheeks as she hung there in the straps, waiting numbly for the touchdown.

Ten metres above the ground, a cluster of impact bags inflated out from the base of the exopod. They hit and immediately deflated, cushioning the landing. The exopod rocked about sharply, gouging out a shallow crater in the sand before slowly coming to a halt, tilted over at about twenty degrees. The main chutes fluttered away for several hundred metres before collapsing.

Laura took her time unhooking herself from the straps. She was hanging slightly face down, and didn't want to fall on her damaged ankle. Slowly she lowered herself onto what was now the floor. The hatch was level with her head. All the port showed was a patch of sandy ground in the shade cast by the rest of the exopod.

She reached up to one of the small consoles and studied the display screen. Power was down to fifteen per cent. She shut down the flight systems. All that was left now was the beacon, sending out its call for help, and the environmental unit. It could recycle her air for another three hundred hours with the remaining power.

'Bollocks to that.' Laura turned the environmental unit off, and pulled the hatch lever. There was a loud hiss as the pressure equalized, then the hatch swung open. A wave of warm dry air rolled in. She breathed it down, not too worried about spores or any other alien microbes. Even without functional biononics, her immune system was enhanced by Advancer genes; it could cope with a lot of dangerous biological crud. In any case, she was past caring. It wasn't going to be bugs which killed her now.

She crawled out of the exopod and looked round. It really was a desert, a flat expanse of gritty sand with meandering rills rippling away in every direction. She crawled round the exopod to be sure, but nothing broke the desolate span of ochre sand except for the red-and-yellow striped fabric puddle of the chutes. There were no clouds in the sky. No wind. No humidity. Nothing alive apart from her.

'Oww, bollocks.'

The sunlight was intense; she was already sweating. If she stayed out for much longer, she'd burn. Probably get sunstroke too.

She squirmed her way back through the hatch, only to find the interior of the exopod was now hotter than outside. The damn thing was acting like an oven under the midday sun.

Oh, just great!

The environmental unit came back on with an unhealthy clanking sound. It settled down soon enough, producing a slightly strained whirring. Laura didn't care; she wormed herself into a sitting position with her face under one of the vents, enjoying the cool air blowing across her skin. When she checked the display screen above her, she saw the power levels dropping already. At this rate, the power cells didn't even have enough charge to keep the environmental unit going until evening.

With a groan, she lumbered up out of the hatch again and scuttled round to a small panel in the base of the exopod. The emergency planetary survival kit was inside, but streaks of molten metal from some sensor or antenna had solidified over the panel, practically welding it shut. She tried prising at it with her telekinesis, but she certainly wasn't strong enough to shift the metal bonds. She looked round, and found a sharpish rock. Flakes of the blackened metal broke off as she hammered away. The irony made her grin fiercely: a rock hammer to open a spaceship, surely the ultimate clash of primitive against sophistication.

She was sweating profusely by the time she finally managed to clear the panel and tug it open. The case slid out, containing basic supplies – four water bottles with built-in purification filters, another medical kit, a couple of array tablets with high-power transmitters, two insulated one-piece suits (which would be useful in this heat, she admitted), some simple tools, including an axe and multifunction knife not dissimilar to the Swiss army knife, two force-field skeleton suits (their processors didn't even respond to her u-shadow's ping), a pair of high-density power cells and an amazingly thin photovoltaic sheet that just kept unrolling. She spread that out, holding it down with rocks on each corner, and plugged it in to the high-density cells, then plugged them into the exopod's power circuit.

Back inside, she gulped down a litre of water after her exertions.

The photovoltaic sheet alone was producing enough electricity to keep the environmental unit going. Her exposed skin was starting to smart from sunburn, so she slathered on some salve. She spent a long minute staring at her damaged ankle. It hadn't got any worse, but sun exposure definitely hadn't helped. If she was going to put an insulated suit on she'd have to cut the trouser leg open first.

She turned to the two array tablets. They had black solar cases that would recharge their cells. So she set them to broadcast a distress signal at full power for ten minutes then charge up for fifty minutes before signalling again. As they were solid state, they should be able to maintain that cycle indefinitely.

After she'd set them outside she ate another tube of pasta and checked the sensors. There was no trace of the *Vermillion* or the other starships. The sky was clear of any signal. It made her wonder how far she'd travelled into the past. Not that it was possible. But *if* . . .

Four hours later the sun dropped below the horizon. After another hour it was cool enough for her to turn the environmental unit off. She looked out of the hatch without venturing outside. Above her, the Void's nebulas dominated the sky. Below them, the desert was perfectly still – a silence that was unnerving now the environmental unit had stopped its wheezing and rattling. Looking at that vast unyielding stretch of grainy sand, she knew there was no way she could get across it on her own. The solar sheet would supply power long after her food and water ran out. All she could do was stay put and keep alive until *Vermillion* arrived. There was nothing else. Just wait and pray that, against all logic and science, Joey had been right.

*

In the morning she started an inventory of food. She refused to cut down on her water intake. That would be dangerous, but she could afford to eat fewer calories, especially as she planned on doing nothing.

She settled back in the tiny cabin and began reviewing the

science data she'd assiduously stored in her lacuna. The molecular pathways inside the distortion tree were truly extraordinary. Mapping them properly was going to be a serious task. But it would stop her thinking about Ayanna and the others.

Seven hours after dawn, the environmental unit packed up. Laura just laughed at the silence. 'What's next? A tsunami?' She was beginning to believe the Void's controlling intelligence was taking a personal and very macabre interest in her. This catastrophic mission was her very own rat maze. *And I can't find the cheese.*

She'd got the top of the environmental unit open when a sonic boom hit the exopod.

The harsh sound made her jump. She dropped the tools and stuck her head out of the hatch, searching the sky.

High above her, a small black speck was falling at terminal velocity, producing a grubby vertical contrail filled with twinkling embers. The contrail shrank away to nothing, and the speck fell in silence. Then a couple of drogue chutes shot out.

Laura's heart thudded hard. 'It can't be,' she murmured. 'I killed you. I killed you, damn it! I killed you.'

It was as if her own memory was false. She closed her eyes and saw the tumbling wreckage of Shuttle Fourteen, its rear quarter shredded. It had happened. She knew it had.

But the drogues pulled out the main chutes. Three big red-and-yellow striped circles bloomed across the clear sapphire basin. An exopod hung underneath them, floating gently to the ground.

'No,' Laura said numbly. 'No no. This can't be right. This isn't my cheese.' Even to her own ears she sounded as if she was cracking up. Then she noticed her time display. Twenty-seven hours, forty minutes since she'd landed. Which was weird, because the descending exopod probably had about a couple of minutes before touchdown.

She shielded her eyes and frowned up at it. It was coming down close. Very close. Directly above now, and –

'Shit!' Laura heaved herself out of the hatch and started

crawling frantically across the hot grainy sand. She'd made probably nine metres when there was a soft pop of impact bags inflating out of the base of the exopod. It landed smack on top of hers and tilted sharply sideways, thudding to the ground. The main chutes fluttered away.

Laura's time display read twenty-seven hours and forty-two minutes since she'd landed. Exactly.

'No way,' Laura said, too stunned to move. *Out of an entire planet, it lands on top of my exopod. Precisely on top!* 'What the fuck do you want from me?' she yelled into the empty sky.

She started crawling back to the two exopods, snarling as the grainy sand scratched her knees and wrists raw. She didn't care. She had to get to the exopod, to face down whatever fresh horror the Void was taunting her with.

The newly arrived exopod was lying on its side. Laura picked up the axe from the planetary survival kit and clawed her way up to the hatch which was at shoulder height. Putting all her weight on her good foot, she pulled the lever. There was a hiss of pressure equalling, and she swung the hatch back. She raised the axe, expecting to see the copy-Rojas or the copy-Ibu – most probably both. But it wasn't them.

A perfect Laura Brandt hung in the webbing straps, squinting against the brilliant sunlight flooding in. She was flawless, even down to the discoloured, badly swollen ankle and slit shipsuit trouser leg.

Laura screamed long and hard.

The other Laura screamed back at her.

Laura brought the axe down with manic strength, burying the edge in her doppelganger's skull.

BOOK TWO

Dreams from the Void

July 9th 3326

Nigel Sheldon woke up. He was immediately aware of feeling warm and cosy, exactly how it should be after a good night's sleep. Then he remembered the last thing that had happened—

His eyes snapped open. There was a face looking down at him. It was his own.

'Welcome to the world,' said the grinning Nigel at the side of the bed.

'Oh, hell,' Nigel groaned.

'Yeah. 'Fraid so.'

Two Months Earlier:

May 17th 3326

New Costa: a megacity that once sprawled for more than four hundred miles along the coastline of Augusta's Sinebar continent, then extended almost as far inland. At its peak, home to a billion people, all of them devoted to one ideal: making money. In those days, the city boasted over a million factories, producing every consumer product the human race had ever dreamt up. The heavy industrial plants consumed the minerals ruthlessly strip-mined from Augusta's other continents, spewing their contaminated effluent out into the oceans. Its wormhole station, New Costa Junction, with its strategic connection back to Earth, boasted fifty wormhole generators creating permanent gateways to the thriving, ambitious new H-congruous planets still further away from the old homeworld. Gateways that were the perfect export routes, enabling those Halcion worlds to develop cleaner greener societies by transferring their industrial pollution debt to Augusta, where no one cared. Multiplanetary corporations, entrepreneurs, financiers – all of them spent their work-addict life in New Costa's endless, centreless chequerboard of industrial districts and residential zones. And when it was all over, when they were burnt out and prematurely aged, they'd re-life and do it all over again – and again – forcing themselves a little further up the corporate ladder each time in a way that would have made Darwin shudder.

Augusta's commercial expansion was performed with a ruthless imperial nonchalance, conquering all it reached out to. That was back in the era of the Starflyer War, nine hundred years ago: the Commonwealth's first and, to-date, only interstellar conflict. Victory came in no small part thanks to the terrible and sophisticated weapons developed, then mass-produced on Augusta.

All of which made New Costa as rich in history as it was poor in culture. If you looked down on the ramshackle old road grid and chaotic layout of neighbourhoods, it was a history that could be read like the rings of a terrestrial tree.

Flying away from New Costa Junction, Nigel Sheldon had a perfect view of all that living archaeology as he turned his capsule's forward fuselage transparent. For all that the megacity was in a period of drastic reduction, the old CST (Compression Space Transport) station was still as busy as ever. The three ancient terminus buildings were still standing, each one with a roof that spanned a square mile. Today it was mainly people who used the wormholes that knitted the Central worlds together. When he'd started the company, it was trains that zipped through the wormholes, carrying freight and passengers between disparate planets. Nowadays, with fabricators and replicators reproducing most things, including themselves, consumerism was effectively dead on the Central worlds. Anybody could assemble whatever they wanted in their own home. In practice, though, there were limits. Large or sophisticated machines were still built in New Costa. The megacity had even held on to its lead in starship manufacture, accounting for nearly thirty per cent of the Commonwealth's total.

The capsule headed north, keeping parallel to the coast, its ellipsoid shape pushing through the air at just below subsonic speed. Right on the shore he could see the big airbarges hovering above the waves, with dozens of smaller earthmover bots loading them up with soil. It was the Port Klye peninsula – now crater, he acknowledged wryly. In the good old days there had been thirty-five massive nuclear fission reactors sited there, providing cheap energy to almost ten per cent of the city. Today the clean-up was almost complete. Before long, the giant hole would be filled in and turned into a wildlife park. Not that Augusta had much native vegetation or animal life, which was one reason he'd chosen it as the ideal location to build his corporate fiefdom.

His u-shadow told him he had a call from his wife. 'I'm not going to make it tonight,' she told him.

'Why not?' He tried not to make it sound petulant. He and Anine Saleeb had been married for eighty years now, a record – for both of them. She was only four hundred and thirty, while he was now close to his one thousand three hundredth birthday. That meant that being together all of the time wasn't as important as it had been even six hundred years ago, back when he still had a harem and lived a ridiculously lavish multi-trillionaire's lifestyle to the full. But they had been apart for a month now. He missed her.

'There's been some hanky-panky going on at our McLeod facility,' she told him.

Nigel blinked in surprise. 'Hanky-panky?'

'The managers think the smartcore has been compromised.'

'Why?' he asked in genuine puzzlement. The Sheldon Dynasty's McLeod facility had been tasked with building a hundred and fifty huge exospheric stations that would float just outside Earth's atmosphere, ultimately providing the entire planet with a T-sphere, allowing practical teleportation anywhere on the surface. It wasn't a controversial project; ANA: Governance had only commissioned it after a long and no doubt tediously parochial debate amid the many political factions that flourished within humanity's down-loaded personalities.

'Production hasn't been disrupted, so it wasn't sabotage,' Anine said. 'Admiral Kazimir believes it may be the Knights Guardians movement.'

One thousand two hundred and ninety-six years old he might have been, and possessing all the phenomenal emotional control only a life so long could bring, but Nigel still let out a sigh of dismay. 'Not Far Away again? Will that planet never stop being a problem?'

'Apparently not.'

'What do they want with the McLeod smartcore?'

'Navy Intelligence suggests the Knights Guardians want to build their own T-sphere.'

'Why don't they just ask us for one? ANA hasn't restricted the technology to the Central worlds. It's just horribly complex. I can barely understand the operational theories myself.'

'Probably because we wouldn't give them one that's weaponized.'

'Oh, that goddamn psycho woman. She's been in suspension for six hundred years already, and she's still casting a paranoid shadow.'

'Never mind, darling. Three more years and our colony ships will be ready.'

'Yeah.' It had taken him long enough, but five years ago Nigel had finally decided to do what so many others had done, and leave the Commonwealth behind to start a fresh civilization a long, long way away. The Sheldon Dynasty had sent out trans-galactic colonies before, and Nigel had almost gone with them. But there was always one more problem to deal with, one more political fight, one more . . . Until now. Now he was finally going to turn his back on it all for good and find time for himself. This time . . .

'I'll see you in a few days,' Anine said.

'Good.'

Nigel's u-shadow ended the link. As the capsule raced away from Port Klye, he saw one of the airbarges lumber up into the sky and fly towards New Costa Junction. It would be using the zero-end wormhole at the station, which opened in deep space, the most convenient and safest place to dump radioactive waste, or some other industrial contaminate material. These days it was used almost exclusively to dump Augusta's toxic legacy where it would do no harm. That hadn't always been the case. The zero-end was originally built for discreet disposal to assist the commodities market. Back in the day, surplus harvests or an excess of rare minerals had been quietly shoved out into oblivion, assisting the market price, reaping bigger profits for the financial sectors at the expense of the consumer.

'What were we doing?' Nigel murmured as he visualized millions of tonnes of golden grain streaming off into the inter-stellar night. Cheap food that could have made ordinary people's lives just that little bit easier and reduced the wealth of people like himself by micro-percentage points.

Those economics were thankfully over. At least in the Central worlds, almost all of which had switched to Higher culture. So many of the External worlds continued to follow the old-style economic and financial patterns. Their politicians claimed it gave them freedom – which Nigel just laughed at. Fortunately, there was a steady migration of citizens inwards, firstly to lead calm and easy lives on the Central worlds before inevitably download-ing their minds into ANA, which was the closest the human race had come to a technological version of heaven. So maybe those conniving politicians did have a point. He was too much of an individualist to contemplate a download. It was interesting that most people retreated into ANA after three or four centuries knocking about the Commonwealth, whereas those who pressed on over six or seven hundred years tended to stay in their (heavily modified and enriched) bodies, almost as if ANA was some kind of illicit temptation and if you avoided it you could reach true maturity.

The capsule curved inland, following the main airborne traffic stream for the Cromarty Hills. Other capsules formed a fluid matrix around him, shiny metallic ellipsoids ploughing through the hot clear air, shining so brightly under the star's blue-white glare that they appeared to have their own halos. Beneath him was the long serpentine ribbon of the ten-lane Medani freeway, standing above the slender river on thick pillars as it followed the floor of the shallow meandering valley all the way back to the hinterlands. Most of the road had been converted now, mutating from a sturdy grey and black ribbon of enzyme-bonded concrete to a weird botanical symbiot colony. With the advent of regrav capsules, New Costa had been quick to abandon its roads. Roads needed annual maintenance dollars spent on them. Air traffic only needed a smartcore controller.

Now bots crawled along the Medani freeway, laying a complex

weave of biological arteries around the concrete. More bots tunnelled into the ground below the support pillars, creating a root network to feed the modified freeway. Nutrients pulsed along the new arterial plexus, supporting an incredible diversity of vegetation. The native plants from hundreds of worlds had been genetically adapted so that they could all be sustained by the same nutrient fluid. The end creation was a wild river of jungle winding its way through the shrinking city, curving down to parks along the old off-ramps and intersections in a strangely exotic three-dimensional growth curve that nature could never produce.

Nigel could still remember meeting with the bunch of crazy artists who'd begged him for the opportunity to do something other than the standard flatten-and-replant policy that gripped so many of the Central worlds' shrinking cities. He'd agreed, not just because such a revamp might well be a truly spectacular art statement, but as a kind of acknowledgement of how different their environment could become. It was also an oblique tip of the hat to the enigmatic Planters, who had left behind truly huge hybrid organic constructs on the worlds they'd visited. Nigel's Dynasty had finally cracked their nanotech inheritance, adapting it into the biononics which the Commonwealth knew. Biononics gave any and every user command of the very molecules which made up their own bodies, as well as making new generations of replicators possible. Ironically, the technology incorporated within the bots was now also rendering whole swathes of New Costa obsolete.

Yet, for all its population was reducing on a daily basis, New Costa was still home to over a hundred million people. The residential districts with smaller mass-grown drycoral homes where all the low-level company workers used to live had been reduced and turned to parkland connected to the synergistic freeways. But the districts with the larger mansions and elegant condos – those round the fringes of the city, away from the worst industrial excesses – still remained. That was where the majority of people lived now.

Nigel had an estate in the heart of the Cromarty Hills, two hundred square miles of manicured gardens and immaculate old-style parkland on the edge of the megacity. The palace in the very middle was a ludicrous anachronism now, effectively a single-building town that had been capable of accommodating his entire household. That was back when he had a vast immediate family and an entourage of managers and lawyers – all of whom had their own staff – who would travel between his lordly residences on many planets, settling for a few months in one then moving on like some royal procession in medieval times. A life lived in a fashion which made the old French Sun King seem cheap and small.

The estate's smartcore ran a final check on the capsule and its solitary passenger as it decelerated across the threshold. Enlightened he might be – relatively speaking – but Nigel was still quite assiduous about his privacy. Especially on this day.

His u-shadow directed the capsule to land outside the lake house. A lake three miles long and two wide, with islands of rock pinnacles whose crests were covered in a thatch of verdant vegetation. They'd taken years to craft and carve from local rock, and as far as cost was concerned, it was trivial compared to the sum his CST co-owner Ozzie had spent converting an asteroid into his habitat home. The only normal, flattish island was in the middle, with a semi-circular white marble pavilion structure above the shore. Most of the island was well-tended forest, but it had a lush verdant lawn stretching between the water and the building. That was where the capsule came down.

'Who's here?' he asked the smartcore as he stepped out onto the lawn. Weeping willow leaves rustled softly in the warm El Iopi wind that blew out of the heart of the continent. The humidity was as strong as always. He started to perspire almost at once.

'There are forty-two Dynasty members currently in residence, along with a hundred and seventeen associates and estate personnel. They are occupying twenty-six buildings. As requested, the lake house is empty, as are all buildings around the shore.'

'Good.' Nigel put on a pair of mirrorshades and squinted up into the sky. The glare point that was Regulus was poised above the rolling mountain crests and sinking slowly. It would be night in a couple of hours. 'I will be having a visitor in three hours. Their starship will be diplomatic coded. Let them through the security screen on my authority. Do not inform anyone else of their arrival.'

'Understood.'

Nigel hurried inside where the aircon would be on and he could get ready.

*

Five hours previously, Nigel had been on Nova Zealand, a Central world that just about qualified as H-congruous. Recella, one of his great-great-great-granddaughters, was getting married for the first time. As Nigel had two hundred and thirty-eight children (that he knew of), it wasn't exactly a rare event. But her mother, Koloza, was on the Dynasty board and had also signed up for the latest colony project. Family obligation . . .

It wasn't unknown to receive a call from the *High Angel*, just extremely rare. CST had discovered the alien arkship in orbit around the gas giant Icalanise back in 2163. It looked like an unusually regular asteroid, except for the twelve giant crystal-roofed domes on stalks sticking out from the rocky surface. Closer inspection of the transparent domes revealed that they contained cities. It was a Raiel ship, though there were other species living in the domes. At the time, the Raiel didn't reveal what the *High Angel*'s purpose was; that only became clear four hundred years later, once the *Endeavour* was turned away from the Wall stars around the Void. The Raiel had built *High Angel*, and countless other arkships, to evacuate representative populations of sentient species from the galaxy should the Void begin its terminal expansion phase.

Ever since first contact, the Raiel had enjoyed excellent diplomatic relations with the Commonwealth, even propagating New Glasgow, a dome city on *High Angel* for humans to live in. Then, after the *Endeavour* encounter, the Navy had been invited to join their observation of the Void. The Raiel didn't release any of their advanced technology, despite numerous requests, claiming they

didn't want to disrupt the Commonwealth's natural sociotechno-
logical development. Even with constant contact, they remained
an enigma.

'Accept the call,' Nigel told his u-shadow. The wedding ceremony itself was over by then, and the relatively modest reception
had just begun. Koloza had hired an entire resort village in the Fire
Plain, a crater in the arctic surrounded by active volcanoes that
heated the land to tropical levels.

'Thank you for talking to me,' the *High Angel* said courteously
in a smooth male voice.

Nigel grinned as Recella and her new wife took to the open-
air dance floor; both girls looked blissfully happy. Somewhere
beyond the resort's armed perimeter, the cries of mighty dinosaur-
equivalent creatures rolled across the swamps. 'You knew I would.
Who refuses a call from you?'

'Ozzie has been known to.'

'Of course he has. What can I do for you?'

'I would like you to meet a Raiel representative. She wishes to
discuss an important topic with you.'

'Interesting. Why didn't she just call me direct?'

'Your unisphere is relatively secure. However, I would expect
the Commonwealth Navy Intelligence office to monitor all calls
originating from me, especially one from a Raiel.'

'Fair point. All right, I'll meet her. Where?'

'We would suggest somewhere that affords some privacy.'

'I know just the place.'

*

After he'd taken a spore shower, Nigel got dressed in the lake
house's master bedroom, choosing a simple pale brown silk suit
with a semiorganic lining that contracted snugly round him.
Check the mirrors to see blond hair that was still pleasingly thick,
though he could do with a cut. Jaw nicely flat, cheeks not too
rounded. His one concession to cosmetic sequencing was green
eyes; otherwise he'd kept his own features. Unlike everyone else
these days, he didn't hold his biological appearance in his twenties,

preferring mid-thirties to give a touch of maturity. Even today people passed judgement on purely visual clues. It mattered not that his brain was genetically and biononically enhanced beyond anything nature could ever achieve, and the ancillary lacuna now stored every memory from his life; before such advances he'd had to edit entire decades from his mind each time he underwent rejuvenation to avoid the inevitable clutter confusion such an excessive accumulation of experience produced. But today, with secondary routines handling recollection, every day of those thirteen hundred years was instantly available – every mistake, triumph, love, heartbreak, political manoeuvre, discovery, disappointment, wonder and grubby deal that made his personality what it was.

'The Raiel ship has entered Augusta's atmosphere,' the estate's smartcore told him.

'Thank you. Let it land, then shield and screen the estate. No exceptions.'

'Understood.'

The interior of the marble lake house always made Nigel think of some Scandinavian church. It was all down to the high vaulting ceilings and plain lines, complemented by simple curving furniture in white and grey. It was as if the place wasn't quite finished, but they'd started using it anyway. The principal lounge had a big arched window wall looking out across the dark water beyond the shore. The centre of the glass parted to allow Nigel out onto the lawn.

Trees from Illuminatus had been planted on the rock pinnacle islands; at night, after Regulus had departed the sky, their bioluminescence came alive, crowning the islands in a soft blue and purple phosphorescence. Long reflection ribbons shimmered across the water like icy flames, the only visual beacons guiding visitors down.

Nigel's enriched vision showed him the Raiel craft while it was still fifteen miles high. He fed the estate's sensor data into his sight, amplifying the image.

The craft was a twenty-metre sphere with a flat base. It was emitting gravitational distortions similar to a Commonwealth regrav drive.

Nigel watched it land in the centre of the lawn. His biononic fieldscan function caught a T-sphere expanding, and a Raiel was teleported onto the grass in front of him.

He arched an eyebrow. *Very dramatic. Overuse of technology, though. What's wrong with a simple malmetal hatch?* 'Welcome to Augusta,' he said out loud.

The Raiel was larger than a terrestrial elephant, with a tough looking grey-green hide. That was where any equivalence died. For Nigel, standing directly in front of the alien, it was like looking at the crown of an octopus. The wide rounded head was surrounded by tentacles that varied from the pair closest to the ground, which were long and strong, clearly evolved for heavy work, up to clusters of smaller, more agile, appendages. Behind the array of tentacles, odd ropes of flesh dangled down like flaccid feelers, weighted by heavy knobs of technology – or maybe just jewellery, he conceded.

'Thank you for receiving me,' the Raiel said from a mouth that was all damp folds. 'I am Vallar, *High Angel*'s designated liaison with the warrior Raiel.'

'Indeed? Please come in. I am delighted to grant you the freedom of my house.'

'You are most kind.'

Vallar walked over to the lake house. She had eight short legs along each side of her body; devoid of joints, they moved in pairs, tilting up and forwards to move her along in an elegant undulation. Nigel had to lengthen his stride to keep up.

The entrance in the window wall widened further to accommodate Vallar, then closed behind her. Nigel ordered the smartcore to activate another layer of privacy shielding around the building.

'I hope we are secure enough now?' Nigel asked. He remained standing. Somehow flopping back into a chair in front of the imposing alien would have seemed vaguely rude.

Her eyes were clusters of five separate small hemispheres that swivelled round in unison to focus on him. 'Completely. I thank you for the courtesy.'

'So what can I do for you?'

'We are extremely interested in the latest development in the Commonwealth concerning the Void.'

'Ah,' Nigel murmured, and started to relax. 'Of course. Inigo.'

Inigo was a human who had allegedly started to have dreams about a life lived by an adolescent named Edeard, living on a planet called Querencia inside the Void. Edeard's story was of an idealist making his way through some quasi-medieval society but with telepathic powers thrown in. So far Inigo had released four of these astonishingly detailed dreams through the gaiafield and was just starting the fifth. A lot of people thought they were perfect forgeries, fantasy dramas produced by some External world company who were enacting the mother of all product placements. But a lot more people – tens of millions already, and increasing daily – were utterly convinced by the visions Inigo alone had been mystically granted. Living Dream was a growing movement that wanted to live the same life as Edeard, and people flocked to Inigo to await further revelations. He was rapidly turning into the human race's latest unnervingly plausible messiah, offering a glimpse into a very strange universe indeed, where you lived a simpler, yet very different life.

Nigel looked up at the Raiel's eyeclusters. 'I can't vouch that those dreams are real. Humans are capable of very ingenious deceptions, for a variety of reasons, not all of which make sense.'

'The fourth dream shows Edeard travelling to the city of Makkathran.'

'Yes, it does.' Nigel didn't quite blush, but he felt a mild embarrassment at admitting he'd accessed all the dreams – a twelve-year-old caught sipping his father's beer. 'It was an odd city. Built by aliens.'

'It is one of ours.'

'What?'

'Makkathran is one of the warships that formed our armada. It was part of the invasion we sent into the Void a million years ago.'

'You're *shitting* me!' Nigel blurted.

'I am not.'

'No. Of course. Sorry. But . . . are you sure?'

'Yes. It is what convinced us that the dreams are genuine, that Inigo is somehow connected to Edeard. And that Edeard himself is real. How else would he know that name? Even we had almost forgotten it. And then there is the shape of the city, as well as its crystal wall.'

Nigel flinched, angry with himself for not seeing the obvious. Makkathran was circular, with a crystal wall running round it. 'Sonofabitch. It's perfectly circular, and the city wall is the base of a dome. How obvious. Then the rest of the ship must be buried underneath. I didn't know you had canals in your cities.'

'We don't. Our ships have an integral mattershift ability. Your species witnessed *High Angel* shape New Glasgow to suit you. This is what has happened here. Some other species lived in Makkathran, and the ship crafted itself to their needs.'

Nigel sat down in one of the lounge's oversized couches. 'And then they all got carried off by Skylords to live in the Heart of the Void, isn't that the local religion?'

'Yes.'

'Wow. So that's what's inside the Void? A spacetime continuum that permits mental powers? How the hell does it do that?'

'We do not know. Nigel, this is the first glimpse we have ever been granted into the Void. Our armada failed. No ship ever returned. We thought they were all dead, that the Void had defeated them. Now it seems at least one has survived.'

'Okay,' he said, becoming wary. 'So what do you want?'

'I have come to you because you are the leader of the Commonwealth.'

Nigel held up a hand, palm outwards. 'Hardly. I drove a lot of its development and policy at the start, back when wealth mattered. But that was a long time ago. ANA: Governance bosses the Central worlds around now; as for the External worlds, hell, they've got political parties to pounce on every grudge. And as a species, we're prolifically inventive when it comes to grudges.'

Vallar didn't move. 'Nonetheless, you remain the single most powerful individual alive in the Commonwealth today.'

'I have influence outside the norm, yeah.'

'We need to investigate Inigo's dreams. It is urgent.'

'There are certain resources available to me,' he admitted slowly. 'But . . . You turn back every ship from the Wall stars. I know this. I accessed the Navy reports on the stealth ships Admiral Kazimir has tried to slip past you. So how did humans wind up in there? And that civilization Edeard lives in is – what, a couple of thousand years old? Was the Void snatching people from Earth back in medieval times? No, wait; don't Edeard and Salrana talk about ships falling onto Querencia?'

'We do not know how humans got into the Void. This lack is greatly disturbing to us. However, one of your inter-galactic colony fleets disappeared two hundred years ago.'

'Disappeared?' Nigel barked. 'What do you mean, disappeared? And if you knew that, why haven't you informed us?'

'It was the second Brandt fleet, consisting of seven starships. The warrior Raiel who guard the Wall stars monitored it flying past the galactic core at considerable distance. Then they lost track of it. Please understand the monitoring was not constant. The warrior Raiel are only concerned with starships that venture close. It is possible that the fleet changed course, or decided to settle a pleasant world they found in this galaxy – and we are looking for that right now. However, it is equally possible they were somehow taken inside the Void.'

'If that's right, then time inside the Void is different – faster,' he mused. 'Well, why not? Giving people telepathic powers is a lot weirder. Temporal flow is a much simpler manipulation of space-time; we've done it enough inside wormholes.'

'The method by which humans got inside the Void is possibly a higher concern to us than even the existence of Makkathran.'

'How so?'

'A fleet of starships two hundred years ago, or a pre-technology civilization on Earth. Either would mean the Void has an ability to bring sentient species inside that we did not know about, and cannot detect. Frankly, we are very worried. Our million-year vigil may have been for nothing.'

'Huh, yeah, I see that.' Nigel took a breath and stood up again. 'Vallar, I will be happy to help you investigate Inigo as thoroughly as needed. And you were right to come to me; playing by the rules would mean Inigo could stall any normal government disclosure request for decades in the courts if he wanted.'

'I thank you. There is another aspect we would also request your assistance with.'

'Which is?'

'We would very much like to know how those humans got into the Void. Their arrival myth needs to be determined. Makkathran itself may be able to help.'

Nigel gave the huge Raiel a puzzled look. 'Yeah, but how can you accomplish that?'

'Someone has to go inside the Void and ask it.'

May 19th 3326

In all her seventeen years Alicia di Cadi had never seen anything as lovely as the isle of Llyoth. It was one of over a thousand tiny coral islands that made up the Anugu Archipelago, stretching for three hundred miles across Mayaguan's Sambrero Ocean. The C-shaped ridge of coral was barely a kilometre long. Thanks to Mayaguan's large close-in moon, low tide pulled the waves back for five hundred metres, exposing a shallow beach of the finest white sand, while on the other side of the isle a circle of low dragonspine polyps produced a shallow lagoon whose water was bath-hot. Native cycads clinging to the slender ground between had saltwater roots, allowing them to produce towering stems with emerald fronds that rolled out like sails every morning.

There were twelve wooden vacation shacks spread out along the curving shore. Deceptively ramshackle looking from the outside, but their interiors were a plush boutique design, promising the clientele a break of unashamed luxury.

Darrin had rented one of the shacks for a week. Darrin was twenty years old, a Natural human like herself, as were most of Mayaguan's population – a stubborn little External world rejecting both Higher culture and the more prevalent Advancer ethos that so many in the Commonwealth adhered to. Darrin, who had moved to her mainland village only four weeks ago, taking up a position as assistant manager at the local Walland general store franchise. Darrin, who was simply a dream of perfection with his lean dark-skinned body, flat face with a wide smile and soft brown eyes that every girl in town wanted to have gaze at her.

But Alicia was the one who he made a special effort to talk to. And he was slightly shy, and funny, and had the same simple dreams as her. He seemed to understand her so well, the frustration of living in a backwater, her timidity of venturing out into the Commonwealth with all its wonder and strangeness.

'Just don't rush,' he'd told her. 'It's been there for a thousand years, and it'll last a lot longer. Wait until you're confident enough. That's what I'm doing. I will see it all, but when I do it'll be on my terms.'

Darrin, for whom it took four whole days before she'd dumped Tobyn, her steady fella of seven months. Darrin, who she went for long walks with. Darrin, who encouraged her to keep up her schooling. Who seemed to understand her battleground relationship with her sixty-seven-year-old mother who was set in ways that belonged in some distant anachronistic century. Darrin offering support and advice and sympathy. Who was so unselfish and empathized with her own insecurities.

Darrin, who she was completely and utterly in love with like no boy and girl had ever been before, who she wanted to live with forever and give him as many children as he asked for. Darrin, who she would willingly die for.

He'd never made a move on her in those three weeks. Not that she would have said no to him. But instead he talked openly and honestly about them becoming true lovers. And then he'd suggested this week together.

With only a mild reluctance, her mother had agreed she could go. And so they took his ageing fifth-hand capsule to Llyoth's discreet landing lawn in the middle of the isle that afternoon.

Their shack had a huge circular bed. Alicia blushed in delight as she looked at it; just considering all the possibilities it offered for naughtiness that night made her deliciously excited. Then they changed quickly and went out exploring the sublime isle, running down the vast deserted beach, where they splashed about in the waves. After that they took a paddle board lesson in the lagoon, constantly falling off, they were laughing so much. Holding hands during the walk back through the lush foliage, they discovered a number of sweet little secluded glades. Every time they stopped in one, they kissed, taking longer and longer each time until she just wanted to rip his swimming trunks off there and then.

'Tonight,' he said, his gorgeous eyes never leaving hers. 'I want it to be just perfect.'

She nodded, nearly biting through her lower lip in frustration.

Dinner was served on a big wooden platform at one tip of the cove, with tables for two that had living canopies of scarlet flower vines. The only light came from candles.

Servicebots waited on the tables, but it was a real human chef working at the grill, cooking the fish. Alicia had put on her navy-blue polkadot dress, the one with a very short shirt and a neckline deep enough that Darrin just couldn't stop staring. It was heavenly being able to entrance him like that.

There were five other couples on the platform that night. But the tables were placed well apart to grant each of them solitude. Alicia smiled round at how fine everyone looked. There was only one person dining on his own, a really old man – like almost thirty or something – with shaggy blond hair, wearing a dinner jacket that was as black as she'd ever seen – but even his table was set for two.

'A tiff, do you think?' Alicia asked with a giggle.

Darrin raised his small frosted beer glass. 'Here's to us never having one.'

She sighed; it was all so delectable. Until she'd met Darrin, she'd never really understood the term *soulmate*.

Another man and woman came in. She was wearing an expensive business suit, in complete contrast to all the very feminine dresses being worn by all the other women. Her partner was in an equally sober brown suit.

'What . . .?' Alicia began. She didn't recognize the woman, who had thick jet-black hair styled primly round a very elegant face that had a strong Filipino heritage. A face that looked seriously determined. She turned to Darrin, startled to see how he had stiffened; his expression was no longer suffused with happiness. It unnerved her. She reached over the table for him, but he didn't move.

The woman stopped at their table. 'Darrin Hoss, birth registered name Vincent Hal Acraman, I am Senior Investigator Paula Myo of the Commonwealth Serious Crime Directorate. I am placing you under arrest with the preliminary charge of multiple illegal cloning. Please deactivate all your enrichments and accompany Probationary Agent Digby to our capsule. You will be taken in custody to Paris, Earth, where you will be brought before a judge.'

'What?' Alicia gasped. 'This is all wrong. Darrin never did anything illegal.'

'Unfortunately, Alicia, your assumption is incorrect.'

'How do you know my name?'

'Vincent, will you cooperate?'

'Wait!' Alicia said as her anger grew. 'This is crazy. Darrin can't have cloned anyone. He works at the Walland store, for Ozzie's sake. Everyone knows that. You've got the wrong person.'

'No,' Paula Myo said. 'I haven't.'

Darrin calmly finished his beer and stood up. Agent Digby applied a small circular patch to the side of his neck.

'Darrin?' Alicia asked. But he wouldn't look at her. 'Darrin!' She was too stunned to move. This couldn't be happening. Not to her – not to her beloved Darrin.

'Constable Gracill will escort you home,' Paula told her as Agent Digby took Darrin away. 'Your local clinic administrator has been informed of the situation, and a specialist psychiatric counsellor will be available for you.' She gave Alicia a sympathetic smile. 'Best you see them.'

'Wait! I don't understand,' Alicia cried with rising distress. 'Darrin couldn't have cloned anyone, he's just a store assistant. That's all.'

'He's not. Trust me. We opened a case file on Vincent Acraman eight years ago. We suspect he has been engaged in this cloning activity for a lot longer.'

116

'But . . . Who did he clone?'

Paula Myo's stare was unflinching. 'You.'

*

There were tears. A lot of tears. Paula had been ready for that. Not that it made watching any easier; poor Alicia's suffering was awful to behold. She cried so hard. Sobbing uncontrollably as the constable from her hometown helped her up from the table.

'It can't be right,' Alicia wailed dismally as she was gently led off the platform.

Paula let out a long breath and pinched out the candle flame in the middle of the romantic table for two.

Somebody started a slow handclap. A deliberately mocking sound that was disturbingly loud amid the silence of the remaining stunned diners.

Paula turned round, about to order her u-shadow to run an identity scan. Then she saw who it was sitting all by himself. She'd walked right past him earlier, she was so intent on Vincent Hal Acraman, her constant low-level fieldscan reporting no immediate threats.

'Well done, Investigator,' Nigel Sheldon said. 'You got your man yet again.' He held up a wine glass towards her. 'Here. I chose a Camissie; you always like a fruity white. Nicely chilled, too.'

It wasn't often Paula found herself lost for words. 'Nigel. What are you doing here?'

He played the mock innocent well, gesturing at his table with its two place settings. 'Waiting for you.'

'Nigel . . .'

'Oww, come on,' he grinned. 'It's a beautiful night, on a planet that's a little wild and invigorating. You closed another case perfectly. Don't waste the moment. Celebrate with me.'

Paula sat down opposite him. 'You're not going to propose again, are you? That's so old.'

He poured some of the Camissie into his own glass. 'Of course not. I'm happily married.'

'You always have been.'

'Monogamously now.'

'Hummm.' She raised a questioning eyebrow.

'You're such a cynic.'

'How did you know I was going to be here?'

'I have a few people who still owe me favours; they checked with your office.' He nodded at the weeping Alicia's departing back. 'That was bad timing on your part.'

'It was in-the-nick-of-time timing, if you ask me,' Paula corrected.

'Poor Alicia doesn't think so. But surely 'tis better to have loved and lost . . .'

'Vincent Hal Acraman has been doing quite enough loving, thank you.'

Nigel smiled appreciatively. 'So you still don't compromise?'

'You know the answer to that.'

'Yes, but – this is really what you're spending your time doing these days? Chasing after an illegal cloning operation?'

'It was a weird one.'

'And you do like your weird, don't you? They're the best challenge, I suppose. But, still, isn't this a bit *small* for you?'

'Why do I get the feeling you're building up to something?'

'Because you're the best detective there's ever been. So come on: chill, tell me, brag a bit to someone who appreciates you, how bad has dear old Vincent been?'

Paula took a sip of the wine, and it was a good choice. 'Bad. He's cloned Beatrice Lissard twenty-eight times that we know of, but he's good at covering his tracks. Digby will give him a memory read when they get back to Paris. I almost don't want to know what the true number will be.'

'And who's Beatrice?'

'An old girlfriend of his. Very old. I interviewed her a while back. She and Vincent grew up on Kenyang three hundred years ago. And when he was twenty and she was seventeen, they fell in love. It was as wonderful as it always is at that age, then it fell apart.'

'As it always does at that age.'

'Quite. He was starting to get obsessional as well as over-possessive, so she moved on and found someone else. He never did.'

Nigel's green eyes widened in understanding. 'So he cloned her and lived the romance all over again.'

'And again, and again, and—'

'Then Alicia . . . ?'

'Is Beatrice, yes. The latest one. He's a Higher, so biononics maintain his body at biological age twenty.'

'So every time the clone girl reaches seventeen . . . Urgggh.' Nigel wrinkled his nose and took a large drink. 'Definitely a weird one. So just to complete the creepiness, does he raise them himself?'

'No. That's why he only operates on the External worlds. He finds some Natural human woman who's having second thoughts about her impending demise. It's common enough out here. Faith often wavers in the face of death when you can see other Factions of our species carrying on partying for centuries. He poses as a representative from a Higher-sponsored charity that offers her money in a trust which will pay to have Advancer genes spliced in during a rejuvenation. That way she'll get a couple of extra centuries without even enriching with biononics. But the price of the trust fund is raising a poor little infant orphan girl.'

'Weird and sick.'

'Yeah. I'm not even sure what you call this. Serial first-lover?'

'How did you catch him?'

'Not all the Beatrice clones turned out devout Naturals after their affair burnt out. Some of them started to migrate towards the Central worlds and got themselves some good new Advancer genes spliced in. Two of them wound up on Oaktier – twenty-three years apart.' She raised her eyebrows significantly. 'Eight years ago, when the second one checked in at a clinic and got herself assayed – surprise, her genome was already registered in the government archive.'

'I'm curious: what specialist?'

'Excuse me?'

You told Alicia you've arranged a specialist counsellor for her. What specialist?'

'Troubled adolescents.'

'Ah, right, no shortage of them. So when the memory read gives you the identity of all the clones, will you put the numerous Beatrices in touch with each other?'

'I've no idea.' Paula started to read the menu. It was printed on a sheet of card, which was a novelty; it reminded her of her official homeworld: Huxley's Haven. 'That one I can comfortably kick upstairs.'

'Paula, you don't have an upstairs. Even ANA does what you ask. It recognizes your value.'

She grinned. 'Ah, is this when you tell me what tonight is all about?'

'I'm leaving the Commonwealth, did you know that?'

'Your Dynasty's latest colony fleet will be finished in three years.'

'Of course you know that,' he said sourly.

She smiled demurely. 'Unless you bottle out again.'

'That's a little harsh, don't you think?'

'Everybody thinks you left on your Dynasty's big colony fleet in 3000. Why didn't you?'

'There was some . . . *stuff* I needed to do. Besides, living in obscurity has its advantages. Do you know how wonderful it is to be able to walk about in public without anyone bugging me? For a start, I can invite a beautiful woman to dinner and it's not an instant shotgun event right across the unisphere.'

'Wait, you weren't going to ask me to go with you? That's worse than marriage.'

'Hey, I'm not that awful.'

'No. Sorry. That came out wrong. I don't want to leave, Nigel.'

'I understand. I'm proud of you, you know that, Paula?'

'Proud? What am I, a pet?'

'I made the Commonwealth possible with wormhole technology – well, me and Ozzie. And only something as wondrously crazy as the Commonwealth could create you.'

'Yeah, I was inevitable right from the moment Ozzie set foot on Mars.'

'Hey, I was the first one who set foot on Mars, thank you! Ozzie didn't trust the spacesuit we'd cobbled together. Believe it or not, he was a conservative little nerd in those days.'

'Oooh, sensitive.'

'Touché.' He raised his glass.

'So why are you finally leaving? Getting bored with your creation?'

'Exasperated, more like.'

She loaded her order into the isle's tiny network. Pan-fried choonfish in a garlic butter sauce, with crushed new potatoes and sugarsnap peas. Behind the counter, the chef gave her an approving nod. 'So we're at fault?'

'Now we have biononics, we have effectively killed death.' His hand gestured irritably at the other diners on the platform, all lovingly lost in each other. 'And what have we done with it?'

'Taken over this whole section of the galaxy, discovered alien life and other wonders, built ANA, given people the ability to live exactly how they please. Sure,' she teased sarcastically. 'So terrible it's a wonder we're not all fleeing.'

'The Central worlds are fine. People are civilized, responsible. The rest—'

'Drag you down. Oh the ingrates.'

'Why do they need you, Paula? Why should they need you? Because they're unhappy and try to get ahead the wrong way.'

'Ah, now I get it. If only everyone knew their place and just did as they were told. You're still the great dictator.'

'I was never a dictator, I just had a huge amount of political clout. I still do. And just to be the devil's advocate, Huxley's Haven was all about knowing your place. And it produced you.'

Paula smiled as she twirled the wine glass in front of her face. She might have known he'd bring up her formative years. Huxley's Haven had been a unique, and massively controversial, experimental society, where its citizens were sequenced with genes that fixed specific psychoneural profiles. In short, their personality and professional aptitude were established before they were even born. Paula had been genetically designed as a policewoman, with an obsessive compulsion to solve puzzles. She'd been taken away from Huxley's Haven, and adapted to life in the Greater Commonwealth, because there were always crimes to solve. 'I had to evolve to survive,' she reminded him. 'Those old profiling genes were sequenced right out on my fifth rejuve – or was it my fourth? Who knows? Point is: nothing stays the same. Our species has become a living free-will Darwinian organism; we are in a constant state of evolution towards post-physical status. The External worlds will become Higher eventually. Don't tell me you're finally becoming impatient?'

'And when the current External worlds are Higher, there will still be some other planets or new Faction causing trouble.'

'Of course they will. That's being human for you.'

He poured himself more wine. 'Yeah, well, I'm going to found a uniform society. Everyone agreeing to the same philosophy and goals before it starts. There'll be no dissent because we won't be taking any dissenters.'

'I can't believe you're being that simplistic. Yes, the first generation will all have the same noble goal, living worthy lives in accordance with the Party rules. But differences will creep in; they always do. By the time the third or fourth generation is born, you'll have a hundred different factions, just like the Commonwealth.'

'I disagree. Differences used to creep into societies because of unfairness and inequality. If you eradicate that, and the potential for it, right at the start, then society will remain uniform. Our technology is finally capable of that; we're effectively a post-scarcity society, Paula. We should be better than what we are.'

She sighed. 'Go get yourself reprofiled and live on Huxley's Haven; they're all happy. Or they were last time I checked.'

'It's a goal worth aiming for, Paula.'

She raised her glass to him. 'I'm proud of you for thinking and acting selflessly. A thousand years ago, who'd have thought . . . Now you're true evolution.'

He laughed as they touched glasses. 'I'll miss you.'

'All right, so now you've duly plied me with alcohol. And you've grabbed my attention with all this philosophy. Please tell me why. You know, tormenting me with this kind of suspense normally gets people thrown directly into memory read.'

'I would like to hire you.'

She pursed her lips coyly. 'Are you sure you can afford me?'

'On a consultancy basis. There's something I personally have to do, and I need your expertise to pull it off.'

'All right, I am officially intrigued. What expertise?'

'I need to know how to commit a perfect crime.'

May 22nd 3326

Golden Park was massive. Paula hadn't quite appreciated how big Makkathran2 was until she walked the mile and a half over the greensward which surrounded it. Because there were no capsules on Querencia where the original was sited, Inigo had imposed a no-overflight law which extended for ten miles around his city, which she thought was taking realism a step too far. The only way into the construction site, which was the full-scale replica of the city on Querencia, was in a ground vehicle, or on foot. She and Nigel had arrived at the project's landing field in a scheduled commercial capsule, then taken a bus to the greensward – actually a misnomer; the ground that would one day mimic the forests and meadows outside the Void's Makkathran was currently a muddy swathe of freshly ploughed and planted earth. From there they'd walked, as all the Living Dream followers did the first time, emulating Edeard who came to the city as a traveller with the Barkus caravan.

Two thousand square miles of empty government land on the eastern coast of the Sinkang continent had been signed over to Inigo by the Ellezelin government eighteen months ago. Paula suspected a great many election campaign donations (among other payments) to local and national politicians by Inigo's wealthier backers had secured it. The official explanation was that the quasi-religious movement would bring a huge influx of followers, who would boost the planet's economy. Ellezelin had been founded as a capitalist Advancer culture and was quite devout in the pursuit of money.

They trudged in through the North Gate (just as Edeard had) – although this gate was less impressive than the one cut through the wall by Rah. The wall of golden crystal around the real Makkathran was nothing more than a three-metre-high mesh fence here – so far. Inside it, the High Moat was another strip of flat grassland. Then came the North Curve Canal – two parallel trenches with slim trickles of brown water along the bottom marking where the excavation was scheduled to be. There was a bridge over the unborn waterway, leading to the Ilongo district. In Edeard's city, it had small boxy buildings with walls that leaned at precarious angles. Here it was like a refugee camp of plyplastic tents and malmetal cabins. The tracks between them were laid with a mesh of carbon fibre through which mud was oozing. The long sections were being slowly tramped down by the sheer amount of foot traffic. It was like being in some pre-Commonwealth bazaar, appropriately enough.

Three hundred metres above her, a realistic semiorganic ge-eagle was keeping pace with them, scanning the neighbourhood. Paula controlled it through a heavily shielded link. Several of the impressive-looking birds soared on the thermals above the proto-city; Inigo's followers had resequenced them from terrestrial avian DNA, duplicating the birds that so many Makkathran citizens possessed. They competed for airspace with Ellezelin's native seabirds. It wouldn't be long before other replica Void creatures appeared.

'I didn't realize there were this many ardent followers,' Paula said quietly as they stood back to allow a young goatherd to lead his animals past them. The other thing she'd noticed was the way people dressed. It was all natural cloth in old styles, some amazingly elaborate, like a costume convention; there was no semiorganic fabric or modern garments to be seen. For herself she'd chosen a simple green cotton skirt, a white blouse and a leather jacket with a satchel slung over her shoulder. Nigel had gone all out in the tunic of an Eggshaper Guild master, complete with fur-lined robe.

He was gazing to the east. 'They're doing that wrong,' he muttered.

'What?' Paula followed his gaze, seeing a tall tower surrounded by scaffolding that swarmed with constructionbots. The ge-eagle performed a fast scan of the incomplete structure. 'That's Blue Tower, the Eggshaper Guild headquarters. I recognize it from the Fourth Dream. It looks pretty accurate to me.'

'The tower is fine,' Nigel said as they started walking along the twisting tracks. 'What I mean is, when you've got a project like this, you complete the drudgework first, then build the landmarks. That's how you make sure the donations keep coming in.'

Paula had her gaiamotes open, receiving the emotional wash of the eager followers and the general emissions of the city's confluence nests. The gaiafield was an excellent simulacrum of Makkathran's telepathic buzz, reproducing the same sensations of busyness and determination that Edeard experienced. 'I don't feel there's going to be any shortage of donations.' A couple of days previously, they had run a sweep through Living Dream's official accounts. The figures involved had surprised her. Some seriously wealthy individuals had made large donations. Living Dream had refined its recruitment techniques to a degree which put most External world cults to shame. She'd almost assumed a degree of illegal coercion, maybe some advanced version of the old narcomemes, except for the sheer number of mid- and small-level devotees also handing over money – in some cases, everything they owned. It wasn't entirely limited to Advancers and Naturals either: a significant percentage of Living Dream was made up from Highers.

That level of universal commitment couldn't be written down to fraud and dirty practices. Edeard's life held genuine appeal, and from the four dreams she'd witnessed, she could actually sympathize with that. It helped that Inigo was now releasing the Fifth Dream, slowly unveiling it a few minutes each night.

And that was what made her extremely suspicious. Those perfectly self-contained sequences were being offered up a little bit too neatly for a mythical vision which was supposedly gifted, and over which he had no control. It was one of the reasons she'd agreed to help Nigel. That and the whole mystery of Makkathran being a warrior Raiel armada ship – a puzzle she just couldn't resist.

They walked from Ilongo over into Isadi, across a hologram of the Pink Canal – a wide ribbon of blue light stretching across the ground. Then Ysidro district, where the first phase of genuine Makkathran buildings were being laid out. The ge-eagle looked down on foundations of enzyme-bonded concrete forming an intriguing jumble of shapes in the raw earth. There were as many constructionbots as there were people working on the site. Large trucks were being driven at speed along makeshift roads, shifting subsoil out and material in.

'Those aren't automated,' a surprised Nigel protested as they had to scuttle quickly across one of the roads to dodge a ten-wheel digger. The driver gave them a long angry blast on the horn as he thundered by.

'You have to admit, Inigo's going for authenticity.'

'No he's not. Makkathran is actually a technology even we haven't mastered.'

Paula shook her head wryly. 'Yeah, but he doesn't know that. Or at least, if he does, he's not admitting it yet.'

Upper Grove Canal, which marked the boundary between Ysidro and Golden Park, was a giant gash in the ground six metres deep. Extruderbots were working their way slowly along the floor and walls, chewing up a thick stratum of the earth, and squeezing out a seamless sheet of enzyme-bonded concrete behind them. The ge-eagle showed her that the Zelda district was covered in big biovats breeding enzymes; Living Dream was going to need an awful lot of it to complete this remarkable homage, she thought.

They made their way over a rickety temporary bridge and into the featureless expanse that was Golden Park. Holograms of the white pillars that lined the real thing appeared insubstantial under Ellezelin's hot late-afternoon sunlight, flickering into translucency every now and then. Over on the other side of the park, the Outer Circle Canal had been completed and filled. The intersecting roofs of the Orchard Palace rose up beyond it like a giant primitive crustacean left behind by a treacherous tide, engulfing most of the Anemone district. Insect-like bots crawled over the curving edifice, dismantling the scaffolding.

'Now what?' Nigel asked.

'We wait.'

Long open-sided marquees had been set up along the side of Outer Circle Canal, protecting tables from the elements. As the sun went down, people started to congregate there. Some tents were kitchens, others served drinks. A few had stages where acoustic bands started to play. The gaiafield was conducting some very mellow emotions.

Paula sent the ge-eagle over to Orchard Palace as they found themselves a bench under one of the marquees. It circled low over the steep domes and dispensed several batches of tiny semiorganic microdrones. Modelled on *Tetranychidae* mites, they began to invade the massive headquarters of Living Dream, penetrating deeper and deeper into the maze of rooms. A three-dimensional map began to build up in her exovision.

'These can't be the actual rooms,' she murmured. 'It's just a grid of cubes made from lokfix panels. Standard cheap throw-it-up construction material. Nothing fanciful here.'

'I guess we'll see the interior in one of the dreams eventually,' Nigel said. 'In the meantime, something that can be changed easily makes sense.'

'Yes, I suppose so.' She sent the ge-eagle back for another pass, scattering more of the microdrones.

The cube rooms formed a stack of offices, living quarters for the senior disciples of Living Dream, kitchens, lounges, some labs where confluence nest technology was expanded, kilometres of identical corridors, store rooms, small replicators, a well-equipped clinic . . . It was like a government administration complex on a frontier planet. Every amenity present and correct, but basic.

'Ah, the man himself,' Paula muttered.

As the sun dipped below the horizon, Inigo had appeared at

the marquee next to the one they were using – a tall ginger-haired man with pale skin and a lot of freckles. He had the appearance of a fit Natural Faction human in his mid-thirties, with an easy, sincere smile.

People were rising from their meal to greet him. He was polite and welcoming, working the crowd like a professional politician. When Paula checked his gaiafield emissions, he seemed genuinely to appreciate the attention – an emotion mixed in with just the right humility. *I am not the chosen one, just the humble messenger.*

'He's good,' she admitted.

Nigel had turned to look. It wasn't something he had to be circumspect about. Everyone in their marquee was craning for a glimpse of the man who offered them a vision of a different exist-ence. 'How old is he?'

'Seventy,' Paula said.

'Then he's got some excellent Advancer genes to look that good at seventy.'

'He's not Higher,' Paula said, 'so maybe he had a quiet rejuve. People like their leaders to have youthful vigour.'

'Yes, you truly are a professional cynic.'

'Why else would I be here?' she countered. 'We both know that this is all too good to be true.'

'Yeah.'

They watched Inigo for several minutes until he finally accepted an invitation to sit with a group of people, most of them female and dressed like the daughters of Makkathran's nobility, all low tops and skirts fluffed out by petticoats.

'Let's go try the local food,' Nigel said.

One of the kitchen tents was doing a hog roast. They queued up and collected their paper plate, piled high with meat and apple sauce and a wedge-chunk of bread. Both of them chose a fruit juice. Nigel paid with a gold coin, stamped with the Eggshaper Guild crest: egg-in-a-twisted-circle. When they'd bought a supply of the coins at the landing field, the exchange rate had proved exorbitant.

'They must have a big problem with forgery,' Nigel decided as they sat back down again. He held up some of the brass and copper coins he'd been given as change. 'Any old fabricator could churn these out. Hell, even an old-style printer could manage it.'

'I expect they'll enrich them eventually. Right now, why would you want to come here and cheat people?'

'Good point.'

Paula stabbed a slice of meat with a wooden prong she'd been given in the kitchen. 'I'm more worried about the lack of vegetables. I know they had them in Makkathran. The whole Iguru Plain was a giant fruit and vegetable nursery.'

'Did you get any crackling? I didn't get any crackling.'

'You'd think after two thousand years they'd have a better diet.'

Nigel gave her a curious look. 'Would you really turn down the chance to join a colony?'

Paula chewed on the meat, which she had to admit was rather good. 'You're not exasperated with the Commonwealth. It's your greatest triumph to date. It's a spectacular triumph for our whole species, actually. But you are flawed by your insatiable drive. People think I'm obsessive, but I'm an amateur compared to you. Founding a whole new society is a challenge that's just about worthy of you. Plus there's the opportunity to explore a new galaxy – I assume that's where you are heading?'

He tipped his head. 'Of course.'

'And then there's this ego trip.'

'This?'

'The Raiel, guardians of the galaxy – a race so advanced they probably know more than a post-physical species – flummoxed by the Void. And who do they turn to for help? Yeah, you could turn *that* request down so easily.'

'Just like you could.'

'Granted.' She closed her eyes to study her exovision map closely. 'Ah, interesting. There's a very secure room right behind Inigo's private chambers. It has a lot of shielding.' She studied the telemetry from the microdrones which were starting to cluster around the room, combining their fieldscan. The room's shielding was high-level, brought in from the Central worlds, but Paula's microdrones were custom made by the Serious Crime Directorate's technical division based on ANA's designs. 'It's got a confluence nest inside,' she reported.

'Now why would a messiah who shares his precious gift openly and honestly need a private confluence nest?'

'That isn't actually contributing to Makkathran2's gaiafield,' Paula concluded as she studied the data.

They turned to look at Inigo again. He had just finished his meal and started saying his goodbyes. A final wave, and he was walking back to the bridge that led over Outer Circle Canal. He was accompanied by five of the wannabe-noblewomen, who giggled and chattered contentedly as they went. The whole group was giving off a very definite carnal vibe into the gaiafield.

'Oh, that takes me back to the good old days,' Nigel said wistfully.

'I thought you were happily monogamous now?'

'I am. But a guy can remember his youth, can't he?'

'Men.' Paula shook her head in disapproval.

They waited another hour then started walking round the Outer Circle Canal, eventually coming to the small pool which joined it to Second Canal, which curved inwards alongside Anemone. They were out of sight from just about everyone on Golden Park. It was a dark area, and very silent. Paula activated a scan distortion effect in her biononics. To visual sensors and anyone watching, she would have faded from view as the air around her thickened into a dark haze. To a biononic fieldscan, she would simply have vanished.

'Ready?' she asked.

The indistinct patch of dark air which was Nigel said: 'Yes.'

Paula activated her biononic force-field function, and slipped over the side of the pool. She sank straight to the bottom. For such a short immersion she didn't bother with a breather gill; her biononics could supplement her blood oxygenation for hours if necessary.

Even her enriched retinas were useless in the water, apart from showing her a wavering infrared image of her arms as she used them as ineffective paddles. She had to use her biononic fieldscan function to sense her surroundings properly. Nigel was dropping down the concrete wall behind her. Once he reached the slimy bottom, they both started walking towards the other side of the pool, then carried on along Second Canal. Even with the force field reinforcing her limb movements, it was slow going.

Second Canal ended at an even smaller pool, which connected it to Centre Circle Canal. Paula inflated the force field out into a four-metre sphere and simply bobbed to the surface. Both of them stepped out onto a pavement that boarded the rear of the Orchard Palace. Her force field switched off, leaving her standing there in perfectly dry clothes, looking up at the scaffolding which clung to the wall in front of her. Loud clanking sounds were coming from the bots high above as they dismantled the struts. Over to her left, a huge set of perron steps curved up to a high arching doorway that was the main entrance from this side. She slipped through the chunky mesh of struts up to the wall where there was an ordinary door.

Her u-shadow took care of the lock codes, and the door swung inwards. It opened into a corridor. The lights were all off in readiness for their covert exploration. She checked her u-shadow's subroutines had taken care of the alarms as well, and stepped inside.

'Cool,' Nigel said. 'This is so much better than sitting in my office telling people what to do all day.'

Paula sighed. 'Until we get caught. This isn't a game, Nigel.'

'Would you have to arrest yourself?'

'We're on a legitimate intelligence-gathering operation, so no. But it would be damn embarrassing.'

'Enough to make you leave the Commonwealth?'

'Nigel!'

They walked unseen through the Orchard Palace, going up two floors and approaching Inigo's private suite of rooms from the back. Paula unlocked a room which wasn't used for anything. Once they were inside, they shimmered back into view. She went over to the rear wall and took a couple of small plastic rectangles from her satchel. She placed them on the wall, above conduits that ran inside the composite. The modules sent active fibres worming their way through the composite to penetrate the conduits; tips insinuated themselves into the delicate optical data cables.

'Good protection,' she murmured as she read the alarm schematics building up in her exovision. A batch of subversive routines were dispatched, neutralizing the various sensor webs that covered the private room. 'Here we go.'

She stood next to the wall and ordered her biononics to produce a valency disrupter effect, focusing the energy flow into a neat ring on the composite. Behind her, Nigel started humming cheerfully.

'What the hell? Nigel!'

He gave her a roguish smile. 'Sorry. It's the theme tune from *Mission: Impossible*. It just seemed appropriate.'

'What?'

'Way before your time. It's only us true oldies that—'

'Nigel. Either behave or go wait outside.'

'Yes, ma'am.'

She let out another exasperated sigh, and concentrated on the disrupter effect. A two-metre circle of wall came loose. She caught it and rolled it to one side.

Inigo's private vault didn't contain much. An old wooden chest, which a quick fieldscan revealed contained clothes along with a lot of infusers loaded with various semi-legal sensory booster drugs, and some old-style memory kubes. The confluence nest sat in the middle of the room, a plain burnished aluminium cylinder a metre and a half high, and sixty centimetres in diameter.

'Are you going to cut that open as well?' Nigel asked.

'No.' Her u-shadow broke the service lock, and the top of the cylinder rose up silently.

The confluence nest was mostly biotech, consisting of eight long segments like desiccated muscle tissue connected with a tangle of small tubes and fibres. Its routines remained closed to every stimulus Paula directed at it from her gaiamotes. So she took the syphon from her satchel. It looked like a liver, with a slick glistening dark-red surface that pulsated slowly. She stuck it on one of the nest's segments. Its cells began to bond with the artificial neurones of the nest segment, leaching out the contents directly.

'I didn't even know that was possible,' Nigel said.

'I thought you were the great techno-nerd.'

'I do theories and strategy. I don't get down and dirty with actual hardware.'

Paula grinned. 'Devil in the detail, huh?'

Nigel was glancing round the vault. His gaze finished on the door, which was perfectly ordinary. 'Is his bedroom on the other side? I swear I can hear giggling.'

'So he's taken his pants off, then.'

'Ouch, you are one cruel lady.'

'Getting some data from the nest.' She ordered the syphon to run pattern recognition. 'Well, what do you know? We were right. There's more than four dreams stored here. Inigo has had a whole load of visions he hasn't released yet.'

'Of course he has. You don't pull a con like this without being completely sure you can see it through. And Living Dream has got to be one of the biggest cons ever.'

'We'll soon find out. I'm copying the contents.'

May 29th 3326

Inigo's Forty-Seventh Dream concluded and Nigel lay on the couch in the lake house's lounge, unmoving as he abandoned the thoughts and sights and feelings of Edeard for the very last time. He stared up at the white arching ceiling, blinking away the haunting mental afterimages of the Void's nebulas.

'Ho-lee crap!' Nigel didn't want the dream to end. He wanted to return to Makkathran, to stand with Edeard atop the tower in Eyrie as the Skylord came to carry his soul away into the Heart of the Void. He wanted a life that was as fulfilled as Edeard's had been. Enemies and wickedness defeated, decency and hope flourishing across the whole world. And the Heart of the Void: welcoming the incorporeal souls of anyone who had lived a fulfilled life, guided there by the amazing Skylords.

It took a long while for the daze of *otherness* to diminish and for him to find the strength to move again. He looked across the lounge to where Paula lay on another couch, staring ahead blankly. There were tears in her eyes.

'He did it,' she said. 'He gave them his gift in the end. What a life!'

'The entrapment potential of Edeard's life is undeniably intense,' Vallar said in a strong whisper. 'I experienced appreciation for the desire myself. Fortunately, the Raiel are immune to such emotional triggers.'

'Lucky you.' Nigel grunted and swung his legs round to a

sitting position. He tried to shake off the sensation of being bereft.

Paula exhaled loudly as she massaged her temples. 'That was a mistake.'

'You mean Edeard shouldn't have told people about the Void's time travel ability?'

'No. I mean accessing all forty-seven dreams one after the other like this. It's too much. I've lived someone else's life, centuries of it, in one week. No wonder I'm totally sympathetic to what he underwent. Vallar is right; Inigo's dreams are a narcomeme, the best there's ever been. Anyone who undergoes that is going to want to be a part of Edeard's existence. Inigo understands that perfectly. That's why he's building Makkathran2, to deliver what the faithful desperately need: to live that life, to immerse themselves in it, to believe that they will be rewarded with guidance to the Heart if they fulfil themselves.'

Nigel shook his head, amazed by Paula's ability to be so analytical in the face of the overwhelming emotional journey of Edeard's life which they'd just undergone. 'Are you saying what Edeard achieved is irrelevant?'

'No. It was astonishing. What I'm saying is that we shouldn't fall into the trap of trying to follow or emulate him. Those circumstances were unique, and they are not our circumstances. We shouldn't try to attain them.'

'Right.' Nigel could see her logic, but right now he didn't like it. What he wanted was to go back to the first dream and live them all again in sequence. 'Living Dream is going to be trouble for the Commonwealth,' he said quietly. 'Inigo has millions of devotees right now with just four dreams released. When people have experienced all of them, he's going to have billions of followers wanting to belong.'

'Is that all of the dreams?' Vallar asked.

'Yes,' Paula said. 'There was nothing else in his private confluence nest.'

'So Edeard hasn't sent anything from beyond the Heart,' Nigel said. 'It's over.'

Paula sat up and took a mug of hot chocolate from a maidbot. 'So what do we know that's going to help find out what happened to Makkathran and the others?'

'Time is strange in the Void,' Vallar said. 'The human ships arrived there two hundred years ago, and yet inside the Void two thousand years had passed before Edeard was born.'

'No,' Nigel countered, making an effort to focus on the project, to analyse what he'd witnessed. This part felt almost as good as living Edeard's life. 'Go back a stage to what the Void actually is.'

'The end purpose is to devour human minds,' Paula said slowly, 'once they've reached a certain level of rational development, or fulfilment. The environment they experience is designed to achieve that – a forced evolution if you will. Then they are taken to the Heart.'

'So it absorbs minds, and then . . . what?' Nigel said. 'Physically it expands, consuming more stars?'

'More mass,' Vallar corrected. 'Presumably to power its internal continuum.'

'It consumes mass, it consumes minds,' Paula said with a shudder. 'Your warrior cousins are right to guard the galaxy from it, Vallar. The Void is the greatest evil possible. It seeks to dominate the universe. Why? Why would such a thing be built in the first place? I don't understand.'

Nigel gave her a slightly surprised look. 'Let's consider this logically. It has layers. There's the physical Voidspace itself where the planets and nebulas exist. But there's also a layer which reacts to thought, that empowers the telepathy and telekinesis.'

'And a memory layer,' Paula said. 'Remember when Edeard travelled back in time to correct his mistakes? He could see the past; the Void had stored it somehow.'

'You can't actually travel backwards through time,' Nigel said. He raised an eyebrow at Vallar. 'Can you?'

'No. It is a fundamental of the universe that time flows one way.'

'So how does Edeard's time travel work, then?' Paula asked.

'There's another layer, a creation layer,' Nigel decided. 'Edeard's

ESP, his farsight, could perceive the whole of his life if he concentrated hard enough. And when he saw the moment he wanted to go back to, the creation layer recreated the whole Void again at that specific instant. Only he knew it was the past, because he was the one who travelled there. It's like the ultimate solipsism. Sonofabitch, no wonder the Void wants to consume the galaxy. The energy that must take . . .'

'This is like a post-physical entity,' Paula said.

'Yet it remains resolutely physical,' Nigel said. He gave her a humourless smile. 'Which is a problem. You're good at them.'

Paula took another drink of her hot chocolate, and steepled her fingers. 'Inigo served six months at the Centurion Station science base observing the Void. That's only just outside the Wall stars, so we can surmise all his dreams were received there.'

'Yes,' Nigel agreed.

'The dreams themselves are now irrelevant; Inigo is simply using them to promote and develop his Living Dream cult. Who knows, he might even believe in the Void's Heart as a solution for where the human race goes next.'

'Most likely,' Vallar said. 'Before our invasion and blockade, we heard of entire species descending into the Void; there were many rumours among the sentient races in the galaxy that it contained a spiritual resolution for biological entities. This lure it exerts was one of the reasons we built the armada.'

'So we're not going to get any more dreams,' Paula said. 'Edeard and whatever weird ethereal connection he had to Inigo is gone. It died with Edeard's body.' Her gaze flicked to the Raiel. 'You were correct, Vallar. If we want to find out how humans were taken into the Void we have to go in to find out.'

'The Void is hostile to Raiel,' Vallar replied. 'Humans appear to thrive there.'

Nigel looked at Paula again.

She pulled a face. 'So who do we get to go in?' she asked.

'Someone who's been prewarned about the Void's nature. Someone who's smart enough to ask the right questions. You would be perfect.'

'As would you. But I'm not going to flip you for it. In the Starflyer War, we took criminals out of suspension and offered them the opportunity to serve the Commonwealth in return for a reduced sentence.'

'Oh, yeah,' Nigel said, surprised she'd even mentioned that. 'Psychopaths and loons are just the kind of people we should be sending into that environment.'

'Ask Living Dream followers. Every one of them would happily volunteer.'

'Again, a great choice to represent us. We both know I'm the one that's going to have to go in.'

'I thought you were leaving the Commonwealth.'

'I am. But dear old Vincent Hal Acraman has shown us how we get round that little problem, hasn't he?'

July 9th 3326

The chrome-blue capsule descended out of the glaring Augusta sky to touch down on the lake house's lawn. Nigel Sheldon walked out and immediately put on a pair of sunglasses. In this new body, everything seemed brighter and louder. That or his old thought routines were simply jaded and faded, unused to perceiving the universe through sharp eyes. It was a better theory; those old routines were having trouble controlling this body with its increased strength and reaction times. He had to concentrate hard just to walk. This body's muscles were strong enough to lift him off the ground at each step, as if he was in lunar gravity, not Augusta's point-nine-three Earth standard.

He stood on the lawn and took a long deep breath. The El Iopi wind was blowing strongly today, bringing the continent's heat with it. Inside his grey-green onepiece coverall, he started sweating. His original came out of the capsule behind him, wearing a purple silk suit. He slipped a pair of mirrorshades on with exactly the same gesture Nigel had just used.

Paula Myo was standing on the lake house's veranda, along with Vallar. She gave him and the original Nigel a sardonic grin. Nigel licked his lips and walked over.

'Welcome to the world,' Paula said directly to him.

Nigel guessed it was the hair which separated them. His original still needed a haircut, while his had barely grown more than a short frizz. 'Did he tattoo the number *two* on my forehead?' he asked.

Her mouth twitched. 'Do you remember me?'

Nigel took both her hands in his, and gave her a fulsome grin. 'Nothing could banish you from my mind.'

'That's very sweet.'

'So I was thinking, as the chances of me coming back are about a million below zero, how about you and I spend the last few days I have in this universe together? Condemned man, and all that.'

She opened her eyes wide with mock adoration. 'The night you come back,' she breathed huskily, 'I'll fling myself at you like Ranalee on Edeard.'

'Ah, dammit. They used to say it was impossible for you to lie,' he said, remembering the young Paula who had caused such a stir when she started working for the Commonwealth Serious Crime Directorate all those centuries ago.

'Come back and find out,' she told him.

'Thank you, but I remember what fate Ranalee had in mind for Edeard.'

'Yeah, but what a way to go.'

The original Nigel cleared his throat, his expression mildly disapproving. 'If you two have *quite* finished . . .'

They all went into the lounge, and the window wall glass swept shut behind them. Nigel sat next to Paula on one of the wide grey couches, while his original sat opposite them – like some kind of nineteenth-century chaperone. Vallar stood in the middle of the room.

'How do you feel?' Paula asked.

Nigel gave his original a smug look. 'Better, stronger, faster than before. I should have downloaded into a re-life clone centuries ago.'

'And how fortunate: you managed to keep your ego intact, too,' she said drily. 'What could possibly go wrong?'

Nigel laughed. 'So how have you three done while I was being grown?' he asked. 'My memory stops five weeks ago, just after we'd gone through Inigo's dreams and decided on this – me.' He cocked his head to glance at his original. 'And the Dynasty's network is sealed against me.'

'You wouldn't find what we're doing on the Dynasty's network anyway,' his original replied. 'This is a very private operation.'

'The ship is ready,' Paula told him.

'How biological is it?' Nigel asked.

'About seventy per cent,' his original said. 'We've even managed to construct some ultradrive systems out of semiorganics.' A slight pause. 'Mark Vernon is in charge of construction.'

Nigel smiled in delight. 'Wow, we're really reverting to the good old days. What did Mark have to say about being brought in?'

'He's loving it, of course,' his original said. 'Between moaning like hell. But there really is no one better for integrating odd systems like this.'

'Excellent.' Before Nigel's new body had been fast-grown in a vat at the Dynasty's private clinic, his original had agreed with Paula and Vallar that organic systems were the most likely to retain functionality in the Void. Something in that weird continuum seemed innately hostile to most technology. 'Anything new come up?'

He watched his original and Paula exchange a glance.

'Not really,' Paula said.

'But . . .' he prompted.

'We've been trying to understand the Skylords. They seem to be independent; they're certainly sentient in a savant fashion. But at the same time they only exist to guide souls, or fulfilled minds, to the Heart. That's a little puzzling.'

'Paradoxical,' his original said.

'So?' Nigel asked.

'We're uncertain if you can rely on them,' Paula told him. 'They don't seem to be antagonistic, more like aloof, which again is contrary, given the function they perform.'

'I'm not sure something like that can evolve naturally,' the original Nigel said. 'They were probably created by the Void Heart or its controlling mechanism, whatever that is. But they do seem a little odd.'

'Unlike the rest of the Void,' Nigel observed.

'The Void is odd, granted, but it's all integral, and even has a kind of internal logic.'

'You said it,' Nigel said. 'They serve a function, guiding fulfilled souls to the Heart.'

'It just doesn't quite seem right,' Paula said.

'You can't seriously think the Skylords evolved outside and then fell into the Void like other species,' Nigel countered. 'That's even more illogical.'

'Our neural bioware is artificial,' Paula said. 'It is technically machinery, yet it can hold sentience. And we've seen AIs become sentient.'

'Don't remind me,' Nigel muttered.

'So they might be external artificial organisms, AI starships or an alien variant of ANA, which have adapted to the Void,' the original Nigel said.

Nigel looked over at Vallar. 'Is that what Makkathran has become?'

'Makkathran sleeps. That is all we have seen. It seems to respond to Edeard at some autonomic level. We have composed a stimulant that you may download into it. We hope this will trigger its awakening.'

'That has got to be one giant needle.'

'It is a thought routine that you should be able to deliver through the "longtalk" telepathy which Querencia's human citizens use. In a worst-case scenario, your ship could make a physical connection to Makkathran's network. The conduits would be relatively easy to identify.'

'Okay, and after it awakes?'

'If there is a way out, it will use it.'

'And if not?'

'The information it has gathered simply by being in there for such a period of time will be invaluable.'

Nigel exhaled a long breath. 'And we're still hoping a gaiafield connection will get that information out?'

'It did for Inigo and Edeard – somehow,' the original Nigel said. 'So it ought to allow me to dream you. The gaiafield function was sequenced into you, every neurone has it. If that doesn't work, I don't know what will.'

'We made you as best as we could to survive the Void environment,' Paula said. 'Your brain is faster and smarter than normal. With luck, that should give you a stronger psychic ability than everyone else. You have weaponized biology in case it's not.'

'What about my backups?' Nigel asked. They had all decided he would need help he could trust implicitly.

'They're ready,' the original Nigel said. 'Modifying a standard ANAdroid was relatively easy, certainly compared to growing you. We managed to build in every ability I thought of. They're fully feature-morphic. Mentally, they can operate independently, or you can go multiple with them as soon as you activate them; their neural structure is compatible with your routines, and they have gaiafield access capability, too. We don't think anyone's ESP can tell the difference between them and a standard human.'

'Right.' Nigel looked at Paula. 'Anything else? You don't look happy.'

'I'm confused by the genistar animals,' she admitted.

'What about them?' Nigel recalled how prevalent they were on Querencia. A native species that humans had learned how to shape into various subspecies to help with simple manual labour. It was Edeard's Eggshaper Guild that was responsible for them. The genistars had several subspecies, which could be telepathically selected just after egg fertilization by someone particularly skilled in the art.

'How do you evolve that function naturally?' Paula asked. 'Granted, it's a big strange universe out here, but I don't believe that could ever happen. They have to be artificial, which is slightly contrary, because that ability to manipulate their final shape can only happen in the Void. As they're not sentient, that has to be performed by someone else, someone with an excellent telepathic ability. Simply put, they were developed as a slave species. And I'm not sure how you'd do that in a technology-free environment like the Void.'

'That's a lot of conjecture you've come up with, there,' Nigel said bluntly. 'I'm not going to prejudge them.'

'It's a logical extrapolation. Edeard's civilization never encountered the slavers themselves. I'm assuming they were the ones who lived in Makkathran before humans, but that doesn't necessarily mean they all vanished into the Heart. I just want you to be extremely careful around genistars, that's all.'

'Got it.' Nigel looked round the three conspirators, feeling a buzz of excitement he hadn't known in centuries. 'So we're basically ready to go, then?'

'Indeed,' his original said.

Nigel regarded Paula slyly. 'What about my emergency fall-back? The fabled plan B?'

She sighed reluctantly. 'The package is ready. But you have to *really* need it. If I find out you activated it without any kind of disaster looming . . .'

'Yeah, I know. And thank you,' he said sincerely. 'All right then, I guess I'm ready. Let's go kick some Void butt.'

'Oh, I knew it,' Paula said disapprovingly. 'Nigel, that's completely the wrong attitude. This is an information-gathering mission, not a war party.'

'Hey, you're getting seriously gloomy; I'm just trying to lighten things up. You know me.'

'I certainly do. That's why I came up with plan B.'

'Have a little faith. This calls for me being smart and sneaky. That I can manage. I won't call for the intellectual cavalry unless I really need to.'

'Are you sure you want to do this?' she asked. 'Really sure?'

Nigel did his best to lower his gaze, but the stare she was giving him seemed to be looking into his mind far more easily than any telepathy. 'It's a simple mission,' he said earnestly. 'Land as close as I can, try and wake Makkathran. Dream whatever I find back out to you. If the ship still works, try and follow a Skylord to the Heart and dream that back for you as well.'

'And if it doesn't work?' Paula asked.

'Then I'll go live a quiet life somewhere in the countryside. Maybe teach them better medicine.'

'Don't do anything—'

'Stupid?' Nigel asked.

'I was going to say, dangerous,' she said. 'And to that we can add: foolhardy, reckless, irresponsible—'

'Okay! Hell, I get it, I'll be good.'

Paula gave him a mournful smile. 'That would be nice.'

'Mark has a whole load of instructions for you,' his original said. 'Take as long as you want to familiarize yourself with the ship, and after that we'll leave.'

Paula leaned over and gave him a light kiss. 'You take care. I mean it. You'll have me to deal with if you don't.'

'I am aware of that.'

She grinned. 'You have the naming privilege. What are you going to call the ship?'

Nigel grinned back. '*Skylady*, of course. What else?'

July 11th 3326

The *Skylady* rose silently up into Augusta's night sky. A fat ellipsoid twenty-five metres long, with rounded delta wings. Her nondescript grey-green fuselage soaked up the starlight, making her very difficult to see.

Umbaratta flew beside her, Nigel Sheldon's personal starship – a sleek teardrop ultradrive, capable of flying anywhere in the galaxy at fifty-six lightyears an hour. Two thousand kilometres above Augusta, they both rendezvoused with Vallar's spherical starship, and all three went FTL.

*

Eighteen hours later, a long way outside the Commonwealth, they dropped back into ordinary space. The nearest star was three light-years away.

Sitting in the *Umbaratta*'s circular cabin, Nigel Sheldon told the smartcore to scan round. The starship's excellent sensors could detect nothing. He'd been expecting a Raiel starship of some kind to be waiting for them. One of their colossal warships, he'd hoped. They were still over thirty thousand lightyears from the Void, and he was extremely interested in how the Raiel were going to transport them there. The Commonwealth had never managed to produce anything faster than ultradrive.

Vallar opened a link. 'Stand by,' she told him.

Nigel opened his gaiamotes, and detected his clone's thoughts. Like his, they reflected a quiet anticipation.

'How much faster do you think their ship will be?' he asked.

'It won't be a ship,' the clone replied.

'How do you figure?'

His clone's thoughts turned smug. 'We only use starships inside the Commonwealth because of politics, and outside because it's practical. The Raiel are evangelicals devoted to saving the galaxy, and they were more technologically advanced than us a million years ago.'

'Well argued.'

'You really do need to get a better brain.'

'Smartass.'

'Thankfully, yes.'

They shared a mental smile.

The *Umbaratta*'s smartcore reported an exotic energy distortion manifesting five hundred kilometres away. Nigel linked in to the external sensors, and his exovision showed him the wormhole opening across the starfield. It was a large one, measuring three hundred metres in diameter.

'This will take you to your destination,' Vallar told them. 'The warrior Raiel are waiting for you. Nigel, I would like to thank you for your help.'

'Anytime,' Nigel replied airily. He could feel a spike of irony rising in his clone's thoughts at the polite response.

Umbaratta and *Skylady* flew into the wormhole, emerging a second later in a very different part of the galaxy. Hundreds of lightyears away, a shimmering band of giant stars formed a magnificent archway across space. The Wall stars, *Umbaratta*'s smartcore confirmed, a bracelet of intense blue-white light surrounding the galactic core – not that there was much left of it. The Void was slowly expanding into the massive Gulf which the Wall surrounded, the dangerously radioactive zone of broken stars and seething particle storms. Not far away – in galactic terms – was the loop: a dense halo of supercharged atoms that orbited the Void. It burnt a lethal crimson across the Gulf, though that was only the visible aspect of its electromagnetic emissions; its X-ray glare was powerful enough to be detected clear across the galaxy.

Nigel hurriedly reviewed the flight data in his exovision, with particular emphasis on the force fields. They were protecting the hull against the prodigious flood of ultra-hard radiation outside, but it was taking a lot of power to maintain them.

Three massive Raiel warships were holding station behind the wormhole, their shielding only revealing dark spectres, like globes of solidified smoke that were hard for the sensors to focus on. And behind them . . . 'Sonofabitch,' Nigel muttered. A Dark Fortress sphere glowed an intense indigo from the swirl of exotic energy it was manipulating. The size of Saturn, the sphere was a lattice of dark struts. Its external shell was wrapped round a series of concentric inner lattice shells, each possessing different physical properties, with a core that was full of extremely odd energy functions.

'No wonder they can produce a wormhole that reaches half-way across the galaxy,' the clone Nigel said. 'The size of the damn thing!'

Humans had first encountered the awesome machines during the Starflyer War. The Raiel had used one to encase an entire solar system in an impenetrable force field, imprisoning the psychotic alien Primes inside. The starship crew who first encountered the sphere that was generating the force field had named it, somewhat quixotically, the Dark Fortress.

It was only later, when the Commonwealth was invited to join the Raiel in observing the Void, that the Navy discovered it was the Raiel who had built the Dark Fortress. At which point the nomenclature was diplomatically shortened to DF sphere. There were a dozen DF spheres in the Centurion Station star system, and many thousands more positioned all the way around the Wall. All the Raiel would say about them was that they were part of their defence against the Void should it start its long-feared catastrophic expansion phase.

A link opened from one of the warships. 'I am Torux, ships-captain. Please stand by for teleport on board.'

'Thank yo—'

The *Umbaratta* was abruptly sitting in an empty, softly lit compartment the size of a CST terminal just as Nigel's exovision icons were telling him a T-sphere had manifested. The *Skylady* sat next to it. Nigel had to smile at the guilty thrill his clone was emitting into the gaiafield; it matched his own.

'We are proceeding to the insertion point,' Torux told them. 'Transit time, seven hours fourteen minutes.'

Nigel's excitement was instantly replaced by a twinge of anxiety, also matched then surpassed by his clone.

'Welcome aboard, Nigel Sheldon,' Torux said. 'You are welcome in my habitation section. Please deactivate your ship's force fields.'

There was a moment of hesitation, the petulant thought: *What if I don't?* Which he knew his clone would also be having. *Umbaratta* was just about the pinnacle of Commonwealth technology, yet it was nestled here in some obscure corner of this monster warship and he finally knew what the NASA astronauts had felt after they landed on Mars to plant their flag, only to find him waiting there beside a prototype wormhole laughing at them because his technology was oh so superior. No human had ever been on board a Raiel warship. It was a historic moment on many levels.

He switched off the force fields and a T-sphere manifested in the cabin. He was snatched away . . .

. . . to a Raiel's private chamber similar to those he'd visited in the *High Angel*. His link to *Umbaratta*'s smartcore remained; he had courteous hosts, then. The room was circular, fifty metres in diameter, with a ceiling that was lost in the gloom above him, making it seem as if he was standing at the bottom of some giant mine shaft. The walls rippled as though they were a single sheet of water; small coloured jewels glimmered behind the idiosyncratic surface effect casting a wavering sheen of phosphorescence.

A warrior Raiel stood before him. Nigel was expecting it to be larger than the Raiel on *High Angel*. *If you've spent a million years breeding for war, everything should be bigger and tougher.* But this one was actually smaller than Vallar, although its skin had meta-morphosed into an armour of blue-grey segments with tiny lights sparkling below the surface like entombed stars.

'I am Torux,' it said in a high-pitched whisper. 'Welcome aboard our ship, *Olokkural.*'

'It is impressive.'

'I would like to personally thank you for helping us.'

'The Void affects all of us, ultimately,' Nigel said. 'Helping you was the least I could do; your vigil is truly selfless. I will do what I can, though I have to say I am not terribly confident.'

'Paula Myo considered this to be a worthwhile attempt.'

'Yes, indeed. Do you know Paula?'

'We have heard of her from our cousins on *High Angel.*'

And why does that not surprise me? Nigel could feel his clone laughing.

'We have a link that will enable you to observe the external environment,' Torux said.

'Thank you,' Nigel replied as his u-shadow reported that a connection to the ship was opening.

*

Seven hours after coming aboard, Nigel watched the *Olokkural* and its two sister warships drop out of FTL and slow to a relative halt half a million kilometres from the lightless boundary of the Void. Greater than the distance from the Earth to the Moon, and it had taken millennia for humans to bridge that gap, but the scale unveiled before him was severely intimidating to Nigel's primitive core. This was the eater of stars, of cultures beautiful and terrible, consumer of hope. The one true enemy of all species across the galaxy.

Five more Raiel warships were already waiting for them, along with seven DF spheres. When he saw what else was out there, Nigel gave a smile of complete admiration.

'Oh, yeah,' he heard his clone say in the *Skylady*'s cabin. 'Win or lose, this is going to make it all worthwhile.'

The DF spheres were using an intricate mesh of gravitational forces to suspend three blue-white supergiant stars, preventing them from the final plunge into the infinite gravity tide of the event horizon which would tear them apart. Even here, half a million kilometres out, surrounded by a cage of inverted gravity fields, their incandescent coronas bulged and writhed, spitting out brutal flares that played across the boundary, dissolving into meta-cascades of radiation as their individual particles were sucked inward and crushed into their sub-atomic components.

'Please stand by,' Torux said.

'Are you sure this is going to work?' Nigel asked. 'Even an ordinary event horizon is impossible to break.'

'This is the method by which we inserted our armada.'

And look what happened to them, Nigel thought.

'We begin,' Torux announced.

The DF spheres changed the quantum characteristics of the cage. Nigel could sense the forces alter even though he couldn't comprehend their nature. The surface of the stars, already impossibly hot, bright and violent, began to burn still brighter as their atoms lost cohesion and transformed into pure energy. For over a quarter of an hour the compression wave grew, travelling inwards, while the coronas mutated to relativistic barbs of raw energy stabbing out in every direction through the cage bands. Subjected to the artificial implosion dynamics even their own incredible gravity couldn't absorb, the three supergiants went nova.

Instead of allowing them to detonate in a radiative blast of energy and superdense hydrogen, the DF spheres did something weird to local spacetime. The power of the novas was converted into negative gravity, and directed in one direction. Straight into the Void's boundary.

'Ho-lee crap,' Nigel grunted, his arms instinctively waving round trying to find something to hold on to as the *Olokkural* accelerated fast across the horribly short distance to the Void. *Skylady* was teleported outside, held in place by a gravity node. The warship's force fields protected it from the cosmic energies wrecking local spacetime.

Ahead of the *Olokkural*, the Void's perfectly smooth black boundary began to distort upwards, as if some kind of tumour was growing inside. Up and up it was stretched by the terrible stress of negative gravity, forming a single grotesque mound.

Nigel held his breath. He could feel his clone closing his eyes, hands gripping the cabin's acceleration couch.

At the peak of the distension, the Void's boundary tore open. Elegant nebula light shone out into real spacetime. The *Olokkural* released *Skylady*, then veered away at two hundred gees, whipping round in a hard parabola and heading back out away from the shrinking rent.

Skylady slipped in through the gap, and thirty seconds later the Void's wounded boundary closed up behind it.

Nigel gulped down air again.

'Did he survive?' Torux asked.

'Yes.'

BOOK THREE

Revolution for Beginners

1

An hour after the patrol squad broke camp, the morning mist still hadn't lifted. Grey haze clung to the ground, swirling slowly round the big ecru-shaded tree trunks, keeping the temperature pleasantly low. All across the densely wooded valley, native birds called to each other in their strange oscillating whistle, competing with the incessant rustling sound of bussalore rodents creeping through the undergrowth. Bienvenido's hot sun was nothing more than a blur-patch above the eastern horizon. Nonetheless, its intensity fluoresced the mist, making it difficult to see more than ten metres.

Slvasta dragged his boots through the feathery lingrass that grew lavishly between the trunks of the quasso trees, ripping the twiny blades apart. It was easier than picking his feet up; the lingrass came halfway up his shins. Dew slicked his stiff regiment-issue canvas garters; he knew that by midday that damp would be soaking his socks and rubbing his feet raw. An hour into the sweep, and he was bored and irked already.

'Crud, Slvasta, why not just ring a bell to tell the Fallers we're here?' Corporal Jamenk chided.

'This stuff is everywhere,' Slvasta complained, as he carried on tearing the wispy strands apart. 'I can't help it.'

Jamenk drew an annoyed breath, but decided not to push it. Slvasta gave Ingmar a desperate look, but his friend wasn't about to take his side in any dispute with the corporal.

Slvasta was peeved by the betrayal. The two of them had signed on with the regiment in Cham three months ago. Slvasta could have done it earlier, but he'd agreed to wait for Ingmar's seventeenth birthday so they could do it together. Signing on was all he'd wanted to do since he was nine, and his father and uncle had vanished after a Fall. The regiment had never found the bodies, not in all the sweeps they made of the county during the following month. Even at school, everyone knew what *that* meant.

Two years later his mother had married Vikor; he was a decent man, and Slvasta now had two little half-brothers. But the loss of his father – the way he was taken – was a fire which burnt his very soul. He knew he would never be fulfilled, never be guided by the Skylords to the Giu nebula where the Heart of the Void waited, not until he had exorcized his demons. And that would only happen when he had his vengeance on the diabolical Fallers, smashing up every one of their eggs that plagued the world.

Joining the regiment was the first step in achieving that. Slvasta had dreams of rising up through the ranks until he was Bienvenido's lord general, commanding troops across the globe. He would show the Fallers no mercy until the Forest which birthed them eventually realized it could never defeat him, and retreated from Bienvenido forever. Now that would be true fulfilment.

However, the reality of regimental life was altogether more mundane that he'd been expecting. Uniform to be painstakingly maintained. Horses to muck out. Food you wouldn't even use as pigswill back home on the farm. Drill – endless drill, marching round the headquarters' yard. Flamethrower practice against mannequins representing Fallers – now that was exciting, the two times he'd got to do it. Search exercises that were basically little more than camping trips out in the wilds beyond the county's farmland.

Then finally, the beacon fires had been lit. There had been a Fall in the lands around Prerov, six hundred miles east along the Eastern Trans-Continental line, the main railway track that bisected the continent from west to east. The regiment had swung into action. They'd deployed their full strength of five hundred troops in less than three hours. Along with all their equipment and mods, they'd embarked the special train laid on for them. Half the town had come out to cheer them off.

He had spent most of the journey with his face pressed against the train carriage window, watching the beacon flames roaring away in their huge iron cage braziers. So big they took days to burn out. He could almost feel their heat every time the steam train raced past one, helping to raise his excitement and determination.

The bulky iron engine had finally pulled in to Prerov's station along with several other troop trains. Eight regiments had been called out to help sweep the estimated Fall zone for eggs. It was the first time Slvasta had ever been outside his own county – his first time anywhere, really. The station was in the middle of the commercial district at the foot of the striking mountain town on the western end of the Guelp range. Slvasta stood on the platform and stared up at the regional capital in delight. Prerov was over two thousand years old. Humans and mods had spent generations hacking into the stony slopes, producing terrace after terrace cluttered with buildings that had whitewashed walls and red clay tile roofs. Most of them were shaded under huge tomfeather and flameyew trees growing in their courtyards. And, perched right at the top, without any trees close by, was the great observatory dome of the Watcher Guild, whose eternal vigil helped protect Bienvenido from Falls. He was desperate to climb the steep winding steps that knitted the terraces together and explore the ancient town, with its wealth and colour, and lots of well-to-do girls who would probably be appreciative of regiment troops risking their lives.

As it happened, the regiment didn't even spend one night billeted in town. A squadron of Marines had arrived from Varlan, the capital, as soon as the beacons were lit. Smart tough men in their imposing midnight-black uniforms, they'd quickly claimed the authority of the Captain and started organizing the regiments. It was important to get the sweeps underway as soon as possible, before the eggs had time to ensnare anyone. So an hour after the train pulled in, Corporal Jamenk's squad, which comprised just Slvasta and Ingmar, had been assigned to sweep the whole Romnaz valley. Slvasta had been proud of the responsibility – it was a huge area. Until Captain Tamlyan had sneeringly pointed out that they were on the very fringe of the estimated Fall zone; it was an assignment to keep the new recruits and an untried corporal out of the way and out of trouble.

A convoy of farm carts had taken them and eleven other squads out of Prerov, the humans rattling round in the back while the regiment's mods trotted alongside. The farmland immediately outside the regional capital was like an extended garden, with the fields and meadows and groves immaculately tended by mods and their human owners. Lovely villas sat in the middle of each estate, larger and grander than any of the houses back in Cham. Streams and canals were meshed together, providing excellent irrigation and drainage. Pump houses clattered away, puffing smoke into the blazing sapphire sky as the engines spun big iron flywheels, maintaining the all-important water levels. It was the only noise the troops could hear. No one else was on the broad road with its guardian rows of tolmarc trees. The villages they passed through had sentries – the old men and stout women; the younger, able, men were in the local regiment reserve, out helping to sweep.

On the second day, the farms were larger, and less arable. Cattle, sheep and ostriches roamed across bigger and bigger meadows. Abandoned quarries disfigured the land. Slvasta was amazed at how much ore, sand and rock had been dug out in the past. The hills to the south grew steeper – precursors to the distant Algory mountains. Active quarries were still and silent, their mod workforces penned up in corrals while their wranglers waited for the sweeps to finish and give the all-clear. Forests began to dominate the rolling landscape, most of them with big square areas eaten out of them where logging operations were felling timber. Farms were further and further apart, and most buildings were made from wood rather than stone.

Trees lined both sides of every public road on Bienvenido,

forming leafy avenues the whole world over. It was a law dating back to Captain Iain, who ruled seven hundred years after Landing, so travellers could always see the route ahead. Here, they were just icepalm saplings, the hope of a road to come rather than a definitive path. The convoy began to split up, with carts rolling off at junctions down tracks marked by even smaller saplings. As the sweltering afternoon stretched out interminably, Jamenk's squad rattled on until they finally left the sentinel trees behind. All that marked the way to Romnaz valley now was a couple of wheel ruts in the ground. Their driver dropped them off at the head of the valley. The last village they'd passed was half a day behind them.

'I'll pick you up back here in eight days,' he told them. So their sweep began.

*

The squad's equipment and supplies were carried by a regimental horse-mod and a pair of dwarf-mods. Slvasta was never entirely comfortable around the creatures. They were different from most of Bienvenido's native animals, which bolstered his suspicions. He just found the whole thing weird – the way their embryos could be moulded by skilled adaptors into any form. In their neut form they were simple six-legged beasts half the size of a terrestrial horse, but fatter. Six odd lumps along their back were vestigial limbs which the adaptors could coax out in the various mods if they were needed. He simply didn't see how that could be natural.

For the mod-horse that carried the bulk of the squad's kit, adaptors had produced something not dissimilar to a basic neut, but larger and with stronger legs. More subtle internal changes gave them colossal stamina; they weren't fast, but they could carry a load for days at a time. And the simple thoughts in their brain could be easily controlled with 'pathed instructions.

The mod-dwarfs were loosely modelled on a humanoid form. With four legs and four arms kept in vestigial form, they were bi-pedal, though clumsy with it. Their heads came up to Slvasta's elbow. Jamenk had given them the flamethrower cylinder backpacks to carry. If they did find any Fallers, the mod-dwarfs could hand over the weapons quickly. In an emergency they could even fire them – though Slvasta wasn't entirely convinced about how good their aim was.

Flamethrowers were supposedly a fool-proof method of dealing with Fallers. They could cover themselves with much stronger protective teekay shells than most humans; bullets didn't always get through. Even so, Slvasta felt reasonably confident that the carbine he carried on a sling would give any Faller a pretty hard time of it. If the weapon worked, that is; they jammed all too often in practice firings.

The mist began to lift, long tendrils winding up lazily into the sky, where they vanished amid the delicate indigo twigwebs of the quasso trees. Bright beams of sunlight filtered down past the blue-green leaves, dappling the lingrass. The sky above became very blue again, with no clouds.

Slvasta took his tunic jacket off, and 'pathed a mod-dwarf. The dumb creature trudged over and took the jacket from him.

'Did you ask permission to do that?' Jamenk asked. 'Regiment uniform will resist an eggsumption.'

Slvasta didn't let his contempt for the corporal show through his teekay shell; he was too used to the idiot's insecurities for that. Jamenk had been a corporal for four months; he was twenty-two with all the maturity of a twelve-year-old. The youngest son of the Aguri family, who owned some land in the county, which was why he was in the regiment in the first place; he wasn't going to inherit anything. And also why he'd got a promotion while better men languished in the ranks.

'Sorry, corporal,' Slvasta said in a strictly level voice. 'It's getting warm. I was worried the jacket might slow down my reactions when we come across the eggs.' And he was mighty dubious about the jacket being resistant to eggsumption; it was just ordinary tweed soaked in mythas herb juice.

'All right,' Jamenk said. 'But nothing else, okay?'

'Yes, corporal.' Slvasta made sure he didn't look at Ingmar. They'd both smirk. No telling how Jamenk would react to that.

Half the time he wanted to be their friend; the rest of the day was spent trying to lord it over them. Inconsistency: another sign of a truly bad NCO.

After another half-hour the mist had vanished altogether. Jamenk and Ingmar had both taken off their jackets. Plenty of sunlight was filtering down through the trees, heating the still air underneath. Even the bussalores had stopped rushing round as the heat built. Thankfully the lingrass was shorter here, or it would be exhausting work just to walk.

Jamenk unrolled the map Captain Tamlyan had given them, then closed his eyes. Somewhere high above, his mod-bird was gliding on the thermals, keen eyes scouring the bedraggled tree canopy that smothered the rumpled valley – a view which skilled ex-sight could borrow. Slvasta wondered why the regiment didn't give all of them a mod-bird and train them to see through it; the ungainly things had excellent eyesight and actually did most of the searching during a sweep. But it was a status thing, of course. Officers and NCOs only, distinguishing them from the ordinary troops. That would be one of a very, *very* long list of things Slvasta was going to change when he was lord general of the regiments.

'I can see where they've been logging,' Jamenk said, his eyes tight shut. 'Another couple of klicks.'

The track was easy enough to follow. It wasn't used much, but there must have been some traffic. Trees had been chopped down where there were particularly dense clusters. A couple of streams they'd crossed had been forded by trunks laid across the bed. According to the Prerov mayor's office, the Romnaz valley was claimed by the Shilo family, who were foresters by trade.

Jamenk nodded in satisfaction and rolled his map up. 'Come on.'

The mods began plodding forwards again. Slvasta started to follow the corporal. He knew he should be looking round for any sign of a Fallen egg. Smaller trees broken, strange tears in the canopy of larger forests, long furrows in the ground, dead fish in ponds. But none of that was going to be visible in this wild forest. It was impossible to see twenty metres on either side of the track.

He just kept trudging on, remembering to take regular sips of water from his canteen. The air was horribly humid, but he was sweating hard. It was important to keep hydrated. That was one of the few things he remembered his father telling him when they were out in their smallholding's fields.

'This has been used recently,' Ingmar said. He was looking at the track as it passed across a runnel.

Ingmar was a skinny youth whose limbs seemed to belong to someone even taller, with glasses that had the thickest lenses Slvasta had ever known. They made his eyes implausibly large, showing up the milky stains in his irises. In another ten years, Ingmar was going to be using his ex-sight alone – just like his father before him, who'd been eye-blind for the last eleven years.

He shouldn't be able to qualify for the regiment, either, Slvasta thought guiltily. But Ingmar had been so desperate to prove himself capable of living independently from his family, and the recruiting sergeant was always keen for new troops.

'It's a cart track,' Slvasta pointed out reasonably. 'The Shilos use it to get in and out of the valley.'

'I know that,' Ingmar said defensively. 'I mean this cart was here in the last couple of days.' He pointed at some wheel ruts in a patch of damp ground. The lingrass had been crushed into the mud. 'See? The breaks are fresh.'

'Well that's good,' Slvasta said. 'It means they're still around.'

Ingmar gave the ruts another glance. 'Nobody moves round after a Fall. All the farms and villages wait for the all-clear.'

Slvasta threw his arms wide and gestured at the immense forest. 'Because anyone living here is really going to know what's going on, right?'

Ingmar ducked his head.

'There aren't any beacons out here,' Slvasta persisted. 'The Shilos won't even know there's been a Fall.'

'Okay,' Ingmar said sullenly.

'Come on, you two,' Jamenk said. 'You're arguing about crud. We can ask the Shilos if they came in or out when we get to the croft.'

'Yes, corporal,' Ingmar said. He stood up, not looking at Slvasta.

After a minute of silent walking, Slvasta used a private 'path to say a very direct and humble: 'Sorry,' to his friend. Before they'd signed up, they would sometimes spend days on end squabbling about the most ridiculous things as they learned about the world: Did Skylords drop Fallers? Was there an outside to this universe like the first ships claimed, and if so where was it? Why was maize yellow? Would Asja kiss either of them? Was rust a disease from space? Would Paulette kiss either of them? How could coal possibly be squashed wood? What gave every nebula its own shape when stars were all the same? Mynea was a great kisser – oh no she wasn't – yeah, how do you know? Why do tatus flies always go for blond hair to spawn in? Crud like that. It didn't mean anything, and Ingmar with his logical brain won most disputes anyway; Slvasta just got in a whole lot of fun from trying to ruin his friend's argument.

He sighed. Life in the regiment was a fast lesson in growing up.

'It's okay,' Ingmar 'path spoke back, equally direct, so Jamenk couldn't sense their conversation. 'I just didn't understand, that's all.'

'Understand what?'

'If they were leaving the valley, going to town for supplies or something, then we would have known, either passed them or that last village would have told us they'd driven out of the valley. If they were coming in, then why?'

'Why what?'

'Why come in? The whole county knows there was a Fall; surely they would have stayed in the village until the Marines announced the all-clear.'

Slvasta grinned at his friend. 'Because they really believe this squad is going to make the valley safe for them.'

'Oh. Yeah,' Ingmar's expression was sheepish. 'You have a point there.'

'I always do.'

'So can't you tell which way the cart was going?'

'No not really. It was just luck I saw that rut.'

'Do you think they train Marines to read a trail properly?' Slvasta asked wistfully. He'd been awestruck by the Marines back in Prerov. They were smart and decisive and overloaded with genuine authority; no screw-ups in their ranks. And those black uniforms had looked amazingly cool. When they walked down a street, girls didn't even bother glancing at anyone wearing a regimental uniform. Marines were the toughest troops on Bienvenido, responsible directly to the Captain himself. Slvasta desperately wanted to ask how you joined. But even he knew he should wait until he had a couple of successful egg hunts under his belt. Maybe even axed one open himself.

'Not that again?' Ingmar moaned.

'Why not? Don't you have any ambition?'

'Sure I do. What I lack is delusion.'

Slvasta licked along the bottom of his teeth. 'Hey, corporal?' he asked loudly.

'What?' Jamenk said.

'How do you get to join the Marines?'

'I . . . What are you talking about?'

'I was thinking of joining.'

Ingmar laughed out loud. Slvasta dropped the shell round his thoughts to feign hurt feelings.

'They wouldn't take you,' Jamenk said irritably.

'Why not?'

'Firstly, you have to be sponsored by a Marine. Do you know any?'

'Ah. No.'

'Well, then. Now keep watch, please. This isn't a drill.'

Slvasta smirked at Ingmar, who winked back – amplified enormously by his glasses. They both started studying the surrounding woods with mock alertness.

It was the longest two kilometres Slvasta had ever known, taking an age to stride through the lingrass and then tougher undergrowth as the ground became wetter. The slope they were walking down became more pronounced. Stones and boulders were more prevalent. It grew even hotter, the humidity climbed ever upwards. There were thick vines tangled in the gaps between the trees, black creepers with tattered moss-like sponge for leaves. They gave off a sharp salty smell.

Slvasta was cursing Jamenk for his piss-poor navigation skills – they'd done at least five klicks, surely – when the forest ended abruptly. A huge swathe of trees had been felled, leaving a field of pointed stumps sticking up out of the muddy ground, softened by the puffy fungus that had smothered them. They were over a kilometre from the swift-flowing river which cut a curving line along the floor of the valley. The forest rose up in wide undulations on the other side of the water, its canopy seemingly untouched. Native birds drifted about overhead, long black and green tri-angles with upturned wingtips. He was sure the specks right at the end of the valley were mantahawks; anything smaller would have been invisible at that distance. His ex-sight wasn't nearly powerful enough to perceive them and confirm the sighting. But he gifted Ingmar his optical sight anyway; one of their big arguments as kids was that the mantahawks were just a myth, that nothing of their alleged size could actually fly.

'Neat,' Ingmar muttered.

Slvasta took a good long look round Romnaz valley, taking in the size, the steep undulations, the trees that packed every square metre. There was *no way* the three of them were going to sweep it properly for Faller eggs, not in eight days, not even with the mod-bird's keen eyes.

'Oh, crud.'

The track was more distinct through the expanse of felled trees. Jamenk set off with long strides, allowing a degree of confidence to show through his shell. He certainly hadn't shown much conviction before.

A hundred metres into the clearing, and Slvasta saw his first waltan fungus. It was a huge fan-shaped piece, looking like perished leather the colour of sour milk, moving terribly slowly as it crawled across the track. It had taken Bienvenido's botanists and entomologists a long time to agree, but the botanists had ultimately triumphed. The waltan fungus was an ambulatory plant, moving between lumps of rotting cells. They mostly digested dead vegetation, but some varieties also consumed animal flesh.

'There's the croft,' Jamenk said. He frowned, looking down at the track they were on as if seeing it for the first time, then looking round the slope of tree stumps to the river at the bottom. 'How do they haul so many trees out along the track?'

Slvasta and Ingmar exchanged a look.

'I think they tie them together in rafts and float them out on the river, sir,' Ingmar said. 'It's a tributary to the Colbal, so they can go all the way down to Varlan if they want to.'

'Ah, yes, right,' Jamenk said. 'Of course.'

The Shilo family's compound was on the edge of the clearing, three hundred metres above the river. There was a sprawling lodge in the middle. The original cabin had clearly been added to over the years, with new sections getting progressively larger and more solid, until it now formed a disorderly E-shape. The only stone structure was a chimney stack in the middle, sending up a ribbon of blue-grey smoke. Sturdy wooden stables and barns formed two sides of the compound, with a slat fence marking out the rest of the area. The ground within it was laid out in the green strips of terrestrial vegetation.

Slvasta could see over a dozen mod-apes shambling round inside the fence, while bulky mod-horses were snorting away inside one of the barns. Just the kind of creatures a family would wrangle to help with cutting down the trees and hauling the trunks down the slope to the river.

As they approached, Jamenk sent his mod-bird swooping low over the compound. 'Ah, someone's there,' he said.

Slvasta watched curiously as the corporal immediately began to straighten his clothes, slicking back his sweat-damped hair.

Two mod-apes opened the big gates at they approached. They swung back to reveal a girl smiling in greeting. She was probably about twenty, with the blackest skin Slvasta had ever seen. In contrast, she wore a white shirt with only a couple of buttons done up; he tried not to stare. A pair of suede trousers clung to long legs, tucked into boots which came up to her knees. A thick mass of curly ebony hair framed a delightfully spry face. The smile was just perfection.

He felt his heart start to beat faster as he smiled back at her.

'Hello, guys,' she said in an amazingly sultry voice. 'My name's Quanda. I live here with my parents.'

'I'm Corporal Jamenk from the Cham Regiment. There's been a Fall in this district. But don't worry, my squad has been assigned to sweep this valley. We're going to make sure you're safe.'

'That's wonderful. Come in, please,' she said, and turned to walk towards the cluster of outbuildings. As they passed the ramshackle wooden lodge building, Slvasta gave it a puzzled look. It was large enough for a lot more than just three people. And he was sure the farmer who'd brought them to the top of the valley had said three branches of the Shilo family lived in the valley.

The mod-apes shut the gates after them.

They walked past the chicken run – though there were no chickens anywhere. The vegetable garden had a lot of weeds growing up among the terrestrial plants.

Slvasta didn't know why, but he suddenly felt even hotter as he walked across the compound. It was a good heat. He couldn't take his eyes off Quanda's powerful legs. And that shirt, with just a couple of buttons done up – so provocative. She must know that, he thought. It was a nice thought.

'Are your parents here?' Ingmar asked; he was glancing at the long croft house.

Quanda stopped and turned round. She had the most delectably naughty smirk lifting her lips. 'No. They're on the other side of the clearing, marking out a new batch of trees for felling. They won't be back until the sun goes down. So that means I'm going to be here alone with three of you for the whole time. How's that for a turn on?'

For a second, Slvasta thought he'd misheard that husky voice. His heart was still yammering away inside his chest. It was making him feel lightheaded in a very pleasurable way, as if he'd just glugged down a couple of beers in quick succession. That, and he was getting rather seriously aroused by Quanda.

'What?' Jamenk said in a strained voice.

'You heard.' And she walked right up to the corporal and kissed him.

Slvasta gazed on in astonishment and not a little jealousy, feeling his erection growing.

She broke away, grinning. 'You heard and you understood. We're alone for the afternoon. That means you can do whatever you want with me.' She turned to Slvasta and kissed him. He'd never known a kiss so full of dirty promise. Her teekay closed around his cock, and slowly tweaked *just so*.

Slvasta's eyes were moist when the kiss ended, making the world misty and out of focus. His ragged breathing produced an overwhelming sense of anticipation. Her scent was thick and sweet, enchanting. He wanted more. A lot more. To crush her to him, and inhale until he burst.

Quanda moved on to kiss Ingmar. 'I never even get to see a man for months on end,' she murmured hoarsely. 'Do you have any idea how frustrating that is? And now, when I'm by myself, three of you appear all at once, like a gift from Giu itself.' She stood before them and undid both the buttons on her shirt.

Slvasta moaned in delight as she lifted the cotton aside. He took a helpless step towards her, just like Jamenk and a befuddled Ingmar. Quanda laughed, and danced away from them. 'Come on,' she beckoned urgently. 'We'll do it in the barn. You don't have to take turns. I want to know what it's like to have all three of you inside me at the same time. I want that so bad.'

Slvasta could barely hear or see anything else, just her, the hottest, most perfect girl he'd ever known. He was drunk on lust and it was fantastic. Her shirt fluttered to the ground. When he walked over it, his erection had become so hard it was almost painful.

From somewhere a long way off, he heard Ingmar say: 'Where's your cart?'

'Away,' Quanda rasped dismissively.

'Shut up, Ingmar,' Jamenk sneered.

Quanda's nimble teekay hadn't let go of Slvasta's cock. 'You're the one I want to take me from behind,' her private 'path told him. Then her laughter was echoing round him as he whimpered in furious desire.

Slvasta started to run after her. He had to get to her fast. To fuck himself senseless with that lean body. The carbine bounced annoyingly against his side.

'Get rid of it,' Quanda said in sympathy. 'It'll only be in the way when you bend me over.' Her teekay slid down to begin playing with his balls.

He started fumbling with the awkward strap as he ran. The barn and its long afternoon of sexual paradise was so tantalizingly close now.

'But we didn't pass a cart on the track,' Ingmar's whiney voice complained.

'They left a while ago,' Quanda said; she sounded irritated. That upset Slvasta. Pathetic, pedantic Ingmar was ruining the state of delirium he'd been elevated to.

'I thought your parents were marking trees.'

'My aunt took the cart.'

Slvasta shook his head angrily so he could concentrate and tell his so-called friend to shut the crud up. When he turned his blurry vision on Ingmar, he saw three mod-apes shambling towards them. He blinked in confusion; shambling wasn't the right description. They were running. 'Uh, hey!' Raw Neanderthal predator-fear instinct kicked all the joy out of his body at the sight of the approaching alien beasts. He used his 'path to shove an order to halt directly into the closest mod-ape's mind. It paid no attention – which wasn't possible. His orders were strong; the creature's mind should have received and obeyed immediately. He instinctively strengthened his own shell, teekay shifting from a basic protection against prying ex-sight to a barrier that would deflect any physical strike. His hands tugged at the carbine, trying to bring it round towards the clearly deranged mod-creatures. 'Come here,' he 'pathed one of their pair of mod-dwarfs. It responded sluggishly. 'Deploy the fire weapon.'

Quanda was laughing still. But the timbre had changed drastically. It was an awful sound now, devoid of any humour or happiness.

'What is wron—?' Jamenk began. He was tugging his revolver out of its holster when Quanda struck him with a backhanded blow, and he went tumbling through the air, crying out more from surprise than pain. Two of the mod-apes landed on him.

'Faller!' a terrified Ingmar wailed.

Now Slvasta finally understood: it had been the egg lure which had bewitched him, corrupting his thoughts, with Quanda's lustful promises lulling him still further. He used his teekay, shaping the invisible force into a blade-shape and stabbing it straight at the eye of the mod-ape that was almost upon him. Blood burst out and the creature dropped dead.

He fumbled the safety catch on the carbine, pulling back the loader lever on the side, preparing the firing mechanism. It was taking forever. Quanda moved fast, sprinting straight at him. He tried to get his teekay inside her skin, into her ribcage where her heart was, desperate to squeeze, to tear arteries – even Fallers had those. But her teekay shell was as hard as iron.

Slvasta fired the carbine. It wasn't even aimed at her to start with, more like panic shooting. The recoil shoved him about, and he brought the carbine back under control. A couple of shots must have hit her as she raced forwards. They didn't get through her shell. The magazine ran out of bullets. He turned, lunging away desperately. Her fist lashed out, and he wasn't quite out of reach. His shell saved him from the worst of the blow, but it was still strong enough to send him sprawling. One of the mod-apes loomed above him, its thick muscular arm raised ready to hammer smash . . . 'Crud!'

A jet of flame seared into the mod-ape's head, flowing like liquid down its torso. It shrieked, radiating its pain in a pulse which made Slvasta groan. Tears flooded his eyes as he tried to tighten his shell against the outpouring of agony.

The mod-dwarf was standing firm, playing the flamethrower over the mod-ape as it thrashed about, legs collapsing. And

Ingmar was standing a little behind it, hands pressed to his temples, eyes shut tight in concentration as his 'path directed the mod-dwarf. Concentrating so hard he didn't see one of the mod-horses charging.

'No!' Slvasta yelled with voice and 'path. 'Ingmar, look ou—'

The great beast was going fast, lowering its head like a battering ram. It struck Ingmar in the small of his back, launching him into the air. Slvasta felt his pain and shock at the crippling blow. Even that faded as Ingmar lost consciousness. Then Slvasta was instinctively rolling over himself as Quanda's booted foot kicked at his head. She missed, and he rolled again. A smeared image of Jamenk lying on his back, with one of the mod-apes pummelling him, its hoof-fist smashing his face again and again. The semiconscious corporal's blood running everywhere – over his cheeks, chin, nose, mouth, neck – soaking into the ground.

Slvasta just managed to get to his feet, swaying about. He slapped an order into the mod-dwarf's mind, telling it to aim the flamethrower at Quanda. But it simply stood there, then slowly brought the nozzle round until it was lined up on him. And Quanda was walking quickly towards him, her face blank. Slvasta charged right at her. He had nothing else. Swinging his fist, ready to follow up with a savage kick.

Her hand grabbed his. She was so *fast*. They'd told him Fallers were quick, but he never expected anything like this! Strong, too. It was like being clamped in an iron vice. Then she twisted. Slvasta was spun round by the incredible force. Quanda's heel smashed into the back of his knee.

He thought the bone had broken. Certainly something tore. The pain was horrifying. He dropped to the ground, wailing.

'This is what they send?' Quanda asked in a mocking tone. 'The finest warriors on the planet?'

'Fuck you,' he managed to croak.

Sunlight was in his eyes. It vanished as she walked round him. He blinked up fearfully. *Is she going to eat me?*

'No. I'm not.'

A hand grasped the front of his shirt and tugged him up to his knees. Her beautiful face was centimetres from his. She studied him intently. 'I'm not hungry. Not right now.'

He tried to strike out with his teekay, going for her eyes just as he had with the mod-ape. But the blow rebounded from her shell, and she didn't even flinch. Still her eyes were looking into his. He felt the toe of her boot shove at his good knee, pushing his legs apart.

'You things barely have thoughts,' she said in a dry growl. 'Just instincts. You are animal. I almost pity the one who will absorb you.'

He had to concentrate to understand her voice – Fallers had broken, gravelly voices, it was right there on page five of the Institute manual. 'We will burn you from our world,' he snarled defiantly. 'I swear it. No matter what the cost.'

Her free arm swung back, then powered forward. Slvasta saw her eyes widen in anticipation just as her fist slammed into his balls. He thought the pain would fracture his skull open, it was so intense. There was nothing else but the pain. He knew he was vomiting. Tumbling down. She stood above him, magnificent and terrible.

Then a mod-ape dragged him across the compound towards the barn he'd been so eager to reach just moments before, his face bumping along the ground, stones shredding his cheek. That pain was infinitesimal compared to the rest. Another mod-ape tugged Ingmar along behind him. Slvasta didn't care. The pain was too great. His eyes fell shut. And he was in darkness, him and the pain, alone together. Falling.

*

Consciousness was more pain. It also brought the overwhelming misery, a loathing of simply being alive.

That's not going to last for much longer, he knew.

Slvasta didn't want to open his eyes. Didn't want to scan round with his ex-sight. He was too afraid of what might be revealed.

'Are you awake?' Ingmar's 'path asked him softly.

Slvasta opened his eyes, blinking away sticky tear-diluted

blood. They were in the barn Quanda had been leading them to, with light filtering in through high windows. There were empty animal stalls, while the floor of the aisle where he lay naked was hard-packed soil covered in filthy straw.

Directly in front of him were two Faller eggs. Slvasta whimpered in dread. All the stories and descriptions were true. The things were spherical, almost three metres in diameter, with a dark crinkled skin. A naked Jamenk was spread eagled against one, like a comedy *splat* on a wall.

Tears started flowing freely down Slvasta's torn cheeks at the sight of him. The corporal's face and chest had already sunk below the surface. Ingmar, also stripped out of his clothes, had been shoved sideways against the second egg. His leg and arm were already inside, with his ribcage just starting to sink in; he was craning his neck to keep his head away from the surface.

'No!' Slvasta groaned, and tried to get to his feet despite his ruined knee. He couldn't move. His bare skin suddenly became ice cold and started sweating. He turned his head. The third Faller egg curved above him. His right arm had sunk in almost up to his elbow. He let his head fall back, and let out a wretched death-howl as he pissed himself.

'It's okay,' Ingmar was saying. 'It's okay.'

'Okay?' Slvasta burbled hysterically. 'Oh-fucking-kay? Okay? Okay? How the crud is this okay?'

His friend gave him a sad smile. 'We can kill each other.'

Slvasta let out a demented giggle.

'We can,' Ingmar insisted. 'We can use a teekay grip on each other's heart. Squeeze together.'

'Fuck the Skylords. Ingmar, no!'

'Please, Slvasta. As soon as my skull reaches the egg, it'll be over for me. It will have me. I'll be a Faller. Is that what you want?'

'No.'

'Then let us do this. Together.'

Slvasta sent his ex-sight probing into the egg, trying to see what kind of grip it had on him. There wasn't much he could perceive beyond the surface, just dense shadows. Yet there was some kind of mind in there, steely thoughts he could make no sense of other than a simple glow of expectancy. Nothing like the bright colourful tangle of unguarded human thoughts, forever discordant with emotion.

Although he could sense its outline, he couldn't feel his lower arm, but it wasn't cold, or in pain, there was just . . . nothing. He tried pulling. Of course, it didn't move. He shrank his teekay down to a point, like the tip of an axe, and stabbed repeatedly into the shell around his arm. Nothing. The shell didn't bend or crack. His attack had no effect whatsoever. He realized his arm was slightly deeper inside, the shell was now up to the top of his radius and ulna.

'We have to do it,' Ingmar said. He was making no attempt to spin a shell round his thoughts. Sadness and exhaustion were emanating out of him. 'We can deny them this. We can deny them us. It's our last weapon.'

'Is it?' Quanda walked down the aisle towards them. She paused at Jamenk's prone form, and inspected him before moving on to Ingmar. 'What a fearsome weapon that is. Can you feel my fear?'

'Rot in Uracus, bitch,' Ingmar said.

She put her hand on his cheek and glanced down at Slvasta. 'Do it. If you want him dead.'

'Yes,' Ingmar pleaded. 'Please, Slvasta. Once it gets to my brain, that's it. Please.'

Slvasta watched through a fresh agony. He formed his teekay into a hand and slowly extended it out towards Ingmar. So close, waiting to push it through his friend's body and crush his heart.

'Do it,' Ingmar shouted.

Slvasta could sense Ingmar's teekay hovering above his own ribs. 'I . . . I can't,' he admitted woefully. 'I'm sorry. I can't.'

'I thought you were my friend,' Ingmar wept. 'How can you leave me to Fall?'

Slvasta shook his head, hating himself for his weakness.

With a mirthless grin, Quanda slowly began to push Ingmar's head. He fought her, every centimetre of the way. His neck muscles stood proud. Teekay scrabbling at her impervious shell, then trying to reinforce his own muscles. It made no difference; the Faller was too strong. She pushed the side of his face against the egg surface. It stuck there immediately. Ingmar started wailing. 'Slvasta, please Slvasta. It will take me. It will take all of me. I will never be fulfilled, I will not be guided to the Heart. Help me. Kill me.'

'Monster,' Slvasta hissed. 'Why are you so evil?'

Quanda squatted down beside him and cocked her head to one side, studying him, always studying. 'You make us; we are formed by you, your body and your mind. This – what I am, the way I think – it is inherited from your kind. It is vile. You, your species, is animal, brutal, despicable. Once we have exterminated you, it will take a generation to breed you out of us. But we will be free in the end.'

'You will never defeat us. Freak monster. The Heart is for us, not you. You will never be fulfilled.'

'We have been before. We will be again.'

Slvasta heard the words, but they didn't make any sense. He tugged at his arm again, but the egg gripped it with a hold stronger than a century-old tree root. 'Crudbitch.' He looked up, and examined the rafters and beams holding up the barn's roof. A lot of the timbers were thick and heavy. Maybe . . . He used his teekay to try and shift one above Jamenk's egg. Just to loosen it would be enough. In his head he had a vision of a huge joist crashing down, crushing the egg.

'You can kill Jamenk?' Ingmar yelled in outrage.

'Because he's already dead. Fallen,' Slvasta shouted back.

Quanda chuckled. Then stopped, her head coming up, eyes staring at something outside the walls. 'Were you alone?' she snapped.

'Go fuck yourself,' Slvasta told her.

There was a burst of gunfire outside.

'In here!' Slvasta shouted, making his 'path as powerful as he could. 'There's a Faller in here!' He sent out Quanda's image, twined with all the hate in his body.

She smacked him on the side of his head. The world didn't make sense for a long moment. There was more gunfire. Mod-apes were chittering in fury and panic. The soft roar of flamethrowers.

'There,' a voice called. 'She's there!'

More and more gunfire. Bullets punched through the barn's timbers, sending small splinters whizzing through the air. Slim beams of sunlight punctured the gloomy interior, shining through each bullet hole.

'Die, you bitch!' Slvasta shouted jubilantly. 'Uracus awaits you!' His smile was more a snarl as he turned to Ingmar. That was when his elation died. Ingmar's cheek and ear had sunk below the egg's surface. He was silent, his bright familiar thoughts slowing and dimming, somehow drifting into the egg. 'No. No, no, no! Hold on, Ingmar, fight it. They're almost here.'

Strong ex-sights played through the shack, examining every solid object. Slvasta dropped his shell, welcoming the scrutiny. The doors burst open.

Marines were running in. Fantastic black-clad figures, holding small carbines, their ex-sight probing hard now.

One of them, a captain, walked over to Jamenk first, then Ingmar, looking closely at his head.

'I couldn't do it,' Slvasta sobbed. 'He's my friend and I couldn't do it.'

'Look away, lad,' the captain said sternly.

Slvasta did as he was told, closing his eyes and withdrawing his ex-sight. A single shot rang out. He glanced at his arm. His elbow had been swallowed by the egg surface now. 'Is she dead?' he demanded. 'Is the Faller bitch dead?'

The captain stood over him. 'Yeah. We got her.'

'Then I'm fulfilled,' Slvasta declared, with very brittle bravado. 'Will the Skylords guide me?'

'Were there any more of them?' the captain asked. 'Any more Fallers?' Marines were manoeuvring a large cart through the barn's open doors.

'No. No, sir, I don't think so. We only saw her. How did you know? How did you find us?'

More Marines were coming in. They carried heavy axes. Blades fell on the egg Jamenk was stuck to, swung with fierce enthusiasm. Before long, a thick milky liquid started to spray out of the tiny splits. Flamethrowers began to play across the egg fluid, boiling it as procedure demanded. According to Captain Cornelius's manual, even the egg fluid was dangerous.

'A regiment patrol intercepted the Shilos' cart a day and a half ago,' the captain said. 'They were all Fallers. Uracus of a fight, by all accounts. Looks like this nest has been established here for a while – there are quite a few human bones left in the house. We came as soon as we got word. Shame we didn't get to you in time.'

'I understand.' Slvasta took a breath and closed his eyes. 'Do it, sir, please.'

He didn't mean to use his ex-sight, but he perceived one of the Marines coming up behind him. Braced himself –

But there was no shot to the head. No deliverance. The Marine started wrapping a slim rope round his eggsumed arm, just below the shoulder, tying it in an unusual knot.

'What?' Slvasta grunted in confusion.

'Bite on this,' the captain said in a sympathetic voice, and pushed a small length of wood towards his face. 'It'll do till you faint.'

'What?'

A Marine handed the captain a saw.

Slvasta started screaming. The wood was jammed into his mouth. The tourniquet was tightened.

He tried to squirm free. But the egg held him resolutely in place.

The grim-faced captain started sawing.

2

With Varlan situated just over a thousand kilometres south of the equator, every day in Bienvenido's capital was a hot one. Even now, close to midnight, the cobbled streets and stone walls were still radiating out the heat they'd been punished with during the day.

Kervarl looked out of the cab's windows as it trundled along Walton Boulevard, trying not to appear like a complete neophyte to the person who rode the cab with him. He was an important man back in Boutzen county, two thousand kilometres south at the end of the Southern City Line. But Boutzen was just a county capital, dwarfed in scale by Varlan.

The cab pulled up in front of the Rasheeda Hotel, which itself was probably larger than the Council chamber in Boutzen. Kervarl frowned, angry with himself for falling into such a depreciative mindset.

I'm here now. I'm making my own impact on this world. I'm as good as any capital merchant. Better, for I have more opportunity.

'Relax,' the man sitting opposite said, with a kindly smile.

Kervarl forced a smile. It had taken two weeks, and considerably more coins that he'd wanted to spend, but he'd finally won an appointment with the National Council's First Speaker in his private annex. The First Speaker had agreed to sponsor him with the palace. Again for more coinage than he'd planned on. But that was Varlan for you: everything was on a bigger scale.

It didn't matter, he kept telling himself. Here he was in a cab with Larrial, the First Speaker's chief aide, on his way to the palace to see the First Officer himself. The mining licences were in sight. *Just keep your nerve.*

He jumped when the cab door was pulled open.

'Calm,' Larrial urged.

Kervarl tightened his shell and looked out. A man and a teenage girl were standing on the pavement. The girl was pleasant enough, with broad features and a good figure outlined by the flimsy white cotton dress she wore. Kervarl would have preferred a prettier one. His uncertainty must have leaked out.

'She's fine,' Larrial said reassuringly. 'Just what he likes.'

'Okay.'

The man with the girl held his hand out. His face was fuzzed, but nonetheless Kervarl got the impression of bulk and malice. He dropped some coins into the waiting hand. It stayed there, open with the coins glinting in the light radiating out of the hotel's grand high windows. Kervarl resisted the urge to sigh, and produced yet more money. The hand finally closed, and the girl was allowed to climb into the cab. She sat next to Kervarl.

Larrial 'pathed an order to the cab driver, and the mod-horse moved forward, back onto Walton Boulevard. 'Couple of minutes to the palace from here. Perhaps a good time for your gift . . .' He gestured at the girl.

'Right.' This was where it got slightly different to the deals he was used to at home. Kervarl prided himself that he was a man of the world, that he understood how things worked. After all, that was how he'd clawed his way up to his current status. This, however . . . He steeled himself against any doubts. This was the capital. Their rules. If you weren't going to play by them, there was no point in being here.

He produced a small phial from his jacket pocket and offered it to the girl. Her eyes widened in delight and surprise. He could sense the greed in her thoughts.

'Take it now,' Larrial said. There was an edge to his voice.

'Thank you, sir,' the girl said. She removed the sealed lid with a practised twist and stuck the phial's long neck into a nostril, inhaling deeply. Switched nostrils, inhaled once more.

'I think there's some left,' Larrial said.

A sublime smile rose on the girl's face. She inhaled again.

Kervarl watched anxiously as the narnik gripped her, for a moment it seemed she might swoon. She seemed barely conscious.

'A much purer form than she's used to, I expect,' Larrial said, studying the girl's lolling head. 'She'll thank us for that in the morning.'

Kervarl said nothing. He'd heard all the rumours about the First Officer.

Walton Boulevard led directly up to the Captain's Palace. Kervarl tried not to be impressed, but the building was massive, like a whole town in one structure. An officer of the Palace Guard came over as the cab drew up outside the huge iron gates. He clearly knew Larrial and gave permission to enter.

The cab went through a two-storey archway in the façade, and into a courtyard. A footman in emerald and gold livery was waiting. He led them through another smaller archway, and out into the palace gardens.

'Please refrain from using your ex-sight here, sir,' the footman said in a deep, dignified voice.

The gardens were just as impressive as the palace itself. Long pathways webbed perfectly flat lawns. Topiary trees twice Kervarl's height stood sentry along them. There were high hedges curving round secluded grottoes. Ponds with fountains were outlined by exotic blooms. Dozens of sweet scents mingled in the night air. Lanterns flickered gracefully, forming their own nebula. Kervarl hadn't even known you could get oil that would burn in different coloured flames. The lights added the final touch, making the whole garden astonishingly beautiful.

He heard the sound of laughter as they walked. It seemed to be coming from one of the grottoes. There were the fainter rhythmic cries of sex. Cheering. Then came a yelp of pain. He focused on watching the stoned girl, making sure she didn't stumble.

The footman led them into one of the grottoes, surrounded by an impenetrable rubybirch hedge. Smaller ornamental trees were inside, bark gnarled with age, and chosen for their night-blossom. Tiny pink and white petals snowed silently onto the spongy grass. Fountains played outside a pavilion of white cloth whose drapes fluttered softly in the warm breeze. Lamps inside made it glow with a golden hue, as if it were some kind of giant ethereal lantern. A harpist was playing.

The party inside was exclusive. Kervarl recognized Aothori, the First Officer. The Captain's eldest son was in his thirties, though his exceptionally handsome face made him appear a lot younger. His fine features were framed by thick curly red-blond hair, with a neat goatee beard styled to emphasize the already-prominent cheekbones. A loose toga revealed a perfectly muscled torso as he lounged on a couch behind the table. Despite that strong physical presence, Kervarl could only think of him as dandyish. His friends around the table, from the highest echelons of Varlan's aristocratic society, were equally youthful and vibrant. One couple in the corner of the pavilion were having sex on a mound of cushions, with several more standing over them, sipping wine as they watched. All the serving girls wore long skirts, but were naked from the waist up, and just as beautiful as the female guests. The two serving boys wore loincloths, their oiled skin glistening in the hazy lamplight.

All Kervarl's inferiority came rushing back. He felt old, shabby, poor.

'My dear chap,' Aothori said. 'Welcome.'

Some of the partygoers deigned to look at Kervarl, only to instantly dismiss him. That was when anger started to replace his timidity. Who the crud were they to look down on him? Aristos who'd inherited everything. Who accomplished nothing.

Larrial made the slightest sound in his throat.

Kervarl bowed. 'Thank you for receiving me, sir.'

'Not at all. The First Speaker speaks very highly of you.' He turned to the beauty lounging next to him. 'You see what I did there?'

She grinned indolently, then fixed Kervarl with an icy stare.

'I brought you a token of my appreciation, sir.' Kervarl applied his teekay to the girl's back and pressed her forward, praying she wouldn't trip over. Narnik-glazed eyes blinked heavily as she walked up to the table with its piles of rich food. Once again, Kervarl wished he'd brought a prettier girl.

'How generous of you,' Aothori said. 'I'm sure she'll be most entertaining.'

All Kervarl heard was the First Officer's mocking tone.

Aothori clicked his fingers. 'Get her ready,' he told one of the serving boys. The girl was led away, still in a narnik stupor.

'Now, I understand you have some kind of commercial proposition for me?' Aothori said.

A couple of the guests laughed at that. Over on the cushions, the sex was getting louder. Another man shrugged out of his toga and joined in.

'Indeed, sir. I have lands in the Sansone mountains. I would like a licence to mine there. The Captain controls mineral rights across the planet; I understand you can sign a licence for my company.'

'To mine what, exactly?'

'Silver, sir.'

Aothori raised a perfectly manicured eyebrow. 'I didn't know there was silver there.'

'My surveyors have found it, sir,' Kervarl said proudly. He wanted to explain how difficult it had been, how expensive, how much effort had gone into the venture. The risk. But here in this ludicrously decadent setting his prepared speech was rendered utterly pointless. All he wanted now was the agreement, and to leave.

'That's very enterprising of you,' Aothori murmured.

'Thank you, sir.'

'And why exactly should I grant you a licence?'

'I would like to propose a joint venture.'

'Ah. Delightful. And very smart. I can see you and I will get along wonderfully. What sort of percentage did you see me taking?'

Kervarl hoped he wasn't sweating. This was crucial: get the

184

figure wrong . . . The First Speaker had advised fifteen. 'Seventeen and a half, sir.' He cursed himself all the way to Uracus for being such a coward.

'That's a very generous offer,' Aothori said. He poured some wine from a flagon and gave it to a serving girl. She carried it over to Kervarl.

Everyone round the table was waiting, watching. Several knowing, predatory smiles were growing. Over on the cushions the vigorous threesome were drowning out the sound of the harp.

Aothori raised his own glass. 'I do believe we have a deal.' He drank his wine. The guests applauded.

Kervarl fought against showing any relief. *Play it cool. Play his game.* 'Sir.' He raised his glass to the First Officer and drank.

'Here's to the two of us,' Aothori announced loudly. 'My new business partner.' Everyone at the table raised their glasses in salute.

'Well done,' Larrial private 'pathed.

Kervarl smiled round and drank some more wine. It wasn't as good as he'd expected. But that didn't matter. Nothing else did. *I've got the licence!*

'My office will sort out the boring legal part with you tomorrow,' Aothori said.

'Yes, sir.' Kervarl said. He didn't quite know what to do now. The First Officer was giving him a mildly expectant gaze. 'Do we stay?' he private 'pathed Larrial.

'Great Giu, no. Say goodbye. The likes of us don't get to socialize with the First Officer.'

Kervarl bowed again. 'You've been most kind, sir. I don't wish to take up any more of your time. My lawyers will contact your office, as you suggested.'

'Indeed,' Aothori gave a casual magnanimous wave of his hand.

Kervarl turned and left. It took a lot of willpower not to dance out of the grotto.

*

Aothori watched the southern landowner stride across the palace gardens. He shook his head in bemusement at all the contentment spilling out of the man's relaxed shell.

'Amazing,' he grunted.

'That they found silver in the Sansones?' Mirivia asked as she scraped her forefinger round a bowl of honeyed acral seeds.

He gave her a disappointed look. Mirivia was this week's favourite, but not for being the sharpest thorn on the firepine. 'That someone smart enough to find silver there could be so stupid. It's the southern mentality, of course. Their pride in their work ethic will be the death of them.' He grinned. 'See what I did there.'

She pouted, and made a show of sucking the gooey black seeds from her finger. 'You're so cruel.'

'I try.' His ex-sight observed Kervarl slow to a halt, and give Larrial a puzzled look. 'If only he'd been one of us instead of having the stench of the Shanty on him. A gentleman would have sent staff to deal with something as vulgar as a licence. But of course that involves spending money and having confidence in your command of others. It would seem Kervarl is too cheap for that.'

Across the garden, Kervarl had dropped to his knees. His hands scrabbled desperately at his throat. Panic and fright poured out of his shell-less mind.

'And as well as not being a gentleman, he's ambitious,' Aothori said as Kervarl pitched forwards, face down onto the neat path. 'We really don't want to encourage that kind of thing; it'll end up in another Jasmine Avenue.'

'Well, nobody wants that,' Mirivia agreed.

Larrial stood over the prone body, and turned to face the grotto. 'He's dead,' the aide 'pathed.

'Jolly good,' Aothori 'pathed back. 'Have the tax people overload the family with death duties. My office will purchase his estate. It looks like we're in the silver-mining business.'

'Yes, sir.'

Aothori picked up the flagon of poisoned wine and handed it to one of the serving girls. 'Get rid of this; we don't want any accidents.'

'Sir.'

'And is Kervarl's gift ready? Shame to waste her.'

The girl carefully avoided his gaze, keeping her shell impervious. 'Yes, sir.'

'Jolly good.' He kissed Mirivia. 'I'm keen to see what you can do with her first. Then I'll show you mine.'

3

When he reached the top of the hill, Slvasta was a good twenty-five metres ahead of anyone else. He hadn't jogged, but he'd set a very fast pace. It had taken an hour and a half to get to the summit. The first thing he'd done when he made lieutenant eight months ago was start his own training schedule for the seven squads he commanded. That training included a ten-kilometre run twice a week, wearing a full deployment pack. His fellow officers – those who'd been oh so reasonable and supportive during the twenty months between the Marines rescuing him and his promotion – hardly ever saw their troops on a day-to-day basis. It was considered bad form for people of their class to mix with the ranks; they left it to their NCOs to implement orders. And they certainly didn't take physical exercise with their men, not after the amount of food and drink they consumed in the mess. Slvasta thought that stupid. He wanted his troopers to know he wasn't some backroom oaf, appointed because of family wealth like most officers. They needed to see that he was just as capable as them when it came to sweeps. They needed to have trust and confidence in him. He also wanted to know their strengths and weaknesses; that way he knew how to deploy them: who could be trusted with what tasks, what skills they had. The only way to ascertain that was to observe them in action first hand.

He stopped and drew down deep breaths. It was almost noon, and the sky was cloudless. The sun was a fierce glare above him, its warmth permeating the air. His shirt was soaked with sweat. He took a canteen from his equipment belt and swigged down water.

The rest of the men started to arrive, grinning and panting, proud of themselves for keeping up with the lieutenant. Above them the air was clotted with spiralling mod-birds. Slvasta had made sure the regiment gave one to every soldier under his command. Now when they were deployed on sweeps, every square metre of ground could be examined for traces of a Fall. After the initial grumbling from senior officers, other squads were asking for mod-birds to be issued to every trooper, too. A new aviary was being built at headquarters to accommodate the expansion. Even less popular among his fellow officers, recruits were asking to serve under the notorious one-armed lieutenant.

'Sergeant,' Slvasta called.

Sergeant Yannrith came over. A big man in his mid-sixties whom troopers obeyed without question. A scar down his throat had given him a liquid whisper for a voice. When he spoke, no matter what he was saying, it sounded like a low menacing threat. Slvasta had never asked about the scar. Rumour in the mess was a husband who'd come home unexpectedly early; other talk was of a youth misspent in a town gang. It wasn't important. Yannrith was the best sergeant in the regiment – that was all that mattered.

'Sir?' Yannrith saluted.

'Ten minutes' rest, then we'll start the sight search. Make sure they have a drink.'

Yannrith gave a curt nod. 'Sir.'

Slvasta sat on a rock, pushed back his wide-brimmed hat and started to examine the vista laid out before him. The hill wasn't particularly high, but it showed him the lands stretching south, a rumpled expanse of forests and savannah. Shining silver rivers sliced through it. Lakes were dark gashes. He could pick out several hints of cultivation, ranches and cane farms, but the majority was wild and unsettled. Beyond the horizon, the river Colbal wound its lazy way south-west towards the capital.

They were two days south of Adice, now. Behind him, the land was heavily populated with big estates and a mosaic of prosperous farms. Towns and villages were connected by good roads. Long strands of smoke from the beacon fires still wound their way up into the sky above the worried residents. Slvasta wasn't interested in that kind of territory; any eggs Fallen there would have been spotted immediately. But out here, in the hinterlands, where roads were few and people fewer – that was a different proposition altogether.

The troopers were settling down, taking snacks from their packs. Slvasta didn't permit his squads to use mod-dwarfs, not after he'd witnessed Quanda's absolute control over mods, so everything they needed during an active sweep had to be carried in their backpacks. The bulk of their field camp equipment was carried on four mod-horses and two new proper terrestrial horses he'd acquired; he was in the process of changing the remaining mod-horses for more terrestrial horses. In the meantime, he didn't allow the mod-horses on any forward deployment during a sweep where they might encounter a Faller. Mod-birds were the only exception he'd grant, and he was still trying to figure out how to replace them. Most native birds were too small and skitty, nothing like as docile as a mod. Some people, mainly in Cham's pubs, claimed mantahawks could be trained; rich estate lords in Rackwesh Province used them for hunting boar and razorback, allegedly. Quite how you'd catch one, even a fledgling, was something which eluded Slvasta, though.

Trooper Tovakar, who was still on punishment duty after his screw-up unloading equipment from the train, tethered the goat he'd been assigned to bring. His notoriously short temper made him an ideal handler for the grumpy animal that was snorting and tugging at its leash, cross about being forced up the hill. Slvasta grinned to himself at that. Nobody in his squads complained about bringing the tough animals along any more, and the five new recruits would understand why soon enough.

Slvasta called an end to the rest, and his NCOs came over. The group used telescopes to study the area they'd been assigned to sweep. Slvasta had requested this area, which the colonel had been quick enough to grant. No one else ever volunteered to sweep the difficult wild territories.

They divided it up into sections. Slvasta and Yannrith designated individual squads. Sweep patterns were discussed. Expected progress was matched against the actual state of the land, as opposed to a section of map. Overnight camp locations were agreed.

The squads set off back down the hill, gradually moving apart as they neared the bottom, and struck out for their individual sweeps.

Slvasta accompanied Yannrith's squad. The area they'd chosen to sweep was reasonably flat, but covered in a native bamboo reed with a tough stem that produced a wide floppy magenta umbrella frond a couple of metres above his head. Sunlight ploughed through the downy mess, to be stained violet in the air underneath where the squad walked.

They spread out in a long line, spacing themselves three hundred metres apart, enough so their 'path voice could reach between them. Some troopers hacked at the stems with machetes. Slvasta used his teekay to snap them away. The hollow stems were a lot thinner than tree trunks, but the sheer mass of them reduced his visibility considerably. The mild claustrophobia didn't bother him. He concentrated on his ex-sight, pulling in his mod-bird's eyesight as it flew above the rippling ocean of purple fluff. His 'path directed it along a grid pattern, parallel to everyone else's. Between them, the squad were sweeping an area over two kilometres wide.

'Sir!' Trooper Andricea called excitedly. 'Is this one?' Her 'path sight was showing a gifted view from her mod-bird, where a clump of the bamboo canes had fallen together.

'Wait,' Yannrith told her. Several mod-birds closed on the break in the swaying purple cover. Slvasta thought it was too small for an egg impact, but circled his mod-bird carefully before letting it flutter down onto the broken stems. There was no egg, and the wispy undergrowth had already recovered. His guess was some kind of fight between ventaus bulls; the thuggish bear-like creatures enjoyed the shade, and normally kept to themselves. But it had been the mating season a month ago.

'Clear,' Yannrith's 'path-voice told the squad. 'Good call, though, Andricea,' he added.

Her mind sent out a burst of satisfaction before she tightened her shell. It was her first sweep, and she was determined to get things right. Slvasta had been worried that her height (lanky limbs put her a few centimetres taller than him) and youth (she was barely twenty) would prove a distraction to the men under his command. But Andricea had proved she could keep a level head in most situations, inside and out of the barracks.

The squad resumed its steady tramp forwards.

The ventaus bulls had clearly had a busy time of it. It wasn't just Yannrith's squad that kept checking out the smashed-up bamboo stems; the calls were constant. Then late that afternoon, Tovakar hailed everyone. 'This is strange. I've found a trail, but I don't know what made it. There are hoof marks and everything.'

Slvasta sent his mod-bird over to check. Tovakar could be a hothead, but out here in the field he was reliable enough. Sure enough, the trail was unusual – a long scar through the bamboo, three or four metres wide. The mod-bird didn't give him the clarity he wanted, so Slvasta told the squad to take a break, and he shoved his way through the stalks to Tovakar. It took a good twenty minutes to cover the distance, during which he sent his mod-bird scouting on down the trail, which seemed to cut right through the bamboo and out into the scrubland beyond.

When he caught up with Tovakar, it was as if someone had cut a road through the bamboo. The trail was straight, with the bamboo snapped off just a few centimetres above the ground. Undergrowth trampled down in an interestingly uniform fashion. There were also several small continuous ruts. No wheel had made them, and just for a moment his imagination flashed up the crazy vision of a miniature plough being tugged along.

'Something heavy has been pulled along here,' Slvasta said. He examined the hoof prints in the damp soil; some were terrestrial horses, while the others were mod feet. When he ran his hand over the crushed blades of grass and shoots of whakwerry reeds, his skin was covered in sap. 'Not long ago, two or three hours at most.' He stood up and looked along the trail. Everything had been bent or snapped in one direction, south-west. 'Sergeant?' he 'path-spoke. 'I want every squad to converge on me. We're following this track.'

'Yes, sir,' Yannrith replied.

The aether was abruptly full of 'path shouts.

'Come on,' Slvasta said to Tovakar. The pair of them set off down the track.

'What do you think it is, sir?' the trooper asked, tugging on the goat's leash.

'I'll tell you what I do know,' Slvasta said. 'Nests of established Fallers gather new-Fallen eggs and take them clear of the Fall zone where we're sweeping. That way the eggs are safe and eggsumption isn't left to chance.'

Tovakar looked down at the crushed vegetation he was walking on. 'This was made by someone dragging an egg along?'

Slvasta shrugged. He sent his mod-bird spiralling high, trying to see what the track could possibly lead to. The land ahead stretched out like a mirage across his eyevision. Now, if he projected a straight line from the edge of the bamboo . . . A broad river cut across the scrubland maybe five or six kilometres ahead, meandering away in big ox-bow curves and odd bends round irregular hillocks. Stretches of rainforest began to build up the further west it went.

That's got to be a tributary to the Colbal, he decided. The biggest river on the whole Lamarn continent, stretching from the Guelp mountain range north-east of Prerov, all the way west to the capital, Varlan, and beyond to empty into the Gulf of Meor, over three thousand kilometres away. Its complex tributary network snaked back through a good portion of the central lands. Hundreds of towns were sited on the banks. Even with the advent of the railway over the last fifteen hundred years, river traffic still carried the bulk of Lamarn's cargo and people.

A boat could travel just about anywhere, a great deal more easily than any cart, and without any of the attention. It was perfect for a nest.

Over the next half-hour, the other squads caught up with him. By the time they left the bamboo behind, he had his whole command with him. Thirty-eight troopers, eager and excited.

Out of the bamboo, they began to pick up the pace. Clouds were streaming across the sky, long white strands at first, clawing their way across the bright cobalt vault. Then the northern horizon began to darken as the rainclouds built up.

The goat was starting to complain and wrench at its leash. Tovakar was having trouble pulling the bolshie animal along.

'Tether it,' Slvasta ordered.

The trail ploughed into a strip of dense trees, an easy kilometre wide, which skirted the river. They reached it just as the rain started. Mod-birds were sent on ahead. Slvasta kept the pace fast, following the route that had been trampled down through the trees and undergrowth.

'Sir,' Jostol called. 'Boats!'

Slvasta's ex-sense picked up the trooper's mod-bird, seeing through its eyes. A pair of large stream-powered boats were anchored in the lee of a curve. Close to the bank, where big wanno trees hung over the water, they were almost obscured by the bushy weeping boughs. Unless you were really looking, you'd never know they were there. Cargo barges, he thought.

He began issuing orders to the corporals, detailing their approach. The other mod-birds were called back, leaving Jostol's as their sole sentry to avoid alerting the nest of Fallers. The mod-bird circled high, keeping as unobtrusive as possible. The rain was heavy now, making it difficult to see much. Slvasta could just make out several human shapes, along with mod-horses and mod-apes. They also had some terrestrial horses with them.

Four hundred metres from the water, the squads began to fan out. Slvasta along with Corporal Yannrith, Tovakar, Jostol and five other troopers slowed down as they closed on the mooring point, allowing the others to circle round, surrounding the group of people at the boats.

'Weapons ready,' Slvasta ordered when they were a hundred metres from the river. He drew his own carbine, using his ex-sight to check the mechanism was working as his teekay pulled back the loader lever.

'Well, hello there,' a strong 'path hailed them cheerfully.

Slvasta flinched. He'd known a wholly secret approach was impossible, but even so he'd hoped they might get a little closer first. 'Who are you?' he demanded.

'Rangers.'

'What?' Slvasta was running now. He sent his ex-sight out, perceiving seven men and one woman standing casually under the great awning of an ancient wanno tree, out of the heavy rain. They weren't carrying any weapons he could detect.

'Rangers,' repeated the man standing at the front of the group. 'We're from the Erond county regiment reserve. Just doing what we can to help. And who are you?'

Slvasta cleared the last of the trees. The riverbank was twenty metres ahead of him now, with the two long wooden-hulled barges sitting calmly on the water. Smoke was drifting out of their tall iron stacks.

He approached the group cautiously. 'Lieutenant Slvasta, Cham county regiment. And we're assigned to sweep this area.'

'Didn't know that. We've swept as well as we could, of course.' The man gave him a smile that was on the verge of mockery. He was tall, probably in his late twenties, with a shock of shaggy blond hair and the greenest eyes Slvasta had ever seen. His raincoat was long and brown, almost like waxed suede, but a lot thinner and lighter; raindrops rolled off it easily. The metal buttons were small and odd, somehow. Slvasta hadn't seen a coat quite like it before. The man's accent was foreign, too; he drawled each word.

'Who are you?'

'Sorry, should have said. I'm Nigel. This is my wife, Kysandra. And these are my grunts.'

Slvasta pushed back his hat's soggy, sagging brim to get a better look. 'Your what?'

'Grunts: soldiers. Under my command.'

'I need to know if you're human.'

'Fair enough, I'll drop my shell. Pervade away.'

'No. That's not good enough. Fallers have the same organs as we do.'

'Then how do you suggest we proceed?

Slvasta slipped the carbine's safety on and let the strap hold it loosely at his side. He drew his knife from its scabbard.

'Ah,' Nigel said. 'If you insist.'

'Cover me,' Slvasta told his troopers. By now, the entire mooring area was surrounded by the squads, with troopers taking position behind trunks, their carbines aimed at the rangers from Erond. He walked up to Nigel, feeling a slight ex-sight flow questingly over his stump. 'Your thumb, please,' he said.

Nigel held his hand up, thumb extended. Slvasta nicked the skin with the tip of his blade. Sure enough drops of red blood came out of the small puncture. He nodded in satisfaction. 'Faller blood is dark blue,' he explained.

'So I've been told,' Nigel said. 'Nice confirmation. Fool-proof, even.'

Again Slvasta had the impression he was being mocked. But the man's thoughts were calm and composed. The only emotional content Slvasta could pick up on was of a serene confidence – which was probably where his own notion of mockery originated from. He did his best to ignore it and beckoned Kysandra forward.

The 'wife' held her hand out. Slvasta thought she was around sixteen or seventeen, a sweet-looking girl with plenty of freckles and a mane of thick dark ginger hair, tied into a single tail. He felt sorry for the poor thing, but refrained from comment. Arranged marriages were relatively common out in the countryside, and Nigel's odd clothes were clearly expensive. Her attitude was a copy of Nigel's, but with less emotional control. The contempt she felt for him and his troopers was a whole lot easier to ascertain. She was human, too.

'Gentlemen,' Nigel gestured the rangers forward. They walked over to Slvasta one by one to be checked.

Slvasta didn't know what recruitment was like in Erond county, but the rangers looked more like a town's gang of thugs

196

than troopers. And they made no attempt to hide their scorn of him, a couple of them openly sneering at his stump.

'All clear,' Slvasta announced after the last one dripped red blood into the rain. He couldn't keep his puzzlement from showing. 'What in Uracus are you doing out here? This is nowhere. We only just arrived.'

'Chance, really,' Nigel said. 'I'm a trader. My boats were in Dural with a cargo of folax. I was looking to exchange it for hethal seed. We saw the beacons light up and volunteered to help sweep. Everybody does what they can, right? The regiment captain in the town sent us upriver.'

A large bird came swooping through the rain to land on one of the boughs above them. The whole bough swayed under its weight. Slvasta had never seen anything like it before. It had broad wings, well over two metres across, and the face was definitely mod. Yet the size and grace was way beyond anything any adaptor he knew had ever produced. 'Is that a mod-bird?' he asked.

'A ge-eagle,' Nigel said. 'Yes.'

'A what?'

'A type of mod-bird, a very good one,' Nigel glanced up affectionately at the bird, who stared unblinkingly at Sergeant Yannrith and the troopers round him. Its claws were metal tipped, Slvasta saw.

'Where did you get it?'

Nigel's smile was sardonic. 'A man from Ashwell village used to craft them. But that was long ago and far away from here.'

'I see.' Slvasta was aware he was losing face in front of everybody. 'We'll need to search your boats.'

'Of course,' Nigel said.

Sergeant Yannrith took a squad on one boat, wading out through the shallows. Corporal Kyliki took the other.

'You trampled down a pretty big track across the countryside,' Slvasta said. 'That's how we found you. What were you carrying?'

'Just us,' Nigel said.

'It looked like you were dragging something. Something large.'

'A couple of the horses were hitched up to stone boats, yes. We piled them up with our camp equipment. Something wrong with that?'

'What's a stone boat?'

'A flat sledge. They move quite quickly, allow us to sweep more ground. After all, you can't use a cart out here, lieutenant. No wheels will work in this kind of country.'

The way it was said – emphasizing the completely obvious, as if Nigel was explaining to a class of five-year-olds – made Slvasta feel stupid. Which was probably the intention.

'Check for sledges,' he told Yannrith and Kyliki.

'If you don't mind me asking,' Nigel said. 'The arm?'

'I fell into a Faller nest,' Slvasta replied impassively. 'I was being eggsumed when the Marines arrived.'

Nigel gave his nicked thumb a quick glance. 'I haven't met anyone who escaped that before. You were lucky.'

'Yes.' Slvasta tried to block out the memory of Ingmar, the awful pleading.

'And so now you understand the threat as few ever do, you're one hundred per cent committed to the regiment, to defending Bienvenido. That must worry your senior officers.'

'Why do you say that?'

Nigel looked at him as if judging from on high. It was all Slvasta could do to return the stare.

'You're better at the task than they are. They know that and so do your troopers here. Your level of dedication will also unnerve them. Belief always does that to old men grown comfortable in their position and privilege. Comfort is the enemy of change. Comfort is easy. It's a good meal and nights in a warm bed. Anything that challenges that is seen as dangerous.'

'Brigadier Venize is an excellent commander.'

Nigel smiled knowingly. 'I'm sure he is. But consider this: is he as good as you would be if you had command of the regiment?'

'I . . . That's a ludicrous question. I've only just made lieutenant.'

'And yet I've known ambition like yours, lieutenant. You, of all people, must realize that the Falls will never end. That the regiments and even the Marines, Giu bless them, are nothing other than damage limitation. If the Fallers are to be defeated, first this sheep-like attitude of acceptance must be broken. After that, after the status quo – so welcome to old powerful families – has been swept away, new attitudes can prevail. Then, and only then, can we dare to dream once more, as someone said long ago. And if that ever happens, life on Bienvenido can change.'

Slvasta was aware of just how uneasy the troopers were with this talk. For himself, it was unexpected, yet Nigel spoke the right of it. These were the very thoughts he never dared to voice. He would have very much liked to sit down and have a long, long conversation with this enigmatic man. Yet . . . something about the whole encounter was wrong. Nigel seemed about as far from a gang boss as you could get – cultured, suave, self-assured beyond even a National Councillor – yet the men with him were a type Slvasta knew so well. And he still didn't get Kysandra. The girl was clearly no simple submissive trinket Nigel owned. In fact, she didn't seem fazed by any of this, just stood there, tired and trail-dirty, but with a superior knowing smile on her face. *The way Quanda looked at me. Could some Fallers have red blood? Uracus, I'm paranoid.*

'They have sledges, sir,' Yannrith's 'path voice announced.

Slvasta couldn't decide if that was a good thing or not. Nigel was giving him an expectant glance – waiting patiently for him to do the right thing.

'Stand down,' Slvasta told his troopers.

'Thank you,' Nigel said as the carbines were returned to their slings and holsters. 'Now, if you have a map, I'll be happy to show you the area we've swept. Duplication is waste. And every day an egg lies free is a day it can lure someone to Fall.'

'Of course.' Slvasta went further under the huge wanno tree, where it was practically dry. He took out his map and unrolled it. 'Did you get a good price for your folax?'

'Haven't sold it yet,' Nigel said. 'I'll try again, downstream.'

'You must be a good trader. Those boats don't look cheap.'

'I have a rich family.'

'But you struck out for yourself?'

'Yes. Estates can provide you with a very comfortable life, but it's a life that doesn't change. There's never anything new. You never go anywhere or see anything fresh; you're never challenged. That means you can never achieve anything.'

'You're very keen on change, aren't you?'

Nigel raised an eyebrow. And for once his smile wasn't mocking. 'Don't tell me you're not. I haven't seen any regiment squads as motivated as yours. That's a substantial achievement, especially on this world. I know what it's like to push against the dead hand of inertia and tradition. If I have any advice for you, it would be: don't let the bastards grind you down. Keep pushing, lieutenant. That and the obvious, of course.'

'What obvious?' Slvasta asked, feeling helpless to stop the conversation.

'Old law: for every action there is an equal and opposite reaction. If you keep going the way you are – and I hope to Giu you do – then the effect you will have on those around you will grow larger. Ripples, my friend. People will look at you, what you're doing, rewriting the regiment rule book, and they'll want to do the same for themselves. That's when you'll start to run into resistance. That's where the politics begins. And that's the dirtiest fight there is.'

'Right.' Slvasta nodded seriously. It was as if his brain was fizzing from the impact of these words. He'd been waiting his whole life to hear them.

'Don't be afraid of your future,' Nigel said earnestly. 'You have principles. Stick with them, but don't think that you can fight fair to achieve them. Make the deals, build alliances with anyone who'll support you, walk away from people when it's convenient or they've outlived their use. Because, trust me, your opponents will use those same skills to bury you. That's the game. The only game. Play it well, and you can achieve miracles.'

'That sounds . . .'

'Cynical? Damn right. It's a big bad world out there. Kill or be killed, son, that's nature. But I don't have to tell you that, do I?'

Slvasta saw Yannrith and Kyliki wading ashore. 'Thank you.'

'Pleasure.' Nigel shook his hand. 'Good luck. Axe one of those bastard eggs apart for me, huh?'

'I will,' Slvasta was smiling, and he couldn't say why. This was still all very weird.

He stayed on the riverbank, watching Nigel and Kysandra wade out to the boats, holding hands. The last three horses were taken on board and settled in the mid-hold. Then the hawsers were untied. The boats puffed out steam from their aft vents as the pistons began to pump away with a loud clattering.

Slvasta waved solemnly as the boats chugged out to midstream. Nigel waved back before he and Kysandra went below deck.

Sergeant Yannrith came up beside him. 'Orders, sir?'

It was like the breaking of a spell. Slvasta glanced up at the sky. The clouds were thinning out. Sunlight haloed the treetops, producing a perfect double rainbow. He checked his pocketwatch with a scan of ex-sight. 'Dark in three hours. We need to connect with our horses and make camp. We'll resume the sweep first light tomorrow.'

'Yes, sir.' The sergeant looked at the map Slvasta was holding. 'Will we be sweeping the area the rangers cleared, sir?'

'Every damn centimetre of it, sergeant.'

'What were they really doing here? You can't get any closer to nowhere.'

'I have no idea.'

As the troopers picked their way back along the track Nigel had made, Slvasta sent his mod-bird flying as high as he could. His ex-sight was strong, allowing him to sense a good distance. The bird could see the two boats sailing down the river, three hundred metres away now. He hadn't realized they were that fast. Two large specks floated effortlessly in the air above them.

Two – what did Nigel call them? Ge-eagles? Slvasta started to wonder just how long Nigel had known the squads were chasing him.

How would you prepare if you had that kind of warning?

'Andricea.'

'Yes, lieutenant?'

'Send your mod-bird as far downstream as you can. Tell me what you see.'

'Yes, sir.'

Her mod-bird soared away, gaining altitude as it headed west. She had the longest ex-sight reach in the squads, as well as a prodigious 'path voice. Slvasta sought out the mod-bird's eye-sight, seeing the meandering river slicing through thick bands of jungle and broad swathes of scrub. Far ahead of the two boats, a smudge of smoke was wafting up from a jungle which hid the river.

Slvasta groaned in dismay. There had been three boats. By waiting for them at the river, letting them check out him and his rangers, Nigel had pulled off a perfect delaying tactic.

'What in Uracus is on that boat?'

*

Slvasta had them break camp at first light. He was grumpy and un-sympathetic to the troopers' grumbling. It had been a despondent night. Sleep had been elusive as he'd wrestled with the problem for hours.

Nigel was engaged in some kind of dubious activity. That was in no doubt. Slvasta's only active option was to send one squad back to the nearest sheriff's office in Marlaie, a day away, and alert them that there may be something illegal on a boat – only he didn't know what the boat looked like or where it was by now. The sheriff was probably out on a sweep, and if he was there he would probably laugh it off – after all, what could he do? Even if by some miracle a law officer caught up with Nigel, that dazzling charm would be played to the full, and there would be nothing incrim-inating on his boat, that was for sure.

It was like facing down Quanda all over again, just without the life-and-death stakes. There was simply no way he could win this one. All he cared about – as Nigel had so smartly determined – was running a successful sweep. By comparison, Nigel's activities were petty and irrelevant. But it galled him that he'd been suckered like that. He was furious with himself for being so gullible. And maybe, that nasty unquiet thought at the back of his head kept insisting, it was because Nigel was so obviously from the landowner class – smart, intelligent and confident. The background Slvasta lacked and had been taught to respect.

Yet Nigel told me to kick against that. Very convincingly.

He made an effort to rein in his frustration as he called Yannrith and the corporals over. A breakfast of hot tea and honey bread was served. They spent ten minutes discussing how the squads would be dispersed across their area. He was keen to make up for the lost hours yesterday.

Tents were packed up. Equipment stowed on the horses. Packs loaded.

Nebulas were still visible in the dawn sky as they set off. Giu was at the zenith, the scarlet crown of the heavens, with translucent prominences radiating out in all directions, captured stars within their gauzy veils twinkling brightly. The gold and turquoise flower that was Tizu was sinking below the horizon as the sun rose, while Eribu's misty spiral contained many ruby-tinged stars. And the Forest was visible if you squinted against the sun's glare, like a scintillating equatorial tumour in the corona. Thankfully, Uracus was on the other side of the planet. Having that scarlet and sulphur gash casting its benighted glow down on him would have been too much like a bad omen this morning.

Once they were underway, Tovakar came over. He looked somewhat on edge, with a hard shell round his thoughts. Slvasta waited patiently, knowing the man would speak his mind eventually. Trusting officers didn't come easy to Tovakar.

'I have a cousin, sir,' Tovakar said. 'A third cousin, mind, we're not close.'

'Of course not. And what does this cousin do?'

'Nothing much. He's a bit of a layabout, in truth. Got a cabin out in the Noldar wetlands.'

'That's good soil, so they say.'

'Yes, sir, when it's drained properly. Thing is, some farmers out that way grow narnik.'

'I see.' Slvasta had tried smoking the herb when he was younger, just like every teenager did, probably right back since the Landing. Ingmar had sneaked a wad from his older brother's stash, and the two of them had bunked off school one afternoon. It hadn't been what he'd expected. The loss of control had scared him, and he'd been sick most of the next day. He found out later they'd smoked far too much at once.

His second taste came from the Marine doctor back in Prerov, who had dosed him up with the plant's refined extract to deal with the pain from his amputated arm. This time he'd welcomed the weird dreams and visions that replaced rational thought. So afterwards he could appreciate the pull it exerted, taking the edge off an impoverished existence. It would have been easy for him to slip into a life bolstered by that sweet narcotic smoke. But those last haunting minutes with Ingmar were stronger than any cravings to annul self-pity. He had been spared, one of very few who had ever escaped being eggsumed. And in return for that gift, he was determined to be guided to the Giu nebula a fulfilled man. Throughout all the weeks of misery and pain, lying there in hospital, he had sworn that to himself.

Narnik's subversive, life-wrecking appeal had resulted in the Captain's Council banning its use outside medicine during the reign of Captain Leothoran, two thousand two hundred years ago. Which of course meant there was a lot of money in its underground trade.

'The farmers, they bale it,' Tovakar said. 'Big bales, sir.'

'Ah. Big enough that you'd need a stone boat to carry one?'

'Can be, sir. Or so I've heard.'

Slvasta grinned understandingly at the trooper's anxious face. 'Thank you, Tovakar.'

They were almost back into the wretched purple-tufted bamboo again. Slvasta pushed the first stems aside automatically. It was hard to believe Nigel was a narnik trader. Unless, of course, he was the junior son of some noble estate family who didn't want to let go of his expensive lifestyle. Narnik was easy money if you had the nerve to go for it. Even so, that was a hard stretch. Nigel just didn't seem the type; that self-belief of his was like nothing

Slvasta had encountered before. Though he was something of a rebel. Or at least preached it. Which might have been part of his cover.

What in Uracus was on that third boat?

Slvasta was desperate to find out. He certainly had enough leave time built up, as the regiment's adjutant was always pointing out. You didn't rise from the ranks to reach lieutenant inside five years without putting in some long and difficult hours. It would be easy for him to take a month off any time he wanted.

Somehow, he just knew, you didn't find a man like Nigel in a month. Not unless Nigel wanted you to find him.

*

'Fallen egg!'

The 'path shout from corporal Kyliki came down the line like wildfire. Good training and better discipline saw the squads close on the egg's location in the pattern Slvasta had drilled them in. Nobody, *nobody*, was to approach within two hundred metres alone: those were his standing orders. So they formed up in a circle, two hundred and fifty metres away. Only after a check to make sure everyone was present, did Slvasta ask: 'Where's the goat?'

'I have it, sir,' Trooper Jostol answered.

'Keep a good hold,' Slvasta replied. 'Sergeant, move us in.'

'Aye, sir. Everyone, mod-birds back and on the ground. Once they're down, move forward. Watch your advance-partner for signs of lure.'

Slvasta ordered his mod-bird back with the rest. Through its eyes, he'd seen the tear in the bamboo's purple canopy, sent the bird skimming fast for a confirmed sighting. The egg was there, sitting at the centre of a small impact zone. What he saw could have been a piece of ridiculously elegant artwork, with the dark globe of the egg in the middle, surrounded by bamboo stalks flattened radially, as if they'd transformed into some kind of freakish earth flower.

It was invisible to his eyesight as he pushed forwards through the thick stalks, but his ex-sight remained fixed on it during his approach, alert for any treachery. The squads emerged cautiously from the upright bamboo into the impact zone. Slvasta felt it then. An aroma that made you want to step forwards and get a better smell, then a taste – all you had to do was lick the dark surface. A sensation hinting of unparalleled joy if you just stepped forwards and reached out. An elusive melody so sweet that you had to hear it properly, if you just stepped close enough to put your ear to the surface of the sphere it emanated from. As always, his heart began to race as his body reacted to the promised pleasure of the lure. If only someone had taught him this was what happened when you encountered an egg. Then Ingmar would still be alive – and Quanda with her devious incitement, manipulating the lure with the addition of sexual provocation, would have died in a blaze of flame and pain. If only . . .

'Hold fast.' Yannrith's stern warning barked round the small clearing.

Slvasta hadn't quite been going to take a step, but the appeal the egg's strange thoughts radiated was darkly enticing every time. 'Remember this, all of you,' Slvasta said. 'Look at your enemy and know its treachery, know its lust for your flesh.' He glanced round the faces of the troopers, seeing each of them fight their own battle to resist. The new recruits were having the worst of it. Several were having to be physically restrained. 'I need you to be strong enough to resist this bewitchment every time. We are going to stand here until you learn to scorn its trickery and lies. That promise you feel is death. It will kill you forever; it will consume your soul. If you Fall, there will be no fulfilment, and you will never be guided to the Heart of the Void. The Skylords do not come for the Fallen. They come for humans alone. They come for the worthy. And that is who I want in my squads. So will you show me that? Will you show me you are worthy?'

'Yes, lieutenant,' they chorused.

'I cannot hear you. Are you worthy?'

'YES, LIEUTENANT.'

'Do you wish to discover the false wonder it offers?'

'NO, LIEUTENANT.'

'Good.' He looked around the clearing again. The new recruits were standing firm. Nobody moved. 'Trooper Jazpur.'

'Yes, lieutenant?'

'Release the goat.'

Jazpur let go of the leash. The goat, which had been silent as soon as it emerged into the impact zone, trotted forwards. It reached the egg and looked up at it, then pushed the side of its head affectionately against the dark surface. And stuck.

'Now watch,' Slvasta commanded.

The egg's powerful psychic lure died away as the goat's grubby hide began to sink below the surface. As always, Slvasta moved closer, probing with his ex-sight, trying to sense what was happening, trying to understand the process. As always, he was baffled. He perceived the surface structure, the thick living fluid inside. The strange uniform thoughts circulating within. The fizz of activity around the goat's skin and skull as it sank into the bizarre yolk.

'Once you have touched that surface, you are stuck,' Slvasta said. 'You cannot pull away.' He thrust his stump out. 'You can be cut free, but only if your friends are quick. If your chest is eggsumed, you are Fallen. Once your head is inside, you have Fallen. Now, despite the rumours you have heard, no cloth you wear can prevent eggsumption, no herbs can make it spit you back out, no teekay can lift you free. Fire will not make it let go. If a friend is Falling, be a true friend and kill him!' Slvasta drew his pistol and shot the placid goat in its head. 'Sergeant, axe the egg.'

'Aye, sir.'

The recruits were given the first chance to swing their axes. It was hard work, for the blackened, rumpled surface was tough enough to survive a plummet through the sky. But they persisted, hacking away until cracks began to appear. Dribbles of pale white goo started to leak out. Then the second batch of troopers moved in and began swinging. The cracks were widened. The goo began to spray out in thin jets.

After twenty minutes, the holes were large and the internal

pressure had been released. The peculiar substance of the egg simply poured out, forming big puddles on the ground.

'Burn it,' Slvasta ordered.

Five troopers with flamethrowers moved in. They began to play their fierce arcs of flame over the egg. The stench of burning jellyoil and roasting egg churned through the air. Slvasta had smelt it enough times before, but several of the troopers were gagging.

'We've found one,' Slvasta announced to his squads as the hot stinking flames incinerated the dead egg. 'That means there will be another three or four somewhere close by, maybe even more. The eggs never Fall alone. So we're going to go back out there, and we're going to sweep this whole county if we have to. We will find those eggs, and they *will* be axed and burnt before any human Falls. Now, let's get to it!'

*

Thirteen days later, Slvasta stood outside the tall glossy double doors of Brigadier Venize's office. He was still in his field uniform, filthy from travelling and camping. The NCOs had led their squads back to the barracks to unpack and clean up and get themselves a decent meal in the headquarters' long mess hall. They were the last of the regiment's troops to return from the sweep. It had been a civilian passenger train which had brought them back to Cham; the troop train with the rest of the regiment had returned a week before.

One of the doors opened, and Major Rachelle came out. She was the regiment's adjutant, in her late nineties, with silver-grey hair wound into a tight bun. Her skin was leathery from decades spent out in the sub-tropical sun commanding sweeps. Slvasta had to respect the service she'd put in. But that time was over, and now she was just another outdated officer clogging up headquarters. There were dozens of them, soaking up the region's budget to pay for their extravagant salaries – money that could have been better spent on front-line troopers, in his opinion. And as for the regulations they invented that sapped the regiment's operational performance . . .

'He's ready for you,' she said curtly.

Slvasta followed her back through the doors. Brigadier Venize's office was another indulgence. A huge tiled room with arching windows that reached up to the high roof. Large fan flaps swung gently above the open shutters, their cord pulled by a mod-dwarf who sat in the corner, rocking back and forth. More irrelevance, Slvasta thought, as he walked the length of the room to the brigadier's desk. It wasn't as if the fans made any difference to the heat. But he kept his shell smooth and impregnable, unwilling for anyone to know his sense of frustration and disappointment at the failure of the sweep.

'Sir.' He reached the desk and stood to attention, saluting.

Venize was pretending to read a thick folder. The previous month had seen a regimental dinner celebrating his one hundred and twentieth birthday, with the nobility from across the county filling the officers' mess and two pavilions set up on the parade ground. Slvasta had seen the final bill, which presumably was one of the major reasons the regiment hadn't yet bought terrestrial horses to replace all the mod-horses.

The brigadier looked good for his years. Still fit and active, with a set of thin wire-rimmed glasses to compensate for short-sightedness, and a slim moustache to add to the dignity of age. He looked up from the folder and extended a finger, pointing to one of the two chairs in front of the ancient leather-topped desk. 'Sit down, lieutenant.'

There was nothing in the voice to give away what tone the meeting would take, and his shell was even sturdier than Rachelle's.

Slvasta sat, keeping his back straight. Major Rachelle sat in the other chair, looking at him.

The brigadier slid the folder onto the desk, next to a pile of similar ones. 'So, lieutenant, would you care to tell me what happened?'

'Sir, we intercepted some kind of criminal called Nigel operating in our designated sweep area. It's my belief he's captured some Faller eggs.'

'Indeed, and why is that?'

'He was dragging something behind his horses. He claimed it was their own camping equipment, and that they were helping with the sweep. I couldn't prove otherwise at the time, so I let him go. Then we found an egg.'

'Well done. Go on.'

'One egg. We both know that *never* happens.'

'Nobody escapes from eggsumption,' Rachelle said. 'Another well-known fact. There are always exceptions.'

Slvasta gave her an irritated glance. 'We swept that area thoroughly. There were another two impact zones, but there were no eggs in them. However, each zone had been visited; we found the tracks. He took the eggs.'

'So this Nigel is actually a Faller?' Venize asked.

'Sir. Not him personally, no. His blood was red.'

'Then the people with him are?' Rachelle pressed.

'No,' Slvasta said. 'I checked them all. But one of the boats he used was downstream. We didn't know at the time.'

The brigadier blinked. 'I can accept that a nest could reach the eggs before our squads. You of all people are aware of that behaviour. But what kind of criminal gang takes Faller eggs? They have no black market value. Not that I'm aware of. Do they, major?'

'No, sir. They do not.'

'Lieutenant, are you aware of their having any monetary value?'

'No, sir,' Slvasta admitted.

'Then why would Nigel take them?'

'I don't know, sir.'

'The only humans who ever move an egg are the Marines, nobody else is qualified or authorized. And that's a rare event; they only ever take one back to Varlan when the Captain's Faller Research Institute needs one to examine. Isn't it more likely that a nest got to them and carried them away?'

'It is possible, sir.'

'And you're using Nigel as an excuse for your failure to find them?' Rachelle said.

'No! There was no other activity in the whole area. Nigel took them.'

'If you're right, then we must assume he is such a piece of lowlife that he's actually in the pay of a nest,' Venize said. 'How extraordinary. I never thought I'd live to see such a thing.'

I . . . know that's not true, Slvasta thought. *Nigel is no one's puppet.* 'That is an explanation, yes, sir.'

'Very well,' Venize said. 'We will alert the Captain's Marines that a nest has acquired a Fall. I hope you understand what such a notice will do to this regiment's reputation and status.'

'Yes, sir. I do.'

'Now, moving on. Tell me about the Bekenz farm, please, lieutenant.'

Slvasta did his best not to wince. 'That was where we discovered one of the empty impact zones, sir, in the wild just outside the farm's boundary.'

'How did you confirm that?' Rachelle asked. 'You just said there were no eggs.'

'I know what an impact zone looks like, thank you,' Slvasta said.

'It was quite a long way from the Bekenz farm's boundary, actually, wasn't it?' Rachelle said.

'The farm was the closest human habitation,' Slvasta replied tightly. 'I had a duty to ensure they were safe.'

'And you checked everyone in your usual fashion, correct?' Venize asked.

'Yes, sir. They were all human.'

'Yes, they are human, and Bekenz, it turns out, is the seventh son of Hamiud, the largest estate owner in Prerov county.'

'So he claimed, yes, sir.'

'In fact, he told you that when you ordered your troops to slaughter every neut and mod-animal on the farm, is that correct?' Rachelle asked.

'Yes.'

'Yet you still went ahead with the slaughter?'

'Sir, the Fallers can control the mods much better than we can.

I know that for a fact. There's no telling what kind of orders the egg might have given the mods. They could have murdered every one of Bekenz's family. There were children on that farm.'

'Lieutenant, I have lost count of how many times I have had this conversation with you,' Venize said. He patted the pile of folders on the desk. 'Others, however, have not.'

'Sir, the way Fallers can control mods is on record—'

'I know. But are you aware of how much compensation the county council has been obliged to pay out recently, thanks to your dogmatism?'

'I'm saving lives, sir. I'm sorry if that's not popular.'

'Lieutenant, I have every sympathy for you, and everyone admits you are one of the best officers we've had in a generation. It's just that some of your methods are too severe for this part of the world. You have your critics, and they include some very important people. Even the mayor's office has been in touch, expressing concern at your culls.' Venize held up a hand to stop the protest Slvasta was about to make. 'Not me. I appreciate what you've done for the regiment, and we'll be adopting your methods in future – the fitness, the training, all that stuff. In addition, twenty terrestrial horses are to be purchased at the town beast market next week.'

'That's good news, sir,' Slvasta said.

'Absolutely. That'll show those damn civilians I will not be pushed around. This is my command and it will remain so until they prise it from my cold dead hand, eh?'

'Sir.'

'And you, Slvasta, are to be promoted.'

'Uh, sir?'

'You heard.' He picked up a scroll from the desk; the regiment's waxed and ribboned seal was affixed to the bottom. 'I've already signed the warrant. Congratulations. Captain.'

'I . . . Thank you, sir.' He accepted the scroll, bewildered and happy.

'My pleasure. After all, we can't have a lowly lieutenant as our liaison officer, now can we?'

Slvasta's delight vanished instantly. 'Liaison?'

'Yes,' Rachelle said. 'You will be our representative in the capital. You'll sit on the Joint Regimental Council and contribute to policy. You can explain all about your methods and have them applied across Bienvenido. When you arrive, you'll also notify the Marine commandant about this Nigel fellow.'

'Sir, no, please. I need to be out in the field. I can't—'

Venize's expression didn't falter. 'It is a considerable honour to be appointed to this important post. Don't let the regiment down. You are dismissed, captain.'

Slvasta just stared at the brigadier for a long moment. He'd lost and he knew it. The only question now was how badly he let them beat him. If he protested, refused the posting, they'd have an excuse to bust him down to the rank of trooper for insubordination. All he could think of was Nigel's words about unsettling his superiors; the man had practically predicted this.

So he got to his feet, saluted, and said: 'Thank you for the opportunity, sir. You won't regret it.'

Venize's urbane composure remained unblemished, while Rachelle's shell couldn't quite contain her suspicion at his easy submission.

Slvasta turned and marched out of the office. *When I come back*, he promised them silently, *it will be to fling you straight into the depths of Uracus itself.*

4

The study was as extravagant as only those in the Captain's Palace could be. Bright and cool in even the worst of Varlan's summer days, it was on the first floor in the state wing, with huge arched windows providing a view along Walton Boulevard and the sprawl of the city's roofscape beyond. Chandeliers like crystal moons hung the length of the study, interspaced with huge eight-blade fans turned slowly by mods in a hidden cable room. Oil paintings depicting heroic scenes of earlier Captains leading regiments against Fallers covered the wall, their gold frames glinting in the sunlight that was streaming in.

There was little by way of furniture. A marble and applewood desk five metres wide and three deep was situated a quarter of the way along the shining black and white tiled floor, its one ornate gilt-edged chair with its back to the huge fireplace. Two chairs for visitors were placed in front of it, velvet cushions unused – nobody sat before the Captain, not for official appointments; tradition had the chairs reserved for family only. Pedestals with busts of yet more esteemed ancestors filled the alcoves. At the far end of the room, ancient vases held impressive arrays of fresh cut flowers.

Captain Philious sat behind the desk while two aides stood at one side, holding folders full of papers which required his signature. Both of them were young women in specialist versions of the usual smart palace staff uniform, tight fitting with a deep-cut neckline that extended down to the navel. Philious might be approaching middle age, but at seventy-seven he still enjoyed all the physical pleasure the flesh could provide. Thankfully his distinguished bloodline hadn't let him down: the Captains remained blessed with a high resistance to illness, giving them a lifespan that usually got to see them comfortably into a second century. Unless their heirs grew impatient. That particular misfortune had befallen several ancestors during the last three thousand years. And Philious was under no illusions about his own son, Aothori.

'Sir?' his permanent secretary 'pathed from her office outside. 'Trevene is here to see you.'

Philious looked up from the stack of papers he'd already signed. 'That's a wonderful excuse to stop. Ask him to come in, please.' He put his ornate fountain pen back into the gold holder. 'We'll finish these later, thank you.'

One of the aides picked up the signed papers. Both smiled at him, and walked the length of the room to the double doors at the far end. Philious watched them go contentedly.

Trevene came in just before they reached the doors. A man approaching a hundred and twenty, whose receding jet-black hair revealed a skull of olive skin that shone in the study's thick sunbeams. He wore a simple grey suit, as unobtrusive as men of his profession always were. It was as if he had a natural fuzz, obscuring him from notice. Thin features were becoming creased as age dried his skin, while small silver-framed glasses perched on a long nose.

'Do sit,' Philious said, as he always did. Trevene was technically family, a second cousin – he had to be, only family could be trusted to run the Captain's police.

'Sir,' Trevene bowed slightly as he reached the desk. As always, he stood.

'So how are we doing with Jasmine Avenue?' In three months it would be the centenary of the Jasmine Avenue rebellion, the last serious civil disturbance on Bienvenido – an unfortunate year for his grandfather, where a disappointing crop coincided with a demographic surge. It had been put down swiftly, of course.

Possibly too swiftly. There were a number of deaths, and a lot more sentenced to the Pidrui mines. A year later, the martyrs' names had been carved on the avenue's walls. The borough council had swiftly removed them, repairing the wall, and then a year later they'd reappeared. Removed. Replaced. Removed. And so it went on for decades, despite sheriffs guarding the avenue at anniversary time. The families of the dead were quite tenacious. It had become a ritual, annoyingly keeping the cause alive.

'There's a lot of talk about commemorating the rebellion at the university, sir.'

'Oh, there's always talk there. Damn students.'

'Yes, sir. Not students of good family, obviously. But provincials and middle classes may be a slight problem. They're unusually persistent.'

Philious raised an eyebrow. 'The radicals are organizing?'

A note of uncertainty coloured Trevene's thoughts. 'Not the radicals. This is something milder – an expanding seam of discontent, if you like. There is no defined leadership, which is peculiar. Yet my assets in the halls of residence report that some kind of loose organization is forming. Nothing formal, nothing official, there's no name for what they are, but someone or something has stirred them up. They have developed a common purpose and support each other.'

'By definition an organization has to be organized. Someone must be behind this.'

'Yes, sir.'

'But you can't find them?'

'If they exist, they are elusive.'

Philious leaned back in his chair, far more amused than worried. 'They're outsmarting *you*? A bunch of students?'

'Inquiries are being made. If there is a leader, they will be exposed and neutralized.'

'I'm glad to hear it. What about the rest of the city?'

'The Shanties are full of talk, sir, of course. But it is just another grumble to the content chorus. No one else is remotely interested.'

'The Shanties,' Philious said in disapproval. It seemed as if every problem his Captaincy faced originated in the Shanties. That same demographic quirk which had seen the sharp population rise hadn't been matched by increased economic activity. Now every city and town on Bienvenido had Shanties on its outskirts – squalid shacks full of the jobless who couldn't afford the rent for a tenement, or to send their children to school. The only thing they were any good at doing, it seemed, was breeding.

Experts from the Treasury and banks constantly claimed that the economy would grow to accommodate them. Philious wasn't so sure. It was a hundred years since they first appeared, and every time he passed a Shanty on the way out of the city, it was larger than before.

'A suggestion, sir: Jasmine Avenue is old; it's my belief that the road surface needs repairing. If the cobbles were pulled up ready to be relaid, the whole avenue would have to be closed off. And it's a long, wide avenue. The work would likely take months.'

Philious smiled. He did so like Trevene. The man was constantly five steps ahead of anyone else, and brutality was always a last resort. 'Excellent. Have a word with the borough's mayor. Let's see; the Skylords will be here in two days, so shall we say work begins the day after, while everyone's still too hungover to question anything?'

'I'll see to it, sir.' Trevene adjusted his spectacles. 'There is one other issue, sir.'

'Yes?' Philious asked wearily.

'There's been *another* girl, sir. It would appear the First Officer's foibles got the better of him again.'

'Oh great Giu, what happened?'

'The hospital says she will live. But she wasn't a working girl like his usuals. This one was from a middle-class family in Siegen, attending the university here. Her parents have arrived, and naturally they're somewhat distressed. They've retained Howells as their lawyer.'

'Oh crudding Uracus.'

'Quite, sir. It may be hard to get his suit dismissed in court without an executive order. And I understand the *Hilltop Eye* pamphlet has acquired the story. It won't reflect well on the Captaincy. Your reputation must remain unsullied.'

'Right. Send someone from the Treasury's legal department round to see the family. Pay them off. Whatever it costs.'

'Yes, sir. And the First Officer?'

Philious pressed his teeth together and took a breath. 'I'll speak with him.'

5

It was the day the Skylords were due to arrive – eighteen months to the day since Slvasta had arrived in Varlan. As customary, the mayor had declared it a public holiday. The city was packed with departer families, coming to witness the fabulous ceremony, which signalled the start of their friends and relatives receiving guidance to Giu.

By midmorning the streets leading down to the city's long waterfront were packed. Many people had eschewed their guesthouses and hotels to camp out along the quayside that ran the length of the city. The psychic sensation that filled the aether above Varlan was one of anticipation and delight.

Slvasta walked along Walton Boulevard, the wide central thoroughfare that led all the way from Bromwell Park to the sprawling Captain's Palace that lay at the centre of the government district – block after block dominated by grandiose ten-storey buildings. Today, the scuttling drab-suited officials that usually swarmed the roads and alleys and intersections were all absent, at home with their families or preparing for the evening's festivities. Even the carts and carriages were fewer, though the flow of cyclists was as thick as ever.

He reached the junction to Pointas Street, marked by the fountain statue of Captain Gootwai, and turned down it past the Ministry of Transport. Holat trees lined the road, their long red and yellow variegated leaves fluttering in the humid breeze. It was always humid in Varlan, something Slvasta still hadn't accustomed himself to. This far south of the equator, it wasn't anything like as hot as his home county of Cham, but the clamminess from the Colbal, which at this point was over three kilometres wide, was extraordinary, and unrelenting.

Pointas Street ended at Okherrit Circus, and the buildings became slightly less stolid, with elaborate carvings on the stonework, and larger windows making them more open and welcoming. This was a commercial district, with fashionable stores and many family offices. Today, of course, the businesses were all shut. He began the steep walk up Longlear Road, with its notorious open stream bubbling and gurgling down a channel cut into the centre of the flagstones.

Major Arnice was waiting for him outside the Burrington Club, his scarlet jacket and white breeches seemingly glowing in their own little haze of extra-strength sunlight. But then, Arnice was utterly faithful to the mould of a dashing officer and gentleman. He caught sight of Slvasta and raised a solemn hand in greeting. 'There you are,' he 'pathed.

Arnice was one of the very few people in the city Slvasta considered a friend – a fellow sufferer of duty on the Joint Regimental Council, and only a few years older than Slvasta himself. They were the two youngest officers on the Council, with a shared contempt for its painfully bureaucratic workings.

Slvasta greeted him with a firm handshake. 'Thanks for this.'

'Delighted to help, old chap.'

They went into the club. And at once Slvasta felt a resurgence of that nagging insecurity he'd experienced since the day he arrived at Varlan. For a boy who grew up on a farm of modest means in the countryside fifteen hundred miles from the capital, a sense of social inferiority was the inevitable fallback position. It didn't help that the dark wooden panelling of the club's hallway, with its classic black and white marble tiled floor, reinforced his impression of the city's casual wealth. Even his own dress uniform, a dark-blue tunic with discreet brass buttons and olive green trousers, was far less ostentatious than Arnice's resplendent Meor Regiment regalia.

'The ladies are waiting,' Arnice said as they made their way up the stairs to the lounge restaurant. There were no mod-dwarfs in the club, which was one of the main reasons Slvasta had accepted the invitation. Here old men and women in stiff black suits with snow-white shirts served the members' every whim with quiet efficiency. None of them would dream of taking a holiday, not even on this day.

The club's lounge restaurant had a wide balcony, with two dozen tables under an ancient wisteria canopy providing a grand view across the rooftops to the river Colbal itself. As such, it was proving very popular with the members. Every table was occupied.

'Best view in the city,' Arnice said from the corner of his mouth. 'Excepting Captain Boorose's pavilion itself, of course.'

Slvasta followed his friend's gaze. Down on the waterfront, the stone dome of Captain Boorose's pavilion stood out against the more utilitarian warehouses and boatyards. It was on a raised mound just behind Chikase's wharf, a simple building open at the front where fluted pillars supported the roof. Palace Guards in full green and blue dress uniforms stood round it, carbines held tightly across their chests. The elaborate black and gold coaches of the Captain's family had just pulled up outside.

Captain Philious was the first to emerge, waving at the crowds, who waved back, every hand grasping a colourful blossom. It looked as if he was swimming in a wildflower meadow. His wife followed, and they held hands and walked up the short steps to the pavilion, where a long table had been set up, allowing them to picnic while gazing out across the fast brown waters of the Colbal.

His family followed, the smaller children giggling and waving enthusiastically back at the good-natured crowd. Then Aothori, the First Officer, climbed out of his carriage, the Captain's eldest son, clad in the suave black of a Marine colonel. The cheering quietened. Even from the Burrington Club, Slvasta could sense the mood of the well-wishers darkening.

'Giu help us when that one becomes Captain,' Arnice muttered discreetly.

Slvasta said nothing as he studied the young man through the

221

public gifting. He'd heard talk about Aothori. About the extravagance and the arrogance. How people who complained about *incidents* involving their daughters or missing property and unpaid bills left the city unexpectedly.

He kept a neutral smile in place as they approached the table Arnice had reserved. There were two young ladies standing waiting for them – dressed, inevitably, in the yellow and blue that Varlan's younger aristocracy had decided was in fashion this season. He recognized one, Jaix – a nice girl in her late twenties whose features showed a strong Chinese heritage. She was the fifth daughter of a merchant family, and as such a likely fiancée for Arnice, though they had only been courting for a month. Slvasta had spent the last three weeks listening to Arnice talking endlessly about her – up until last week, when Arnice had withdrawn from social evenings in the city's clubs and pubs and theatres. Now all Slvasta heard was how he spent every evening visiting Jaix at her day villa over in the Gonbridge district. For propriety's sake, the unmarried daughters of good family were supposed to return home by midnight.

Arnice introduced the other lady as Lanicia. She was tall and slender, the same age as Slvasta, with long strawberry-blonde hair arranged in elaborate curls. Her smile as he took her hand was fixed and emotionless, like all women of her class. Slvasta didn't really care; all he could focus on was her nose, which was petite with an upturned tip. On such a narrow face, it was striking. He managed to look away before his stare became blatant.

But then she was directing her ex-sight at his stump. It didn't help that he pinned the tunic's empty sleeve across his torso, drawing attention to it. He wanted a jacket tailored so the sleeve could be folded down his side, making it less obtrusive. And like so many things in Varlan, he hadn't quite got round to doing it. Time seemed so very different here; the city's languid pace was insidious. People spent so much of their day in the pursuit of such small goals. But they did know how to enjoy themselves, he admitted.

Slvasta used his teekay to pull Lanicia's chair out, as a gentleman should. Her eyes widened in appreciation.

'That's a very powerful teekay you have,' she said as she sat down.

Slvasta caught the glance she and Jaix exchanged. 'It's a compensation,' he explained.

'How did it happen?' Lanicia asked, without any of the usual semi-embarrassment most people had.

'Slvasta's a genuine hero,' Arnice said loudly. 'Don't let him tell you otherwise.' He turned to a waiter. 'We'll start with champagne, thank you. The Bascullé.'

'Sir,' the waiter bowed.

'It wasn't heroic,' Slvasta said. 'I was caught by a nest.'

'Giu, really?' Lanicia asked, her hand going to her throat. 'You've met a Faller?'

'Yes. She and her mod-apes captured my squad. Then we were stuck to eggs. The Marines arrived just in time for me, but not my two friends.'

'How dreadful. I don't know what I would do if eggs Fell on Varlan. Flee, I expect.'

'That's the worst thing you can do,' Slvasta said. 'Arnice's regiment is the one that will sweep the city for eggs. It's a well-planned exercise. Unless one lands in your house, just stay put and wait for the all-clear.'

'Why shouldn't we run?' Jaix asked.

'Because then there's a chance you could stray into an egg's lure and be drawn to it.' All he could think of was Trooper Andricea staring at the last egg they'd found, filthy from days on the sweep, determined never to succumb to the egg's bewitchment, then swinging the axe furiously when it was her turn. So very different to these two refined daughters of the aristocracy, who probably didn't even know how to boil water on a cooker.

'But don't you gals worry,' Arnice said. 'There hasn't been a Fall on the city for seven hundred years. And there've only been three since the landing.'

'What about a nest bringing eggs inside the city?' Lanicia asked apprehensively.

'The sheriffs remain vigilant for any signs of nest activity. There is none in Varlan, believe me.'

Slvasta held his tongue. There were always rumours of nests established in cities and towns, preying on the poor and friendless, people that no sheriff would care about. In some cases, like Rakwesh Province, he knew it was a lot more than rumour. Reports from local regiments that crossed his desk were full of 'disappeared' people the sheriffs had compiled.

'So do your family have an estate in Cham county?' Jaix asked.

'I gave the land up so I could serve in the regiment,' Slvasta said. 'I intend to spend my life fighting the Fallers.' He hated replying in such a fashion – a vague truth that didn't actually answer the question. It was another unwelcome trait he'd come to adopt in the city. But, as Arnice constantly reminded him, if you were going to accomplish anything in Varlan, you had to be accepted by the aristocracy. And the greatest barrier to that was being poor. As a serving officer with a position on the Joint Council, he could bypass that requirement to some degree – except probably marriage.

'That's so noble,' she said in admiration.

Arnice gave him a quick ironic smile as the bottle of Bascullé arrived. They toasted the day.

'To Guidance.'

'And Fulfilment.'

Slvasta would rather have had a decent beer, but sipped the champagne anyway, conceding to himself that it was actually rather nice. Sometimes he wondered if it was only his own prejudices which were holding him back.

'Oh, look, the boats are setting out,' Jaix said.

From the quayside, thousands of pyre boats were casting off, pushed out into the fast flow of water by teekay from teary relatives. They varied from large and expensive craft with high pyre platforms where those who were seeking Guidance waited on their comfortable beds, down to simple rafts with their owners sitting atop a pile of firewood.

Captain Philious stood at the front of the pavilion and waved graciously to the departing boats, smiling widely. The city's harbour-master boats were trying to steer the irregular flotilla out away from the quays and slipways. There hadn't been a blowback fire for over nine hundred years, and the city authorities were keen to keep that record going.

As the four of them sipped their champagne, the boats moved out and the current started to carry them downstream. Nonetheless, they maintained a loose formation, with few stragglers.

'How many?' Lanicia asked.

'The mayor's office estimated about seventeen thousand people,' Arnice said. 'They come in from eight counties, after all.'

Slvasta sent his ex-sight slipping over his pocketwatch. The Skylord was due in another three minutes. The sound of the water-side crowd waving and cheering was audible even on the balcony.

'Do you think it will come?' Jaix said.

'The Watcher Guild reported five approaching,' Slvasta said. 'Their calculations are usually accurate.'

'So how come they can never be as accurate about the eggs?' Lanicia asked.

'You're talking about two very different objects to spot in space,' Slvasta replied. 'The Skylords are vast and glow. They are easy to see at night, especially with the large multi-mirror tele-scopes the guild uses at its primary observatories. But the eggs, now they're as black as the space between the nebulas. The only way we can have any advanced warning is if they're spotted tran-siting during the daytime, and for that you have to have keen eyes and get very lucky. Usually, we only get advance warning for about one Fall in five; otherwise all the guild sees is the descent contrail through the atmosphere – and we only get that if there aren't too many clouds.'

'I thought you couldn't see space during the day,' Lanicia said.

'It's the sun which is the problem,' Slvasta said. 'The Forest is directly between us and the sun. And you absolutely cannot look at the sun through a telescope; you'll burn your eyes out in a frac-tion of a second.'

'Then how do they see the eggs approaching?'

'Filters and a giant screen,' Slvasta said, remembering his trip to the guild's Polulor Observatory. 'The telescope is rigged to shine the magnified image of the Forest onto a giant screen, and I do mean giant. It's a white wall probably half the size of this building.'

'What did they look like, the trees?' Lanicia asked.

'Smudges, really,' Slvasta admitted. 'To me, anyway. A trained Guild observer interprets them a lot better. And they're the people who detect the eggs falling from the Forest. I was told they're like grains of sand, a fleck of darkness which shoots across the screen so fast that if you blink you miss it. That's why they always have a minimum of five observers watching at all times.'

'That's fascinating,' Lanicia said, staring at him over the top of her champagne glass. 'I'd love to see the projection of the Forest.'

'Ah, well, you're in luck there,' Arnice said cheerfully. 'Slvasta can arrange a tour of an observatory for you; he has the authority.'

Which was utter crud, but Slvasta resisted glaring at Arnice. He didn't mind the occasional blind date, but being set up like this . . .

'It's here,' Jaix said quietly.

Like everyone on the balcony, the four of them stood up to watch. The first of the Skylords rose out of the north-eastern horizon. A vast ovoid of crystal sheets folded in amongst themselves in the most extraordinary warped geometry. Slivers of pastel light glimmered within the massive curving furrows, slithering and sliding about as if they were alive. Under Bienvenido's dazzling sun they should have been washed out, yet they perversely maintained their intensity.

As always when one of the mighty creatures appeared, silence fell across the city as its true size became apparent. The leading edge of its giant shadow rippled across the land and river below as it blocked out more and more of the sky. Birds warbled in distress as they flapped frantically, trying to outrun the impossible umbra. Tufts of strato-cumulus were torn apart by the wind roaring out in all directions as the Skylord ploughed through the air.

Down amid the flotilla of pyre ships, those seeking Guidance sent their last 'path goodbyes to everyone watching from the city.

Captain Philious raised both arms beatifically, wishing his subjects a successful Guidance, looking for all the world as if he personally had conjured the Skylord into existence. Before him, the would-be astral travellers crushed their little capsule of etire juice and swallowed the sickly fluid. Within seconds, the toxin had stopped their hearts. As their bodies died, they used teekay one last time to start whatever method of ignition was on board. Flames began to lick at the pyres as the Skylord swooped low overhead, as if the flames could help propel the departing souls upwards.

It took a particularly sensitive ex-sight to perceive souls as they departed their physical body. Slvasta had never even come close to sensing such a delicate essence. Today he didn't have to. Today, those with the greatest ex-sight ability were standing along the city's waterfront, minds open to share their gifted perception with everybody.

The souls began to glide up out of dying bodies; ephemeral spectres taking on the idealized form of the corpse they had just departed. No longer old and frail, bloated or withered. These were themselves as they best remembered, young and vibrant. Delight radiated outwards as they slipped fluidly through the growing flames and tendrils of smoke. Phantom hands were raised in farewell to those they once loved. In response, the cheering and shouts of encouragement from the shore grew ever louder.

The flames engulfing the flotilla of boats rose higher, becoming bright enough to be refracted from the vast crystalline sheets hanging above the river. More and more souls ascended into the Skylord, absorbed into its translucent mass, where they could journey safely – though Slvasta was sure he perceived several slip off the surface of the crystal, those the Skylord didn't consider worthy. The unfulfilled – tragic souls whose lives had left them bitter or broken. They were left behind to make their own way across space to the Giu nebula, which was the entrance to the Heart of the Void.

Even so, he joined the cheering, applauding wildly as the souls streamed into the Skylord. So many were going; so many had reached fulfilment. He was genuinely proud of a world that provided so much opportunity despite the constant adversity of the Fallers.

Then the Skylord was moving on, slipping across Varlan's rooftops towards the next city. Slvasta looked upwards as the massive bulk glided smoothly through the air above him. Weird bands of coloured light played across his face, and the air swirled energetically. There was a part of him that wanted to join the Skylord there and then, to be taken away to the Heart, circumventing the difficulties he knew he was going to face during his mortal life. His hand came up and saluted the alien angel. He wasn't surprised to see tears glinting in Lanicia's eyes, while sadness and longing oozed from her mind. She caught him looking and gave a modest little shrug as she hardened up her shell.

They ate a lunch of pasta and fish while the abandoned boats on the Colbal burnt in spectacular style, thousands of flaming hulls drifting downstream, pumping out clouds of lively sparks which swirled and twirled above the choppy water. The current was strong enough to carry them past the city boundary, and the river wide enough so they never came too close to the banks. By mid-afternoon the last flames had expired in puffs of dirty steam as one by one the scorched hulls were swallowed by the water.

They were just finishing dessert, a heavy walnut sponge coated in thick toffee syrup, when a batch of Arnice's friends came in. Slvasta didn't even have to use his ex-sight to see who was making their way up the club's broad stairs. He heard them a long time before they reached the restaurant. Their braying voices carried through the club, full of sneering and self-confidence. Slvasta never did understand how someone as basically decent as Arnice could ever talk with such people, let alone actively seek out their company.

The three of them blundered into the restaurant and, as one, yelled greetings to Arnice, sauntering over, stealing spare chairs from other tables. Their breath smelt of narnik smoke and whisky.

Slvasta stayed for a tactful five minutes, then excused himself. Arnice barely noticed. As he headed down the stairs, Slvasta saw with some dismay that Jaix was laughing heartily at the anecdotes of the youthful aristocrats. She would make Arnice an excellent bride, he thought.

'Are you really going?' Lanicia 'pathed him.

'Yes, 'fraid so.'

'Wait.' She appeared at the top of the stairs and hurried down towards him. 'You weren't going to leave me with *them*, were you? What kind of officer and gentleman does that?'

He grinned. 'Sorry.'

'Sometimes I wonder how we ever survive the Fallers. I thank Giu we still have men like you, to protect us.'

'We all play our part.'

'Ha.' She rolled her eyes and made a remarkably obscene gesture towards the floor above. 'They don't.'

Slvasta began to re-evaluate Lanicia in an altogether more favourable light – and realized he was staring at her divine face again. 'There are always ways round people like that.'

'So what party are you going to tonight?' she asked as they walked across the entrance hall.

'I won't be. I have some work to do. It's a good time to catch up.'

'Oh, Slvasta, that's terrible. Everybody parties the night a Sky-lord arrives, from the stevedores up to the Captain himself. We deserve it. Don't you think?'

'It would be nice, but, like I said, someone has to remain vigilant.'

They reached the door, and the concierge clicked his fingers, calling a carriage from the waiting rank.

'I will be attending the Kayllian family party tonight,' she said as the carriage pulled by a black terrestrial horse drew up beside them. 'But until then I shall probably take to my bed to rest. I keep a day villa on Fortland Street. Would you care to escort me there, captain?'

Given his pause could only have lasted a second, Slvasta was impressed with himself for just how many thoughts for and against ran through his mind. 'I would be delighted at such a duty.'

*

As always, Slvasta woke at six o'clock, just before his alarm clock was set of go off. His teekay reached out and flicked the little toggle on the top of the clock so it wouldn't ring the hemispherical copper bells. He was glad to find it there beside the bed; indeed he was glad to find he was in his own lodgings, for he couldn't really recall much about travelling back here last night. He'd certainly taken a cab from Fortland Street, but he'd kept dozing off during the ride home. An afternoon in Lanicia's bed was as exhausting as a week of Faller combat exercises. She'd been very keen to explore the potential for wickedness his strong teekay could accomplish, casting off her shell as fast as she did her clothes. And his missing arm certainly didn't seem to bother her.

He lay there in bed as the usual sounds of the morning city washed over him, remembering their repeated couplings through-out the afternoon, some dreamy part of his mind wondering what life would be like if they were wed and *every night* was spent like that. He sighed ruefully at the impossible thought. By now he'd learned that his status condemned him to being nothing more than an audacious dalliance for girls of Lanicia's upbringing, some spicy sexual shenanigans before her inevitable society wedding. Still, there were worse things, he decided. And Lanicia had seemed different to the normal debutantes – more independ-ent, smarter, more curious about the world. Not so . . . pointless. He shook his head at such whimsy and went into the little bath-room.

Slvasta had lodgings in Number Seventeen Rigattra Terrace, a nice four-storey white stone building overlooking Malvine Square, in the centre of one of Varlan's more affluent districts. A proper gentleman's residence. The landlord (from an old metropolitan family) had been delighted to accept a bachelor officer, even though Slvasta was only from a county regiment. The rent alone was equal to his captain's salary, but of course that was paid for by the regiment.

Water gurgled in the pipes as he turned on the brass tap; as always, he had to wait a minute for it to warm up. There was a communal boiler somewhere in the building, burning logs loaded by the landlord's mod-dwarfs. Everybody in Number Seventeen had one or two of the mods as servants. The practice was so well established that the building actually incorporated their pens in the basement, with a separate warren of passages and little doors opening into all the residents' rooms. But Slvasta, of course, refused to have any kind of mod in his lodgings and had bolted the little door from the inside as well as putting a heavy dresser in front of it.

He still had a couple of clean dress shirts in the wardrobe. The pile of dirty linen was getting unreasonably large again. Without mod-dwarfs cleaning the rooms and taking care of such things, he had to organize his own laundry service.

The last of the dawn river mist was drifting away as he left Number Seventeen. A team of civic council mod-dwarfs were busy in the street, extinguishing the flames in the street lamps, trimming the wicks and refilling the little reservoirs with pressed yalseed oil ready for the night. He nodded to their wrangler and made his way down Tandier Avenue to Rose's Croissant Café. It was his first stop every morning. Inside, he joined the usual bunch of early risers, plus a few nightshift people on their way home. These were working people, and he felt comfortable around them. It had taken a while for the other regulars to grow accustomed to him, but he was now accepted as one of them.

Rose herself was serving this morning: a big woman in her eighties, wearing a floral-print dress. 'Half my girls are late,' she complained as she brought his orange and mango juice over. 'Out partying last night, no doubt. So it might take a moment longer this morning, sorry.'

'Guidance is worth celebrating,' he assured her.

She gave his face a shrewd look. 'And they weren't alone,' she decided. 'I think someone had a nice time last night.'

'I'll have scrambled egg and smoked lofish on brown toast, Rose, please. With tea.'

'She's a lucky girl,' Rose declared as she left.

Slvasta grinned and opened one of the news sheets Rose provided for her clientele. The rack beside the door held both official news gazettes and pamphlets from the smaller political parties. Rose had been nervous the first week he started visiting her café when she saw him reading through the pamphlets, most of which were critical of the National Council, or the Captain's officials (never the Captain himself, which Slvasta found interesting). But he was interested in the genuine grievances that were raised in the pamphlets – the way cheap old housing was kept in such bad repair, the rising cost of food, the lack of jobs and the low wages among the poor, the slow but noticeable increase in people drifting to Varlan from various outlying provinces, particularly Rakwesh. And always the rumours of nests – though most of those were satirical attacks on suspicious ties between merchant families and councillors. Then there was *Hilltop Eye*, a relatively new pamphlet that always contained some highly embarrassing stories of the aristocracy and their corrupt involvement with officials, or some family's semi-legal financial affairs. Twice in recent months, the city sheriffs had tried to track down the 'citizens' collective' that produced it – to no avail. Distribution was clever, with civic mod-dwarfs counter-ordered and given the pamphlets to take to cafés and pubs and theatres. Nobody knew who or what the citizens' collective was, though the best rumour Slvasta had heard in the Regimental Council offices was that the Captain's family was behind it, using public condemnation as an excuse for cracking down on families that didn't pay their full taxes. The latest *Hilltop Eye* had arrived overnight while everyone was out partying (good tactics, Slvasta thought admiringly). Its main story was about the hundred-and-twenty-eight-year-old mayor of New Angeles, Livanious, who it seemed was diverting a lot of city funds into his own coffers to pay for outrageously decadent parties and keeping a seventeen-year-old mistress, Jubette, in a luxury villa on an offshore island – safely away from his (seventh) wife. Livanious, as everyone knew, was Captain Philious's uncle.

So much for *Hilltop Eye* being produced by the Captain's family, then, Slvasta thought cheerfully as he ate his scrambled eggs. There were quite a few people in the café chortling over the pamphlet as they had breakfast. It was a bold story to put into print, confirming what everyone 'path gossiped anyway. The problem the authorities had with *Hilltop Eye* was the way it encouraged other pamphlets to be equally audacious. Questions about the activities it reported were already being asked in several district councils. Nothing in the National Council yet. But if it carried on exposing theft and fraud like this, people would want to know just what Captain Philious was going to do about it. Probably a question the good Captain would be asking himself this fine morning.

*

Slvasta arrived at the Joint Regimental Council building just after eight o'clock. It was a monolithic stone building on Cantural Street, whose three lower floors were a maze of corridors leading to hundreds of small offices occupied by junior staff. Slvasta, at least, had an office on the fourth floor, with a broad arching window that gave him a view out into the central quad, with its fountain and topiary flameyews.

Keturah and Thelonious, his assistants, were waiting for him as he settled behind his desk. Both of them held bundles of files and papers, which made him shudder inwardly. Thelonious had bruised-looking eyes set in a pale face, and his shell was none too stable, allowing little bursts of nausea to trickle out – clearly badly hungover. Slvasta chose to ignore it.

'What have I got?' he asked.

'Transport policy sub-committee meeting at ten,' Keturah said. She checked her clipboard. 'Aflar nest incursion briefing at fifteen hundred hours – the Marine Commandant will be chairing that one himself. Inter-region communication and cooperation budget sub-committee meeting, seventeen hundred hours.'

It was an effort, but Slvasta managed not to groan. 'Okay. Reports?'

Thelonious stepped up to the desk and put his pile of files down on the oak top. 'Two Falls in the last ten days. We're just getting the notice from Portlynn. The other was way down south in Vondara.'

'Thanks. I'd like the final Portlynn report when it comes in.

For now, just get me some tea, please, and remind me about the transport meeting a quarter of an hour before it starts.'

'Yes, sir,' Keturah said with a hesitant smile.

Slvasta waved them both out. When the heavy door had shut behind them, he looked at the map of Bienvenido, which took up an entire wall. It was covered in tiny yellow pins, indicating Falls. They were denser in the tropics, becoming progressively sparser further from the equator. According to the Watcher Guild, the Faller eggs, which always came from the section of the Forest closest to Bienvenido, would naturally fall along the equator; it was only little inaccuracies in their trajectory as they left the trees, and the way they drifted on the long flight through space, that left them peppering the whole planet.

He went over and stuck two yellow pins in the new Fall zones. His map had several clusters of red pins for sweeps in which their officers had reported suspected impacts devoid of an egg. And, according to the Marine Commandant's office, the Faller Research Institute hadn't issued any requests for a new egg to experiment on for years now. He'd sent Keturah over there to check; she'd come back with a date with one of the junior clerks and his promise to report any such request when it happened.

The first red pin Slvasta had ever put in the map, the day he arrived, was just below Adice, where he'd encountered Nigel. Black pins were based on reports of people disappearing without explanation. He'd set the criteria as three or more people in one area to qualify. The heaviest concentrations, naturally enough, were in Rakwesh Province and the Aflar peninsula, west of the Spine mountains.

As always, he stared at the 'Nigel' pin. There were few other red ones near it, and no black ones within two hundred miles. If Nigel had taken any more eggs, it wasn't anywhere within five hundred miles of Adice. In fact, Slvasta hadn't read any report of missing eggs that matched the profile.

'Where *are* you?' he asked the map.

*

The transport policy sub-committee meeting was held in one of the big conference rooms on the fifth floor. Twenty-three officers (seven of them majors) sat around a long mercedar table; that left another seventeen chairs empty. Age-darkened oil paintings of past regimental commanders gazed down at them from the walls. Aides and staff bustled round, served tea and coffee to the officers, then took their seats around the wall, notepads open and pens ready.

Arnice sat next to Slvasta and told his staff to fetch him a coffee. 'My third this morning,' he confessed. 'How about you? Did you have a good night?'

'Very pleasant,' Slvasta said, keeping his smile to a minimum.

'You sly old dog, you. Jaix said Lanicia told her you both had a great time together.'

'That's what I like to hear – first-hand information.'

'In this city? Listen, that's like a licensed news gazette. So when are you seeing her again?'

'No real plans.'

'My dear fellow, you must strike while the iron's hot. Her family owns part of the South-Western Rail Line company. Admittedly, she's only the fourth daughter, but nonetheless there'll be a handsome dowry for you there.'

'And what about the person herself?'

'You really do have a lot to learn about society, don't you? I now officially consider it my personal challenge to see you wed properly by year's end.'

'Really? Then do please tell me what her father is going to say when he meets a one-armed pauper.'

'And that is going to be the first part of your education. Do away with your modesty, learn to emphasize your finer points. None of the chaps in this town is a tenth as honourable or heroic as you. Admit it, you're a fine catch. And, married well, you could go back to Cham and take over the regiment.'

'In another fifty years.'

'Ah, great Giu, that's clearly my second challenge. You're in such a hurry to get things done. Life here has a pace, a rhythm.'

'One that suits you, not me.'

'I'm on your side. Come now, shall I 'path Jaix to set up a meal tonight? A splendid, fun double date? What do you say? And don't try and claim you're frightfully busy, for I know you're not.'

'I'll think about it.'

'Excellent answer. We're meeting the gals at the Piarro restaurant at eight thirty.'

Slvasta shook his head, grinning ruefully. 'You are impossible.'

'My pleasure.'

Colonel Gelasis from the Captain's Marines called the meeting to order. There were twenty-seven items on the agenda, from the provision of trains and increasing the cooperation of the rail companies (by National Council law if necessary) to boot leather selection for tropical-based regiments. The only item Slvasta cared about was fourteenth, the one he'd proposed; he'd had to back numerous other items and policies to even have it considered. That had been a hard and rapid introduction to political horse trading. Item fourteen was the legal requirement for all regiments to abandon mod-horses in favour of terrestrial ones when engaged in a Fall sweep.

'Excellent notion,' Colonel Gelasis said. 'Especially in view of Captain Slvasta's testimony concerning abnormal Faller control of mod-animals. I trust everyone read the report?'

There was a general wave of amusement round the table, which Slvasta did his best to play along with. He didn't need dropped shells to know the answer to that one: no. It was his own response to all the other appended reports on the items. It was always a puzzle, given that he spent his days achieving nothing, that he had no time for anything.

'If I may,' Major Rennart said.

Slvasta looked at Rennart with interest. He wasn't a regiment officer, but on assignment from the Lord General's staff.

Gelasis gave him the floor.

'I'd like to second the proposal, and move that it is forwarded to the Treasury for a detailed cost–benefit and implementation timescale analysis.'

'Is that good?' Slvasta 'pathed privately to Arnice.

'They're taking it seriously, if that's what you mean.'

'How long will that take?' Slvasta asked out loud.

'I will see that it gets a top team,' Rennart replied.

'Yes, but how long until they finish reviewing it?'

Rennart glanced round the table, with a *what-can-you-do?* mien showing through his shell. 'Those of us serving for a while are familiar with the progress of review teams.'

That brought several chortles from the officers. The aides were starting to watch keenly.

'Could you tell us newbies?' Slvasta asked impassively.

'The preliminary report shouldn't take more than a year.'

'A *year*?' Slvasta couldn't believe it. Aside from his attempts to try and spot any sign of Nigel within the myriad of reports he could request, Slvasta had devoted all his efforts to engineering a switch to terrestrial horses. It was the first stage in what he considered the essential modernization of regimental practices. 'Why does it need a year? And why involve the National Treasury? This is a matter for individual adjutants, surely? My own Cham regiment was instigating the change when I left.'

'That's very commendable of them,' Rennart said. 'But if we start to issue advisement notices that involve any sizeable purchase, those same county adjutants will send the bill back to the Treasury. And, believe me, young captain, you do not want to be held responsible for annoying the Captain's Chief Chancellor.'

'But—'

'I'd advise you to listen to Major Rennart,' Colonel Gelasis said. 'We have a way of doing things here. I understand that they are slow and irritating to any serving officer recently brought in from the field, but nonetheless this is the way that three thousand years of government has produced as best method. You cannot argue with that much history. Now, captain, you have an excellent opportunity to see your proposal move forward towards enactment. If it is not approved for Treasury review, I will have no choice but to strike it from Council policy. How do you wish to proceed?'

Arnice didn't move. He wasn't looking at Slvasta, and his face was perfectly impassive. 'Take it,' he 'pathed privately. 'For the love of Giu, Slvasta, be practical. The more paperwork you create, the harder it is for the administration to ignore it.'

Slvasta nodded formally to Major Rennart. 'My apologies, I meant no disrespect. I am indeed accustomed to faster decisions. But, given this opportunity, I would like to second the proposal for Treasury review.'

'Splendid,' Colonel Gelasis said. 'Vote, gentlemen, please.'

Everyone raised a hand.

'Excellent. Major Rennart, kindly see that through. Now, item fifteen, provision to increase sweep deployment remuneration for reserve forces' daily food consumption.'

Slvasta didn't even bother to listen. Once again he hated himself for being beaten, for playing their game. He hated Arnice for being right, too. There was only one way to do things – the same way there'd always been. Friends of the Treasury officials who owned stud stables would be brought up to speed about the proposal, allowing them to prepare their responses to the official request to purchase bid, when it was eventually issued. *In about ten years' time.*

'You did well,' Arnice assured him as they walked down the stairs together afterwards.

'It doesn't feel like it,' Slvasta told him.

'Nonsense. You've only been here eighteen months, and you've already got the Lord General reviewing a proposal.'

'I suppose . . .'

'Well, not the Lord General himself, more like his staff.'

'Right.'

'Actually, if we're being realistic: his staff's clerks.'

'You're always such a comfort, aren't you?'

'Look at it this way: I've never had an item moved up to that level.'

'All right. So what happens now?'

'They'll spend a year and a vast amount of money messing it about and watering it down, then it'll be shown to one of the

Chancellor's junior under-secretaries, who'll add his own notes and send it back for further review. After it's been bounced around for a while with everyone contributing to show their own worth and importance, it'll be sent up to the National Council financial review board for a final vote. Oh yes, and you'll be the one who presents it to them. A wife like Lanicia will give you greater kudos when you do.'

'Water it down?' Slvasta asked incredulously. 'We either buy the horses or we don't. How can that be watered down?

Arnice raised an eyebrow. 'You'll find out. Treasury chaps can be rather inventive when it comes to purchase proposals. Always have been. That's just the way of it.'

Slvasta wanted to bellow in frustration. To think, when he woke this morning he'd assumed he would finally be making progress. 'Then maybe it shouldn't be the way of it.'

'Ah, a *revolution*,' Arnice said. 'Now there's a true goal for you. Be nice to your old upper-crust friends when it comes to putting us aristos in front of the firing squad, eh?'

'I certainly won't forget what you've done for me.'

'I should think not. Starting with the Piarro at eight thirty tonight. Don't be late.' Arnice patted him on the shoulder and hurried on down the stairs to hail another group of officers.

Slvasta watched him talk to them, the easy chat and smiles. He almost envied the way Arnice knew everyone, knew what to say and how to comport himself. If it had been Arnice putting the proposal forward, it wouldn't be diverted by Major crudding Rennart. He had the connections, knew the way to smooth progress. The embodiment of the very system that was thwarting Slvasta.

'I'm out for the afternoon,' Slvasta told Keturah and Thelonious when he reached his office.

'But, sir, you've got—'

'Don't argue,' he snapped at Keturah. 'Rearrange things.'

'Yes, sir.' Her shell didn't quite harden fast enough to conceal her resentment at the way she was being treated.

Join the club, he thought, and stomped out.

*

It wasn't that far to the National Tax Office, a walk down Walton Boulevard towards the palace, then cross over at the junction with Struzaburg Avenue where the statue of the Landing Plane stood – a weird triangular sculpture, badly worn by time and constant bird droppings. Half a mile along Wahren Street, the granite façade of the Tax Office's hall of records loomed over the delicate bundwine trees with their ruddy spine-leaves waving in the wind. Eight storeys of offices and archives with small dark windows that didn't open. He'd been told there were more archives below it as well – ten basement levels, apparently.

The circular entrance galleria was clad in a drab brown marble, with broad stairs spiralling up all eight storeys, where it was topped by an elaborate glass cupola. There were two receptionists behind the curving desk, and five civic guards. If it hadn't been for his uniform, he doubted he would have been allowed through the door.

'Do you have an appointment, captain?' one of the receptionists asked. He was an elderly man in a black tailcoat with a grey striped waistcoat. His glasses were thick pebbles. The whole place with its silent, timeless existence was draining Slvasta's anger and determination away fast.

'I'd like to see a clerk called Bethaneve, please,' he said, hoping his rank was enough to ensure compliance.

'Is she expecting you?'

'She is dealing with a case for me. It has become an urgent matter for the Joint Regimental Council.'

'I see.' The receptionist wrote something on a small chit and handed it to a mod-dwarf, the smallest one Slvasta had ever seen. The creature disappeared into a little archway behind the desk. 'If you'd like to wait, captain.'

Slvasta sat on one of the two wooden benches, which looked out of place in the big space. By the time the mod-dwarf returned, all his early determination had gone, evaporated into the cool air, and he was feeling slightly foolish at his impetuosity. But the setback in the policy meeting had been infuriating. He wanted to *achieve* something today. Just for once.

'Bethaneve will see you,' the receptionist said. 'Office five-thirty-two.' He gestured to one of the guards.

The five flights of curving stairs made Slvasta realize how long it had been since he'd done a run. He was breathing heavily when they started walking down one of the long corridors on the fifth floor. They must have passed fifty doors, his ex-sight revealed clerks sitting behind desks in their individual offices. The long rooms between them contained row after row of shelving, with every centimetre crammed with files and ledgers.

'No ex-sight perception, please,' the guard told him. 'Tax material is classified.'

Slvasta almost protested that ex-sight couldn't read entries on paper even if he could distinguish individual sheets, but of course that was one of the rules. It didn't matter if it was relevant or not.

The guard knocked on a door.

'Come in,' a 'path voice said.

The guard opened the door. 'I will wait until you've finished, then escort you out,' he told Slvasta, and indicated a wooden seat back at the last junction.

Bethaneve was a surprise. He'd been expecting someone at least as old as the receptionists downstairs. Instead she was about his age, with thick unstyled auburn hair that hung just below her shoulders. She wore a green cardigan over a shapeless blue polka-dot dress which had a slim white lace collar and a skirt that fell almost to her ankles, but allowed a view of her black leather shoes. It was the kind of outfit he would expect to see on a centenarian. But then it fitted the location, no matter how young and bright the wearer.

'Thank you for seeing me,' he said.

'I've been here seventeen months, and nobody has ever asked for an appointment before,' she said with a small smile. 'Actually, I don't know anyone on this floor who's ever had a visitor. I'll be talked about for weeks in the canteen.'

He smiled back. Bethaneve wasn't as pretty as Lanicia. Her features were too broad, and her nose larger – which was an unfair comparison, he told himself sternly. For Bethaneve had a lightness which was especially noticeable in this small dreary office with its single high window.

'Sorry,' he said. 'It was just that I did put in a review request four months ago. You sent me an acknowledgement and said it was underway. I'd appreciate a progress report.'

'Yes, that was unusual. We've never had a request from the military before.'

'Is that a problem? I was told I had the authority to make the request.' It was Arnice who'd suggested it as a way of tracking down his elusive quarry after he'd found nothing in the Erond regiment personnel records. Everybody on Bienvenido had a Tax Office file, the one inescapable constant.

'As one of the Captain's officers, you do, yes.'

'So? How's it going?'

She gave him an awkward look, then gestured to one of the shelves which covered two walls of the office from floor to ceiling. Black and red leather ledgers were piled up all along it, looking as if they were about to slide off. By the archive hall's standards, it was akin to anarchy. 'This is my investigation. I'm working through every variant of Nigel I could think of registered in Erond county.'

'And you haven't found him?' Slvasta sighed.

'No. Certainly not a trader as you described. However, there are some boatowners who have similar businesses, although none of them is called Nigel.' She smiled.

Slvasta liked that smile, it animated her. 'Ah, excellent. Can I see their files?'

'These are just the registration ledgers,' she said. 'The actual files are still in the vaults. I haven't requested them yet.'

Slvasta looked at her, seeing the smile fade. Looked round the woeful office. 'You have a lot on. I understand.'

'Oh,' she blushed. 'Yes. I'm sorry. If it's really urgent I can order the files up. They'll be here in a week. My supervisor has to approve the request.'

Slvasta started laughing. 'Rushing it through, huh?'

'It's really quite quick.' She shrugged. 'By archive standards, anyway. It's just . . . things are done in a certain way.'

'Because that's the way they're always done.'

'Yes.'

'Then I thank you for putting in the request. Can I ask another favour?'

She nodded quickly. 'Yes, of course.'

'I'd like to take you out to dinner. Tonight, if you're not doing anything.'

Bethaneve blushed again as she gave him a startled look, but her gaze didn't stay on his empty sleeve for very long. 'Um, well . . .'

'Please say yes. I'll have to go out with my fellow officers if you don't. Would you really wish that on anyone?'

'That's a trick question,' she said, her voice challenging, not a clerk's voice at all.

'Not really. I'm just a country boy, posted to the city and finding it hard. Take pity on me, please.'

'My landlady locks the door at ten thirty.'

'Quite right, too. Can I pick you up at seven?'

'Yes. Thank you. That would be nice.'

And so very worth enduring Arnice's dismay at abandoning their double date.

*

Bethaneve had lodgings on Borton Street, an area where housing was a lot cheaper than anything on Rigattra Terrace. But not quite working class, he decided as the carriage pulled up outside the neat three-storey blue-brick house. Borton Street was formed by old, classically tasteful houses, with cracks running up the brickwork and walls starting to bulge. In another century or two they'd be demolished and replaced, as they had replaced those that stood here before. Such was the cycle of continual regeneration. The city didn't get any bigger, though Arnice claimed each cycle built a little higher than the last. Like the society it housed, Varlan craved stability.

The landlady answered the door when Slvasta pulled its bell cord. Now, *she* would have been perfectly at home in the hall of archives, he thought. A puffy face that looked perpetually miserable, dark dress made out of stiff fabric, greying hair in a tight bun. Her gaze and ex-sight ran up and down Slvasta's plain grey suit. 'This door is locked at ten thirty,' she said primly. 'I insist that my girls are back by then. If they're not, I will assume they no longer require residence here – and frankly if that is how they choose to behave, I wouldn't want them under my roof anyway.'

'An admirable philosophy,' Slvasta assured her.

Bethaneve appeared in the hallway. She'd changed into a green dress with a skirt whose hem hovered around her knees, and a white cobweb shawl wrapped tightly round her shoulders. There was a pink rose in her hair. Hints of mischievous thoughts slithered about beneath a shell that was tantalizingly thin.

The landlady gave a snort of disapproval and closed the door.

'You kept a straight face,' Bethaneve said as they walked to the cab. 'Well done.'

'She does seem rather imposing.'

'She used to work at the Tax Office. You develop a certain attitude if you stay long enough.'

The cab driver opened the door and helped Bethaneve up. When she sat on the bench and removed her shawl, Slvasta did a classic double take. The green dress had a square neck cut almost as low as the one Lanicia had worn yesterday. He cursed himself for being so obvious, but Bethaneve grinned knowingly.

'So, where are you taking me?' she asked.

Slvasta paused on the verge of answering; was he imagining a *double entendre*? 'I've heard good things about the Oakham Lodge.'

'I'm in your hands. Oh—' Her hand covered her mouth, and she blushed. 'Slvasta, I'm so sorry. I didn't mean—'

'Trust me. After having your arm amputated without narnik, figures of speech don't really register as terribly upsetting.'

'*Without* narnik?'

'Uh huh.'

'Great Giu, tell me all about it!'

*

When Bethaneve smiled, her lips curled up. It made her look delightfully impish, he realized. Her laugh was husky. She didn't have the formal restraint and coldness of the aristocratic daughters he'd met, a difference which was so *refreshing*. She knocked back beer, not wine. She was animated on a number of subjects, such as the three dams on the Yann river which ran through the city and provided water for nine districts – how the pumps were constantly breaking down and the owners weren't obliged to compensate the households when supplies were cut off. Or the lamplight company that had the contract for Borton Street, which was doing such a sloppy job. And how the meat inspectors at Wellfield market were so crooked. And . . . And . . . And . . .

'I shouldn't be telling you things like this,' she said as the main course was cleared away. They'd both had the steak-and-kidney pie that was the lodge's specialty.

'Why ever not?'

'Well, you're an officer.'

'That hardly makes me part of the Captain's police.'

'No.' She raised her beer glass and gave him a shrewd look over the top of it. 'You're not what I imagined an officer to be, either.'

'How did you imagine an officer to be?'

'Stuck up, like the rest of the aristos. Uncaring.'

'Regiments have a difficult job, you know. Being an officer is no sinecure. It's tough out there sweeping the countryside. And . . .' He glanced at his stump. 'Tougher if you fail.'

'I get that now. It's the uniforms, you see, all bright and expensive. I just identify you with the rich families who run everything.'

'Some of their younger sons take commissions, mostly with the Meor regiment. That way they get to stay in Varlan – admittedly on the other side of the river. I heard there's almost one officer for every trooper. And the Meor does pay officers about ten times what any other regiment pays. It's called the capital weighting; life here is more expensive.'

'Whose fault is that?' she said sharply.

'But there are more opportunities in a city than out in the countryside. That attracts people.'

'Which puts up the prices, which takes opportunity away from the poorest.'

'But you live here. You managed to get a good job.'

'That's a good job? Eight o'clock till five thirty, with forty minutes' lunch break which you have to take in the canteen, which just happens to be run by the senior clerk's family? Every day for a hundred and ten years, that's the requirement to qualify for a full pension.'

'Do you think you'll last that long?'

'No. I'm going to find me a rich landowner who'll take me away from all this.' She raised an eyebrow in scorn. 'That's what's supposed to happen, isn't it? Sorry, do I sound bitter? I don't mean to be. It's just that nothing changes. And there's so much injustice on Bienvenido, and nobody seems to be doing anything about it. Certainly not the Captain and all our Councils. The money they receive – sweet Uracus! I see some of the public expenditure files, you know.'

'Doesn't surprise me. And I'm afraid I'm not landed. My mother has a farm, but my half-brothers will inherit that now. I'm going to spend my life fighting the Fallers.'

Bethaneve slid her hand across the table and grasped his fingers. 'You're a good man, Captain Slvasta. You stick to your beliefs. Don't let them take that away from you.'

'I won't.' Somehow he didn't have the courage to tell her about the committee meeting that morning, how they'd *already* thwarted him.

'So who's this Nigel person?' she asked. 'You must want him very badly to resort to the Tax Office for help. What's he done?'

He explained what had happened, how angry he was at himself for being tricked.

'That's very strange,' she said when he'd finished. 'I can't imagine anyone working for a nest, no matter how much they were paid.'

'Me neither,' he admitted. 'But what else could it be?'

'Did you know that Captain Xaxon used to destroy an egg in public every year?'

'No.'

'He was the seventh Captain, I think. There'd be a big mid-summer ceremony at the palace, and they'd bring out this giant steam-powered guillotine device he'd had specially built for the event. It could slice a Faller egg clean in half. There were bands, regimental parades. The whole works. Quite a spectacle, so they say. Ten thousand people used to turn up.'

'Why did it stop? There's nothing this world likes better than its traditions.'

'One of his granddaughters had a puppy. It slipped its lead and ran towards the egg – the lure, you see. She ran after it—'

'Oh, crud.'

'They had to amputate three of her fingers when she got stuck.' Bethaneve squeezed his hand a fraction tighter, and gave his stump a thoughtful look. 'I don't suppose they had time to administer narnik, either. Poor girl.'

'Yeah.'

'Anyway, that's the only time I know about an egg being moved anywhere by humans. Maybe this Nigel is planning some kind of victory ceremony. Is he a politician?'

'I suppose he could stand for a Council office. It makes as much sense as anything – except this was over a year and a half ago.' He realized they were still holding hands, and made no effort to stop.

'I'll do you a deal, Captain Slvasta.'

'Go on.'

'I will order up all the files on boatowners in Erond county and go through them for you. See if any of them fit what you've told me about Nigel.'

'That sounds good. What's my side of the deal?'

Her smile became fierce. 'You take me to a bait.'

'A bait?'

'Yes.' She was looking at him intently, ex-sight examining his shell for hints of his reaction.

'Very well.'

She drained her beer glass, then dropped the pretty rose from her hair into it. 'Come on, then.'

*

Slvasta had never been to the city's Newich district. Never had a reason to. It was a jumble of derelict warehouses and factories, broken up by bleak tenements the owners had built to house their workforce. A canal had been dug through the middle, channelling a powerful flow from the river Gossant before it emptied into the Colbal. Big factories were built on both sides of it, forming a dark artificial canyon. Each of them possessed two or three water-wheels, turning the looms and lathes inside.

The bait was held in one of them, an abandoned cloth works. Most of the building's upper floors had been stripped out years ago as part of the demolition and replacement schedule for the whole canal – which hadn't yet happened. Their absence left a single large enclosed space, with the remnants of the upper floors clinging to the walls forming precarious balconies. The uneven brick floor was broken up by deep, narrow trenches where the whirring leather pulley belts used to run day and night, and had now been colonized by manky, disease-laden urban bussalores. Big iron bearings were still affixed to the walls, the last remnants of the mighty looms which used to fill the factory.

Dozens of slates had slipped off the roof, allowing wide beams of moiré nebula-light to shine in. But the main source of illumination came from hundreds of oil lanterns hanging from the jagged edges of the balconies. They shone down on the bait pit in the centre of the brick floor, an arena seven paces across, made from thick timbers.

There must have been over three hundred men and women crammed inside. Slvasta had expected it to be mostly working class, residents from the nearby slum houses. But no, there were many shiny top hats and ornate dresses; he even saw a few regiment uniforms amid the crowd. The noise was brutal, the air rancid and filled with tatus flies. People were sitting along the edge of the balconies, dangling their legs over the side, tankards and wine glasses in hand. Spilt drink was a constant drizzle as they cheered on their animal down in the pit.

Slvasta stared round in amazement, letting his ex-sight drift about. One end of the factory was stacked with cages containing the animals yet to fight. There were barrels of beer set up, the brewers charging double the price of any pub, tables with wine, even some narnik traders blatantly walking round with trays of wads and fresh pipes. And bookmakers lurked in the corners, surrounded by guards armed with knives and pistols that you didn't need to probe with ex-sense to discover.

'Everything out in the open,' he said, unsure if he approved or not.

'True democracy,' Bethaneve replied. Then she waved to someone at a small table on the other side of the pit. 'This way.'

Her friends turned out to be Javier and his boyfriend Coulan. Javier was a big, heavily muscled thirty-year-old with ebony skin almost as dark as Quanda's. Slvasta fought down that shameful comparison. The man had a Rakwesh accent, and the way he was hunched over the table made it look as though it'd been built for children. In contrast, Coulan was a tall lad with short-cropped fair hair and skin so pale Slvasta first thought he was albino; with his endearingly handsome features it was easy to like him at first glance. However, his shell was completely impervious, allowing no aspect of his thoughts to escape.

They greeted Slvasta with a modicum of suspicion at first, even with Bethaneve vouching for him.

'Your first time at a bait?' Javier asked as he beckoned a barmaid over.

'Yes.'

'Thought so.'

Slvasta didn't know how to take that. Now he was sitting next to Javier, he was beginning to realize just how large the man was.

'Any tips?' Bethaneve shouted above the din.

'Initie's hound,' Coulan said. 'It's a mean beast. Worth some coin.'

'Putting it up against two mod-dogs in a while,' Javier said. 'I got Philippa one of them.'

'Philippa runs the bait,' Bethaneve 'pathed, as she nodded towards a ninety-year-old woman in a filthy silk kimono, sitting in a big armchair close to the arena.

'Do you keep mod-dogs?' Slvasta asked.

That earned him a snort of derision from Javier. 'No. I find them for Philippa. Owners shouldn't be so fucking careless.'

'People shouldn't own them at all,' Slvasta replied levelly.

It clearly wasn't the answer Javier had been expecting. He gave Slvasta a dark smile. 'Then what would we all use?'

'Who the crud cares? I just don't want mods and neuts on Bienvenido.'

Javier grinned and nodded at Slvasta's stump. 'One of them get a bit snappy, did they?'

'No, I lost the arm to an egg. The mods helped stick me to it; they belong to the Fallers. People can't see that.'

Javier rocked back on his stool. 'Crud!'

A roar came from the arena's audience. A wolfhound had been dropped into the arena, along with three mod-cats. The wolfhound charged at the mod-cats, slavering furiously. The crowd cheered loudly as its teeth closed round the first mod-cat. But the other two mod-cats, 'path goaded and in a terror-frenzy, started snapping at the wolfhound's legs. Teeth which adaptors had formed to slice clean through rodents ripped through the dog's flesh. The wolfhound snarled in pain and fury and clamped its jaws on a mod-cat. Locked together, all three animals jumped and slung themselves around against the wooden wall, growling and shrieking as blood made the floor slicker.

Slvasta used his ex-sight to observe the carnage. Bethaneve stood so she could see the whole gory spectacle. A barmaid delivered three tankards to the table. Javier raised his. 'To killing mods.'

'Wherever they are,' Slvasta responded. They knocked their tankards together and drank.

Bethaneve rolled her eyes. 'Boys!' Grinning, she drank a big slug of beer, then resumed her yelling at the arena.

'So it's a cushy office job for you now, is it?' Javier asked.

'Temporary. I'll be back sweeping for eggs soon, I hope.'

'Politics, then? They pushed you out because you were too dedicated to your job? I can appreciate that.'

'That obvious, huh?'

'It's how the rich always work. Anyone who comes along that can upset the way things are done gets taken down fast. How else are they going to keep what they have?'

'The Fallers keep them in power,' Coulan said. 'This constant fight against them means people accept the social and financial structure of this world without question. We need the regiments to perform the sweeps and root out nests; therefore we pay the government to protect us. Who's going to argue? Without that protection, you either Fall or get eaten. It's a great incentive.'

This world – a phrase Slvasta had heard before, though he couldn't think where. 'But there will always be Fallers,' he said. 'The Forest sends them. We can't do anything about that.'

Javier leaned over the table, suddenly animated. Mostly by drink, but anger played its part. 'People came to Bienvenido on ships that flew through the Void – some even say they came from *outside* the Void. No matter; once we could fly like Skylords. Can you imagine that? Now we just sit here and cower as the eggs Fall on us like Uracus is taking a shit. How our ancestors must despise us! We abandoned all the marvels they had, we shrank and listened to the weasel words of men like the Captains who promised us this false shelter. What we should be doing is declaring war on the Forest. Take the battle up there, into the Void itself.'

'People flying into space?' Slvasta asked. 'You're talking about ship's machines, and they don't work on Bienvenido. Our ancestors came here so they could live simple lives, lives that brought fulfilment. That is the way to the Heart of the Void.' He frowned, barely able to believe he'd just quoted such orthodoxy. It was supposed to be him who argued against the establishment's restrictions.

'Really? Did any of your first ancestors tell you that directly? Or was it the teachers in schools paid for by the Councils? Councils that are ruled by the Captain and all the rich families who support him and beg his patronage. We don't know what happened three thousand years ago, not really. But does it make any sense to you that the ships would choose to come here, a world under permanent siege? Why would they do that when they had a whole universe to choose from? Got an answer for that?'

Slvasta had to shake his head and admit defeat. 'No. Not if you put it like that.'

'Is there another way I should put it?'

'Hey, I'm on your side.'

'Yes. I can see you're kept down just like all the rest of us dumb peasants. But is it the side you'd choose? If you were allowed to choose, that is? Which you're not.'

'I'm doing what I can.'

Javier clapped him on the shoulder. 'Of course you are.'

Which he actually wasn't, but that was down to a harsh self-judgement.

'Enough,' Bethaneve said. 'We're here to enjoy ourselves. Slvasta, fancy a flutter? Javier talks way too much, but he does know his beasts. Initie's hound might be worth it.'

'Quite right,' Javier said. 'Ignore my bullshit. I apologize. Put your money on Initie. You'll double it at least.'

'All right then,' Slvasta said, suddenly realizing he was genuinely enjoying himself for the first time since he'd arrived in the city. 'If it loses, I'll claim you are a Faller and send the Marines after you. Still think it's going to win?'

Javier roared with laughter. 'Put my coin on with yours. We'll find out the hard way.'

*

'Would you like to start with the bad news?' Bethaneve asked. It was Saturday, a week after the night at the bait. Bethaneve had agreed to meet Slvasta for lunch, and he'd chosen Davidia's, a fresh-fish café halfway along Captain Sanorelle's Pier. The pier was actually the start of what the poor Captain had hoped would be a bridge across the Colbal – a folly doomed from the moment the first stanchions were sunk. The river beside the city was over three kilometres wide, with a fiercely strong current even outside the rainy season. The bridge had reached four hundred metres on five massive stone arches before the end collapsed. Scaffolding and masonry alike were washed away by a surge, taking over two hundred workers with it.

Three arches remained now, and what had been planned as the wide road and railtrack they supported was now covered by a chaotic array of wooden shacks containing fish merchants, cafés and pubs. The air was thick with smoke from the curing houses.

Slvasta grinned. 'You're married?'

'No. I went down into the vault containing tax returns from Erond county. There's nothing that matches a trader with three or more boats.'

'Ah, well, thank you for trying.'

'I can expand the search.'

'To where? There are hundreds of counties.'

'Seven hundred and fifteen, plus eighty-two governed territories waiting to be elevated to regional status; then they'll be split into about twenty counties each.'

'That many? I didn't know. Well, it was a valiant try. I'll just have to find another way of tracking him down.'

'I didn't like to say it, but if he is a criminal, or he's sided with the Fallers, then he probably won't have a tax file.'

'You're probably right.'

'Of course, Javier doesn't have a file.'

'Now why does that not surprise me? Your friends are quite intense.' So far he and Bethaneve had been out in the evening on three occasions, two of which had seen them ending up in a pub with Javier and Coulan. He'd enjoyed the men's company, though he was starting to think he'd like to spend slightly less time with them and more with Bethaneve.

'They talk a lot,' Bethaneve said as she ate her grilled marrobeam. 'So do a lot of people. It's harmless.'

He examined his beer. 'Shame.'

'Really?' She grinned. 'Do you think Javier would make a good Captain?'

Slvasta smiled back and drew in an exuberant breath. 'No!'

She laughed. 'He's more like you than you realize.'

'I don't quite see that.'

'Of course you don't. That big-man bluster act of his covers up a lot. He was ten or twelve, I think, when his parents were eaten by Fallers. That's what drives his contempt for the Captain and the Councils – just like you.'

'I didn't know that.'

'We all have reasons for what we do, and the way we think. You want to change the way the regiments do things because that old way nearly got you eggsumed.'

'True, things needs shaking up and modernizing. That's progress.'

The look she gave him was almost sad. 'We both know that's a pile of crud. Progress stopped on this world three thousand years ago, the day our ancestors landed here.'

'Is that what drives you? The quest for progress?'

'I have a friend . . .'

He was slightly worried at the way her shell tightened, allowing no shade of emotion to show. Whatever she felt, she wasn't prepared to share. 'Go on.'

'Had a friend, I suppose. We were young, and we came to Varlan together. Usual stupid story: we thought a life here was rich and exciting. Which it is when you're young. Then I learned it wasn't, not really. It took a while for me to realize that. It took the First Officer to make me see it.'

'Aothori?' he asked in surprise. 'You know him?'

'My friend did. A landowner from the south took her to the palace one night. She didn't want to go, but she had problems in her life.'

'Problems?' Slvasta queried; he didn't like to, it was obvious that talking about this was tough for her.

'Narnik,' she said resentfully. 'What else? So she wasn't in a position to say no. When she got there, Aothori enjoyed how vulnerable she was. Thankfully he gets bored quickly, which was probably the luckiest thing that ever happened to her. Too long with him, and . . . well. You've heard the rumours about him?'

'Yeah.'

'They're all true, and that's not the half of it. He's evil, Slvasta. Really, truly, evil. If they ever cut him open, I wouldn't be surprised if he bled blue.'

'That bad, huh?'

'Oh Giu, yes. I want him gone. Dead even. It's the Captaincy that allows people like him to do whatever they want, to ruin lives. They rule the world for their own pleasure and profit, and it's wrong. The day they and all their kind are brought down will be the happiest day of my life. So now you know – that's what drives me.'

'You're not alone there. And your friend? The one who knew the First Officer? What of her?'

'Gone away somewhere,' she said with a sad sigh. 'I suppose you have to know at some time.'

'Know what?' he asked in sympathy, thinking he could guess what was about to be said.

'It wasn't just my friend who used to do narnik.'

'We all did,' he said, a little too cheerily.

'No, Slvasta, I had a real problem. It just took over. But I've been clean for a couple of years now. I'm never going back to that, not ever. It's a dark place, and you don't see it, not from the inside. And before you know it, the dark closes in and covers you. It's like being buried alive, and the only way out is another wad. That's when you think you can see the light again. But it's not light, not really. It's just the narnik lifting you, fooling you.'

He reached over the table and took her hand. 'I'm sorry. But you're clean now? That's good.'

'Yes. It was Coulan; he found me. He helped me see how bad I was. He helped me kick it. There's not many people manage that, not when they're as far gone as I was. But he knew what to do, how to help me. It was amazing, building up my self-esteem again. I owe him a lot. Everything, actually. He was so sweet, so generous. He didn't have to do it, to help a stranger, but he did because that's the kind of person he is.'

Just for a moment Slvasta could sense some of her memories, a few hazy images rich with emotion. He was proud of the way he kept hold of her hand. 'You and him, then?'

'Yes,' she said quietly. 'But it's over. It has been for a long time. He's with Javier now.'

'We've all got a past in that respect,' he assured her.

'I know. But I'm still friends with him. Slvasta, I really hope that doesn't bother you. It's not in my nature to turn my back on someone who was so important to me. Without him . . . I don't know where I'd be now. Dead, possibly, or just another house girl down at the bad end of Gamstak district.'

'But you're neither of these things. And I'm very grateful to him for that.'

'Really?' Her hand tightened on his.

'Yes. Whatever you've been through, it made you what you are today. And that's a very special person, Bethaneve. One I'm pleased I know.'

'You're so sweet. I can't believe you do the job you do.' She leaned over and kissed him. They'd kissed before – pleasant end-of-the-evening kisses when teekay strokes became playfully naughty – but not like this, not with this hunger. His shell immediately tightened round his thoughts, preventing anyone's ex-sight from sensing them directly. Nothing he could do about the other café customers' eyesight, though.

They moved apart, sharing the same knowing smile. It gave Slvasta real hope for the future for the first time since Ingmar's death.

6

It was the following Thursday when the news reached Varlan. It must have come in by special messenger to the palace some time during the night, the kind of news the Captain and his Council kept quiet about until the official gazettes could print clever sanitized reports that minimized the level of damage.

But when Slvasta walked into Rose's Croissant Café, he knew something was wrong. Even the regulars were giving him disapproving stares, and the unguarded thoughts his uniform kindled in some were downright hostile.

'Is everything all right?' he asked Rose when she came over to take his order.

'You pay them no heed, captain,' she said, her voice growing loud enough to carry across the café. 'Everybody here knows you're from the Cham regiment, and they do all right by their county. You're not like those others.'

'Other what?'

'You might want to look at the *Hilltop Eye*.'

When she'd taken his order, Slvasta used his teekay to pluck the *Hilltop Eye* from the rack beside the door. The pamphlet was easy enough to find; the rack was stuffed full of them that morning. It slid through the air above the heads of everyone sitting at their table.

He was slightly surprised to see it was a new one; normally the pamphlet was printed every month or so, and the last one had come out barely five days ago. Also, this was just a single sheet. 'NEST UNCOVERED' was printed in bold across the top. With a growing sense of dismay he read down the report. Wurzen, the southernmost town in Rakwesh province, had discovered a nest. All the Fallers had been killed by sheriffs and regimental reservists from the town. No thanks to the authorities.

The nest had taken over the Lanichie family, some local land-owners who had a grand townhouse. How long they'd managed to carry off the charade was unknown. Rumours had been rife for years – true, Slvasta knew, he'd seen classified reports of suspi-cions from the Wurzen sheriff's office – but one of the Lanichie daughters was married to the Captain's district governor; the county regiment's commander was a cousin. The family employed hundreds of people in its estates, and half the businesses in the county depended on its patronage. Official reports into the disap-peared, and qualms about the increasingly reclusive occupants of the townhouse with its strangely persistent fuzzing, had been quashed for years.

Two days ago, at one o'clock in the morning, a drunk group of sailors had waylaid a covered cart trundling quietly through the town. It had a brewery logo on the side, and they were hoping to help themselves to some barrels. What they found was two eggs. The Faller who drove it made a desperate dash for the Lanichie townhouse, with the rapidly sobering sailors in hot pursuit.

A 'pathed alarm surged through the town, and a mob emerged. Every mod-animal in Wurzen went wild, attacking the entire human population.

'I knew it!' Slvasta exclaimed out loud as he read that part.

But fear and anger had taken hold now, and the mods were swiftly killed by teekay assault, physical battery and pistol shot. Sheriffs and reservists, who had weapons, led the charge against the townhouse. What they found inside, after they killed the Fallers, was what everyone imagined Uracus itself would be like. Human bones, gnawed clean, filled every room. Initial estimates were that over three hundred people had been eaten.

The Wurzen nest was an atrocity on a scale nobody had even

conceived of before. And it had all been brushed aside and kept quiet because the Lanichie family was of good stature – land-owners, aristocracy, rich. The ruling class. Those rulers had allowed it to happen because they'd never dream of questioning their own.

Other houses and the town Council offices were fired as the mob sought revenge, a physical outlet for their horror and fury. Landowners, merchants, anyone living in a large house, govern-ment officials – they were chased out of their homes, out of the town, beaten, robbed, brutalized. The Captain's district governor was supposed to have been lynched with help from his own sher-iffs . . .

The mob still ruled in Wurzen, *Hilltop Eye* claimed, and the discontent was spreading to the surrounding towns and villages, where the families of the disappeared were taking up arms in search of vengeance.

'Great Giu,' Slvasta muttered. His dismay was tempered by a grim satisfaction. *The regiments will have to change now.*

He dropped a few copper coins on the table and left. As he walked down Walton Boulevard, he grew aware of the unusually light amount of traffic for the time of day. At the same time, his ex-sight was gathering up the emotional atmosphere starting to engulf Varlan. That was the thing with 'path whispers. Given the right spark of gossip, they could spread across the city in a matter of minutes. *Hilltop Eye* wasn't a spark, it was an eruption; shocked 'path conversations between families and friends over-lapped, multiplied to streak along streets and canals at the speed of thought.

The city's cab drivers, those masters of urban gossip and innu-endo, understood all too well what the growing mood spelt, and turned to head back to their stables. Their absence added to the expanding feeling of anxiety; ire towards authority was building fast. Once or twice, Slvasta sensed individuals urging people to take their frustrations out on the government – fast sharp 'path voices that swirled for a few seconds amid the mental clamour, only to vanish again after a few seconds, untraceable even to the

259

best psychic detective. But each little burst of encouragement was absorbed and disseminated, adding to the citymind gestalt.

Keturah was in the Regimental Council offices, radiating worry – a state shared by just about all the staff. Thelonious hadn't come in yet. Slvasta sat behind his desk, not knowing what to do. The 'path babble filling the aether outside precluded any work. Everybody, it seemed, was waiting for *something* to happen. He told Keturah she could go home if she wanted, but she said, no, she'd ride it out, although she did want to go home early.

At nine o'clock, Arnice stuck his head round the door. 'This is getting a bit beastly,' he said.

'I told you we should be taking those reports of the disappeared more seriously. And did you read about the mods attacking humans in Wurzen? I wonder what Major Rennart makes of that?'

'Oh, come now, be gallant in your victory.'

'I don't think anyone has won anything here. Three hundred people!'

'Humm. Don't tell anyone, but it was probably closer to four hundred. The Captain's police chief, Trevene, was saying the Lanichie family probably Fell five years ago.'

'*Five years?* Hey, wait a minute, how do you know what the police chief is saying?'

Arnice winked. 'Trevene is my sister-in-law's uncle.'

'Did he know?'

'No, of course not. The idiot governor was too stupid to question anything.'

'Bloody typical.'

'Quite. Anyway, I'm off to change into my combat uniform.'

'What? Why?'

Arnice pointed at the window. 'You need to stretch your ex-sight. There's a nasty little bunch of peasants congregating in Bromwell Park, fizzing with anti-Captain thoughts – as if he knew what was happening in Wurzen. We're worried they'll march on the National Council chamber, or worse, the palace. So the Meor regiment will deploy across Walton Boulevard and, shall we say, *discourage* them.'

'Ah.' Slvasta frowned. 'Can they get here in time? Your men are all barracked on the south side of the Colbal.'

'Not as of three o'clock this morning when the news reached us. They're in various forward deployment bunkers, including the one under this building.'

'We have a deployment bunker here?'

'Oh, yes. But don't spread the news around.'

'Right.'

'Don't worry. The chaps train for civil disobedience suppression. We'll crack a few heads, chuck some of the would-be revolutionaries in jail, and the rest will slink off back to their hovels and drink themselves stupid all night. And if the worst comes to the worst, well, we've got all the guns, haven't we?'

Slvasta didn't trust himself to answer; it was difficult enough to keep his shell solid. He'd never known regiments were used to keep order, let alone trained for it. But then the Meor was always regarded as an elite regiment, directed by the National Council. And . . . guns? Fired at civilians?

'You can take me out for a drink tomorrow evening,' Arnice said cheerfully as he left. 'I haven't seen you properly for ages. I want to know all about her – whoever she is. This girl you're spending all your time with and ignoring your best friend in the city: your loyal friend, your drinking friend, the friend who showed you round right from the start, your friend who managed to get you laid a lot, the one friend who—'

Slvasta smiled sheepishly. 'Bethaneve. Her name is Bethaneve.'

'Lovely. And I've got some news, too. Tomorrow.' A final wave, and he scurried out.

*

The mob was over a thousand strong as it finally spilt out of Bromwell Park. Shared ex-sights allowed the whole city to watch as they started to make their way along Walton Boulevard. Jeering and chanting, they launched half-hearted teekay attacks at statues of historical dignitaries. The surprisingly large number of the protestors encouraged more hesitant people to join and make their opinion known to the arseholes in charge. A steady stream of fresh supporters swarmed in, bolstering the scale and determination of those leading the push up Walton Boulevard. Government buildings along the road were now locked and sealed. Teekay punches from the sneering crowd slammed into the windows. Blizzards of shattered glass began to rain down onto the broad pavements.

Troopers of the Meor regiment filed across Walton Boulevard, forming a resolute barrier, five deep, blocking the approach to the palace. The first rank carried long batons, as did the second. The third rank was made up of strong teekays, well practised in cooperative techniques, shielding their comrades. The fourth and fifth ranks were armed. Sheriffs and marshals scurried onto the road behind them, bringing jail wagons. Officers used strong 'path shouts to order the mob to disperse.

The two sides faced each other for several minutes, with the mob flinging taunts and the occasional teekay-boosted lump of stone. Then a clump of protestors broke off and started running down Cantural Street, shouting, 'There's the regiment offices, they're all in there.' More hate-inflamed protesters were pouring out of alleys and side roads – those who were genuinely aggrieved by the disaster and blamed the regiment for not stopping it, and others who simply fancied giving the sheriffs and troopers a good kicking, revenge for a life lived at the bottom end of society.

'Oh, Uracus,' Slvasta grunted as it became clear that their target was the Joint Regimental Council offices.

'What do we do?' a terrified Keturah asked as she ran out of his office.

'Stay in here,' he barked at her. 'Lock the doors and don't let anyone in that you don't know.'

Officers were running out into the main corridor, the majors trying to shout orders. The chaos was ridiculous.

'We have to coordinate our teekay to defend the building,' Slvasta said.

Nobody paid him any attention. Cursing, he ran for the stairs.

The building's big front doors were shut and bolted, but the broad windows would be easy points of entry once the glass and shutters had been smashed down. They had to be reinforced. 'Come on,' he 'pathed to some of the junior officers he knew. They acknowledged his intent and started to follow him. Outside, the shouting was getting louder.

Four squads of Meor troopers came up the narrow stone stairs from the deployment bunker in the basement of the Joint Regimental Council offices. Arnice led them out through a small door at the side of the building. They came round the corner to confront the mob swelling across Cantural Street.

*

'This has been declared a restricted area,' Arnice announced, 'pathing as strongly as he could. 'Disperse and return to your homes.'

The squads lined up in single file all along the front of the long stone office building. They were spaced wider than he would have liked, but then they were a reserve force. The main body of the Meor was still guarding Walton Boulevard.

'Get some wagons here,' Arnice 'pathed the local sheriff's station. 'We need to make arrests, show these bastards they don't have free rein.' He stood at the top of the stone steps, his back to the office block's sturdy double doors, obviously trying not to let any concern filter out through his shell. Behind him, the teekay of the officers inside the building insinuated its way into the doors, strengthening the wood. On either side, more teekay was weaving into the shutters and glass of the windows.

'We're sealing it up,' Slvasta's 'path assured him.

Bolstered by the support, Arnice bellowed: 'Go home!' at the mob. 'This is your final warning. I have been authorized by the police councillor herself to use force.'

That was greeted with a chorus of booing and obscenities. Stones began to fly through the air, accelerated and guided by teekay. Several were aimed at him. His own teekay batted them away. Just.

'Stand by to fire warning shots,' Arnice told his squads.

He was appalled to see women in the frenzied crowd, and even some children. All of them animated with hatred, letting loose vile 'path images of the Captain and First Officer.

Someone with disturbingly strong teekay wrenched the glass oil reservoir from a lamp post, sending it arching towards the office. It ignited at the top of its trajectory and smashed against the stone wall just above the front door. Flames cascaded down. Arnice ducked, flinging his teekay around himself for protection.

The mob yelled its approval. More reservoirs were snatched from lamp posts.

'Aim high,' Arnice instructed. 'Fire!'

*

Her name was Haranne. She was twelve years old, and jumping up and down amid the crowd in Cantural Street, enthusiastically chanting the new and wonderfully rude song about rich boys loving an egg up their bottom. She was there with her father and older brother, Lonnie, caught up in the excitement and drama of an extraordinary day. She stopped singing as the first flaming oil bottles went flying overhead. Pointing and going: 'Look, look, Dad.'

The bottles from the lamp posts smashed against the front of the big office building, and bright flame went ripping across the stone wall. That drained the smile and joy away from her face. The sheet of flame was scary, with long streamers pouring down close to the regiment soldiers standing along the base of the wall. She was worried one of them might get burnt.

But they were all raising their guns in one hand. A volley of terrifically loud shots crashed out. Haranne ducked instinctively, hardening her shell around her at the same time as her dad snatched her and held her tight as he crouched down.

'Go home!' a strong 'path voice commanded.

She recognized the regiment captain again; he'd been telling them to leave as soon as he emerged. People in the crowd around her groaned and shouted in antagonism. An astonishing sensation of anger washed against her mind. There were more shots.

'This way,' Dad ordered. They started to run, hunched down.

'Together now,' a calm 'path voice commanded. And she could sense teekay slithering through the air, many strands combining into a tight bundle like some invisible giant's arm. It lashed out at the regiment captain, knocking him sideways. Blood poured out of his broken nose and torn cheeks. Then one of the glass yalseed oil bottles smashed on the ground beside him; flame burst out.

Haranne cowered away from the brutality, retracting her ex-sense. 'Daddieee!'

More shots rang out. They seemed closer, different somehow. Then the soldiers were shooting again, and they weren't aiming up into the air any more. Her father pulled her along frantically. 'Bastards, bastards!' he shouted. 'Out of the way, I've got childr—'

An incredible force smashed into Haranne's side, actually lifting her off the ground for a moment before she crumpled onto the granite cobbles of the road. 'Dad?' She was completely numb, staring up into the warm sapphire sky, somehow removed from all the frantic activity churning around her. The angry voices and 'path shouts were becoming muffled. 'Dad?'

His face slid across the sky. And the way he looked down at her was frightening.

*

Shock and dread hit Tasjorka as he stared down at his daughter's wound. Blood was running from the appalling hole the bullet had torn in the side of her ribs, and her gorgeous eyes were dazed with confusion and trust as she tried to grab him.

'Haranne!' Adrenalin and terror gave his voice and 'path shout a power far beyond normal. Everyone within two hundred metres winced as the image of Haranne burst into their consciousness. A pretty girl with dark hair and rich olive skin, lying awkwardly on the cobbles, her dirty old green dress soaked with blood. More blood starting to glisten on the cobbles beneath her, spreading out. Eyes filled with uncomprehending tears. Breath coming in jerks as shock set in.

'Help me!' he commanded. 'Help!'

The conflict along Cantural Street faltered.

'Stop the bleeding.'

'Put pressure on the wound.'

'I'm a nurse, let me through.'

'Help her breathe.'

'You have to stop that bleeding – here—' Tumbling memory images of how to apply teekay to human flesh.

Too many people crowding round. A hundred different haunting images of the shot girl rippled out across the city, the gifting passed from shocked mind to shocked mind.

'A girl. They shot a little girl!'

'I'm a doctor, damn you!'

Tasjorka, along with two others, was trying to staunch the flow of blood with their teekay. He was crying, his mind too frenzied to direct teekay accurately.

'Let me through!'

'Please.'

A circle of tough angry men had formed a guard around tragic Haranne. They parted with snarls as a young regiment officer pushed through. He was carrying a fat satchel with a red cross on the side. He fell to his knees beside the girl.

'Stop doing that,' he said. His teekay reached out, and flowed over the wound. Pinching and squeezing in clever little pulses. His 'path voice spoke quietly and calmly to Haranne. She managed a brave smile. He opened the satchel and dressings rose out of it like a slow-motion explosion, hovering in the air. He began applying them to the wound. The nurse arrived and helped tie them properly. A phial of amanarnik was broken under Haranne's nose, and she sighed as the narcotic hit. Her eyes closed.

*

Along with most of the city, Slvasta watched through other eyes as Haranne's travails were gifted openly. How the mob parted for her, using combined teekay as a protective umbrella from the stones and firebombs arching overhead. How the Meor regiment blocking Walton Boulevard opened their ranks so she could be carried through to the Captain's Free Hospital on Wallace Road. How the hospital staff clustered round and transferred her onto an iron gurney. He clenched his teeth, his thoughts riding in tandem with Tasjorka's anguish as the surgical team elbowed everyone away from his precious daughter, now desperately pale, her breaths coming in short gasps. A father's fright as needles were slipped into arteries, and foreign fluids started to seep along veins.

Then the hospital's senior doctor hurried in, snapping instructions, and the entire building fuzzed, giving Haranne her rightful privacy.

Every Varlan resident not involved with the riot waited anxiously for news on Haranne's progress. They endured three fraught hours while the battle of Walton Boulevard raged with escalating violence. There were dozens of further injuries and even two deaths, but it was little Haranne's plight that had captured everyone's heart.

Finally, Tasjorka emerged through the fuzz around the Captain's Free Hospital, and announced in a shaky 'path that Haranne was out of the operating theatre, and the doctors were confident she would recover. He thanked everyone for their help and support. 'And please, no more violence. No one should suffer as she has.' With that, he turned round and walked back into the hospital.

The clashes reduced after that, flaring sporadically throughout the afternoon before people finally drifted away as the sun sank below the horizon.

*

Slvasta stayed on at the office that night, helping to clean up and secure the building. The deployment bunker was now serving as a triage post for regiment troopers who'd been injured, which was most of them.

Oil lamps hanging from the bunker's brick arch ceiling cast a pale yellow light and filled the air with fumes. Slvasta ignored the groaning as he walked along the line of cots, trying not to flinch at the troopers with bloody bandages. Arnice was lying motionless on the cot at the end, his head swaddled, leaving only narrow slits for his eyes and mouth. The white linen was stained crimson in several places. Slvasta's ex-sight probed below the bandages, revealing the disturbing extent of burnt, ruined skin, the missing part of his lips. A drip bottle hung above the cot, a rubber tube snaking down to his arm, where an intravenous needle had been taped in.

'I was wondering where you were skiving,' Slvasta said, keeping the tone just right, the joshing bluster – nothing wrong here, no allusion to the disfigurement and thick scars Arnice would be left with even if the surgeons did a good job.

Arnice didn't reply. His shell was tight, allowing no emotion to show.

'The girl's all right,' Slvasta said. 'Haranne. The Free Hospital staff are sending out general 'path reports every hour, reassuring people. It's helping, I think.'

Arnice stiffened, his muscles tensing up. 'We didn't do that,' he 'pathed. 'My squads are good men; they wouldn't shoot into the crowd. Not a girl. A child.'

'I know.'

'That's what everyone's saying. I can hear them, the whole city felt her, they saw her through her father's eyes. They knew a father's pain. And they blame us. Me. They hate me for giving the order.'

'You didn't give that order. We all know that; your last order was to fire into the air.'

'And who's going to remember that?'

'There'll be an inquiry. There's got to be one. You were struck by the mob's teekay well before the shot was fired; I'll stand in the witness box myself and swear it. Everyone will know you're completely innocent.'

'Officially. That's what it'll be: officially vindicated. And we saw today what everyone thinks about *official*, didn't we?'

Slvasta gripped Arnice's hand. 'We know the truth. That's what matters. I know. Your friends know. You know.'

'Slvasta, you're a good friend. Thank you.'

268

'You don't have to thank friends. Ah, here are the ambulance wagon fellows. Can you walk?'

'I'm not sure. These damn drugs. I hate them. But there's not much pain now, thank Giu.'

'Would you like me to come with you? Or shall I go get Jaix?'

'No!' Arnice lifted himself from the cot, and created a thick fuzz around himself to deflect any ex-sight. 'No Jaix. She can't see me, not like this. Please, Slvasta, promise me, you won't let her see me.'

'Yes. All right, I promise. I have to say, I think you're under-estimating her, though. She's a lovely girl; she's not going to be turned away by a few scars.'

Arnice clenched his fist and started hitting it on the side of the cot. 'Scars? *Scars?* You moron, I have no face left! I'm going to be a freak. I'm going to be a fucking freak! I can't live like that. I can't.' His voice rose to a frantic shout. 'What is there now? I shot a girl! I shot her!'

Slvasta tried to grab his fist as it pounded the cot. 'You didn't! You didn't shoot anyone. Nurse!'

'She's dead!' Arnice cried. 'I'm dead! I can't live like this. I'm a monster. A monster without a face!'

'Nurse!' Slvasta bellowed.

The doctor came running down the aisle.

'They hate us. Everybody hates us! Kill them. Kill them all. I've Fallen, Slvasta, I've Fallen! Kill me. Somebody, please!'

Arnice started to thrash about. Slvasta had to use his teekay to pin him down on the cot as the doctor fiddled with the mechanism on the bottom of the drip bottle. It took a few moments, then Arnice subsided. Slvasta looked on in anguish as his friend began to sob.

'Slvasta. Don't leave me! Don't . . . ' Arnice sank back, uncon-scious.

The doctor patted Slvasta on the shoulder. 'Don't worry. It's the drugs talking. I've seen it a hundred times. He won't even remember in the morning.'

'Of course. Thank you, doctor.'

'They're taking him to the Hewlitt Hospital now. I know some of the surgeons there, good chaps. They'll fix up what we can of his face. Damn savages, doing that to him.'

'Yes, quite.'

*

Slvasta watched Arnice's unconscious body loaded onto the canvas-covered ambulance wagon. The driver was an ordinary cabby, volunteering to help out. 'Don't you worry, gov, I'll get the major there okay,' he assured Slvasta. 'I haven't lost one today.'

'Thank you.' Slvasta hadn't realized his shell was so flimsy that it was allowing his worry to show.

Keturah hurried across the rear courtyard. 'Captain?'

'Why are you still here?' he asked in surprise.

'Because you are,' she said.

'Oh, Giu, Keturah, you should have gone home hours ago. I'll get a trooper to escort you.'

'That's very kind, sir. But there's someone here to see you. Says she's a friend. She was very insistent. The building guards are holding her in the main entrance.'

Slvasta sent his ex-sight out into the building's main entrance hallway. It was Bethaneve sitting on the bench between two suspicious and tired guards.

'It's fine,' Slvasta told the guards as he walked across the marble floor to her. 'I know her. Well done for being vigilant. Dismissed.'

Bethaneve hugged him as the guards went back to the front door. 'I'm sorry,' she said, sniffing and clinging tightly, 'but I didn't know where else to go.'

'Are you all right?'

'I'm okay, yes. I managed to dodge the Meor troopers when they were beating the crowd.'

Slvasta gave Keturah an awkward look. The woman's surprised gaze darted between him and Bethaneve.

'Ah, right,' he answered, then cursed himself for his own cowardice. 'Come on up to my office.'

'There's no time. They've arrested Javier, Slvasta. The sheriffs beat him terribly and threw him into one of their jail wagons.'

'Crudding Uracus. When was this?'

'About five o'clock. They took him to the Ganuzi Street Station. There's a judge gone there already. They say the judge is using suspension powers to pass sentence.'

'What's suspension?' he asked.

'The Captain can order suspension of civil laws in an emergency,' Keturah said. 'The order came through from the Captain's Palace this morning. It allows the Meor to use armed force against whoever the local commander believes is threatening the state.'

'What?'

'There's a copy on your desk. I put it there.'

Slvasta just stood there. Too much was happening. He didn't know what to do or say.

'They'll sentence him to the Pidrui mines,' Bethaneve said. 'And there'll be no appeal allowed because the sentence was issued during suspension. Slvasta, he'll never get out of there. They won't even admit he's been taken there. Uracus, they won't admit they've even arrested him.'

Slvasta wanted to ask what the Pidrui mines were; he didn't like the way there were so many things he was ignorant of. 'All right, can we get a lawyer? A civil rights one?'

'There are no civil rights under suspension,' Keturah said. 'That's the whole point of it.'

He gave Bethaneve a desperate look. 'Then what can we do?'

'I don't know. I thought you . . .' She struggled against her tears. 'You're an officer.'

Slvasta tried to think. One thing he knew for certain: Javier wasn't going to be freed using any legal means. He turned to Keturah. 'This suspension order, it allows any Meor officer to do what he wants?'

'More or less, yes.'

'Can you find that copy for me?'

She took a moment. Her shell flickered, allowing him to sense her thoughts, how much she hated the day's events, her contempt for the organization she worked for, the haughtiness of the officers. 'Yes.'

'Thank you. Please bring it to the back courtyard.'

Keturah gave Bethaneve a quick timid smile. 'Good luck.'

'Where's Coulan?' Slvasta asked. 'Did he get arrested as well?'

'No. He's outside, fuzzed. We thought I had more chance of getting in here.'

'Good call. Now, listen: he has to get us a cab. Do either of you know a driver who'll be sympathetic?'

'Probably. Coulan knows a lot of people.'

'Good. Now go and tell him to arrange it, fast. And tell him I'll meet him on the corner of Enuie Alley and Conought Square in fifteen minutes.'

'Okay. What are you going to do?'

He gestured down at his filthy uniform. 'Get spruced up.'

*

In the end, it was so much easier than Slvasta had expected. The mildly fuzzed cab, driven by Coulan, pulled up outside the Ganuzi Street Sheriff Station – a strictly functional four-storey building with three underground levels containing cells. Set back from the road, it was built from a dark brick, with narrow barred windows. The sheriffs inside maintained a constant fuzz, adding to the forbidding atmosphere.

There were five sheriffs standing guard outside, watching keenly when Slvasta's cab drew up. He didn't get out, simply stuck his arm out of the door window and beckoned.

One of the sheriffs went over. 'What in Uracus do you want?'

Slvasta leaned forward so the pale light from the streetlamps revealed he was wearing the uniform of a major from the Meor regiment. Arnice wasn't quite the same size, but the fit was good enough for tonight, with little illumination and some strategic fuzzing. The sheriff couldn't even tell he only had one arm – that would have been a complete give-away.

'Tell your station commander I want to see him.'

'Uh . . . sir?'

'You heard. Get him out here now.'

'But—'

'Now!'

The sheriff wasn't going to argue. Not today. He hurried into the station.

A few minutes later the station commander came out.

'He looks happy,' Coulan 'pathed privately to Slvasta.

'What is this?' the commander demanded. It had been a long bad day, and it was far from over. He clearly didn't need any further complications.

Slvasta still didn't come out of the cab. He simply held up the copy of the suspension order. 'You are familiar with this order and the authority it gives me?'

The commander barely read the first few lines. 'Aye.'

'Good. You have a Javier in your custody. Big man, arrested on Walton Boulevard around five o'clock. I'll take charge of him now.'

'You've got to be joking. The judge has already sentenced him. We're about to ship a whole bunch of these rebel bastards out to Pidrui.'

Slvasta hardened his voice, exactly the way so many officers in the Joint Council did, lifting himself up an entire social class. 'This is not a joke, commander. My uncle believes him to be one of the ring leaders. He will be questioned quite firmly on that matter.'

'Your uncle?' a tone of uncertainty had crept into the commander's voice.

'Trevene. I trust you're familiar with the name?'

'Yes, sir.'

'Good man.' Slvasta waited until the station commander had turned round. 'Oh, and, commander?'

'Sir?'

'This never happened. Understand?'

'Completely.'

Two minutes later, a pair of sheriffs dragged a limp Javier out of the station. Coulan hopped down and opened the cab's door. All three of them bundled the big man onto the floor at Slvasta's feet.

Only when the station was out of any reasonable ex-sight range did Slvasta let out a cry of disbelief. 'Oh my crudding Giu, we did it! We crudding did it.'

'You were brilliant,' Coulan replied. 'You've got to have balls the size of melons.'

'Interesting compliment. Thanks.'

'How is he?'

Slvasta's ex-scan swept along Javier. There was plenty of bruising, both eyes were almost swollen shut. A multitude of cuts and grazes had clotted and scabbed, leaving a lot of dried blood on his skin and clothing. Several ribs were cracked, and one knee was badly wrenched with fluid building round the joint. 'Alive.'

7

The sub-basement was a long way underground, and old, a maze of corridors and small cells whose original stone walls were frequently patched with crude bricks and crumbling mortar. Slicks of blue-green algae ran down from oozing cracks, while spiky clumps of small pale stalactites protruded from arching ceilings like petrified fungal blooms. The air was cold, rancid and stale from being unable to escape; just to breathe it in was immediately dispiriting to anyone who was brought down here, sapping all hope.

Aothori accompanied Trevene down the interminable spiral stairs, making sure the hem of his natty embroidered evening cloak didn't drag along the worn steps. He rather enjoyed the smell of bussalore shit and human sweat; it always accompanied a sense of fear. The central chamber into which they emerged had three small oil lamps on iron brackets high on the wall. Their meagre light left the apex of the chamber in shadow, but did manage to illuminate the figures shackled to the wall with iron manacles, their mouths filled with wooden gag balls held in place by leather straps. He counted seventeen, of which seven were female. As soon as they recognized him, their already apprehensive thoughts became panicky.

He smiled in acknowledgement of just how weighty his reputation was these days, and began a circuit. His shell was tight, not that he was in any real danger from a teekay strike. They had all been fitted with a collar of etor vine. The vine, which was as strong as leather, had a peculiar property: when soaked in water a cut length expanded to nearly twice its original size. In that state a braided collar could easily be slipped over a human head. After that it began to dry out, and shrink. If you were wearing one, it took a vast amount of teekay to hold the savagely constricting braids off your throat. Any lapse in concentration, any teekay diverted somewhere else meant the collar would tighten fast and choke the wearer. It left the prisoner without any ability to spin out a shell, their body was devoid of protection, their thoughts unscreened.

'Students,' Aothori concluded, allowing his contempt to show. The clothes, the age, the outrage that mirrored their fright, the broken arrogance. He knew the type well enough – all from the university.

'Indeed, sir,' Trevene said.

'Radicals?'

'Possibly.'

'Are these the same ones who wanted to kick up a fuss over the Jasmine Avenue anniversary?'

'We know two of them have been outspoken about the Jasmine rebellion on occasion.'

'Disgraceful. We provide a wealth of opportunity for them, and this is how they thank us. Were they all plotting today's pitiful demonstrations? Are they the ringleaders?'

'This group was acting together, certainly. The sheriffs arrested them all in Bromwell Park after my people pointed them out.'

'So this was planned? I'm curious. How? Nobody knew about Wurzen until a couple of days ago.'

'"Plan" might be too strong a concept here. I prefer to think they were primed ready to react to a scandal. Wurzen simply came along; if not this, it would have been something else.'

'Really? So they were being prepared for general rebellion? That speaks of serious organization.' Aothori walked over to one of the girls. Her green dress was torn and filthy, her ebony skin grazed along one arm and leg – presumably where she'd been dragged. She began to shake as he stared at her; tears welled up in her eyes.

'Your name?' Aothori asked.

'Oeleen,' she 'pathed. 'Please, the collar's so tight.'

'I know.' He studied the thoughts spewing out of her frantic mind, the images, her deep terrors. 'My, my, what an imaginative little thing you are. So are you the ringleader of this wretched band?'

'No, no, there is no ringleader. It's not like that. We were just protesting about Wurzen, that's all. I'm sorry, I'm so sorry.'

'Ah, so many people are always sorry after the event. Unfortunately, that doesn't help anyone. So who is "we"? All your friends here?'

'Yes. Yes.'

He grinned at Trevene. 'Well, how's that for camaraderie? Everyone here! I can't say I'm terribly worried about the Captaincy being overthrown if this is the best radicals can do.'

'We'll get lists of everyone they've 'pathed and received political 'paths from, and when,' Trevene said. 'It will take time, but my clerks will draw up a register, then we can cross-reference and analyse it, see if we can find a pattern, some kind of hierarchy.'

'Sounds terribly dreary.'

'Please,' Oeleen 'pathed. 'The collar. Please. It's been on for hours. I can't . . . I can't hold it back much longer.'

Aothori studied her face, savouring the way her pretty youthful features were distorted by strain and panic. 'Then we'd better not waste any time, had we?' He turned back to Trevene, whose lenses were reflecting the flickering orange oil lamps, occluding his eyes. 'I'll take her, and this one, and this one,' he indicated two other girls.

'As you wish.'

'You're not going to go running to father? That's refreshing.'

'They aren't ringleaders, and frankly there are too many for us to process properly. However, there can be no public knowledge of the outcome. Everyone is focused on Haranne right now. I don't want that attention diverted.'

'A good point.' He stroked Oeleen's cheek tenderly. 'Not that I would ever send anyone as special as this to the Pidrui mines. I'll 'path the professor when I've finished with them.'

*

Slvasta took a cab to the Hewlitt Hospital at midday the next day to visit Arnice. He knew something was wrong as soon as the driver turned on to Lichester Street. Several people were standing together outside the entrance, their minds flashing with shock and distress. In growing alarm, he realized two of them were Jaix and Lanicia. Jaix was sobbing uncontrollably, her shell gone, her thoughts incoherent with grief. He climbed out of the cab.

'What's happened?'

The look Lanicia gave him was brutal; without any 'path it told him what a useless, worthless piece of human-shaped shit he was. And not just because he'd turned her down. 'It's Arnice,' she said.

Slvasta just stared at the wailing Jaix. He didn't want to know. Didn't want to be told the horrible truth. 'What?'

'I'm afraid Major Arnice has passed away,' the man in the doctor's coat said gently.

'Oh, no. Jaix, I'm so sorry,' Slvasta said. He stepped over to hug her, to offer his meagre comfort.

'You were good to him,' Jaix said through her tears. 'He really liked you. He said you were real, not like the rest of them.'

'He was a wonderful man. Truly.'

'We were engaged,' Jaix said. 'He proposed to me two days ago. I said yes.'

Slvasta closed his eyes in grief. 'The news. He said he had news for me. He was going to tell me today.'

'Arnice wanted you to be his best man.'

Slvasta turned to the doctor. 'What happened?'

It was the wrong thing to say, he knew it at once. Jaix immediately stiffened inside his embrace.

The highly agitated doctor said: 'I'm afraid the major committed suicide.'

'What? No!'

'He didn't,' Jaix snarled, she turned and pointed at the other man standing with them. 'You murdered him!'

'Jaix—' Lanicia began.

'No! I will not calm down, and I will not recant the truth. Slvasta, *this* man murdered Arnice.'

'Who are you?' Slvasta asked.

'Davalta. I'm an assistant attorney for the city prosecutor's office. And I do understand, and sympathize with, Ms Jaix's grief. However, I must insist that this calumny is not to be perpetuated.'

'I'll perpetuate as much as I like, you boywhore scum,' Jaix spat. 'You think working for the prosecutor is going to save you? When my family's lawyers are through with you, you'll wish you'd plea bargained for the Pidrui mines and a nightly gang rape! It'll be a trip to Giu compared to what I'll have done to you.'

'Ms Jaix—'

'All right,' Slvasta held his hand up. He gave the assistant attorney in his smart expensive suit a suspicious gaze. 'What are you doing here? Why is Jaix blaming you for my friend's death?'

Davalta took a breath. 'I was serving papers on Major Arnice. Soon afterwards, he jumped from the fourth-floor window.'

'Papers? What sort of papers?'

'The prosecutor decided he should be charged with Haranne's shooting.'

'You've got to be out of your Uracus fucking mind!' Even as he said it, Slvasta could put together the tricky political reasoning behind it. Someone had to be the scapegoat for the girl's ordeal, someone in authority. You couldn't blame the mob in this case, that would only aggravate the resentment – and enough people were being carted off to serve in the Pidrui mines to keep that cranked up high right now. The other side had to take a hit, too; there was always a penance to be served in order to restore equilibrium. From a strategic point of view, Arnice was a perfect candidate. The Meor officer in charge of the troops when the shot was fired – even though he'd been knocked unconscious and was having his face burnt off at the time.

'I assure you, captain—' Davalta began.

'You served papers on a man who'd just had his face fire-bombed? What did you think that would do to his state of mind?'

'There was no legal reason to delay the court summons.'

'Legal . . .' Slvasta shaped his formidable teekay into a giant fist.

Davalta sensed it and took a frightened step back. 'I assure you, sir, assaulting an officer of the court is a serious offence and will be pursued vigorously.'

Slvasta gave him an icy smile, then turned to Jaix. 'Make sure your lawyer collects my statement on Arnice's mental state, and how he should not have been persecuted by a malicious lawsuit. I'll also be giving testimony that he was unconscious when Haranne was shot, and that I personally witnessed his last order, which was to aim above the heads of the crowd.'

'Thank you,' Jaix whispered.

Slvasta gave Davalta a final contemptuous glance. 'You are not fulfilled, and your profession will prevent you from ever becoming so. Your soul will spend eternity lost amid the nebulas, diminishing with every passing year.' With that he climbed back into the cab. As his teekay shut the door, he caught Lanicia's approving gaze. It didn't make him feel any better.

*

Slvasta walked down the east side of Tarleton Gardens, a terraced square on the edge of the Nalani borough, with a small iron-fenced park in the middle where ancient malbue trees dangled long skirt branches of their dark grey-red leaves from crowns twenty metres above the cracked pavements. The brick house he stopped at was no different from the others which made up the terrace walls of the square. Five storeys high, with bay windows up the front and a wide wooden door painted a cheerful blue. Like most around the square, each floor had been divided up into separate apartments. The structure had a simple psychic fuzz, no different from any other home in the city, preventing anyone from casual prying with their ex-sight. He felt a faint perception wash across him as he went up the three steps to the door.

'Come on up,' Bethaneve 'pathed.

The inside was more timeworn than the outside, with a stone stairwell that echoed to the sound of his feet. With whitewashed walls and a grimy roof lantern high above, the air was noticeably cooler than the square outside. He climbed up to the third floor. Bethaneve opened the door and beckoned him across the small landing, her ex-sight sweeping round.

'Nobody followed me,' he said.

'The Captain's police use mod-eagles,' she replied. 'Mod-dogs and cats, too. There are rumours of other adaptations we've not seen before.'

He almost said: *So how do you know that, if you don't know what they look like?* But for once he had the smarts to keep his mouth shut.

The flat was as bare as the stairwell outside. Its walls had been painted a pale green decades ago, and had faded further under layers of dust and dirt. Dark floorboards creaked under his feet. There was no furniture. Javier was lying on a mattress in the back room, covered by a thin sheet. Coulan sat on a fold-up chair beside him. The young man looked exhausted, his hair limp, stubble shading his chin and cheeks, shirt criss-crossed with streaks of dried blood.

'Hey, you,' Javier 'pathed. There was a strong seepage of distress within the simple thought, despite his tight shell. The amount of tissue bruising was worrying. On his dark skin, the swelling was like a purple and bronze stain, leaving every limb puffy and discoloured. Wounds still leaked pustulant fluid, though they were drying out and scabbing over. Both eyes were completely swollen shut from the bruising, and his cheeks had ballooned out as if his mouth was full of nuts.

Slvasta smiled and held up the satchel he'd taken from the office's deployment bunker. 'Brought you something.'

'Is that amanarnik?' an incredulous Coulan asked.

'I got hold of some phials, yes. Clean bandages and dressings, too; they're important.'

'Thank you,' Coulan's hand was trembling as he took the satchel. 'He spends so much energy fighting the pain.'

'Ha, you don't have to tell Slvasta about pain,' Javier 'pathed. 'This is just a few bruises. You had it worse, right?'

'The doctors kept telling me it wasn't as bad as kidney stones,' Slvasta said. 'I pray to Giu every night I never have any of those.'

'Doctors!'

Coulan knelt beside his lover and prepared a syringe of amanarnik.

'I don't know the dosage,' Slvasta said.

'Don't worry, I do,' Coulan said.

'He's like a walking encyclopaedia,' Javier 'pathed. 'Despite that, I still quite like him.'

Clearly fighting back tears, Coulan slid the needle into Javier's arm. 'There. That should shut you up. Honestly, the whingeing I've had to put up with . . .' He caressed the big man's sweat-soaked forehead.

It was only a short while before Javier sighed. A profound sense of relief pulsed out from his thoughts. 'Oh, wow, that feels better.' A minute later he was asleep.

'I'll change his dressings while he's out,' Coulan said. 'I don't want to risk infection. There are some nasty germs on this world.' He smiled up at Slvasta. 'Thank you so much. Without you . . .' he choked.

Bethaneve put her arm round his shoulders, and gave him a reassuring hug. 'He'll be okay, the big old fool.'

'Yes.' Coulan started to busy himself with the satchel.

Bethaneve inclined her head, and Slvasta followed her out. The front room was a lot bigger, with warm afternoon sunlight streaming in through the big bay window. Like the rest of the flat, the room was devoid of furniture or decoration. There was a single mattress on the floor, covered by a rumpled sheet. Bethaneve sat on it and patted her hand for him to join her. He did, with a sigh of his own.

'You did good,' she said. 'Strike one against the system.'

'And the system strikes back even harder.'

She put her hand on his cheek. 'What's happened?'

'My friend. My one and only friend in the office, Arnice. You remember, the major who got burnt by a firebomb?'

'I remember him, yes.'

'He's dead.'

'Oh, Slvasta.' She hugged him tight. 'I'm so sorry. But you said the burns were pretty bad.'

'It wasn't the burns,' he said hoarsely, and told her what had happened.

'Those people!' she said in dismay when he'd finished. 'He was one of them, and they were going to use him like that?'

'Yeah.' Somehow they had wound up pressed together, holding each other. 'That little shit Davalta, who served Arnice with the summons, he didn't even care. Suicide was actually more convenient for *them*. Now everything can be blamed on my friend, and nobody will clear his name. Jaix will try, but they'll stall her and discredit her, I know it. If she ever does get her day in court, everyone will have forgotten. This whole disturbance, everything that happened, will be blamed on Arnice.'

'They can't blame the Wurzen nest on him.'

'No. That was the district governor, who conveniently for the Captain is swinging from the end of a mob's rope. Nothing will change. Everything will carry on as before.'

'Not you,' she said with conviction. 'I know you won't give up. You won't, will you?'

'Give up what?' he asked bitterly. 'Trying to get the regiments to use terrestrial horses instead of mod-horses on a sweep? Yeah, that's going to change everything, isn't it? It's just so petty, a pitiful act of bureaucracy. *I* am pathetic. I can't change a Uracus damned thing. I might as well join them, all those families and officials that rule this world. That way, if I'm going to live a worthless life, at least I'll be comfortable doing it.'

'Stop it. Stop thinking like that. I can't take them winning. They always win, Slvasta, every time. They broke my friend, they killed yours, and there is never any justice, not for people like us. Why? Why can't they be brought down? Why can't the world change?'

'It's all right,' he said, stroking her neck. 'I'm just messed up by Arnice. I won't give up.'

'Promise me! Promise, Slvasta.' Her face was pushed up against his. Desperation and urgency were swelling out from a mind which no longer had any shell.

He kissed her. 'I promise.' He kissed her again. 'I promise I won't give up.'

Her hands were fumbling with his shirt. He used his teekay to lift her dress off. They fell back onto the mattress, touching and caressing skin as it was freed from the restriction of clothes. When they were naked, she straddled him, surrounded by bright sunlight pouring in through the bay window behind her. He used his teekay to pull her down, impaling her. The sunlight seemed to flow around her, turning his world to a glorious white blaze as she cried out. Then she was riding him, letting him into her thoughts to reveal her body's secret demands, pleading with him to perform them. He responded with equal intimacy, sharing his physical appetite. And a completely uninhibited Bethaneve used her hands and mouth and tongue and teekay to delight him in all the ways he'd always fantasized she would.

He held nothing back from her, and felt no shame in exposing himself in such a fashion, for she reciprocated with equal enthusiasm.

All that afternoon in the hot light they made love on the slim mattress, intent on just one thing: satisfying each other's cravings. And all the while, thoughts churned in his mind, notions he'd thought impossible. Everything was free for consideration now, liberated from his reticence, rushing out of its cage amid the sunlight and joy.

*

'I'm scared,' he told her eventually.

Bethaneve was lying on top of him, hot sweaty skin pressed into his. The smell of sex in every breath. The feeling of intimacy was unsurpassed.

'Don't be,' she told him. 'This will happen again and again. As much as you want. Because I want it too – you know that. I held nothing from you.'

'Yes. I know. But that's not what scares me.'

'Then what?'

'What we both know and are too afraid to say.'

'Then say it. To me. You can say anything to me.'

'If there is to be change, I know of no one who is going to bring it about.'

'So many want it. Someone will—'

'No,' he said firmly. 'Not *someone*. If this is to be done, then we must do it. Right here. Right now. This is where it begins. This is the revolution. We will organize, and we will overcome.'

Bethaneve lifted herself up so she could look into his eyes. Her own were moist with emotion. 'I am with you to the very end,' she swore. 'Whatever that brings us.'

BOOK FOUR

Cell Structure

1

Slvasta resigned his commission the week after Arnice committed suicide. He gave no reason, nor indication of where he was going. On his way out of the Joint Regimental Council building, he paid a quick trip to the forward deployment bunker, where he quietly removed a couple of pistols and four boxes of ammunition, carrying them out in a satchel he fuzzed. Just as he expected, no one questioned an officer.

'We need to organize,' Bethaneve said that evening. 'That's obvious.'

Slvasta had turned up at the house in Tarleton Gardens carrying just a single suitcase that contained all his civilian clothes. It was a symbolic arrival, he thought. He'd left his uniforms behind at Number Seventeen Rigattra Terrace. Bethaneve, too, had left her lodgings on Borton Street.

They sat on the bare floorboards in the back room, with Javier propped up on pillows which Coulan had arranged. The worst of the big man's swelling had just started to go down, and one of his eyes was starting to open again. Amanarnik had reduced a lot of the pain, though Coulan was worried about the long-term damage to his knee.

'Just how many people is this going to take?' Javier asked.

'Is what going to take?' Coulan asked. 'Exactly what is the aim here?'

'To get rid of the Captain and the National Council,' Bethaneve said. 'Right?'

'Yes,' Slvasta said. 'And then what?'

'Democracy,' she said indignantly. 'Proper democracy, with courts that are open and honest. And government officials who are accountable. That's for starters.'

'So we have to physically kick the bastards out,' Javier said. 'That's not going to be easy. They'll put up a fight. We'd need an army.'

'Or a mob,' Coulan said. 'We've just seen how powerful that can be. The Meor was hard pressed to defend the government buildings.'

'You can't control a mob,' Slvasta said.

'Don't be so sure about that. A mob just needs the right leader.'

'But if anyone establishes themselves as a mob agitator, the Captain's police will pounce on them,' Javier said. 'If they're lucky, they'll escape with being sent to the Pidrui mines.'

'So their identities need to be kept hidden,' Bethaneve countered. 'That's simply a question of maths.'

'Maths?' Slvasta queried – and maybe a little too much scepticism leaked past his shell.

'Of course.' She grinned tauntingly at him. 'What we need is separate groups of agitators, kept in isolation from each other, but using private 'paths to keep in touch. Lieutenants that don't know each other, so they can't betray anyone, and nobody knows us. Maybe some kind of pyramid structure, with instruction coming down from us and relayed through the groups.' She closed her eyes, her thoughts alight with geometric shapes designated by lines and nodes. 'Humm, let me think on that.'

'I like it,' Javier said. 'So if we're group one, right at the top, all we have to do is just recruit the layer of groups below us. After that, the groups we found go on to establish more groups. The layers build up.'

'Sounds good,' Slvasta admitted. 'If only we knew someone who could organize that?'

Bethaneve gave him an obscene finger gesture.

'We'll leave that with you, then,' Coulan said. 'Our official communications officer.'

'Not officer,' she said sharply. 'Regiments have officers.'

'Comrade then?'

'Yes. I like that.'

'Our biggest problem is going to be motivating people,' Javier said. 'There are so many people who just accept the status quo.'

'Water,' Bethaneve said eagerly. 'Everyone knows how badly the water companies maintain the city pipes. It wouldn't take much to bugger up the pump stations. The Captain's family owns half of them. We can put it about that the failures are all down to him, squeezing profit out for himself and not spending enough to repair and replace essential parts.'

Slvasta gazed at Bethaneve with a growing admiration. He'd never seen her this animated before; angry with the First Officer and the Captain, yes, but this – this was a whole new aspect of her. He rather liked her fierceness, and how smart she was being.

'We also need to think about how to get our message out to people,' Coulan said. 'A reason why our way is better than the existing system.'

'Money,' Slvasta said, determined to make his own contribution.

They all looked at him.

'Everyone wants more money, right?' he said. The idea that was blooming in his mind was only just keeping ahead of his speech, so he just let himself flow with it. 'So we have to show them we can give them that. They have to know that opposing the Captain is going to end in better times, especially money-wise.' He paused, slotting the aspects together, feeling a great deal of satisfaction at breathing some life into his personal goal.

'Go on,' Javier said.

'There are a lot of people in Varlan on the breadline right now, and not just the ones in the Shanties. And every day there's more drift in from the provinces in search of work. Well, why don't we make sure they get that work?'

'How in Giu's name do we do that?' Bethaneve asked.

Slvasta smiled round at all of them as the perfect solution bloomed in his mind. 'By taking it away from the mods.'

*

It took Javier a couple of weeks to recover well enough to walk. He had to use a cane and support himself with teekay. But once he was able to leave Tarleton Gardens he got Slvasta a job at Coughlin's stall in the Wellfield meat market. Coughlin was a hundred and sixty-three, so he relied entirely on Javier and two lads, Pabel and Ervin, as well as three mod-apes in their third decade – it wasn't kind keeping the creatures on that long.

Every morning, an hour before dawn, Javier would take one of the lads with him to collect their meat from the Plessey station goods yard where the night trains delivered it. Along with dozens of other stalls, they'd load carcasses – some fresh, some salted – and cart them back to Wellfield, where the meat would be cut up and packed for their clients. Coughlin had taken some convincing that a one-armed man was up to the task. But once Slvasta had demonstrated just how strong his teekay was, the old man relented.

'This is a stall suspended in history,' Javier confided when Slvasta arrived on his first day.

Slvasta took a look around the poky clutter of huts sheltering under the massive roof and thought Javier was being generous: the stall should have been relegated *to* history and a new one built on its foundations.

*

They had to wake up at four o'clock every morning to be at the Plessey station. So getting up an hour and a half earlier wasn't too much of a hardship. Bethaneve had tracked down the addresses of the major adaptor stables across Varlan without any trouble. 'You just have to know which public registry to search,' she said brightly. Slvasta hadn't been surprised to find there were thirty-seven stables on her list; and plenty of people had smaller stables, too. There were a lot of mods in the capital.

The Dawa family's stable was on Hatchwood Road, barely a quarter of a mile from the riverfront in the Oxlip district. A neat block with ten-foot-high brick walls, surrounded by spindly voxin trees whose chaotic black and grey tufts waved about in the breeze.

A six-storey townhouse stood beside the main entrance, with a neat little front garden and deftly trimmed pinku vines scrambling up the front. Inside the walls was a traditional layout of barns and two exercise yards. The birthing manger was in the middle, long enough to hold twenty-five pregnant neuts, with the hatchery at one end where their newly laid eggs would sit on clean straw. Two of the barns housed the hundred-strong herd of female neuts, where they were bred with the stable's ten male neuts. The remaining barns were for the young mods, with specific stalls for mod-apes, dogs, dwarfs, cats, birds and horses of various sizes. Right at the centre was the adaptor stockade, where those with the talent sat for long hours beside a neut whose egg had just been fertilized and used their teekay to bring on the required traits in the embryo.

Slvasta and Javier turned down an alley at the back of the Dawa stables and hurried along it. There were no streetlights down the narrow passage, and the nightly river mist was reducing visibility to a couple of yards. Nonetheless they both clad themselves in a subtle fuzz to deflect any ex-sight that might chance to sweep the alley. Not far from the corner, they found a sturdy little wooden door which hadn't been opened for years. It was secured with a Ysdom lock – still the finest anti-teekay lock on Bienvenido, with multiple springs and levers designed to thwart the most skilful burglar. You could break it, of course, but the main bolt was solid iron an inch in diameter, so you had to either have the strongest teekay on the planet or bring a sledgehammer along. Either way, chances were that an assault that blatant would be noticed. They'd found that out the hard way during their first couple of attempted incursions.

So Slvasta concentrated his ex-sight on the door's hinges and used his teekay to turn the screws. They were old and practically welded into the wood, but he persisted. It took ten minutes and eventually they all came free, methodically winding up from the hinges, and Javier lifted the door aside.

They crept into the stable complex, keeping up their fuzz. There were oil lamps on the corners of all the buildings. Slvasta reached out with his teekay to snuff the flames on some of them so they could slink past unseen. Then they were at the barns. That was where they split up. Slvasta crept into one of the low buildings, wrinkling his nose up against the smell of neuts and their manure. The creatures were all huddled together, sleeping on their feet. He sent his ex-sight into the body of the first, and followed with his teekay.

Slaughtering every mod they encountered would be easy. A quick spike of teekay into the brain or heart would kill the defenceless animal instantly. But that would be noticed, and the authorities put on the alert, so they were going for a more indirect approach. A small pinch of teekay in the right place in a female neut's ovaries and the creature was barren for life. After a few weeks, the city's supply of new mods would dry up, and all those jobs they were intended for would have to be done by humans instead.

Of course, new neuts could be bought and brought in from other towns and cities, but that would take time. By then, Slvasta was hoping the movement would have built enough momentum to cause a lot of problems for the adaptor stables everywhere.

It took twenty minutes for Slvasta to sterilize all the female neuts in the barn. He and Javier crept out of the stable unseen, and fixed the door back into place behind them.

*

The Great North-Western train company had built Plessey station in Varlan's Narewith district, the terminus to a main line that ran almost three thousand miles north, crossing the equator to reach to New Angeles at the tip of the Aflar peninsula. Its goods yard sat behind the grandiose passenger terminal, with row after row of sheds whose steep roofs stood on iron pillars covering the slender loading bay platforms. Every day, hundreds of goods trains brought raw materials into the capital and dispatched manufactured goods out across the north-west. The money which flowed through the station on a daily basis formed a goodly portion of the city's overall economy. Many people relied on it for their jobs.

Slvasta and Javier drove their carts into the goods yard at just after half past four, merging into the usual procession of carts belonging to various stallholders. They already knew something was wrong before they passed the tall stone gateposts. The aether was bubbling with disgruntled 'path comments suffused with emotion.

There were a lot of carts pulled up in the loading bays which ran along one side of platform 8D, which handled the meat trains. Big yalseed oil lamps hung from the rafters, shining a meagre yellow light down on the men milling along the narrow platform, but Slvasta couldn't see the trains. Just about every platform was empty.

'What's going on?' he asked Javier.

The big man just shrugged. There were no station officials anywhere, though Slvasta could sense the engineering crews in their shops, radiating disgruntled and in some cases nervous thoughts. He scanned a little deeper, trying to identify individuals whose resentment burnt hotter than the others. By now he recognized most of the night-shift station workers.

'Check it out, I think we might have three,' he told Javier, his thoughts indicating the specific people hunkered down in the engineering shops. They avoided recruiting anyone from the Wellfield these days. Bethaneve said a concentration of activists in the same place would be suspicious if the Captain's police ever stumbled onto those cells.

Wherever they went now they were on the lookout for the resentful and sullen among the city's residents. When a possible emerged, a day later that chosen one would receive a quick private 'path from someone they didn't know, asking them if they'd like to actually do something about the focus of their ire. Responses were graded against a chart Bethaneve had drawn up. 'To see if we've got a talker or a doer,' she said as she supervised their growing network of activist cells. Some of their best assets were cells of one – a person broadly known as a political activist (criminal record preferred) who would happily take an order to cause a little physical havoc.

Testing Bethaneve's pyramid of cells had so far resulted in

water being temporarily cut off to certain streets (in one case for two days), allowing them to gauge the efficiency and preparedness of the repair teams. That information, along with their growing map of the city's main water pipe network, would allow them to cut off water to nine individual districts through just seven small acts of sabotage, throwing the proverbial spanner in the ageing, rickety pump mechanisms of substations.

'Good. Tag them for Bethaneve,' Javier replied. His own ex-sight and intuition wasn't as developed as Slvasta's. He gestured around at the throng of unhappy stallholders waiting for the overnight meat train. 'This doesn't look good.' He 'pathed Vladja, another Wellfield stallholder, waiting in a bay further down platform 8D.

'There's been no goods train come in since midnight,' Vladja told them.

'What about passenger trains?' Javier asked.

'Some, but only from the local stations.'

'What's happened?'

'Nobody knows, but it's got to be some kind of major accident somewhere up the line.'

Finally, a station official had appeared at the end of platform 8D; a young man in an assistant platform manager's uniform, surrounded by a big scrum of stallholders. He looked terrified and his superiors had clearly sent him out with the purpose of saying one thing: we don't know when the trains are coming.

'Come on,' Javier said. 'This is pointless.' He jumped back into the cart and picked up the reins. Slvasta followed him out of the goods yard. As they passed through the gates, his ex-sight showed him two more stallholder carts leaving.

*

Wellfield market had been on its current site, barely a mile from Plessey station, for over two thousand years. It had been completely rebuilt seven times, the last being two hundred and eleven years ago, though there had been many refurbishments since. This latest version covered six acres under a series of long curving glass-and-slate roofs that could easily be mistaken for one of the capital's railway stations. Heavy iron girders supported the roof; every five years they had their rust scraped off so they could be given a fresh coat of red and green paint to protect against the humidity; some claimed it was just the paint layers holding it all together these days. Most of the sides were open, allowing a breeze to carry through, cleaning out the damp clingy smell of butchered meat. Over a hundred wholesale merchants had Guild permits to operate in Wellfield, supplying meat to the trade across the capital city.

After a month working there, Slvasta was completely immune to the smell and sight of raw meat in the form of freshly slaughtered carcasses. They left the carts in the stables with Pabel. Javier started scanning round with his ex-sight. 'We need to buy stock, quickly,' he said. 'Most stalls have some in reserve. Once they all hear there's no train, they'll cling to it like gold.'

He started to hail people, using a confident, slightly amused tone to wheedle a carcass out of them. Never more than one per stall, for fear of arousing suspicion. Slvasta, Pabel and Ervin hurried around the market with barrows, collecting the meat. Their good fortune came to a halt about thirty minutes later. Slvasta was hanging up a salted pig carcass in the cool brick-lined store when Javier came in sighing.

'Game's up,' the big man announced. 'Great North-Western have just announced their main line service is suspended for today, and possibly tomorrow as well. Every stall is hanging on to what it's got now.'

'What happened?'

'There's something wrong with the bridge over the Josi. That's about four hundred miles north of Varlan. It's a big river, merges with the Colbal just outside the city.'

'There must be other bridges,' Slvasta said.

'Not for the main line. There are plenty of branch lines out in the counties. So I suppose they can divert trains round onto the south-west main line, but nothing like the regular traffic. This is really going to bugger things up for a day or two.' He looked round the store, which had a dozen carcasses hanging up. 'We should have enough for today and some of tomorrow's orders. After that . . .'

They set to with cleavers, preparing the orders. A lot of people started to arrive in the Wellfield as the news of the trains spread across the waking city. Surprisingly, Coughlin was one of them, turning up a little after six.

'I haven't let anyone down in a century,' the old man said, looking round the market in distress. 'Time was when we'd always keep four days' worth of meat in the store, but the damn account-ants put a stop to that. Dead money, they said. It should be in the bank accruing interest. Damn them all to Uracus.'

'We can supply our regulars tomorrow,' Javier said.

'Yes, yes, you did well there, my boy,' Coughlin said. 'But now we have to take care of the days after that. I want you to accom-pany me. We'll take a local train to Chelverton; it's only about an hour outside Varlan on the local line, which – thank Giu – is still running. There's an abattoir there we buy from.'

'I remember the invoices, sir,' Javier said.

'Yes, indeed. They're expensive, but beggars can't be choosers. We'll go there and buy a week's worth of carcasses. It can be deliv-ered by cart if that's what has to be done, and Uracus damn the cost. If we sell it at a loss, so be it. But I will not allow my good name to be tarnished by this wretched railway. My reputation is all I have left.'

'I understand.'

'And you, er . . .'

'Slvasta, sir.'

'Slvasta, yes, yes, of course. Are you capable of looking after the stall until I get back?'

'I can do that, sir, don't you worry.'

'Good man. Thank you. Come now, Javier, we'll get over to the bank first, and take out some sovereigns, eh? People will always take good hard coins over a cheque any day of the week.'

'That they do, sir,' Javier winked at Slvasta as he untied his apron.

*

In the middle of the afternoon, Great North-Western announced it would take a day to bring in replacement track to repair the warped rails on the Josi bridge, then a further day or possibly two to get the trains back on schedule.

'It's caused chaos,' Bethaneve said that evening. As always, after they'd had their supper, they sat and discussed strategy.

'Chaos, yes,' Coulan said. 'But no hardship outside the merchant classes. Who cares about those Fallerloving bastards?'

'There's a knock-on effect,' she said earnestly. 'If the merchant's business suffers, you can bet he'll pass the pain down to his workforce.'

'And customers,' Slvasta pointed out.

'But one of the main train lines goes down for a couple of days, and . . .' She nodded her head in admiration. 'It causes a lot more financial damage than knocking out the water.'

'There are four main trans-continental lines into Varlan,' Javier said. 'They all have bridges, a lot of bridges. Bridges can fail.'

'You're saying we should sabotage the rail lines?' Slvasta asked.

'Uracus, yes! It would be much more effective.'

'But obvious,' Coulan said. 'We could hardly blame the woe that brings on the Captain. It would be us hurting people.'

'Only if we do it continually,' Bethaneve said. 'We could maybe shut down the rail lines as the final twist of the knife.'

'Makes sense,' Slvasta conceded.

'I'll get some level elevens to look at possible bridges,' she said. 'There are enough of them.'

'Level eleven,' Javier mused. 'Recruitment is going well, then? How many do we have?'

'We're recruiting for level fifteen now,' she said. 'But I'm not using a pyramid structure any more.' Her mind showed them a complex geometric structure mimicking some kind of crystal. 'The inter-cell connectivity is difficult to crack, and I've started arranging loops which we can initiate but then they just feed back on the cell we imparted that initial instruction to, so there's no way the Captain's police can ever intercept us.'

Slvasta tried to get his head around the concept of passing

instructions round the cells with loops and cut-offs, and realized he was never going to be the mathematician Bethaneve was. *Giu, but I'm lucky to have her.*

'Good,' Javier grunted. 'But, back to the merchant classes. How is making their lives more difficult going to benefit the cause?'

'Hurting them financially weakens them and reduces their power over the workers they exploit. The point is that individual ownership of the method of production – or its distribution – is stealing from those who work to produce goods,' Bethaneve said. 'It results in an uneven distribution of wealth, which ultimately ends up in the unfair society we have today.'

Slvasta and Javier exchanged a glance. There was no arguing with her when she was in this frame of mind. 'Where do you get this stuff from?' Slvasta asked.

Bethaneve raised an eyebrow. 'Books. I read books. I can read, you know.'

'Oh. Yes, of course. Sorry. I should maybe start reading some of those myself.'

'Coulan tracked down some useful ones for me.'

'I found some very old political texts in the university library when I was working as an archivist there,' Coulan said. 'I can probably get you some of them.'

'You used to work as an archivist?' Slvasta asked. Now he thought about it, he knew very little of Coulan's background. Just about all he did know was that the man worked for the Ministry of Industry, regulating chemical companies.

'While I was a student, yes. They say the vaults under the university library are almost as big as those under the palace where the Captain's ship is entombed. There are thousands of books and journals in there, and most of them are falling to pieces they're so old. Looking after them helped bring a few coins in during the holidays.'

Which must have been when he and Bethaneve were together, Slvasta realized – *so don't go there.*

'That could be very useful,' Javier said. 'We need to offer

people a practical alternative to the government we have now, not just tear it all down. That would give us legitimacy.'

'Form an opposition party, you mean?' Coulan asked. 'Risky.'

'As opposed to what we're doing now?' Slvasta said.

'People have to know there is something concrete to challenge the Captain,' Javier said, 'something that they can rely on and trust. Not Citizens' Dawn, that's never going to stand against the Captain, it's just an extension of the aristos' power. It's got to be a new political party, one that supports the poor and the workers.'

'Aren't we a bit early for that?' Slvasta said.

'Not for the groundwork,' Bethaneve said. 'If we're legitimately established before the Captain's police realize we're a problem, it'll be a lot harder for them to dislodge us.'

'Start small?' Coulan suggested.

'A borough council,' Slvasta said.

'That could work. Borough councils are almost powerless. Nobody cares about them. But it would give us a solid foundation to build on.'

'One problem,' Javier said. 'We need to win an election.'

'Preparation solves that one,' Coulan said. 'Never fight a battle until after you've won it. We have to be sure that if our party stands, then all the candidates will get elected.'

'How?'

'We need to have a pre-existing power base.'

'Not the cells,' Bethaneve said quickly.

'No. What I'm talking about is an alternative political organization, one that's mutually beneficial to a democratic party. I'm thinking maybe Slvasta and Javier could start a union in Wellfield. There hasn't been one for two centuries. Not since the weekend payment accord was signed by the guild. Then the union could sponsor candidates for the borough elections.'

'That doesn't give us much time,' Bethaneve said. 'The borough elections are only five months away.'

'Mod shortages should be noticeable by then,' Javier said, 'and this train bridge problem is an excellent starting point. Everybody in Wellfield is going to work harder to get round the problem. Half the stall owners did the same as Coughlin and I today, and visited abattoirs outside the city to secure meat for tomorrow. Do you think anyone is going to be paid extra for all that overtime?'

As always at these discussions, Slvasta was annoyed with himself for not seeing the obvious until after someone else had voiced it. *How come I'm always so far behind with ideas?* 'That's excellent,' he said. 'We can use it to stir dissatisfaction.'

'You mustn't be the leaders,' Bethaneve said. 'Not at this early stage. There are three cell members working in the Wellfield. We'll instruct them to start the union. You can be staunch supporters.'

'Puppeteers,' Slvasta said contemptuously.

'Just like the Captain,' Bethaneve shot back. 'He protects himself from any criticism with layer after layer of scapegoats. Starting with Arnice. Well, that's what we're going to do with you.'

'*Me?*'

'Yes, you. You're the perfect figurehead for this revolution. A regiment officer, a genuine hero who's been out there on the front line slogging through the wilderness to scan for Falls. You've encountered Fallers, and escaped. And you rejected the Captain and the regiments because you know they haven't got the interests of the people at heart – just themselves. And you're not an aristocrat or from the merchant class; you're an honest working man who will be a true representative of the people. People can sense that decency in you; I did the second you walked into my office. They'll believe in you. You're our secret weapon, Slvasta. You're going to be this world's first democratically elected president.'

2

It was a big day. Auspicious, even. The Watcher Guild had seen Skylords approaching ten days ago, and predicted their arrival accurately. A lot of people in Varlan were talking about the co-incidence that they'd arrive on the exact centenary of Jasmine Avenue. A couple of pamphlets actually used the word: omen.

It was also a week since the Josi bridge failure. The chaos and financial strain it had created in the Wellfield market proved too much for poor old Coughlin. He chose Guidance, taking a pyre boat out onto the Colbal and freeing his soul to be Guided by the magnificent crystalline creature.

That evening, Slvasta, Bethaneve, Javier and Coulan went to the bait Philippa was running to celebrate the Skylords' visit. It was for cover, making sure that Slvasta and Javier were seen by hundreds of witnesses, putting them beyond suspicion. Trevene's people were already alert for any sign of protests or demonstra-tions of solidarity for Jasmine Avenue, Bethaneve reported. She didn't want to give them the slightest excuse for arrests.

Slvasta conceded the logic in needing cover, even though he privately thought she was leaning towards paranoia. 'Javier's a stallholder now,' he told her. 'People aren't going to think he killed his own mod-apes.'

'Not now, no,' she said. The two of them had claimed a table by themselves for once, leaving Coulan and Javier to join a group of friends clustering round the arena. 'But when you two start to rise to prominence, the Captain's police will investigate you thoroughly. We need to be sure they don't find anything they can use to charge you with.'

A big cheer went up as a mod-dwarf and a pair of terriers were released into the arena. The mod-dwarf started to bleat with terror and tried to climb the smooth walls to escape. One of the terriers snapped its jaws around its foot.

'Uracus-be-damned,' Slvasta said. 'You really do think of everything, don't you?'

'Thinking ahead is the most important part of this. I'm good at it because it's logical – like the ultimate practical application of maths.'

'Yeah. So what do you extrapolate in our future?'

'You'll get elected to Nalani council, all right. I've got thirteen cells covertly campaigning for us, and there are over fifty union members and their families openly canvassing the vote. Democratic Unity will win a majority, and that puts us in charge of the borough. The Citizens' Dawn party won't know what hit it. Actually –' she grinned aggressively – 'they will. Two cell members work for them, and the feedback I've got is that the Nalani branch are already worried – so worried they haven't dared tell their district officers that they might lose to us.'

'Bethaneve.' Slvasta took her hand, and gazed right at her face with its slightly wild hair. Her cheeks were flushed from excitement and determination. 'I meant: what about us? You and me?' There was a real tumult in his mind. The quiet success they'd been having positioning themselves and their movement's activists was exhilarating. They'd built a clandestine organization that could accomplish acts of sabotage without the Captain's police realizing anything was amiss. His rage at injustice had taken on physical form, which was an almost frightening accomplishment, like discovering a new psychic power.

'Slvasta,' she said in dismay, 'you and me are what this is all for. So our children won't have to grow up in the same kind of world we did. How can you question this?'

'I'm sorry,' he said instantly. 'It's just that this is all happening so fast. I guess I get a little overwhelmed at times.'

A roar of jeering and chants broke out all around the cavernous old factory as the terriers finished off the mod-dwarf. People started clustering round the bookies. More drinks were ordered.

'I know what you mean,' she said, her shell dropping enough to show him the sympathy colouring her own thoughts. 'Sometimes I can't believe what we're doing, too. It's like—'

'Go on,' he urged.

'I'm not sure. We've done so much without the sheriffs or Trevene noticing. I sometimes think that maybe they have, that they're just waiting until we commit some really blatant act, then they'll have the excuse they want to give us life sentences at the Pidrui mines. And in a public court, too, not using some suspension order.'

'They'll make an example of us, you mean?'

'Probably?'

'If they were watching us, I'm pretty sure we'd know about it. We are being careful, and my paranoia is a big old beast.'

She touched her beer glass to his. 'You're the sensible one.'

'But you have made me wonder what happened to all the previous attempts to oust the Captain. There must have been some. I don't recall ever hearing about any in history class. Not that it was the greatest school on Bienvenido.'

'Apart from the Jasmine Avenue revolt I haven't heard of any. Coulan probably knows; he went to university, after all.'

'I'll have to ask him some time.'

'Do that.' She drained her beer in one.

'Another?'

'No.' She thrust her face towards him, not caring about the wisps of loose hair that slipped across her eyes. 'I think we should say crud to caution. We've been here at the bait as agreed. Everyone has seen us if the sheriffs ever ask them. So let's go home now. Just you and me. And I'll do my best to convince you how much you mean to me.'

'Sounds good,' he croaked.

*

At a quarter to four, Slvasta and Javier arrived at the Wellfield market, ostensibly to pick up the carts to take them to Plessey station as usual. As they drew closer, they could pick up the furious 'path shouts that were flying about under the long parallel roofs. Three sheriff's cabs were drawn up outside the main eastern side entrance. Two senior sheriffs were surrounded by a group of stallholders, all of whom were trying to shout over each other. Yalseed oil lamps on the iron pillars cast weak pools of illumination, revealing the corpses of several mod-apes lying in the aisles. When Slvasta followed up with a sweep of ex-sight, he perceived dozens more corpses lying in stall buildings and aisles right across the market. None of them had any surface injuries. They looked as if they were sleeping.

'Thank Giu you're here,' Pabel said, coming out to greet them. 'This is bad. Really bad.'

'What's happened?' Javier asked.

Slvasta was impressed. Not only did Javier sound puzzled, he even managed to affect considerable concern and interest.

'It's terrible,' Pabel said, leaking dismay into the aether. 'Someone's murdered all the market's mod-apes.'

'What?'

'It's true. A whole bunch of them ran through the market last night. They used teekay to kill every mod they could find, jabbed 'em inside the heart or the brain. It's . . . It's like . . .'

'A slaughterhouse?' Slvasta asked innocently.

Javier flashed a glare at him. 'Did they get our mod-apes?'

'Yes. I'm sorry, sir. I didn't turn up till after it'd happened. There was nothing I could do.'

'All right. Come on; let's see what the sheriffs have to say.'

The senior sheriffs were having a tough time saying anything. Even Ryszard, who ran the Wellfield's Meatcutter Guild, was having trouble getting the stallholders to calm down.

'Has anyone been threatened recently?' one of the sheriffs shouted.

Nobody had.

'Did the killers 'path anything when they came through? Anything that could identify them? A reason?'

They hadn't.

'Did anyone recognize any of them?'

All of the killers had been heavily fuzzed.

The sheriffs didn't seem to know what else to do or say.

'What do we do?' a stallholder called Calik asked Ryszard.

'We came through the train delivery crisis just fine,' Ryszard 'pathed strongly. 'This is no problem. We work a little harder ourselves this morning, and by tonight we'll all have ordered new mod-apes from the adaptor stables.'

'Will the guild insurance cover us for the cost of replacements?' Javier demanded.

'I, er . . .' a nervous Ryszard stammered. 'That will have to be looked into, but obviously all claims will be given a great deal of sympathy.'

'That's no answer,' someone else shouted.

'I pay my dues,' Javier said. 'We all do. What are they for if not for calamities like this?'

Ryszard gave him a glance of pure hatred. 'Can we all just keep calm, please? I've lost mod-apes, like everyone else.'

'Then give us the guild insurance.'

'I will do everything I can. And I will also be meeting with the chief sheriff to urge him to do whatever he can to catch these criminals.'

'Urge?' came a derisory 'path.

'Insist!' Ryszard sucked down an anxious breath. 'Now I am off to Plessey to collect my meat. I will not let this heinous crime beat me. And neither should you.'

'Politician,' Javier grumbled loudly as the guild leader hurried off towards his stall. Several of his fellow stallholders heard and muttered agreement.

Without mod-apes, everyone struggled to cut their orders

in time. Clients turned up, dismayed to see the mod-ape corpses lying round, but waited stoically for their orders to be completed.

Then men started to appear, asking if anyone wanted to employ them to help. Javier took on two, promising them work for a week. But first he sent them to Bryan-Anthony, the leader of the newly formed Wellfield union, to sign on with the organization. Other stallholders grumbled about him setting a bad example. Few followed his lead. By mid-morning, several stall-holders had gone off to visit nearby adaptor stables and buy themselves new mod-apes. That was when they received their second shock of the day.

*

'Every adaptor stable?' Captain Philious asked in astonishment. He was standing in the garden room at the rear of the palace. It resembled a small Hellenic temple, but with glass sheets filling the gaps between the pillars, then curving back and merging to form a seamless roof. That glass was supposedly the last thing ever manufactured by the ship's machines before they failed. Philious believed that; the glass was ancient, yet still stronger than any metal made in Bienvenido's foundries today.

'Yes, sir,' Trevene replied. 'The owners have been keeping very quiet about it, of course. But once the first couple of rumours leaked out, I had my people investigate thoroughly. The Adaptor Guild was *reluctant* to cooperate, but I insisted. There isn't a neut in the city that hasn't been sterilized.'

'Crud!' Philious made an effort to keep his temper. He looked out across the lawns where the annual afternoon garden party was underway. Varlan's aristocracy and wealthiest merchants, all dressed in their finery, sipping tea as they waited for the Captain's family to walk among them and murmur thanks for supporting the regimental widows and orphans fund. 'How could such a thing happen? Is it a disease?'

'No. This is deliberate. Three separate vets confirm it. Teekay destroyed their ovaries.'

'Every one?' he repeated incredulously. 'But there must be thousands.'

'Yes, sir.'

'Crud.' Philious stopped gazing at all the society girls with their colourful dresses cut to show off cleavage and legs. 'Who did it?'

'I'm investigating that.'

'Investigating? That's it? That's your reply? There's never been a crime this big before. You're the chief of my police, for fuck's sake! How can you not know? There must have been something? Dammit, half this city spies for you; the other half is terrified of you. You must know!'

'This is something new, something different.'

'What do you mean?'

Trevene pushed his glasses up his nose. 'It could be a rival adaptor guild, Uracus knows there's no love lost between any of them. But, as you rightly pointed out, the level of this goes beyond anything we've seen before. I can't believe this is the work of jealous competitors seeking to take advantage of the city stables' misfortune with high prices. I believe this has to be political.'

'Political? Are you serious? The radicals at the university are dumb middle-class children playing at being important. As soon as they get their degrees they go home to work for daddy. And Shanty-dwellers are thicker than mod-ape shit. They couldn't organize a fuck in a brothel, let alone this.'

'Indeed. As I said, sir, this is different.'

'Crud!' Philious's anger drained away as fast as it had risen. 'So who are we left with?'

'There are new workers' unions springing up across town. And yesterday a team of unknowns rampaged though the Wellfield market, killing all the mods. Every one of them. It was butchery, plain and simple. An interesting coincidence, considering the people who will most benefit from the shortage of new mods will be the working class.'

'And the Wellfield is unionized now?'

'One of the first, yes.'

Philious realized he was actually smiling. 'Clever. It would seem we have someone dissatisfied with my rule.'

'Yes, sir.'

'A hundred years since Jasmine Avenue, too. Which speaks to me of small minds with big memories. How very apt. This is going to be interesting.'

'I expect so,' Trevene said impassively.

'Right. I want to know who they are. Do you understand? You infiltrate them, you find their names and what they're planning next. Giu, this attack on neuts is going to hit the city's economy hard. That's all we need right after the Josi bridge disaster.' He gave Trevene a sharp glance. 'Was that part of this?'

'Unlikely. It was an old bridge.'

'Nonetheless . . .'

'I'll look into it.'

'There's going to be unrest, no matter what we do to the leaders, and this time it won't be limited to the Shanties.'

'I'll speak to the captains of the sheriff stations.'

'Do that. And I'll call in the First Speaker. He needs to knock heads together in the Adaptor Guild. Our priority must be to restock the stables. Dammit, my estate has shares in several of them.' He squared his shoulders and returned his attention to the genteel throng walking all over his lawns in high heels. His wife was over by one of the fountains, chatting to a group of old women in hats that were mostly plumage. 'I'd better get back out there before my sons claim all the fuckable daughters for tonight.'

3

'Look at this,' Coulan said, slapping down a copy of the *Hilltop Eye* on the table as he came in that evening.

The pamphlet had broken the story about the sterile neuts.

'They got everything,' Coulan continued. 'How there hasn't been a new mod in the city for a month now. How the stables have been conspiring to keep quiet about it. They've told the whole story.'

'I should hope they have,' Bethaneve said indignantly. 'We keep feeding the pamphlets enough information. I'm never really sure how good our connection to them is. Does it say what the stables are doing about the neut shortage?'

'No. But *Hilltop Eye* also found out that the towns around Varlan have the same problem. The stables are going to have to import from the regions we haven't reached.'

'That'll cost them,' Bethaneve said in satisfaction.

'But the mods will return,' Coulan said, 'and now the stables will be on their guard against the neuts being sterilized again.'

'We'll be in power by then,' Slvasta said.

'In Nalani borough council,' Bethaneve retorted scathingly. 'Our timing was all wrong. We should have been winning elections in district councils before we hit the neuts.'

Javier clapped his hands down on both their shoulders. 'I say this is fortuitous timing. Tomorrow morning, every stallholder in Wellfield is going to be taking on new workers. Human workers.'

'That are all going to become union members,' Slvasta said. 'And there were more mod-apes than humans at the Wellfield.'

'Uracus, the unemployed will be out there tonight asking for work if they have any sense,' Coulan said. 'We have to make sure they all know to sign on with the union.'

'I don't,' Javier said. 'I'm a stallholder now, one of the oppressor class.' He smirked. 'Slvasta should go.'

'Bryan-Anthony knows what to do,' Slvasta said. 'He's at the Wellfield right now, with several loyal union supporters, making it very clear to stallholders that any new cutter has to be signed up with the union first.'

'And Ryszard is still at the sheriff station,' Coulan said. 'There's some senior Citizens' Dawn members there as well; two of them came along from the district headquarters. People in high places are getting very nervous about the Nalani borough elections.'

'Now, there's a sentence you don't often hear,' Bethaneve said with a relaxed smile.

'It's still three weeks away,' Slvasta said. 'There's a lot can go wrong before that.'

She shook her head ruefully. 'You're such an optimist.'

'Anyway, Javier and I are off to Coval Road tonight. We're addressing a meeting, pulling in a few more voters.'

'Isn't the Ellington pub on Coval Road?' Bethaneve asked.

'Life is a constant Uracus for us politicians.'

*

Even though it was election day, Slvasta still kept to the usual routine. Up early, take a cart with Pabel to Plessey station to collect the day's meat. Back to Wellfield to package it for customers. He didn't get to vote until after midday.

His local voting station had set up in a shabby old community hall on Footscray Avenue, just round the corner from Tarleton Gardens. A bored, uniformed sheriff standing outside nodded impassively as he went through the doorway.

The election officials had set up five voting booths inside. Two women were sitting behind a desk, with a huge leather-bound voting ledger. The line to vote stretched the length of the hall, which apparently was rare. Normally turnout was about twenty per cent. Slvasta joined the queue. One or two people recognized him as a candidate and nodded or grinned. It took five minutes for him to reach the desk; the line behind him was still back to the door. 'Busy?' he said to the woman who checked his name off before handing him a voting slip. She gave him a disapproving look and beckoned the next voter forward.

As he drew the flimsy curtain across the booth he realized how much he wanted Bethaneve here with him, how much nicer it would have been for them to have voted together. But she was busy, and appearances must be kept to protect themselves from discovery and danger. Slvasta looked down at the voting sheet. There were eight parties competing to run Nalani's borough council. Citizens' Dawn and Democratic Unity were the largest and best organized, followed by the usual collection of eccentric independent candidates who had some burning local issue to promote. It was an unusually large number. Even some of the pamphlets they didn't have contacts with had noted it. Everyone was interested in the emergence of a workers' union again. Many thought Bryan-Anthony was a political genius for developing a political base so quickly.

It was a strange feeling, seeing his own name on the ballot. This, then, was the leap into the abyss, he thought; after this there can be no going back. He just had to have the courage – another reason he wished Bethaneve was here. How she would scorn his pathetic doubts. He closed his eyes, and saw Ingmar's face.

I was weak before. I will not be again.

He placed his cross against his own party, pressing the pencil down hard so it left a firm dark mark that could never be disputed.

The world outside was so ordinary for such a momentous day. Bright sunlight shone down, prickling his face as he left the hall. A few high strands of cloud ribbed the sapphire sky above the city. As Slvasta started down Footscray Avenue, he saw a man at the end of the road, sitting on a bench which gave him a perfect view of everyone going into the hall. He'd been there when Slvasta walked to the hall as well: ordinary clothes, ordinary features, unobtrusively reading a gazette. Not quite fuzzed, but giving off a subtle psychic impression of insignificance. A tiny 'path that wheedled: *ignore me*, just below conscious thought – unless you hunted for the emanation.

A small smile lifted Slvasta's lips and he scanned round with his ex-sight. Sure enough, there was a mod-bird perched on a chimney stack, its keen eyes gazing along Footscray Avenue, exposing the road's traffic to its hidden owner.

So you are worried about us, Slvasta thought as he walked past the watcher, studiously disregarding him. *As you should be.*

4

Looking round the Nalani council chamber, Slvasta wasn't quite sure they'd won such a big victory after all. The chamber had a pretty standard layout, but degraded by age and cheapened by generations of dispirited councillors. Those councillors who did turn up sat in rows at long benches, facing a dais from which the mayor ran the proceedings. The wood panelling on the walls was old and dark, helping to amplify the gloom, while the glass cupola in the middle of the roof was so grimy it barely let any light through. The borough clerk had given Slvasta a copy of the council's current financial accounts. Which, after one of the most depressing hours of his life reading it, Slvasta was surprised the council could afford to print in the first place.

Bethaneve and Coulan were up in the public gallery, along with over a hundred Democratic Unity supporters and several reporters from gazettes across the city. Slvasta winked up at Bethaneve just as the county clerk called the meeting to order. First order of business was to appoint a new mayor. Out of the seventeen seats, fourteen had been won by Democratic Unity, with Citizens' Dawn keeping just two, while one had gone to an independent road-improvement campaigner. Bryan-Anthony was nominated to be mayor, and quickly seconded. The vote was unanimous, and Bryan-Anthony walked up to the dais amid a lot of cheering and applause from the public gallery. He was given the robe with its fur-lined collar, and a heavy gold chain of office.

Then he was sworn in as a faithful and loyal subject of the Captain, an oath he recited without any trace of irony.

'Well done,' Slvasta muttered under his breath. Bryan-Anthony was a good choice as their frontman, though he was impressively passionate about the cause, with a heated radical streak which too often manifested in tirades against authority, especially after a few pints. But tonight he was stone-cold sober – Javier had made sure about that.

There was an official agenda for the meeting, starting with the appointment of new councillors to the borough's various portfolios. Slvasta himself was given the office responsible for drain and sewer maintenance (which gave him access to a lot of information on the water utilities), and a second portfolio for the maintenance of public trees. Bryan-Anthony even graciously allocated one of the Citizens' Dawn councillors the office which was responsible for licensing the borough's cabs.

Then there was a debate on the accounts. Five Democratic Unity councillors spoke condemning the financial state which the last council had left the borough in. 'We're effectively bankrupt,' one stormed.

At which both Citizens' Dawn councillors stomped out. Cue booing and jeers from Democratic Unity supporters in the public gallery.

It was agreed to form a special task force to review finances and the options available, which would report back to the full council in a week. Slvasta was one of the five members of the task force. It was tough keeping his shell hard enough to contain his dismay.

'I now open the floor to any new business,' Bryan-Anthony said.

'I would like to propose a licence suspension,' Jerill said.

The crowd in the public gallery finally perked up. Slvasta kept his face and mind composed, while inside he was praying to Giu that Jerill wouldn't screw up; they'd certainly spent long enough briefing him for this moment.

'I represent a ward with, like, a great load of . . . um . . .

unemployment,' Jerill continued, glancing round edgily. 'Them families live under a . . . er . . . hardship unknown and unrecognized in them boroughs stuffed with rich toffs. Nothing is done for them. The sheriffs are bloody harsh when any of us, like, fall behind on our rent. The city doesn't give a toss for us. Well, I do care, see, for I know what hardship is really like. Er . . . Yeah, I was elected to help the poorest folks, and that is what I will do, no matter what vested interests I have to fight.'

Jerill was given a couple of loud whoops from the public gallery. Slvasta wished they'd given him a shorter speech; the man wasn't the best orator, and clearly hadn't rehearsed enough.

'In light of that, mayor, I would urge this council to support a moratorium on issuing any further mod-keeping licences for newly purchased mods in this borough. If, and only if, full human employment is restored, then we can consider approving any new licences.'

They didn't get it. Slvasta smirked to himself as he glanced round the blank and puzzled faces in the public gallery. The only one smiling was Bethaneve. But then, she was the one who discovered there was a city-wide law that said you needed a licence to own and keep a mod, with every borough responsible for enforcing it within their boundary.

The law had been introduced by Captain Ephraim two thousand five hundred years ago, when mods were nothing like as common as they were today. It had never been repealed, but as mod usage increased, the licence fee was reduced under political pressure from adaptor stables and business owners and most householders, until eventually the cost of collecting the fees far outweighed the monies it raised. It remained purely as a historical quirk on the statute book, along with other relics like the Brocklage Square horseshoe tax or the Taylor Avenue flower tithe.

As Bethaneve told them, an existing law – especially one as old as this – could never be challenged legally. All the council had to do was carry out its duty and enforce the law. And, as no one had a licence, the next stage was going to be setting the licence fee and forcing people to apply for the mods they already had. The money due would solve the borough's financial woes at a stroke – providing they could collect it, of course. But there were plenty of unemployed people who would relish the job of licence regulation officer – especially when they were encouraged by the cells and the unions.

The proposal was seconded, and passed.

That was when Slvasta caught sight of him. The same man who'd been sitting on Footscray Avenue. He was standing at the back, not far from Bethaneve. His eyes were narrowed slightly, as if he was just coming to the realization of what had happened.

*

Trevene stood in his usual place, between the two plush chairs in front of the Captain's desk, waiting while Philious absorbed that latest news. Delivering unwelcome announcements was becoming a habit he didn't like. He was reacting to events, not controlling them as he should be.

The last few weeks had seen some definite progress. His informants had embedded themselves in both the Wellfield union and Democratic Unity, they'd even been out on the streets canvassing for votes. Two of the newly elected Democratic Unity councillors belonged to him. There was nothing the party said or planned at their meetings that he did not know about within the hour.

But that was one of his biggest problems. Nothing Democratic Unity did was surprising or relevant. They were a political party for poor people, which was rare enough, but apart from having absurd quantities of ambition and deluded goals of rivalling Citizens' Dawn and becoming a major opposition party, they weren't planning anything untoward. That left him with what they'd come to call *the core*: Slvasta, Bethaneve, Javier and Coulan. He'd built comprehensive files on all of them. Had them under constant surveillance. Interviewed people who used to know them before they turned political. Slvasta was the key, of course. A good ex-officer (he'd read the reports from the Cham regiment, and how his diligence was a problem for them) galvanized by his friend

Arnice's death. Which, when Trevene read the Justice Office file, he had to agree with Slvasta, was a phenomenal act of stupidity on officialdom's part. The others were basically a support group to their leader – and Slvasta was smart enough to keep in the background. Bryan-Anthony, for all his good intentions, was a simple figurehead.

It was the core who planned everything in private, who pulled the strings that controlled Democratic Unity and the ever-expanding unions. They were impressively good at it, too. Slvasta was clearly a natural politician. Trevene had even slipped into a public meeting in a pub to observe the man first hand. By the end there was no doubting Slvasta's genuine commitment to improving life for the underdog.

It was the methods that were proving a giant headache.

Captain Philious looked up from the file Trevene had delivered. 'But . . . I never signed an order to license mods.'

'No sir. That was Captain Ephraim.'

'Er, which . . . ?'

'Two thousand years ago. He was Captain for seven years. Not terribly remarkable, by all accounts. Unfortunately, his law hasn't been removed from the statute books. It's still valid. Nobody has bothered enforcing it for centuries.'

'Oh crud!' Philious dropped the file on his desk and slumped back in his chair. After a moment's contemplation, a grin of admiration lifted his thin lips. 'He's good, isn't he?'

'Yes, sir.'

'Shame, he'd make a superb First Speaker for me.'

'Slvasta has his own agenda. It's not one which embraces you or me.'

'So I'll just remove the assent from poor old Captain Ephraim's mod licence. Take the wind out of Slvasta's sails.'

'That's an option, of course, sir.'

'Ah, here we go. What would your advice be?'

'They're a one-borough protest party, unregarded by the rest of Varlan, let alone Bienvenido. Cancelling the mod licence calls their action to prominence. It says you're worried about Citizens'

Dawn being challenged. The Captaincy mustn't be seen to be dabbling in grubby politics.'

Philious gave him a curious look. 'Do nothing? Look out there.' The Captain's arm gestured at the big windows overlooking Walton Boulevard. It was night outside, with nebula light effervescing out of a cloudless sky. Their gentle radiance shimmered on the rooftops. Windows glowed yellow. 'No streetlights. For the first time in thousands of years, Varlan's lights are going out. And its my Captaincy! This wretched *core* has done that. But that's a mild disaster compared to what I'm reading in the Treasury reports. Prices are rising, banks are nervous. That cannot stand. We need the new neuts the guild is arranging to bring in, and we need the mods they'll produce. Unrestricted, unlicensed mods.'

'Yes. But this clever little manoeuvre of theirs confirms what I've said all along: the core is behind the whole neut situation. Slvasta has a weakness: he is obsessed by Fallers and mods. It consumes him – understandably. That is what ultimately lies behind all this.'

'Then he should have stayed in the regiment; fought the Fallers head on.'

'But he didn't, sir. And we have to deal with him. He and his friends have become public figures. Not so easy to quietly dispose of any more. Questions would be asked. Nobody wants a martyr.'

'What, then?'

'They have made their move. It is a public message of defiance to you personally. We have to make a counter-move. Make them understand this is not some easy game. They must be taught there are consequences to challenging the authority of the Captain.'

'Very well. Send them a message. And Trevene, make it a firm one.'

'Yes, sir.'

5

'We did it.' Bethaneve said. 'We started it.'

It was half an hour after the end of the council meeting, and the four of them were sitting in the garden at the back of the Bellaview pub on the other side of Tarleton Gardens from their flat. Four beers on the table, and a mild fuzz around them to prevent any eavesdropping. Clouds were beginning to thicken in the twilight sky above.

'A good beginning,' Javier agreed. 'But now our biggest task is to keep the momentum going.'

'The word is out with every cell,' Bethaneve said. 'There's going to be a lot of dead mods across this city by the end of the week.'

'The sheriffs are going to be busy,' Coulan said thoughtfully. 'They'll work out there's an organization of some kind behind it. And, as it all started with the Wellfield, I expect they'll start poking around.'

'Maybe not,' Bethaneve said. 'Once you've struck a spark, some fires flash out of control. If all the unemployed see that dead mods mean jobs for them, we won't have to keep feeding the cells with orders to kill. It'll start to happen naturally.'

'I like it,' Coulan said. 'The sheriffs might blame Nalani council for the spark, but the deaths will look spontaneous. They won't be interested in us.'

'Someone already is,' Slvasta said. 'And it ain't the sheriffs.' He told them about the observer he'd spotted.

'Uracus!' Coulan exclaimed. 'He was really standing that close to me in the public gallery?'

'Yes.'

'You should have warned me.'

'Why, what would you have done? Turned and stared? How would that help?'

'Is he here now?' Bethaneve asked.

Slvasta took his time and looked round the pub garden. At one time it might indeed have had a view, but now the only thing behind the garden was a high stone wall covered in viricote vines whose large papery white flowers were furling up now the sun had gone. 'Not him, no,' Slvasta confirmed, checking all the tables. 'But if they're smart they'll rotate their watchers so we don't start to recognize them.'

'You already have,' Coulan said.

'I was lucky, or they got careless. It's not something we can count on.'

'You're implying they have a big team on us,' Bethaneve said in a subdued tone.

'If they're watching us already, then we are in trouble,' Javier said. 'If they're watching anyone, it should be Bryan-Anthony. He's really embracing his role as chief radical. Even I believed he's in charge, the way he ran that meeting.'

'About that meeting,' Bethaneve said. 'Next time you introduce a proposal, make sure the speech is better rehearsed. It was painful listening to Jerill.'

'Yes, but it made him sound honest. A natural first-time request, well intentioned and guileless. Nobody wants professional politicians taking over Democratic Unity right now.'

'I'm not saying professional, just a little more coherent.'

'We'll all grow into the role.'

Slvasta 'pathed an order to the barman for another round.

'We have to be careful,' Bethaneve said. 'This is a critical time. We have to get a groundswell of support behind us. So far, all we control is one of the poorest boroughs in Varlan. And the next round of elections isn't for another eight months.'

'Is there a time when it won't be "critical"?' Javier asked.

Bethaneve raised her glass and gave him an amused glance over the rim. 'I can't think of one.'

*

The second Nalani council meeting was much more boisterous than the first. They'd been expecting that. What the gazettes were condemning as the slaughter of the mods had taken on a fervour that left even Slvasta and Bethaneve surprised and not a little concerned. The cells had been told to limit their killing to the mods used by business, but no one else felt that constraint. Household mods were targeted with as much glee as those in commerce. In some of the wealthier boroughs, sheriffs were patrolling all the roads leading into the area, demanding proof of residency before they let pedestrians and cabs through. Citizens were determined to keep undesirables out – a policy which quickly resulted in a few ugly incidents when the sheriffs were overzealous. Pamphlets and 'path gossip feasted on those for days.

Then there was the problem of the bodies. Dead mods were simply thrown out onto the streets. Bussalores emerged from their secluded warrens; people reported packs of the sleek rodents swarming over this bounty of rotting food. They became brave protecting their carrion, snapping at human children. Tatus flies formed huge clouds that clogged the air along alleys and narrow streets. Public health was becoming a serious issue.

Bryan-Anthony's opening statement was that the borough considered clearing the bodies away to be the highest priority. Twenty new human workers would be taken on to clear the streets.

'How will you pay for them?' asked Oriol, one of the Citizens' Dawn councillors.

'I propose charging one shilling for each mod-licence,' Jerill said. 'That should see a considerable rise in the borough's income.'

'Your lot are killing all the mods,' Oriol shouted back. 'There won't be any left to buy a licence for, you cretin! You didn't work that out before you started this, did you?'

'Keep it civil, councillor, please,' Bryan-Anthony said.

'Five of my mods have been murdered by your supporters. Is that civil? I will be ruined!'

'Employ a human,' someone shouted from the gallery.

'Criminal scum,' came the answering shout.

Bryan-Anthony started banging his gavel as the shouting and accusations in the gallery grew louder and more heated. 'Order, please. Order!'

Insults were followed up by mild teekay jabs. They didn't stay mild for long. A full-scale brawl broke out. The sheriffs were called.

It took twenty minutes, but the public gallery was cleared and the rest of the meeting was conducted without any physical observers. As no closed sessions were permitted in Varlan, the borough clerk allowed any interested party to see and hear through her senses.

'Did not expect that,' Slvasta admitted as they walked home.

'We should have done,' Bethaneve said. 'After all, the whole point of getting rid of mods was to hit people where it hurts most: in the wallet. Start taking money away from the privileged, and they can turn just as savage as any animal that gets shoved into Philippa's arena.'

Her nose wrinkled up as they turned onto Onslo Road. It was a commercial street with plenty of shops and businesses. Dead mods were piled in the gutter, although the corpses were hard to see without ex-sight. None of Onslo Road's streetlights had been lit; the only illumination came from the nebulas and the occasional upper-floor window. Mod-dwarfs made up most of the capital's lamplighter teams, and they'd proved an easy target. Gossip 'path claimed that less than twenty per cent of the city's lamps were currently being lit at night.

They hurried along the pavement. The dark mounds in the gutter shifted about as if they were ripples on some murky lake, emitting slithering sounds as they sloshed against the kerb stones. To begin with, Slvasta thought the bodies weren't quite dead, then a quick sweep with his ex-sight showed him they were all smothered by dozens of bussalores – big brutes, he perceived in dismay; he'd always assumed rodents that size were an urban myth, but then they'd enjoyed plenty to eat this last week.

His arm tightened round Bethaneve's shoulder, and they all hurried along.

'We really will have to do something about this,' Javier said, clamping his hand over his nose to ward off some of the stench.

'Another unintended consequence,' Bethaneve 'pathed as she held her breath. 'It's too expensive to pay humans to light the streetlamps and refill them again in the morning. Maybe we should start to put in some exemptions in the licensing ban.'

'It wouldn't matter any more,' Javier said. 'The streetlight companies couldn't afford new mods right now. Have you seen what a three-month-old mod-dwarf is going for today? That's if you can import one. The sheriffs are talking about providing armed guards when stables bring them into the city.'

'It's starting to hit the economy, too,' Coulan said. 'Food prices are going up.'

'I could have told you that would happen,' Slvasta said. 'All the Wellfield stalls have raised their prices. We had no choice; people cost more to employ.'

'Wages will have to rise to take that into account,' Bethaneve said. 'Which, of course, they won't. Maybe Nalani should intro-duce a minimum wage level?'

'No,' Slvasta said. 'We have to be realistic. Even if we could enforce it, every shop owner and business would challenge it in the courts, which would just shut down the borough's commercial affairs. That would cause even more hardship.'

'Okay,' she said. 'That will have to come after, when we can enforce it planet-wide.'

'Good call,' Slvasta said. Once again he was impressed and disturbed by her devotion to the cause.

*

A squad of sheriffs were waiting in the Wellfield market when Slvasta and Ervin drove their carts back from Plessey station. Five of them were standing round Javier's stall, strong shells preventing any emotional leakage.

Slvasta saw Javier standing in front of the main display cabinets, in deep conversation with the squad's sergeant.

'Get the carts unloaded, please,' Slvasta told Ervin and the new workers as he pulled up outside the store rooms. 'I'll see what's going on.'

Javier gave him a tight smile as he went over. 'This is Sergeant Becker. He needs us to identify someone.'

'Identify?' Slvasta said.

'If you wouldn't mind, please, councillor?' Becker said. He was in his late sixties, a rotund man with a big walrus moustache. The polite yet firm attitude told Slvasta he was a career sheriff used to dealing with human extremes.

'I'll be happy to help the sheriffs,' Slvasta said.

All that earned him was a quiet grunt. Three of the squad fell in behind them as they walked out of the Wellfield to a couple of cabs waiting outside.

'Are we under arrest?' Slvasta asked.

'No, sir. My men are here for your protection.'

When Slvasta checked with Javier, all the big man could do was shrug.

Doyce Street was barely ten minutes away. Slvasta had a bad feeling as they pulled up outside an old tenement. He remembered Doyce Street, and couldn't think why. More worrying, his ex-sight caught a glimpse of mod-bird circling high overhead. It wasn't just the sheriffs involved in this . . . whatever this was.

Two sheriffs stood guard outside one of the tenements. They opened the door to allow Becker through. He tried not to let any censure show through his shell, but the place was bleak. Bare brick walls whose mortar was eroding to fine sand which drifted down the walls to contaminate the floorboards. Odd stains discoloured bricks at random. Long, poorly lit corridors of doors on every floor looked like the image created by two mirrors reflecting each other, they were so monotonous. Identical doors opened into single-room lodgings; communal bathrooms at the end of each corridor were ornamented by leaking pipes and cracked basins. Cool air was heavy with the smell of sewers that drained badly. It was all a stark reminder of the life he was barely avoiding by living with his friends, of how every farthing from his wage was important.

They followed Becker up to the third floor. Slvasta didn't need any ex-sight to know there was death in the miserable lodgings Becker finally showed them to. An eerie sensation of gloom pervaded the walls, so much so that Slvasta wondered if there was a tortured soul clinging to the building's structure. The drab cube of a room had paper on the walls, so ancient and damp it was barely more than a grey skin of mould. There were just two pieces of furniture: an iron-framed bed and a recently repaired bussalore-proof wooden chest full of clothes. Tall piles of extremist political pamphlets cluttered the floor, their curling pages yellow and damp.

A body was sprawled on the bed. A lot of blood had seeped out of the multiple knife wounds to soak into the mattress and drip onto the floorboards. Two bright oil lamps had been set up by a coroner's assistant who was waiting patiently, reading a copy of *Hilltop Eye*. He rolled the pamphlet up when Becker showed them in.

Slvasta looked at the body then hurriedly looked away, fighting the urge to throw up.

'Sorry about that,' Becker said in a detached voice. 'The bussalores had chewed quite a lot of his face before we arrived. They're getting bold right now. I guess that's what eating well does for them.'

'Crudding Uracus,' Javier grunted.

'If you wouldn't mind, gentlemen, I would like a formal identification, please. You were his colleagues.'

Slvasta clamped his teeth together and made himself look at the body again. The facial features – even with half of the skin missing – were easy enough to place. And the bussalores hadn't touched his hair. 'Sweet Giu. It's Bryan-Anthony.'

'Are you sure, sir?' Becker asked.

'Yes.'

'Thank you. And you, sir?'

'It's the mayor, yes,' Javier said.

'Officially confirmed.' The coroner's assistant scrawled something on his clipboard. 'Thank you, gentlemen.'

'What happened?' Javier said.

'As far as I can make out, it was a teekay violation in his cranium during sleep,' the coroner's assistant said. 'There's a small but noticeable tear inside the frontal lobe, with no corresponding external trauma.'

'But the stab wounds . . .'

'Done immediately following death. Presumably to make a point. Whoever did this didn't want us to write it off as a misidentified mod killing.' He pulled back the blanket. The words UNION WAGE had been sliced into Bryan-Anthony's chest.

'Crud,' Slvasta exclaimed.

'Did anyone sense his soul?' Javier asked.

'No, he's ascended to Giu,' the coroner's assistant said. 'I couldn't find his soul when I arrived. If they can resist the song of Giu, then the souls of murder victims tend to linger long enough to tell us who killed them. That's why my profession has to have a very sensitive ex-sight.'

'My station commander would like to meet you now,' Becker said. 'He wants to talk about giving all of you sheriff bodyguards.'

'All of us?' Javier asked. Who's us?'

'Democratic Unity councillors.'

'I see,' Javier said. 'Tell him we'll be happy to meet him later today. I must discuss this with my colleagues first.'

Becker glanced down at the corpse, then back at Javier. 'As you wish. Do you have any idea who might have done this?'

'No. but we both know a lot of business people aren't happy with our party right now. Do you have any leads?'

'No, sir, none. We only found out about the body a couple of hours ago. The bussalores made enough noise to wake a neighbour; she used her ex-sense and found his body.'

'Body temperature gives me an approximate time of death around midnight,' the coroner's assistant said.

'I see.'

'Where were you at midnight, sir?' Becker asked.

'You can't be serious?'

'Murder is as serious as it gets, sir. It would help if we could eliminate you from our inquiries.'

'I was at home. My partner Coulan will confirm that. As will Slvasta.'

'Indeed. So you all live at the same address?'

'Yes.'

'That's very convenient. Did anyone else witness you going home?'

'The neighbours, probably.'

'Of course. I'll check with them. Routine, you understand.'

'Yes,' Slvasta said. 'I understand very well.'

*

Bethaneve was getting ready for work when Slvasta and Javier arrived back at the Tarleton Gardens flat.

'Dead?' she asked incredulously. 'Bryan-Anthony is dead?'

'Yes.'

'Oh, great Giu.' She clung to Slvasta, struggling to keep her grief and fear under control. 'Who did it?'

'The sheriffs don't know.'

'Ha!'

'They don't,' Javier said. 'Not the ones who talked to us, anyway. They were just the locals. The Captain's police wouldn't include them in anything.'

'You think *they* did it?' she asked.

'I don't know.'

Slvasta's ex-sense showed him Coulan hurrying up the stairs. When he burst into the room he was carrying three gazettes.

'Bryan-Anthony—' Javier began.

'I know,' Coulan waved the gazettes above his head. 'They're all leading with the story.'

Slvasta gave Javier a concerned look. 'That was very quick. When do they print?'

'Middle of the night, so they can get them on the racks by breakfast.'

Bethaneve had grabbed a gazette from Coulan. 'This is awful,' she said. 'They're saying it was poetic justice, that the anti-mod league mistook him for a mod-ape. What anti-mod league?'

'This one says that he was skimming union funds,' Javier said. 'And that the union is a gangster organization that murdered him because he wasn't paying the gang bosses their full cut. Bastards!' He scrunched up the gazette.

'The union doesn't have any funds,' Slvasta protested.

'What did you expect?' Coulan looked round at them. 'Welcome to the opening salvo. You wanted the Captain's attention, and you got it.'

'They killed him!' Bethaneve said.

'And we want to overthrow them. Do you think that's going to happen without blood being spilt? How did you think this would play out, that they'd just hand over the keys to the palace? So far it's all gone our way. Last night it didn't. We knew it was dangerous being a frontman in this city; that's why we pushed Bryan-Anthony out there. And it's going to happen to the next guy, and probably the one after. This is a war. You know that. So now it's our turn to strike back. The pamphlets are on our side, so we get them to counter all the crud Trevene's people are peddling to the gazettes. People aren't *stupid*; they're going to realize there was something wrong about Bryan-Anthony's death. And next Tuesday we can use that to our advantage.'

Slvasta nodded, though he felt bad. They had known it would be dangerous fronting Democratic Unity. But this . . . It was shocking, being reminded just how high the stakes were, how serious this was. He couldn't even call it a game. Not any more, not now he had blood on his hands. 'So are we still doing this?'

'Fuck, yes,' Bethaneve snapped.

6

The Eastern Trans-Continental Line was one of the four principal railway lines which stretched out from Varlan to cover most of the Lamaran continent. From Doncastor station in the heart of the city, it ran north for nearly a thousand miles to Adice before heading due east for another two and a half thousand miles across the continent's central lands to Portlynn at the bottom of Nillson Sound – the vital spine of a hundred branch lines (themselves substantial) that nurtured the economy of the cities and towns that cluttered the provinces.

It wasn't just Lamaran's economy that was dependent on its railways; it was such a vast continent there was no other way the human society it hosted could hold together under one governmental authority. As Slvasta's cabal had discovered, organizing anything at a distance was tough. To date their influence didn't extend outside the capital, and even there they had no traction in the wealthier boroughs. As a result, Varlan's beleaguered adaptor stables had only to travel a few hundred miles along the tracks to find stables with plentiful stocks of neuts.

Those county stables that suddenly found themselves on the receiving end of bountiful orders to resupply the city with female neuts soon realized their advantage and hiked their prices up. It was a seller's market. Varlan's Adaptor Guild gritted its collective teeth and paid. The guild president also insisted that the new stocks be guarded; he was very firm about that, and the Captain's private estate owned quite a few shares in the adaptor business. So all the roads around Doncastor station goods yard were closed at six o'clock on Tuesday morning. Every sheriff from the surrounding five boroughs was on duty at the station to reinforce the barricades. More sheriffs were deployed at the station to escort the animal wagons back to their stables.

The Adaptor Guild had arranged a train of thirty cattle trucks, each containing fifty new female neuts. It was enough stock to refill every stable in the city, and to restart mod breeding. Already the stables were being strengthened – fortified, according to the pamphlets – by surviving mod-apes and human labourers. Men with strong teekay were being employed as guards, most of them brought in from outside Varlan to be sure they weren't tainted by this new anti-mod fanaticism infecting the city.

Gossip 'path began as soon as the sheriffs started to put up the barricades. By seven o'clock everyone awake in Varlan knew the train was due in today.

Bethaneve sent a private 'path to five people. It was forwarded to eight more. Then seventeen. Forty-three . . .

Cell members began to agitate each sympathizer they knew to go and protest. People with newfound jobs. People who were now unionized and anticipating higher wages. People who'd realized that their lives would have more opportunity without mods. And, as always, the ones spoiling for a fight, any fight. They all converged on Doncastor station as the sun rose over the city and the night's river mist burnt away.

Cab drivers outside the borough refused to take anyone there, no matter if they had legitimate train tickets. Cabs already in the borough headed out.

Bethaneve took up position a quarter of a mile away from the station, sitting in a little café on Rycotte Street. Her ex-sight located Slvasta, Javier and Coulan, all of whom were closer to the station, but at the rear of the swelling crowds. She sent out quick private 'paths to each of them, checking they were in range. In turn, they were in contact with all the level two, three, four, and five cells, and confirmed their location. Those cells were the cut-offs, inactive and unseen, they'd never be asked to perform any physical action, never do anything to draw Trevene's attention. They were the communications strata, in touch with dozens upon dozens of other cells scattered throughout the crowd, relaying orders and receiving observations. Her mind held the beautiful geometry of inter-cell communications, positioning them in her ex-sense visualization of the area.

'Are we ready?' Slvasta 'pathed at half past nine.

Bethaneve sipped her hot chocolate and picked up a gazette, the perfect image of an innocent bystander. 'We're ready.'

'Then let's do this.'

The train pulled in to the goods yard at eleven minutes past ten. It was greeted by stable owners from across the city. All of them had caged wagons to transport the female neuts, most of them hurriedly altered with planks of wood affixed to the bars, offering a flimsy level of protection and anonymity to the animals they were intended to transport. Waiting alongside the wagons were guards, tough men whose loyalty was to the shiniest coin.

Bethaneve sent out some instructions, sensing them dissipate across the cells. Several mod-birds fell from the sky, striking rooftops with nasty thuds – dead long before they landed. The remaining mod-birds started to flap hurriedly away from the area, withdrawn by their owners.

*

Excitement and animosity began to build in the crowd waiting outside the barricades – a psychic wave that washed across the station and began to unnerve the placid neuts. As they were led out of the cattle trucks and into the boarded-up wagons, they began to buck about, anxious to escape this new and frightening environment. Handlers were hard pressed to cope with them.

'Is that a truck of mod-apes?' Bethaneve asked in surprise.

Cell members (level twenty-eight) were close to the train, sharing their perception. Sure enough, two of the trucks seemed to be full of mod-apes.

'Those stables are greedy,' Slvasta murmured.

333

'More like desperate,' Coulan said.

Jeers rippled across the protesters jamming the streets outside the station as they picked up on the shared ex-sight. The new surge of antipathy made several neuts rear up and run frantically. Stable Guild workers ran after them, trying to calm the terrified animals.

An insidious teekay began to open the locks on the cattle wagons. The neuts crammed inside, already frantic and oversensitive to the psychic storm boiling from the hostile crowd, burst out and stampeded across the station's marshalling yard. Amid the chaos, more truck locks were opened. The mod-apes broke free. The humans in the marshalling yard yelled wildly as the tide of alien animals raced about chaotically, hooves kicking at anybody in the way. Guild workers tried to halt the mod-apes that were rampaging amid the neuts, but their 'path orders had no effect.

'Oh crud,' Slvasta gulped. 'Did we do that? Did we set them free?'

'We didn't plan it,' Bethaneve said. 'But it looked organized to me.'

'One of the cells innovating, maybe?' Javier said.

'Maybe.'

'Irrelevant right now,' Slvasta said. He was standing a little way up Cranwich Road, surrounded by the crowd. The atmosphere had begun to change from confident aggression to unease. A hundred metres away, the sheriffs on the barricade across Knole Street, which ran along the side of the station, were turning round nervously. Behind them, one of the tall cast-iron gates leading to the marshalling yard began to shake as neuts hurled themselves at it. Individually, a neut was a modest animal without a great deal of power, but now there were hundreds of them hurtling along, goaded by their own fear. Herd instinct, enhanced by a shared crude psychic distress, made the flight imperative utterly dominant. The impact as they flung themselves heedlessly at the gate was like a battering ram. Then a couple of hulking mod-apes hit the gate.

Slvasta was perceiving it with his own ex-sight, so there was no mistaking the force and coherence of the telepathic orders which frantic Stable Guild members were thrusting into the minds of the mod-apes to stop. Yet they made no difference.

The gates burst open. Hundreds of panicked frenzied neuts burst out into Knole Street and began to run for freedom.

'That's *wrong*,' Slvasta whispered. 'Why can't the wranglers get control of them . . . ?' Bad memories began to percolate into his conscious thoughts.

Anxiety started to flare through the crowd around Slvasta. Over by the barriers, the sheriffs were trying to combine their teekay before the onrush of hundreds of crazed neuts bearing down on them. The neuts at the front of the rampaging pack were felled as the sheriffs lost discipline and sent spikes of teekay into the animals' brains, shredding the neural cells. But it took time, and the corpses were immediately swarmed by the rest of the inflamed herd. Several sheriffs broke and sprinted for the relative safety of the buildings on either side of the road.

'Slvasta, you need to move,' Javier said.

The crowd around him seemed to be sharing that opinion. People were turning, pressing towards the buildings lining the streets that had been locked up against trouble since first thing that morning. Teekay and boots thumped into locks on sturdy wooden doors. The equally frantic residents and storekeepers inside used their strength and teekay to keep them out.

Slvasta turned and let the alarmed crowd push him along. Once he felt the flow of bodies surging round him, he started to push in the same direction as those heading back along Cranwich Road. The road opened into some sort of square ahead, he remembered; the pressure would ease off and the crowd could disperse down half a dozen alleys and lanes that led away from it.

Behind him, the neuts and mod-apes reached the abandoned barricades. Their weight and speed sent the metal and wood rails crashing to the ground, and hooves sped over them. Slvasta was concentrating on running with the crowd – he could sense the street opening into the small square ahead while flashes of shared ex-sight showed him the torrent of neuts and mod-apes pouring along Knole Street. People were clinging to windowsills to get above them; some had even scaled iron lamp posts, hanging on for dear life as the animals thundered past underneath. He perceived one man drop, to be pummelled under the hooves.

'Oh, that's all we need,' Bethaneve declared.

'What's happened?' Coulan asked.

'The bastard Meor regiment. They're coming out of the government buildings. Must have been waiting since last night. Our people missed that.'

'What in Uracus do they think they're going to do?' Javier asked.

'If the officers are smart, they'll take out the neuts and mod-apes,' Coulan said.

'Those bastards are more likely to kill people for running away,' Javier said.

'It doesn't look as if they're well organized,' Bethaneve said. 'And there are more coming out of the station.'

'Too late!'

The front of the stampede reached the junction of Cranwich Road. 'Oh, crudding Uracus!' Slvasta exclaimed. Over half of the neuts and seemingly most of the mod-apes peeled away to charge along Cranwich Road. The screaming began all around him – high-pitched shrieks and bass roars combining into a wall of sound that hammered against his brain, amplifying the primeval fear that was rising all along the road. The last dregs of civility shattered in that single moment. The crowd became a mob, with everyone looking out for themselves, no matter what the cost.

Slvasta came hurtling out of Cranwich Road into Eynsham Square, a pleasant cobbled area with tall blue-leafed arctan trees lining the small central garden. Stalls with striped canvas canopies defending food and clothes from the sun were clustered together along one side, the vendors fleeing away down side lanes along with the mob.

Then Slvasta saw them, pressed up against the railings round the garden not twenty metres ahead. 'No,' he yelled, his mind emitting a burst of horror. Instantly, Bethaneve, Javier and Coulan were querying him, anxious for his personal safety. The image that blasted into his eyes flashed out, shared openly by his distraught mind, imbued with a terrible flood of urgency and fright.

*

Josanne's Hill junior school had begun that Tuesday like any other. Most of its middle-class parents had picked up on the expected trouble growing round Doncastor station, but the school was eight streets away. Safe enough, surely? Besides, they all had to work. Protesting was all very well for the feckless louts and union militants who lived by sponging off the edge of society, but those who had to earn money to support their family couldn't afford to take a day off. They dropped their children off at the school gates at eight thirty, as they did every day, kissed them goodbye, then went off, gossiping with other parents as they went.

At ten o'clock, as they did every Tuesday without fail, Josanne's Hill's full contingent of eight-year-olds, all thirty-two of them, were led out of the school grounds by seven harried teachers for their weekly swimming lesson at the lido pool on Plaxtol Street, an eleven-minute walk away, taking them directly through Eynsham Square. This Tuesday, the walk took a lot longer, with the teachers having to wind their way round the clutter of protesters assembling in the streets around the station. It was all good-natured then, but the children picked up on the excitement, and their teachers had to keep special watch to make sure everyone stuck together. By the time they eventually made it into the square, the neuts had broken loose.

The terrified mob moved like a solid wavefront. Nobody cared that there were children in the way. The teachers gathered their charges together, sheltering them with teekay and arms hugging close. They were clumped against the railings around the garden, with several children crying as they were repeatedly pummelled against the thick trunk of an arctan tree.

Slvasta needed all of his strength just to stop, his strongest teekay shell forcing people to surge round him. He was three metres away from the schoolchildren. The braying cries of the neuts were rising above the human screams as the stampede approached the square.

'They're going to smash straight into the kids,' Slvasta told his friends. 'Where's the Meor regiment?'

'The nearest squad to you is in Arlington Lane,' Bethaneve 'pathed. 'They'll never reach you in time.'

Slvasta turned and faced the end of Cranwich Road. It was barely visible beyond the frantic charging bodies. Curses and threats were hurled at him as people lurched past. He drew the revolver he'd been carrying – so carefully obscured by a psychic fuzz. It was the one he'd taken from the bunker below the Joint Regimental Council office, a world and a life ago. There were five bullets in the chamber, another dozen in his inside pocket. His teekay clicked the safety off. He took a breath. Steadied himself.

He was aware of Bethaneve's distant 'path producing a string of instructions; they were passed along the convoluted command channels of the cells. Then someone else was standing beside him, a man in his fifties in a shabby jacket, struggling against the throng of people desperate to escape the square.

'Kolan,' he said, with a thick Siegen county accent.

'Slvasta. Thanks for this.'

'No worries, pal. We'll not let them get the kiddies, eh?'

Slvasta just had time to say, 'Right,' when a frightened young woman came to stand on his other side. She was trembling as her surprisingly strong teekay pushed running people away.

'Teekay spike directly into their brains,' Slvasta told them.

Another youthful lad joined them. Slvasta almost laughed. Four people standing firm against an onslaught. It was suicide.

'There are more comrades in the square,' Bethaneve 'pathed. 'I'm trying to get orders out. They'll help.'

The mob was thinning out fast. It was mostly the elderly now, wheezing as they half-limped, half-staggered along, crying with fright as they tried to stay ahead of the feverish neuts hot on their heels.

Then there were no more humans, and the neuts came

thundering out of Cranwich Road. Slvasta hadn't known the stupid creatures could actually move that fast. He stared at the one directly ahead, and lashed out with his teekay. It died instantly as his invisible blade sliced into the brain, tumbling across the cobbles and tripping two other neuts as it went. He stabbed out again, and again. The cell comrades standing by him were doing the same. He perceived similar spears of teekay reaching out from other places in the square, directed at the neuts.

One cell was standing just at the edge of Cranwich Road when the first half-dozen mod-apes charged out. The big shambling beasts managed to protect themselves from the teekay assaults with basic shells, snarling in rage as they did. 'Pathed orders to stop had no effect on them at all. And Slvasta's memory was all too horribly clear on that. 'Faller!' he warned Bethaneve. 'There's a Faller controlling them.' He raised the pistol, forcing himself not to hurry. Slain neuts were plummeting to the ground, peeling away from the thundering herd. But the mod-apes kept coming. Slvasta fired.

The noise of the shot overrode every other sound in the square. For a second, there seemed to be nothing but silence. Then the yelling and screaming redoubled. One of the bulky mod-apes crashed to the ground, blood pouring from the fatal head wound. Slvasta moved his arm, lining up on the next . . .

He fired. Again. Again.

Around the square, people pelting into the relative safety of the lanes began to slow, glancing back. The tiny band of stalwarts standing resolutely in front of the sobbing, wailing children instigated a great deal of shame. Slvasta's one arm was raised to shoot with calm accuracy. A mod-ape fell with every bullet. Neuts were collapsing from teekay strikes that were coming from all directions. As people stopped fleeing, they began to add their own mental power to the strikes.

'Can anyone see the Faller?' Javier asked.

'We don't know who it is,' Coulan 'pathed urgently.

'They're here for a reason,' Slvasta told them. His teekay was slapping fresh rounds into the pistol. 'This is the perfect cover to snatch a few people.'

'So what are we looking for?' Bethaneve asked. 'I've still got contact with most of our cells.'

'They're strong,' Slvasta said as he lined up the pistol again. And two mod-apes were slavering as they rushed him, powerful hands raised to grab and claw. He fired. A perfect shot, catching the lead one in the centre of its head. The back of its skull blew off; gore and blood exploded out.

Nine cell members across the square combined their teekay and penetrated the remaining mod-ape's crude shell, decimating its brain. The bulky creature toppled to the ground, momentum skidding it along for several metres. It scrunched to a halt a metre short of Slvasta and the other defenders.

Slvasta took a deep breath, trying to stop the shakes. 'The Faller will be carrying someone away.' He aimed at a rampaging neut. Fired. Two bullet left in the chamber, two in his jacket pocket.

'They'll be unconscious,' Coulan added, 'so it'll look like they're trying to help a friend.'

'Tell our comrades to search for that,' Javier said. 'And quick.'

Slvasta shot another neut as he sensed Bethaneve's frantic instruction spreading across the cells amid the agitated crowds. In Eynsham Square, the stampede had now stalled. People were turning round and emerging from the side roads, directing teekay strikes at the petrified animals that mewled in bewilderment as they jostled about. They fell in silence, adding to the distress of those remaining.

Humans closed in on them from all directions, seeking retaliation. The mods that lay dead were kicked at, stomped on, spat at, had their softer flesh ripped by vengeful teekay twists.

The scene vanished behind a deluge of images dispatched by every cell member in the area as they hunted around for people being carried away by others. There were many: men hauling women and children along, their faces distraught, pleading, urging . . .

'Look for someone who doesn't care about who they're taking,' Slvasta urged. For a second the montage was overwhelmed by the vision of Quanda's face, beautiful and terrible, her mouth parted in a wide victorious smile as she loomed over him.

'There!' Coulan exclaimed.

Slvasta focused on the sight gifted by a comrade from a cell at the far end of Cranwich Road, where a relative peace had fallen. People who had leapt out of the way of the stampede were beginning to re-emerge onto the street, as were the sheriffs. At the junction was a big thickset man in late middle age wearing a filthy tweed jacket and stained brown trousers. He carried the limp form of a teenage boy over his shoulder. His walk was methodical, inexorable, as evidenced by the determined expression on his squat face. One hand only had two fingers.

'Got to be him,' Slvasta breathed.

'Challenge him,' Bethaneve sent to the nervous cell member who was watching from a safe distance.

The possible Faller was going round the corner into Knole Street and heading away from the station and the sheepish sheriffs. In all the turmoil no one else was paying him the slightest attention.

'Faller,' the cell member said in a feeble voice. Nobody even heard her, let alone paid attention.

'Back her up,' Bethaneve's instruction went cascading through their erratic communication web between cells.

'Faller.' This time the cell member sounded a little more confident. She raised a hand and pointed. 'Faller!'

The call was taken up by other cell members along Knole Street.

'You, hey, you!'

'Stop.'

'Faller! He's a Faller.'

'Stop him.'

'Sheriff, sheriffs! Do something.'

Now people were starting to look. The Faller – if that's what he was – had quickened his pace.

A sheriff stepped towards him. 'Just a moment, you.'

He was ignored.

The sheriff was only five metres away now, his arm held up, palm outwards as if he was directing traffic. 'Right, you—'

The Faller flung the unconscious teenager he was carrying right at the sheriff, who collapsed under the impact, crashing to the pavement. He screamed in pain. The Faller started running, moving incredibly fast for a man his size and age.

It seemed as if everyone on Knole Street was shouting. A cacophony of alarm and fear that was swiftly supplanted by shrill sheriffs' whistles, calling for help. Some people tried to stop the Faller, lashing out with teekay. Others – stronger, confident men – attempted to tackle him physically. They were smashed aside as if they were rag dolls.

Then a couple of Meor regiment squads raced into Knole Street.

'Get down,' their officers bellowed – an order backed up by shrill 'path shouts. The soldiers brought up their carbines. Everyone dropped to the ground, parents clawing at their children, forcing them onto the cobbles; even the sheriffs ducked down. The only person moving was the Faller, pounding along at an inhuman speed, still looking directly ahead as if he hadn't noticed what was happening. Even treading on cowering bodies as he went.

The carbines opened up with a devastating roar.

7

Philious never enjoyed visiting the Faller Research Institute. Even in childhood Fallers triggered an instinctive discomfort, but his father had insisted he see one as part of his training. Time hadn't lessened the reaction.

The black carriage he rode in with Trevene and Aothori was larger than an ordinary cab, but unadorned with any heraldic crest. There were several of them in the palace stables for the family to use when they wanted to travel about incognito. Two ordinary cabs followed them through the streets, filled with Palace Guards in civilian clothes.

East Folwich was a wealthy borough dominated by the clothing trade, so although it had a large industrial park the factories didn't belch out smoke and chemical effluent as many did in Varlan. Pleasant houses formed quiet leafy streets, while larger residences surrounded the two parks. The majority of factories were built along both sides of the Dolan Drop canal, a channel dug specifically to divert half of the river Erinwash in a two-kilometre semicircle. Water surged down the brick-lined canal with considerable force, powering dozens of water wheels. Pollution here amounted to the tremendous clattering of big looms that reverberated through the air for sixteen hours a day.

To an observer, the institute looked like a small exclusive factory, wedged between an underused railway marshalling yard and the edge of the Dolan Drop factory zone. It was surrounded by an unusually high wall which was well maintained. No sign announced what was contained within. There was only one entrance, through heavy wooden doors into a short tunnel that had another set of identical doors at the far end. They were linked mechanically, making it impossible for both to be opened at the same time.

With the inner doors open, the Captain's carriage trundled out into a bare courtyard. The institute building's sombre purpose was reflected in its plain design, a long two-storey rectangle with narrow iron-barred windows and no adornment at all. Philious believed it was the only part of Varlan where you could see no vegetation. Even the weeds were scoured regularly from the courtyard's cobbles by the staff. Human staff. There were no mods permitted inside, ever. Of all the places on Bienvenido, the institute remained steadfast in following the guidelines laid down in the original Faller manuals it had produced almost three thousand years earlier. Fallers, those pages warned, could exert total control over mods and neuts, rendering any human instruction worthless.

As he alighted from the carriage, Philious reflected on the irony that the other most devout believer in that tenet right now was Captain (retired) Slvasta.

The institute director, Professor Gravin, bowed gravely at his distinguished visitors. He was well into his second century, an enormously heavy man whose midnight-black skin served to highlight his remaining wisps of silver hair. Shaking the professor's damp hand Philious also noticed how much sweat was glinting on that skin. It wasn't from stress; moving such a bulky frame just a few steps seemed to exhaust Professor Gravin.

'I'm so very glad you came, sir,' the director wheezed as he led them inside. 'What we have found is remarkable. And disturbing.'

'So your letter implied,' Philious murmured. He kept glancing at the director's white coat. Everyone at the institute wore one, it was their uniform. But the buttons on the oversized director's lab coat seemed perpetually on the point of ripping, they were under so much pressure. Not for the first time he began to question the need for the institute. For all his dedication, the professor and his staff were utterly inferior to the scientists who had accompanied Captain Cornelius, those stalwarts who had investigated the Fallers as their ship's instruments decayed and died around them, who had determined so much of their nature and ability. Since those first two centuries, the institute had added very little to their knowledge. These days it didn't do much other than confirm that the corpses of humans and animals brought to them were indeed Fallers, and check that there was no deviation, that nothing new had developed. Pioneering science had given way to a detailed cataloguing mandate as the institute tried to establish any kind of a pattern in Faller activity, because it no longer had anything else to contribute. Any idea that the institute would lead the fight back against the Fallers and their Forest home had faded more than two thousand years ago. Now it was just another government department, locked into the status quo, battling for budgets and staff.

Professor Gravin opened the doors of the autopsy room, barely fitting through the gap. The room was completely clad in shiny white tiles, except for the ceiling, which was all glass, with the late-morning sunlight streaming in. Philious had to squint against the glare.

The broad metal-skinned slab in the middle of the room held a body that had been cut open and spread apart so much that its original human outline was difficult to recognize. He was looking at a butcher's table. It didn't escape him that Aothori leaned forwards keenly.

'The Meor regiment brought its remains to us two days ago,' Professor Gravin said, sucking down air after his exertion. 'We've been examining it ever since.'

Philious was aware of the professor's emphasis, *the institute carries on doing its job as always.* 'The Knole Street Faller, yes. I took the gifting, along with most of the city.'

'Our first point of interest was the missing fingers,' the professor said. He pulled on some rubber gloves and picked up the Faller's hand. The index and middle fingers were missing, reduced to tiny stumps from which several sections had been sliced away. 'In itself there's nothing too unusual about that. An eggsumption will always duplicate the person it absorbs, right down to moles, blemishes, hair pattern. If our man had lost two fingers, than that's what will come out. The egg won't grow replacements.'

'I am aware of this,' Philious said, looking at the hand. The dead flesh was abnormally pale in the bright light. 'So what is unusual?'

'The surgery.'

'Excuse me?'

The professor tapped the Faller's index finger stump with his thumb. 'We noticed the ends were unusually smooth. Normally when someone is unfortunate enough to lose a finger – some kind of industrial accident or just simple carelessness with an axe – the doctor will trim the torn flesh and stitch the wound together. It will heal, leaving scar tissue. This man had none.'

'So it was a congenital condition,' Aothori said. 'He was born without those fingers.'

'No, sir. We don't think so. In both fingers there was still a section of the proximal phalanges remaining, about a centimetre long, extending from the knuckle. I consulted with the dean of medicine at the university – that isn't a congenital defect we're aware of.'

'Then how do you explain it?' Philious asked.

'The tips of the phalanges had been smoothed, yet I don't know how that would be achieved. And we examined the skin of the tip under a microscope: the wound had healed over in a uniform fashion. There is no scar tissue, no anomalies in the dermal layer at all. If he lost the fingers in an accident, he was given a perfect treatment afterwards. A treatment we are not capable of providing.'

'Occam's razor,' Aothori said. 'Just because you haven't seen that congenital condition before doesn't mean it doesn't exist. Or perhaps the egg made a small alteration during duplication this time. More likely, the Faller lost those fingers in some kind of fight and you're seeing the way their bodies heal.'

'Yes, sir. We considered those options.'

'But?' Philious continued. 'We're not here because of the fingers, are we?'

'No, sir. When my deputy reported the irregularity I took it upon myself to continue the autopsy personally.'

'Commendable. And?'

The professor pointed at the open skull. The brainpan was empty. 'Its brain. I dissected its brain. Please.' He beckoned them over to one of the long benches running down the side of the room. There were several glass jars with flesh sealed inside, and a large brass microscope. A Faller brain was splayed open on a small metal platform, the grey-brown mass peeled apart like a fruit, its segments pinned down at the tips. A brass stand with various magnifying glasses curved over the dissected tissue, providing various enhanced views of the stringy organ. 'Fallers copy human organs very precisely,' the professor said. 'Except for the brain. It is the most distinctive difference outside of blood colour. Their brains are a single array of identical neural cells. Ours are a composite of clusters and lobes and glands, while theirs are uniform and regular. This one was different.'

Philious studied the splayed brain open before him; his distaste suppressed by curiosity, he moved in closer. The big magnifying glasses provided weirdly distorted images. 'How so?'

'There were minute fibres interlaced within the structure. I only just spotted them because I was using the strongest lenses.'

'Fibres?' Philious peered closer. The biggest lens showed him a landscape of grey-brown hummocks threaded with collapsed tubules – which he took to be capillaries.

'Here, sir,' the professor indicated the big microscope. 'They're considerably thinner than a human hair. As I say, it was mostly luck I spotted them. And they were terribly difficult to extract. We've only succeeded with a few sections so far.'

Philious looked into the microscope. The vision field was a simple white expanse, with what could have been a slender translucent grey blemish running from top to bottom: the fibre. He saw tiny spikes radiating out from the main strand, as if it had bristles. It was fascinating. 'What is that?'

'We don't know,' the professor said bluntly. 'You saw the secondary filaments branching?'

'Yes.' Philious reluctantly moved away; he could sense Aothori's eagerness to view the thread.

'They appear short, but actually we don't know how extensive they are. They get thinner and thinner until they vanish from the microscope's sight. We're guessing, of course, but they could wind up as molecular strings. In which case they're presumably connected to individual neurones.'

Philious glanced back to the body on the slab. 'And they're part of its brain? Some kind of second nervous system?'

'We simply don't know.' The professor dabbed a handkerchief across his brow to soak up some of the perspiration. 'There has never, ever, been anything like this recorded in the institute's history.'

'You said yourself you got lucky.'

'Yes, sir. I did. But the institute's founders, the scientists who had ship's machines, I don't believe they'd have missed something like this, yet it isn't described in any of the texts they published. And I've had staff re-examining microscope slides of Faller brain tissue for the last thirty hours. We have hundreds of valid samples dating back two hundred and fifty years. As yet, no one has spotted any threads like this.'

Philious licked his lips and glanced over at Trevene, who as always guarded his thoughts impeccably. 'New,' he said slowly. 'And different. Sounds familiar?'

'Not coincidence,' Trevene said. 'A new kind of Faller?'

'Why bother speculating?' Aothori said. 'Let me bring Slvasta in. I can have answers out of him in a day – two at the most if he wants to play tough. You know I can.'

'The Hero of Eynsham Square?' Philious asked sarcastically. 'The man who stood up to rampaging neuts to save a bunch of adorable schoolchildren in front of the whole city? You want to snatch him from his home and interrogate him until his mind and body are broken? Really?'

'The Fallers manipulated that stampede,' Aothori said. 'And it made Slvasta look like the greatest thing on Bienvenido since we discovered how to adapt neuts. Is that also coincidence?'

'Slvasta loathes Fallers and mods more than anybody,' Trevene said. 'His hatred consumes and drives him. It verges on the irrational. He is responsible for the neut sterilization. His followers are the ones slaughtering mods.'

'You hope,' Aothori sneered back. 'Father, we need answers. I can get them. If our world is facing a new threat from our enemy, we must expose it.'

'Not like this. These are troubled times. Our position, our status, must not be questioned.'

'There were other people standing with Slvasta to face the neut charge,' Trevene said. 'Slvasta would naturally stop and make his stand: despite everything he's an officer, regiment trained and sworn to protect Bienvenido's citizens. But those others, it was almost suicide to stand with him. Their reasons for doing so might be a more profitable avenue of investigation. They have slunk away again, which is curious in itself.'

'I remember the girl,' Aothori said.

Philious held up a hand. 'Not a girl, not this time. As I recall the gifting, there were at least two other men – one was quite young.'

'I'll find them,' Trevene said.

'Good. Now, professor, what do you think these fibres could be? Do they make the Faller's teekay stronger, perhaps?'

'Anything is possible, sir. All we know is that it's new.'

'Which is what this institute is actually for: discovering information about Fallers.' He gave Aothori a pointed look. 'So I'm assuming, professor, your next step is to find out if this Knole Street Faller is unique, or the start of some new development.'

'Yes, sir,' the professor said.

'Right then, Aothori, you're to speak to the Marine Commandant. From now on, every Faller the regiments kill is to be brought here for further research. Understood? All of them, no exceptions – not just the human ones, but the animals as well. The professor and his colleagues will examine every brain to see if there are more fibres.'

'Yes, father. What about Slvasta?'

'He's chosen politics as his arena, so that's the arena where we'll deal with him.'

8

It had rained for half the morning, leaving the city's cobbles and bricks slicked and shining. Now, a noon sun seared down on the streets, creating long wisps of vapour as the residual rainwater evaporated. The humidity was intense, making Slvasta sweat just walking a few metres from the cab to the entrance doors of the Westergate Club. Inside the grand building on Mortemer Boulevard, the marble walls and pillars and floors calmly absorbed the heat, taking the air down to an altogether more reasonable temperature.

The doorman was frowning as Slvasta came up the steps. Then recognition kicked in, and the doorman suddenly smiled.

'Captain Slvasta, sir! Welcome.'

Slvasta gave the man a small nod, half-embarrassed. This had been the way of it for the whole ten days since the Doncastor Station Stampede (as everyone now referred to it). He hadn't realized at the time, of course, but the shared vision from everyone in Eynsham Square had been perceived clean across the city. The one-armed man, standing resolutely in front of a group of terrified school kids, aiming a pistol at the charge of rampaging neuts and fearsome mod-apes. Calmly picking off the mod-apes while his teekay lanced into the brains of neuts until the children were safe. A few other people stood with him, but no one noticed them. Pamphlets and gazettes alike had been effusive in praising the 'Hero of Eynsham Square'.

'Thank you,' Slvasta said modestly.

A footman was waiting by the reception desk just inside. He bowed in greeting. 'Colonel Gelasis is waiting for you in the Nevada suite,' he said. 'Please follow me. It's such an honour to have you here.'

And how do you answer that and its variants twenty times a day?

The Nevada suite was a private wood-panelled room off the club's second-floor dining hall. Colonel Gelasis was sitting at the head of its long polished table, wearing his uniform. But not full ceremonial dress, Slvasta saw; no silk sashes or spiky oversize medals, just discreet gold braid and a line of ribbons. For the colonel, that was almost being in civvies.

'My dear chap.' Colonel Gelasis rose and shook Slvasta's hand enthusiastically. 'So good to see you again. Thank you for coming.'

Slvasta inclined his head politely. 'Thank you for inviting me.' His first instinct when the runner arrived with the invitation had been to refuse – with a vulgar reply. The others had talked him out of it.

'We need to know what they want,' Bethaneve had said.

'We need to know what they think you are,' Coulan countered.

'What I am?'

'If they know you're the true head of Democratic Unity.'

'We are the party leaders,' Slvasta said, almost desperately.

'In here among ourselves, yes,' Javier said. 'But after Eynsham Square, you're the public face.'

'Like Bryan-Anthony?' he grumped.

'That's not going to happen. Not to the Hero of—'

Eight days, and he was already cringing at the term.

Bethaneve stroked his cheek possessively. 'They won't kill you,' she said. 'They want to seduce you. That's why your old boss wants to see you.'

'So what do I tell them?'

Looking at Colonel Gelasis as they sat down, Slvasta couldn't think of anyone less likely to be a political agent. The colonel had served the Captain's Marines with distinction. The damage to his leg was cleverly fuzzed, and he could walk with just the slightest limp; only if he attempted to run was the injury apparent. But then that was probably why he'd been chosen as the one to make contact, someone Slvasta could relate to.

'I have to tell you,' Gelasis said, 'we were all shocked by your resignation. Personally, I was very disappointed.'

'Really?' Slvasta wasn't going to let him off that lightly. 'They were going to crucify Arnice. He was going to be blamed for everything. If that's the kind of loyalty the Meor regiment shows, then—'

'That *wasn't* the regiment, and you know it,' Gelasis snapped immediately. 'Some little prick working in the basement of the National Council thought he could shift the blame away from his masters. The Meor commandant would have had that charge revoked by the end of the week, that or the regiment would've marched on the Council. Arnice was one of their own, dammit, a brother officer. Politicians don't get to blame the regiments for their stupidity and incompetence.'

'It wasn't just that,' Slvasta mumbled, annoyed with himself for being put on the defensive. 'That was just the last straw.'

'Ha.' Gelasis poured him some wine. 'Paperwork, eh? Now that I do understand. The number of times I've been tempted to tell the Treasury maggots to stick their triplicate forms up their arse . . .'

'One reform. Just one. That's all I wanted. And it wasn't exactly a tough one.'

'Well, if it gives you any satisfaction, it's going to happen now. And sharpish. Doncastor station was a lesson too close to home for some. I mean, I knew Fallers have a better control of mods, but that . . .' He shook his head and took some wine. 'Bad business. And you did a superb job protecting those children. Commendable. You know, recruitment in the city has nearly doubled in the last week. That's all down to you.'

'I'm a private citizen.' Though it hadn't escaped his notice that all the gazettes kept calling him Captain Slvasta.

'That was a regimental officer I saw out there. Saving Bienvenido's citizens from the Faller menace, without fear, totally selfless. You made me proud, my boy.'

'What menace? I haven't heard a damn thing about the nest since. You and I both know he couldn't have been alone.'

Gelasis grimaced. 'That's the bloody Captain's police. There hasn't been a nest in Varlan for five centuries. They're shit scared one slipped through somehow. There's a lot of backstabbing going on up at the sheriff's office right now. And to their credit, there's a lot of hard searching going on, too. Right now, you can't get into any government building without having a needle jabbed into your thumb to see the colour of your blood. They'll find the others, don't you worry. Failure simply cannot be tolerated, not when it comes to nests.'

'Glad to hear it.' Slvasta was well aware of the political pressure right now. Even the gazettes had been scathing about the authorities allowing a nest into Varlan.

Their soup was brought in by two waiters in starched white jackets – tomato and red petter with crusty bread still warm from the baking oven. Slvasta had to admit it did taste good; the Westergate Club wasn't just about status.

'Nice,' he conceded.

'My pleasure. Enjoy it while you can; the economy is going to take a real beating now. We're all going to have to tighten our belts.'

'Why?'

Gelasis paused with the silver soup spoon almost at his mouth and gave Slvasta a stern glance. 'Please don't pretend to be that naive. Besides, Democratic Unity supports the killing of mods. Your public policy is quite clear and explicit about that.'

'We support severing our dependence on them, yes.'

'You're talking genocide.'

'I've faced Faller-controlled mods twice in my life now. That's two times too many. Both times I was lucky to escape alive. I don't want it to happen a third time. The odds aren't in my favour any more.'

'That's understandable. And now you may well have your wish. People were badly shaken by the stampede. Two of the smaller stables in town have already closed. It's only a matter of time until the rest collapse.'

'You expect me to show sympathy?'

'No. But you have to admit, we're off the map with this one. The Treasury doesn't even know if the economy can remain intact without mod labour.'

'As you said, everyone will have to tighten their belts.' Slvasta raised his spoon to make the point. 'Except the people who had nothing to start with and now find themselves overwhelmed with offers of jobs. The underclass finally has new opportunities opening up.'

'And the votes for Democratic Unity will flood in, no doubt.'

'Here's hoping.'

Gelasis nodded sagely. 'What do you want?'

'You're the one who invited me.'

'I did, didn't I? May I speak plainly and in confidence?'

'Frankly, it would be a relief. If I've learned anything from council meetings, it's that I'm not the world's greatest politician.'

'I'm surprised you're not mayor of Nalani, now.'

'Are you? Look what happened to the last mayor.'

'Touché. All right.' Gelasis pushed his soup bowl to one side and gave Slvasta an intent stare. 'I have friends in the National Council who are keen to come to an accord with Democratic Unity.'

'Members of Citizens' Dawn want an agreement? I find that hard to believe.'

'Very senior members, yes.'

'Ha. Who don't like losing backwater boroughs like Nalani.'

'Slvasta, face facts, nobody gives a crud about Nalani. Uracus, your party might even do some good there! Giu knows, nobody else cares about it. But the mid-term elections are coming up in less than eight months. A third of Varlan's boroughs, many of them poor ones. There are also seats on the National Council up for grabs, too.'

'And your friends are getting concerned about that, right?' Slvasta asked. Bethaneve and Coulan were already recruiting potential candidates to stand in the boroughs. They weren't short of volunteers; everyone was fired up after Democratic Unity's recent success. And, just possibly, they were impressed by the Hero of Eynsham Square, too.

'Some of those boroughs could be yours,' Gelasis said. 'Maybe even a National Council seat. Langley, for example.'

'What?' Slvasta desperately wished it was Coulan or Bethaneve sitting here in his place. Politics and its labyrinthine deals and bluffs and weasel words was something he could never quite grasp. He was always worried he was being played for a fool when convoluted clever deals were suggested. And, as for making equally smart counter-offers . . .

'Hear me out,' Gelasis said smoothly. 'I really did mean *yours*.'

'Ours?'

'No: you. Personally. You would be a superb addition to the National Council. Think about it. You're not from a wealthy family, which brings so much resentment among a huge proportion of the population, but you served your regiment with distinction. The city witnessed you going head to head with Fallers. You have integrity. People trust you, rightly so. You're a perfect candidate.'

Slvasta thought back to a similar conversation not so long ago, how his friends were just waiting to push him forward as the head of Democratic Unity. 'I can't believe Citizens' Dawn is offering this.'

'You're the right type, Slvasta – a decent cove who wants the best for people. All the people. And having you on the National Council would make the recessive elements of Citizens' Dawn sit up and take notice. They've been excluding and ignoring the poor for too long, don't you think?'

'Well, yes. That's why we formed Democratic Unity.'

'Tuksbury holds Langley, has done for the last thirty-six years. He's a stupid, petty, vain little man, running a rotten district, serving his family and their companies before everything else. The worst type of Bienvenido politician. If you were to stand, I have been given assurances that Citizens' Dawn support for Tuksbury would be non-existent. You'd win. It's that simple.'

'And Citizens' Dawn are happy with that?' he asked sceptically.

'Listen, Slvasta, you're a reasonable, rational man. You understand what should be done, and you're not a raving hothead about it like all the other hate-the-rich dissenter rabble. People who run the world need to be sensible and cogent, to understand give and take.' Gelasis gave him a friendly smile. 'And think how many friends you'd have in the regiments. You could give us a direct voice in the heart of government, instead of trying to worm progress through the Treasury one request form at a time. That is the ultimate aim for all of us, isn't it? To give the regiments the ability to defeat the Fallers once and for all? After all, if not, we're all doomed.'

'I think that would take more than one lone voice.'

'You have more supporters than you think. Your party only existed for a few weeks before the Nalani election, and look how many votes you got. And we both know you're building support in new boroughs, ready for the next elections. You know full well that nothing will be accomplished if your candidates are just a collection of firebrands and ideologues. Building a reputable party capable of achieving your aims will be tough. If you don't step up, it will be damn near impossible, eh?'

Slvasta let out a long breath. 'You don't have to tell me how tough it is.'

'So you'll consider it? Standing for Langley?'

'I'd be foolish not to.'

'Excellent. So, let's get those steaks in here, shall we?'

*

Bethaneve waited in a small clothing store on Vesuvian Street opposite the six-storey tenement. The monolithic building was a couple of centuries old, and completely covered in the heavy blue-white leaves of a skirs vine. She didn't know if the walls were brick or stone – even the windows were slowly shrinking behind the vigorous shoots. Hordes of children played lively games on the street outside, their exuberance a reaction to the tiny rooms they were forced to share inside.

It wasn't that she didn't want to go into the tenement herself;

her reluctance came from a deeper place, the need to avoid exposure. The revolution might be undeclared so far. But that didn't mean it had gone unnoticed. And the First Officer was often seen at Trevene's headquarters at Fifty-Eight Grosvner Place. The risk—

Bethaneve put a fast stop to that line of thought and glanced at the tenement again. Coulan was coming out of an open archway, walking briskly across the road. His thoughts as urbane as ever. She left the shop, her ex-sight scanning for any mod-birds. This level of vigilance was routine now.

'Well?' she asked.

'Kolan's not been home for two days now,' Coulan said, maintaining his neutral face and shell.

'Crud!' Yesterday she'd heard that Trevene's weasel teams were asking about Kolan, the man who'd stood with Slvasta in Eynsham Square. Kolan, a fifth-level cell member whom she'd instructed to help defend the children. Not directly, the request came slipping and slithering through three other cells before it got to him. But still . . .

Her people told her the questions were closing in on Vesuvian Street, then they had the name. They were good, her people. Special. Quiet. Clever. Elites, a group chosen by her from various cells for specialist tasks. Not the kind of aggressor duties Coulan was training his militia for; her elites were used to tracking people across the city, to ask discreet questions, to follow rumour to the source and gain the truth. They were developing into a useful asset in the unseen quiet struggle with Trevene's informers and spies and thugs. She hadn't quite got round to mentioning them to Slvasta. The arrangement was that she handled details, leaving him free to lead the revolution.

'Do you think they've got him?' she asked as they walked away. Not in a hurry, not drawing attention. Further along the street, three elites were watching people and mods, alert for anything out of place.

'Oh yes,' Coulan said. 'He has a wife and three kids. He's not going to vanish without telling them.'

'Has she reported it to the sheriffs?'

'Yes. As you can imagine, they just leapt into action.'

'Dammit. Nobody can hold out against what they'll do to him. He'll give them passwords, places, times. Everything. He probably already has.'

'Yes, but what is everything? What does he actually know? He gets an occasional 'path from someone he's never met, a suggestion that this or that might help stick it to the Captain every now and then. Harmless enough stuff.'

'I ordered him to stand with Slvasta, Coulan. It's a disaster. Trevene will know we're organized way beyond a simple political party.'

'If he's half as smart as he's supposed to be, he knew that a long time ago.'

'But now he's got names.'

'A name. One.'

'There were others with Slvasta. They need to leave Varlan. For good. And the other four in Kolan's cell, too: he can identify them.'

'So warn them. That's why we have the cells set up the way they are. It's a network Trevene can't hope to crack as long as we take the right precautions.'

'Yes,' she nodded, his composure making her own fluttery thoughts calmer. 'You're right.'

He grinned. 'I'm always right.'

Bethaneve started to private 'path specific warnings. With luck, the recipients would take them seriously. It took a lot to up and leave your home. She added a few details, emphasizing the danger. The First Officer's face was often a subliminal addition to the messages.

Do what I ask. Please. Get out while there's still time. You won't live to regret it if you don't.

⋆

'Hotheads and ideologues, huh?' Javier snorted in contempt.

Slvasta grinned at him over his tankard. "Fraid so.'

They were all in the Bellaview pub's high walled garden, huddled round a table to discuss Slvasta's lunch.

'And they'll give you Langley?' Coulan queried.

'That's what he said.'

'I wonder who he really represents?' Bethaneve asked.

'Some faction of Citizens' Dawn that's backed by the regiments,' Javier said. 'There's some heavy-duty fallout from the Doncastor station stampede. The politicians and the regiments are each blaming the other. It's getting ugly in the government district.'

'It's getting ugly everywhere,' Coulan said. 'People have been reminded how dangerous mods are when they're controlled by Fallers; their complacency has been shaken. We need to capitalize on that with the right candidates, who can stand up in public and make a smart argument for our policies.'

'Why are we even talking about this?' Bethaneve said. 'It's the cells that will overthrow the Captain, not spending twenty years working up through the corrupt council system.'

'Really?' Javier said. 'There were hundreds of comrades at the stampede. We managed to get three to stand with Slvasta. We were helpless when the neuts charged. We turned and ran when the mod-apes joined in. It was the Meor that actually brought that Faller down. We did the groundwork, but they have the power, them and the sheriffs.'

'Power,' Slvasta said. 'You mean weapons.'

'I do.'

'We'll never achieve anything until we can physically take on the regiments and sheriffs,' Coulan said.

'You're talking about killing people,' Slvasta said wearily.

'We have to arm ourselves,' Javier said. 'What happened to Bryan-Anthony made that very clear.'

'Maybe,' Slvasta said. He hated the whole idea, though he had to admit that unless they could fight the establishment out on the streets, the odds against them were overwhelming. 'But Trevene will certainly know if we start buying guns. Even if we had that kind of money.'

'Maybe not,' Bethaneve said. She tried not to grin as they all turned to look at her. 'I had an interesting message today; it came up through the cells. One of the comrades was trying to recruit someone from out of town. Turns out this person claims he can put us in touch with some kind of weapons merchant.'

'Trap,' Javier said immediately. 'Trevene and the Captain are closing in. You're popular now, Slvasta, they can't just disappear you like they do everyone else. So they set you up, then come crashing through the door just when you're holding the guns and handing over the money. A gift for the whole city to perceive.'

'Nice idea, but we don't have the money,' Slvasta said. 'And before anyone suggests it, I really don't want to use the cells to start robbing banks – we'd be nothing more than gangsters then.'

'It wouldn't come to that,' Bethaneve said. 'The weapons merchant is sympathetic to our cause.'

'There's no such thing as a sympathetic merchant, let alone one who sells weapons,' Javier said forcefully.

'We can't afford to ignore this,' she replied, meeting Javier's stare levelly. 'It could be the difference between success and the dungeons underneath Fifty-Eight Grosvner Place.'

'Trap,' Javier repeated stubbornly, shaking his head.

'Possibly,' she conceded. 'In which case we need to send someone who's smart enough to see it coming and walk away, someone they can't arrest on suspicion alone. But at the same time, someone who can deal directly with this weapons merchant if it turns out legitimate.'

They all turned to look at Slvasta.

'Oh, come on,' he exclaimed, his tankard frozen halfway to his mouth. 'Seriously?'

'Yeah,' Bethaneve said. 'Seriously.'

9

The Southern City Line express was scheduled to take sixteen hours to complete the thousand-mile journey from Willesden, Varlan's over-the-river station, to Dios, the capital city of a sprawling agricultural county. After that it would carry on to Port Chana on the southern coast, a further two thousand miles and thirty-five hours away.

Slvasta sat in a second-class carriage, a window seat giving him a view out across the farms and forests that cloaked the landscape. Long brick viaducts carried the train lines across broad valleys where tributaries of the river Nubain meandered their way through the land. Streamers of steam and smoke churned past the glass, temporarily obscuring the view. At first he'd paid a lot of attention to the panorama, then as the monotony grew, he turned to the books Bethaneve had supplied for the journey. Three biographies of first ministers of the National Council: 'Pay attention to their campaign strategies,' she instructed; and two weighty tomes on economic theory, 'because we have to get a grip on the fundamentals'. He read the pages dutifully, wishing she could have slipped a decent modern novel into the stack; he enjoyed sheriff procedurals.

The carriage was mostly full of salesmen and junior government staff. Some families were travelling, their restless kids prowling the aisle. At the far end an infant cried in hour-long outbursts despite everything its fraught mother could do to quiet it, triggering weary, knowing expressions from the rest of the adults each time the wailing started.

Slvasta's travelling companion took a seat further down the carriage. The meeting had been set up by a cell in the Hicombe Shanty. A cautious introduction in the middle of Lloyd Park, with Javier and Coulan keeping a careful watch for any signs of the Captain's police lurking in the bushes. The sky overhead appeared to be free of mod-birds, and no one suspicious was strolling across the rolling expanse of grass. And as agreed, the man had been waiting by the big stone and crystal fountain at the centre of the park, wearing a dark blue hat.

He called himself Russell, and Slvasta couldn't tell if that was true or not. His shell was impeccably maintained. He was middle aged, wearing a simple white shirt, dark blue trousers and sturdy boots. 'Captain Slvasta, a pleasure,' Russell said.

'Just Slvasta, now. I resigned from my regiment some time ago now.'

'Of course. But I am glad it's you who's here.'

'You told a colleague you might be able to help Democratic Unity.'

Russell smiled gently. 'We both know that's not true, but I understand your caution. So, yes, I know a man who can greatly assist your cause.'

'In what way?'

'The way every politician craves. He would like to donate. The kind of donation that will ultimately guarantee your success.'

'I see,' Slvasta said. 'And what is it this benefactor wants in return? Democratic Unity is not rich.'

'I have no idea what his price is.'

'Then what— ?'

'This meeting is simply to assess your level of integrity.'

Slvasta's face hardened to match his shell. 'Oh, really?'

'He would like to meet you. That way you can have the opportunity to appraise him. He hopes, that way a deal can be agreed.'

*

So, a week later, here he was on the express, travelling to an unknown destination to see someone who may or may not have guns for sale. It was about as unlikely as you could get. Not to mention potentially lethal. If this was a set-up by the Captain's police, he wouldn't be coming back.

Though, if it was a set-up, he had to admit it was flawless. Everyone at the station had seen him get on the train by his own free will, no coercion involved. He wasn't yet Democratic Unity's publicly acknowledged leader, not a true public figure. So who would ever ask what happened to good old Captain Slvasta if he didn't come back? And if you were stupid enough to persist in asking, you'd most likely experience a similar journey. All he wondered about now was if the Captain's police were really *that* good.

It was half past ten at night when the express finally drew in to the main station at Dios. There were eight platforms sheltering under four long arched roofs whose glass was blackened by soot from the big engines. Russell brushed against him on the platform, and Slvasta was left holding a new ticket. A local train for Erond at the end of a branch line, two hundred and fifty miles east. It departed in twelve minutes from platform seven.

Slvasta hurried over to platform seven, where the slightly smaller engine was puffing away enthusiastically. Behind him the express let out a sharp whistle blast as it rolled out of the station on its way south. As far as he could tell, he and Russell were the only passengers from the express to board the Erond train. Once again, they sat in the same carriage but not next to each other.

Erond was the end of the line – a simple station with two plat-forms but no grand overhead roof. A considerable quantity of cold rain washed across Slvasta as he stepped out at two thirty in the morning. He hurried for the cover of the wooden canopy that arched out of the main ticket office like a stumpy wing. A lone platform agent inspector stood by the gate, stamping his feet against the chill as he examined the tickets of the disembarking passengers. Outside, sparse oil lamps on wall brackets emitted a weak yellow glow, revealing a bleak street of terraced houses and small shops. A couple of listless mod-monkeys moved along slowly, clearing rubbish from the gutters. Slvasta stared at them almost in shock; he hadn't seen a team of mods performing civic work for weeks now. No one here had heard of the anti-mod campaign that thrived in the capital. Erond was a market town, but not especially wealthy. Here people needed all the help they could get. He suspected that it would be a lot harder to wean them off mods, even though the countryside population ought to be natural Democratic Unity voters.

If we overthrow the Captain and the National Council, how many of the counties will recognize a new government? he wondered. *But they can't afford to ignore us. Defending Bienvenido from Faller eggs has to be a joint venture, with everyone cooperating.*

Russell walked past. 'Follow me,' he 'pathed.

The street led into the town's waterfront district, which had been colonized by warehouses and large commercial buildings. Walking along the gloomy streets between the high uncompromising brick walls, trying not to lose his mysterious guide, Slvasta hadn't felt so isolated and lonely since the day he arrived in Varlan, full of resentment and completely alone. At least, back then, he knew where he was going; here there could be anything waiting for him in the bleak warren of lanes and alleys. He wasn't sure if he was frightened or excited by that.

When he arrived at the docks, the cold rain had wormed its way under his jacket, turning his skin numb. Slipways alternated with wharfs, almost half of which had cargo boats birthed for the night, dark and silent except for one.

Russell had stopped at the gangplank of the only boat that had its running lamps lit, a longbarge that was fully laden judging by how low it was in the water. Slvasta could hear the engine chugging quietly below decks; a tall iron stack puffed out thin streamers of smoke.

Then he sensed someone emerging from an alley between two warehouses behind him and turned to see a dark figure in a rain hat standing in the meagre glimmer of a street lamp. Slvasta was

365

sure he hadn't been on the train. Russell gave the watcher a silent wave of acknowledgement. 'We haven't been followed. You can come on board.'

'More travelling?' Slvasta asked with a groan.

'If you want to meet him, yes. Not much further.'

Slvasta shrugged; he'd come this far. He stepped onto the gangplank, impressed by the way Russell's boss had arranged the trip and watched for any signs of pursuit. Clearly, the network of cells they'd painstakingly built up in Varlan wasn't the only subversive organization on Bienvenido. He wasn't sure if that was a good thing, or not.

*

Slvasta didn't know how long he slept. When he woke it was raining again, the big drops drumming loudly on the taut canvas tarpaulins covering the longbarge's holds. His cot was in a tiny alcove in the cabin, barely more than a shelf, a curtain closing it off. He pulled it aside and swung out. A weak grey daylight shone through small portholes just below the roof. His clothes were stretched across a stool in front of the galley's small iron stove. The heat from the coals glowing in the grate had dried them out overnight, and he put them on, allowing his ex-sight to sweep the longbarge.

Their cargo was grain of some sort, big nut-like kernels filling each of the five holds. Behind the cabin, two mod-monkeys worked in the engine compartment, methodically shovelling a mix of coal and wood into the furnace while long brass pistons pumped away on either side of them. The compartment's upper hatch was closed against the rain, and the only light came from the flames. Neither of the mod-monkeys appeared bothered by their harsh environment.

Slvasta went up the narrow stairs at the end of the cabin, which took him to the tiny wheelhouse. The bargemaster was at the wheel. Slvasta had met him last night when he came aboard – a tall fellow with greying hair and thick mutton-chop sideburns, a black Dutch cap seemingly part of his head. He nodded at Slvasta but said nothing.

'Morning,' Russell said. He was standing beside the barge-master, staring through the narrow windows. Dark clouds hung low in the sky, scudding along quickly in the strong wind. Meadows and forests on both sides of the broad river were glistening under the deluge.

'Where are we?' Slvasta asked.

'Coming up on Brewsterville,' Russell answered him. Which, of course, told Slvasta nothing.

'Am I allowed to know where we're going?' he asked with a heavy irony.

Russell grinned broadly. 'Adeone. It's a town at the western end of the Algory mountains. Nice place.'

'I'm sure it is.'

*

There were plenty of towns along the river, all of them with docks and warehouses. In this part of the world, the river was an important trade route, used by a great many boats; he saw coal barges, grain barges, ordinary cargo boats, some private yachts, even trains of log rafts being steered carefully downstream.

Slvasta helped the crew operate the locks they came to, which were built along the side of great stone weirs where river water churned and foamed vigorously as it dropped several metres. He marvelled at the massive wooden doors as he pushed hard at the long oak balance beam to open one, the size and ease of the operation putting into perspective the engineering and labour that had gone into taming the river over the centuries. With the economics texts fresh in his mind, he could comprehend the effort that generations had expended to develop this quiet corner of Bienvenido into a steady agricultural and mining community. Once again it forced him to confront how big the world was, how difficult to govern. The Captain's rule might not be enlightened, but it did work. Now here he was, coming along to change an evolutionary development, motivated by little more than exasperation. *If we succeed, so much will change, and no doubt there are going to be deaths, too. Do I have the right to instigate such an upheaval? Perhaps it is just fear that makes me think violence is the only way to transform the system. Violence: the brutish solution of the ignorant who know they could never get enough people to vote for them.*

Bethaneve certainly thought theirs was the only way. The right way. She never had these moments of self-doubt the way he did; because of her job at the centre of government, she could see how the Captain and his allies had corrupted the system so nothing could change. It was the chaos and suffering which would surely swarm the capital that Slvasta dreaded most. When he examined his life, there were times when he simply didn't understand how he had come to be in such a position.

*

Adeone was a pleasant enough market town, grown up around the original stony river crossing where the pioneers forded the water to reach the Pirit Wolds. It was a natural point for the farmers who'd arrived back during Arnithan's captaincy to cultivate the rich loamy soil around the edges of the wolds, to bring their produce to the boats. Then later when modest malachite deposits had been found in the Algory mountains to the east, the wharfs had been extended to carry the mineral downstream to the larger towns and cities where smelters awaited.

As the longbarge tied up at a wharf, Slvasta admired the impressive stone bridge that had long since replaced the ford. Warehouses formed a near-solid cliff behind the waterfront. The brick and timber houses that spread out beyond were pleasant, though hardly extravagant. Adeone was just another provincial copy of Dios. Smaller and shabbier, but with a sense of purpose, its citizens knowing they were secure in their position, that nothing was going to upset their way of life.

Two horses were waiting for them in the stables of the local coaching inn. Slvasta mounted a terrestrial chestnut mare while Russell claimed a stolid mod-horse with a bristly grey hide which could take his weight easily.

As they rode out of Adeone he realized there were none of the usual Shanties cluttering its outskirts, which surprised him; rural areas were notoriously short of jobs. Here, the road was lined by terrestrial cedars, the tallest of which were easily two hundred years old. Their unique flattened branches arched out high above Slvasta's head to merge across the track of muddy stone, filling the air with their distinctive sharp scent after the rain. Where some of the ancient titans had fallen, new trees had already been planted; the local council was clearly quite efficient, taking its obligations seriously.

It was late afternoon when they began their trek. Behind him, the sinking sun produced red-gold rays that cut down at a low angle past the thick tree trunks. Slvasta had to ride to the side of the road, there were so many carts using it. He enjoyed the bustle and confidence he sensed radiating out from people. The whole area put him in mind of his early childhood, when the world was a pleasant and happy place.

The sun was setting when they came to a major junction. Two big greenswards split off north and south – one carrying on with the line of cedars, the other marked by the drooping pink leaves of thrasta trees. There were also two new roads, their trees barely three metres high. Russell set off down one defined by blue-grey follrux saplings whose prickly leaves were already folding up as the sunlight shrank away. The land was wilder here, with deeper valleys; the farms were smaller, and the forests larger. Directly ahead, he could just see the snow-tipped crowns of the Algory mountain range catching the last of the sun, like glowing beacon fires against the darkening sky.

Although they were now clearly at the frontier of civilization, the road they travelled was extremely well used, with fresh stone laid to keep the mud at bay. Russell turned off down a track unmarked by trees, winding through a wide gash in a forest. Slvasta saw an ageing sign nailed to a tree, with vines already coiling round the edges. BLAIR FARM was carved crudely into the wood. The ground began to rise on both sides, and nasty clouds of small tatus flies emerged from the thick trees to buzz round Slvasta's head. He extended his shell to ward them off; they clearly had a thirst for human blood.

Finally, they rounded a curve, and a valley unfolded ahead. The land along the bottom had been cleared of trees and laid out in a chequerboard of fields. A large farm compound stood just short of the treeline, with long wooden barns in perfect rows. For an unpleasant moment, Slvasta was back on patrol approaching the Shilo compound.

As they approached, Slvasta let his ex-sight range through the buildings. The timber barns were all new. Indeed, one of them was a timber mill, with a steam engine powering a couple of saws. Four hulking traction engines were puffing their way home from the fields they'd been ploughing, pistons clanking loudly in the still evening air. Nearly half of the barns were full of stalls or cages with a huge variety of mods, which made him even more uneasy. He was astonished by the amount of activity and the number of people out here. A couple of the barns were dormitories. One was nothing more than a coal store. Other barns housed heavy machinery, stamping out shapes of metal which were carried to long benches where dozens of mod-dwarfs sat assembling odd pieces of equipment. Furnaces burnt hotly, powering all sorts of unfamiliar devices. Then there were the long sheds at the far end of the compound, protected by the most effective fuzz he'd encountered.

The farmhouse itself was a normal two-storey affair, with a veranda along the front and roses climbing up the gable ends. A bright light shone welcomingly out of every window. It was a lot whiter than the oil lamps he was familiar with. He tied his horse up on the rail beside the paddock. With a grin, Russell showed him through the front door. That was when Slvasta realized he'd never actually jabbed a pin into Russell's thumb to check his blood. So much for him being the smart one, as Bethaneve claimed, but at least he had his pistol. *While walking into the home of a weapons merchant.* Anxiety made his stomach churn as he crossed the threshold.

The centre of the house was a large hallway with a curving stair that led up to a long landing. By now Slvasta wasn't at all surprised by how pleasant the interior of the farmhouse was, with plush furniture and thick carpets. The too-white lights hung from the ceiling, strange glass globes that shone with a uniform mono-chrome brilliance.

Someone was coming down the stairs. A man shedding his fuzz to smile knowingly, allowing a certain degree of lofty amusement to radiate out through his shell.

Recognition locked Slvasta's muscles tight. 'You!' he grunted in shock.

'Good to see you again, lieutenant,' Nigel said.

BOOK FIVE

Those who Fall

1

It was two days before Kysandra's seventeenth birthday when the *thing* plunged flaming through the night sky. She was sitting by her bedroom window on the top floor of the farmhouse, eyes a blotchy red from another bout of crying. The argument with her mother had been epic, even by their standards, starting that morning and carrying on all afternoon. The ancient mod-dwarfs that helped out around the farm whimpered softly and crawled under the dining-room table, folding their arms over their heads as the air filled with screams, insults, threats and denouncements, and 'path emotions saturated the aether like firework bursts.

'I *hate* you. You're the worst mother ever! I hope you die!' was just a mild opening salvo.

None of the insults made any difference, nor the pleading, nor the anguish. Sarara, her mother, was too skilled in this battle-field. Anger was answered by scorn and fury. Threats came thick and fast from both sides. More of the kitchen's dwindling stack of crockery had been hurled. Sometimes by hand, often by a near-involuntary teekay reflex, thought becoming deed without restraint.

By mid-afternoon the argument had become so fierce that Sarara had inevitably turned to her pipe of narnik. After that, the dispute became surreal as the drug amplified and soothed the woman's thoughts in random surges. Sometimes she'd be sobbing, moaning, 'sorry, sorry, sorry,' while at other times her eyes would be focused with manic hatred and she'd hold a carving knife dangerously in her shaking hand as Kysandra unleashed another torrent of abuse.

Exhausted and distraught as the sun dropped behind the valley where Blair Farm nestled, Kysandra had run upstairs and slammed her bedroom door shut, then pushed the old chest of drawers across it. Mother and daughter had shouted at each other through the wood for a further ten minutes before Sarara had stomped off downstairs for another pipe.

Kysandra had cried pitifully as her mother fumbled her way into another night of mad narnik-fuelled dreams. Ex-sight showed her Sarara's comatose form sprawled across the parlour's settee. Every so often she would jerk about and yell something incoherent as the drug sparked a fresh hallucination in her brain. Then she'd sink back down again to resume a soft snoring and sniffling. The cold empty pipe had fallen onto the bare floor-boards beside her.

Adding to Kysandra's misery was the hunger. She hadn't eaten since breakfast, and that had just been some apples and a glass of milk. But she refused to go downstairs to the kitchen. Even though there was no chance of her mother waking before morning now, she was powered by a stubbornness which had governed her whole life.

'Girl, you have an attitude from Uracus,' her father used to say, half in delight, half in dismay, as she refused to back down or apologize for whatever mischief she'd performed.

But that was years ago, before her father had gone off with the Adeone county militia to help sweep after a Fall. Eight years. And he'd still not come back.

Kysandra was still waiting for him, refusing to give up. That had been one of the first massive battles with Sarara, when she found her mother getting rid of Dad's clothes. It was around the time Sarara had started smoking to cover her own grief and the difficulty of looking after a farm by herself. Those diffi-culties had just kept getting worse as the fields turned fallow, the mods grew old and the buildings in the compound started to deteriorate.

After eight years without Dad, they could just about keep the compound's vegetable garden going, along with maintaining a couple of pigs, an ageing cow for milk and a chicken coop – which the bussalores kept getting into. It was hard to feed themselves some days.

That was why Kysandra was due to marry Akstan in two days, as soon as she was seventeen and it was legal (with parental permission). Sarara hadn't simply given permission; she'd eagerly agreed to the whole dowry arrangement with Akstan's grubby family. It was simple enough. In exchange for Blair Farm (and Kysandra), Sarara would get three rooms of her own above one of the family's stores which sold cloth to the town. With an easy job behind the counter, she'd finally be rid of her whole night-mare inheritance problem. In her more hurtful moments, she'd screeched at Kysandra that without a brat daughter and a crap farm holding her back, she'd be able to find herself a decent man again. Kysandra had hurled the last remaining china jug at her for that one.

So there she was that clear night, looking out at the splendid nebulas whose moiré radiance dusted the Void. Their remarkable intricate shapes and glowing colours did nothing for her. She simply stared at them, trying not to think of how Giu had claimed her father's soul. She alternated that with malicious snarls at the idea of Uracus taking her mother and Akstan, and the rest of his wretched family – including their matriarch, Ma Ulvon, whom Kysandra was secretly rather scared of.

Tonight Uracus glowed brightly high in the night sky, its malevolent carmine swirls surrounded by tattered amber veils curling back into the empty gash at its centre, like a raw wound across space. *An omen*, she thought miserably, *signalling how crudding bad my life is going to be*. Something moved across the evil nebula. A smudge of amber light, racing out of the north-west. And growing brighter.

Kysandra stared at it. Puzzled to begin with. She'd never seen a nebula like it. And she'd certainly never heard of a nebula moving. The thing began to elongate, a thin perfectly straight line of hazy salmon phosphorescence stretching out behind it.

That's not a nebula!

There were only two things that moved in Bienvenido's skies. The Skylords gracing the planet with their awesome presence, or—

'F . . . F . . . Faller!' she yelled in shock.

An utterly pointless shout. Sarara was deep in her narcotic sleep, and the mod-dwarfs were still curled up under the table.

Kysandra kept watching the glowing spectre. It was a lot brighter now as it streaked closer, heading almost directly for Blair Farm. A second equally pointless shout of warning died on her lips. Faller eggs dropped straight down, or so she'd always believed. And they were dark. Nothing like this.

A new kind of Faller?

Curiosity overcame her initial burst of fear. The glowing object was changing somehow. Its glow diminished as it soared above the valley, yet the orange light expanded as it drew ever closer to the farmhouse. It was big, she realized – far, far bigger than any Faller egg. The weird shimmering tail of luminescent air started to shrink, like smoke wafting away.

Kysandra could barely turn her neck fast enough as the glimmering thing shot overhead with a roar almost as loud as a thunderclap. She managed to catch a swift glimpse of its shape: the body of a giant egg, with stiff curving triangular wings. It was as if a shipwright had tried to build a boat that flew. For the last eight years Kysandra had been steadily reading her way through her father's huge library of books (another bone of contention with her mother), and she couldn't recall anything remotely like this in any of the manuals and accounts published by the Faller Research Institute.

The impossible thing shot away over the river, sinking swiftly out of the sky. Its glow vanished as it reached the treetops. Only the writhing streamers of iridescent air were left, ghostly indicators of its path. They ripped away to nothing just as the noise reached the farmhouse – a cacophony of crashing and snapping as trees were smashed apart from the impact.

Then everything was still. The night sky was clear, the nebulas shimmering exuberantly as normal. Nothing moved.

Kysandra stared at the woodland on the other side of the river. But the trees were an impenetrable tangle, webbed with tenacious vines. Her ex-sight certainly couldn't reach that far.

What do I do? Should I run?

It had to be some kind of Faller. A huge one. That boat-bird shape had been as big as the farmhouse. She couldn't imagine the horror it would unleash upon the county. *Worse than being married to Akstan, even.*

She didn't dare go outside and walk down to the river to see what had crashed into the trees, nor did she have the courage to make a break for the town, for she'd have to leave her mother, which she realized she couldn't actually do. Getting the mod-dwarfs to help haul her narnik-saturated mother out to the buggy and then harnessing their one remaining mod-horse to it would take forever. The new Fallers would be able to overwhelm them before they even started racing down the road.

By law, each farm was supposed to have a Faller fire beacon, a pile of wood ready to light at a moment's notice, sending a warning blaze shooting up, visible for miles around should they catch sight of an egg Falling. Her father had built one just outside the compound – a marvellous pyramid of branches standing over four metres high at the apex, built in a clever lattice allowing air to be sucked though and help accelerate the flames.

That had been before he left, and the wood had been exposed to many years of rainfall since. Mildew and fungus had gnawed at the sturdy branches, reducing them to crumbling fibres swamped by vines.

It would never catch light now, anyway, she thought.

Kysandra stared at the dark mass of the wood beyond the water. Still nothing moved. She used her 'path to order the mod-dwarfs to fetch her the shotgun from its place in the cabinet downstairs. While she was at it, she added an instruction to bring the remainder of the bread from the kitchen. And some milk.

With her stomach mollified slightly, and the weight of the cold metal gun resting reassuringly against her side, she settled down to begin her vigil.

*

'Wake up, you idle girl!'

Kysandra's body jolted painfully. She opened her eyes to see her mother framed by her bedroom door, holding the shotgun with a wary expression marring her thin, lined face. It was daylight outside, well into the morning if she was any judge.

'What were you going to do with this, then?' Sarara demanded, her grip tightening on the shotgun as she held it up. 'Shoot me in my sleep?'

'I saw something,' Kysandra said defensively. She turned to stare out of the window. The wood on the other side of the river was almost as dark in the morning sun as it was at midnight. There was no hint of anything awry, no dread invading army of Faller creatures marching out of the trees. No massive shape taking flight.

'What?' her mother sneered.

It was that *tone*, the one which always made Kysandra's shoulders hunch in reflex, annoyance and contempt contracting her muscles. 'I don't know.' She thought about how to explain what she'd seen.

'Get yourself ready. Julias is here.'

'What?' Kysandra hated Julias. He was one of Akstan's brothers, an even bigger slob than her intended groom. Ma Ulvon had him running one of the abattoirs in Adeone, yet another of the family businesses over which she ruled with supreme authority. 'Why is he here?' she asked in surprise.

'I must have dropped you on your head more than once when you were a baby. You're to be married tomorrow, remember? All our lives are going to get better then.'

'I'm not getting married!' Kysandra snarled. 'Not to *him*.'

'Now you listen, and you listen good, you ungrateful little bitch. We owe Ma Ulvon a lot of money. How do you think I've supported us for the last few years? This farm isn't worth crud

380

without someone working it. And I couldn't do that, not with you running round like a wild bussalore all day.'

Kysandra's anger drained away into shock. 'We owe Ma Ulvon?' She couldn't believe it. You had to be crazy to take a loan from Ma Ulvon – everybody knew that. Interest payments never ended, and Ma's sons and grandsons and nephews were punctual and forceful when it came to collection time. 'Why?' she demanded, suddenly suspicious. 'What did you buy? We've grown enough food for ourselves. Always have.'

'The farm needs plenty of things that don't grow on trees, and your father spent every coin we earned on those stupid books when he should have invested it properly. Now, pack your bag and get ready. Julias and I will drag you out of here if we have to, make no mistake about that.'

'Narnik!' Kysandra cried in horror. 'You've been buying your narnik from her, haven't you?'

'Don't you judge me,' Sarara shouted back. 'You don't know how I've suffered, not since your father left.'

'He's coming back.'

'He was fucking eaten by a Faller, you stupid girl. When will you ever get that into your dopey cloud-filled head? He's dead! He's not coming back. Not ever. His soul wasn't even strong enough to come visit us after. So he didn't love you that much, after all. Did he?'

Kysandra screamed incoherently at her diabolical tormentor. Her teekay lifted the empty milk bottle and shoved it forward through the air, aimed directly at her mother's head. Sarara swung the shotgun round and pulled the trigger – completely missing the bottle.

The shotgun blasted a hole in the ceiling. Long splinters exploded out of the planks. Kysandra's shell was barely strong enough to ward them off. She twisted round, diving for cover. Two slivers of sharp wood cut through her dress along her ribs, slashing hotly at her skin.

There was no pain, not immediately. Kysandra stared down at the slim rents in the fabric. Blood began to stain the cloth.

Sarara had a nasty red graze on her forehead where the bottle had struck her. She dabbed at it while she peered in dismay at Kysandra's wounds, as if she couldn't believe what she was seeing. The two of them looked at each other wordlessly for a long moment.

'Wash and dress those cuts,' Sarara said flatly. 'Don't let them get infected. I'll get our things into the cart.' She turned on her heel and rushed out. Kysandra heard her sobbing as she stumbled down the stairs.

And there was nothing else left to be done.

*

Normally Kysandra enjoyed visiting Adeone. The town with its big solid buildings and busy docks and bustling streets was always a welcome break from the farm, and the Shanty outside was small enough not to worry her. But this time when the cart rolled in, she wished it dead and ruined. She cursed its people. Everyone who saw the cart (and they all quickly looked away again) knew she was being brought to the town hall as payment to Ma Ulvon. None of them protested. They didn't even dare offer her any sympathy.

Once they were in the centre where the roads were paved, the ride became a lot smoother. She'd spent most of the time wincing at every jolt. But the pain from the splinter cuts was nothing to the one in her head. They crossed a junction. The road on one side led to the central square, where the town hall with its bright red brick walls and white stone-outlined windows stood two storeys higher than all the rest of the buildings. The place where they'd take her tomorrow and sign her up for a life of suffering – if they had their way. She knew damn well the county registrar wouldn't help her. The ceremony would go ahead, no matter how many times she said no.

'You've turned me into a whore,' she told her mother stonily. 'Are you proud?'

'You know,' Julias said from the front of the cart where he was directing the mod-horse with 'path instructions, 'it seems to me you should show some respect when you talk to your mother. Some gratitude to Ma would be welcome, too. She's doing you a favour.'

Kysandra glared at the back of the obese oaf, seeing the way the seams on his red and black checked shirt strained to contain his great rolls of flesh. She allowed all the hatred to shine through her shell. 'You're going to die,' she told him triumphantly. 'You're going to die pissing your pants while your soul screams as it's consumed by Uracus. And I want you to know, here and now, that I played my part in making that happen.' She was never going to tell them about the huge new Faller in the forest beyond the farm. Not now. Never going to warn the town and all its passive compliant people. The arseholes deserved to be eaten for what they'd allowed to take control of them. Ma's family was worse than any Faller nest.

Afterwards, when the Fallers had devoured everyone, the regiments would finally come and burn the whole stinking place to the ground. When that happened there wouldn't even be a grave to bury the mounds of broken bones in.

Good!

'Uracus, she's got a mouth on her,' Julias grunted.

'You need to know not to speak to your husband like that,' Sarara said. 'Wives don't.'

'I'm not to be his wife; I'm to be his whore. Thanks to *you*, Mother.'

'Shut up!' Sarara shouted.

They drew up in front of the Hevlin Hotel on Lubal Street. Low, dark clouds were scudding across the sky. Kysandra knew that weather; the rain that was coming would last the better part of a day. She looked up in loathing at the hotel. It was a sprawling white-painted building with a wide three-storey frontage obscuring a labyrinth of ill-matched extensions at the back; it had even merged with another couple of dwellings behind. This was where Ma Ulvon lived, and ran her collection of legitimate businesses alongside a wider network of altogether darker activities.

'Come on,' Julias said. His teekay tipped her bag off the back of the cart.

Kysandra thought about refusing, but she could perceive several of Ma's people in the lobby. Bulky men who didn't give a crud that she was just a girl; they'd spill out onto the street and drag her inside, no matter how much she yelled and fought. None of Adeone's fine residents would lift a finger to help her. So she gave Julias an evil grin. 'Screaming as you die,' she said victoriously as she climbed down. 'You'll see.'

'You are one screwed-up girl,' he muttered sullenly, and 'pathed the mod-horse to walk on.

Kysandra watched the cart roll past. Her mother didn't look round as she was taken away to her promised new life above the cloth store.

'Welcome,' a voice said.

Kysandra jumped. The woman had been well fuzzed, so much so she hadn't noticed her in the lobby nor coming out of the hotel entrance. Ma Ulvon was big, over a head taller than Kysandra, but without the weight her sons were notorious for. She wore a classy cream-coloured linen business suit and shiny black shoes. A strange quilted cloak was wrapped round her broad shoulders, held in place with a gold chain; the kind of garment Kysandra imagined the fancy aristocratic women of the capital would wear. Auburn hair was trimmed in a neat style that gave the appearance of a forty-year-old – though everyone knew Ma was closer to seventy. Jewellery was minimal, just a few rings and a slim diamond necklace. Kysandra glowered resentfully at her, tucking some dirty strands of hair behind her ear, and very conscious of her threadbare dress. Ma Ulvon was so elegant in comparison, the most sophisticated woman in Adeone.

'I won't do it,' she snapped.

Ma Ulvon raised a plucked eyebrow. 'Do what, my dear?' Even the voice, so smooth and cold, was intimidating.

'Marry Akstan. You can have the farm, I don't care, but I won't do that.'

'Really?' Ma gestured at the lobby. 'Shall we go in, or do I need to have you carried in?' She turned and started up the short stone steps to the glossy doors.

Kysandra considered simply running, but again doubted she'd get very far. She walked after the daunting woman.

'Don't forget your bag,' Ma said.

The lobby was dark after the street outside. A rich burgundy and gold wallpaper seemed to shimmer in the yellow light of the oil lamps. Settees and chairs were all upholstered in lush velvet. Its assault on the senses announced that the Hevlin had aspirations way beyond Adeone's provincial status.

Ma was waiting beside another woman. This one was dressed in extravagant colourful clothes, with a great deal of black lace frill. Her bodice was open halfway to her navel, showing off a lot of cleavage. Kysandra tried not to stare, but it was pretty obvious what her profession was.

'This is Madeline,' Ma said. 'She's the Hevlin's madam.'

'Hiya, kiddo,' Madeline said with a wink.

Kysandra put on her best belligerent expression, not understanding what was happening.

'So,' Ma said. 'You have a choice now, Kysandra. You either work for Madeline, here – you'll be popular, a pretty young thing like you. We'll dose you up at the start so you don't struggle too much, then after a while you'll be used to it. Or you marry Akstan and lead a normal life, with money, comfort and children. And believe me when I say I am very protective of my grandchildren. Nobody will mess with you or disrespect you, not even Akstan.'

'And when are you going to tell me what the choice is?' Kysandra sneered sarcastically. She managed to look at Ma without flinching.

Ma chuckled. 'I think Akstan should be the nervous one.'

Kysandra tipped her head back, staring defiantly at Ma. *I can afford to be bold, because you'll be dead within a week. Eaten alive. If I can, I'll make sure you know I'm the one who's responsible.*

With only a small flicker of uncertainty at this unexpected resistance, Ma turned to Madeline. 'Take her upstairs and clean her up for Giu's sake. She looks like something they dragged out of the river mud. Every girl should look splendid for her wedding day, especially my future daughter-in-law.'

Kysandra allowed herself to be led upstairs by Madeline. She was given one of the larger guest rooms at the back, with its own bathroom. The boiler at the farmhouse which was part of the range stove hadn't worked too well for a couple of years now. She stared in guilty longing at the enamelled rolltop bath as abundant hot water poured out of the tap. Soaps and salts were added by Madeline, producing a marvellous lavender scent in the air. The water was covered by a thick layer of white bubbles.

'Enjoy,' Madeline said as she left the room. 'I'd suggest at least half an hour soaking. Honestly, kiddo, you need to treat your pores a lot better. When you're out we'll start on the hair. It may take a while.'

When the door shut, Kysandra turned the Ysdom lock, then spun out a big fuzz, which was quite reasonable for a girl getting undressed in a public building. There didn't seem to be anyone's ex-sight pervading the room.

Her skirt came off. Underneath she was wearing a pair of tough denim shorts that came down to her knees. Her frilly blouse followed. The T-shirt worn below was one of Dad's, saved from her mother's cull; it was baggy but acceptable. This was hardly usual attire for a teenage girl, but nobody in this town would be bothered. And the docks were only a quarter of a mile away. She had five silver shillings. That was more than enough to buy her passage on some boat. She didn't care where it was sailing to, just that it left Adeone behind.

The bathroom's sash window slid up easily enough. She swung a leg out over the sill. It was six metres to the ground, but a drain-pipe was only a metre to one side. She grabbed it and began to shin down into the alley.

With just a couple of metres to go, the window slammed shut above her. She glanced up, but it didn't matter. Then the fuzz in an arched doorway below faded out. Three of Ma's people were waiting for her. Their combined teekay yanked her off the drainpipe. She hit the ground painfully and yelped.

'Oh, you are so predictable,' Ma 'pathed mockingly. 'Bring her back, boys.'

Kysandra screamed as they closed in on her, but there was nothing she could do. They were big and strong and didn't care how much she squirmed, kicked and shouted. They picked her up and held her so tightly she knew she'd have bruise rings around every limb.

She was carried unceremoniously inside. Madeline was waiting, a small bottle in her hand. 'Hold her down.'

Kysandra started to fight as hard as she could. It made no difference. She was shoved onto the floor and immobilized with a combination of hands and teekay. Then Madeline pinched her nose shut. Teekay expanded in her mouth like a ball that was inflating, a very prickly ball. It forced her jaw open.

'You're all going to die, and I made it happen,' her 'path blazed at them.

They just laughed as the neck of the bottle was shoved between her teeth. The liquid glugged out. Kysandra tried not to swallow, but it was impossible. The bitter liquid went down her throat. Madeline withdrew the bottle.

After a minute, the men let go of her. Kysandra stood up; it was difficult. 'What was that?' she asked, or thought she did. Her words sounded strangely slurred. Then her legs wobbled. Madeline grabbed her, stopping her from falling. 'Bitch . . . What . . . ?'

The world seemed to dissolve into really pretty colours, so nice she cooed enthusiastically at them. Then they started spinning, which made her dizzy. 'I need to sit.'

'Of course you do,' Madeline's voice said somewhere off in the distance.

There was a strange ripping sound, like cloth being torn. Lovely cool air glided like silk over her bare skin. Kysandra smiled at the sensation. Then frowned. This was all wrong; she shouldn't be enjoying this. She frowned harder, which sent purple waves swishing through the air. Madeline bent over her as the bathwater warmed her skin. The soap bubbles came alive. Each one popped and released a tiny Faller. Kysandra started screaming as they wriggled over her body, miniature teeth snapping.

*

'. . . Do you take this noble woman as your wife, to love and cherish during your mortal life, and then to take Guidance with her into the loving embrace of Giu?'

'I do.'

Kysandra blinked slowly, barely able to stand. Nothing had made sense for . . . well, a while now. The universe had become weird and blurred, sometimes warm and nice, sometimes sharp and terrifying so that she screamed and screamed. They kept making her swallow the bitter liquid. A lot of the time she was cold and shaking. She dreamt, or thought she did, or maybe her dreams had surged out of the night to live in her head permanently.

And now there was a dress. A white dress with a ridiculous puffy skirt, and gold silk bows, and a veil. *Is that still over my eyes? Is that why everything looks so odd?*

'And Kysandra, do you take this good man as your husband, to love without question during your mortal life, and then to take Guidance with him into the loving embrace of Giu?'

'Say yes,' the man said.

Swaying about, Kysandra peered at the man standing beside her, holding her arm. 'Who the crud are you?' she blurted. Even with the drug buzzing loud and warm in her blood, she knew this wasn't Akstan. He wasn't old enough, certainly wasn't fat enough, and anyway he had blond hair. His green eyes were looking expectantly at her.

'Just say yes,' he said with so much sympathy and kindness she thought she might cry. Nobody had looked at her like that. *Not since Dad . . .*

Thoughts that weren't entirely her own produced a word that simply had to push past her lips. 'Yes.'

'I now pronounce you man and wife from this day forth. May Giu bless your immortal souls.'

Kysandra started to laugh. 'You're all going to die.'

'You may kiss the bride.'

The man settled for giving her a quick hug, patting her back. Over his shoulder she saw Ma Ulvon, and Akstan and Julias and Madeline and two more of Ma's sons with their wives. All of them lined up in a row along the side of the registry office, not saying anything, their faces blank. Kysandra's laugh became hysterical. 'Yes! Oh yes, you're already dead, aren't you? They got you. They ate you already. You're not you, none of you is. I didn't warn you it'd landed, see, I didn't tell you. I did this to you.' She giggled exuberantly. 'This really is the happiest day of my life.'

'That's my girl,' said the man holding her, the man she was married to.

Her legs started to buckle. 'Are you going to eat me now?'

'No. Time to go home, Kysandra.'

'Oh, goodie.' She passed out.

∗

There were new planks spliced into her bedroom ceiling. Four of them, fresh wood neatly cut, forming a square not quite a metre on each side. Kysandra frowned up at them, not understanding why they should be there. *Shotgun blast.* Then the memories came rushing back. Julias arriving. That last day she'd argued with her mother. The shotgun. Ma. Trying to escape through the Hevlin's bathroom window. Drugs forced down her throat. The wedding. *Man with blond hair!*

She gasped and sat upright in bed. She was still wearing the wedding dress, though someone had removed the skirt, allowing her to see the frilly knee-length bloomers covering her legs. It was a ridiculous sight.

Very conscious of the way the drugs had messed with her, she tried standing up. There was no dizziness, no shaking limbs. In fact she felt amazingly clear headed and refreshed, as if she'd just had the best sleep of her life. And she was very, very hungry. To emphasize the point, her stomach gurgled like bad plumbing – because there was the most incredible smell of cooking bacon drifting through the farmhouse.

Kysandra took a step towards the door. Stopped. Looked round properly. Her bedroom wasn't just tidy, it was immaculate. And the sheets on the bed were clean. New! She touched them gingerly, marvelling at how soft they were. A dress was hanging over the back of the chair. Not her dress; she'd never seen it before. This was a nice dark blue cotton with a square-cut neck – brand new and looked like her exact size. Fresh underwear was folded neatly beside it. A decent pair of dark-brown ankle boots.

'What the crud?'

The landing outside was clean. Furniture polished. The glass in the windows was perfectly transparent; someone had washed the dirt and mould off.

She went downstairs. *He* was in the kitchen: the man with the shaggy blond hair and green eyes. The quite good-looking man, who was probably in his mid- to late twenties. He wore a simple white shirt and green denim trousers. And his smile when she came in was . . . *nice*.

'Hi,' he said. 'Big shock for you, I guess. Don't worry, you're doing fine. Sit down, I'll get you some breakfast. You must be hungry. I gave you a sedative so you'd be able to sleep off the drugs they forced into you.'

'Whaaa—?'

'It's okay. Sit. I'm not going to hurt you. Promise. After all, I am your husband.' He grinned. 'Formal introduction: my name is Nigel.' He stuck out his hand.

Kysandra stared at it, worried she was going to start crying.

'Oh, hey, please. I really don't mean you any harm. I know we started off . . . strangely. But I want us to be friends at least. Now come on, eat; it'll help.'

Kysandra sat down heavily. It was one of the kitchen chairs, but clean, just like the table. He fetched a plate from the warming surface on the range stove. And, yes, the stove had been completely repaired, the iron brushed to a dull sheen. A lively fire burnt behind its lower grate door. *I wonder if we have hot water again?* She hardened her shell so he wouldn't know she'd just thought that. His own shell was incredibly solid, stronger than anyone she'd ever known.

The plate (new) had bacon, scrambled egg on heavily buttered toast, grilled folberries in thick tomato sauce, sausages, and . . . 'What are those?' she blurted.

'Hash browns. Potato, but done – well, like that. You shred them and fry them. Try it. But I won't be offended if you don't like it.' He smiled hopefully.

The smell was just too strong, and her stomach was reacting loudly. Kysandra tried some of the scrambled eggs. She'd never known they could be so creamy.

'Tea, coffee or orange juice?' Nigel asked.

'Tea, please.'

One of the farm's mod-dwarfs put the cup down in front of her. It had been spruced up as well, its short fur washed and brushed.

'What's happened?' she croaked. 'I don't understand.'

'Short version,' Nigel said. 'I'm new in town. I want a remote place to live where I won't be bothered, and Blair Farm fits that requirement perfectly. I'm also very rich. So I paid off your mother's debts to Ma Ulvon and bought the farm. I admit I wasn't quite expecting you to be part of the deal, but you have title to the farm and, frankly, I thought you'd prefer me to Akstan. My apologies if I was wrong.'

Which was a mad story. Kysandra wasn't sure she believed it. She gave him a surly look. 'Are you going to fuck me?' she asked with as much defiance as she could manage.

'Oh, hell, *no*. No. Look, I know we're officially married, but I want you to think of me as your guardian; you're really still a child despite what the law here says. Sex isn't part of the arrangement. I just need the farm. Okay?'

She nodded, still uncertain. 'Okay.' And some small bad part of her brain was asking: *Why not? All the boys in town would, and most of their dads, too.* She pouted. 'Thank you. Er, what about my mother?'

'Living above the cloth store, as agreed with Ma Ulvon. Why? Would you be happier if she moved back here?'

'Uracus, no!'

The bacon was cooked to perfection as well. Kysandra had another large helping of eggs, then suddenly stopped and stood up, glancing nervously out of the window. The river was just visible, as were the woods on the other side. It all seemed normal. But it wasn't, of course – it couldn't be. 'How long was I asleep?'

'Nearly eighteen hours. It's the day after we got married.'

'Uracus! We have to leave. Now!'

'Would you like to tell me why?'

'Something . . . A Faller egg, but bigger, a new type, big enough to carry a whole nest of them. It came down in the woods on the other side of the river three nights ago. They'll eat us, Nigel! I didn't tell anyone. I know I should have done, I'm sorry, but I didn't. I was so angry about the wedding, about everything.'

He sat at the table opposite her, hands wrapped round a mug of tea. His smile was reassuring. 'Ah. Yes. Don't worry. Actually, that wasn't from the Forest. It's not a Faller invasion. You're safe.'

Her skin chilled as she looked at him. Slowly, slowly, she tensed her leg muscles, ready to make a dash for the door. *Is the shotgun back in its cabinet? Has he found it?*

'Now try and keep calm,' Nigel said. 'This is the biggie coming up: that thing you saw land was my spaceship.'

'Riiiight—' Kysandra sprinted as fast as she could in those stupid bloomers. Straight through the hall and out into the compound. The ground with its small sharp stones stung and cut her bare feet, but she didn't stop. Refused to let the pain distract her. Ahead was the gate in the sagging fence round the overgrown garden. Except the vegetable garden was now in good order, with the soil beds freshly dug. Someone was kneeling to sort out the tangle of runner beans on their bamboo canes. Someone dressed in simple dungarees and a rust-red T-shirt.

Someone who was standing up and turning to face her. And his face was—

Kysandra screamed and lost her footing, tumbling over in a flurry of flailing arms. Pain shot up both knees.

'Are you okay?'

She looked round fearfully. Nigel was coming out of the house, his expression full of concern. She looked from him to the *thing* by the vegetables. It was human shaped, but its face – it was completely devoid of any characteristics. *Like an adult-size doll*, she thought. Waiting to take someone's identity. 'Fallers,' she cried. 'You're Fallers!'

'Kysandra, please,' Nigel said. And his shell softened to let her perceive his thoughts; the genuine compassion, and more, a trace of amusement at her reaction.

A spark of anger fired into her brain. 'You think I'm a crudding joke?' she shouted.

'No. I think you're holding up well . . . given the circumstances. How do you think Akstan would react? I met him, remember. I think he'd have fainted clean away by now.'

'You're going to eat me!'

Nigel sighed, and knelt down beside her. 'No, Kysandra. I'm not going to eat you. I'm human, just like you.'

She twisted her head round to look fearfully at the doll-man. 'That's not.'

'No. It's not. It's what we call an ANAdroid. It's a machine. Biological, but manufactured. Think of it as a giant mod-dwarf, just a little smarter.'

'Oh, thank you,' the doll-man said. Its pale lips curved up, approximating a smile. 'I apologize if my appearance startled you. I assure you I am not hostile. Nigel is correct, I am a biological machine.'

Kysandra started crying.

'Come on,' Nigel said kindly. 'Let's get you back inside. Those cuts need cleaning.'

Kysandra stared up helplessly at him as he stood above her. She was all out of fight. *I can't stop them. I'm already dead.* So she didn't resist when he picked her up and carried her back inside.

As he walked back to the house she saw another of the doll-men up on the roof, fixing the shingle. *There is no escape.*

Nigel put her down on the settee in what had originally been the dining room until her father had covered the walls with shelves which he filled with his treasured books. The room hadn't been refurbished yet. Somehow that made the worn cushions she lay on quite comforting. She'd often sat on this same settee with her father when he read to her.

A mod-dwarf brought in a small green bag with a white cross on the top. Nigel knelt beside her and put an old towel underneath her heels. Kysandra watched dully. Blood was staining the bottom of the bloomers, and her feet were a mess, too.

Nigel took a slim tube from the bag. 'This may sting for a moment,' he warned. Kysandra shrugged. The tube hissed as he brought it close to the torn skin on her soles. He moved it in a strange motion as if he was painting her feet.

He was right: it did sting. She sucked down some air sharply at the biting sensation. Then her feet became numb.

'Antiseptic and a mild anaesthetic,' Nigel said quietly. 'Let's see, the dermsynth should work here.' He took out another tube.

Kysandra peered down curiously now, just in time to see a faint blue mist spray out of the second cylinder. The substance stuck to her skin, flowing over it and foaming to form a thin, even layer.

'Good. I was worried the Void wouldn't permit that.'

'What?'

'The Void inhibits a whole range of electrical functions. I didn't know if it would affect the dermsynth. But that's mostly a biochemical reaction.'

'Oh.' She didn't really understand.

'I need to get the fabric clear from your knees.'

Kysandra realized he was asking permission. 'Whatever.'

His teekay ripped through the bloomers' cotton as if it was air. *Faller teekay is stronger than ours.*

Then he was spraying the stuff from the first tube on her

gashes. Her knees stung, then there was nothing again. She let out a sigh of relief. The blue substance was applied. It was like a layer of skin, but tougher.

'There we go,' he said happily. 'All finished now. The dermsynth will help regenerate your own skin. It'll peel off when it's done. Couple of days, maybe.'

'Right.'

'Kysandra.'

'Yes?'

'Have you ever seen anything like that before?'

'No,' she admitted.

He gestured round at the books which surrounded them. 'I've had a bit of a crash course in your history the last two days. Mainly I've been learning about the Fallers. But, tell me, do you know that humans came to Bienvenido from another place?'

'Yes, of course.' Kysandra nodded at the five thick Landing Chronicles – she'd read every one. 'Captain Cornelius brought us here in his ship.'

'Good. Okay. Then is it too much to ask you to believe I came from the same place as that first ship?'

In her mind, the image of the boat-bird falling through the night sky was very clear. She stubbornly refused to admit anything, but her racing thoughts were chaotic, surging with so many conflicting emotions. She could not let hope dominate. Hope betrayed her every time. That he'd flown to Bienvenido was too much to believe. *It would be wonderful, though.*

'Is it at least possible?' Nigel persisted.

'I suppose so.' *Flying through space is in the books, it's real history, so we used to be able to do it.* 'But—'

'Incredible, I know. This must be very shocking. So take a quiet moment and try to relax a little. Why don't you get dressed? And when you're ready, I'll take you over to see my spaceship. That should finally convince you. If it doesn't, I don't know what will.'

'Then what?' she asked.

'Then we'll talk. Once I know you believe, I'll answer all your questions. And, trust me, you'll have a lot of questions.'

She looked down at the patches of blue . . . *stuff* on her knees. It was like nothing she'd ever seen before. Instinct told her it really was something from beyond this world. And a Faller wouldn't treat her like this. 'All right,' she said cautiously. Because if there truly was such a thing as a spaceship, she simply had to see it.

*

The blue dress did fit perfectly. It felt wonderful, too – clean and fresh. She couldn't remember the last time she'd ever worn anything new. Sarara had always collected her clothes from a charity house in town, sewing patches onto worn cloth, darning sweaters. Badges of how poor they were. But this dress . . . Kysandra stood in front of the mirror and simply couldn't stop the smile lifting her lips as she admired herself. Her red-gold hair fell over her shoulders in long waves, without any of the normal tangles that were so devilish to tug out. It was as if she'd spent a week in a salon. She hated Madeline with all her might, but had to admit the woman knew a lot about taking care of hair. *I must make an effort to keep it like this*, she thought. Then she instantly hardened her shell so *he* didn't pick that up. When she looked a little closer into the mirror, she saw the zits on her nose, with more on her chin, one on her cheek. She sighed; would they ever stop?

Nigel was waiting in the hall when she came down the stairs. They'd been fixed, too; not one of them creaked when she put her weight on them.

'Right, then,' he said. 'Ready to visit your first real live space-ship?'

'I want it to be real,' she said. 'I do.'

'I know. Come on.'

They walked down to the river, through the old pattern of fields that were now just squares of tangled weeds and vines separated by hedges that had grown wild. A small boat was tied up on the shore. Not a kind of boat she recognized. This one was circular and seemed to be made of orange fabric. It was *alien* – no other word for it.

There was a rope running across the river, tied to trees on either side. Nigel knelt in the bottom of the boat and used the rope to pull them across.

Kysandra had only crossed the river a handful of times. The wood that occupied the other side of the valley was gloomy and unwelcoming. Its great dark trunks had grown packed close, and they leaned against each other, seemingly merging together several metres off the ground to give an unbroken canopy of aquamarine fronds and verdant fan-leaves. Those trees that died stayed upright, buttressed by their neighbours, so they simply became pillars of vibrant orange and grey fungi. The narrow crooked gaps were filled with vines, as if some giant arachnid had turned the wood into an oversized feeding trap.

A passage had been cleared through the dense web of creepers, the cut ends still bleeding gooey sap. The ground underfoot was a springy loam that smelt vinegary. Tatus flies and larger stikmoths fluttered about in the shade. She could hear bigger creatures rustling through the creepers, though her ex-sight only ever perceived bussalores slithering down into their dank underground burrows.

Then her ex-sight perceived the *thing* up ahead. It must have come down almost vertically at the end, for there was no long trail of smashed trees. Instead it was in a small clearing of broken trunks.

She'd been right about the shape: a large bulbous oval with triangular wings on both sides; she thought the wings had been a lot bigger when it flew over the farmhouse. As she stood at the edge of the clearing looking at it, the surface was an intensely dark green where the sun struck; otherwise it appeared to be coal black. Surprisingly, her gaze was drawn to the twenty or so neuts that were milling about passively.

'Why are they here?' she asked.

'I need manual help to restart the farm,' Nigel replied. 'They're having their eggs shaped into useful genistars.'

'Into geniwhats?'

'You call them mods.'

'Oh. Do you know how to adapt neut eggs?'

'I know the theory, but the ship's smartcore – its brain – is doing the actual shaping.'

'The ship?' She looked at the smooth foreign artefact that had ended its flight in such an ungraceful fashion by thumping to the ground here, and realized she wasn't afraid any more. No, that had been replaced by very strong curiosity. And wonder.

'Come on.' He held out his hand.

She held it tight as a hatch opened in the side of the ship, a circular area which seemed to contract somehow, revealing a short white corridor that was lit as brightly as if the sun was inside. 'It *is* real!'

*

Nigel was from the Commonwealth. The union of human worlds that existed outside the Void. A universe that was very different. He had come to find out what had happened to the ships that Captain Cornelius had flown into the Void.

'Why?' Kysandra asked. She was sitting on a round chair that had grown out of the floor in the blank circular chamber he called the main cabin. And Nigel had been right; there were so many questions her head was in danger of bursting open from the pressure of them.

'We don't know how they came through the barrier that guards the Void from the rest of the universe.'

'But you came through.'

'That was different. Some alien allies tore the boundary open temporarily, just long enough for me to slip inside. I've spent seven years in suspension – that's a long sleep – while a Skylord led me to this world.'

'You flew through space.' It was just the most wonderful thing ever to think that humans could still do such a thing – that it wasn't only Captain Cornelius who travelled between planets. Out there in the Commonwealth, where there were hundreds of worlds, all filled with marvels, people flew between them all the time. 'Please take me out there, back to the Commonwealth you came from. Please, Nigel. I'll help you however you want while you're here, but afterwards . . .' She gave him the most entreating plea she could, letting her yearning thoughts free so he could taste them.

'Getting out is difficult,' he said awkwardly. 'I didn't expect I'd be doing that.'

'But you can do it,' she insisted. Her hands gestured round the magnificent spaceship with its clean air and bright lighting. A machine that could fly! 'You're so clever. You know everything there is to know.'

'Ha!'

His bitter laugh shocked her.

'I'm the stupidest person in the galaxy, actually.' He glanced meaningfully up at the blank ceiling. 'Though I'm not alone.'

'I don't understand.'

'We thought there was only one planet in the Void where humans lived – Querencia. How wrong we were. We should have known, should have worked it out, but we didn't; we assumed – which is always a foolish thing to do. We did it because all our power and knowledge brings a huge dose of arrogance with it. Well, thank you, universe: lesson in humility well and truly learned.'

'There's more than one planet in the Void?'

'Apparently.'

'And do people live there, too?'

'They used to, Kysandra. That's all I can tell you. They managed to get a message out to us. But it was a very long time ago. And I'm *here* now, not on Querencia.'

'So what are you going to do?'

Nigel massaged his temples. 'My original goal was to get to Makkathran – which is a living alien spaceship that's managed to survive on Querencia – and send all the information it gathered back to the Commonwealth and its own species. But that's going to be quite tough now. My ship can't fly any more. The Void has affected its engines – or part of them, anyway. The closer you are to a planet, the worse it gets.'

'So you can't fly me to the Commonwealth?'

'I don't think so. I'm going to research the Void from here for a while. Maybe if I can analyse its structure, I can learn to fly again. But right now I'm more interested in the Fallers. I don't understand what they are at all. They don't plague Querencia like they do Bienvenido.'

'They've always been here,' she told him. 'Right from the start. It's in the Chronicles. Captain Cornelius saw what they were as soon as the ship landed. He founded the first regiment, the Meor, to fight them; then he set up the Watcher Guild to warn everyone when the eggs fall. And the Research Institute so we could learn how to fight them. Without him we would never have survived.'

'Did you learn that at school?'

'Yes.'

'Interesting. So the Fallers were here already when the colony ships were sucked in. They're probably prisoners, just like us.'

'Prisoners?'

'Yes. Haven't you worked that out yet? The Void is a prison; it consumes your soul for its own twisted purpose. People. Their thoughts. Their minds. They're like a kind of food that gets sucked up into the Heart.'

'They live for ever more in glory. Everybody knows that.'

'Do they indeed? Have you ever seen this glory? Always demand proof of nirvana before you start following messiahs who're selling it to you. Those guys don't exactly have the greatest track record in the universe.'

'You doubt the Skylords' Guidance?' she asked, shocked.

'I doubt any system that won't reveal its purpose, that only offers promises of a better tomorrow. But then I'm just a thousand-year-old cynic. You have to make up your own mind, Kysandra. And to do that, you need information. A lot of information.'

She looked round the cabin, surprised she could feel so deflated on the day she'd discovered the truth of the universe. 'I want to learn,' she told him, 'it's all I ever really wanted.' Somewhere at the back of her mind a hope was burning that the ship would carry a library, maybe even bigger than the public one at Adeone.

'I can help you do that,' he said. 'I might not be able to take you to the Commonwealth, but I can certainly bring the Commonwealth to you. Think of it as payment for you providing me with cover here. How does that sound?'

Kysandra smiled in a way she hadn't for the last eight years.

*

'Lie back, this won't hurt,' Nigel said.

Kysandra didn't believe him. But she lay back anyway. The medical chamber – a cylinder like a silver coffin – had slipped out of the cabin's wall. Its oval top had done that magical contraction thing, revealing a padded mattress inside.

'I'll keep it open,' Nigel said. 'It can be a bit claustrophobic in there if you're not used to it.'

Kysandra didn't trust herself to speak. All she concentrated on was the very firm belief that this was nothing to do with the Fallers. She wasn't going to get eaten. *Probably.*

'Here we go.' Nigel's grin was reassuring. The silver sides of the capsule sprouted slim tendrils that moved like serpents. They began to prod and poke at her body. She'd removed the dress for the chamber to do whatever it did, but Nigel assured her she could keep her underwear on. More of the tendril things were emerging round her head, a dense cluster of them wriggling through her hair. She swallowed hard, trying to be brave.

'You're doing fine. Keep still.'

'This is your doctor?' she asked.

'Sort of, yes. Though it can do a lot more than just cure you.' He closed his eyes, but his expression was one of concentration, as if he was reading something.

Can it get rid of zits?

'Interesting.'

'What is?' she asked.

'You said Captain Cornelius landed three thousand years ago?'

'Yes.'

'That gives us a conservative estimate of a hundred and twenty generations. There's been some drift in your Advancer sequences; several of them have broken down. I can't believe the Void's been screwing with your DNA on top of everything else. Of course, we haven't had a hundred-generation baseline in the Commonwealth to compare it with, and most of our generations are still factoring in improvements every twenty years. But that level of reversion will be something for the geneticists to watch out for.'

'Oh.' *Whatever that meant.*

He opened his eyes and grinned. 'Commonwealth citizens have certain additional biological . . . er, abilities built in to their original bodies. They're specialist cells which help you communicate over distance, like a 'path voice but a lot faster and more sophisticated. Memory can be organized, too, rather than nature's rather random method.'

'And I don't have them any more?'

'You do, but they're slightly degraded. And disconnected from your brain.'

'So I can't learn Commonwealth stuff like you said?'

He grinned at her disappointed expression. 'There are always alternatives. I'll insert some replacement neural pathways into the macrocellular clusters to integrate your secondaries. That's a standard med repair. Then there are new vectors for the other Advancer features. It will be a while before the reseqencing takes effect.'

Nope: still don't have a crudding clue what you're saying.

It had been a year since Kysandra had stopped going to Mrs Brewster's school every other weekend. She really missed it; school had been the one part of her life that had carried on as normal. With the teacher's clever gifts and tutelage she'd quickly mastered the basics: reading, writing, arithmetic. Mrs Brewster was the only person left she could talk to about the amazing things she read in her father's books. And the teacher had told her all about the university in Varlan, where people did nothing but read and learn all day long. That sounded pretty much like a piece of Giu to

Kysandra. 'It's worth applying,' Mrs Brewster had suggested as her sixteenth birthday approached.

To which Sarara had retorted: 'She'll do just fine as a farmer's wife, so don't you go filling her head with dreamy nonsense. She needs to get ready for real life.' That was the last time she'd been allowed to go to the school.

Now Nigel promised her knowledge beyond anything she'd ever read on Bienvenido. The truth about the whole universe.

Something pinched the back of her skull.

'Ouch.'

'Sorry,' Nigel said absently.

Obscurely, Kysandra felt better. *I knew it would hurt.*

Nothing much happened for a few minutes, then all the silver tendrils withdrew and flattened out against the sides of the capsule, blending into the metal casing.

'You can get dressed now,' Nigel said.

She turned her back to him to put her dress on. *Ridiculous.*

'So this is going to be like 'path gifting?' she asked.

'Sort of, yes.'

When they left the spaceship, she was sure there were more neuts milling round outside than when she went in.

'What sort of mods are you adapting?' she asked as they took the fabric boat back across the river. And to think, an hour ago she'd been impressed by *that*.

'Ge-monkeys and chimps, mainly. Like your dwarfs and apes. They'll be the most useful to start with.'

'So ge-forms come from the other planet the ships landed on?'

'Yes.'

She looked up into the sky with its high drifting cloud ribbons. 'Where is it?'

'Querencia? I'm not sure. Some of the nebulas are the same. Your Giu is their Odin's Sea, and Uracus is Honious to them. But nothing else is the same. The Void may have different internal pockets, like segments in an orange, if you like; or the quantum geometry spacetime equivalent here is folded more than we realized.'

'I think I need to wait for the Commonwealth giftings. Tell me what life was like on the other Void world.'

'They found Makkathran, which had a city section modified by a species that came to Querencia before humans. It was abandoned, so I guess they were all consumed by the Heat, whoever they were. Makkathran made life a little easier for the Querencia humans, so it shaped their society slightly differently to yours, from what I've seen so far.'

'Was that earlier species the Fallers?'

'No. Like I said, I don't understand them at all. I wish I'd taken time to study the Forest during my approach. It had a very unusual quantum signature.'

'A what?'

'Space was different there, somehow. Don't worry. I'll get to the bottom of it eventually. There was another abnormality, too, but that was here on Bienvenido.'

'There's a Forest on the planet?' she asked in alarm.

'No, no. As I was coming down, the *Skylady* detected something unusual, way to the east of here, a sensor return that didn't make a lot of sense. I don't suppose you know where the original ships came down?'

'Captain Cornelius landed where Varlan now stands. His palace was built over his ship.'

Nigel raised an eyebrow. 'Really? I wonder if another colony ship came down in the east. The sensor return showed processed metal and metalloceramics, a lot of it.'

'I don't know anything about it,' she said, then paused. 'There is the Desert of Bone.'

'The what?'

'The Desert of Bone; that's nearly at the east coast. Nobody goes into it. It's supposed to be haunted. The first explorers who tried to cross it came back mad.' She shrugged. 'Just a rumour.'

'Curioser and curioser. And why would you give that name to a desert? Is there a map anywhere in the house? I'd like to see if my signal came from around there.'

'There's an atlas in the library. I think the Desert of Bone is about three thousand miles away.'

'That's not a problem. We can visit the anomaly once I'm established here. I can set up a trading business; that'll be good cover to travel anywhere.'

As they approached the farmhouse, she realized the man-doll on the roof had nearly finished repairing all the shingles. 'Don't they ever stop?'

'No.'

*

They were sitting at the dining-room table that evening, eating the fish pasta supper Nigel had cooked. At first Kysandra thought something was flashing. Nigel had brought several slim solid boxes the size of his hand into the farmhouse. *Modules*, he called them. They didn't seem to do anything. A couple of them had tiny lights shining out of insect-eye lenses. But they weren't the source of the light. It seemed to be coming from inside her eyes.

The flashing steadied to five hazy stars in a simple pentagon formation, then they started to change.

'Nigel!' she exclaimed. 'What's happening?'

Patterns were forming out of the stars, patterns that had nothing to do with what Kysandra's eyes were seeing. Like ex-sight, they hovered in the centre of her perception; unlike ex-sight, they were precise and coloured. Concentric circles that slowly expanded and deepened as if she was looking down into a cylinder with ring walls. Green lines blossomed, outlining a pyramid. Spheres made up of spheres that kept multiplying, like the soap bubbles in the Hevlin's bath.

'The pathways I inserted have established themselves. They're activating, that's all. Don't panic. It's perfectly normal.' He held her hand.

The touch was a comfort, but she was still startled. Then someone whispered into her brain – soft nonsense words. She yelped in panic.

'It's okay,' he said instantly. 'Pay attention to the voice. It will tell you what to do next.'

She bit her lip, but nodded. Tried to calm down and stop jerking breaths into her lungs.

'Can you understand this?' the foreign, soundless voice asked. 'If you can, please say yes out loud.'

'Yes.'

'I am the basic operational memory package for macrocell cluster operation. Follow these instructions. There is a red diamond icon positioned at the top of the display in your exovision. Please locate it.'

'I can see it.'

'In order for this package to download into your cluster, you must visualize the diamond expanding. When it has done this, rotate it one hundred and eighty degrees clockwise. To cancel the download altogether, rotate it the other way. Do you understand?'

'Yes.'

'Please make your choice.'

Choice? You're crudding joking. Like I'd choose not to!

The diamond expanded and turned clockwise as if Kysandra had shot a 'path order into it.

Something like a cross between the fastest 'path gifting ever and a jet of ice-cold water shot into her mind. The strange thoughts broke apart and snuggled down into her memories. It was as if the operating icons suddenly came into proper focus. Every function snapped into alignment. And she *understood* them all. How to connect to datanets, how to call someone, how to accept data, how to receive entertainment forms, how to construct her own address code, how to . . . how to . . . how to . . . 'Crud on Uracus,' she grunted. Most of her body's Advancer functions were registering inert, but a medium-level medical analysis was available. She could read her blood toxin content, oxygenation, nerve reception, muscle efficiency, heart status, hormone levels, neural activity.

'So much,' she exclaimed, her hands waving around like a flightless bird's wings. 'How do Commonwealth people live knowing so much all of the time?'

406

On the other side of the table Nigel was sitting back in his chair, watching her in amusement. Exovision icons were superimposed across him, yet they didn't interfere with his image. It was very strange. A call icon flipped up, with a code identifying it as Nigel Sheldon. She allowed a connection – not really having to think how to make that happen, just willing it. Icons rearranged themselves as she thought of them.

'It can be overwhelming,' Nigel told her. 'You just need to learn how to filter. The secondary routines will help you.'

She grinned in delight. His lips hadn't moved, and he hadn't 'pathed, either. This was new, a direct datalink. 'It's fantastic,' she sent back. 'I want to learn more now. I want to learn all about everything.'

'I think we'd better begin with some primary grade educational packages, and move on from there.'

She laughed in delight. 'Let's get started.'

2

'I can zoom,' Kysandra declared loudly as she came running down the stairs. Her ex-sight showed her Nigel was in the library, trying to instruct the farm's oldest mod-dwarf how to turn the pages of a book one at a time. The poor old thing didn't have much dexterity left in its thin hands and kept turning several pages at a time. A simple memory module had been rigged above the table on a wooden frame, where its camera could scan in the text.

She and Nigel had taken a trip into Adeone yesterday to get a cartload of general supplies, food and other essentials. 'We can't use the ship's semiorganic synthesizers for everything, even if they stay glitch free,' Nigel said. 'And I can't afford Blair Farm to have a reputation for being the place where some odd rich bloke hides out. I don't want to attract attention. We have to be accepted as just another farm.'

Maybe the ship couldn't extrude absolutely everything from its neumanetic systems, but Nigel had certainly got it to counterfeit Bienvenido's coins perfectly. Kysandra carried a huge heavy purse round the stores, choosing a dozen dresses and more practical clothes (no shoes, though; ship-produced footwear couldn't be beaten). Then she showed him which merchant to order coal from, a decent timber yard, ironmonger, stables, the town's live-stock market . . . None of them had any connection to Ma Ulvon. Nigel had spent a small fortune on the kind of things they'd need to return the farm to productivity. People were pleased to hear it.

So he was right; a rich newcomer settling in was interesting but not suspicious. They were happy for her, too. Old schoolfriends had stopped to congratulate her.

When they were done with spending, they went to the library; Nigel registered himself and borrowed a dozen books on history and law.

'Why law?' she'd asked. The farm library didn't have any legal books; her father hadn't been interested in that subject at all.

'Building blocks of society. If you want to understand how a government works, the laws tell you.'

Now all he had to do was load all the text into the ship's smart-core. The mod-dwarf was pleased at being given a job which involved sitting down all day, but frustrated with its inability to perform as instructed. Nigel was spending half his time soothing its thoughts. He looked up as she rushed into the room. 'Zoom where?' he asked.

Kysandra wrinkled her nose up at his odd sense of humour. 'My eyes, stupid. Their zoom function is working.'

'Excellent. The resequencing is progressing nicely. Nice to confirm the Void allows genetic modification to work. How about infra-red function?'

'Yes,' she confirmed – though that image was just plain weird. Everything a different colour, with brightness depending on how hot an object was. Still it was better than light amplification for night use, which was even stranger than ex-sight perception. 'Got it.'

'Great.'

'You're good at calming mods,' she said, indicating the dwarf, which was concentrating hard on the book.

'I had a good teacher.'

'I'm going out to take a proper look at the third barn,' she told him. 'I still think we'd be better off demolishing it and beginning again from scratch.' Nigel had big plans for expanding the compound, starting with building a barn large enough to conceal the spaceship from casual sight. Developing a modest industrial base was all part of his mission to gather as much scientific data on the Void as he could. And *Skylady* was the key to it. The ship's smartcore could control dozens of mods simultaneously, using them as remote manipulators. But the 'path its bioprocessor smartcore generated was range-limited. They needed the ship at the farm.

'Sure thing,' he said.

'I had a carpentry memory implantation this morning,' she assured him. 'I should be able to tell which purlins and rafters are still solid, if any.' Commonwealth memory implants were a complete revelation. She'd been accepting four a day – which was as many as Nigel would allow her. The first three days had been spent bringing her knowledge base up to the equivalent of teenagers in the Commonwealth. She understood so many concepts now, but details remained to be filled in. For the last couple of days she'd divided her allowance between practical skills like carpentry and general information.

'Just go easy,' he told her for the hundredth time. 'You need time to assimilate all the new data. It has to settle in properly.'

'I'm using my storage lacuna so I don't get brainburn, like you said. I'll be fine. Besides, I know all about native wood anyway; the carpentry knowledge just adds technique.'

'Well, listen to the neural expert,' he muttered sarcastically.

She grinned. An icon flipped up into her exovision. One of the sensors they'd placed round the valley was showing a big cart turning off the public road three miles away, turning down the track to the valley. With the Void distorting electromagnetic communications, bandwidth was poor over such a distance. She couldn't get a clear picture of the people riding in the cart.

'We weren't expecting a delivery until next week,' she said automatically. 'The coal's supposed to be first, and that isn't old man Steron's wagon anyway.'

'That's not a delivery,' Nigel said.

Normally, Kysandra had some clue about a person's emotions, even with a decent shell wrapping round their thoughts. But with Nigel's impenetrable shell she was completely lost. Looking at him, sitting perfectly still as he sent out a stream of encrypted code to the smartcore, she was suddenly struck by how menacing this man from another universe could be.

A second sensor, further down the track, gave a better image of the cart and its three passengers as it trundled past. 'Oh, no,' she groaned. It was Akstan, Julias and Russell – another of the brothers.

'My fault. I shouldn't have left such a big loose end,' Nigel said. 'That was stupid of me. Maybe I have been a little cautious about exposing myself. Shock, I expect. Well, that ends now.'

'Are you going to kill them?' she asked quietly. The weapons available to the Commonwealth were truly astounding, even though half of them probably wouldn't work in the Void. Ma's boys with their pump-action shotguns and hunting knives wouldn't stand a chance.

'No. That would be a waste.'

'Waste? So what are you going to do?'

'Recruit them.'

'Er, Nigel, they're pretty loyal to Ma.'

'Did I say I was going to offer them a choice?'

The cold intensity of his voice made Kysandra shudder. Her u-shadow accessed the feed from various sensors around the farmhouse, building their images to a single picture across her exovision.

*

The wagon came to a halt just outside the gate set in the compound's ramshackle fence. Julias frowned at the farmhouse, taking in the repaired roof, freshly painted gable bargeboards, fixed windows, pruned climbing roses, the kitchen garden with rows of newly planted vegetables, the half-refurbished first barn.

'It wasn't like this a week ago,' he said. 'He might have brought in some help.'

'So have we,' Akstan said, and patted his shotgun.

The *Skylady* had a small flock of semiorganic ge-eagles stowed on board. Nigel activated one and downloaded a set of instructions which its small smartcore could follow easily enough. It loaded its ordinance and flapped up quickly into the sky.

Akstan primed his pump-action shotgun with a single powerful motion and climbed off the cart. His brothers followed him down, their own weapons held ready. They kept their shells strong, but neither made any attempt to fuzz themselves. None of the brothers noticed the big artificial bird swooping quickly and silently through the air towards them. To ex-sight, its semiorganic components were identical to living tissue. Only its controlling bioprocessor might have betrayed it, with routines that were fast and precise rather than a bird's natural impulse-instinct thoughts. But the difference was so tiny that they probably wouldn't have noticed even if they had examined the bird.

Akstan directed a strong 'path shout at the farmhouse. 'Kysandra, hey, Kysandra, you want to come out here? Be easier that way.'

She didn't even turn round.

Akstan looked at his brothers. Russell shrugged.

'Come on now, girl, you belong to me. Everybody knows that. Your new man in there, we gonna see him off today. He ain't gonna be around no more.'

A shadow flashed across the group of men as the ge-eagle passed five metres overhead. Julias frowned up at it, clearly puzzled by the strange powerful shape. He was completely unaware of the aerosol it released.

'You come out here now, Kysandra,' Akstan 'pathed, his thoughts colouring towards anger at the defiance. 'If you don't, we gonna come in and get you. Ain't gonna be pretty.'

'What—?' Russell murmured, and fell unconscious.

'Huh?' Akstan grunted, then joined his brother in an inelegant heap on the ground.

'Now what?' Kysandra asked as the ANAdroids carried the three comatose men into the farmhouse and laid them out on the floor of the front room.

'I used a mild domination on them last time, so they'd agree to giving me you and the farm,' Nigel told her as he stared down impassively at the sleeping figures. 'Too mild, apparently.'

'Domination?'

'It's a kind of mind-control technique they developed on the other world. Someone called Tathal perfected it.'

'Mind control? You mean you can order them round like mods?'

'Not quite. You subvert their loyalty, which makes them want to do everything you ask.'

Kysandra hoped she was keeping her shell firm, because, if anything, that sounded even more unpleasant than simply ordering people around. 'And you know how to do that?'

'Oh, yes. I tried it out on Ma and her family when I followed you into town. I just wasn't forceful enough, and I was in a hurry. This time I'll get it right.'

An ANAdroid walked in carrying a large medical kit. Nigel selected an infuser and applied it to Akstan's neck. 'This will elevate his brainwave activity to borderline consciousness. We have a few techniques in the Commonwealth to subvert personality, dating all the way back to the Starflyer War, some more brutal than others. I think I'll start with a modified narcomeme; that's soft enough. It should help subdue any instinctive resistance. Then I'll use Tathal's procedure.'

Kysandra watched Akstan moan feebly. Thoughts grew out of his unshelled sleeping mind. She perceived her own face tumbling through the phantasms his semi-conscious brain was producing, the disturbing sexual obsessions she featured in, his anger at being thwarted mutating into perverted revenge fantasies.

All the lingering doubts she had about what Nigel was going to do dried up like field dew in high summer. Instead, she stood above the insensate Akstan, and used her ex-sight to perceive the complex stream of 'path that Nigel directed into his naked brain. It was interesting.

*

Heavy clouds swept in from the south-west to cover Adeone at eleven o'clock at night, obscuring the nebulas and bringing a cold persistent rain. By two o'clock in the morning, the town was asleep; pubs and clubs had closed, the docks were silent, the teams of civic mod-dwarfs had gone back to their stables. The miserable rain had even curtailed the activities of its more nefarious citizens.

Oil lamps along Lubal Street flickered and went out one by one, allowing the shadows to swell out and embrace its entire length.

Standing at the end of Lubal Street, with her shell deflecting the swirling raindrops, Kysandra looked at the Hevlin Hotel. In infra-red, the broad white façade was a dull luminous blue as the rain washed down the walls, cooling the structure.

Nigel stood directly to her left. Her ex-sight couldn't perceive him at all. Naturally, Nigel had a far superior fuzz technique than anyone, which he'd gifted her, too. Concealment, he called it. It was only infra-red which showed her where he was, a green and blue profile where the rain dripped off his big brown coat. Infra-red also allowed her to see the others they'd brought with them: Akstan, his brothers and three ANAdroids, standing motionless behind her.

'He's good,' Nigel admitted as the ex-sight swept along the street, as it did every couple of minutes. Their fuzz deflected it easily, but they were still forty metres away.

Someone was awake in the Hevlin's lobby, faithfully watching out for trouble. Ma had too many enemies to leave the place unguarded, even on a night like this.

'Akstan?' Nigel queried.

'It's probably Snony,' Akstan said. 'He's got good ex-sight. Reliable, too.'

'We need to get inside without anyone raising the alarm.'

'Leave it to me,' Akstan said eagerly.

Kysandra had to press her teeth together and strengthen her shell so her feelings didn't betray her. It had taken Nigel twenty minutes to turn the surly Akstan into an over-friendly eager-to-please disciple. She'd watched all of the sullen, sulky brothers start to behave with the kind of adoration that a puppy would exhibit.

Akstan and his brothers deserved no less; she wasn't arguing

414

that. But it was a sharp reminder than the man who treated her so kindly could also be completely ruthless. It made her glad she had been shown trust. But equally, she wondered if that appreciation was all her own. Had he used domination on her while she slept that day after their wedding? *But . . . if he'd done that, would I ever question if he had? Unless that was part of it, making me doubt so I think I am free . . . Uracus.*

'Did you do that to me?' she blurted as Akstan walked steadily towards the Hevlin.

Nigel turned and frowned. 'What?'

'Did you use Tathal's domination procedure on me?'

'No.'

Infra-red showed him grinning, his teeth glowed ruby red under the wide brim of his hat.

'But I get that making you believe that is practically impossible,' he said. 'Ask yourself: why would I give you the Commonwealth memory implants?'

'So I'm more useful.'

'Ah, okay; good answer. So the second question is: why would I risk leaving you free?'

'I don't know. Why?'

'Because I have great-great-great-great-great-granddaughters your age or younger. Because I am many bad things, but enslaving teenage girls isn't one of them. Because I won't have many genuine friends here, but you could be one. And, face it, I am kind of overwhelming, which is a sort of domination.'

She nodded slowly. 'Are you really that old to have great-great – whatever – granddaughters?'

'Oh, yeah. They're all out there, on the other side of the barrier. Judging me.'

'Uracus. So what bad things?'

Nigel chuckled. 'I used my power and money to build an empire. Opponents got pushed aside. Pushed hard.'

'You ruled people, like the Captain does?'

'It was a commercial empire. Which, given its size, translates into political power. So yes, I ruled people. Just like the Captain does here. I choose to believe I was a reasonably benign dictator. Hardass, fanatical dictators never accomplish anything, and for all my faults I'm proud of what I achieved. Along with my friend Ozzie, I helped open the stars for our whole species, Kysandra; I was one of the founders of the Commonwealth. Long time ago, though.'

'If you're really that important, why are you here? Why did you come into the Void?'

His glowing grin widened. 'Who else you gonna call?'

Her own lips lifted in response. That was Nigel. Odd yet reassuring.

Akstan walked into the lobby. The man behind the reception desk looked up, jerked his head in recognition. Akstan pulled out the air pistol Nigel had given him and shot the man in the throat. The sedative in the pellet worked fast. Surprise and shock had just registered, he was starting to 'path out an alarm, when his eyes rolled up and he collapsed.

'Good work,' Nigel 'pathed.

Akstan looked ridiculously pleased with himself.

'Gas masks on,' Nigel said.

Kysandra took out the slippery triangle of fabric and pressed it to her face. It adhered to her skin, covering her mouth and nose. She took a cautious breath; the filtered air was very dry, but apart from that perfectly normal.

'Let them go, Russell, please,' Nigel said.

It had taken *Skylady*'s synthesizers most of the afternoon to produce components to graft onto the small semiorganic ge-cats it had in storage. But after a solid three hours work, eight of the slick little creatures were now rodent-like enough to pass as bussalores. They were in a box carried by Russell, who put it down on the wet cobbles.

Kysandra's ex-sight followed them scampering over to the Hevlin. Three of them went in through the front door Akstan was holding open. The remaining five veered off down the alleys on either side of the hotel. They entered through air bricks set level with the pavement, through cellar windows, through drainpipes.

Pre-loaded directions sent them racing along corridors and through rooms. As they went, gas sprayed out through their anus vent, permeating the entire building. Sleepers drifted into an even deeper sleep, unaware as their dreams faded to nothingness.

Nigel waited outside in the rain, observing the creatures' progress with his ex-sight. Ten minutes after the last artificial bussalore entered, he said: 'All right, let's go.'

He started to walk towards the Hevlin Hotel and the unconscious bodies it contained. Kysandra and the others followed.

3

Kysandra was desperate to start the expedition to the Desert of Bone. She'd never even seen a train before, let alone travelled half the length of the continent on one. And then an adventure was waiting for her at the far end. Yet at the same time, it was so hard to leave Blair Farm. In the six months since Nigel had arrived, crashing into her life, turning her existence into something extraordinary, the farm looked as she'd always imagined it would be if Dad had come back and run it properly. Teams of perfectly coordinated mod-apes and mod-dwarfs had built a waterwheel-powered timber mill beside the river. Then with the planks and posts cut from trees they'd felled, new barns were constructed. Hedges had been hacked back into shape, and fields ploughed and drilled ready with the seed crops they'd bought from town. Sheep, pigs, cows, chickens, goats, llamas and ostriches had been delivered from the local livestock market, and thrived under *Skylady*'s excellent proxy husbandry. The stable of mods expanded constantly. Machine shops were being put up. Each day there was something to help with and accomplish.

There were some days when she looked round at what they'd achieved and wondered if it was all real. But, of course, it was all Nigel. He knew exactly what to do, how things were built, the components, the tools they'd need. He knew how to handle people. He wasn't afraid of being forceful when he had to be. He was focused in a way she knew she'd never be, not even with all her bright bubbling Commonwealth knowledge. Which made her slightly envious.

She found herself watching him more and more. He was over a thousand years old – so he claimed – even though he didn't look much over his mid-twenties. That youthful appearance was . . . nice. It helped conjure up certain daydreams. Not that they were anything but daydreams.

He teased her a lot, which was cool that he felt so comfortable with her. It meant she could tease him back, ask questions she'd never dare ask Mrs Brewster. She'd never known that kind of honesty before. It made her feel good, on a lot of levels.

It was a time she'd have been happy to stretch on and on, but Nigel was keen to find out what had caused the peculiar signal from the Desert of Bone. So with Blair Farm functioning smoothly, they set off as the dry season arrived, leaving *Skylady* and three ANAdroids in charge.

They had to take a boat to Erond first, which had the closest branch-line station. Nigel hired the whole longbarge to ferry them and their luggage along the Nubain tributary from Adeone. Before they started, he'd ordered five brand new trunks from the general store, which had taken three weeks to arrive from Varlan. Lovely brass-cornered boxes with heavy-duty Ysdom locks, so large Kysandra could practically fit into one if she curled up tight.

Russell and Madeline came with them, as valet and maid respectively, along with two of the ANAdroids who had now modified their faces, giving them real human characteristics. One had acquired Asian traits and had aged himself to about eighty, complete with a receding hairline – nice touch, she acknowledged. Who would ever suspect anything abnormal about that? The second had turned his skin as pale as the Algory mountains' snow-caps and toned his hair to a matching light sandy shade. She'd spent a few days suggesting facial elements he might want to incorporate, watching in delight as they slowly manifested, until a week later they'd wound up with a wonderfully handsome twenty-year-old's countenance. Sure enough, every time he visited Adeone, all the girls directed sight and ex-sight his way.

'You're projecting,' Nigel had commented, in not-quite-disapproval.

She and the ANAdroid had laughed at that behind his back. All the ANAdroids had distinct personalities, and this one had a dry sense of humour she enjoyed. 'What do I call you?' she asked. Because now that he had a real face, it was impossible to think of him as a machine.

'I am Three.'

'That's not a proper name, and I can't call you a number in public. Nothing that draws undue attention, remember?'

'I can't forget anything, remember?'

Kysandra giggled. 'Then I'm going to call you Coulan, after one of Mum's nephews. I always liked him.'

'I accept the name with gratitude.' He gave her a short bow. 'What are you going to call the rest of my batch?'

So it was Demitri, Marek, Valeri and Fergus.

'Fergus?' Nigel sighed and rolled his eyes. 'Seriously?'

'Yes, Fergus.' She linked arms companionably with the newly named Fergus, who generated a quick pulse of smug amusement from his bioconstruct brain.

'All right. But when I start using them as embedded scouts, he might have to be called something else if that's what it takes to blend in.'

'Fine,' she said airily.

But he was Fergus when he accompanied them on the expedition. With their luggage and servants and first-class tickets, they really did fit the ideal of an aristocratic couple taking a grand trip.

The first train took them all the way up the Southern City Line and into Varlan's Willesden station, which stood on the Colbal's southern bank. Kysandra had pleaded to spend a few days in the capital before setting off east. Surprisingly, Nigel had agreed easily enough. 'I need to look around at some point,' he said. 'Can't put it off forever.'

So they booked in to the palatial monolith that was the Rasheeda Hotel on Walton Boulevard, with its diamond-patterned bricks and stone oriel windows, where their fifth-floor suite had a balcony that overlooked Bromwell Park. Kysandra laughed in delight at the ornate rooms, which had wood panelling and lush gold and scarlet wallpaper, then gasped at the size of the four-poster bed in the master bedroom. She couldn't resist running across the room and jumping onto the vast mattress, giggling as she bounced about. 'This bed is the same size as my whole bedroom back home!' She rolled over and ran the tip of her tongue along her teeth. 'It's a perfect bridal suite, don't you think?'

Nigel gave her a faux-lofty glance. 'I'm sure a lot of brides have had a happy time here.'

'You say you're a thousand years old,' Kysandra retorted with her best coquettish pout, 'so you must have had a lot of wives.'

'Kysandra: you're seventeen, I'm a thousand. That's just wrong on every level. Just keep thinking of me as your big brother guardian and you and I will be fine. I've told you before, when you see a nice boy who's close to your age, then take him to bed and have as much fun as you want.'

'I don't want a *nice* boy.'

'That's an old argument which isn't actually true. Trust me: you do.'

'Don't,' she insisted stubbornly.

'And I recognize the way that jaw is firming up, so let me tell you now before you turn any more daydreams into plans: I get that this is all tremendously exciting for you, but I will not offer you any kind of false happy ending. I may have to leave, I may get imprisoned or lynched, I just don't know. So understand this: you and I are not going to grow old together and watch our grandchildren take over the farm. I'm glad I met you, and I'm pleased that your life has improved because of that, but I have obligations to the Commonwealth and the Raiel that have to be met. Everything else is secondary.'

Her pout turned grouchy. 'Fine. Okay.'

'Damn, I'd forgotten what teenagers are like. I love that you know everything and don't need any help in the world.'

'Stop being such an arsehole.'

'Yes, ma'am.' He gave her that grin that admitted he was

actually really fond of her. 'You know, if they'd chosen Ozzie instead of me, it would have been very different. He would have taken you to bed without any hesitation.'

'Is he likely to come? After all, you crashed on the wrong planet. Will he come and rescue you?'

Nigel burst out laughing. 'Hell, no. Sorry. I'm all you've got.'

'So who is Ozzie, anyway? You keep mentioning him.'

'My oldest friend. I can't even begin to tell you all the things we've done together. Not that you'd believe them anyway.'

'Try me.'

'Maybe on the train to Portlynn. It's going to be a long trip.'

'And he really won't come to rescue you?'

'No. He'll likely laugh and say: I told you so. But he won't come. I'm on my own.'

*

For two days Kysandra toured the centre of the capital, relishing every moment. The huge stately buildings, the wide tree-lined boulevards, public parks, galleries, theatres, the people, rich and poor – there were more walking along a single street than lived in the whole of Adeone. But as much time as she could wrangle out of Nigel was spent visiting the grand department stores and couture houses. She was dazzled by the furnishings and fittings the stores offered, and constantly asked Nigel if they could have pieces for the farmhouse. Nothing the county carpenters produced could ever come close to this elegance and comfort. He laughed and said perhaps they could order some on the way back.

And the clothes. Oh, the clothes! She could have emptied every trunk of their silly expedition equipment and filled them with fashionable gorgeous clothes to take home.

However, there was a price to pay. Nigel insisted they take a look at the government institutes and offices. 'To get a feel of their abilities.' It turned out that half of Varlan's central district was a government building of some kind.

They started by strolling up Walton Boulevard to the granite statue of Captain Cornelius that stood outside the palace gates.

There they joined the schoolkids and curious tourists lining up outside the four-metre high iron railings that surrounded the broad cobbled ground in front of the palace. Several Palace Guards patrolled the perimeter in fours, marching along like heavily ordered mods, humourless, perfectly shelled, the silver buttons on their yellow and blue tunics shining in the morning sunlight, rifles shouldered.

Nigel ignored them, staring at the six-storey façade on the other side of the open ground. This section of the palace was over three hundred metres long, built from a stone that had an odd blue hue. Tall Italianate arched windows surrounded a grand archway in the centre which led into the first of many courtyards. There were several ornate turrets and domes rising amid the steep roofs.

'I wonder what it's like living there?' Kysandra mused wistfully.

'Pretty awful. I've lived in mansions this size myself. Ninety-five per cent of it is given over to staff and offices. You spend so much time mediating their internal politics, you get distracted from the real job. And it's no place for a family. I wound up with some pretty screwed-up kids at one point. Five of them still aren't talking to me.'

'You lived . . .' Kysandra's hand gave the palace a limp wave.

'Oh, yeah. Won't make that mistake again. This Sun King monstrosity tells me all I need to know about how wealth and power is consolidated on this planet. My guess is that the court here will exercise absolute power. And to do that you have to have a political system that doesn't permit dissent. Give the people the illusion of democracy, with a few elected councils that've been given power over local trivia, while you control anything that really matters directly through the economy. He who pays the piper calls the tune; then, now, and forever. The Treasury will be the true seat of power on this world, trust me. And somewhere in the Captain's multitude of honourable titles will be something like: Chancellor of the Exchequer, or Lord of the Treasury, or Governor of the National Bank or Chief Revenue Officer. That's how it's done.'

She looked from Nigel to the palace and back again. 'You know all that by how big and gaudy the palace is?'

'Yeah. Pretty much. I've seen it enough times to know what I'm facing.'

'But we have elections.'

'I wasn't criticizing. Given the Faller threat, you've got a pretty good arrangement here. Government is always a balance between liberty and restriction. Back in the outside universe, political systems evolved as technology and understanding grew, and that generally brought a liberalizing democracy with it. The problem here is a near-perfect status quo – though perfect isn't quite the right word for it – and all the Shanties are a new development that can't be helping the economy or the crime rates. The Fallers aren't ever going to stop Falling. If anything, they have the advantage. Your society is probably stagnating in a lot of subtle ways that'll start to mount up, and with that comes decadence and corruption. The Fallers only have to wait until your vigilance falters.' He pursed his lips thoughtfully. 'Then again, fear keeps you on your toes, and you have kept society going for three thousand years.'

'You think the Fallers will win in the end?'

'Time and human nature is on their side. But only because the Void restricts us. If we could get up there to the Forest and deploy some decent Commonwealth technology, it would be a very different story.'

'Us?' she taunted. 'So you do consider yourself human, then? I was wondering.'

Nigel grinned back. 'Occasionally.'

'Anything else you've decided just from looking?'

'Not really.' He turned back to stare at the palace, sending his ex-sight to examine it closely. As expected, the whole structure was fuzzed. 'You said this is where the ship landed?'

'Yes. They built the palace around it.'

Nigel studied the façade closely, then turned three hundred and sixty degrees. 'Around and over, I'd guess. Especially if they came down anything like the way I did. You see this landscape? The palace is two thirds of the way up an incline; those big gardens at the back slope up. And this last mile of Walton Boulevard itself is actually a shallow valley, see, running up a slope? Unlikely in nature. No, I'd say the ship hit somewhere down where our hotel is and kept on going, ploughing a groove through the earth until it came to rest here. So once it was down, the ship would be Cornelius's headquarters. It also contained all the resources; those ships carried everything you needed to start a new society on a fresh world. A lot of it wouldn't work here, but there was enough, clearly, and the metal from the superstructure would have been valuable back in the early days. And Cornelius had control over it. The start of the Captain's economic authority. He wouldn't have moved away from that. No. He secured it. Built walls around it, buried it, closed it off to everyone else.' Nigel licked his lips and frowned. 'I wonder what happened to everything they didn't use. Is it still here? I mean, why move it?'

'You think bits of the ship are still here?'

'Could be. We need to get inside to see for sure. But not today.'

'Shame. I'd like to go inside.'

'Come on. Let's go check out something else.'

'Okay. What?'

'I thought the courts; I'd like to observe a trial. Then the Treasury. I'd say the security sheriffs, too, but I don't think any public sheriff station is going to be the kind I need to know about.'

'I don't get it.'

'Government always has its own special police. The kind who really don't like people sniffing round in places they shouldn't. The kind who make sure that anyone complaining about life and saying, *Something should be done*, are quietly dealt with.'

'The Captain has his own police squad separate from the sheriffs,' Kysandra said, trying to remember details from Mrs Brewster's history lessons. 'They're mostly ceremonial body-guards.'

'Ceremony my ass. They'll be the ones.'

It was a ten-minute walk to the central justice courts, back down Walton Boulevard to the junction with Struzaburg Avenue. Nigel stood admiring the Landing Plane statue for a while. 'I remember those brutes; they made them on Oaktier. Cargo capacity about two hundred and fifty tonnes. Aerodynamic flight only, no ingrav propulsion. The Brandts were lucky to have them in the Void. If they had any sense, they'd have ferried their people down in them before they tried to land the big colony ships themselves.'

Kysandra walked on, shaking her head in bemusement. Nigel claimed to know about or be connected to absolutely everything. It was a weird quirk.

*

The courts were another grandiose government block, with narrow windows running up the whole six storeys. The front was classical architecture with heavily stylized columns running along the front. A green copper dome dominated the roofs of its various wings, the apex supporting a fluted pillar where gold scales stood on the top. 'Pretty standard,' Nigel proclaimed.

The trials listed beside the main entrance were all fairly minor ones. They sat in the public gallery of a dispute between a merchant and a rail freight company over the price of grain. The merchant claimed the grain was low quality, the rail company lawyer said the quality wasn't their responsibility. But it was the rail company's agent who had secured the load, the merchant's lawyer protested.

'Nothing ever changes,' Nigel muttered with a sad smile.

They went back to Walton Boulevard, past the plane monument. Before they reached the Treasury at the end of Wahren Street, Nigel stopped outside the looming granite wall that fronted the National Tax Office. Kysandra sensed his ex-sight probing. He walked to the far end of the vast building and looked down the tiny alley running up the side. Several high enclosed pedestrian bridges connected it to the stolid office block next door.

'No wonder the government can afford to build the way it does, as well as fund the county regiments,' he said. 'I'm impressed. That is one big mother of a tax office.'

'They say that the Captain has an agreement with the Skylords, that if you haven't settled your taxes when you seek Guidance, the Skylords will take you to Uracus instead of Giu.'

'Interesting.'

'I don't think it's true, Nigel.'

'Not that. Both Bienvenido and Querencia have the same myths about those two nebulas. Uracus is the doorway to hell, Giu is the route to paradise. That has to come from the Skylords. They're the only connection.'

'Did the Skylords Guide the people from Querencia as well?'

'Yes.'

'Then it's not so strange.'

'Good point.' He gave the Tax Office one last disapproving look and headed off towards the Treasury.

That night they visited the Grand Metropolitan Theatre to see *A Midsummer Night's Dream*.

'What's the matter?' Kysandra asked afterwards as they sat in a corner booth of the Rasheeda's lounge bar for a nightcap. Half of the booths had their black velvet curtains drawn, their occupants fuzzing themselves effectively.

'The play has changed slightly, that's all,' Nigel muttered.

'How could it change?' She closed her eyes, summoning up the memory. '"The moving finger writes; and having writ, moves on."'

'Very good. But somebody else's finger has written over the top, believe me. There were no vampires in the original *Midsummer Night's Dream*.'

'I liked the vampires.'

'They're a metaphor for the temptation of refusing a spiritual afterlife in exchange for flawed physical immortality.'

'Can't you ever just kick back and enjoy things? You always analyse stuff to death.'

He grinned and his retinas zoomed in on the labels of the long line of bottles arranged behind the mirrored bar. 'I'm going to get a drink. What would you like?'

'Double bourbon. Neat. No ice.'

'Okay. One white wine spritzer coming up.'

Kysandra pulled a face at him. She settled down in the booth, a small smile elevating her lips. Life was pretty much perfect right now. A girl, probably twenty years old, left one of the curtained-off booths, and walked over to the bar. Kysandra instantly knew her. It wasn't the dress, which was an elegant tight-fitting burgundy silk gown with a big rose-knot at the base of her spine. Not the long auburn hair, styled in waves at the back to leave delicate curls framing her cheeks. Nor even the broad features of her face, emphasized by too much mascara. No, it was the brittle determination which propelled her across the floor that Kysandra could sense without any ex-sight at all. Exactly the same as her mother's. Determination to get the next shot, no matter what the cost.

She watched the girl sit on the stool next to Nigel in a slinky movement that was akin to a snake flowing into its nest. Long fake eyelashes were flapped slowly. Small inquisitive smile. Toss of the head. A few words spoken.

'Well, hi there,' Kysandra mocked facetiously. 'Do you come here often? Why, yes. Oh, good, so do I. Can I buy you a drink? That would be nice, until my friends turn up.' She lowered her voice to a growl. 'Well, pretty thing, I hope they don't. Perhaps we could wait in my room? That would be simply splendid, I used to wait in rooms all over the Commonwealth, you know.' Open mouth wide and poke a finger in, making a retching sound.

At which moment Nigel turned round, holding a crystal brandy tumbler and a wine glass. Kysandra frantically turned the gesture into rubbing the side of her lips. Too late. Nigel's eyebrows had risen in that irritatingly disdainful put-down he'd clearly spent centuries perfecting.

'Who's your new friend?' Kysandra asked as he sat back down in their booth, what with offence being the best defence, and all.

'Why? Jealous?'

'Sure, if you like narnik whores,' spoken just a little too loudly.

Nigel's teekay slid the booth curtains shut smoothly. 'I think you're being a little judgemental, don't you?'

'Sorry.'

'Your mother's going to be fine. The domination variant I used just compelled her to straighten her act out, not turn into one of my cronies.'

'I know,' Kysandra said in a small voice. The whole domination technique both fascinated and repelled her. Ma's entire family and organization had flipped in that one dark rainy night, becoming Nigel's unquestioning acolytes. They talked the same, walked the same, but he owned them now, sure as if they were a batch of mods. They actually had a rivalry going among themselves to be the best, the fastest to perform his bidding.

It creeped her out. Ma Ulvon's ex-madam, Madeline, might be her maid for the trip, but Kysandra avoided talking to her as much as possible. She was afraid she'd blurt out something like: 'Don't you remember what you were like, what you and Ma were going to do with me?' which might be enough to shatter the spell.

'Aren't you worried about that?' she asked.

'About what?'

'Nobody on this world has ever cured narnik addiction before. Someone might get suspicious about Mum overcoming her problem.'

'Someone in Adeone is a qualified psychologist?'

Kysandra sipped her spritzer sheepishly. 'All right, smartarse.'

'I'm sure people have turned their lives around, even here. If you're determined enough you can achieve miracles. Family support is a big help, too. And I'll bet rich people have sanatoriums that take in wrecked younger members to—'

'All right! Uracus, you know everything always. I get it. I'm just saying it's not so common in Adeone.'

He settled back, looking thoughtful. 'I appreciate that, but don't worry about your mother. If anyone does start asking questions, then Demitri will steer them off topic. Frankly, I'm more concerned about the Tax Office.'

'What?'

'The Tax Office. Even Kafka would envy the size of the place we saw today. And they'll have regional offices, I imagine. I may have been spending a little too freely.' His grin was knowing. 'After all, taxes is how they got Al Capone in the end.'

'Again: nonsense words. Stop it.'

'Sorry. The point is, all the locals in Adeone are happy to accept me as a rich newcomer, especially the ones I spend so many of my counterfeit coins with. To the town, I'm obviously throwing family money around. But when the Tax Office comes calling, the bureaucrats will want to know where that money came from. And I'm not in their existing records.'

'Just dominate the tax inspector. Simple.'

'Yes and no. We need to get politically strategic.'

'What does that mean?'

'I've slightly underestimated this society. That can be corrected by a presence here in Varlan.'

'What sort of presence?'

'I'm going to leave one of the ANAdroids here to embed himself.'

'What will he do?'

'To start with, I'd like to know what's inside the palace. If there's anything left of the ship's network, we might just be able to access some of the flight logs. Unlikely after three thousand years, but you never know. Then a few people working for me in the Tax Office would be advantageous. And it's always good to have political contacts . . .'

'That's just to *start*?'

'Yeah.'

'Giu. So what happens after that?'

'Whatever needs to happen. That's the whole point of being strategic.'

*

This version of his personality was strange. Not unpleasant, but definitely different. Nigel knew they were his own thoughts running through the ANAdroid's bioconstruct brain. The inbuilt gaiamotes still connected him to his real self as he went upstairs to the hotel suite with Kysandra, just as they simultaneously linked him with the second ANAdroid sharing a room in the hotel's servants' quarters with Madeline and Russell. Identity wasn't the problem. It was the responses that were difficult. For all its excellent duplication of his own neural pathways, the bioconstruct brain didn't facilitate spontaneous emotion. Instead he had to analyse situations and extrapolate what he should be feeling. The bioconstruct brain was fast enough and the secondary routines good enough to produce appropriate expressions without delay. Ironically, of course, not having emotions didn't bother the ANAdroid; he simply knew that any real version of himself would be bothered.

There was also the problem of ex-sight perception. Without a shell (which this artificial brain could generate perfectly), anyone on Bienvenido would know his thoughts were different, wrong. Best case scenario they'd think him a psychopath, unfeeling and cold, disconnected from his fellow humans. More likely they'd assume he was a Faller. But then, as the ANAdroid didn't sleep, he was never likely to be caught with his shell down. In fact, maintaining it constantly was handled by a secondary routine.

He was confident he could pass for human in the city. Kysandra had certainly never realized the ANAdroids were all Nigel-copy personalities. A subtle variation in the emotional responses of each one was easy enough, making them appear distinct and different. But she was young and naive. Living in Varlan would be the real test.

As Nigel and Kysandra said goodnight and retired to their separate rooms upstairs (Kysandra claimed the huge bed in the master bedroom, of course), he walked into the Rasheeda's lounge bar. At this time of the evening, coming up on midnight, the room was quite full, with most of the booths occupied. He sat at the bar, choosing the middle one of three empty stools.

'Dirantio,' he told the barman. An almond-flavoured spirit his real self enjoyed the taste of. Taste made no difference to him, and the ANAdroid body would never metabolize the alcohol, but he should sound as if he knew what he liked.

'Ice with that, sir?' the barman asked.

'Yes, please.'

There was the distinctive *swish* sound of silk as she sat on the stool next to him. He turned to look at her. Fresh mascara had been added. He wondered if she'd been crying, slapped about by her pimp back in the booth for her earlier failure.

'Now, where's that barman gone?' she asked, not quite to herself.

'Getting me some ice. He'll be back in a moment.'

'Oh, good. I like my drink chilled.'

'Really? What do you like to drink?'

'Me? Oh, white wine, mostly. Sometimes a Finns. When I'm in the mood.'

'I would love to buy you one of those.'

She did the slow appraising blink. 'Can you afford one? You seem rather young.'

'I've just arrived in the city today. It's kind of a tradition for the men in our family. We spend a couple of years at the university partying and making contacts and maybe even going to a lecture or two before we get dragged back home to manage the estates like every other boring ancestor since the landing.'

'Oh, really? Where is home?'

'Kassell. Ever been?'

'No.'

'Well, maybe one day. I'd be happy to show you round.'

'If that offer is still open, I think I'll risk a Finns.'

'Glad I caught you in the right mood, er . . . '

'Bethaneve.'

'Hello, Bethaneve. I'm Coulan.'

4

From Varlan, they took the express to Portlynn, which sat at the end of the Great Central Line, three thousand miles as the manta-hawk flew, but the track headed north to Adice first, then curved round the Guelp mountains as it sliced through the middle of Lamaran. By the time they finally pulled in at Portlynn, the train had travelled closer to four thousand miles, stopping twenty times and taking four days.

Portlynn had sprung up as a trading town at the end of Nilsson Sound, a huge inlet slicing deep into the heart of Lamaran. It was also the estuary to the river Mozal, whose massive tributary network multiplied across the wetland basin which stretched right across to the Bouge mountains a thousand miles to the east, and down to the Transo mountains in the south. This close to the equator, and with guaranteed rainfall, the rich soil was perfect for stonefruit, banana, breadfruit and citrus plantations, as well as extensive rice paddies. The river network made travel easy and cheap, with no need to invest in expensive train lines that would have needed a multitude of bridges.

The regional capital extended over across dozens of estuary mud islands. Its buildings were all wooden, which came as quite a change for Kysandra after all the stone and brick towns the express had just travelled through. Wood imposed natural limits on the height of the buildings, so instead of going up, the town sprawled outwards, colonizing the marshy ground. There were bridges between the islands, but there was no logic to their positions, and they were all narrow – for pedestrians, not carts. Sometimes you'd have to go round three or four islands before reaching the one neighbouring the one you started at. All real travel in Portlynn was by boat along the channels, which were constantly being dredged clear. The buildings themselves were all built on stilts, thick hardwood trunks driven deep into the alluvial silt to provide stability and protection from the monsoon season floods.

Nigel booked them into the Baylee Hotel, a big three-storey structure close to the east bank docks, where the town's largest warehouses stood at the end of long wharfs. Fast sailing clippers and steam-powered sea barges were berthed along them, with teams of mod-dwarfs and stevedores loading and unloading cargoes all day long.

It took two days to gather supplies then hire a boat to take them upstream. But at daybreak on the third morning Nigel, Kysandra, Fergus, Madeline and Russell walked along the rickety bridges to Kate's Lagoon at the south end of the city. Nigel had hired the *Gothora*, a sturdy steam-powered cargo boat, with a hull built out of anbor planks, one of the hardest woods on Bienvenido. A tiny crew cabin at the rear had berths for Captain Migray and his three crew: Sancal, Jymoar and the engineer Avinus. They certainly couldn't fit Nigel and the rest in with them, so they'd rigged the first of *Gothora*'s two holds with a simple bamboo frame covered in canvas, allowing the passengers to spend the trip under cover, along with their trunks and supplies. The other hold was rigged with a simple open-sided awning, and used as a stable for the five terrestrial horses which they would ride across the desert, and the three mod-horses that would go with them, carrying their provisions.

Portlynn was just coming to life when Migray cast off and steered them out of Kate's Lagoon into the three-kilometre-wide mouth of the Mozal. The water was a thick ochre red from the silt it carried, and it flowed so swiftly at the centre that boats going upstream had to travel close to the side where the current wasn't as tenacious. Even so, *Gothora* burnt a lot of logs and didn't make much headway for the morning of the first day.

The riverbanks for the first fifteen kilometres up from the mouth were still wild despite the heavy cultivation a few kilometres inland. *Gothora* chugged past a continuous wall of marshes and jugobush swamps, one boat in a long procession of cargo vessels setting off upstream. Five hundred metres to starboard, vessels laden with freshly picked crops were racing past, catching the current downstream to dock in Portlynn where their payload would be transferred to trains or the big seagoing ships.

By mid-afternoon they were seeing the first plantations and pastures encroaching through the flood meadows. Big white-painted manor houses were glimpsed amid the dense groves. Then the villages began to appear on the banks; like Portlynn, the houses were all built from wood and stood on stilts. Landing jetties extended out into the river, with boats docked and stevedores busy.

'It all looks so lovely,' Kysandra said wistfully as the pretty little communities slid past. Nearly all the original jungle had been cleared, surrendering the land to cultivation. Rigid lines of citrus trees stood proud in their groves. Small armies of mod-dwarfs moved through them, picking the colourful globes. Big carts stacked high with wicker crates full of fruit wound along the dirt tracks lined with tall fandapalms to the jetties. Paddy fields glinted rose gold in the afternoon sun, with even smaller mod-dwarfs wading through them, planting rice. Cattle and ostriches grazed long lush meadows. Humans walked about or rode horses, all wearing wide-brimmed hats against the powerful sun. It looked such a settled, easy life.

'Would you like to live here, señorita?' Jymoar asked.

Kysandra gave a small furtive smile and glanced round. Jymoar was standing beside the small wheelhouse, looking at her. He caught her eye and grinned happily. She blushed and turned back to stare at the riverbank. Jymoar was maybe nineteen, serving his apprenticeship with his uncle Migray. Cute enough, but . . . *No thanks.*

'I already have a home, thank you.' Even as she said it, she regretted it. The lad gave her an apologetic nod and turned to go.

'But I could be persuaded to move.' She gave Nigel a sly glance. 'My guardian won't be able to order me around forever.'

'Guardian?' Jymoar said in confusion.

Nigel tipped his hat at Jymoar. 'That would be me. But I'm going to check on the horses, or something; you kids have fun.' With a private 'path, he added, 'Play nice, now,' to Kysandra.

'So have you travelled this far east before?' she asked.

Jymoar hurried forward to be with her. 'Never so far, no. But I have only been on the *Gothora* for seven months. One day I will have my own boat.'

She gave him an encouraging smile. 'Really? What sort?'

*

As night came, lights from the villages and more isolated manors shimmered across the fast quiet water as the *Gothora* kept a steady course upstream. They stopped at a village the next day to replenish their logs and buy fresh food for the galley. After less than four hours, they set off again.

It took eight days to navigate the length of the Mozal. Fortunately the main river extended almost all the way to the southern end of the Bouge mountain range, a thousand miles due east from Portlynn. Only the last fifty miles saw them turning down a tributary river, the Woular, heading north again. The mountains had grown steadily up from the horizon for the last two days.

The land on either side of the Woular had reverted to long stretches of raw jungle and scrub. Estates and villages were spaced further and further apart. This was wilderness country, devoid of any terrestrial vegetation. Native natell and quasso trees grew tall along the riverbanks, festooned with vines decorated in an abundance of white and purple flowers. The water was getting clogged with rotting fallen branches and long vine tendrils. Tough bakku weed grew along the edges, forming large wiry mats. Captain Migray had to reduce speed, while he and Sancal used their ex-sight diligently, probing the river for snags. They hadn't seen another boat for hours.

Finally, Croixtown slipped into view round a long curve. The village was made up from about fifty houses, none of which had a second storey. They were huddled together at the centre of an array of big pens, whose high, strong fences contained bison and wild boar. Smaller pens contained neuts. Kysandra craned her neck forward, her retinas zooming in.

'Are those camels?'

'You have good eyes,' Jymoar said, smiling worshipfully. He'd spent most of the voyage flirting hopefully with her and was now badly smitten.

'Thank you.'

'And, yes, those are probably camels. The rancheros, they don't care what they drive into their corrals, as long as it fetches a shining coin from the markets.'

'That's a lot of livestock out there,' Nigel said, regarding the pens attentively.

Jymoar didn't flinch quite as much as he had at the start of the trip whenever Nigel said something. 'Si, señor. The savannah is home to many beasts; they run wild here. There are few predators, just mantahawks and roxwolves and dingoes – and the rancheros hunt them down to protect the herds.' He looked round furtively, then lowered his voice. 'I've heard that the people of Shansville like dingo meat.'

Kysandra stared past the pens. Beyond them, the land rose slowly to the foothills of the Bouge range, a vast open region of savannah where the blue-green native gangrass rippled away like some sluggish sea. The occasional ebony whipwoor tree stood proud, thorny blemishes speckling the endless shifting gangrass. 'Is that where the Desert of Bone is?' she asked.

'Beyond the mountains, yes,' Jymoar said. 'I wish you were not going there, señorita. It is a bad place.'

'Why do you say that?'

'Everybody knows. Not even the Fallers dare to travel there. They say there are ten thousand bodies piled up in the centre, their bones are a monster's treasure hoard and their souls haunt the desert, weeping tears of grey light into the sand.'

'Fascinating,' Nigel said. 'What sort of monster?'

'Nobody knows, señor. If you encounter it, you do not survive. Those that do manage to avoid its clutches are scarred for life by what they have seen; many go mad afterwards.'

'Ten thousand bodies? That's a lot of people. Where did they come from?'

'Nigel,' Kysandra chided, frowning at him. It wasn't fair to mock the poor boy's superstition.

Jymoar shrugged. 'You doubt me, but those people have died in the Desert of Bone, señor. I will not go there, not even for the señorita.'

'And I would never ask you to,' she told him kindly.

Gothora tied up at Croixtown's single jetty. The townsfolk were disappointed it wouldn't be taking any of their livestock down river to the big markets, but Nigel was paying Captain Migray to stay there until they got back.

'For a month,' the captain said. 'Your coins are good, señor, but the *Gothora* is my life and my living. I cannot chain her to the land; she must travel the river.'

'I understand,' Nigel said. 'We'll be back before the month is up.'

'I will wait,' Jymoar 'pathed privately to Kysandra, 'until you return safely.'

'Don't worry about us,' she 'pathed back. 'Please.'

Nigel whistled happily as he led his horse down the jetty. 'Ahh, shipboard romance. Finest kind.'

'Oh, shut up,' she growled at him.

5

It was hard riding across the savannah. Kysandra was almost in tears the first night, she was so saddle sore. Even the nerve blocks her secondary routines established to ease the pain didn't seem to help much. They set up camp in two tents that *Skylady* had fabricated to resemble ordinary canvas, but were actually lightweight thermo-stable sheets. 'They'll keep the temperature just right in the desert,' Nigel explained. 'Nights can get exceptionally cold. Explorers have been caught out by that before.'

Kysandra lent some half-hearted help putting them up. She didn't want to sit down, and watched Fergus disapprovingly as he showed her how to use the valve on her self-inflating mattress.

'It'll be soft enough,' he promised.

'Nothing could be,' she assured him.

But because the mattress was some fancy Commonwealth fabric, it was indeed soft enough to lie on without wincing and cursing. Madeline came in with a large tube of cream from the first-aid kit and told her to roll onto her front.

'I'm going to need this as well as you, kiddo,' she admitted to Kysandra as she rubbed it on red-raw skin. 'That was a long ride, and I haven't been on a horse in years.'

Kysandra sighed in relief as the mild analgesic took hold.

'We should put some dermsynth on that,' Nigel announced. 'It'll strengthen your backside for tomorrow.'

Kysandra *yiped* in shock and hurriedly pulled a towel over her bare buttocks. She glared up at him. 'Don't they have privacy in the Commonwealth?'

'Hmm.' Nigel scratched the back of his head, seemingly bemused. 'It kind of depends which planet you're on.'

'Out!'

He chuckled as he left the tent. Kysandra glared at the flap for a long moment. Her u-shadow told her Nigel was sending a file, which she accepted reluctantly. It was a list of dermsynth properties.

'Always got to be right,' she grunted. 'Madeline, fetch the dermsynth spray, would you?'

'Sure thing, kiddo.'

Russell started a small fire and cooked their rations. As the sun finally went down, Kysandra was suddenly very aware of animals snuffling about through the long gangrass at the periphery of her ex-sight where she couldn't quite identify them. Cries of lone rox-wolves began to sound further off across the savannah, answered by the challenging howls of dingo packs.

'They won't come near the fire,' Nigel said, picking up on her concern.

'It's not the genuine animals I'm worried about,' Kysandra said. 'It's the Fallers. The eggs don't get to choose what they egg-sume.'

'Interesting,' Nigel said. 'They must have some basic parameters. I mean, eggsuming a roxwolf I can understand, but there's no point in them becoming bussalores or flies.'

'They call it the first forty rule,' Kysandra said. 'I read it in the Research Institute's manuals. If an animal weighs less than forty kilos, it doesn't get attracted to the egg in the first month, but after that the egg gets less fussy and starts to attract smaller creatures.'

'So they're smart even at the egg stage,' Nigel mused.

'Not smart,' Russell said. 'Cunning, like all evil things.'

Kysandra grinned at the man's certainty. Even this new Russell liked his world simple.

'We're going to have to examine an egg at some point,' Nigel said. 'See what makes it tick.' Then he cocked his head to one side.

'But the Faller Research Institute must have done that already; and they would have had the best equipment – if it worked. We need to get their results, if they ever published them.'

'Coulan will find it,' she said confidently.

'If it's there.' Nigel gave Kysandra a sharp look. 'So, do Faller animals eat humans, too?'

'No. They only ever eat what they've become, it's in the manual.'

'Curiouser and curiouser,' Nigel muttered.

'The animals know,' Madeline said in satisfaction. 'They can always tell if one of their own is really a Faller. They attack instinctively. Bienvenido would be overrun otherwise.'

'But Faller animals kill humans, they always have,' Kysandra said. 'They know we're their real enemy. That's why . . .' She gestured into the night.

'I'll be on watch all night,' Fergus assured her. He patted the high-powered hunting rifle *Skylady* had fabricated to look like a normal Bienvenido-manufactured weapon. 'You'll be perfectly safe.'

Despite the worry about possible Faller animals, and the nagging pain from her thighs and bottom, Kysandra fell asleep quickly.

It was another two days' ride over the savannah before they reached the foothills. This was the southernmost point of the Bouge range. Three hundred miles directly east lay the coast with the Eastath Ocean beyond, while to the north the Desert of Bone rolled away for nearly eight hundred miles before eventually breaking up against a small range of hills that dipped down to the northern, equatorial, coast. The north-eastern boundary of the desert was formed by the Salalsav mountains; while not as high as the Bouge range, they formed an effective barrier to any rainclouds coming off the Eastath Ocean. So only the southern edge of the desert was unguarded by highlands, and it was a rare wind indeed which blew any rainclouds in that way.

They trekked round the Bouge foothills until the scrubland grew arid, gangrass giving way to tufts of succulent weed which itself soon became sparse. Loam turned to gritty soil. The first of the dunes were visible a few miles ahead, and with the sight of them came fine particles of sand, blown by the parched wind that came off the Desert of Bone, stinging Kysandra's face.

'There's a stream over there,' Nigel said, standing up in his stirrups. 'That's where we'll camp and prepare.' He flicked the reins, reinforcing the 'path order to his horse. The rest of them followed.

The stream was barely more than a winding line of rushes in the grit, betraying the damper ground. When they parted the sharp blades to expose the water, it was brackish and slow moving. 'It should be enough,' Fergus said. He took a spade and started digging.

'I'll help,' Russell said, always keen to prove his worth.

Nigel, Kysandra and Madeline opened the trunks the mod-horses were carrying and unloaded the extra bundles of rods, laying them out on the ground in the pattern they'd all memorized from the countless rehearsals they'd gone through before setting off. Had anyone examined the thin composite struts, they would have assumed they were just more tent poles.

Once they had them in the right order, they clipped them all together, forming three simple square framework platforms. Kysandra slotted the curving struts together to form wheels and fitted the tyres to them – superstrength fabric tubes that weighed less than a kilogram each. There were six of them. She twisted the footpump hose into the valve of the first and started inflating. It was hot, exhausting work that had her sweating profusely after the first minute, but she kept going determinedly. Nigel took over and inflated the second. Once all six tyres were inflated, they fixed the wheels to the platform axles, and they had three small carts which the mod-horses could pull.

Russell loaded them with the water bladders made from the same fabric as the tyres.

'Now the tough pumping,' Nigel declared.

They used a second, larger, footpump to siphon water out of the hole Fergus and Russell had dug, impelling it through a

442

sophisticated filter and into the bladders. There were three on each cart, holding a hundred and fifty litres each.

'Isn't this too much?' Kysandra asked, a question she'd asked often enough back at Blair Farm as they put their equipment together.

'It's a desert,' Nigel had explained patiently. 'Eight hundred miles long and three hundred at its widest. We have to find the one point that produced the anomaly, and I've only got an approximate coordinate for that. Now I have no idea how many days this search will take, but I'm budgeting a couple of weeks. A horse will consume a minimum of twenty-five litres of water a day under normal circumstances, but this is a desert, not normal circumstances. And we need a good three to four litres a day ourselves. Even carrying thirteen hundred litres, we'll have to go back to the foothills and refill every few days.'

'All right, all right,' she surrendered.

They'd only pumped three of the nine bladders full when Fergus said: 'Oh, yes, look at this – there, where the air's cooler.'

Kysandra looked in the direction he was pointing. High on a slope about three miles away she saw some grey specks moving slowly round the gradient. When she zoomed in, she realized just how big the animals were. 'Are those elephants?' she asked. She'd always wanted to see one of the big animals.

'Mammoths,' Nigel said, with a knowing smile. 'Hell, I remember when the first one was born. San Diego Zoo was swamped for months after; even baby pandas got ignored by the media.'

'Are they artificial?'

'Oh, no. Well . . . not exactly. They were terrestrial animals that died out during Earth's last ice age; then the Genome Structure Foundation sequenced their DNA from mummified remnants dug out of the Siberian permafrost. Controversial at the time, especially given what that particular foundation morphed into, but we wound up taking them to half the planets we settled, them and the crudding dodo – though what the point in recreating that was I'll never know. Dumbest creature ever, and as ugly as sin too.

Plus, it tastes exactly like chicken, so that wasn't a valid reason, either.'

'It sounds very worthy, bringing the species back from the dead. I know Earth was in big ecological trouble at one time; that was in my general history memory.'

'Yeah. We had a bit of a guilt overreaction to that. It's called Sanctuary: the only world we ever terraformed from scratch. Two hundred years dumping billions of tonnes of microbes and biogunk onto it to prepare its atmosphere and sand for terrestrial plants. Another century bombing it with seeds and insects before we went all Noah on its ass and released our animals two by two. Every species but humans – oh and wasps, I think. It's the only true pure copy of Earth's biosphere in the galaxy, and we're the one lifeform that's banned from it. Brilliant! But hey, there are lots of whales in Sanctuary's oceans. Always whales. We have such an ingrained collective culpability trip over them. So that's okay.'

'You sound so cynical.'

'That's self-deprecation,' Fergus said. 'He's not sorry about Sanctuary at all. Who do you think paid for it?'

'That was necessary,' Nigel said. 'An experiment.'

'Experiment?'

'Yeah. See, there's a lot of H-congruous worlds in this galaxy; the biochemistry is different, but not lethally so.' He gestured round. 'Like here, we co-exist happily; there's even some native plants we can eat. But if our colony fleets got to another galaxy and the majority biochemistry was incompatible, we'd have to know how to terraform, and get it right. Best we find out how before we go.'

'Another galaxy?' Kysandra pressed her hands to her temples. 'Is there really no way I can get out of the Void? I want to live out there. I want to be *free*.'

Nigel gave her a sorrowful look. 'Sorry – me and my mouth. I've got to learn when to shut the crud up.'

'No,' she said. 'Don't do that. Not ever.'

*

In the morning they dressed in their desert robes – a silverwhite cloth that had the same thermal properties as the tent fabric. It was also used in the wide floppy hats they made the horses wear to protect their heads from the direct power of the sun.

Kysandra carefully wrapped the turban round her head, making sure she tucked all her hair away from her face. With the cloth wound tight, it was difficult to make sure her darkened goggles fitted properly.

'I can hardly move my jaw,' she complained.

'I'll refrain from the obvious comment,' Nigel said, and stood in front of her, adjusting the strips of turban she'd wrapped below her chin. 'How's that?'

'Good, I guess.'

'You ready?'

'Uracus, yeah.'

They rode their horses out past the foothills, where the last tufts of vegetation clung to the floor of shallow gullies, and moved out into the dunes of the desert itself. Nigel and Fergus checked how the tyres were dealing with the hot grey sand, but they appeared to be coping okay. Certainly the bladder carts rolled along smoothly enough.

An hour after they started, Kysandra was glad of the desert robes. She'd felt as if she was swaddling herself when she put them on, they seemed so restrictive. But, sitting in the saddle as her horse plodded along, she didn't have to exert herself. The cloth's shiny surface reflected the sun's heat away, while the thermal shielding prevented the hot air from scorching her skin. Except for breathing. The air was hot in her mouth, almost painfully so, quickly drying her throat out. She sipped constantly from the tube that snaked up from the flask strapped to her stomach under the robes. As the morning progressed, the desert's eternal heat was something she was highly aware of, enveloping her completely, yet never managing to break through her protection. It felt exciting, defying such a hostile environment. She began to wonder if those audacious early explorers had actually found anything. Surely no one would be mad enough to trek to the middle of the desert as they were doing. *Are the legends of bones just heat fever dreams?*

The dunes began to grow larger, the sand looser. The course Nigel set, taking them to the heart of the desert, was always on a slope, going up, then down. Never following a flat gradient. Soon the foothills vanished from sight; only the Bouge mountains remained, implausible pinnacles of snow glinting above the desert.

The fiery air was saturated with minute particles, stirred by the mild but constant breeze. Despite the robes, they began to creep in through the folds to scratch her skin. She was blinking a lot now, small tears flushing her eyes clean. Her horse shook its head constantly at the irritation, whinnying protests at the awful heat. She had to send constant 'path orders, keeping it on track, soothing its mounting agitation at the harsh white-glare landscape. Only the mod-horses plodded on, unperturbed by their ordeal.

After four hours, Nigel called a halt in the lee of a tall dune. 'I miscalculated,' he announced. 'This temperature is getting dangerous to the animals. It's crazy to travel in the day, especially midday. We'll make camp here until evening, and travel at night.'

Kysandra didn't complain. She wanted to get on and reach the centre of the desert to solve its mystery. But her horse was becoming increasingly skittish, and she was picking up its genuinely distressed thoughts. As she climbed down she was startled by the sudden outbreak of noise from the poor animal. The desert had been devoid of any sound since they entered it. When she pushed up her goggles to wipe her eyes, the brightness was shocking.

They rigged up a big awning, and tethered the animals – not that they would have run off anywhere. Then she helped Madeline and Russell pitch the tents while Nigel and Fergus inspected the axles on the bladder carts, injecting fresh oil into the bearings to compensate for the sand that had got in.

Kysandra was impatient to get the tents up. The bizarrely contradictory feeling of claustrophobia the robes produced as she walked around slotting poles together and screwing pegs into the sand was making her edgy. As soon as she had watered and fed her horse, she hurried inside and stripped down to her underwear. The air within the tent was hot, verging on unpleasant, but she didn't mind that; the absence of the robe was liberating. She took a long drink from the chillflask, gasping at how cold it was – only just above freezing.

'Coming in,' Nigel 'pathed.

Kysandra pulled a shirt out of her duffel bag and slipped into it.

'How are you doing?' he asked as he started to take his robes off.

'I'm going to need more ointment,' she admitted. The backs of her legs were still red and sore despite the salves she'd used every morning and night.

'Me, too.'

'Do you think the horses will be all right?'

'The temperature is a lot lower under the awning. They'll cope. And it should get cooler in here too, as long as we don't keep opening the flap. Give it an hour.' He dropped his robe on the floor.

'Good.' She unrolled her bedding and waited for the self-inflating mattress to plump up. 'And you were worried about us freezing at night.'

'Even I can be wrong. Who knew?'

She lay back on the mattress, telling herself she was slightly cooler. 'So we're just going to stay in here together for the next seven hours?' Even now she couldn't bring herself to share a tent with Madeline, or Russell. And Fergus was outside under the awning with the horses, keeping watch, as always.

'Yeah. We'll have a meal before we start off again. With all the senses we've got available, it'll be perfectly safe riding at night.'

*

Despite her expectations, Kysandra managed to doze quite a lot as the unrelenting sun blasted the desert, taking the midday temperature close to fifty degrees Celsius. In the tent, it never rose above twenty-five.

447

She wasn't hungry; she didn't want to do anything. But Nigel insisted they eat towards the end of the afternoon. Her meal was some jibread, which was baked so long it was as tough and dense as a biscuit, but could be carried for weeks, and a meat paste chosen because it also could last for a long time without putrefying. She forced it all down and drank a lot more water from the chillflask. The high point was an apple, one from a sack they'd bought in Croixtown. It didn't taste of much, and she thought the skin was starting to wrinkle up already.

They put their robes back on and went outside to break camp. The rest of the day continued in the same fashion as the morning's journey. A steady measured progress. Up a dune, down the other side. Then again. Again. Tiny runnels of sand slipping away from the hooves. A track of churned-up sand in their wake. Twin grooves of the bladder carts' wheels stretching out behind them, dwindling into the distance.

After an hour the sun sank behind the Bouge mountains, leaving the desert encased in a rosy twilight. The hard-packed sand turned a dull rouge colour. That shaded down to a murky grey before long. The clear sky darkened, allowing the frail nebula light to shine down. Air temperature began to drop towards the low forties Celsius.

Within her little cocoon of protective Commonwealth gear, Kysandra became more and more convinced that no one had ever come this far inside the Desert of Bone before. Explorers must have skirted the edges. Nothing more.

As the night wore on, the size of the dunes began to reduce, their height shrinking, slopes flattening out. She realized the breeze was fading away, too.

An hour after midnight, Nigel led the way over the last true dune. On the other side, the desert became tediously flat; washed by the insipid phosphorescence of the nebulas, it resembled a lacklustre becalmed sea. But it did allow them to pick up the pace as they started moving across the dreary terrain.

*

They stopped at three o'clock to water the horses. The animals were tired, but hadn't protested at the night march.

'At least nothing can creep up on us here,' Russell said as they filled the water sacks. Even the dunes, barely ten miles behind, were lost to the dark horizon. The sensation of isolation was formidable.

'There is no monster,' Nigel assured him.

She wished she could believe so easily, but the Desert of Bone was a strange place.

Dawn arrived two hours later, a blazing crescent of gold light sliding up fast from behind the Salalsav mountains and pushing a pale blue haze ahead of it. By then Kysandra was feeling desperately weary. Even with a long rest yesterday afternoon, the night trek had left her drained.

'Do we stop now?' she asked. It was practically a plea.

'When the temperature rises,' Nigel replied impassively.

Kysandra's horse kept walking as the day bloomed around them; the steady rhythm had become her whole universe. The heat increased inexorably, punishing the air. She could taste it in her mouth again.

Vivid sunlight revealed nothing, only how vast the Desert of Bone was. Today, even the surrounding mountains were lost to sight in the quivering miasma of roiling air that shrouded them.

'Stop,' Nigel 'pathed.

The order broke through Kysandra's hypnotic stupor. Nigel had reined in his horse ten metres ahead. She hurriedly ordered her horse to halt behind him.

'Anyone else see that?' he asked.

Kysandra stared at the wobbling horizon, unsure where the land ended and the sky began. But there was a definite dark knot in the contorted air, and not even her reactivated Advancer-heritage eyes could focus on it. 'What is that?' she asked plaintively.

Nigel raised a module, pointing it at the dark smudge. 'Mirage. There's something over the horizon. Something big. Too far away for a reading.' He lowered the module.

'That's lucky,' she said. Navigation icons slipped across her exo-vision, linked to the small inertial guidance OCtattoo the *Skylady*'s medical module had printed on her shoulder. 'Old technology,' Nigel had said. 'But we thought it might work here.'

He was right. The exovision data confirmed that the object, whatever it was, was situated east of the course they were taking to the epicentre of the desert.

Two months ago, the post had delivered the most expensive, elaborate atlas available on Bienvenido: a huge tome with fold-out charts which Nigel had ordered directly from the Captain's Cartography Institute. The world's main features had supposedly been copied from images originally captured during the approach of Captain Cornelius's ship, with additional details supplied by various Geographical Association expeditions over the centuries. It certainly gave a reasonably accurate plan of the Desert of Bone, which they'd faithfully copied into their storage lacuna. There were no features within the desert, no hills no canyons; according to the atlas, its topography was blank.

'I don't think that's entirely luck,' Nigel said slowly. 'It's simply large enough to be refracted across a long distance. Which isn't necessarily a good thing.'

'Is it one of the other ships, do you think?' she asked. 'Did one crash here?' The idea was frightening. What would it be like to stumble out of a wrecked ship and find yourself in this utterly inhospitable terrain? *And everyone says there are a lot of bodies.* A chill rippled over her skin, making her shiver inside the robe.

'Possibly,' Nigel said. 'Though I'd expect a decent population centre to emerge close to anywhere a ship came down. And this end of the continent is one of the last areas to be developed. There are some fishing villages on the other side of the Salalsav mountains, but nothing major.'

'Because they never got out of the desert.'

'Cornelius wouldn't have abandoned them.'

'Then—?'

'This is why we're out here, remember? To find out. Come on, we'll camp here for the day.'

This time, Kysandra fell asleep almost as soon as she stumbled into the tent. Nigel woke her late in the afternoon for a meal, which she ate enthusiastically.

It was still appallingly hot when they set off again in the unremitting glare of low sunlight. Nigel and Fergus said the mirage had been visible for most of the day. It skipped about in the distorted air, but the direction hadn't varied by more than a few degrees.

That was the course they followed, with the mirage flickering directly ahead of them like some black sun poised on the horizon. Then it sank away in tandem with Bienvenido's real sun, leaving the uniform desert stretching away to the infinity edge, where it blended into the sky. Kysandra's exovision projected a single purple guidance line towards the vanishing point. She stared down it obsessively as the horse plodded obediently onwards into the night. The gentle phosphorescent light of the nebulas shone across them, as unchanging as the desert.

'There's something,' Fergus announced.

It was long past midnight, and Kysandra's determination and eagerness had abandoned her quite a while back when it became obvious that the mirage object wasn't waiting just over the horizon. Now she was simply enduring the tedium of the trek, waiting for dawn and the tent to appear in her life.

She waited without real interest as Fergus dismounted and walked across the grainy sand to a small stone. Her retinas zoomed in. He bent down and picked something up. A scrap of cloth? But it disintegrated as soon as his fingers plucked it off the ground. Except for a small metal ring left sitting in his palm, which he stared at curiously. A direct channel opened to her u-shadow, and exovision threw up Fergus's sight, complete with spectrographic analysis.

It was a ring, measuring three centimetres across. Made of titanium.

'Commonwealth artefact,' Nigel said.

'Not jewellery,' Fergus said. 'It was fixed into the fabric.'

'Any more of them?'

'I can't see any, no.'

'All right, let's keep going.'

They began moving forwards. Ten minutes later Nigel called a halt. He dismounted and picked up another scrap of cloth. Like the first, it disintegrated as soon as he touched it.

'Ancient,' was all he'd say. 'Very ancient.'

There were more tatters of the frail cloth scattered over the desert. Snagged on stones, half buried under tiny rills in the sand. One they saw had a cable attached, which was twisted round a flinty rock.

Nigel and Fergus knelt beside it, examining the find. 'Mono-bonded carbon filament,' Nigel said. Fergus gingerly started pulling it. More fabric puffed into dust. The filament was ten metres long, one end connected to a metal clip of some kind.

'So did a ship crash here or not?' Kysandra asked.

Nigel kept his shell perfectly opaque. 'Maybe. These fragments are certainly left over from that era. The wind must have blown them about from whatever's out there. I just don't quite get what the fabric was. Maybe some kind of tent?'

For another two hours they kept going. More and more torn ribbons of the ubiquitous cloth were scattered about. They saw one patch that was over three metres across, draped tightly over several stones and rills, age and sun conspiring to tighten it into a skin that revealed every crack and blemish it covered. Under the eerie nebula light, it shone a pasty blue-grey against the dark sand, as if it was a lost smear of bioluminescent lichen.

'How long can fabric survive out here?' Kysandra asked.

'This stuff is a polymer residue; there's no telling what it decayed from, so I don't know the timescale,' Nigel said. 'But there's a hell of a lot of it.'

'Got something,' Fergus called out. 'Switch to infra-red and look at the horizon.'

Kysandra switched to infra-red. It was a mode she'd avoided: turning the desert ground to a speckle pattern of pink and yellow in the middle of the night was disorientating, especially with the blank sky above. But there it was before her now – an exquisite level plain of glowing colour, fluctuating in slow undulations as residual heat leaked back out into the mild air. She frowned. Out there at the very limit of the gentle tangerine illumination, where heat gave way to emptiness, a green blob straddled the rim of the desert. She tried to zoom in, but the higher the magnification, the more blurred the thing became.

'What is that?' she asked cautiously.

'Something a different temperature to the desert,' Nigel said. 'Something big.'

'The monster?' Madeline asked fearfully.

'There is no monster,' Nigel said.

'Let's go,' Fergus said. 'We might reach it before dawn.'

They tried hard, urging the horses forward in a fast walk. But after another forty minutes, the green glow didn't appear any larger and dawn spread a brilliant sheen of monochrome light across the desert. As shadows thrown from them and the horses stretched out across the ochre sand, they stared at the horizon directly ahead. A small conical hill rose out of the barren terrain, its shallow slopes a curious slate grey, turning to a lighter ash shading as the sunlight slithered down it.

'That's not a ship,' Kysandra blurted.

'Doesn't look like one,' Nigel agreed. 'But it's definitely metallic. That has to be the spectrum *Skylady*'s sensors detected. This is what we're here for.'

Even as he was talking, Kysandra was studying the ground around them. The shreds of fabric were everywhere. Hundreds – thousands – of tattered streamers lying without order, from the size of a handkerchief up to sheets that would have covered the bed back in the Rasheeda Hotel; lacing the sand between them was a multitude of thin filaments, some stretched out flat, others tangled in knots. There were also little chunks of tarnished metal – clips and bolts which the filaments were attached to. The ubiquitous rings.

'How far to the metal hill?' Kysandra asked.

'Difficult to measure,' Fergus said.

Even as she zoomed in again, Kysandra could see the desert stirring. The air swelling and flowing as the sun began its tremendous bombardment.

'Let's press on,' Nigel said. 'We might get there before we have to make camp.'

Kysandra thought that unlikely, but said nothing. The little convoy rolled along, with puffs of dust swirling up whenever a hoof or a wheel ran over a patch of cloth, causing it to disintegrate instantly. At the beginning, they were dismounting every couple of minutes to remove filaments that had tangled round the legs of the horses. After that, whoever took point used teekay to clear the strands away.

Now, the track they left behind was like a path of destruction, a trail anyone could follow. When Kysandra scanned round, she couldn't see any other furrow through the delicate scraps of cloth.

'Nobody else has been here,' she decided.

'Not for a long time,' Nigel agreed.

The hill was definitely larger when they stopped two hours later. Her zoom function still wasn't much use through the wavering heat, although she was convinced the sides of the hill were exceptionally knobbly. She was also intrigued by the uniformity of colour. The cone shape was nearly perfectly symmetrical, too, though it was odd, with a wide base, as if it had sagged at some time since its formation.

'Why would you cover a hill in metal?' she asked as they put the tents up.

'There is no reason for that,' Nigel said. 'But then, I don't think it is a hill, either.'

'What then?'

'Some kind of ship. Nothing else it can be.'

'Is that what the colony ships looked like?'

'No. At least, not any human one I know of.'

That made her shudder.

Despite a hard night in the saddle, Kysandra could only doze through the long day. She was bursting for them all to get back on the horses and ride to the hill. *Solve the mystery!* Though some deeper, more cautious, part of her mind was urging her to turn round and gallop for Croixtown, sail cleanly down the river and be safe.

'Do you want to go home?'

Kysandra snapped fully awake, staring belligerently at Nigel, who was lying on his mattress next to her. She tightened her shell immediately, annoyed that she'd been spilling her drowsy thoughts. Irritated with him, too, for studying them. 'No!' she snapped. 'This is a mystery that even you don't understand. I want to find the answer. I want to *know* what's out there.'

Nigel grinned. 'That's my girl.'

They watered the horses and packed up the tents. This time the pace was less frantic than it had been that morning. They'd been travelling for ninety minutes, with the sun dropping close to the mountain peaks, when they found the first body. It was sprawled on a crude cart, made from what looked like a circular door of some kind with a glass porthole in the middle. Solid-looking hinge mechanisms had a melted appearance. Wheels were circles of crudely cut metal that were twisted and cracked, stuck on axles that were lashed to the hatch with filament. A couple of tarnished boxes lay nearby.

Kysandra didn't want to look, but couldn't resist. The wizened body was strange, its skin grey and taut, as hard as stone; wisps of straw-like hair swirled round the skull. Remnants of clothes seemed to be fused with the skin. There was only one boot, on the left foot; the right foot was bare, twisted at an odd angle.

'Mummified beautifully,' Nigel said to Fergus as she approached. The two of them were examining the body enthusiastically, poking modules into it. 'That's kind of inevitable, given the location.'

'Is it . . . ?' Kysandra took a breath, calming herself. 'Is it human?'

Nigel turned to frown at her. 'Of course.'

'I mean: is it a Faller?'

'Oh. Hard to tell. There's not much left to do a biochemical analysis on. And, in any case, I still need to get my hands on a Faller to find out exactly what their biochemistry is.'

Kysandra shuddered. Who else but Nigel could casually say: *I still need to get my hands on a Faller*? She gave the metal hill a pensive glance. It was closer now, just over eight kilometres away. They'd determined its size, too: u-shadows working it out as five hundred metres wide at the base, and two hundred and sixty three metres high at the precarious-looking apex.

Nigel and Fergus turned the body over. Its arm broke off with a dull *crack*. Kysandra flinched and clamped her jaw together. *Come on, you can do this. Don't be weak, not now.*

'Female,' Fergus proclaimed. He ran a scanner over the skull with its empty eye sockets. Heavily creased lips ringed a wide-open mouth, making Kysandra think the woman had died screaming – a last action steadfastly preserved by the desert environment.

'Picking up traces. She had biononics. Commonwealth citizen, then.' He gave Kysandra a reassuring grin. 'Human.'

Russell opened one of the boxes. The lid crumbled out of his fingers. 'Nothing much in here. Metal bottles and some dust.'

'Food and water,' Fergus said. 'Too bad she didn't make it very far.'

Nigel knelt beside the rickety cart, his eyes closed as he reviewed data from the modules he'd placed on the body. 'Crud. She's been out here for three thousand years. Whatever happened here, happened when the colony ships arrived.' He stood up and faced the hill, squinting against the dying sunlight. 'What the hell is that thing?'

Fergus ran his hand over the hatch/cart, tracing the broken hinges. 'This is from some kind of space vehicle. A shuttle? Exopod, maybe?'

Kysandra saw it, actually saw the shock flare on Nigel's face. She'd never seen that before. It was hard to believe he could be shocked. As if that wasn't bad enough, his shell weakened enough to let out a corresponding pulse of dismay. He stood up slowly and pulled his goggles down to stare at the hill. 'Oh crap,' he said quietly. 'The profile. Look at the profile. It's segmented. That isn't some geological rock spike, it's a pile.'

Fergus made no attempt to hide his flinch. 'It can't be. That size? There'd be . . .'

'If it's solid,' Nigel said. 'Well over a million of them. Which means the fabric is all parachutes – not tents. It fits, dammit! Where the hell did a million exopods come from? The Commonwealth never manufactured that many.'

'What?' Kysandra shouted. 'What are you two talking about?' The way they were sharing thoughts, how weirdly unified they were, frightened her. Because they so clearly knew something was wrong. Very, very wrong. 'Tell me!'

'Jymoar was mistaken,' Nigel said sombrely. 'It's not ten thousand bodies out here. There's going to be more, a lot more. You need to be ready for that.'

They found the next body ten minutes later. Female again. It was on a cart almost the same as the first: identical hatch, but with different improvised wheels. There was no sign of them; they'd flaked away to dust down the millennia.

Over the following kilometre they encountered another eight of the carts with bodies. Those were just the ones lying along their path. Retina zoom showed them similar carts scattered across the desert.

'All female,' Fergus announced as he examined the sixth. 'And they all have the same severe damage to their right ankle. The fracture patterns match perfectly, which is absurdly odd.'

There were few carts after that. Now the desert sand was littered with the same identical female body. She'd crawled along through the sand and pointed stones with her ruined ankle, always hauling along a box or bag. *And how desperate would you have to be to do that?* Often, the woman had died with her arms outstretched, as if reaching for something. Many were curled up. *In defeat?*

Kysandra cried quietly to herself for a couple of kilometres as the sun went down. The night obscured all the bodies lying away from their direct route, but the horses were having to weave about constantly to avoid stepping on the desiccated carcasses.

So she rode on in silence, her tears all dried up. She was completely numb, her feelings banished to somewhere deep in her mind. This much death was impossible to grasp. Instead she ignored it, and focused only on following Nigel's horse as it picked its way across this pitiless land of corpses. In front of her, the metal hill grew steadily closer. She imagined this was what it must be like for a soul arriving at Uracus itself. Eternal anguish was unavoidable. You could watch it coming, and there was nothing you could do to stop it. Nothing.

With the nebulas shimmering sweetly in the clear air above, they halted the horses five hundred metres from the base of the hill. The bodies were lying so close together now that the animals would be unable to avoid walking on them.

'Wait here,' Nigel said kindly.

'I'm staying with you,' she replied firmly.

So she and Nigel and Fergus walked the remaining distance to the hill, treading round the bodies where they could. As they grew closer, they couldn't avoid stepping on the limbs any more, they were packed so close together. She felt them crunch and crumble beneath her boots. The baked three-thousand-year-old bodies were tragically brittle, shattering at the slightest touch.

Soon they were trying to dodge venerable, deteriorating pieces of equipment as well as corpses. The ground was jamming up with survival equipment cases, their contents of bottles and tools and cracked powercells and wisps of clothing and tarnished axes and ragged photovoltaic sheets spilling out, amalgamating to form a rigid hardware stratum for the bodies to sprawl across.

They stopped before they reached the base, where the bodies were piled up on top of each other, producing an embankment five or six times her own height. Here the majority had clearly fallen to their death from the tricky slopes of the hill above, to be mummified in contorted positions, legs and arms snapped and bent in grotesque angles, necks and spines broken. Every awful lonely death perfectly preserved by the desert.

Kysandra lifted her gaze above the gruesome mound of desiccated skin and bone that was melding together, up to the metallic structure of the hill itself. It was a stack made up from spheres about three metres in diameter, though it was difficult to distinguish them. This close to the base, the weight of the spheres above had crushed and squeezed the lower layers out of shape. But like the female body they'd brought to this world, they were all the same, all with a single bulging oval window at the front, a circular hatch that hung open, and inert clusters of disturbing tentacles that Kysandra's implanted memories identified as electromuscle. Her ex-sight probed into a few of the artefacts, finding a maze of wires and pipes, the heat-wrecked hardware of complex systems.

'What are these things?' she asked.

'They're exopods,' Nigel told her. 'Larger spaceships carry them to perform maintenance work outside. In an emergency, they can aerobrake into an atmosphere, and land.'

'So they all landed here together?' Kysandra asked, desperate to understand. If she understood, she knew she wouldn't be so afraid. 'Why did they all bring the same woman? Is she . . . ?' Her memory implants held the concept, one she'd never bothered to consider, it was so . . . so, Commonwealth. 'A clone? Did she clone herself?'

'I don't know,' Nigel said as his shoulders sagged in defeat. 'I don't understand any of this.'

6

They made camp half a kilometre from the hill of exopods. Fergus and Russell cleared an area of the dissolving bodies as best they could, creating an unpleasant cloud of gritty dust in the process. Once that was done, Kysandra actually welcomed the distraction that came from setting up the awning and the tents. It was familiar, something useful she could abandon herself to.

She'd just started to give her horse some water when Nigel and Fergus both looked up in unison. That fast nervy reaction made her worry, but then everyone was edgy. Her u-shadow was telling her one of Nigel's sensor modules was sending out an alert, supporting a stream of fresh data. Displays appeared in her exovision, but even with the u-shadow tabulating them neatly they were incomprehensible.

'What's happened?' she asked.

'Localized quantum field fluctuation,' Nigel answered. 'Spike's over. They've reverted.'

'Oh right.' His casual, confident answer was obscurely re-assuring after days of uncertainty. Of course, what it actually meant was another thing altogether. Her physics memory implant wasn't terribly helpful, something about quantum fields underpin-ning spacetime, and some reference codes for further memory implants. 'Does that happen much?'

'Never. Not in the outside universe, anyway. In the Void – who knows?'

That was when the sound began – a distant clattering and banging. It made Kysandra jump. The desert had been devoid of sound since the moment they started trekking across it. Sound was alien here. Shocking.

They all stopped what they were doing, staring round, trying to pinpoint the noise. Kysandra realized it was coming from the exopods, and well up the hill if she was any judge. The clattering went on for a few moments more, then stopped.

'What caused that?' Madeline asked anxiously. 'It's the monster, isn't it?'

'No monster,' Nigel said. 'I'd say an exopod shifted about. It certainly sounded like that.'

'Has another one landed?' Kysandra asked. She studied the top of the hill, her infra-red scan trying to find an exopod that was a different temperature to all the others. They all remained stubbornly identical.

'No such thing as coincidence,' Nigel said. 'Whatever instigated the quantum fluctuation knocked the exopods about.'

'The monster,' Madeline said in dread. 'It's coming for us.'

'Now listen, all of you,' Nigel said forcefully. 'There is no monster. These corpses, everything we've seen here, it's all three thousand years old. Whatever happened, happened back then. Today, here, now, you are perfectly safe.'

Whatever the sound was, it didn't come again. They carried on putting the tents up. Kysandra kept using her ex-sense and infra-red vision to scan around, making sure nothing was creeping out of the darkness. Just in case.

Once the tent was up, she went inside and took her robes off, slipping into the baggy white shirt. Nigel came in and unwrapped his turban, but left the rest of his sand-encrusted robe on.

'What now?' she asked, sitting on the mattress, hugging her knees.

'We wait until daylight. Even with all the senses I'm enriched with – nice irony, that – I do need to have a clear field of vision to assess things properly.'

'And when it's light?'

'Fergus and I will start a decent, detailed investigation of the exopods. There are well over a million of them piled up out there, stuffed full of solid state components. Sheer probability is that some processors and memory blocks can be salvaged, especially those that haven't been crushed. And I saw a lot of array tablets jumbled up with the bodies. There have to be some files somewhere I can retrieve and download into my storage lacuna.'

She managed a weak smile. 'I'm so scared,' she confessed, on the verge of tears again. 'Something killed that woman. All of her.'

'That's the bigger puzzle,' he said. 'Why so many? Nobody has over a million clones. It's insanity. Whatever happened to her, it wasn't as simple as a monster.'

'Is it going to get us?' she asked, hating how pathetic she sounded.

'No.' And he actually grinned, squatting down beside her. 'I really meant it when I said we're perfectly safe. This is probably the time to tell you. You see, the people on Querencia found out something else about the Void. Something utterly amazing.'

'What?'

'There's a kind of time travel possible in here.'

It was no good; her mind had gone blank, unable to process what she'd just heard him say. 'Time travel?'

'Yes. You know, when you travel into the past.'

'You can time travel in the Void?'

'Yes. If you know how, and if your mind is strong enough. I tried it once, the day I landed. I can just do it; it takes a hellish amount of concentration, and I could only manage to perceive a couple of hours. But I went back in time. My first couple of encounters with Ma's boys at the Hevlin Hotel didn't go too well. But the third time, I knew what didn't work, like trying to reason with them, so I just started straight in with domination. And . . . here we are. So you see, if anything does start to go catastrophically wrong, we travel back in time and avoid the danger.'

'No,' she said. 'No, you're just saying that to try and make me feel safe. Nice try, though.'

'Listen, outside in the real universe, time is a one-way flow. We learned how to manipulate that flow in a wormhole, slow it down so we can take a relative jump forward if we want, but it is impossible to go back. Always. But here, the Void is different. Remember I told you it is made up of many layers?'

'Yes.'

'This layer, where we exist, is only one of them. The Heart, where you say your soul lives on in glory after death, that's another. But there are two more layers that are critical here: the memory layer and the creation layer. The memory layer stores everything: you, your thoughts, your body's atomic structure. And the creation layer, well, that can take a version of you from any moment of your life and physically manifest it.'

'I can go into the past?' she asked incredulously. 'You mean I can go back and stop Dad from going on that sweep?' Tears began to prick her eyes.

Nigel sighed. 'I can only manage to go a few hours, I'm sorry. There was one person we knew of who could travel back decades, but he lived on Querencia a thousand years ago.'

'I see.' She dropped her head so he couldn't see the misery that was written there.

'The point is, if you produce a – I don't know what to call it – a short circuit between the memory layer and the creation layer, you basically reset this whole section of the Void to the moment you've chosen. But here's the important thing: anyone who does that remembers the future they just left. No one else does. You quite literally become the centre of the universe.'

'Riiight.'

'Stand up.' Nigel stood and beckoned to her.

She thought about ignoring him, but this was Nigel . . . She stood up, and he took her hands in his.

'I don't know if I can take you with me, but—'

Kysandra perceived him gifting her a complex vision and let it stream into her mind. It was Nigel's mental perception, but so finely focused she could hardly distinguish anything. He was perceiving the tent with the two of them in it, but pushing further, *into* everything. Pushing hard. And there behind the phantasm shapes and shadows that were her eldritch world lay a second image, identical to the first. Nigel's sense probed at that, and another more distant image was revealed. Another, and another. They began to sink through them, and she saw herself shift back down to her knees where she'd been a few moments ago.

Somewhere in the real world she heard a gasp escape from her own lips. Then the images were racing past. Played out in reverse was their whole conversation. Nigel left the tent. Then she was alone sitting on the mattress having a good old wallow in misery. Then earlier still; she was taking off the shirt. The robe rose up from its puddle on the floor into her hand. And the perception froze. Her mind *twisted* through the image until she was looking out through her own eyes. The real world came rushing back in and she dropped the robe to the floor. Hot air licked over her skin. Kysandra yelped in shock.

'Told you so,' Nigel said.

He was standing at the far end of the tent. He'd *materialized* there.

Kysandra screamed. Then stopped, her hand flew to her mouth and she stared at him in astonishment. She gave a feverish little giggle. 'Crudding Uracus!'

'Are you all right?' Fergus 'pathed from outside.

'We're doing just fine,' Nigel 'pathed back.

'It's real,' she grunted. Then gave a start. She was standing there in front of him in sweaty underwear – and nothing else. One arm hurriedly slapped across her bra, and her teekay yanked her baggy shirt from the duffel bag.

'Pardon me,' Nigel said in amusement and turned his back.

She slipped into her shirt.

'So now do you believe me when I say we're not in any danger?'

'Yes!' she exclaimed. 'Oh, crudding yes, do I ever!' This was more fantastic than finding out he was from another universe, that he had a spaceship, that she could learn all the knowledge of the Commonwealth. More fantastic than anything.

'So . . .' She grasped at words. 'So, like, that piece of time we just lived through, stopped? And we came back here?'

'Yes, and only you and I know those five minutes ever happened. Everyone on Bienvenido who died in those five minutes is alive and about to die again. Every baby that was born is about to come into the world again. Every drunk falling over – bang, ouch. Everyone who got kissed . . . is going to get kissed again.'

'But they don't know.'

'They don't know because it hasn't happened for them. It never did.'

'Nigel?'

'Yes.'

'Please, don't ever go back to before you met me. Don't let me live that life. Please.'

'I won't.'

'Thank you,' she said.

'But if you ever become strong enough to go back to rescue your father, then you go right ahead.'

'Uh huh.' She was already trying to use her ex-sight the way he had. It was unbelievably difficult. She could barely perceive an instant ago.

'So, do you understand that we're not in any immediate danger out here?' he asked.

'Yes.' She smiled, actually meaning it.

Nigel sat down on his mattress. 'There's another reason I told you about that ability.'

'Yes?'

'The creation layer. I think it's glitching somehow. I think that's what's happened here. Somehow, for some reason, it recreated the exopod and the woman time and time again. Only on this occasion, it doesn't reset everything else.'

'Why?'

'I have no idea. But it's the only logical explanation. Her body has the same ankle damage every time; that tells me she was constantly recreated from one specific moment.'

'So the Void must still be doing that?'

'I'm not sure. All the bodies we've seen have been here for the same length of time. That's a paradox – or it would be in the universe outside. There's something very strange happening here. And that's what I'm going to try to understand. Anything which can affect and alter the structure of the Void is tremendously important.'

*

In theory, Nigel declared next morning, the exopods at the top of the pile should be the newest. Their systems would be in better shape than their squashed and smashed cousins at the bottom. They might be able to get some useful data from them.

So Fergus started off at first light. He clambered slowly up the pile, gingerly testing every foothold to make sure it could take his weight, that the whole mound wouldn't suddenly shift and an avalanche of pods come tumbling down on top of him.

Kysandra couldn't bear to watch. She winced at each move. Constantly scanned the surrounding exopods with her ex-sight for any signs of instability. Sent 'path after 'path telling him to be careful.

'Go away,' Nigel told her eventually. 'You're distracting him, and more importantly, me. Leave him alone and go find me some intact array tablets.'

She and Madeline started walking a circuit of the exopod hill. The embankment of the woman's mummified bodies was the same all the way round, as was her tight-packed sprawl over the cluttered caseloads of emergency survival hardware.

'There might not be a monster here,' Madeline said, 'but this place is cursed. The women that died here, their souls screamed and screamed their bitterness and fear as they were cast into Uracus. That anguish will linger here even after her last corpses have turned to dust.'

Kysandra gave her a sullen glance, but couldn't disagree.

Nothing responded to the pings sent by Kysandra's u-shadow – not that she'd expected any replies. As they made their way round the hill, she let her ex-sight flow over the technological wreckage, searching for array tablets. Unopened cases were her best chance, Nigel had decided. She located several buried amid

466

the debris, and she and Madeline had to grit their teeth and walk over mummies that were pulverized beneath their boots. Once they pulled the cases out, the arrays they contained didn't seem any different to those exposed to the desert, their electronics no more active than the sand, but she put them in her bag and carried on.

She almost missed it. One more axe amid the jumble of survival supplies and the horror of merged bodies. Nothing unusual there. But this axe blade had slammed through one of the skulls. Kysandra focused her perception. She wasn't wrong. The mummification process had welded the axe in place.

Now she'd seen one, she started to look for more. Quite a few mummies had similarly damaged skulls, some with the axe still in, some without. Other mummies had loops of filament wrapped round their necks. Strangled.

It took them nearly fifty minutes to complete a circuit. When they got back, Fergus was at the top of the hill, studying the exopods there.

'Nothing different,' he 'pathed. 'The decay is identical. They've all been here the same amount of time. But they must have landed one after the other.'

'Paradox,' Nigel sent back, indecently cheerful.

'She was killing herself,' Kysandra told him as she handed over the bag full of arrays. 'She was an axe murderer, among other methods.'

'This place,' Nigel said. 'There's too much death here. It's haunted.'

'I don't think her soul stayed behind, not any of them.'

'Not that kind of haunting, not a Void-engineered one. This is purely human. She left her imprint on the sand and in the exopods. How could she not? There were so many of her. Spiritually, this reeks of her.'

'Madeline said something similar.'

'Did she now? Maybe there's hope for her yet.'

'Do you need me for anything?' Kysandra asked. 'I thought I might go back to the tent.'

'Sure,' he said gently. 'Have a rest. I don't think there's actually much more we can do here. We'll gather some memory processors from exopods and see what we can do with them when we get back to the *Skylady*.'

Inside the tent, Kysandra stripped off her robes, trying to contain the sand that fell out of them. By now, there wasn't a square centimetre of the tent that wasn't contaminated with sand. It was even in her sleeping bag, despite her best efforts to shake it out.

She lay down on top of the mattress and withdrew her ex-sight. It wasn't that she couldn't help at a practical level; there were a dozen housekeeping jobs that needed doing every day while they were camped. In truth, she simply didn't want to spend any time outside where she couldn't ignore the mound of corpses. In here, confined by the bright walls of the tent fabric, she could shut out the horror. Pretend her little bubble of existence was somewhere else entirely.

'You were right,' her whisper told the memory of Jymoar. 'This desert can drive you mad.'

Her u-shadow produced a list of books she'd loaded in her storage lacunas from *Skylady*'s memory. She picked one called *The Hobbit*, and started reading.

*

It was past midnight when the noise woke Kysandra. The same as the previous evening – a pronounced clang, metal scraping raw against metal. Then silence.

She was sitting upright, heart pounding, sending out her ex-sight to probe the night beyond the tent.

'It's all right,' Fergus said. He was sitting close to the tent, rifle cradled across his lap. 'Nothing here.'

'Humm,' Nigel said. He was lying on his mattress next to her. A module close by had a purple light winking steadily. It was sending out a stream of raw data.

Just like last night.

'Was that another quantum event?' she asked as the nonsense tables slipped across her exovision.

'Yes. The same as yesterday. Except it's not precisely a daily event. The last one was twenty-seven hours and twenty-nine minutes ago.'

'Is there something inside the exopod pile, some piece of machinery that's still working?'

'I'm not ruling anything out, but if it's there, it was amazingly inert during the day for us not to detect anything at all.'

'Sorry.'

'Hey, it's okay. This place freaks me out, too.'

'When are we leaving?'

'Tomorrow. Promise, okay? Fergus and I will finish off during the day, then we'll pack up and start the trek back. We'll be back at Blair Farm in three or four weeks.'

Kysandra exhaled loudly. 'Thank you.'

*

Most of Croixtown turned out to greet them as they rode back into the village. Sitting up in her saddle, her clothes filthy, sand itching everywhere, a sunhat flopping down over her eyes, Kysandra couldn't help but grin at the sight of them. Men, women and children gathering around, gazing up, half in awe, half in fear.

The mayor stood in front of them, flanked by several tough-looking men. She saw Jymoar hurrying through the crowd behind him, smiling in relief and delight. She grinned at him, gave a small wave.

'We are happy to see you again, señor,' the mayor said to Nigel. He looked awkward. Apprehension was leaking through his shell. 'Nobody has ventured into the Desert of Bone in living memory.'

'It is not a place you want to go,' Nigel replied solemnly. 'I will never return there.'

'Is it true? Are there mountains of bones at the centre?'

'There are bodies there,' Nigel said loudly. The villagers let out a collective gasp. 'A great many bodies. Thousands, probably.' He gifted them the image of the mummified face, forever arrested with its mouth open, teeth amalgamated with the lips. 'They are incredibly old, killed thousands of years ago. We don't know by what.'

'Were they eaten?'

'No. The bodies were all intact. There are no Fallers in the Desert of Bone, no nests.'

A few people applauded. Everyone was smiling openly now, and began to press forward, eager for details – mainly about the monster. 'We did hear strange sounds at night,' Nigel said gravely, 'but we never saw anything.'

Kysandra shook her head at his consummate showmanship. He would say nothing that was an outright lie, yet by the time he was finished, no one from Croixtown would ever travel into the desert, and the word would spread among the other ranchero villages skirting the savannah, reinforcing the legend. The exopods would remain inviolate for another century. Or, 'Long enough for me to sort this mess out,' as Nigel said on the trek back. She thought that pure bravado. But . . .

She climbed down from her horse wearily and handed the reins to Russell before slipping though the crowd. Jymoar was standing in the same place as she'd seen him, his face anxious, yet optimism burnt hot behind his shell.

'Told you I'd make it back,' she said with a taunting grin.

He took an uncertain step forward. 'You did. I never doubted you, señorita. Not you.'

She leaned forward quickly and gave him a small kiss. And he was the one who blushed. 'I'm a mess,' she said ruefully.

'Never!'

Kysandra laughed, and gestured down at herself. The brown suede riding skirt was creased with mud and water stains. Her long boots were coated in sand, inside and out. White blouse had turned grey, made worse by the unpleasant sweat stains. 'Stop being gallant. I haven't washed since we left, and that was weeks ago.'

'You've been through a desert,' he said. 'And you still look amazing.'

'Come on.' She started walking towards the *Gothora*. When she took her floppy hat off, her hair barely moved, it had so much dirt caked in.

Arriving at the gangplank, she was inexplicably glad to see the old steamship. It resembled a stability she hadn't known she missed, a stolid representative of her world and the way she had lived before Nigel.

'So what was it like?' Jymoar asked.

'Bad. Remind me to believe you next time.'

'Next—' He gave her an appalled look, which made her smirk. For all he'd travelled a lot more than her on boats up and down the Mozal, he was the naive one.

Kysandra walked round the wheelhouse where she was hidden from the shore and the rapt crowd gathered around Nigel – who was still playing them. She cast a mild fuzz and started to undo the buttons on her blouse.

'Uh!' Jymoar grunted. He gave an anxious look round, but he was the only one who could see her.

She kicked the boots off and slipped her skirt down. 'I need this very badly.' She plonked her hat down on his head in a quick playful motion. 'You going to join me?' she asked as she slithered quickly out of her grimy underwear, then jumped straight into the river.

The water was cold and delicious. There had been times, back in the desert, when she'd doubted it ever existed, that water was just some figment of her sun-punished brain. She stayed under for a long moment, feeling the dirt start to flake off. Her hair began to move again, long strands sloughing about languidly in the current. She kicked hard and broke surface. Just in time to see a naked Jymoar leaping off the gunnel.

He swam over to her as she luxuriated in the clean flow of water. 'What did you find out there?' he asked timidly.

'Death. Death and suffering on a scale that really could drive you mad. But, strangely, in the end, it helped me.'

His open features produced a sorrowful frown. 'How?'

'I grew up a bit out there. I think. I know now that I'm not going to live a normal life, Jymoar. And I think what I saw, what I discovered about this world, made me come to terms with that. I know not to waste this life I have. I know so many things are petty and stupid, and that you should grab happiness when you can, for you never know what this universe is going to throw at you. I want to celebrate those moments of happiness. I need to be happy after the desert.' She put her arms on top of his shoulders and twined her fingers through the thick dark hair at the back of his head. Looking unflinchingly into his eyes as she let a lot of her shell drop. Waiting . . .

Jymoar pulled her to him and kissed her. They sank below the surface, then bobbed up together, spluttering and laughing in delight.

*

From Croixtown, it took them just two and a half weeks to reach Blair Farm. Kysandra was disappointed at how fast the *Gothora* made the trip back to Portlynn, but with the relentless current pushing them along as well as the ship's steam engine labouring away, they made it downstream in five days. Nigel had sold their animals to one of the rancheros in Croixtown (at a loss), which left the forward cargo hold empty. They altered its bamboo frame and canvas so it was more like a tent, where she and Jymoar spent most of the trip locked together in sweaty carnal bliss.

Kysandra was worried that, when it was over, she'd be unable to say goodbye. But when they did tie up at a jetty on the west shore of Nilsson Sound, just below the railway station, she just cried a lot and wrapped her arms round him for a long hug. They both promised to write all the time and made elaborate plans and promises for her to visit next year.

It was a lovely fib to end it on. As she walked beside Nigel along the platform to the first-class carriages of the Varlan express, her eyes were still damp. She expected a lot of teasing from Nigel, but there was none. He was supportive and sympathetic, treating her like an equal. *Like he always does, actually*, she realized.

Understanding that was probably the best conclusion the trip could possibly have.

It took the *Skylady*'s smartcore four days to read all the data from the assortment of damaged electronics they'd brought back. Then it spent another two days piecing together coherent sequences from dozens of broken files.

'Are you ready for this?' Nigel asked as he came back to the farmhouse carrying a module with the newly transcribed master file in a simple old-fashioned Total Sensory Immersion format, covering a time period lasting twenty-seven hours and forty-two minutes.

Kysandra was about to give him a boisterous: "Course I am,' but his pensive expression made her hesitate. 'How bad is it?'

'It explains what happened. And from a historical perspective, it's fascinating. You'll actually get to see Captain Cornelius. But I have to warn you, it's not pretty.'

'Worse than the Desert of Bone?'

'The scale isn't quite the same.'

'I'd like to see it. No. Actually, I have to see it. You know that.'

'Yes. I know.'

She settled back in the front room's deep settee and told her u-shadow to access the file. Her nerves tingled, as if someone had stroked a feather over all of her skin at once. Exovision produced a blurred full-colour optical image. And she looked out of Laura Brandt's eyes as the tank yank pulled her roughly back to consciousness.

7

Months of preparation, months of watching and the interminable waiting had finally paid off. They'd intercepted the eggs. Then along came the regiment squad and almost wrecked everything. Kysandra stood on the prow of the steam-powered cargo barge as it backed away from the wanno trees lining the riverbank. Directly ahead of her, clustered in a gap between the trees' big weeping boughs, the idiot one-armed lieutenant and his troops watched as the pistons below deck chugged loudly, taking them away from the temporary mooring and out into the broad channel of fast-flowing water.

'Wave. Smile. Be happy,' Nigel said as he stood beside her. He raised his own arm solemnly.

Across the muddy water, Lieutenant Slvasta responded with a fast, precise gesture – half-wave, half-salute.

Kysandra held back from giving him a mildly obscene gesture and waved her hand without any enthusiasm. 'Wow, I'm amazed we've not been completely overrun by Fallers if that's what passes for officer material these days.'

'I don't think you'll find a more devoted officer, frankly,' Nigel said. 'He's certainly dedicated to exterminating Fallers. And he knows something's not quite right about us.'

'But lacks the courage to do anything about it.'

'That's not lack of courage. You're talking about someone who escaped being eggsumed. I've never heard of anyone being saved before.'

'Captain Xaxon's granddaughter,' she said automatically as they turned from the lieutenant and made their way back to the mid cabin.

'Who?'

'Big part of Mrs Brewster's history lessons. I'll tell you about it one day. But for anyone in the regiment to succumb to a lure is just pathetic.'

Nigel sighed. 'You're becoming very judgemental these days.'

'Can't think why.'

The barge reached the middle of the river and turned downstream. The pistons reversed amid a loud clattering and began to power the boat forwards. They soon rounded a curve, taking them out of sight of Lieutenant Slvasta and his troops.

'You were getting very friendly with him,' she accused. 'I thought you were prepping him for domination.'

'Just planting a few seeds of doubt, that's all. The good lieutenant is seething with righteous indignation at the way things are. That's always to be encouraged.'

Kysandra glanced at the thumb which Slvasta had cut, frowning in disapproval. 'I'm going to get some antiseptic on this. We all should before we die of blood poisoning from your righteous friend's paranoia.'

'He's a good man in a bad world. You never know when you might need someone like that.'

'He's a loser.' She gave Nigel a jubilant grin. 'Forget him. Come on, we actually did it!'

Nigel nodded thoughtfully before breaking into a wide smile. 'We did, didn't we?'

Two hours later they caught up with the third steam barge, the *Mellanie*. 'Old girlfriend?' Kysandra had baited when Nigel renamed the boat after it had undergone a fortnight's refit in Adeone's largest boatyard. Ma had been slowly squeezing the owner out over the past two years – a position Nigel had subsequently regularized to become a sleeping partner.

'Someone I underestimated once,' he said with a certain distant gaze. 'Don't worry; it doesn't happen often.'

In the *Mellanie*'s wheelhouse, Fergus reduced speed so they could come alongside. Kysandra followed Nigel, hopping over the narrow gap while the two barges chugged along steadily. Russell and his team were quite content to stay on their barge, looking after the horses.

Ma Ulvon was waiting for them on deck, dressed in a tailored grey suit under a black longcoat that was still damp from the rain. A pump-action shotgun was slung across her chest on a polished leather strap. 'Any problems?' she asked.

'He knew something was wrong,' Nigel said. 'But we didn't give him a chance to work out what.'

'So my boys behaved themselves?' The men in her old organization, who were now under Nigel's domination, respected and obeyed him eagerly, but they still feared Ma.

'Yes.'

'Good,' she said in satisfaction.

Even now, over a year since Nigel had arrived, Kysandra couldn't quite get used to Ma like this. Nigel or an ANAdroid refreshed the domination every few months, but even so there was a background worry that Ma would one day break free. Kysandra studiously avoided eye contact as she walked past.

Nigel climbed through the deck hatch to the forward hold. Kysandra went down the ladder after him. *Mellanie*'s refit had seen the big deck loading doors elevated until the forward hold was just over four metres high – easily large enough to install the two circular cast-iron cages it now contained.

Yalseed oil lamps fixed high up on the hull walls shone a bright yellow light across the hold. Demitri was waiting for them at the bottom of the ladder, creating a fuzz so strong it was like passing through a curtain of cold mist. Even standing on deck Kysandra hadn't been able to perceive what the *Mellanie* was carrying.

Now, standing in the hold, she gazed in trepidation at the two dark Faller eggs in their cages. It had taken them nearly a day to drag those precious, deadly eggs through the violet bamboo on their stone sledges. Even after all that exposure, she still couldn't get over her fear at being so close to the implacable threat to her whole world. The lure was drawing her in; she wanted to rush to the front of the boat where Jymoar was waiting for her as usual, to tremble in delight at her lover's touch. When she breathed in, she could even smell him. So close.

'Don't,' Nigel said sharply.

Kysandra opened her eyes to realize she had taken a couple of paces towards the first cage. There was no Jymoar, no promise of satisfaction. She was immediately furious with herself for allowing the egg lure to ensnare her, and glared at the dark malign shape. 'Sorry,' she mumbled, red faced.

'It can get to you if you're not careful,' Demitri said sympathetically. Of all the ANAdroids, he was the most sensitive and compassionate, almost as if he wasn't really cut out for this kind of work.

'So what have we got?' Nigel asked, prowling round the cage as if he was studying a wild beast. 'Is there a brain in there?'

'It's fuzzed itself effectively,' Demitri said, 'so there are obviously some kind of thought processes occurring inside. But here's the interesting thing: the ultrasound can cut clean through it.' He pointed at the small electronic sensors stuck to the egg. 'There's no solid cell structure inside. The cells are all suspended in the yolk fluid, and evenly distributed. Just as the institute's papers claimed.'

They'd spent a couple of months scanning in all the research papers Coulan had sent them from the Varlan university library, where he'd established himself as just another unobtrusive student. For a century after the *Vermillion* landed, the scientists who'd been on board had studied the eggs, discovering very little as their equipment slowly failed around them. They didn't understand the method of absorption/duplication, suspecting a mechanism whose principles were similar to human biononic organelles – but the Faller system worked while the human one failed miserably in the Void. They'd also been unable to establish communication with the controlling intelligence residing in the egg.

'So it's a homogenized distribution,' Nigel said. 'Interesting. That suggests an artificial construct to me.'

'You mean the Fallers were made by someone?' Kysandra asked.

'Yes. But I'm more interested in why. I'm thinking some kind of weapon.'

'Against who?' Demitri challenged.

'Any biological species. Think: Primes.'

'Who are Primes?' Kysandra asked.

'Aliens who nearly wiped us out,' Nigel replied. 'We got lucky and defeated them. But it was a sharp lesson that not every sentient species in the galaxy shares our moral viewpoint.'

She glanced back at the ominous dark sphere, determined to try and lose her fear. The cage wasn't there to keep the egg confined, that was ludicrous; the bars were to prevent anyone who succumbed to the lure from being eggsumed. 'Does anything like the Fallers exist outside the Void?'

'We haven't come across them,' Demitri said. 'Yet. It's a big galaxy.'

'I wonder,' Nigel mused. 'If we prevented the egg from eggsuming for long enough, would it revert and form the species it was developed from?'

'Nothing in the institute papers mentioned that,' Demitri said. 'I'm hoping my fusion will provide all the information we need.'

Kysandra shuddered. She'd always thought this plan to be insane, but Nigel insisted it was necessary. They had to understand the Fallers in order to work out what was happening up at the Forest. Only then could they start planning how to defeat them.

'Fergus,' Nigel 'pathed, 'let's get out of here fast before Lieutenant Slvasta figures it out and comes charging after us.'

As she climbed up out of the hold, Kysandra could hear the steam engine picking up speed. It had been modified to Nigel's more efficient design during the refit, giving the *Mellanie* a surprising turn of speed. One of a great many preparations they'd been making.

In the long months since they'd returned from the Desert of Bone, *Skylady*'s sensors had been searching the sky above Bienvenido for Falling eggs. The resolution was nothing like it would have been in the real universe outside, and the radar often glitched, but nonetheless, even with the interruptions and degraded results, they'd spotted nearly a dozen Falls long before the Watcher Guild's whitescreen telescopes. Nigel wanted the advance warning so the team could be in and out of the landing zone before the regiments even began their sweep. What they needed was a Fall in an area with an accessible river nearby; close enough to Adeone that they could reach it before the regiment arrived, yet not so close that people would recognize them.

The Fall south of Adice was the best chance they'd been offered in six weeks. As soon as the *Skylady* detected the eggs leaving the Forest and plotted their trajectory, they rode hard for Adeone and took the three barges out, powering along quickly until they reached the Colbal, then turned upstream. Now the *Mellanie* was retracing that route, but at a more sedate pace than the one used on the outbound leg. The last thing Nigel wanted was to attract attention. However, there were enough logs in the aft hold to keep the engine going for the whole time until they returned to Adeone; there were to be no stops en route.

They took three days of continuous sailing to reach Adeone. The *Mellanie* anchored three miles downstream for the afternoon, while the other two barges docked. Marek and Ma's boys got everything ready for the *Mellanie*'s arrival.

When they did finally tie up at the town's docks just after midnight, the whole riverside area was deserted apart from Nigel's people. Three ge-eagles sculpted by *Skylady* flew high overhead, checking that nobody was venturing close, innocently or otherwise.

Nigel stood on the jetty, supervising the extraction operation. They didn't bother with a crane. Their combined teekay lifted the eggs (in their cages) out of the hold and onto a pair of custom-built carts. The cages were locked in place and quickly covered with a canvas sheet. The ANAdroids maintained their competent fuzz as they drove the carts carefully along Adeone's empty streets, escorted by the rest of the group on terrestrial horses.

Barn Seven had been built to hold the eggs. The outside walls were ordinary planks, but then behind that was a further wall of metre-thick cob, followed by an inner brick wall. The roof was held in place by a series of large anbor beams which held up sheets of beaten tin, followed by a half metre of soil, capped by ordinary shingle tiles. To any observer, the structure was no different to the other farm buildings in the compound, and if they followed that up with a quick ex-sight scan, their perception would never get through the solid walls. The inside had been divided into a pair of large pits, with broad metal basin floors, ready to catch any of the yolk fluid if/when the eggs were broken open.

At four o'clock in the morning Kysandra stood on the rim between the two, yawning heavily as she watched the eggs being lowered into place. Bright electric lights shone down, illuminating them in a stark monochrome which only served to emphasize how disturbing they were. The electric cables run into Barn Seven from *Skylady* also powered a variety of sensors. The ANAdroids set to work fixing them to the eggs. Kysandra yawned again.

'Go to bed,' Nigel said. 'Don't worry; this part is going to take a couple of days. We don't get to the next stage until after we've learned everything we can from passive scans.'

She nodded agreement and went back to the farmhouse.

The results were pretty much as anticipated and added little to their database. Biononic infiltration filaments were unable to permeate the shell, probably due to their instability in the Void environment. Equally, though, a detailed nuclear analysis determined that the shell wasn't organic. There was no cell structure, and the molecular bonds were too complex. It was an artificial construct.

Laura Brandt's doomed science team was right; they were manufactured in the Forest trees.

Two days after the eggs arrived, Kysandra was back on the rim of the pit, along with Nigel and Fergus, looking down fearfully as Demitri walked across the metal floor towards the cage. He was naked, the harsh light giving his pale skin a bright sheen.

'Do you really need to do this?' she asked.

Demitri paused at the cage door, and turned round to look at her. 'I'm not human. Please try and remember that. My eggsumption and conversion will provide a great deal of information.'

'I suppose,' she said reluctantly.

'You don't have to watch,' Nigel said.

Kysandra didn't even bother answering that. But she did let the scorn escape her shell.

Demitri smiled as he put the key into the Ysdom lock and opened the door. Kysandra took a deep breath as he stepped inside and shut the door behind him. Nigel's teekay turned the key, then the little brass cylinder was flashing through the air to land in Nigel's hand.

'Recording,' Fergus said. 'Sensors are at eighty per cent efficiency. That's not too bad.' The egg had thirty-five sensor pads stuck to it, their thin cables snaking away across the metal basin to three management modules. More sensors were clipped to the cage bars, focused on the shell.

'Proceed,' Nigel said.

Demitri shuffled round so he was side-on to the egg, next to a curving sensor band.

'Good angle,' Fergus assured him.

'Deleting now,' Demitri said.

'Deleting?' Kysandra asked.

'The egg absorbs memories as well as the physical body,' Nigel said. 'The institute was quite clear on that. It's like the memory read the Commonwealth Justice Department has. I don't want the Faller to know everything I do. And it certainly can't realize that we're going to download a copy of its memories.'

'It's clear,' Fergus said. 'We're down to basic autonomics.'

When she looked back at Demitri she saw him staring emptily into the distance, as if he was asleep with his eyes open. ANAdroids didn't sleep.

Nigel took a sideways step. Demitri copied the movement exactly, his right arm and leg touched the egg, and stuck.

Kysandra drew in a gasp. 'Uracus!' But she clenched her jaw and stared ahead resolutely. *Use your logic, not emotion*, she told herself sternly. *Observe this as a Commonwealth scientist would.*

It's an experiment, that's all. No humans will be hurt during this research.

Just yesterday she'd laughed and joked with Demitri, sharing the excitement of the egg capture mission. She liked him. Machine body or not, he was still a person.

Was a person, she corrected. Demitri's shell was non-existent now, allowing her to perceive his thoughts. The patterns in his head were little more than an animal's: basic routines that animated the body, but nothing else, no awareness or memories. That had all gone, downloaded into *Skylady*. Death of sorts.

Demitri's shoulder was sinking slowly into the egg, as was his hip. Sensors observed closely as the molecular structure of the eggshell changed to become permeable where Demitri's skin touched it.

'That has to have a specific trigger,' Nigel muttered. 'The internal intelligence must have direct control over the shell structure.'

'Or it's touch sensitive,' Fergus said.

'There's a discrimination effect involved,' Nigel countered. 'There has to be. You'd get stones and raindrops being absorbed otherwise.'

Kysandra concentrated on the datastream coming from Demitri. His medical routines were showing her how the skin that had been drawn into the egg was already starting to break down at a cellular level. It was being penetrated by micro-organisms which were methodically dissolving the dermal cell membrane walls.

Demitri's head reached the egg, and started to sink into it.

'Here we go,' Nigel muttered as he stared raptly at Demitri's eggsumption.

Exovision showed Kysandra the egg organisms devouring Demitri's ear then exposing the skull bone. He sank deeper and deeper into the egg. After another twenty minutes half of his head was inside, at which point the egg finally eroded a small patch of his skull just above the jaw. With the breakthrough complete, the rest of the bone began to vanish like window frost before a warm breath. The organisms began to infiltrate the brain, forming long, superfine threads whose tips pierced individual neurones.

'That is one sophisticated weapon,' Nigel said in a troubled voice. 'Commonwealth biononics are a long way behind this kind of nanobyte ability.'

'Why would we want to build it?' Fergus replied, his nose wrinkled up in dismay.

Nearly half of Demitri's body had been absorbed into the egg now. A status review of his medical routines showed Kysandra that the egg had stripped his arm, leg and torso of skin. It was beginning to consume the exposed musculature. Her ex-sense could perceive the yolk substance thickening around the section where he was being drawn in, with denser folds beginning to accrete, like swirls within a black nebula. Strands began to slither into the missing slivers of muscle. Blood began to pulse out of frayed veins and arteries, to be sucked deeper into the egg. The egg's serene thoughts were also starting to quicken. She glimpsed strange fractured images seeping free, and the sensation of profound cold . . .

'What's happening?' Nigel asked. 'Is that normal?'

The sharpness of his voice made Kysandra start. When she looked at him, he was frowning down at the flaccid ANAdroid protruding from the egg. The edge of Demitri's body where it was being absorbed into the egg was oozing blood.

'He's coming out!' Fergus barked.

Kysandra's mouth dropped open in shock. The whole process was reversing. The egg was expelling Demitri's body. She could perceive the egg's thoughts fluttering, radiating out a sensation close to human panic.

'Dammit,' Nigel grunted.

Blood was flowing freely now as more of the semi-devoured body was expelled from the egg, splattering across the metal basin floor. Egg yolk began to spray out through the exposed muscles and slippery blood vessels.

Kysandra winced. 'Uracus! That's horrible.'

'It's rejecting him,' Nigel said. 'Hell, there must be something in his biochemistry that's incompatible with the egg.'

'What?'

Exasperated, Nigel gave her an almost pitying look.

'Sorry.'

The flow of yolk liquid abruptly increased, forcing Demitri's body out of the gap which the eggshell had created to ingest it. With a sickening fluid crunch, it collapsed onto the floor, heart still pumping strongly to squirt long streams of blood from the unravelled arteries in the leg and arm. Muscles fell off, slithering across the slick basin like gory fish.

Kysandra cried out and shut her eyes, feeling the bile rising in her throat. For a long moment she thought she was going to be sick. She made sure she turned round before opening her eyes again. The brick wall of Barn Seven was directly in front of her, reassuring in its bland normality. While behind her the last of the gurgling sounds faded away. 'Now what?' she asked miserably.

'I'm storing the data in my lacuna,' Nigel said. 'Not that there is much.'

It was as if he hadn't heard her, or didn't care. She frowned at him.

'Give me your hand,' he said.

'What?'

'I'm going to undo this, obviously. I can tolerate losing Demitri if it achieved something. But it hasn't. So . . .' He held out his hand.

Kysandra grasped it, surprised by how warm and sweaty it was. Just like hers. As before, her ex-sense perceived the weird echoes of herself pervading the hidden fabric of this universe as Nigel pushed his thoughts deeper into the memory layer. She glided back through them, through herself, watching events rewind.

'Stop,' Nigel commanded.

Kysandra was standing on the rim of the pit, looking down as a naked Demitri reached out to put a brass key into the cage's Ysdom lock. He paused, and looked up at Nigel.

'It doesn't work,' Nigel said.

There was a long moment while Nigel downloaded the data

he'd saved from the non-existent future to Demitri's u-shadow.

'Damn,' Demitri grunted. He grinned. 'Something I ate?'

'I don't think you're organic enough,' Nigel said. 'Once it started to break down your cells into specific compounds it realized something was wrong. There's got to be a whole load of protective protocols built in.'

Demitri gave the dark egg a suspicious glance. 'Clever. So: plan B, then?'

'Looks like it.'

'What's plan B?' Kysandra blurted. Nobody had mentioned this before.

'We use a body that won't be rejected,' Nigel said.

'A body? You mean a human?' Her voice rose in alarm. 'You're going to let a human be eggsumed? To Fall? That's . . . That's . . . '

'Pretty bad.'

'You can't. I won't let you.'

'Sometimes to do what's right, you have to do what's wrong.'

'Still no.'

'Not even Ma?'

Kysandra blanched. Hesitated for a moment. 'No,' she said, then more firmly. 'No, not even her.'

'Interesting moral dilemma,' Nigel said. 'Given a soul in the Void is effectively immortal, and we desperately need the information. Just who is unworthy enough to qualify?'

*

Proval was lucky. He'd left the safety of the Shanty to visit the public bar of the Kripshire pub, which was at the back of the building with its entrance in the alley leading off Broad Street, when he saw her: the blissfully sweet teenager. Proval didn't like using the main streets in any town, not with all the people walking and riding about. Main streets were all clean and proper, a town's pride, where the sheriffs kept an eye out for trouble and troublemakers. But underpinning them were the smaller streets, where it was possible for a man to walk without drawing any kind of attention. Home to the kind of people and places he preferred.

He'd already pushed the door open when she passed the end of the alley. Late teens. Long emerald-green skirt swishing about, white blouse with plenty of buttons undone to show off great tits. *She knows she's doing that. Slut.* Red hair falling halfway down her back, all clean and glossy. Freckled skin with a wonderful clear complexion. Sunny smile showing off happy confidence. Pretty. Oh so pretty.

Proval got all that in one swift glance before she passed the alley. He did a perfect one-eighty turn and walked smartly away from the bar. You have to grab opportunity when you see it. And he recognized one instantly these days. As he walked back down the alley he 'pathed his mod-bird, which was circling high overhead. The bird banked and glided down along Broad Street. He watched through its eyes.

She was carrying a big shoulder bag that bulged. *Out shopping, then. Bag's full, so she's heading home. Where? Where is home, sweetness?*

Proval hurried along the backstreets, keeping more or less parallel to Broad Street. The exquisite girl kept walking, heading for the west end of town, away from the river. Proval barely knew which town this was, just another set of jetties with houses sprawling along the Nubain tributaries – one of hundreds. The whole river basin was his territory. Travel here was easy, and the sheriffs just minded their own patch.

The girl turned off down a side street, bringing her just that fraction closer to him. He couldn't help the smile. Luck. When you were due it, luck came like a torrent. *Was she heading for the stables? Please, Giu. Please.*

Proval almost ran the last two hundred metres to the livery. He was actually in the saddle of his mod-horse, leaving the main gates when she arrived at the front.

Yes. Oh yes, today Giu is smiling on me.

His horse ambled along the road out of town. A kilometre further on, the neat fields had begun and there was a fork in the road. He hesitated. The mod-bird showed him the sweetness on a terrestrial horse leaving the livery, the bag slung on the back of her saddle. She lived out in the countryside somewhere. Probably a nice well-to-do farmhouse. The sweetness was that type.

Decision. He took the left-hand road, lined with tall goldpines. Behind him the mod-bird glided lazily on a thermal, keeping the sweetness in sight. If she took the right-hand road, it didn't matter: he could ride fast and catch up. But if she turned left – well, that would be so easy.

Giu continued to bless Proval. The girl came to the fork and turned unhesitatingly down the left-hand road.

This close to town there was still a fair bit of traffic. Horses, carts, even a few walkers. Proval carried on, keeping a kilometre or so ahead of the sweetness until he was in a steep valley with heavily forested slopes. The midday sun burnt hot overhead, and the air was dry and still. He was sweating when he finally dismounted. His mod-bird raced ahead, keen eyes searching the road for traffic. The day's luck was amazing. There was nothing about, not a solitary rider or farm cart. They were the only people for kilometres. He could carry the sweetness through the dense trees into the valley and no one would ever see them. He wouldn't even have to gag her like he did some. There was nobody to hear her screams.

Just as she came round the last bend, he bent down as if examining his horse's hoof. Nothing suspicious here. Just another traveller with a bit of difficulty. *And you know, don't you sweetness, that there's nothing bad here. Not on the road home which you've ridden down a hundred times in your lovely young life. Here you are safe.*

'Trouble?' the girl asked as her horse came close.

Proval didn't even have to answer. She swung a leg over the saddle and hopped down.

So strong. So agile.

He stood up in the shade of the tall goldpines and smiled a hungry smile. That was when they normally started to realize something might be wrong. He was under no illusion about his looks. The busted nose, missing teeth, shabby clothes. Most people instinctively shied away from someone like him, certainly young girls. 'Kind of you to stop.'

Her smile was still suffused with confidence. 'That's what you wanted, isn't it?' she asked matter-of-factly. 'Get me off my horse. Middle of nowhere. Nobody around. Perfect for you, right?'

Proval's hand slid down his grubby shirt to the pistol under his jacket. Something not right about this. Not at all. He checked the mod-bird's eyes. But nothing had changed; they were completely alone. 'Perfect for what?'

'You're Demal. Or Proval. Maybe Finbal. I don't know for sure. The name is different most of the time, but the description fits.'

'Who the fuck are you?'

'Do you normally ask any of your victims' names?'

Proval drew the gun, pointing it at her in one smooth movement. Unnervingly, she didn't even flinch. 'Are you some kind of sheriff's trick? Answer me, bitch. I'll make it worse for you if you don't.'

'Uracus, no! If they knew I existed, the sheriffs would probably give you a reward for telling them. The Captain's police certainly would.'

He clicked the safety catch back, enjoying the loud *snik* it made. So she'd understand he wasn't bluffing. Not even the strongest shell could withstand a bullet. 'Start talking.'

'I know you've raped over eleven girls in the last two years. I think you killed three farm families when you raided their houses at night. And the sheriffs suspect another two. There are plenty of highway robberies with extreme violence around the Nubain tributaries, too. Right? That's you?'

'Very smart. But it's seventeen girls,' he snarled. 'And you, eighteen, you're going to be the sweetest of them all.'

She nodded seriously, as if she'd just confirmed a fact with a library book. 'Thought so.'

Proval lost the vision 'pathed from his mod-bird. 'Huh?' He glanced up instinctively. Sight and ex-sight revealed his dead mod-bird dropping from the talons of a huge avian predator that was still plunging down in its kill-dive.

Something smashed into his chest. He was thrown backwards as if the world's strongest teekay had punched him. Arms windmilling helplessly as he crashed to the ground. Then the pain flooded across him from the agony point that was his sternum, and he wailed. But through all the hurt and terror, he still managed to bring the gun up, tracking it round towards the bitch from Uracus. There was some small metallic egg-shaped thing poking out of her blouse sleeve, held steady by what looked like a slender white tentacle. Crazy it might be, but Proval knew a weapon when he saw it. The thing emitted a green flash, and his gun hand ruptured. Blood splattered over his face and jacket. He stared manically at the tattered remnant of his hand, and screamed again – high-pitched and hysterical now.

*

'I said intact,' Nigel complained when he, Russell and Demitri drove the cart up to Kysandra three minutes later.

She frowned up at him. 'You want me to go back in time and try again?'

'No, no,' he said cheerfully. 'This will do. I suppose.' He and Demitri exchanged a quick glance of amusement.

Proval was sprawled unconscious on the dirt. Kysandra had sprayed his damaged hand with a specialist dermsynth, a lot thicker than the usual application. 'He's hardly broken. I think two fingers are still intact. I just set the pulse a bit high.'

Nigel gave her a quick hug. 'That's my girl. Wow, but you're growing up.'

'No choice.'

Demitri and Russell picked up Proval's inert body and carried him over to the cart.

'So?' Nigel asked. 'Does he qualify?'

'Yes,' she admitted. 'He's actually proud of what he's done, what he is. I . . . I wasn't expecting that.'

'I keep telling you, there are a lot of bad people in this universe.'

'You did, yes.'

'You're mad about it? Don't be. I'm always right, you know that.'

'I'm not sure what I'm more worried about,' Kysandra said.

'The fact that Proval exists, or that you knew how to find him.'

'Come on, it's hardly been easy. You've been dressed like that, parading up and down towns for a week now.'

'But you knew which towns he'd probably be in.'

'Patterns,' Nigel said. 'Everything is down to patterns. Once you have them, you can predict what's going to happen. Back in the day, the financial sector turned pattern recognition into a science. Entire national economies were gambled on it.'

'And the sheriff records gave you that,' she said in admiration. 'Amazing.'

'They gave me generalizations. You did the rest. Don't be modest about your part.'

She watched Demitri and Russell dump Proval in the back of the cart and pull a canvas sheet over him. Demitri hopped down. Russell paused, gazing intently at her, then saw she was watching him. He looked away hurriedly, strengthening his shell to block out the tweak of guilt. Irrefutably loyal to Nigel though he was, domination didn't suppress all his instincts.

Kysandra glanced down at her chest, sighed, and began buttoning up her blouse. 'What did you call this thing?'

'The plunge push-up, more commonly known as a Wonder-bra,' Nigel said. 'Invented by a man, I believe.'

'No kidding.'

'They started making them before even I was born. Imagine that, thousands of years old, yet still popular the galaxy over.'

'I'm not surprised,' she murmured. 'I don't quite understand how it does it. I'm not actually this . . . big.' She shook her head in irritation, knowing her cheeks would be red.

'You can get rid of it as soon as we reach home.'

'Yes. Right. I'll probably do that, then.' Kysandra narrowed her eyes in suspicion and scowled at Nigel's horribly smug grin.

*

Two days' travel brought them back to Blair Farm. They put Proval in the medical capsule as soon as they arrived. It repaired his hand to a degree, cauterizing the flesh and repairing the two

490

remaining fingers. Growing replacements for the ones he'd lost would have taken at least a fortnight, even if that had been possible in the Void. Nigel didn't care to find out.

Kysandra looked down at the bandit/rapist/murderer she'd captured, his body half covered in the silver tendrils the capsule extruded, like weird restraints. The kind of thing you'd use to hold down a monster.

'So?' Nigel asked her.

She glanced at him over the capsule. 'You're really asking for my approval?'

'It would be nice.'

'Do it,' she said firmly. Bienvenido would be a better place without Proval. No matter how squeamish she was about what they were doing, that was unarguable.

Nigel gave the medical cabinet a series of instructions. More silver tendrils snaked out around Proval's head and began to infiltrate his skull.

'Just like the egg,' she muttered.

'Disturbingly so,' he agreed, and ordered the capsule's surface to close. The malmetal contracted shut.

Kysandra didn't bother to use her ex-sense to see what was happening inside it. She knew. Personality erasure was an old Commonwealth ability, though rarely employed by the courts in recent times, Nigel assured her.

The medical chamber would infiltrate Proval's brain, its active bionomic filaments seeking out the neurones that contained his memory. Slowly and inexorably, with chemical manipulation, narcomeme subversion and direct physical neurone penetration, his memories would be exorcized. With that, his identity would evaporate. Proval, as a distinct entity, would cease to be. The process would leave nothing but a collection of organs and bones orchestrated by autonomic reflex. A living corpse.

*

One day later, the naked insensate body stood beside the Faller egg in Barn Seven, an eerie replay of Demitri's disastrous attempt at being eggsumed. Indeed, it was Demitri who stood beside the body, his 'path feeding continual instructions into the empty brain, activating the correct muscles to allow the body to stand.

He opened the cage and mentally puppeted the body through the door. The brass key was turned in the Ysdom lock. Following 'pathed instructions, the body turned slowly to face the curving surface of the egg. Its feet shuffled apart, and it held its arms up to assume a spread-eagle pose. Demitri allowed the ankles to hinge forward, and it hit the surface of the egg – torso, arms, thighs immediately sticking fast.

Up on the walkway rim between the two pits, Kysandra shuddered exactly as she had last time. It took the egg forty minutes to fully absorb the body. Sensors followed as much of the process as they could, ultrasound and density scans tracking the body's simultaneous disintegration and mimicked reassembly. Ex-sight gleaned a few extra facts – the way the yolk swirled and mutated, how the Faller's thoughts coalesced out of the wisps of awareness which permeated the yolk.

Five hours after Proval's body sank into the egg, the shell began to lose cohesion. It sagged and began to split. Yolk fluid poured out of the fissures as they tore open. A gooey wave sloshed out across the metal basin, and the final shreds of the flaccid shell split apart around the solid core that now stood upright in the centre.

A perfect replica of Proval's body glistened in the fluid, and drew a deep loud breath. Its psychic shell was strong and resolute, concealing whatever thoughts were flowing within its duplicated brain. Eyes opened. A hand with two fingers wiped the thick fluid away from its face. The head turned slowly, following the probing fan of ex-sight it generated, sweeping round the pit. Then it focused on Nigel and Kysandra and the two ANAdroids standing above.

Nigel smiled thinly. 'Welcome to hell,' he said.

The Faller screeched – an incoherent blast of sound that was too loud for a genuine human throat to produce. It ran at the cage bars, slamming into them. Rebounding. Another screech, and it gripped the bars, tugging furiously.

Kysandra thought the iron might actually have bent slightly. But no way was she going in for a closer look to confirm that.

Demitri and Fergus jumped down into the pit. The Faller dropped to a half-crouch and watched them intently.

'Interesting,' Nigel mused. 'That's a very human defence posture. I guess we didn't vacuum Proval's subconscious as clean as I wanted.'

Kysandra was barely aware of breathing. She watched fearfully as Demitri unlocked the cage door and swung it open. The Faller walked through it, switching its attention from one ANAdroid to the other, ready for them to attack.

Fergus raised a fat metal tube, and shot it with a tangle net. The Faller tried to jump aside, its teekay lashing out to deflect the seething dark cloud of cables. Demitri's teekay was instantly reaching for it, and the Faller hardened its shell defensively, teekay diverted long enough for the net cable to whip round it with a flurry of whistling air. It tumbled to the ground, thrashing against the cables which slowly and relentlessly tightened their grip. After a few seconds, it was reduced to an immobile bundle on the slippery floor. But still very conscious. A strong teekay began to assault the net cables, gnawing at their individual strands.

Demitri stepped up, and slapped a charge-patch on the back of the Faller's neck. Fifty thousand volts slammed through him. His reaction was extremely human – muscles convulsing, teeth clenched, air forced from his lungs in a drawn-out groan of pain.

'Well, that works,' Nigel said in satisfaction.

Demitri zapped him again. The Faller's body vibrated, juddering away inside the restrictions of the net, before he finally lost consciousness. His shell vanished. Demitri 'pathed a neuromeme variant to suppress the Faller's primary thought routines – providing they were close to a human's. The body relaxed further.

'Is he dead?' Kysandra asked anxiously.

Demitri's ex-sight scanned through the Faller. 'No.'

'Uracus!'

'We don't have the time to analyse his biochemistry,' Nigel said. 'For a start, getting a blood sample would be hellishly difficult.

Then we'd have to experiment to find an anaesthetic that worked, and what doses to use. It would be like torturing him. This way is quick and clean.'

'I know, I know.' *Yeah, you're right again. Well done.*

Fergus quickly slipped a helmet over the Faller's head.

If anything was torture, it was this, Kysandra thought. Nigel hadn't wanted to put the Faller into *Skylady*'s medical module. Not after Demitri got rejected by the egg. He was concerned about the Faller's nanobyte functionality; the sophisticated molecular clusters of its cells might be able to contaminate and corrupt Commonwealth technology, especially here. So, *Skylady* had synthesized this, a biononic infiltrator, with active filaments almost identical to the ones in the medical module which had invaded Proval's brain. Except this was a cruder, stronger, quicker procedure. There was nothing subtle about the way these filament tips breached the skull and penetrated the brain.

The Faller's body juddered again as the infiltration started, then stilled. His eyelids opened and the eyes rolled back until only the whites were visible.

Kysandra studied her exovision display, watching the infiltration's progress. A multitude of filaments had made it through the exceptionally hard bone of the skull, to worm their way through the neurone structure. The brain was noticeably different to a human's. Synaptic discharges were faster, more precise.

'More like a bioprocessor matrix than our typically chaotic neural structure,' Nigel commented. 'I'm guessing that allows for operating a wider range of thought routines. The brain looks like one of ours, but it's actually quite homogeneous. There are no regulatory centres, and certainly no hormonal triggers. Clever, given the Faller mind will have to acclimatize to whatever animal form they encounter and duplicate. Basic thought routines will be adaptable to manipulate however many limbs they have, as well as interpret the new sensorium.'

'That's a dynamic flexibility range,' Fergus said.

'They can't be the primary form of the origin species, not any more. This is the expanded version.'

'Just like us,' Kysandra said. She gave Nigel a small smile. 'You said I was an Advancer. Clue's in the name. My genome has been changed from the one my ancestors carried. Improved, supposedly.'

'I was talking about their mentality, but yes,' Nigel said approvingly. 'Nobody goes voyaging across the galaxy without modifying themselves to some degree. It's a bit of a prerequisite among progressive sentient species.'

Demitri coughed. 'The Ocisens.'

'I did say: progressive,' Nigel replied equably.

It took two hours to complete the first sequence of the infiltration procedure, deploying the filaments. Their positioning was guided directly by *Skylady*'s smartcore, which had to probe and examine the duplicated neural structure they were invading. Ultimately, the filaments were as evenly distributed as the brain's regimented neural pathways. Unlike the procedure they'd used on Proval, chemical intervention was impossible. They had to rely on neuromemes and subversive thought routines. Over the next six hours, the smartcore began to decipher the Faller's major thought patterns, distinguishing between active reasoning routines and the deeper incorporated memories that were infused within them, loosely equivalent to a human subconscious.

With the brain's network profiled, the smartcore constructed a digital simulation, and began downloading the Faller's thoughts into it.

*

The Faller didn't have memories in the human sense – the recollection of sights, sounds and sensation with all their associated clutter of emotion; this was more an awareness of being, of purpose. It understood itself thanks to a history that had become the biological imperative of its species, in every branch.

They originated somewhere in the Milky Way. It didn't know where the birth star lay, nor even when its species began to venture out across interstellar space, though there was an echo of immense distance and time within its identity.

In one form, the species became their own starships, carrying their essence across the gulf of space. Vast creatures that drew energy from spacetime itself, twisting gravitational fields to propel themselves along at a good fraction of lightspeed. Expansion was their destiny now, the very purpose of life.

When they arrived at the bright new stars they'd pursued, they found the biosphere of many planets to be incompatible with their original body chemistry. Rather than tackling the immense task of changing these inimical planets, they pushed fusion with their liberating nanotech further, their bodies becoming even more malleable, adapting easily to their new environments. Morphing into direct rivals to the existing lifeforms who struggled against their conquests.

Innumerable conflicts arose from their implacable colonization, instigating more change, more deviation from their original physical identity. The mimicry ability was born, the pinnacle of their nano-derived evolution, allowing a more aggressive and insidious incursion across fresh worlds. Starships orbited high above the newfound planets, dropping swarms of eggs, which would absorb the form of the natives and give birth to a generation of changelings. When they became dominant, eradicating their indigenous rivals, subsequent generations reverted as close to their true form as planetary conditions permitted and lived their lives as masters of their new domain.

Somewhere amid the expansion wave, a flock of starships was taken into the Void. Adaptation here was difficult, but continued anyway, driven by fear, for the Fallers soon understood the Void's purpose. As they had merged with and eradicated countless species across the stars, so the Void would absorb them, and in doing so quicken their development to an elevated state suitable for subsumption into its Heart.

Some Fallers adapted as best their nature would allow. They sought out a niche in this new and strange meta-ecology, assuming a symbiotic role for the Heart, guiding worthy entities to fulfilment, assisting newcomers to compatible sections of the Void: these guides were the Skylords.

Others simply carried on as before, deluging the other luckless biological captives with their eggs, devouring lives and cultures until they could emerge as themselves once more. Living out their lives under the Void's constant pressure to fulfil themselves and contribute their essence to its heart.

One faction of Faller starships struggled against their incarceration. They used their innate ability to warp local spacetime for flight to try and change the nature of the Void, to claw their way out by force. It didn't seem to work.

'The Forest,' Kysandra said softly. She'd joined Nigel out on the veranda. It was close to dawn, and the silver haze of the Forest was visible above the horizon. Nigel was gazing up at it, a brandy in one hand. 'The Forest is the Faller starships that tried to escape, isn't it?'

'Yes.'

'So it is true,' she said. 'Nobody can get out. If they can't do it with all their power . . .'

'They messed up. That distortion they generated created some kind of loop in the local memory layer. They're stuck in the past, or rather what the Forest remembers is the past.'

'Is that what happened to Laura?'

'Yes. As soon as Shuttle Fourteen entered the Forest, it got entangled in the loop. There's a place in the memory layer, a subsection where she repeats that whole experience every twenty-seven hours and forty-two minutes. It creates her, and makes her and the science team relive the same section of their expedition every time. Sonofabitch, they started over every twenty-seven hours and forty-two minutes for the last three thousand years. That's . . . just . . . damn!'

Kysandra frowned, trying not to be too overwhelmed by the horror of it. 'But why are all the exopods and bodies in the Desert of Bone all the same age? She should be landing on Bienvenido every time she leaves the Forest.'

'Paradox. You can't actually travel back in time, so the Void outside the Forest's distortion tries to normalize the event. As near as I can figure it, every time Laura's mission loops, it does so in the Void's memory of three thousand years ago that the Forest has screwed up. It's like a shared solipsism for her, except the person she's sharing it with is herself. And each time one of her dies inside that distorted memory segment, the creation layer manifests what happened as a piece of Bienvenido's history.'

'So it does happen?' Kysandra asked. 'It is real?'

'To her, yes; but not to us. She doesn't exist in this time, in our segment of the Void's reality; what happens to her – to each one of her – is supposed to have occurred in the past. So when her life ends and the loop throws her latest corpse out here, it's instantly transformed to a chunk of a past that never existed. That's how the Void outside the loop attempts to balance the books and make the present correct, to neutralize the paradox.' He grinned savagely. 'It's like the old Creationists claiming God laid down the dinosaur fossils a few thousand years ago. Crud, how they'd love this!'

'Uracus! But she still lives through it?'

'Yes. Somewhere, in some aspect of the memory layer, Laura, Ayanna, Ibu, Rojas and Joey, all of them have been through the same event over a million times now.'

Kysandra closed her eyes, recalling the hill of exopods and their horrifying crust of mummified bodies. 'So right now, in this screwed-up section of the memory layer, there's a Laura trying to escape the exopod landing point, to make it across the desert on a cart?'

'That, or she's waiting at the bottom of the exopod hill ready to kill the next Laura that comes floating down out of the sky; we saw she's done that enough times. Then again, given the height of the hill now, I imagine a majority of her will either die or be badly maimed when their exopod lands on top and goes tumbling down the side. Either way – every time – she dies, and her personal segment of the loop ends.'

'You have to stop it. You have to set her free.'

Nigel took a sip of the brandy. His gaze never left the Forest. 'I know.'

8

Even though Kysandra considered herself so much more sophisticated and experienced nowadays, she was still excited to be visiting Varlan again. The rush and bustle of the city, its smells and psychic effervescence, was something poor old Adeone could never match. The size, too, was impressive; even the Shanties were larger here. Looking at it with new knowledge and understanding, she saw that size gave it power, economic and political. By design, it was the hub of the continent's rail and river trade routes. Ports, train stations, factories, banks, the headquarters of the Marines and the Meor, the seat of the National Council, seat of the civil service – it had them all. Varlan was a true capital.

'You can't change Bienvenido without changing Varlan first,' Kysandra announced. She was standing on the balcony in the Rasheeda Hotel suite, staring out across the lush green expanse of Bromwell Park. On the other side of the grass and trees, buildings and streets smothered the folds of the land in brick and stone. Rooftops stretched away to the riverbank, hard angular waves of blue slate and red clay. A forest of tall industrial chimney stacks populated the north-east of the city, looking like the pillars of some gigantic folly roof that a mad captain had never quite got round to building. They pumped out thick fountains of smoke that cast a palpable shade across that whole district.

'That's my girl,' Nigel said from the lounge.

It wasn't really a revelation. She'd always known. But it had taken this vista for her truly to comprehend the concept. 'There's so much inertia here,' she murmured.

'Start small, and keep pushing.'

Kysandra grinned and went back into the lounge, where it was slightly cooler. 'I thought you were going to say it only takes one pebble to start an avalanche.'

He cocked an eyebrow at her. 'Now who knows it all?'

She sat down on a chaise longue, stretching out her arms theatrically. 'What difference would it make, giving the world true democracy? People will still have to pay taxes to fund the regiments, because the Fallers will never stop. They can't. It's what they are.'

'I have to get back into space. That's the first stage. Once *Skylady* is up there, I might be able to do something about the Forest.'

'But you can't get into space.' She stopped, suddenly alarmed. 'Unless you go back to before you landed here.'

'If I could do that, I would, because then everything would change, even your destiny. But I can't go that far back in time. There must be something missing, some part of Edeard's technique I haven't grasped. Or my mind simply isn't strong enough. Then again, it could just be more difficult in this part of the Void.'

'Because of what the Forest is doing to the memory layer?'

He shrugged. 'It's my best guess. It's also my biggest hope, because that would make the Forest very important.'

'Important how?'

'It's damaging the Void – something no one else has ever done.'

'Does that help us?'

'Oh, yes! We're missing a lot of Laura Brandt's data on the quantum distortion. If I can analyse the effect properly, my allies the Raiel may be able to use it. They have resources far greater than the Fallers.'

'The Raiel can get us out?'

Nigel held up his hands. 'We're talking infinitesimal chances here. But then again, when infinitesimal is all you've got to grasp at . . .'

'Then let's do it. How can we get the *Skylady* back into space?'

'I've been thinking about it. Regrav is the problem. It glitched on me the whole time, and since I got down it's been dead. But ingrav worked. It still does. Not well; it can't generate a full gee of thrust, which is what I need to lift. But it's still operational. If I could just get *Skylady* to a decent altitude, the old girl might be able to accelerate to escape velocity.'

'So you need something to boost *Skylady* to start with.'

'Yeah.'

'Can you get a Skylord to help?'

'I don't see how.'

'Tell them you can help the Forest.'

'Even if they understood the concept, you forget they're the Faller variant that's perfectly adapted to the Void. They're not going to help change a damn thing.'

'Oh.' She pursed her lips in annoyance. 'Yeah. Uracus!'

'I was thinking along the lines of something crude enough that the Void won't glitch it.'

'What?'

His grin was malicious. 'Project Orion. Now that would be something.'

'What's Project Orion?'

'Something utterly beautiful, and completely crazy. It involves a lot of atom bombs. But, don't worry, I'm not actually going to use it. There are a few more rational options open to us. We'll run some experiments and see what's the most effective.

'How long will that take?' It came out more childlike and petulant than she wanted.

'I don't know, because I haven't decided which propulsion systems to test, yet. I need—'

'—more information,' she said in exasperation. 'Yes, I know.'

'Everything costs more and takes longer. You need to get used to that.'

*

They walked along the railings that isolated the Captain's Palace from the rest of the city. At the front, where the grand façade

501

looked down Walton Boulevard, was the big open cobbled square where people could watch the Palace Guards and the Marines strut their ceremonial stuff twice a week. But, as you walked round, the rails gave way to a high stone wall, blocking the palace gardens from casual view. It was topped by firepine – a prickly scarlet and orange bush that resembled a cascade of foam, with a venom in its thorns that was both excruciating and lethal to humans. The stone was also thick enough to prevent most ex-sight perceiving what was going on inside. Mod-birds belonging to the Palace Guard avian squad flew ceaseless patrols overhead, preventing anyone else's mod-bird from getting close and providing curious citizens with a glimpse of the hanky-panky that the Captain's family was rumoured to get up to amid the lovely topiary paths, ornate ponds and shady glades.

Mayborne Avenue was the road which circled the perimeter directly outside the wall: a wide thoroughfare planted with everblue procilla trees, with elegant stone townhouses on the other side; by law only two storeys high so they couldn't see over the wall. The avenue was deliberately designed to draw attention to anyone who lingered.

It was drizzling lightly when Nigel and Kysandra started to walk along the pavement on the houses' side. Originally they'd been built by aristocratic families and wealthy merchants desperate to court favour with the Captain. But the two-storey law prohibited any truly grandiose house from being constructed on the avenue, so time had seen many converted into grace-and-favour apartments for the palace courtiers; several, it was said, were now residences reserved for the Captain's various mistresses, while the remainder became prestigious addresses for company offices, legal firms, banks and charitable societies under the Captain's generous patronage.

They stopped outside one whose yellow dressed stone was aged to grey, its surface pocked with innumerable cracks and patches. The brass sign beside the front door read: Varlan University Bibliographical Preservation Society. Nigel's teekay rang the bell.

A receptionist showed them to a first-floor waiting room, her shell not quite strong enough to contain her condescension. Their appointment was so routine, so predictable. Nouveau riche provincials seeking a contact – any contact – within the palace court. Making a sizeable donation to one of the charitable societies of which the Captain was patron was the start of the long road to acceptability by Varlan society.

After making them wait for a quarter of an hour, the receptionist showed them up to a second-floor office. It was a square room with high walls covered by floor-to-ceiling bookshelves. The only break was a tall sash window looking out over Mayborne Avenue. A broad applewood desk sat in front of it, almost black from age. Coulan rose from his chair and gave Kysandra a big hug and a kiss.

'You look great,' she told him. Which he did, his hair cut shorter and gelled in a conservative style. White shirt and dark fuchsia tie, charcoal-grey suit jacket hanging on the back of his chair. 'A proper city worker.'

'Really? So you mean I look bored, poor and miserable?'

'Not that bad.'

'I missed you,' he said.

'Nice,' Nigel grunted as he sat down. 'We brought a lot of files for you to access. But mainly we've made progress on the Fallers; turns out they're a nasty type of nano, built for planetary conquest.'

'Fascinating. Well, on my side, I've built up a decent network of contacts in Varlan, some actives.'

'Actives?' Kysandra asked.

'Dominated,' Coulan said. 'I need to be able to rely on key people, not just hope they'll do as I ask.'

'Oh.' She looked down, studying the floorboards.

'Once I got her detoxed, I placed Bethaneve in the Tax Office,' Coulan continued. 'Several others report back to her, so the inspectors won't be bothering you.'

'Glad to hear it,' Nigel said. 'What else?'

'A couple of Citizens' Dawn politicians in the National Council were eager for campaign contributions; there's always plenty of internal party bitchfighting going on for secure seats. Technically we're living in a democracy, though in reality this is a one-party state; the Citizens' Dawn party is the only one that counts. There are some opposition parties, but they're a rag-tag bunch with a few borough seats that nobody really bothers about, not even the voters. I'm developing contacts in the radical movement, such as it is, but I have to proceed with caution there; they're all as paranoid as they are committed, but I think I've found a way in.'

'Sex?' Nigel guessed.

'Always: the eternal human weak spot. The other reason for my restraint in that direction is that, surprisingly, the Captain's police are actually quite effective. They monitor all opposition for anyone able to mount a real challenge, or even just garner some popular support. If you want to get on in politics here, you join Citizens' Dawn and spend the next century fighting your way up a very treacherous ladder. Outside politics, I've acquired assets in the banks, and even some in the regiments. Pamphlet editors are always eager to trade gossip, which ties in neatly with the ten sheriffs who will private 'path information to me for a price. And I'm working on identifying possibles in the Captain's police, but they're going to have to be turned by domination. I can't trust anything else; the whole damn lot of them are fanatical about maintaining things the way they are.'

'Sounds like progress,' Nigel said.

'Thank you. Oh, and you'll never guess who's just shown up in town.'

'You're right, I won't guess.'

'Captain Slvasta.'

Nigel's grin was positively dirty. 'Captain, eh?'

'Yeah. They promoted him and booted him over to the Joint Regimental Council where all that bright-burning youthful enthusiasm will be snuffed out by bureaucratic procedure.'

'Poor boy. Can we use him?'

'He's on my watch list.'

'Okay. What about the palace?' Nigel nodded at the wall on the other side of Mayborne Avenue.

'Real progress there.'

Kysandra's u-shadow reported that Coulan was sending over a file. It was a recording from an artificial bussalore that *Skylady* had synthesized. Coulan had taken a week just getting the slippery little drone into the palace gardens, sitting in his Preservation Society office as the ersatz-rodent nosed along the wall, examining cracks. Eventually it found a deep one and slithered inside, then began clawing at the mortar joints, taking days to tunnel through and break out into the gardens.

'It is true what they say about the Captain's family,' Coulan said solemnly. 'It took me three days to navigate across the garden. There's a lot of degenerate nocturnal behaviour going on in there, let me tell you.'

'We should record it,' Nigel said. 'Nothing wrecks a reputation worse than a scandal. It can always be gifted to the city when we need it.'

'I'll send in another bussalore drone tonight.'

The file continued to play, showing Kysandra the interior of the palace. Even though she'd seen the façade, she wasn't quite prepared for the opulence of the rooms within. But Coulan didn't keep it above ground for long. The vast building squatted above an expansive labyrinth of cellars and vaults and tunnels. She found herself in a brick vault with the drone's little enhanced-sensitivity retinas looking up at the far wall. It was a convex curve made from metal that had darkened with age and gathered a dusting of powdery pine-green algae. There was a door in the middle, a big circular affair with an odd collar of torn metal and what looked like shredded rubber, whose stands hung limply.

'Is that plyplastic?' she asked. *Skylady* didn't use much of the substance, but there were hundreds of references in her newly implanted memories.

'Yes,' Nigel confirmed.

'So that's . . .'

'A cargo module, by the looks of it.'

'Correct,' Coulan said. 'I found another eleven of them underneath the palace. The bussalore drone managed to get inside one.

It'd been stripped clean. Even some of the internal structure had been removed.'

'Useful material,' Nigel muttered. 'Probably propping up some aristo's mansion roof.'

'Indeed. Then two weeks ago, I found this.'

The image changed to another large vault, this one annular with a ribbed ceiling. It enclosed a big ellipsoid made of smooth hexagonal panels which stood on its wide end, supported by brick buttresses. Metal struts which protruded from the panel intersections appeared to have been broken off. Tangles of cables and pipes formed a tattered web around the object. Six thick seamless tubes emerged from the panels around the narrow end, extending upwards so they almost touched the vault's curving roof.

'It took a while, but the drone eventually found a way in; some of the conduit mouldings had perished,' Coulan said with a note of pride.

The recording switched to a weird spectrum of cobalt-blue and black. Scale was difficult to make out, and the interior of the ellipsoid was filled with a dense lattice of support struts and cables and wire tubes, which made the picture confusing. Lean lines of scabbed electromuscle had distended from various mechanisms, oozing flaccid knobs that hung limply over dark gulfs, as if it had briefly turned liquid, only to resolidify. Cradles held blurred shapes; spheres, cylinders, discs . . .

'Freeze,' Nigel commanded.

The recording focused on a long cylinder with a wasp-waist middle and a mushroom-profile head.

'Oh, holy crap,' Nigel whispered. His lips parted in a soft lopsided smile.

'My thoughts exactly,' Coulan said.

Kysandra wanted to shout the question at them, but she knew the way this game was played now.

'This changes everything,' Nigel said. 'We have to get in there. I need them.'

'Not going to happen,' Coulan said. 'Not easily, anyway.'

'I could ask nicely.'

'I've studied Varlan's society closely while I've been in the city; it's conservative and sliding down the decadence decay curve. Can you imagine your impact? Hi there, Captain Philious, I'm from the Commonwealth. I have more knowledge than you, so just give me what I need and I'm going to try and get you all out of here, back to a universe where you will have none of your wealth and power, where you're just the same as everyone else.'

'Yeah,' Nigel drawled, and scratched the back of his head. 'So, we put together a crew of master criminals and pull off the crime of the millennium.' He grinned. 'Finally, something to rival the Great Wormhole Heist of 2243. I'd love to see Ozzie's face at that news.'

'It took me nearly three weeks to get a seven-centimetre remote drone into that vault. The palace has about a hundred armed guards on duty at any one time. There's a Marine barracks five minutes away. And the Captain's police aren't idiots or slack. I just don't see how we can realistically get into the vault, let alone take those out through the palace and back to the *Skylady*.'

'So we have to get rid of the guards and Marines and the police, then.'

'And manufacture a time crazy enough so no one will notice them being carted off down Walton Boulevard in broad daylight.'

'Ah, hell. I suppose so. We don't have a lot of options right now.'

Kysandra gave up. 'Right, you two! What the crud is that thing?'

Nigel turned to face her, actually expressing some genuine gusto for once. 'The *Vermillion*'s armoury.'

BOOK SIX

Those who Rise

1

Even though he'd sworn not to return, Slvasta had enjoyed seeing his old regimental comrades again. He'd made the journey back to Cham just ten days after he'd returned to Varlan from agreeing the deal with Nigel. Sergeant Yannrith had written, asking him to be a character witness for Trooper Tovakar. He was to be court-martialled, Yannrith's letter explained: there had been one too many charges of drunk and disorderly behaviour. Major Rachelle was to be the prosecuting officer. If found guilty, Tovakar would be given a dishonourable discharge and stripped of his pension.

That it was Major Rachelle was a big factor in Slvasta's return. That and the injustice. Tovakar was no saint, but to strip a trooper of his pension – a man who'd faced terrible danger to keep his fellow citizens safe – well, that was exactly the kind of thing Democratic Unity and their organization were fighting in Varlan.

His arrival caused a stir. Even provincial old Cham had heard of the Hero of Eynsham Square and looked favourably on a famous son. Ultimately, though, it had made no difference. Slvasta's testimony appealed to emotion; Rachelle deployed cold logic and impeccable legal precedent. Tovakar was kicked out of the regiment and his pension rights revoked.

Afterwards, Slvasta almost didn't bother with the subtle recruiting questions, but routine and paranoia made him ask them anyway. He wasn't asking them with the usual protection of anonymity, and Uracus alone knew how furious Bethaneve would be with him for that breach of security. But Tovakar was absolutely perfect material for their movement, so Slvasta made him an offer to accompany him back to Varlan and help Democratic Unity with certain politically useful acts. Tovakar didn't even hesitate, which got Slvasta thinking. The trooper would be extremely useful when it finally (Giu forbid) came to using the weapons that Nigel had agreed to supply. There weren't many ex-regiment people in their organization yet, and they could really use someone with that kind of experience. In his own way, Tovakar was indisputably loyal and reliable.

So he went and sat down with Andricea, and then Sergeant Yannrith. It helped that the Cham regiment hadn't been having the happiest time since he left. True, they didn't take mods with them on sweeps any more, but most of the other reforms he'd instituted had quietly been dropped. There were more officers, recruited from the county's gentry – junior sons and daughters who received no income from their family estates, and who saw the regiment purely as a way of maintaining their lifestyle. To pay for them, there were fewer troopers. Brigadier Venize was withdrawing from the day-to-day running of the regiment, with Major Rachelle stepping up to fill the gap. So when he made them the offer, Yannrith and Andricea were on the train with him and Tovakar back to Varlan.

It turned out to be the smartest recruiting move he'd made. Even Bethaneve agreed with that. Eventually.

*

As always these days, Yannrith, Andricea and Tovakar were the ones standing with him on Varlan's quayside in the grim meagre twilight, waiting for the ferry to chug its way over the Colbal. It was raining hard, a thin drizzle swirling out of featureless grey clouds that formed an unbroken ceiling over the city. Despite the rain, Slvasta was suffering a clammy warmth. Under his coat he wore a protective waistcoat of drosilk. Bethaneve insisted on that at all times. As the official leader of Democratic Unity he was a public figure, and not all the public admired him. The waistcoat would help against any sudden attack.

Drosilk, which had started to come on the market eighteen months ago, was astonishing: a light glossy thread that formed a fabric with a beautiful moiré shimmer. But it was also fantastically strong; there had been nothing like it on Bienvenido before. At first it had been used by society ladies for their couture dresses. But soon the factory looms had begun to weave tighter fabrics, strong enough to turn a blade. Really thick weaves were supposedly bullet proof. Everybody wanted the stuff, which had first appeared from Gretz county. Slvasta had been mildly alarmed to learn that drosilk came from a mod. Some adaptor stable had produced what it was calling a mod-spider which spun the stuff out. The spider, barely the size of a human hand, was utterly harmless. That was going to add complications for his anti-neut policy. Drosilk was becoming an important commodity, helping the city's battered post-mod economy along. Democratic Unity couldn't afford to be seen opposing it; weaving and tailoring the bales of cloth into finished clothes provided a lot of work. A couple of the old adaptor stables in the city were already bringing in the mod-spiders, adapting their old barns to accommodate them, and nobody was protesting. Slvasta considered that the thin end of the wedge, but Coulan had advised him to say nothing and bide his time over the problem.

Even with the constant downpour of murky rain, the docks carried on as usual. Commerce, the city's great engine, was floundering in these difficult economic times, and simple downpours couldn't be allowed to restrict the flow of commodities. So every jetty bustled with human stevedores using muscle and teekay to load and unload the cargoes from a multitude of different boats – the big three-masted ocean-going clippers docked alongside the longest jetties, sturdy river barges, fishing boats with cold-holds full of their catches, steam ferries which crossed the river several times a day laden with cargo from Willesden station. Several jetties had huge lumber rafts tied up to them after their long trip down river from the mountainous lands in the east, with steam cranes hoisting the thick trunks up onto flatbed wagons one at a time. There wasn't a mod-ape to be seen along the whole quayside, not these days. Horses pulled heavily loaded carts along the jetties, but they were terrestrial animals, not mods.

It was a rare thing indeed to catch sight of any mod now. The sheriffs (and the Captain's police) still used mod-birds drifting on the thermals above Varlan to keep an eye on known and suspected recidivists; and rumour had many grand houses still employing mod-monkeys behind their thick ex-sight-proof stone walls. But the time of civic teams cleaning the streets, or building teams using them for heavy work, were now past. Even cabs used terrestrial horses, raising their prices to pay for the new and expensive animals.

Democratic Unity had ridden the wave of popularity that had come from the employment shift, with new party chapters forming in over a dozen cities. They'd even held their first convention a month ago to formalize their policies for the forthcoming elections. As the democratically elected leader of the party, Slvasta was now a readily identifiable figure right across the city. So as they stood in the lee of a big warehouse at the end of Siebert jetty, he used a mild fuzz to deflect any ex-sight, while his wide-brimmed rain hat left his face shaded. A bulky grey greatcoat also disguised his missing arm. No one who worked on the quayside paid him a second glance as they passed by, allowing him to remain perfectly anonymous amid the busiest district in the whole of Varlan.

The four of them watched silently as the ferry *Elmar* pulled up at the jetty on schedule. Slvasta's ex-sight scanned across the throng of passengers huddled together under the awning pitched across the mid deck. It was a miserable duty, but he didn't complain. They'd been receiving a delivery from Nigel almost every ten days since Slvasta returned from Blair farm. Either Slvasta, Bethaneve, Coulan or Javier would be on hand to collect it – not that they didn't trust anyone else, but . . .

Russell stood close to the back of the ferry, where the wind pushed a quantity of rain under the edge of the awning. Like most of Varlan's citizens that day, he wore a long dark coat slicked with rain, while his teekay brushed the heaviest droplets away from his face and hair. One hand rested on the handle of a large trunk bound with brass strips and a small set of wheels on the bottom.

'Get ready,' Slvasta said. Andricea and Tovakar walked away from the warehouse in opposite directions, mingling with the traffic along the broad quayside road. Their ex-sight scanning round, alert for anything out of place, any police operation. Slvasta himself used his ex-sight to keep watch on the wet sky overhead, alert for mod-birds. Russell joined the queue of people disembarking along the gangplank, walking steadily, his trunk trundling along behind him. An unremarkable figure, indistinguishable from the other ferry commuters that damp evening. As soon as he reached the end of the jetty, he made straight for the warehouse. Slvasta and Yannrith walked back into the loading bay they were temporarily borrowing – courtesy of the stevedores' union – where the cab was waiting. Russell wheeled the trunk round to the cab's door. He was fuzzing it slightly, preventing any curious ex-sight from pervading the interior. Yannrith was already in the cab; he leaned out, gripping the top of the trunk. Slvasta used his teekay and his one arm to help Russell push the trunk up and inside. The thing was excessively heavy, but the three of them managed to shove it onto the floor of the cab quickly enough.

'A fortnight on Friday,' Russell said. 'It'll be mostly ammunition then. I'll use the *Compton*'s five-thirty-five crossing.'

'One of us will be here,' Slvasta assured him. He climbed up onto the driver's bench and 'pathed an order to the horse.

Russell walked away into the dreary evening as the cab rolled out of the loading bay. After a hundred metres, Slvasta stopped and allowed Andricea to get into the cab with Yannrith, who was maintaining a decent fuzz. Less than a minute later, Tovakar arrived and climbed up beside Slvasta. Slvasta ordered the horse forward again, and the cab picked up speed.

*

Bethaneve used a mild teekay shield to keep the drizzle off as she walked into East Folwich. The inclement weather had emptied most people from Varlan's streets, which was an unwelcome development. The city's bustle provided useful cover when she was about some task.

Not this evening. So, after she met Coulan, they had to go into a small café a couple of streets away from the Faller Research Institute. Standing about outside in the rain would have made them conspicuous. The café was pleasant enough inside, and the tea and cakes they ordered were excellent – even though the prices made it very clear you were in East Folwich.

She sipped her third cup and eyed up one of the chocolate cupcakes. The fresh strawberry slices on top made it especially tempting.

'You know you want to,' Coulan taunted.

'Don't. I'm putting on enough weight as it is. All I do every day is sit. And eat. Who knew a revolution made you fat?'

'Rubbish. You look just as hot now as when we met.'

'So much for all of us aspiring to truth.'

'A white lie isn't a real lie.'

'So I am fat?'

'Stop it. You always were the smart one. If you don't have that cupcake, I'm going to.' He reached out.

'Get your hands off!' Her smirk faded as the mod-bird caught sight of the carriage. 'Here it comes,' she warned him.

The low clouds and patch mist provided good cover for the mod-bird. It flew high above East Folwich, slipping quickly from one patch to another. In between, its sharp eyes scanned the wet streets and rooftops, providing an intermittent – but safe – view. The mod-bird belonged to a level nine cell member, and Bethaneve found it invaluable in any observation operation. She hadn't told Slvasta about using the mod. His obsession wouldn't allow exceptions, not even for her.

The two of them sat at the table with the cupcake between them, perceiving the mod-bird's sight. They looked down through the grey swirl of drizzle to see a long black carriage pulled by a terrestrial horse approaching the walled sanctuary of the Faller Research Institute. It paused while the outer doors were opened, then rolled into the tunnel which formed the mainstay of the gate-house.

'I understand they have to be super cautious about preventing Fallers from escaping,' Bethaneve private 'pathed. 'And I'm glad they are. But that entrance is going to be a problem if we ever want to get inside.'

'Depends when you want to get inside,' Coulan replied. 'If you want to sneak in to scout round now, then yes. But when the revolution's in progress, a couple of well-placed explosives will blow the hinges easily enough.'

'The direct approach. I like it.' Bethaneve allowed a sense of admiration to flutter through her shell. Even though she knew him so well, Coulan could still surprise her.

It was risky, sending a mod-bird directly over the institute. Its staff were extremely vigilant. So Bethaneve counted off a minute to allow the carriage time to get past the inner gate and into the courtyard, then sent the mod-bird on a fast pass.

The carriage had stopped in the centre of the bleak courtyard. Two men were helping a figure out. He had a hood over his head and his hands were cuffed. His movements were awkward, as if he was in a great deal of pain.

'There,' she said. 'See? A prisoner.'

'Obvious enough.'

'But why? I don't understand why they bring them here.' It had come to her attention a couple of months ago, when Trevene had seized more cell members. The elites had kept watch on Fifty-Eight Grosvner Place to try and see if their comrades were being taken to the Pidrui mines. There were a lot of people who'd have to be rescued from that terrible place as soon as they liberated Bienvenido. Instead the elites had reported something altogether stranger, so she mounted a discreet observation operation. Every now and then, maybe once every two or three weeks (there was no regular schedule), a fuzzed carriage with a (presumed) prisoner would travel from Fifty-Eight Grosvner Place across half the city to the Faller Research Institute, then drive back empty. 'What's the connection?' she asked. 'What does Trevene's Uracus-damned operation need with the biggest collection of obsolete science nerds on the planet?'

'I have absolutely no idea. But I now understand your obsession to get through the institute gates.'

'It's not an obsession. But you have to admit it's a strange—'

The mod-bird had finished its overflight of the courtyard and was banking to head for the nearest fog patch. Its head turned to provide a last glimpse of the institute. A man had emerged from the entrance, walking towards the prisoner.

Bethaneve stiffened. Then she started shaking.

'Bethaneve?' Coulan asked in concern. 'Bethaneve, what's wrong?'

She tightened her shell as strongly as she possibly could. Hating herself for the weakness. Knowing that, despite veiling her thoughts, her face would be creased with distress. Tears threatened to trickle down her cheeks.

'Bethaneve, for Giu's sake—'

'It's him,' she whispered. 'The First Officer.' Her hands gripped the edge of the table, squeezing hard.

'What's wrong?'

'Ha! You know what he does to people.'

'Yes, and because of that he's up there at the top of our list along with people like Trevene, to be dealt with as soon as we overthrow the Captain. He'll be taken care of.'

Bethaneve didn't like the way Coulan was looking at her, the curiosity in his gaze. Aothori's appearance had been so unexpected, taking her by surprise. 'But why's he here? Why is he involved in this weird prisoner movement?' As deflections went, it was pitiful. But Coulan at least appeared to be considering the question.

'Aothori enjoys the interrogations,' he said slowly. 'He turns up at Fifty-Eight Grosvner Place often enough for them, we know that. So maybe the interrogations carry on at the institute.'

'Why? What can they possibly do here that Trevene's bastards can't do in their dungeons?'

'I don't know. It's not a good question to dwell on.'

'Uracus!'

'Where do the prisoners get taken after the institute?' Coulan asked. 'Is it the Pidrui mines?'

Bethaneve made an effort to focus, to get back to normal. 'I don't know. We haven't tracked them when they leave.'

'Then that's your next step. Find out where they're sending our comrades. Once we know that, we can rescue them as soon as we've got rid of the Captain.' He paused. 'And the First Officer.'

'Yes. Yes, you're right. I'll start organizing that.'

'Good.' He pushed the chocolate cupcake across the table to her. 'You're their best hope, Bethaneve. Don't let them down.'

'I won't.'

'Okay then. We'd best be getting back. I want to know how the latest delivery went.'

'Andricea's with them,' she said, not bothering to hide her disapproval. 'I'm sure she'll make sure everything goes off perfectly.' She bit hard into the cupcake.

*

Andricea's mod-bird circled overhead, watching the cab as Slvasta steered a convoluted route across Varlan. He had very mixed feelings about the mod-bird, but it had been with Andricea since it was born. Keeping it with her was a condition of her coming to Varlan – a very strong condition. He comforted himself with the knowledge that if anything went wrong, a mod-bird couldn't do anything like the damage a mod-ape could wreak; in any case, it was damn useful to have an eye in the sky. The Captain's police hadn't intercepted a weapons shipment yet, but he knew Trevene suspected the rebel cells had access to weapons. Several activists had travelled out of the city to undergo training on the sniper rifles; they weren't the kind of things you could just hand to people and tell them to get on with it. Nor, sadly – human nature being what it was – were they the kind of weapon everyone could keep quiet about. Loose boastful words at the end of an evening in a pub, pillow talk, whispers and hints – it all mounted up over time and became quiet rumour. Informants picked it up and reported it to their contacts.

And Slvasta knew they had, because Trevene was picking up more and more cell members for interrogation. Bethaneve was constantly sending warnings through the network, advising comrades to get out of town. It was becoming a regular migration.

But they fought back. Bethaneve's contacts and lookouts kept an equally keen watch on the members of the Captain's police. She and Coulan had gradually compiled a comprehensive list of names, starting with Trevene, and then addresses, family connections, habits, areas of expertise. Once that was established, Javier started telling subtle lies to cell members known to Trevene's people. Bethaneve called that disinformation. Whatever name you used, their orchestrated deceit caused a great deal of confusion to the Captain's police, and how they interpreted the surge of radical activity in the city.

If the stakes hadn't been so high, Slvasta would have laughed at the mirrored networks of gossips and informers working the capital's streets.

So despite formidable expense and effort since Democratic Unity won their seats in Nalani, the Captain's police still hadn't intercepted a weapons shipment, nor discovered a cache. And Slvasta was determined that record should remain intact. What Trevene's reaction would be if a cache was found made for uncomfortable thinking.

He took a careful ninety minutes winding along Varlan's boulevards and avenues and narrow back roads until they reached the junction into Prout Road in the Winchester district on the western side of town. It was a respectable enough region, with long rows of terraced houses long since converted into multiple lodgings. But there were still individual townhouses and parks, and light industry which didn't belch out pollution into the culverted rivers that ran through it.

'Taxing the poor,' Slvasta 'pathed to the partially concealed man standing on the kerbside by the junction.

'Pays for the rich,' the man 'pathed back.

'Is it clear?'

'Yes. Nobody we don't know visiting, nobody shown an interest for two days. No mods close. Go on in.'

'Thanks.'

Slvasta used his ex-sight to guide the cab along the uneven cobbles of Prout Road. With the rainclouds remaining stubbornly overhead, there was no nebula light shining on the city tonight, and Prout Road's streetlights hadn't been lit for over a year, leaving the road in the pitch dark. The cab rolled up to the broad wooden doors of an old leatherworks yard, and a couple of level seven cell members opened them.

The factory was over three hundred years old, currently awaiting redevelopment. Its owners had moved the vats and rollers and cutting tables out to new premises three streets away when the cracks and bulges in the dark brick walls had become just too alarming to ignore. In the meantime squatters had moved in. To begin with it was families who wanted out of the Shanties, but couldn't afford even the smallest rent, the jobless and the terminally unemployable. Over the last year, those first-generation residents had moved out as job opportunities opened wide across the city, only for their rooms to be taken over by those with drink or narnik problems, people whose mental health had deteriorated. People who didn't care who came and went in the night.

Weak yellow light flickered in a few of the big windows looming over the courtyard. The door closed behind the cab, and the cell members increased their fuzz, obscuring the whole courtyard from psychic perception. Up on the driver's bench, Slvasta increased his own fuzz so they wouldn't realize who he was.

It was a smooth operation. Tovakar and Yannrith carried the trunk with two cell members; Andricea walked behind, gifting her sight to Slvasta, who stayed in the cab. They went down into the factory's vaulted cellars. The bricks were crumbling here, and there had been several cave-ins. The cell members led them to a wide fissure with a steep ramp of rubble on the other side, leading down.

Andricea's ex-sight probed round the cavern behind the opening. The stone walls here were ancient, slicked with algae along the edge of each big block. It had archways along one wall, which were all blocked off. 'What is this place?' she asked.

'Whatever the factory was built on top of,' the first cell member said. 'There have been buildings here for two thousand years.'

The stones in one of the archways had shifted, leaving a gap they could just push the trunk through. On the other side were crude stairs leading down a circular shaft cut into naked rock. By the time Andricea reached the bottom there was so much rock and stone between them that her gifting had become very tenuous; Slvasta could barely make out anything. The little party seemed to be walking through another series of vaults. Empty crates and barrels were strewn across the floor, their rotten wood crumbling apart. A thick layer of gritty dust covered everything, but the air was perfectly dry.

Andricea had to use a lot of teekay to keep the dust out of her nose and mouth. The trunk was lowered to the ground, and Yannrith finally stopped fuzzing it. They all used their ex-sight to perceive the contents. There were twenty snub-nosed carbines inside, with three spare magazines each, everything wrapped in oiled cloth.

'Don't open it,' Andricea said at once. 'The dust down here will screw up the firing mechanisms.'

'Nobody's going to touch it,' the first cell member said. 'We'll make sure of that. It's quite safe here.'

'When do we get to use them?' the second cell member asked.

'Nobody tells us,' Yannrith said in a joshing tone. 'We're just the errand boys.'

'It's got to be soon,' the first one said. 'This has been going on for crudding years. How long does it take to kill the Captain? These fuckers would make easy work of it.' His hand came down possessively on the trunk.

'It's not just the Captain,' Andricea said. 'There's everyone who supports him as well.'

'What? We're going to kill all of them?'

'I dunno,' Andricea said. 'Get them to think again, maybe. Who knows?'

'Some fucker better,' he said giving Yannrith a pointed stare. 'Right.'

As Slvasta drove the cab back to its stables, he was satisfied the weapons would remain untouched until the day came. There were over twenty such caches distributed across the city now. Varlan seemed to be built above a honeycomb of forgotten crypts and cellars for which no map existed. They'd scattered an equal number of secure ammunition deposits underground as well. It was a decision they'd made right at the start: never to put the two together until they armed the cells. There was too much temptation for the people guarding them to sell and make a quick profit. After all, it wasn't as though Bethaneve was going to run an audit. Personally, Slvasta would be satisfied if eighty per cent of the weapons remained when the day came.

After they returned the cab, they went their separate ways. Home for Slvasta now was Jaysfield Terrace – a smart stone crescent that curved round a circular park right in the heart of Langley, a borough that was the closest that anywhere in the city came to a country town. It was on Varlan's north-western outskirts, with tree-covered hills visible from the taller buildings, and much sought after by the middle classes who enjoyed its leafy lanes and fashionable shops and decent schools. Slvasta had to admit he found it a comfortable place to live in despite its distance from the centre of the city. The furnished apartment they were renting occupied the whole of the fifth floor of Number Sixteen Jaysfield Terrace. With its high ceilings and four bedrooms, it was much too big for just him and Bethaneve.

'Essential, though,' she'd laughed as they moved in. 'You have to live in the constituency if you're to contest it at the election.'

For Langley was also the heart of a National Council constituency that stretched for over sixty miles out into the countryside – an area which comprised several old-family estates and their worker villages as well as some thriving towns and smaller farms. It contained a broad social spread of residents, with a great many small business owners, most of whom were dissatisfied by government with its excessive regulation and restrictive trading laws that favoured the established order. Colonel Gelasis had been right: it was a perfect constituency for him to challenge the incumbent.

The long curving terrace had small front gardens confined by iron railings. All the gates which led to front doors were set into iron arches with oil lamps at their apex. Almost half of them had been lit by residents determined to keep up standards and alleviate at least some of the darkness. The public lamp posts on the other side of the road remained dark. Slvasta scanned the plant pots on the steps of Number Sixteen. A tall neatly pruned bay tree on one side and a purple climbing jasmine on the other. The bay tree pot was the right way round. If anything was wrong, Bethaneve would have turned it a quarter clockwise – assuming she had time. By now Slvasta had lived with the prospect of arrest or worse for so long that he didn't bother worrying about it.

The only downside of the apartment in Number Sixteen with its elegant fittings and fabulous views was the five flights of stairs he had to climb to reach it. When he did finally get into the marble-tiled hall the rain had soaked through his coat, leaving his clothes damp and cold. He shivered as he hung the coat up, and started unbuttoning the drosilk waistcoat.

Bethaneve was working in the dining room. She'd taken it over as her office as soon as they arrived; the long marwood table big enough to sit ten made a perfect desk, with papers and folders scattered across it. Strong oil lamps burned on either side of her, casting a bright light across the room. A bulky cabinet with carved doors had been moved across the mod door – not that there were any mod-dwarfs left in Number Sixteen. More thick folders were piled up around the walls, ledgers of the revolution all filled with her writing. Even her accountant's mind couldn't hold all the information on the cells and their activities. The symbols she used made no sense to anyone else; she wouldn't even tell Slvasta what they all meant. 'To protect the cells if we ever get interrogated,' she said. 'I'll die before I betray our comrades, and their identities will be lost with me.'

Now she was making extensive notations in a spread of purple folders. Slvasta watched her in mild concern for a moment. She still kept her job at the Tax Office, a respectable position for the fiancée of a National Council candidate, which meant she worked in her drab office all day then came back to yet more book-keeping here – when she wasn't risking herself on some clandestine activity. As always, he marvelled at her dedication and devotion to their cause. It had been his idea, but she had taken it forward in a way he'd never imagined.

She finished writing and turned to smile at him amid a burst of admiration and love. 'I knew you'd be wet,' she said. 'I ran you a bath.'

'There's a strategy meeting in an hour,' he said in regret. Another session of angst and determination in the local Democratic Unity offices, with him trying to hearten and inspire the devoted volunteers, most of them young, and all of them so desperate for him to succeed, to make a difference.

'It's a filthy night. I cancelled it.'

'But—'

'Go get in the bath.'

Slvasta did as he was told. After all this time, with every second of their lives spent on some aspect of the revolution, to have a break for one night wasn't something he was going to protest at. Since they moved in, he hadn't had a bath more than three or four times; everything was showers and quick meals snatched between events.

Six big double-wick candles had been placed strategically round the blue and white tiled bathroom. Bethaneve must have used her teekay to turn off the brass taps just before he arrived, for the big iron rolltop bath was full of water that was almost too hot. The air was saturated with the orange blossom scent of bath salts. He stripped off his soggy clothes and climbed in. Eyes closed, he leaned back and let the water engulf him.

Some time later Bethaneve asked: 'Is that better?'

He opened his eyes. Not asleep, just resting heavily. Her teekay was snuffing out the candles, leaving just two flickering. The shadows expanded, framing her in the topaz light of the doorway. She was wearing a strikingly erotic long black lace robe tied loosely round the waist.

'Uh huh,' he said with a throat that was suddenly dry.

She walked over slowly and knelt beside the bath. The front of the robe shifted to reveal the slope of her breasts as she bent over to kiss him. Strands of hair fell into the water.

'You're perfection,' he said eventually.

There was just enough light to show the smile on her face. 'Thank you.' She picked up a tall bottle of liquid soap and poured some into her cupped hand. 'Let me do this.'

'You know you're what makes all this possible,' he said, then whimpered as she began rubbing the soap slowly across his shoulders.

'That's very sweet, but we both know you're the one everybody admires. No one would vote for me, or even listen to me. You have a fire; you burn for justice. They all sense that. They sense how genuine you are.'

'Just a pretty figurehead. You do all the work, you and Coulan and Javier.'

'Don't forget the others.' More soap was tipped into her hand; she slid it down his sternum. 'Andricea helps you a lot.'

Slvasta suppressed a smile. Bethaneve had never quite been comfortable around Andricea, with her long limbs and sunny smile and trim figure.

'Are you thinking about her?' Bethaneve's hands had paused.

'Not at all.'

'Hmm.' She sounded suspicious.

Slvasta curled his hand round the back of her head and pulled her down for another kiss. Finally, Bethaneve relented and her hands crept down his stomach. 'Not at all,' he promised sincerely.

'Are you frightened?' she murmured. 'I am sometimes.'

'Not of the Captain's police, no. We're too prominent now, and we have support from some sections of the establishment.'

'I meant the election. It's only a week away.'

'Ten days.'

'Suppose we don't win?'

'The polls are good, and Tuksbury is a fool. Really, I had no idea.' He'd assumed that anyone who'd held on to a constituency seat for forty-eight years would know a thing or two about election campaigns. Not so Tuksbury. At first he'd simply sneered at Slvasta, assuming his own nomination as Citizens' Dawn candidate was good enough to gain him a majority. Then six weeks ago, when he realized that his own party's unenthusiastic support and lack of funds being thrown his way meant they'd abandoned him, he suddenly woke up to the very real prospect that he might lose his Council seat. By then Slvasta had already been campaigning for two months – not just in Varlan where the bulk of the voters lived, but visiting every town and village in the constituency, attending public meetings, setting out Democratic Unity's policies, promising to sweep away the old restrictions and conventions that made society so hidebound. He'd surprised himself at how adept he'd become at handling people, providing smart answers, telling the right jokes, knowing when to listen with a serious face, producing promises that sounded firm. It seemed there was truth in the old adage that you can get used to anything if you do it long enough.

Tuksbury, however, had never really campaigned before, had never engaged with the people he was supposed to represent. So when he finally stood up in public to address people, it didn't go well. He spent family money on lavish spreads of free food and drink, then lectured the people scoffing it down on why they should always vote for him because – 'I come from good family stock, not like this common moron who was so useless in the Cham regiment that he lost an arm to Fallers.' The two open debates with Slvasta which he agreed to also ended badly. The last one had to be halted early when the audience started throwing things at him and trying to make him tumble off the raised platform with their teekay.

The shock and dismay of discovering what people truly thought of him sent Tuksbury to seek solace in the bordellos he discreetly and regularly frequented, while inhaling more narnik than usual to dull the pain of his humiliation – facets of his personality that the pamphlets were eager to print, complete with details. His misery was compounded by the gazettes, which were normally so supportive of Citizens' Dawn, beginning to report the same foibles as the pamphlets.

Tuksbury hadn't appeared in public for the last four days. Cell members had reported him holed up in the Maiden's Welcome, a high-class brothel on Mawney Street, leaving his dispirited and badly underfunded campaign staff to produce leaflets that nobody read. One cell member, a clerk in a solicitor's office, reported that Tuksbury's wife had already filed for divorce.

'We will win,' Slvasta said confidently. '*Hilltop Eye* has the tax returns for Tuksbury's estate, hasn't it?'

'Delivered three days ago,' she confirmed. 'I got them the records for the last ten years. Uracus, those bastards have paid less than you and I did. Can you believe that? *Hilltop Eye* will print them four days before the election.'

'So it would take a Faller egg landing on my head for us to lose now. I just have to keep showing my face and not saying anything too stupid – for which I have you to watch over me.'

Bethaneve's expression was pure wickedness as her hands and teekay reached his groin. As always, he was helpless under her ministrations. She could make his body do whatever she wanted, and the intensity of the pleasure made him cry out, sending the bathwater sloshing across the floor.

Afterwards she made him stand next to the bath while she used a towel to dry him. Then he was taken to the bedroom.

'Marry me,' he said as he lay back on the sheets and watched her move round the room, first to her dresser to dab perfume on her neck, then lighting three candles. They were officially engaged, of course, but that was for the sake of the election. There was no wedding day named nor planned for.

'You know my answer,' she told him gently.

'Yes,' he said forlornly. 'When we've won.'

She came over to the bed and stood there, hands on hips, looking down at him. 'And you know why.'

'Because nobody should bring children into a world as unjust as this one,' he responded automatically.

'After we've won,' she said. 'That's the time to build for the future. Anything before that is just castles made of sand and promises.'

'I know,' he said. 'So if I don't win, do we still arm the cells and march on the palace?'

'No. That would be a complete disaster. We have to have popular support on our side, a clear mandate from the electorate. It must look as if we're doing what the people want.'

'Some of them, anyway.'

'You're having doubts?' she asked. 'Now?'

'No. I'm just tired, that's all.'

'Poor you. It's nearly over. We just need another few weeks, maybe months. That's all. Can you last that long?'

'Do I get a choice?'

'No. I'm sorry, my love. None of us does, not any more. This has grown too big to take the feelings of one person into account.'

'Are we really going to do this?' Slvasta wasn't even sure if he was asking this out loud. 'I mean, overthrowing the Captain? It's just so . . . so outrageous. Sometimes I have to check I'm still real, that I'm not living some dream in the Heart. How did we ever do this? Put all this together?'

'We did it because it was right. And it must be right, because it's worked. Everything is ready.'

'Yeah.' That part was as much a mystery to him as the rest. The four of them had spent so long talking and arguing about what had to be done physically to achieve success. How do you march a force of armed men through a city to take out the top of the existing government, and have that accepted by everyone else? So many ideas dismissed, so many details expanded, strategies planned.

'We just have to wait. Once you're elected to the National Council, you—'

'—become the authentic voice of the disaffected. Up pops my credibility and with it my legitimacy. Yes. Yes.'

'And if we give the underclass enough to protest about, and the Council doesn't listen – because it won't; it's full of people like Tuksbury – then we have the justification to launch the revolution.'

'I know.' Always there was the doubt. The way the rich with their fancy accountants avoided their fair share of taxes made him furious, and proper taxes for all was a priority for afterwards. But *they* were the ones planning on sabotaging the city's water, creating disruption and suffering; it would be *their* activists who blew up the rail bridges, which would increase Varlan's economic woes. Without them, things would carry on as they always did, which wasn't *that* bad . . .

Bethaneve licked her lips. 'Let me see. What I can do to perk you up?'

Even though she'd already satiated him in the bath, he knew he would be erect again when she wanted him to be. Her sexual skill was something he never questioned. No one with half a brain asked about previous loves, but still, some small bad part of his mind kept wondering about her and Coulan – if he'd been the one who'd taught her so much about what men truly enjoyed in bed. If it had been his touch which had encouraged her to cast off her inhibitions.

Fingers caressed him with nonchalant skill, then teekay so soft and slow it was torment plucked individual nerve strands in his cock. His flesh betrayed him immediately, igniting the pleasure pathways directly into his brain. He watched in awe as the lace robe flowed down over her skin like liquid gossamer, inflaming him still further.

'A month,' she whispered as she straddled him. 'A month after the election. That will be the right time. The perfect time. That will be when you lead us forward and take control of the whole world. Does that satisfy you? Is that what you want?' Her teekay crept around his balls like fronds of arctic frost, gripping mercilessly to balance him perfectly on the edge between pain and ecstasy.

'Yes,' he cried, 'Oh Giu, yes!' Not knowing or caring what he was agreeing with any more.

2

Some people simply couldn't be arsed – especially those who looked down on politicians and politics with the same contempt as they would regard a smear of animal dung on their boot sole. But still, many more did care, turning out to vote, making the effort. Outside some polling stations where Democratic Unity had put forward a full field of candidates for borough council seats, the sheriffs were unaccountably missing. In their stead, Citizens' Dawn toughs watched over the free private vote, making sure the cross went in the right place. Wherever that happened, the knowledge slipped through Bethaneve's communication network and local Democratic Unity activists arrived, demanding privacy and freedom from intimidation. Fights broke out, but they were sporadic, with the sheriffs finally turning up only to cart both sides off to the local station where they sat out the rest of the day cooling off in the drunk tank.

Then there were cases of people being told they weren't on the borough voting registry. There was nothing Bethaneve could do about that. But Tovakar, Andricea and Yannrith each had their own missions, running cells to intercept postal ballots that had been in storage for the last month. Citizens' Dawn had been adding to the envelopes with their own false voters – dead or non-existent. Those sacks were discreetly swapped with alternatives full of the same fantasy people, but now voting for Democratic Unity.

Some borough voting forms were in short supply.

Officials never turned up to open voting stations.

Four Democratic Unity candidates were arrested on charges ranging from tax evasion to assault, making their candidacies invalid.

It was another unremarkable election day on Bienvenido.

Despite everything the establishment threw at them, Democratic Unity's vote held solid in their strongholds of the more deprived boroughs. Slvasta, who arrived at Langley's council hall at five o'clock in the afternoon for the count, was 'pathed reports from party officials right across the city. Turn-out had been good. Interference was about what they expected. By eight o'clock, results were starting to come in. With a third of the thirty-three borough councils in the city up for election, five of them were shaping up to be Democratic Unity boroughs, with another three predicted to have no one party with an overall majority, and Citizens' Dawn claiming the remaining three (the richest boroughs). For them it was a disaster.

Five National Council seats in or around the capital were also being contested, along with a hundred more across the continent. In Langley, it was obvious from the moment the first sealed voting sacks were opened who was going to win. Tuksbury hadn't even been seen in public since the day *Hilltop Eye* published his tax records. Thanks to quiet surveillance by cell members, Slvasta knew he was holed up at his family estate just outside Varlan.

By eleven o'clock Slvasta had been confirmed as the new National Council representative for Langley. He gave a short thank-you speech (written by Coulan and Bethaneve) to his delighted supporters. By midnight the results for the Varlan boroughs were verified. Democratic Unity had won five outright, one more was theirs thanks to a coalition agreement with three independent councillors, Citizens' Dawn had four, and one was left without a majority party.

'Seven councils, counting Nalani,' Slvasta said as he walked home with Bethaneve, Javier and Coulan. 'That's amazing. Really, it is.' The dark streets had a lot of pedestrians and cabs for the time of night, all of them going home after the count. High overhead, Andricea's mod-bird kept level with them, its superb eyesight vigilant for trouble. Yannrith himself was barely a hundred metres away, and carrying two pistols. There were other party members close by, ready to rush in at a single 'pathed alert.

Javier had insisted on the precautions.

'You'll have to resign from Nalani tomorrow morning,' Coulan said. 'You can't sit on two councils.'

'You're the only Democratic Unity candidate to get a National Council seat,' Javier said; he sounded regretful.

'Bapek gave them a good run for their money in Denbridge,' Bethaneve said. 'Thirty-two per cent.'

'Denbridge is over the river,' Javier said. 'Large middle- and working-class population. Shame we couldn't win it.'

'We didn't win Langley,' Slvasta said. 'We were given it, remember?'

'Yeah, and are they ever going to regret that,' Bethaneve said happily. 'They think that's a bribe to keep us in line. Well, even if they survi—'

A wide corona of bright orange light flared across the southern skyline, silhouetting the rooftops and chimney stacks. They saw the flickering haze of a fireball ascending at the centre of it, wreathed in churning black smoke. Seconds later, the sound of the explosion rolled across them.

'Uracus!' Javier snapped. 'What was that?'

'It's down near the quayside, I think,' Coulan said. 'Eastwards, too. There are some companies around there that deal in yalseed oil. Big barrels.'

'Crud,' Slvasta grunted. 'Did we order that?'

'No,' Bethaneve said. 'And I don't like the timing.'

*

It took two days to get the warehouse fires under control, and the city authorities were lucky it rained on the second night. Smoke hung over Varlan for another day as the ruined buildings three streets above the quayside smouldered. Exploding barrels had thrown flaming yalseed oil a long distance, and the volunteer fire crews were scared to venture too close for fear of more barrels detonating.

Eventually, when all that was left was a circular area of blackened walls and piles of rubble, hospital staff and fire officers started to pick their way through the tangled debris, ex-sight probing the stone and charred wood and smashed slates, hunting for bodies.

Twenty-three business premises were destroyed. Fortunately, given it was a commercial district, and late at night, fatalities were minimal. Only eight people were known to have died. But it was another blow against the city's economy, with insurance companies hit hard. Everyone's premiums would be going up.

*

Kysandra was deep into the farm's accounts when Russell rode into the compound. His arrival gave her an excuse for her u-shadow to fold the spreadcube files away and free up her exovision. When they'd started planning the revolution, she'd been so enthusiastic and excited, never thinking she'd spend hours – days, weeks – having to manage the basic finances of the enterprise. But as she'd swiftly learned, shoving a government aside wasn't cheap.

'Our insurrection doesn't even have to work,' Nigel had said. 'Not permanently. We just need time to get in and out of the palace. All we really need for that is anarchy.'

'It should work,' she objected. 'Otherwise we've let down so many people.'

'You can't afford to think like that. The radicals who make up the movement are just another set of tools to help us complete the job. Nothing more.'

'But . . . they have to believe that their lives will change for the better to commit to the cause. You're asking them to risk everything they have.'

'And that risk will be repaid a thousand-fold. Not by replacing one set of useless, corrupt leaders with another, but by liberating

534

them from the Void. You have to learn to see the big picture, Kysandra. No more small-town thinking, okay?'

'Okay.' But it was difficult. People, real people, were going to get hurt. She just had to keep telling herself it was all worthwhile, because: this was *destiny* they were working to achieve.

Russell jumped off his horse as his teekay fastened the reins to the paddock fencing. 'Slvasta won the Langley election,' his 'path shout informed the compound. 'Democratic Unity is now a legitimate opposition party.' He waved a couple of Varlan's gazettes above his head. 'It's official.'

Kysandra hurried out of the house and met him on the veranda. 'Let me see,' she said, and took one of the gazettes. It was a large edition, printed yesterday, she noticed – *fast delivery to Adeone*. She kept her shell hard so she didn't reveal the swirl of disappointment that came from reading the results. *Only Slvasta got elected to the National Council? We put candidates up in five constituencies. And just six new boroughs with Democratic Unity in the majority?* In her heart she'd been hoping for so much more. Some public validation from the people they were about to set free.

'I'll go and show Nigel,' she said with a cheery smile. 'You go in and ask Victorea for some lunch; she'll make you up some sandwiches.'

Russell touched the brim of his hat respectfully. 'Thank you.'

Kysandra set off across the compound. It was barely recognizable now. So much had changed, so many buildings added. There were over thirty barns and storehouses, some of them vast, with iron I-beams supporting the wide span of their roofs. Eight of them were used purely for the farm, housing the mod-apes, horses and dwarfs needed to tend the crops and herds of terrestrial beasts that now covered almost the whole valley. The two timber mills were as busy as always. And the bulky steam engines thrummed away at the side of the engineering shops. Labourers and the dominated used two long barns as dormitories, dividing them up into snug but comfortable private rooms, with communal washrooms at one end. The three that housed the weapons factories were quiet now, their machines idle. Enough guns and ammunition had been manufactured and sent to the various radical groups they'd established, with the majority delivered to the capital. The mod-dwarfs that had worked on the production lines were now sitting in their stalls, doing nothing but eating and sleeping.

But it was the launch project she admired the most. Four long sheds lined with racks of ge-spider cages, spinning out vast quantities of drosilk. Nigel had introduced that particular variant to Bienvenido, of course; but not directly. Marek had travelled halfway up the Aflar peninsula to Gretz before teaching the adaption to a small family-run neut stable. That way it wouldn't be yet another innovation emerging from Blair Farm. After some experimentation, Nigel had found that to produce the best drosilk, ge-spiders should eat leaves from the deassu bush. If everyone else was breeding ge-spiders and producing drosilk for the clothing industry, there would be nothing odd about Blair Farm buying deassu leaves in considerable bulk.

After the ge-spider sheds was the booster bunker, which had been dug deep into the soil. Here the drosilk was wound carefully and precisely onto a long iron cylinder (precision milled, which had taken months) and sprayed with resin before being cured in a huge kiln. There were nineteen layers in all, each of which needed to be flawless. Only when sensors linked to the *Skylady* had confirmed that the last layer was unspoiled did the cylinder get taken out of the tube. Despite their very best monitoring and quality control, they only managed to get one perfect cylinder for every three attempts. Finished cylinders were wheeled into the second half of the booster bunker, behind thick iron and concrete wedge-shaped doors so heavy that they needed a set of train wheels to roll across the chamber on their own tracks.

That was where the process was finished, filling the cylinders with propellant, turning them into giant solid rocket motors. She could still remember the first test firing, with the booster standing vertical, its exhaust nozzle pointing up into the sky. Even standing a kilometre away, the roar of sound was like a solid force as it punched across her. The fire plume was incandescent, searing purple after-images across her retinas for minutes, while the smoke jet soared ever higher into the clear sky, reaching for the clouds above. It was as if the universe had somehow cracked open, allowing a gale of elemental forces to howl through the gap.

Afterwards, staring in astonishment at the still-smouldering booster casing while her overloaded senses began to calm, she said simply: 'You cannot sit on top of that. You just can't.'

'They're perfectly safe,' Nigel said contentedly. 'People flew into space on chemical rockets for decades before Ozzie and I put a stop to it.'

'No! Just . . . no!'

But of course there was no choice. So the production of the solid rocket boosters went ahead, despite her fears. Nigel had chosen an ammonium nitrate-based fuel, which was one of the easiest to make – especially given the production method they had discovered. Again it was all about keeping a low profile; he didn't want to add chemical refineries to the farm compound as well as everything else. Fortunately, the Fallers had given them an unexpected alternative in their slave species.

Kysandra walked past the booster bunker and along the rows of mod-pig silos. Out of the whole project, these animals were her biggest headache. They had to be fed a very specific diet of substances which their weird secondary digestive tract broke down and rearranged into faeces pellets that were the fuel used by the boosters. She had to track down suppliers right across the continent, seeking out merchants who dealt in powdered aluminium, hydrochloric acid, sodium, liquid rubber and a dozen types of nitrate-based fertilizers. Then she had to arrange to have them shipped to Blair Farm, but not in quantities that would arouse interest. She and Valeri set up dozens of small businesses in towns along the continent's main train lines, where labels could be swapped and the compounds forwarded in different containers. Then, when they did get here, they had to be mixed in just the right proportions before being fed to the mod-pigs.

The testing shed was two hundred metres past the silos, perched on the riverbank. She plodded over to it, through the shadow cast by the big iron crane of the launch framework. The squat gantries that would support the *Skylady* and her booster rocket assembly when they were ready to send her soaring back into space had been completed several weeks ago. Five red-painted iron scaffold pillars curved upwards in shallow arcs over a big circular pool filled with river water, to merge into a bracelet-shaped cradle where the crane would hoist the starship. Right now, it was a strange empty construction, as if it had outlasted a building it had once contained.

There were filter masks hanging up under the testing shed porch. Apparently exposure to perchlorates could cause thyroid problems in humans. Kysandra put one on before going in. The interior was simple enough, with a broad bench running along one side, filled with the kind of glassware that told anyone they were in a chemical lab. Nigel and Fergus were standing over a jar of greenish fluid, where a couple of thumb-sized fuel pellets were fizzing like bad beer.

'Slvasta won,' she announced.

'Yes,' Nigel's voice was muffled by the mask. 'We sensed Russell. Most of the county did.'

'That means it's going to happen!'

'Yes.' He still hadn't looked up from the sensor module that was scanning the jar and its dissolving pig faeces. 'That's up to standard,' he said to Fergus. 'Load the booster.'

'Slowly and carefully,' Fergus retorted.

Nigel abandoned the bench and put his arm round Kysandra, walking with her out of the test shed. 'Sorry,' he said when he'd taken the mask off. 'Some things just have to be done correctly. I'd hate to wind up sitting on top of a bad batch.'

She nodded earnestly. 'I understand.'

'Those pigs are pretty unpredictable.'

'We get the feed mix right every time.'

'I know, but I doubt the Fallers ever had this in mind when they designed the neuts.'

It had been the final revelation they'd extracted from the Proval-Faller's memory. Neuts were their perfect domestic slave race, biological machines created for one reason – to serve the Fallers. Capable of being moulded into dozens of sub-species, from animals that could perform most kinds of physical labour to immobile organ clumps whose enzymes turned them into simple chemical refineries, neuts eliminated the need for an overly mechanized civilization. You just had to know how to format the embryo. That was the second part of the puzzle.

When they assumed human form, the Fallers had thick bundles of additional nerves stretching down their arms to a small wart-like protuberance on the back of the wrist. It allowed a direct synaptic interface to a corresponding patch of nerve receptors at the back of a neut's head. All mods had an identical patch, through which instructions could be channelled. It was a discovery which had delighted Nigel. 'So that's how they operated outside the Void,' he'd muttered as the *Skylady* displayed the information through their exovision. 'Paula will be happy about that.'

It had taken the *Skylady* a while to work out the sequence, but eventually they got the mod-pig embryo correct. So the fat creatures lay in their stalls, with stumpy legs that were little more than wedges to keep them upright, and a body containing bio-reactor organs that could crap out pure rocket fuel. They didn't live long; the toxicity of the compounds they ate saw to that. But they had enough of them in the silos, and with regular births to replace the dead, the supply of pellets matched production of the booster casings. There was only one booster left to fill now, and they'd have a cluster that could send *Skylady* racing over ninety kilometres high. But it would be a ballistic trajectory; her speed would fall far short of orbital velocity. Achieving that still depended on the starship's degraded ingrav drive providing the final impetus. Nigel swore the figures checked out, and he'd make it to the Forest.

'Will the last booster be finished in time?' she asked as they made their way back to the farmhouse.

'It takes ten days to load the propellant and catalyse the final binding, so yes. Phase one isn't scheduled for another month. That'll give us plenty of time for the final stack assembly.'

She turned to look back at the launch framework. 'What if the weapons are no good?'

'Come on, Coulan has had drones in there examining them for eighteen months. Their integrity hasn't been compromised. They're simply powered down.'

'They're three thousand years old, Nigel.'

'Irrelevant. Their warheads are solid state. All the ancillary components are fragile, granted. We'll have to refurbish and replace quite a bit, but they'll function just fine. Stop worrying. You'll make me jittery, and that's no good at all.'

His arm went round her shoulder, holding her close. She'd noticed him becoming gradually more tactile over the last year or so.

'Sorry,' she said, pouring out insincerity.

'Yeah, right.'

'But I do have a question.'

'What?'

'I was going through the accounts. Who's James Hilton? We've been paying him an awful lot of money recently.'

'Ah. Actually, James Hilton was a novelist back on Earth, pre-Commonwealth era.'

'So why are we paying him a small fortune?'

'He's only really known for one book, *Lost Horizon*; it featured an imaginary valley called Shangri-La, which was sheltered from the rest of the world. I thought that an appropriate name.'

'For what?'

'A refuge, in case anything goes wrong.'

'What can go wrong?'

'Ah, now there you are. That's exactly why I was keeping it quiet. If you start having doubts, you always panic.'

'I do not!'

'Then why are you worried?'

'I'm not worried. I'm curious, that's all.'

'So now you know. If anything happens, there's a place where you, me and the ANAdroids can go and regroup.'

'Right. Thank you. Where?'

'Port Chana.'

'Ah! I thought Marek spent a lot of time there just to buy hydrochloric acid.'

'Clever girl.'

'Don't be so patronizing.'

'You get aggressive when you're worried.'

'I'm not worried. I'm concerned you think something can go wrong.'

'I don't.'

'But—'

'But, I've enough experience with life to know that you should always take precautions for other people screwing up. Look, if everything goes right, in a couple of months from now the Void will be gone, and you, me and everyone else on Bienvenido and Querencia will be on board a Raiel ship heading for the Commonwealth. But if not – if something does come along to screw things up – well there are consequences for the things we've done. Consequences I'd rather not face. So this is an emergency fall-back. *Surely* that's sensible, isn't it?'

Kysandra clenched her jaw. 'Yes.'

'See. What do I know?'

'Every crudding thing.'

*

The weak state of Varlan's economy was of no concern to the Westergate Club. Established for over fifteen hundred years, and rebuilt four times on the same spot, it epitomized how the city's ruling class sailed on serenely through the misfortunes of others, observing their travails the way one might view the antics of a zoo animal. Slvasta arrived at the richly decorated front door a week after the election, wearing the grey suit he'd bought for public speaking during the campaign. Shame he hadn't had the time to get it cleaned. The doorman in his immaculate black tailcoat smiled obsequiously and ushered him in. 'Welcome back, Captain Slvasta, and my personal congratulations on your election.'

'Thank you.'

The receptionist behind the desk gave him a very spry smile, backed up by a sultry private 'path – a wordless pulse but full of invitation. Slvasta hoped he didn't blush too obviously as the footman led him away. As always the huge marbled interior seemed to absorb sound. He was halfway up the sweeping staircase when he saw a young woman coming down towards him. She wore a bright red dress, a colour which emphasized her long strawberry blonde hair; its bodice was tighter than was the fashion among society ladies, and the skirt had a rather daring split all the way up one side, allowing a glimpse of long and very shapely legs. Her face was familiar, which made him struggle to recall—

'Slvasta!' she smiled and embraced him before he had time to react. 'Oh no,' she said theatrically, and waved a hand in front of her face. 'You've forgotten me already. And we had such a good time together.' A private 'path gifted him the inside of a boudoir that kicked off all sorts of enjoyable memories in Slvasta's skull. How he'd spent a long afternoon with her on that big soft bed. How it wasn't just Bethaneve who knew how to have uninhibited fun. How they'd laughed . . .

'Lanicia,' he said. 'I'm sorry. It's been a while.' Though how he could forget that beguiling face even for a moment was a complete mystery.

'It certainly has! I spent simply months pining after you, you mean thing. Fancy abandoning a girl after an afternoon like *that*!'

'Sorry.'

'I'm teasing, silly thing. It's really good to see you. And you're a National Councillor now! That's just brilliant. I bet old conservative men choked on their breakfasts all over town the day after the election. Daddy certainly did. Have you been introduced to the Captain yet?'

'Ah, uh, no, not yet. The Council's opening ceremony was postponed because of the explosion.'

'Oh, Giu, yes, that was so terrible. So! How are you? Married yet?'

'Uh, no.'

'Me neither.' The smile she gave him was downright wicked. 'I've still got my day villa for privacy. I'd enjoy being your mistress.'

All Slvasta could do was stand there with his mouth open. His gaze flicked to the footman, who had suddenly found something immensely interesting to stare at on the landing above. He really had forgotten how society girls behaved, their freedoms and delight in mischief.

Lanicia laughed gleefully at his expression, the confused emotions leaking through his suddenly shaky shell. 'I'll leave that offer open for you to consider,' she said and started walking down the stairs. There was one final saucy wink goodbye.

Slvasta finally managed to close his mouth. He wanted to carry on watching her walk down the stairs, he wanted to go after her, he wanted to have a day, one day, away from stress and fear and anger, to be carefree just as he had been that long ago afternoon when the Skylords had visited. Lazy evenings in her day villa would never be spent full of intense discussions and momentous decisions and ideological analysis. There would be no plotting how to kill people and bring down governments and change the world. There wouldn't be *responsibility*.

He closed his eyes and took a breath, allowing his heart to calm.

The footman was waiting patiently. 'Lead on,' Slvasta told him. The temptation was hard to fight. It wasn't just old flings like Lanicia who were coming on strong these days. There had been interest from women ever since he was publicly elected Democratic Unity's leader – interest which had steadily increased from the moment his candidacy for Langley was announced. Since the election, the offers had been quite brazen. It made him nervous about venturing outside Number Sixteen Jaysfield Terrace with Bethaneve. He could laugh off the attention, while enjoying the flattery. She, he knew, did not have the same liberal view of the phenomenon.

Colonel Gelasis waited for him in the Nevada suite, with all its sombre wood panelling setting the tone to match the colonel's thoughts. This time there was no effusive greeting as he rose from behind the big glossy table. Instead there was a curt: 'Councillor,' and a quick squeeze of the hand.

'Colonel.'

Gelasis waved the footman away, then straightened his uniform before sitting again. 'I believed we had a gentlemen's understanding?'

'Did we?' Slvasta said, wishing he didn't feel quite so intimidated.

'A quid pro quo was certainly implied. That's why you're now the Councillor for Langley. You got what you want, did you think that was free?'

'No.'

'Then would you mind explaining to me why in Uracus's name you blew up the yalseed oil company's depot? The city was crudding lucky that fire didn't spread any further. As it is, the financial damage it will inflict on decent people is quite bad enough. And that's on top of everything else the city is suffering right now because of the anti-mod movement.'

The outright accusation made Slvasta stiffen, only partly in anger. 'I didn't blow up anything.'

'Of course not, not personally, you're not an idiot, but can we say the same thing about your colleagues, eh? What would Tovakar tell us under interrogation I wonder? Or Andricea? How long would it take for her to crack if the Captain's police were to bring her in? Apparently the process is a lot worse for women, especially when they're young and good looking. I believe the First Officer takes a personal interest.'

Now Slvasta was deeply worried. If the colonel was using plain talk, this was no simple horse-trading arrangement any more. This was something a lot more serious. 'Actually, they'd say the same thing. I don't know who blew up the oil depot. Frankly, it's the last thing I need right now.' Which was true enough. It had taken Bethaneve two days of sifting through the scraps of information which percolated up through the network of cells to discover who might have sabotaged the oil company, then a follow-up visit from

Javier and Yannrith had confirmed it. Three members from a cell on level twenty-eight had grown frustrated by the lack of action and decided to take things into their own hands, striking a definitive blow for the movement, hurting the establishment. Yannrith had to pull Javier off one of them; the man was now in hospital with broken bones and heavy blood loss. Such a show of capability and determination could have given the game away. If the Captain's police had caught them, the interrogation would have lasted until they were either dead or confessed everything. As it was, Trevene's interest in the cells and suspected radicals had risen to dangerous levels. His agents were pressing informants hard. Three more cell members had disappeared in the last twenty-four hours. Bethaneve was busy warning their contacts.

'The deal was: you get Langley and in return peace is restored to our streets,' Gelasis said. 'No more acts of sabotage, no more Shanty mobs looting and wrecking, no more union bullying of hard-pressed businesses. Life becomes civilized once more, with you acting as a conduit for legitimate concerns and complaints.'

'That is my wish, too,' Slvasta shot back. 'Come on, I've invested everything in getting this seat. I'm not going to blow it now.'

'I'm glad to hear it. From now on if your lowlife supporters have problems with the world, they take those problems to you. Even with drosilk sales bringing fresh cash in, the economy needs a time of stability to get back to what it was before Democratic Unity's paranoid campaign against mods. You do know the capital is the only place that particular idiocy took hold? Rather like your voter base.'

'People will realize—'

'No, Slvasta. They will not realize. Because nobody is going to stir up that prejudice any more. I'm sorry about your arm. Really, I am. But you need to get over it. Your private obsession is damaging Bienvenido. Is that what you want?'

'We have to eliminate our dependency on—'

'You haven't been sworn in to the National Council yet. Think carefully what you say, and remember the oath you will be taking before the Captain. Specifically, the part about protecting this world from *all* forms of harm.'

Slvasta glared at the colonel, trying to control his temper. He had the distinct feeling Gelasis was deliberately baiting him. This was another test to see if *they* were going to allow him his seat. Democratic votes were an irrelevance to those who held the true strings of power. 'I'm going to bring it before the National Council.'

Gelasis nodded in satisfaction. 'You do that. And at the same time you keep your hotheads quiet. That's also your obligation, understand?'

'Nobody is going to be blowing anything up on my watch.' *And, Uracus, it feels good looking you in the eye and being just as deceitful as you.*

'Glad to hear it. You can have a great life, Slvasta; the rewards for people in your position are enormous. I wouldn't want you to sell yourself short.'

'I won't.'

'So what's going to happen about your engagement? Clever electioneering move that, by the way. She looked jolly pretty on your arm out there on the campaign trail. Won quite a few bachelor votes for you, I imagine.'

The change caught Slvasta by surprise. 'We said we would wait until after the election before setting a date.'

'Indeed. Then consider this: there is a whole city of opportunity opening up to you now. You should enjoy yourself for a while before making a smart choice.' The colonel leaned forwards slightly, studying Slvasta closely. 'You need a girl who will enhance your new status. After all, you do know what your little radical sweetheart did before she met you, don't you?'

'What are you talking about?'

'It's different for her class, of course; we all know that, not like Lanicia. People can judge harshly.'

'I don't understand. Bethaneve is a Tax Office clerk.'

'Of course she is. Well, I'd offer you lunch, but I have a rather pressing engagement. Dull but necessary; I'm sure you remember what responsibility is like. If not, you're going to get a swift hard reminder when you take your seat. Oh, and I forgot to say: congratulations.'

*

'We've underestimated them,' Slvasta said. 'Uracus, did we ever.' After leaving the Westergate Club he'd collected Bethaneve from the hall of records on Wahren Street, and the two of them went directly to the house in Tarleton Gardens, where Javier and Coulan were still living.

'Who?' Javier asked.

'The Captain, the First Officer. The establishment. Especially Trevene. Uracus!' He started to pace up and down the empty lounge. 'They know everything!'

'What do they know?' Coulan asked.

'He told me: Gelasis. He sat there smirking while he told me. It's a warning. They've just been laughing at us. They know it all.'

'What?' Bethaneve asked. 'Focus, please.'

Slvasta gave her a broken look. 'They know about you. I'm so sorry.'

'What do they know about me?'

'That you used to do narnik. How do they find these things?'

'The same way we know Trevene's nephew has gambling debts. That the Captain's second daughter has just had a baby and she's not sixteen yet. That Gelasis and Trevene are both members of the Travington Society. That the First Officer is a psycho nutcase. We hear whispers on the street and ask questions.'

'They know Andricea is helping us, and Tovakar, too; so they'll know about Yannrith.'

'They know the name of every party member and union member. They'll know which of them are activists. Their list of names and all the details will fill a whole floor of Trevene's offices with filing cabinets. You know the one: Fifty-Eight Grosvner Place, his secret headquarters, which extends six levels below ground, and occupies the buildings on both sides.' She went over to him and held his arm to stop him walking. 'We know them, and they *think* they know us. They *think* we are idealists trying to bring justice to the poor through the ballot box and a bit of petty agitation. They know nothing else. They don't know how extensive our cells really are. They don't know about our weapons. They certainly do not know our plans. They do not know they're about to die and we are going to sweep their whole rotten regime away.'

Slvasta looked at her, then at the other two. Seeing their calm, concerned faces, he took a long breath and nodded. 'Okay. Sorry. He was just so crudding confident.'

'He doesn't know anything else,' Coulan said. 'People always fold for him. Nobody's ever mounted a serious challenge to the palace since the Jasmine Avenue rebellion, and that was hardly threatening, not really. All they're used to are small groups of radicals and thugs up from the Shanties who don't have a clue what they're doing. The whole concept of our organization is beyond his understanding.'

'The explosion is a problem, though,' Javier said. 'Our people are getting very impatient. I'm not sure we can keep a lid on things for much longer. They want action.'

'We agreed to a month,' Coulan said.

'That we did. That would suit us. But what about all our comrades? They don't know the plan. They don't know how big this thing goes. All they see is an election where Democratic Unity finally gained some seats, and *nothing* is happening. The Captain's even put off inaugurating the National Council, which demonstrates what he thinks about democracy. We've primed thousands of people, promising them drastic change, and they're still waiting. The idiots in that level twenty-eight cell who bombed the yalseed oil company depot are going to be the least of it if we don't give the membership decisive action soon. And if that happens, if they move without us, without a coordinated plan, then it's all over. The cell network will fragment. The Captain's police and the sheriffs will swoop. We'll probably have to go into exile. The whole movement will be in ruins. We lose. The end.'

Everything Javier had said made perfect sense. But . . . still

Slvasta hesitated. If they started this, there would never be any going back – win or lose. 'Bethaneve? Can we bring it forward?'

'There's no practical reason why not. We were waiting a month to position ourselves politically, to give you some respectability in the National Council. But seeing as how we haven't got a National Council actually sitting yet, that has to be a secondary consideration now.'

'The Captain is opening the Council in three days, if nobody else sets fire to anything. Can we get phase one up and ready for that night?'

'Yes.'

'We need to leave at least a week between phases one and two,' Coulan warned. 'People have to feel the hurt from having their water supply screwed with. They need to become political. Then, once they're angry enough, we frighten them with phase two.'

'And put our people on the streets,' Javier said. He walked over to Bethaneve and Slvasta, putting his thick arms around them. Coulan joined the embrace.

'Together we are strong,' Bethaneve said.

'Together we stand,' Coulan said.

'Together we will succeed,' Javier said.

'I will never turn away from you, my true friends,' Slvasta said. He squeezed them all hard. 'Together we have the courage we need. Now, let us liberate this world.'

3

The Hevlin's orangery stretched along one side of the hotel's neat little central courtyard, where fountains played and fig trees formed a tall canopy to ward off the midday sun. The table where Kysandra sat was right next to the glass, with a gentle breeze drifting down from the open windows above. A snow-white tablecloth was laid out with shining silver cutlery, and the cut-crystal goblets sparkled in the dappled sunlight. It was Madeline who served the fish starter – smoked macod wrapped in kall leaves, and drizzled with a lime sauce.

'Enjoy,' Madeline said in a very knowing tone.

'Thank you,' Kysandra replied levelly.

'Would you like more wine?'

'Not for me.' She looked over the table at her companion.

Deavid smiled happily. 'No, thanks.'

'Madam.' Madeline gave a small bow and left.

Kysandra hoped Deavid hadn't noticed how smug Madeline had been. Every time that happened, Kysandra couldn't help wondering if Nigel's domination technique was slipping. *After all, I have finished up spending a lot of time on my back in the Hevlin's bedrooms recently – just not quite the way she and Ma intended.* The thought made her grin across the table at Deavid's handsome face. His answering smile was worshipful. They'd met five months ago. He was twenty-two, the youngest son in a family who owned a respectably sized carpentry business in Jaxtowe, fifty kilometres to the south. With Adeone's prosperity rising dramatically over the last two years, he was one of many salesmen arriving in town to seek fresh markets. He played football for the Jaxtowe team, which kept him in very good shape, and when she ran her fingers all over him his ebony skin was gorgeously smooth to the touch. Best of all, he made her laugh. His cheery, mildly disrespectful attitude was a rarity among the young men she got to meet, who were all so desperately serious would-be businessmen or entrepreneurs. All on their way up – or believing they were.

Deavid had convinced his father they needed to open an office in town, with himself as manager. And Kysandra suddenly found herself with a lot of reasons to be in Adeone, supervising the flow of goods which the industry inside the farm's compound consumed, as well as overseeing activities among the radical groups Nigel and the ANAdroids had established.

That was during the morning. Afternoons were spent with Deavid in the Hevlin's garden suite, exploring new ways the huge four-poster bed could be used to accommodate their wanton gymnastics.

'This is delicious,' he said.

'They catch macod in the freshwater lake upstream. It's quite the local speciality.'

He held up a fork with a perfectly cooked pink sliver impaled on the tip. 'Can you stay tonight?' His tongue came out slowly and licked the piece of fish off the fork.

'I could be persuaded. I have some meetings tomorrow afternoon which I can reschedule for the morning.'

'Do you really need an excuse?'

'No. I'm just being practical.'

'Of course, you wouldn't need to be practical or have excuses if I moved out to the farm. We could spend every night together then.'

She looked at his eager expression and felt her own buoyant mood start to deflate. 'Deavid . . .'

'I know: your guardian doesn't approve. Strange, considering he doesn't seem to mind you spending as much time as you want with me in town.'

'It's not that.'

'I'd really like to visit. All the wagon drivers who go out there talk about how it's practically a town in itself.'

'We have a few extra barns for engineering, that's all. Nigel's hobby is making things he hopes to sell one day, and we maintain the farm's traction engines ourselves.'

'Really? They say you have hundreds of mods working on the farm. And there's like a train of goods carts that carry stuff out there every day. Weird loads, too, crates of minerals from all over. Barrels full of Giu knows what.'

Kysandra put her knife and fork down. 'Foodstuff for the neuts, and metals for smelting. That kind of thing.'

'Look, I'm not complaining. I think it's wonderful what Nigel has done, all the trade and industry he's brought to this town. The whole region benefits. But it's as if there's a whole part of you that I'm shut out from.'

She almost groaned in dismay. No matter how many times she said at the beginning: *this is just fun, I don't want anything serious right now,* and no matter that they always instantly agreed to those terms, it always wound up with them getting more demanding and possessive. 'Isn't what we have good enough?'

'Oh, Giu, yes. I'm sorry, Kysandra. I just—'

Don't say it. Don't!

Even with her shell rock hard and revealing no hint of emotion, he must have sensed what a mess he was making of this.

'I just want to see more of you,' he finished lamely.

'I don't think there's much you haven't seen.'

He smiled, but she could see it was forced. And now the mood had gone completely. Neither of them seemed to know what to say. She considered talking about the lingerie that had arrived from Varlan, which she'd been planning on wearing for him that afternoon. That always made men happy. *But why should I always have to rescue the moment, why not him?* That was the trouble with being infected with the attitudes and outlook possessed by Commonwealth citizens; it was hard to find anyone on Bienvenido who could meet those expectations. *Perhaps we could talk about*

552

the election, how Democratic Unity won a seat on the National Council. Another glance at Deavid revealed how pointless that would be. Locals neither knew nor cared about politics in the capital. Why should they? It didn't affect them. So they believed.

Just how is he going to react to salvation? How are any of them going to cope? I can barely comprehend what it will mean, and I've been thinking about it for years.

They were finishing the fish course in mildly awkward silence when Russell 'pathed her privately. 'Gorlar's riding the message cart into town. Riding hard.'

Kysandra stopped eating straight away. The message cart wasn't due in until tomorrow. Something important must have happened for a message to be sent outside the schedule. *Great Giu, Coulan's people can't have been blown, can they? Slvasta won his seat, dammit. Everything was going perfectly.* 'I have to go,' she told Deavid.

'No! Please, I'm sorry. I shouldn't have asked to be with you at the farm, it was stupid.'

She stood up. 'This is nothing to do with that. My mother's been a pain, and I have to go and sort it out. Again.'

'Oh.' He reddened. 'Of course.'

'I'll see you tonight,' she promised.

His smile was almost nervous. There was clearly a lot he wanted to say, but held his tongue. 'Tonight, then.'

Kysandra was proud of the way she kept her shell solid. Even if the message was nothing and they spent the night together, everything was about to change. Within a month, they would have the fearsome weapons from the palace. Nigel would launch *Skylady* and attack the Void's structure. She still considered the whole mission crazy dangerous, despite his ability to reset the Void. But – oh, oh – if he was right, if he really did know everything, the Void would be no more, and Bienvenido would be free. But it all depended on events in Varlan playing out smoothly, or at least in their favour for a few days.

She waited with Russell outside the livery on the edge of town. It had a good position at the end of the newly upgraded river road which was lined with tall featherpalms. Deavid's company had been given the contract for the frame of the livery's latest stable – which wasn't the quality she'd been led to expect, but she never challenged it. *It's only for a couple more months.*

The message cart came into view round the final bend in the river road. Russell's ge-eagle had seen it five miles out, and he was right; Gorlar was riding it hard. The horse was flecked with foam, wild-eyed and galloping along as if they were being chased by wild haxhounds.

Gorlar steered it off the road's newly compacted stone surface and slowed down as the horse reached the livery's wide gates. The neat cart was Nigel's design, its narrow bodywork made out of a drosilk-reinforced resin to combine strength and lightness, forming little more than a frame with a seating sling above the axle. People had been amazed by how fast the thing could travel between Adeone and Erond, especially now the road had been relaid. They'd concluded two years back that river travel, which was the usual way of getting between the two towns, was too slow for anything urgent, so Nigel through his expanding commercial concerns had lobbied and used some mild domination on local councillors.

Now the road was level and sound, with fresh or repaired bridges offering a clean route. They'd positioned new stables in towns at reasonable intervals, so the message carts could change horses.

'The buggy express', Nigel called it.

'Ma'am,' Gorlar said as he jumped down. He was out of breath, with an exuberant look on his face at the frantic charge from Erond. Hands rummaged round in the leather satchel and produced the pale-blue envelope. 'It left Varlan yesterday,' he said proudly.

'Thank you.' Kysandra took the letter from him. The big wax seal on the back was intact. Not that it was remotely important.

'Imagine that,' Gorlar said to Russell. 'A letter from the capital here in less than two days.'

'Yeah. Imagine,' Russell said with a complete lack of interest.

'Crud!' Kysandra exclaimed, frozen in the act of opening the envelope. The letter and whatever Coulan had written was irrelevant. The paper contained a small biochip memory which her u-shadow had accessed. Coulan's message was very clear. The political situation was destabilizing; they'd been forced to bring the date forward.

'What—' Russell began.

Kysandra held her hand up, closing her eyes to think. They were going to initiate phase one when the Captain inaugurated the new National Council, and the letter had taken nearly two days to reach her. That barely left a day until the cells hit Varlan's water supplies. *A day!* And only at lunch she'd been thinking they still had several weeks left. There were few options now, but she had to choose. Time was slipping away fast, and Nigel was back at the farm, hours away.

Coulan needs confirmation that we're in position and ready to retrieve the weapons from beneath the palace. So . . .

'Right,' she snapped. 'Gorlar, get yourself a fresh horse: you're riding to Blair Farm with a letter for Nigel. Russell, same for you. I need you to be on the eight-thirty express to Varlan.'

Russell pulled a face. 'That's tight.'

'I know, so let's move it.'

'You haven't even opened the letter,' Gorlar protested. He was just one of their normal employees. Devoted to Nigel but not dominated, which left him free to question.

'I know the handwriting,' she said immediately. 'It's from an old friend, so it can only be one thing, I'm afraid. Important news. So I need you to ride as fast as you can for me. Nigel must get my letter this afternoon.'

'Right-o, ma'am. You can rely on me.' He almost saluted.

•

Kysandra had plenty of time to get changed out of the dress and into some practical jeans with a white blouse under a suede jacket, and some sturdy boots, all worn beneath a decent ankle-length coat of thin leather. Her small backpack had a few additional clothes, along with her basic kit of Commonwealth gadgets. She felt quite the adventurous traveller again.

Four hours after she'd dispatched Gorlar to the farm, she heard *it* clattering along the road. *Now this should be interesting*, she thought as she walked out of the livery.

Madeline was in the livery's yard with her, also in travelling clothes, a happy grin spreading over her face. 'He's riding it.'

'I know. Nothing else on this world makes that racket.'

They faced the road to the farm, which thanks to the ancient cedars on both sides was practically a green tunnel. The mechanical clanking and brief roars of high-pressure steam echoed off the trunks and branches. Kysandra's ex-sight found him just before he came into view. Her grin rose to match the one on Madeline's face.

Nigel was driving the steam car at about eighty kilometres an hour, with Fergus sitting in the front passenger seat. Smoke from the fire tube boiler was shooting out of the back like a grey flame before swirling away in its wake. The wheels with their fat low-pressure tyres were a blur, giving the suspension a hefty workout. Two horses trotting sedately down the road were immediately spooked, and bolted through the line of cedars. Carts and wagons swerved out of the way. Kysandra could feel a great deal of ex-sight swelling out from the town to scan the extraordinary vehicle.

It was beautiful to behold. She'd spent hours in the workshop over the last five months, helping him with the early models. The work was nothing a mod-dwarf couldn't do, screwing parts together, hammering, even painting the bodywork, but she so wanted to be a part of it. The steam car was probably the most advanced piece of machinery to have been built on Bienvenido for a thousand years. They'd constructed two prototypes, testing the whole boiler system, then made three working models.

'Dead-end technology,' Nigel had called them. 'Just like airships and paddle steamers. But romantics never give up on them. You can always find enthusiasts building them somewhere in the Commonwealth. They're really quite evocative, like something from an alternative history.'

She was almost offended by him calling the splendid car a dead end. Driving it round the farm compound had been exhilarating. It had two seats in the front and three in the back, all of which could be covered by a retractable canvas hood if it started to rain.

The car rolled into the livery yard, startling the horses in their stables. Its weight dug deep ruts in the damp ground as it came to a halt. Nigel hurried out, long brown coat swirling round his legs, pushing his goggles up onto his forehead to reveal clean circles of skin round his eyes; the rest of his face was caked in soot and hot oily grime spat out by the engine. 'Right, what's happened?'

'Message from Coulan,' she told him. 'The radicals are getting restless. They've had to bring the date forwards.'

'When?'

'Phase one is planned to start tomorrow.'

'Hell. That doesn't give us any time.'

'Don't worry. I've sent Russell on the express.'

'Which express?'

'The eight-thirty to Varlan. It'll get into the city early tomorrow morning.'

Nigel looked at her for a long moment. 'Okay. And what is Russell going to do when he arrives?'

'He's carrying a letter for Coulan—'

'*Yes!* Saying what?'

She frowned at him. 'Confirming we'll be there, and to activate the external groups to assist phase two. Russell will also tell Akstan to get everything ready for us in Dios, and then he'll contact our station chief in Willesden to make sure the Southern City Line is protected.'

Nigel's shell attenuated slightly, allowing her to sense the lofty amusement colouring his thoughts – along with a steely thread of pride. 'You said yes, then?'

'What?'

He put his hands on her shoulder, giving her a steady look. 'You said yes? You told Coulan to go ahead with the revolution?'

'Well, obviously. Russell absolutely had to make the eight-thirty express. I didn't have any time to consult with you. Why?'

'You realize there's no turning back now? You've fired the

starting pistol – a shot that will be heard all over Bienvenido. Actually, all over the galaxy.'

'Oh. Yes, I suppose so.'

He kissed her on the forehead. 'That's my girl. No doubts. No hesitation.'

'Nigel, it wasn't a decision. This is what we've been preparing for since we visited the Desert of Bone.'

'Quite right,' he said briskly. 'Madeline, the car needs coal and water; get the livery people to bring it out – quickly. Fergus will show them what to do. Then you'll be coming with us.'

'Yes, sir.'

'We'll stay in Dios overnight, and load our equipment onto tomorrow morning's express.'

'That's what I thought,' Kysandra said. 'Akstan will deliver everything from the warehouses to Dios station.' She glanced out of the livery yard. People were drifting along the street outside, anxious to get a real glimpse of the amazing steam car. A lot of them were kids. 'There's really no going back now, is there?'

'No.'

*

It began a few minutes after midnight. The steam engine in the Holderness Avenue pump house suddenly lost pressure in one of its pistons, stalling the massive flywheel it turned. The cut-off valves worked perfectly, allowing steam to escape from the boiler, averting any kind of dangerous pressure build-up. The pump slowly rattled to a halt. Water pressure fell to zero across the whole district.

In the Hither Green Road pump house it was the pump itself which broke, its bearings seizing and disintegrating from the grit that contaminated the lubrication oil. Chunks of glowing metal exploded across the big hall, embedding themselves in the stone walls and punching clean through the roof. Pressure surges burst several feed pipes, sending water jetting out. A few minutes later, it poured into the idling engine's firebox, extinguishing it in a blast of steam that shattered all the windows. Water continued to gush out, cascading down the road outside.

Chertsy Road pump house saw the engine regulator fail, allowing the pistons to increase speed, turning the pump faster and faster. The pressure in the pipes outside increased dramatically. Junctions sprang leaks, sending water fountaining up through the cobbles, breaking the valves on domestic tanks.

It was a domino effect that had been meticulously plotted. No one incident was enough to wreck Varlan's water utility network, but the surges and dips had a cumulative result, affecting subsequent stations, forcing them to either shut down or suffer severe damage.

As pump house demand across the city fell drastically, the Watling, Highbrook and Ruslip reservoirs all had their sluice gates opened to maintain the correct levels. They were supposed to open only a few inches, but instead they kept going until they were fully open. Huge jets of water thundered out. As the small nightshift crews tried to shut them again, the mechanisms broke, jamming the gates in that position. Surge waves ploughed along the emergency culverts down towards the Colbal. But the culverts merged, and they'd never been designed to cope with three simultaneous releases. Water foamed up over the lips of the culverts, turning streets into streams, flooding into terraces and offices and factories.

By six o'clock in the morning, two thirds of Varlan was without fresh running water, and the reservoir sluice discharges had inundated the lower boroughs next to the river. Raw effluent, flushed out of the sewer pipes, bobbed along on the overflow, drifting into buildings on the eddies and swirls.

*

'It is the radicals!' the councillor for the Durnsford constituency declared, glaring at Slvasta from his position beside the First Speaker's podium. 'I say the sheriffs should round them up and send the lot of them to the mines.'

He was given a rousing cheer from across the tremendous marble chamber. Bienvenido's National Council building was centred on the vast amphitheatre where councillors sat in tiers behind huge wooden desks to debate and scrutinize legislation. The walls were supported by thick fluted columns and hung with huge ancient oil paintings that depicted times from the world's first millennium. Statues of past Captains and First Speakers gazed down from their high alcoves on the six hundred councillors. Five hundred and ninety-nine of them were members of Citizens' Dawn. But, as Slvasta had discovered during the Captain's opening ceremony, that didn't actually mean uniformity. The chamber was alive with ever-shifting alliances clamouring for their 'fair share' of the national budget. Town against countryside, finance and industry, regions, the Varlan caucus, trains against boats, farming, the regiments. They all had their interests which had to be protected, urgent projects that needed funding, for which they required support. It was actually a lot more democratic (or at least balanced) than Slvasta had realized. That first day, he'd been approached by five separate factions, all eager to have him vote in favour of their bill in return for support on anything he wished to introduce to the Council.

But right now, differences had been put aside so they could all condemn him. He dropped the fist-sized red ball into the cup at the front of his desk, indicating that he wished to address the chamber.

The First Speaker, on the floor of the amphitheatre, rose from his ornate onyx throne. 'Representative for Langley has the floor; pray silence and respect.'

Slvasta got neither as he walked down the aisle to stand beside the First Speaker's podium.

'Silence!' the First Speaker's voice and 'path declared across the chamber.

'Mr Speaker.' Slvasta bowed to the podium, as was tradition. He stared round at the ranks of desks, most of which had the yellow ball of challenge in their cups. The contempt and scorn radiating down on him was a psychic storm. 'My honourable colleague from Durnsford has levelled a serious charge. I really don't care that he slanders me with association; however, he does immense wrong to the people who simply speak up for a better life. He claims radicals are responsible for the calamity in this great capital city of ours. Could he perhaps name which pump house the sheriffs have confirmed was sabotaged? Of course he cannot, because we all know there has been no such declaration. We are also aware of the perilous state the city's water utilities have been in for a great many years. Have the companies who own this precious utility which is vital to all of us, rich and poor alike, improved their pipes and pumps in the last ten years? Have they heeded the pleas of their engineers for funds and more repairs? Have their vast profits been invested wisely in new facilities that would alleviate any problem such as we now face? Has there been a debate or inquiry by this esteemed chamber in the matter by the very members who now claim to know so much about pipes and engines and reservoirs? Of course not. For complacency has become Bienvenido's watchword – an example sadly set by this chamber. And for which this chamber must take responsibility.'

The torrent of vocal and 'pathed abuse was overwhelming. The First Speaker had to hold up the gavel of silence for over a minute before the honourable representatives quietened down.

'I repeat my question,' Slvasta said when the noise subsided. 'Can you name an act of sabotage? No. This was a catastrophe waiting to happen. I say to you, my honourable colleagues, don't try to cast blame outside; instead look where it truly lies. Any impartial inquiry will find where the fault for this disaster actually falls. If arrests are to be made, it should be among those who own the water utilities, whose uncaring greed is responsible.' He bowed again to the First Speaker and made his way back up the aisle. This time there was no jeering, only sullen glances. Several of the yellow challenge balls were removed.

'Brilliant,' Bethaneve's 'path reached him as he sat behind his desk. 'You smacked it right back at them. Everybody who's receiving the gifting from the Council clerk will know you're the people's champion now.'

Next to the First Speaker's podium, the councillor for Wurzen was demanding that the regions should not be taxed to pay for setting the city to rights. Slvasta watched him with growing respect

– someone who was trying to protect his constituents. 'I think it takes more than one speech to establish that.'

'It was the perfect start we wanted.'

'Besides, who bothers with the gifting from in here? Watching mod-spiders excrete their drosilk is less boring.'

'Stop being so negative. The pamphlets will be all over this. Uracus, Slvasta, you need to focus.'

'Yes,' he sighed. 'I know.'

*

Varlan was the hub of all four of the continent's major train lines; the Great North-Western Line, the Southern City Line, the Eastern Trans-Continental Line and the Grand South-Western Line; each ran out of the city in rough alignment with the relevant compass point. For all their prominence, passenger trains only formed fifteen per cent of the traffic; the rest of it was freight trains, unnoticed by the majority of the residents. The trade they generated was phenomenal, bringing in raw material for the factories, then exporting finished goods out to the furthest province. They were the city's economic arteries, as well as supplying most of the food to markets and homes. Just how essential they were to Varlan's survival had become obvious to Slvasta when the Josi bridge was damaged. The rail lines were a terrible weakness; anyone who could control the flow of goods in and out of the city could dictate their own terms. Of course, the government knew that as well, which was why any such attempt would be met with a swift and extreme response. What was needed, then, was a blockage which took time to repair – a repair which could be prolonged even further with small strategic strikes.

The cells chosen were from the top layers of the network: people who had been recruited right at the start, those who had proved themselves to be loyal time and again, as well as being totally committed. Weapons caches were finally broken open, and explosives distributed. Nine groups met up for the first time in the late afternoon five days after Varlan's water supplies were disrupted. Each of them took a cart out of the capital, riding them to railway bridges, not just on the four main lines but on the nearby branch lines that could be used as alternative routes into Varlan.

After darkness, they crept across the supports and arches, placing bundles of explosives precisely in the places they'd been told – locations that *Skylady* had worked out were the maximum load points. At two o'clock in the morning, fuses were lit. Ten minutes later, explosions crippled seven bridges.

News seeped into the city as the dawn cast a crisp light across the buildings and waterlogged streets. As before, it was markets such as the Wellfield that alerted friends and business colleagues to the absence of trains. Ex-sight began to scan round, perceiving marshalling yards full of the trains that should be heading out. Railway workers were summoned in early, and packed into special trains that headed cautiously along the tracks. Head office staff were called in and swiftly dispatched by horse and cab to further assess the damage. The chief sheriff of every borough was roused; they converged on the Justice Ministry offices, along with senior government officials and Trevene's lieutenant. By seven o'clock in the morning all of Varlan knew the rail bridges north, east and west of the city had been sabotaged. No natural collapse, no derailment blocking the lines, no water surge washing away supports, no structural failure of ageing structures. They'd been blown up. Giftings from people who'd travelled out and returned were shared across the whole city, confirming the destruction. The only communications left open were the roads, the river and the Southern City Line.

'I cannot get anyone to respond,' Bethaneve said in frustration. She was sitting at the kitchen table in Number Sixteen Jaysfield Terrace, fingers pressed against her temple as she sent 'path after 'path into their network. 'I just don't understand what's happened.'

'The trains from Willesden station are leaving on schedule,' Slvasta confirmed, as 'paths came slinking through the complex network strung across the city, relaying messages directly from five separate cell members at Willesden, sent there specifically to tell them what the Southern City Line managers were doing and saying. 'The company's been 'pathing out general reassurances since six o'clock. Three teams of sheriffs have been sent to guard the closest bridges.'

'Uracus! They can't have intercepted all our demolition squads – they just can't. That makes no sense. Trevene either knows all about us or he doesn't. He wouldn't have arrested just two squads and left the rest alone. Where are they?'

'Maybe running for cover. Or they had some kind of accident. It was a lot of explosives they had piled up on those carts.'

'I don't like it.' For the first time, Bethaneve actually showed uncertainty. 'We would have heard about it if the carts exploded.'

'So they didn't explode. They threw a wheel, or a horse spooked and bolted. Who knows?'

'I need to know!'

He wanted to tell her to calm down, but that would be a mistake, he knew. She was running on raw nerves now. And terrified. 'We'll know soon enough. At least they haven't been arrested.'

'How do you know that?' she shouted.

'Because we haven't been arrested.'

'All right. Sorry.'

'It's okay.' He reached across the table and took her hand. 'I have to go.'

She nodded, her hair falling down over her face to hide a forlorn expression. 'Be careful.'

'I will, but I need to be at the National Council.'

'Everyone's in place. They'll gift your message out uncensored.'

They embraced. He could feel her trembling, and assumed she knew he was equally scared behind the hardest shell he'd ever manifested. His ex-sight perceived Andricea, Coulan and Yannrith waiting for them in Number Sixteen's entrance hall below. 'Come on,' he said gently. 'Let's go. I want to know you're at the safe house before I make the denouncement.'

'Let's hope it is safe.'

'Ha! Now who's the cynic?'

She smiled and hugged him closer. '*Please* be careful.'

'You too.'

It took a long moment for them to let go of each other.

At the bottom of the stairs, Coulan and Yannrith looked equally pensive, while Andricea looked positively gleeful.

'How's it going?' Slvasta asked. He and Bethaneve had been so busy with the rail bridges and preparing his National Council appearance they'd left the other half of the operation to Coulan and Javier.

'Distribution's been running pretty smoothly,' Coulan said. 'The caches were opened at four o'clock this morning, and we've armed the majority of grade threes.'

'What are grade threes?' Slvasta asked.

'The comrades we believe can be trusted with weapons,' Bethaneve said as they went out into the road where two cabs were waiting. 'After all, we can't supply every grunt on the street. That would be anarchy, and we want precision.'

'Right,' Slvasta frowned. Something she'd said bothered him, and he couldn't figure out what or why. 'What about the snipers?' He hated the idea of that – it was cold murder – but the others had talked him round.

'They're all active and ready,' Yannrith said.

'Okay, then.' He looked at Bethaneve as she stood poised beside the cab – wearing a simple burgundy-red dress, her hair held in place with clips, those broad features burning with concern – working hard to memorize the image perfectly. Because if this all went straight to Uracus, it would be the last time . . . He grinned at his own pessimism.

She mistook it for encouragement. 'See you tonight, my love.'

'See you tonight.'

Coulan and Andricea climbed into the cab with Bethaneve. Slvasta shut the door, and the horse started off down the street at a fast pace, with Andricea's mod-bird zipping through the air high above. He and Yannrith got into their cab, fuzzing the interior.

'Crud!' Yannrith grunted.

'I know. Every day I have to ask myself if this is real.'

'It doesn't get any more real, captain. Not today.'

Their cab made good time across the city. It was a cloudless cobalt sky vaulting the capital, with the hot sun glaring down. Slvasta didn't know if that was auspicious or not. The morning's river mist began to clear urgently, evaporating out of the wider boulevards and avenues. It exposed the deep puddles and long streams running down the middle of streets, still lingering six days after the pipes had burst and the reservoirs discharged into the city. The water was dank and sluggish now, steaming slightly under the morning sunlight. Whole boroughs were still without fresh water; those living closest to the river took buckets to the quayside and hauled them back home just like people from the Shanties. The northern boroughs had laid on emergency tank carts, rationing each household to two buckets a day. The silt and filth that had been swept along by the tide of water had been deposited in rooms and along roads as the levels fell. Borough council work crews struggled to clear the stinking mess away. Fire carts were helping to drain basements and cellars with their mobile pumps. People were starting to mutter about how it would have been so much easier if they had mod-apes and dwarfs to help. Every engineer employed by the water utilities was working sixteen-hour days as they strove to repair the network and restore supplies.

Two days ago, Captain Philious himself had toured the worst afflicted areas. He even climbed down from his carriage to talk with flooded householders and the owners of ruined businesses, offering sympathy. 'I know exactly what it's like: we have no water in the Palace, either.' Which was a politically astute lie; the Palace had its own freshwater spring. He also promised to punish 'those responsible' and get the city and National Council to pass much stricter regulation so this could never happen again.

The atmosphere of misery and resentment pervading Varlan was as thick and toxic as the stench of the sewage layer clogging the streets. And now with news of the rail bridges percolating between the residents, uncertainty had supplanted stoic misery. Several of the large wholesale markets had shut their gates that morning; without trains coming in, they simply had no fresh food to sell. All the food in city warehouses dramatically increased in price and became difficult to obtain. Retailers that did open sold out fast, although most kept their doors closed. Crowds began to gather at the borough markets, their vocal complaints escalating fast at the sight of empty stalls. Sheriffs arrived, to be goaded by strategically positioned cell members. What started as worry and dissatisfaction began to grow into something more ugly.

As the shock of the transport failures sank in, so businesses large and small began to realize the true extent of the problem. A lot of private 'paths began to flash out. Banks found queues materializing outside before they opened. Sheriffs were called to keep order as the queues steadily lengthened. The first customers that rushed in as soon as nervous clerks opened the doors demanded huge cash withdrawals. Banks didn't keep large amounts of cash at individual branches. On the emergency instructions of the Treasury, managers were told to limit withdrawals to fifty silver shillings per customer. Nice middle-class people got very cross about that. Arrests were made. Branches tried to shut, only to find people forcing the doors open. More requests for sheriffs were hurriedly 'pathed.

By ten o'clock, Varlan's mighty economy was grinding to a noisy and unprecedented halt. Real fear was beginning to gain momentum. It was everything the revolution wanted. Fear was a state easy to exploit.

'Did you know about the grading?' Slvasta asked as the cab arrived at the central government area. Here the avenues were clear and clean, untouched by the flood and disruption – deliberately so, to help encourage resentment.

'Captain?' Yannrith said.

'That we'd graded cell members to find the ones we could trust?'

'I knew instructions had gone out to help decide who to give the guns to. Bethaneve is right; you can't just give them to everybody. Why?'

He shook his head. 'I didn't know. Or I forgot; Giu knows, there's been a lot of planning. Coulan chose his palace militia

567

carefully. I helped him and Javier with the bridge teams – we can't have mistakes with the critical parts of the plan. There are so many details . . .' Yet he knew that wasn't what bothered him.

Two kilometres past the palace, Byworth Avenue ended at First Night Square – a huge expanse of cobbles encircled by snow-white riccalon trees, where it was said the passengers of Captain Cornelius set up camp the night they landed on Bienvenido. The circular National Council building stood at the far end, dominating the whole square with its eight blue-stone fresco rings wrapped round the rust-red brick wall. The green copper dome on top shone a hazy lime in the morning sun. Native birds sat perched on the lip, staring down at the large crowd milling round the square. Over two thousand people had already gathered, mostly men, and definitely no children. The instructions which had come buzzing through the cell network as they woke had been very clear about that. No one wanted another Haranne incident.

The grim psychic aura they gave off matched their demeanour. It was stifling, as if the air temperature had risen ten degrees. Cabs delivering National Council members to the morning's emergency debate were booed and jostled with teekay, making their horses skittish. Badly unnerved representatives hurried into the sanctuary of their grand building, carefully avoiding glancing at the forest of banners with crude slogans and cartoonish images of the Captain.

The horse pulling Slvasta's cab grew panicky as it trotted round the road at the edge of the square. Slvasta dropped his fuzz, allowing ex-sight to pervade the inside of the cab. It was a perception that was quickly gifted round the square. The cheering began.

He opened the door, and grinned round at the smiling faces, raising his arm. 'Thank you for coming,' he 'pathed wide. 'Thank you for adding weight to my lone voice in this nest of ugly bussalores. I'm here to tell the First Speaker and Citizens' Dawn that their way, their privilege and arrogance, is coming to an end. They must listen to you, they must act upon your grievances. You have a RIGHT to be heard. They cannot ignore you forever. Today, they will be made to LISTEN.'

A renewed wave of cheering swept over First Night Square like a gale, breaking upon the walls of the National Council building. Slvasta pumped his fist into the air, then hopped down and strode through the main entrance. Yannrith walked alongside him, motioning the Council guards away. They were mostly ceremonial officers, positions awarded to troopers retiring from regiments so they might spend their last decades in fine scarlet and navy-blue tunics, living in neat apartments and being given three full meals a day before accepting Guidance. They certainly had no contingency to repel large angry mobs.

'Sheriffs are on their way, captain,' the master at arms told Slvasta as he made his way across the ante-chamber. 'Don't worry.'

He nodded briefly, and carried on towards the central amphitheatre.

'Slvasta,' Bethaneve private 'pathed. 'The Meor is mobilizing.'

'Crud.' He couldn't help a worried glance at Yannrith. 'Are you sure?'

'Yes. They're coming out of their barracks. Two ferries have been taken out of public service, and they're docked on the south bank waiting for them. The crowds must have frightened the First Speaker. There's a lot of discontent coming to the boil in the city.'

'It's supposed to, but . . . Crud, I thought we'd have more time.'

'Don't worry. I'll deploy some grade three comrades to the quayside to pin them down. We have several allocated for it. They won't get into the centre of the city today.'

Slvasta knew they had contingencies for everything – well, every screw-up they could think of. *So stick with the plan and trust your people.* 'Okay.'

He made it into the huge amphitheatre, where several hundred councillors were taking their seats. But it was by no means a full session. The disapproval of the crowd outside was penetrating the thick walls, contributing to the worried and sombre mood gripping the tiers of desks. Nobody knew what to make of the city's economy crashing.

Down on the floor of the amphitheatre, Slvasta saw Crispen,

Trevene's lieutenant, in a huddle with the First Speaker, who still hadn't taken his polished throne on the podium. The two of them were having an intense discussion. The First Speaker glanced up at Slvasta, then hurriedly away.

'Congratulations,' someone said.

Slvasta turned round to the tier of desks behind his. Newbon, the councillor for Wurzen, inclined his head. 'That was a nice chunk of theatre outside. Well played.'

'Thank you.'

'What comes next?'

'I meant what I said. I will give those people a voice in here. They can be denied no longer.'

'Quite right. Though I'm curious that they have an opinion on bridges being blown up.'

'Suppressed anger finds many outlets.'

'You really do have integrity, don't you?'

'I try.'

Newbon pressed his lips together and 'pathed privately, 'Be careful. There are powerful people watching you today.'

'Thank you,' Slvasta said quietly. He took his seat, with Yannrith sitting behind him.

It wasn't just the emotions of the crowd outside which could be felt in the chamber; their chanting too was audible, faint but ever present as a disconcerting tremble in the air.

'Sheriffs are moving into First Night Square,' Yannrith murmured.

Slvasta opened his shell to receive various giftings, and watched through another's eyes as long carts filled with squads of sheriffs began to arrive at the back of the National Council building. On the other side of the Colbal, the Meor regiment was marching down to the jetty where the ferries *Alfreed* and *Lanuux* were berthed, waiting for them. 'Uracus,' he muttered. 'There must be over a thousand of them. Their full strength.'

'They can't cover the whole city,' Bethaneve 'pathed privately. 'There are trouble spots erupting everywhere. People are angry and afraid. We were . . . more successful than we expected.'

The First Speaker took to his throne on the podium and held up the gavel of silence. 'I call this honourable assembly to order. You have been summoned to debate the unprecedented acts of sabotage perpetrated against the main railway lines vital to this city, and how we are to advise the Captain to respond. I call upon the representative for Feltham, who sits upon the Captain's security committee, to give us an account of the night's events.'

'There's still nothing from our Southern City Line teams,' Bethaneve 'pathed as the councillor walked down to the podium. 'I'm worried.'

'They must have been arrested.'

'There's nothing from any sheriff informant about that. They've vanished. There were twenty people and a lot of explosives on those carts. How can they just vanish?'

'I don't know,' he admitted.

'Our agents confirm the bridges are still up, and now heavily guarded.'

'Uracus! Should we send more teams, take out bridges further down the line?'

'I talked that through with Coulan. We can't see the point, not now. Trade is completely paralysed, everything is shutting down. We've got the anarchy we wanted.'

'Okay. I'm about to make my stand.'

The Feltham representative was finishing his account. It was clear that he knew only the barest details, just which bridges were down, and how it was triggering great economic hardship to everyone, not only the merchants. 'So I would ask my honourable colleagues to unequivocally condemn those who perpetrated this appalling crime against all of us. The sheriffs and other govern-ment forces should have full authority to search out and appre-hend these terrorists, and sentence them to take immediate Guidance. Let them swiftly discover for themselves if the Heart will accept them, or if they are bound for Uracus.'

'They've done it,' Javier private 'pathed as the Feltham repre-sentative walked up the aisle to his desk. 'The Captain signed a suspension order. It's starting to arrive in government offices.

Trevene's people are already in sheriff stations, telling them who to arrest.'

'Do we have names?' Slvasta asked as he dropped the red ball into his desk cup.

'Union officials and Democratic Unity officers. They're coming for us.'

'Make sure that goes out across the network. Tell every cell member.'

'We're on it.'

'I call the representative for Yeats to address Council,' the First Speaker announced.

Slvasta stood up at the same time as the Yeats councillor started walking down the aisle. Councillors behind their desks looked quite shocked.

'Captain Slvasta,' the First Speaker exclaimed loudly, 'you have not been called.'

'Nor am I likely to be,' Slvasta declared. 'For I know who is responsible.'

Outside, the crowd in First Night Square was cheering.

The representative from Yeats had stopped halfway down the aisle, looking uncertainly at the First Speaker. 'I yield the floor to the representative from Langley,' he said.

Slvasta ignored him and walked over to the First Speaker's podium. Every councillor was silent, leaving the muffled cheers and chanting of the crowd as the only sound in the cavernous amphitheatre.

Slvasta paused, and slowly looked round the tiers of desks, his uncompromising stare demanding the attention of everyone in the amphitheatre. 'I lost my arm in defence of this world. It is a small price to pay for ensuring another nest of Fallers was thwarted. But as to why I lost it? That is down to a multitude of compromises made by my regiment – compromises to the front-line budget necessary so barracks officers could live a comfortable life. Compromises which continue to this day. Compromises supported by the Treasury, desperate to maintain the status quo. Hundreds of people in New Angeles lost their lives – *no*, that is how the gazettes report it. Hundreds of people in New Angeles were *eaten alive* by a nest. Why? Because the Captain's uncle was a corrupt, debauched bastard who cared only for his own welfare, and that of his family cronies.'

Cries of protest rose from the desks, 'pathed calls of *shame* swatted against his shell. Slvasta remained resolute, buoyed by the swell of approval from the massed minds outside.

'*Alfreed* and *Lanuux* just started across the river,' Bethaneve reported. 'I've got some armed comrades in place on the quayside, but I don't know how long they can delay the Meor.'

'Almost done,' Slvasta 'pathed back to her. He caught sight of Yannrith, who had risen from his seat. He nodded at Slvasta.

'The water utilities debacle?' Slvasta declared angrily. 'Not a product of sabotage, as conveniently declared by this very assembly. No. It was caused by greed, by the privileged caring only for themselves. And now, now we are summoned here to make grand empty statements denouncing the destruction of the rail bridges. Well. I. Will. Not. This desperate act was inevitable. This act is a direct result of the oppression, both political and economic, imposed by our government. You crush hope. Yes, you! You destroy opportunity. You eradicate dignity. You do all that so you may maintain your filthy bigoted anti-democratic society. You leave the rest of us no choice. We are not allowed to protest. Any complaint sees you marked down for life as a troublemaker by that tyrannical murderer Trevene. Those explosions today, they are the true voice of the people. And they are loud voices – voices you will not be allowed to ignore, voices you cannot smother, not this time. This is the day the disenfranchised, the weak and the persecuted find their will and say: *No more. You will listen to us!* You ask who is responsible for blowing up the bridges, for hurting the government in the only place it values – its wealth, the method by which it maintains control? I tell you: it is *you*. You: the rich, degenerate, privileged filth. And for that, for your eternal crime against this beautiful world of ours: I denounce you. I will have no part of this assembly, which I declare unlawful.'

The shouts of fury from the desks rose above the jubilant clamour from outside.

'A new parliament will be formed!' Slvasta shouted and 'pathed above the bedlam. 'The Captain's dictatorship will end. I ask all decent people of this world to join me in a democratic congress to establish a fresh constitution. Together we can build a new world based on fairness and democracy. Join me. Everyone.'

His rallying cry was gifted across the unquiet city. Supporters, goaded by cell members everywhere, added their emotional blasts of enthusiasm and confirmation to the psychic maelstrom.

Slvasta turned and gave the First Speaker an obscene finger gesture. Then he opened his mouth to deliver a final insult—

An explosive in the keel of the *Alfreed* detonated when the ferry was halfway across the three-kilometre span of the Colbal. The burst of terror and shock from the seven hundred Meor troopers on board washed across Varlan, swamping the giftings from the National Council. Everybody was suddenly there, on board as the ferry broke in two uneven halves. Through multiple viewpoints everybody seemed to be hurled about by giant forces, slamming them into bulkheads and decks. Lucky ones were tossed overboard to be engulfed by brown river water, arms thrashing frantically as saturated clothes abruptly seemed to be made of lead. People felt them open their mouths to scream, felt the water rushing in, felt them choking. Those still alive on board were over-whelmed by giant waves of water seething through the decks as the halves of the boat sank with incredible speed. The boiler plunged below the surface, and exploded in a giant plume of steam and spume, its blast wave pummelling the hysterical survivors struggling to stay afloat.

The Meor troopers on the *Lanuux* were watching in horror as their squadmates floundered in the treacherous surging water; they started to combine their teekay to pull people from the river. A second explosive blew the *Lanuux*'s hull open beneath the waterline, though it didn't succeed in breaking the ship in half. Thick river water surged in, geysering up through the deck hatches as the ferry rolled alarmingly and began to sink. The aether was filled with anguish and fear as the *Lanuux* slid down, portside first. Troopers jumped to safety, only to be sucked under by the fierce swirling currents of water created by the descending hull. River water slammed into the *Lanuux*'s boiler. The explosion heaved the ruined hull up out of the river, echoing the death throes of some giant creature. It quickly slipped back under, pulling dozens of helpless troopers with it.

Within minutes, both ferries had fallen below perception, leaving the lethal whirl-currents of their descent stirring the surface. Over two hundred troopers were still straining to stay afloat. They were the ones who'd successfully shed their equipment and weapons. Now they had to battle the inordinately fast flow of the Colbal itself. Dangerous undercurrents belied the smooth surface, tugging more to their deaths, their minds gushing out the atrocious sensation of drowning for all to perceive. Desperate panic clogged the aether, reinforcing the feeble screams that washed across the banks on both sides. All around them, ferries and barges and fishing boats tooted whistles and horns as they converged on the survivors. Varlan perceived every nuance of their weakening battle against the devouring water in stunned horror as the whole disaster swept rapidly downstream.

'What the crud happened?' Slvasta demanded as he and Yannrith hurried out of the National Council building by a small lower level service door – an exit route they'd scouted weeks ago.

'I don't know,' a mortified Bethaneve 'pathed back. 'It wasn't us, Slvasta, I swear on Giu itself. We didn't plan this!'

'Fucking Uracus! There were fifteen hundred people on those ferries.'

'Fifteen hundred armed troopers,' Javier 'pathed. 'Deploying to kill us.'

'Did you do this?'

'No.'

'Who? Who could plan such an atrocity?'

'I don't know, but it is a considerable help to us. And people, smart people, will want to know why the Meor was coming over the river. Don't ignore such gifts.'

'Uracus. It just seems . . . wrong.'

'There is no good way to die. What we have started will kill many more.'

'I know.' Slvasta and Yannrith slipped through the door, into the bright morning light. A cab was waiting, driven by a cell member. They got in and fuzzed themselves. The driver set off down Breedon Avenue.

Giftings from cell members in First Night Square showed the sheriffs moving round the National Council building, their faces angry, thoughts eager for revenge, for vengeance.

'It's starting,' Bethaneve 'pathed in wonder and dread.

'Then we must control it,' Slvasta replied. Strangely, after all his doubts and hesitancy, he had never been more certain than he was now. He 'pathed to the members of the level one cells.

'The code is: Avendia. This is our day, comrades. Be bold. Be strong. Together we will succeed. Go now. Liberate yourselves. Reclaim our world.'

4

Bethaneve's elites weren't entirely made up of quick-witted observers and infiltrators and scouts; they didn't all dart about the city watching and gathering information. Over the last few months as the group's plans for the day of the revolution came together she'd quietly gathered up a few of Coulan's rejects for herself. Not bad people, just possibles he'd rejected for final inclusion in his militia, the teams that would storm the palace and Fifty-Eight Grosvner Place. But still good people. Tough people who could handle weapons, who weren't afraid of violence, nor of carrying out orders fainter hearts might baulk at.

There was something Bethaneve needed to do when the great day came. It would benefit the revolution – they'd even included it in their plans. But she had to be completely certain, and the only way that could happen was if she did it herself.

Coulan had been right. Explosives (unobtrusively acquired from the railway bridge teams) blew the hinges on the Faller Research Institute's sturdy doors without any trouble. It was just one more detonation in a city plagued by fire and violence. Nobody really noticed. It barely distracted Bethaneve, she kept sending her messages into the network, marshalling the ecstatic comrades, keeping them on track. It didn't matter where she was, just that she kept on 'pathing. Slvasta, Coulan and Javier all had their own objectives, and were busy leading their teams to achieve them. Coulan the palace, Javier the financial district,

Slvasta the government institutions. They all believed she was sitting safely at the safe house, directing their comrades.

Guarded by her elites, she walked through the short smoke-filled tunnel and into the institute's barren courtyard. Professor Gravin came out to meet her while his staff cowered nervously inside. He didn't rush, but certainly managed to thrust his massive bulk forwards in an impressive fashion. 'What have you done?' he yelled. 'Those gates must never be broken. The risk! Do you understand the risk?'

Bethaneve marched right up to the huge man and smacked him hard across his rubbery cheek.

He stared at her in shock. The blow was so fast, so unexpected he hadn't even spun a protective shell. 'What? Who are you?'

'I am in charge of this institute now, professor,' she told him. 'I am going to ask you some questions. You will answer them without your shell so I can see the truth in your thoughts. Every time you refuse to answer a question, my people will shoot one of your colleagues.'

He gaped in fear as the armed elites jogged past him and started to enter the institute's main building.

'Please,' he moaned. 'Please understand, the work we conduct here is the most valuable thing on Bienvenido. We are not political, we are scientists; we will work with whoever is in charge, but you cannot destroy the institute. You would endanger the whole world, every human alive depends on us even though they never know it.'

'Question one,' she said relentlessly. 'What happens to the prisoners Trevene delivers to you?'

Professor Gravin swallowed hard. 'Oh crud,' he whispered. 'It wasn't my idea. I swear on Giu itself, it wasn't me.'

*

The stench was noxious, thick enough that Bethaneve half expected to see it as a thick rancid miasma contaminating the air. She'd spent the first ten minutes in the pit room almost gagging as she tried to get used to it. She never would, she knew. The reek would stay with her for the rest of her life, as would the memory of what caused it. But she stayed there, resolute, standing beside the railings that guarded the deep rectangular pit cut into the naked rock many centuries ago. The true heart of the Faller Research Institute.

Her elites brought him in almost an hour after they'd blown the gates open. A figure with a hood over his head, hands cuffed behind his back, moving with difficulty. The beating they'd given him hadn't broken anything too important, although his fancy, expensive clothes were grubby and torn, bloodied in several places.

They positioned him carefully in front of the open gate. His shaking body became still then as he guessed where he was.

Bethaneve's teekay removed the hood from his head. Aothori blinked, and glanced round. His jaws were clenched, muscle cords standing proud as the collar of braided etor vine assaulted his throat. But even now, here on the edge of the pit, that terrible arrogance was undiminished.

'I know you,' he 'pathed.

And for the first time she didn't tremble at the sight of him. 'Good. I wondered if you would. There have been so many like me, haven't there?'

'Oh yes, now I remember: the silver man's present. He chose well, as I recall.'

'I hated the doctors and nurses who treated me afterwards. They didn't deserve that hatred. They were good people. It took me a long time to realize that, to accept there were still good people in this world. And now I've gathered them to me. Enough to overwhelm and obliterate you and everything you have.'

'Self-justification, the refuge of the weak. And I know how weak you truly are. I have seen everything you are, I tasted your every precious thought. It was pitiful, as all your kind are.'

'And yet here we are.'

'Because you copy me. Because you admire my power, my strength. You worship me now, as you did before. And secretly you know that to replace me, you must first become me. Will you ever admit that to yourself, do you think? Or will the knowledge break you?'

'Mad to the very end,' Bethaneve said ruefully. She put her hand between his shoulder blades – and pushed hard.

*

The splendid ge-eagle drifted on a thermal high above Varlan, soaring above the disturbed flocks of native birds, unseen by the mod-birds that darted about so frantically. It looked down on the wide pleasant boulevards in the middle of the city, which were now filled with running crowds. Fires began in many boroughs, sending long columns of dirty smoke streaming into the clear bright air. The ge-eagle flicked its powerful wings, curving effortlessly round them. Shouts of fury and screams of terror mingled into a single haze of sound that smothered the city buildings like an invisible fog. Its monotony was broken by sharp bursts of gunfire. They went on all day, then further, long into the night. Darkness didn't quench the screams, either.

*

For two days Slvasta was on the front line, protected by his stalwarts Yannrith, Andricea and Tovakar as he led charges against government buildings and other enclaves of resistance. The sight of him was gifted continuously: dirty, tired, showing sympathy to all those who had suffered in the violence, helping wounded onto cabs heading for hospitals. Wherever resistance flared from remnants of regiment officers and their remaining squads, he was there, fighting for his side, for justice, for change. He was the face of revolution, the inspiration for righteousness. Towards the end, if he simply turned up at a barricade or a building siege, the opposition gave up and surrendered. He made a big point of treating the defeated with dignity, preventing any retaliation or dirty street justice. You didn't need a gifting to know where he was; you just had to listen for the cheering.

He was only granted privacy on the morning of the third day because everyone thought he was finally resting from his heroism. In reality Yannrith and Andricea had shoved him into a fuzzed cab driven by Tovakar. He watched the city roll past through a small gap in the blinds that'd been drawn against curious eyes. The darkness inside the cab was a huge invitation to sleep. It had been so long since he'd even had a rest; he was filthy, aching in every bone, and exhausted.

Outside, people shuffled through the morning river mist with dazed expressions. He was surprised by how many windows had been smashed here, well away from the centre of the city where the majority of the fighting had occurred. Some of the furtive figures carried bulky boxes or sacks with them. Looters, he supposed. Bethaneve had been getting a lot of reports of that. It was ironic, in all their plans to overturn the civic and national authority with their revolution, they'd never thought about the consequences such lawlessness would bring.

There were also families outside, parents shepherding children along, surrounding them with their strongest shells, hurrying in search of . . . Slvasta wasn't sure what, but they all moved with purpose. The families were nearly always well dressed, the faces of the children fearful and tear streaked, parents grim and apprehensive. He would have stopped and asked where they were going – if only he had the energy.

The cab drove into East Folwich, a district which seemed to have escaped the worst of the revolution. Here there was no broken glass, nor smoke rising from firebombed buildings. No blood staining the cobbles. All that marred these charming suburban streets were the hastily boarded-up windows and locked doors.

Slvasta stared curiously at the shattered remains of the sturdy doors belonging to the Faller Research Institute. He couldn't remember them plotting any kind of action here – but Bethaneve had insisted he come.

The courtyard's tall walls helped ward off the low sunlight, allowing the cool grey mist to linger. It eddied slowly around the two parked cabs and a wagon. His curiosity grew when he saw men unloading barrels of yalseed oil from the back.

Then he didn't care any more, because Bethaneve came out of the institute's entrance. They embraced in the clammy mist, desperately checking each other over to make sure they were both intact, that they hadn't lied when they kept breezily assuring the other: 'Yeah, I'm fine,' all through the revolution.

She rested her forehead on his, fingers tracing his features for still more reassurance. 'We did it,' she whispered. 'We've beaten them.'

'We did,' he whispered back. 'Thank you.'

'It was you. I just helped.'

They kissed again.

Finally he leaned back from her, but still smiled. 'Why did you bring me here? You said it was important.'

'It is,' she said, her voice suddenly unsteady. 'We've won, you know that: Coulan at the palace, you with the government offices, Javier with the merchants and companies. The hold-outs can't last much longer. The government is gone. You understand that, don't you, my love?'

'Well . . . yes.'

'Good. And we were right to topple it. I want you to be certain of this when you sit in the new congress. It's important, because that congress will shape our lives, it will determine how our children will be free of suffering and poverty, that there will be justice on our world.'

'I know all this,' he said.

'There is always a danger, because you are a good man, that you will be magnanimous in victory. That cannot happen.'

The joy he'd felt at seeing her was starting to fade; the weariness eclipsed everything. 'I don't understand. The congress starts in a few hours. I'm not going to waver. All I need right now is some rest. Sorry if that sounds selfish, but I'm so tired, Bethaneve.'

'I know. But first you must come with me.'

She led him through the institute, down several flights of stairs, then into the cellars. Like every building in Varlan, they were extensive, and old. As the walls of the passage changed from brick to bare rock, a small bad part of his mind was glad Tovakar and Andricea were accompanying him; that they were all armed with the formidable carbines Nigel had supplied.

'Did you ever wonder what happened to all those people Trevene snatched?' Bethaneve asked. 'Our comrades?'

They passed a group of men who'd been unloading the oil barrels. Slvasta frowned at them – they all looked scared. 'They're sent to the Pidrui mines,' he said. 'It was you who told me. That's one of the first things we're going to do: set them all free.'

'Most would have gone there, yes. But some, the special ones, the ones Aothori took an interest in, they're not there, Slvasta. We can't rescue them.'

'Then what . . . ?'

They reached the end of the passage. There was a single thick iron door set in the rock, secured by several heavy Ysdom locks. 'I'm sorry,' she said. 'But you have to see this before you hold the congress. You must never forget the evil we overthrew.'

Slvasta gave her outstretched hand a worried glance. But he took it and let himself be led through the door.

It stank inside. The room was a simple oblong cut into the rock, with iron rails along the middle, guarding the edge of the pit. In the middle of the rails was a gate. Two comrades stood beside it, holding their carbines ready, the safety catches off.

'This is what they did to us,' Bethaneve said.

Slvasta inched towards the pit, where the awful stench was even stronger. Bethaneve handed him a bright lamp, which he held out over the dark chasm. Shadows shrank down the walls of the pit, as if they were a liquid draining away. Something moved at the bottom. A face looking up.

Slvasta screamed, and stumbled back. The lamp fell from numb fingers, tumbling down into the pit. He hit the rock wall beside the door and crumpled to the floor. 'No! NO!' Tears flooded his eyes as his whole body shook.

'The professor in charge told me the institute doesn't just keep eggs for research; they've been keeping Fallers here from the very beginning as well,' Bethaneve said quietly.

Slvasta gave her an uncomprehending stare.

'When one dies, or they cut it open to examine it in their laboratory, the Marines bring them another,' she continued. 'They don't bother much with the eggs, the professor says, because they don't have the instruments to analyse them like the first scientists from Captain Cornelius's ship did.'

'It's him,' Slvasta croaked. His thoughts were threatening to burn his brain apart, they hurt so much. He wanted to shrink to a foetal ball, away from the universe, to spin a shell so strong that nothing could ever get to him. To seal himself off from *knowing*.

'The First Officer, yes,' Bethaneve said. 'He brought his victims here. He enjoyed watching, Slvasta, when they were cast into the pit. That's what we have destroyed today, the pinnacle of corruption, of power abused. We were right, Slvasta. Everything we have done, the deaths, the damage. We had to do it. Do you understand now?'

'Its him,' Slvasta yelled at her. 'Him!'

'Slvasta?' There was worry in Bethaneve's thoughts now. 'It's all right, my love. We're going to finish this. The oil will burn—'

'Shut the crud up,' Slvasta bellowed. He rose to his feet. His teekay snatched one of the lamps from its bracket on the wall, bending the iron rods holding it. Tovakar and Andricea exchanged a concerned look. 'The Marines who saved me fired one shot,' Slvasta laughed, spraying out spittle. 'I only heard one shot. Why did I never figure out what that meant? It's so crudding obvious. Isn't it? Well, isn't it?'

'Slvasta?' Bethaneve moaned in dismay. 'Please.'

He gave her a wild grin, and his teekay sent the lamp arching through the air. It descended halfway down the pit before he halted it, holding it steady in mid-air. Then he looked down, properly this time.

The floor of the pit was covered in bones – human bones – some of which still had flesh sticking to them. Skulls lay everywhere, smashed open. There were scraps of fabric amid the festering layer of slime which covered the rock floor – clothes from the victims. Boots. Shoes. Buttons and buckles glinted weakly in the lamplight. And there in the middle of it all was the Faller. Looking up, his face displaying that puzzled entreating expression that Slvasta remembered so perfectly.

'Ingmar,' Slvasta whimpered.

'Slvasta. Slvasta, help me,' the Faller pleaded.

'You're not him, not Ingmar. He has Fallen.'

'But I am Ingmar. It's me, Slvasta. The Marines cut me free as they did you. Look, I drop my shell to you, my friend. These are my thoughts, aren't they? Know me. Sense me. This is my essence, my soul. You know that's true. Know I am genuine. You're my friend, Slvasta. My friend!'

Slvasta sobbed as he brought his carbine round.

'No! I have been down here since we were captured by Quanda. In the dark. Alone. They were terrible to me, Slvasta. They torture me eternally. My soul is broken from what they have done to me. Please, Slvasta, please.'

'You know me, Faller?' Slvasta growled at his tormentor. 'Do you?'

'Of course I do. We grew up together, Slvasta. Do you remember the time when—'

'I remember my life, for I lived it. So tell me this. Do you remember me saying *We will burn you from our world*? Ha! Do you, Faller? Do you remember?'

'Slvasta, please.'

'You should do. You were there. It is for you I said it. And in your memory I will honour it. Now and forever!' He pulled the carbine's trigger and held it down until the nonhuman creature at the bottom of the pit was ripped apart.

*

Cell members had been appointed to supervise each borough council after the Captain and his authority had been overthrown. The sitting elected representatives were dismissed, and fresh open elections promised to the residents. That order was irrelevant in many boroughs; the Citizens' Dawn councillors were either dead or had fled with their families.

The National Council amphitheatre was still cluttered with broken desks from when the mob had broken in. Files and folders had been flung about and burst, snowing paper everywhere. Iron bars had hacked big chunks out of the First Speaker's onyx throne, cracking it. Vigorous teekay had pulled statues from every alcove, sending them toppling to the ground, where they smashed apart, inflicting more damage on the chamber's classical decor. The plaster was pocked with an awful number of bullet holes. Paintings had been ripped off the walls to be burnt in a bonfire outside, while slogans were daubed in the empty spaces.

Sitting on a small wooden stool beside the ruined throne, with Yannrith ever watchful behind him, Slvasta couldn't help but be disappointed. Behind Yannrith was Tovakar, a necessary concession; a democratic leader shouldn't need a bodyguard, but there were a lot of people and organizations out there still loyal to the Captain. He'd wanted the first session of the People's Interim Congress to appear a little more dignified, proving its authority with formality and gravity. Grandeur wasn't completely essential, but the damage to the chamber looked as if it had been wrought by teenagers wrecked on narnik. However, the comrades directing the First Night Square mob had achieved their objectives. The National Council was no more; over half of the councillors were now locked up in the cellars of the Merrowdin Street sheriff's station. Some representatives had fled, others had been caught trying to escape and faced immediate mob judgement. Several were still hanging like grisly fruit from the riccalon trees around the square.

Coulan had commanded the mob assigned to storm the Captain's Palace, an operation which had gone remarkably smoothly – mainly down to the perfectly placed snipers from his militia cutting down the guard. Cell members and Coulan's militia were now going through every room, clearing them of furniture and clothes and trinkets and art and fine wines, distributing the booty to a throng of cheering supporters along Walton Boulevard. That was simple cheap popularity politics. Far more important was Coulan taking the Captain and his family into custody (apart from Dionene, his youngest daughter, who'd eluded them), which gave Slvasta tremendous leverage over the government institutions who were still holding out. As the palace had suffered little damage, they could have held the parliament in one of the huge intact staterooms there. Javier had advised against that. 'We have to make a clean break with the old regime; don't be tainted by association.' Slvasta agreed totally. His hand still trembled from the memory of the Research Institute. He wanted the whole monstrosity blown up, the gardens turned into a public park, eradicating the last vestige and symbolism of the Captain's power. But that might have to wait a while. For now, they held the city, but not the rest of Bienvenido.

Messengers had been sent to every city and province, explaining that the People's Interim Congress was the new government, so they had a choice: join us, agree to democracy, or we will enforce the change. It wouldn't come today or tomorrow, but in a few months or a year, the old mayors and governors would awake to find revolutionary forces besieging their city.

In the meantime, despite Bethaneve's claim that they'd won, there were still pockets of resistance to be quashed in Varlan. It was Tovakar who had led a group of comrades against Fifty-Eight Grosvner Place, which was still burning. Trevene's decomposing remains hung from one of the lamp posts just down the street from his broken headquarters. Over two dozen prisoners had been freed from its dungeons before it was firebombed, all of them associated with Democratic Unity or the cells. They at least would never know the Pidrui mines, or the horror of the Research Institute. Their erstwhile jailers and interrogators were either shot during the incursion or left dangling close to their boss an hour later.

Despite that, many government offices refused to acknowledge the legitimacy of the People's Interim Congress. Their staff had ignored orders to report to work in departments where cell members had already installed themselves as managers. Comrades were arranging for each and every one of them to be visited at home by activists to explain why they should.

There were also nine city boroughs (the wealthiest nine) which repudiated Slvasta's claim to government, along with all the outlying National Council constituencies.

He hadn't expected quite so much resistance. Couldn't they see the revolution was a success? That true democracy was coming?

A great many comrades wanted to march on these centres of defiance and bring the rich and privileged to their knees at the barrel of a gun. But there had been enough killing, so after they'd left the institute Slvasta had told Bethaneve to arrange a blockade of the boroughs that refused to cooperate with the People's Interim Congress. After two days of armed struggle, food was already growing short in Varlan. 'Let's see how long the rich can eat their money for,' was Slvasta's message to his supporters.

In the meantime, those Democratic Unity members he'd appointed to represent the boroughs had arrived in the National Council building, and were finding themselves somewhere to sit among the splintered woodwork on the amphitheatre tiers. The number of women was heartening; before they'd been only a tiny number in the National Congress, now it was nearly half. He watched the new delegates jostling about good-naturedly as they hunted around for something to perch on, and he smiled at the three-strong team from Nalani who were shuffling sideways along the front tier. Javier grinned back and gave a quick, half-mocking salute. Slvasta thought his friend looked about as tired as he felt. There had been maybe three hours' proper sleep in the last fifty hours.

'How's it going?' he private 'pathed.

'I think there would have been a lot more opposition to us nationalizing the railways if the railways actually worked,' Javier replied. 'None of the office staff complained when we went into their buildings and told them the government were their new owners – but then, all my aides are armed. They don't quite believe this is real. Not yet. It'll probably be different when the shock wears off.'

'What about the owners?'

'I'm sure they're objecting,' Javier chortled. 'Wherever they are.'

Somewhere at the back of his mind Slvasta remembered

Arnice telling him Lanicia's family owned a lot of Grand South-Western Line stock. *Uracus, I hope she's all right.* 'There are a lot of people leaving Varlan. The roads are full with carts and cabs. And they say every boat leaving the quayside is packed to the gunnels. I didn't expect so many to run away.'

'Uracus take 'em. They're the rich – people with country estates and second homes, crud like that. They're parasites we're better off without. None of the workers is leaving, not people who actually power the economy.'

'The stallholders in the Wellfield,' Slvasta reflected fondly.

'Aye, they're still here. Everybody we need to get the economy back up and running properly. And when we do, the workers will own the means of production.'

'At last.' It came out like a sigh from Slvasta's mouth. It was hard to keep his eyes open in restful moments like this.

'So have you got an agenda, prime minister?'

'Oh, yeah. I think Bethaneve would have *me* carted off if I wasn't prepared for this. We'll start off with a vote on a planet-wide ban of all neuts and mods. Then I'm going to introduce an equality bill—'

'You are crudding joking!' Javier was abruptly on his feet, still private 'pathing, but staring hotly at Slvasta across the chamber.

'What's wrong?'

'A mod prohibition? That's our first law? You can't be serious.'

'What are you talking about? That's what this was all about. Remember? The Fallers are our true enemy. Now that the Captain's gone, we can hit them head on. And we start that war by getting rid of their creatures.'

'Don't be ridiculous. Bienvenido's entire economy depends on them; every farm needs them to bring the crops in. If you want this Congress to be accepted outside Varlan, you have to be realistic.'

'Varlan survived without mods and neuts.'

'Survived, yes, because the city is stinking rich. It certainly didn't *prosper*. Getting rid of the mods was an excellent piece of strategy for us *back then*. No, the first thing we have to do is restart the economy and bring back the prosperity we took away. That's how we gain the support of everyone we've just spent two days scaring the crud out of.'

Slvasta felt his cheeks warming as he glared back at Javier. All he could see was the Ingmar-Faller looking up out of that terrible pit, the lies he pleaded with . . . 'That was no mere political strategy. That was *survival*. No more neuts! They are evil. They are the Fallers' creatures. They will overwhelm us if we don't kill them first. Do you understand nothing?'

'I understand perfectly. Get over your monomania or you will ruin us all! This revolution exists to improve the lives of everyone, and to do that we need mods. Playtime is over. This is life and death now.'

'They will wipe us out!' Slvasta was on his feet now, shouting furiously. 'They will *eat* us. Is that what you want? Because if it is, you're no better than the Captain was. A traitor to us, to your entire species!'

'Fuck you! You didn't lose an arm to the Fallers, you lost your brain! Without an economy, we can't fight the Fallers. How is that difficult to understand? And don't you ever call me a fucking traitor again, you crudding worthless bastard! You lost your arm because you were a shit trooper, too dumb even to recognize a Faller when you met her.'

'*Get the fuck out of my sight.* You do not represent Nalani; you represent nothing. Nothing!'

Slvasta's whole body was quivering in reaction to the argument. Yannrith's hand fell on his shoulder. 'Captain,' he said in a warning tone. 'This should not be happening. Not here.'

Javier spat on the floor, and stormed away. 'This is not your revolution,' he shouted at Slvasta, shaking his big fist. 'It belongs to the people. The only person who'd deny that is a megalomaniac. The Captain would be proud of you.'

Slvasta could just detect a flurry of private 'paths spinning out of Javier's mind. Over a dozen delegates were clambering to their feet, joining him as he stomped towards the nearest exit. 'Bethaneve,' he 'pathed. 'Close the whole cell network to Javier; he's trying to sabotage us.'

'That's not how it works,' she protested. 'What in Uracus is happening in there? What are you two idiots doing?'

'Nothing.' He took a breath to calm his quivering body and stared out at the remaining delegates, who were watching him with incredulous faces. 'Well,' he said, the corner of his mouth lifting in a rueful grimace. 'Welcome to true democracy.'

*

Kysandra leaned on the ferry's gunnel, staring down at the thick mud-brown water of the Colbal. Her ex-sight probed down into it for a couple of metres or so, but that was as far as she could reach. Solids and liquids were a strong barrier to psychic perception, for which she was grateful. Three days ago, she had stood on the south bank, with tears running freely down her cheeks when the *Lanuux* and *Alfreed* had set off. Of all the terrible things that they'd done to manufacture the revolution, this was the most awful. Nigel had told her to wait in the Willesden station hotel where they were staying, but she simply couldn't. Not facing up to this, to the consequences of their actions, was the worst sort of cowardice.

'Other ships will come swiftly to help,' Nigel said. 'There are dozens making the crossing at any given time.'

'We just have to stop the Meor from interfering with the cell comrades,' Fergus said.

'Okay, so why don't we just sabotage the ferry engines?' she'd asked. The Meor troopers weren't bad people; they didn't deserve this.

'They'll commandeer other ferries,' Nigel said gently. 'The Captain and Trevene know something is happening, that there's an organized underground movement opposing them. They need the Meor in the city. We're lucky there are two Faller alerts right now, and most of the Marines are away. They're loyal and tough.'

So she'd stopped objecting, because it was logical and necessary, and she mustn't be a stupid sentimental little girl. The fate of everyone on Bienvenido depended on the outcome of this day, and that was all that mattered. And an hour later she watched the *Lanuux* and *Alfreed* sink below the water, leaving survivors floundering desperately in the river's strong flow and lethal undercurrents.

Nigel had been right; every other ship on the Colbal did rush to help. But the troopers were wearing full uniforms and heavy boots, and the swift water was pitiless. In the end, they reckoned over three hundred troopers were plucked out of the river to safety – three hundred out of one and a half thousand. By then, the even more bloody revolution had kicked off in the city. Kysandra stayed on the riverbank, staring across the water, watching the fires flare, listening to the gunshots. She strengthened her shell against any giftings of the sadness and brutality and anguish that came slithering through the aether, along with the deluge of cries for help and mercy.

Now, three days later, they were crossing the river on a big barge. Ma Ulvon was in charge of the crew, standing in front of the wheelhouse, with her pump-action shotgun on a long shoulder strap, and bandoliers full of cartridges worn over her neat grey and blue jacket. Akstan and Julias were sitting in the two big wagons strapped to the deck that they were bringing to Varlan, keeping the terrestrial horses quiet and soothed. The carts were custom built, with tough suspension, and deep cradles inside their sturdy covered frames, ready to carry their prize back.

'Typical,' Nigel barked under his breath.

Kysandra looked up from the water where the wrecks of the ferries must be lying some ten or twelve metres down. She didn't need a shell to guard against showing her emotions. The luxury of feelings was something she'd forbidden to herself since the revolution began. This must be how the ANAdroids think, she told herself. They saw, they understood, but they didn't sympathize. They kept aloof; neither death nor beauty bothered them. Every response to life's events a perfect forgery. It wasn't a bad way to live. She saw now she'd been striving for something similar ever since Nigel arrived.

'What is it?' she asked him.

'Slvasta. The People's Interim Congress is being gifted in the spirit of democratic openness. He and Javier have had a very public bust-up.'

Kysandra shifted her gaze to the approaching city, seeing the imposing buildings rising up the slopes behind the river, but not really caring. Staying aloof – a high place where you couldn't be hurt. 'Really? I'm not taking giftings right now.'

He went over to her. 'I should have made you stay at home.'

'Made me?'

'Insisted.'

'But everything would still have happened, wouldn't it? Everybody would still be dead.'

'I'm sorry.'

For once she believed the melancholy voice, the sympathy expressed in those mesmerizing green eyes. 'It's not you. I just . . . didn't think it through. I didn't realize how big this was. I really am just a smalltown girl after all.'

His arm went round her shoulder. 'You are so not. You are the smartest, most knowledgeable person on Bienvenido – after me.'

'Pretty rough comment on Bienvenido.'

'That's my girl. Besides, bodyloss is terrible, but not fatal. In the Commonwealth, people just download their thoughts and memories into re-life clones. Here, souls fly to the Heart.'

'Nigel.' She gave him the look that said: Don't patronize me. 'If everything works the way you planned, you're going to rip the Void apart. All those souls the Heart has stolen will die with it, so don't use that to try and comfort me, okay?'

'Quite right. So let's use the truth: Laura Brandt has been created and died over a million times. The soul of everyone who ever made it to the Heart has been imprisoned and adapted into crud knows what to serve the Void somehow. There has never been an atrocity committed against the human race on this scale before, not ever. And that is what all the millions of people born here on Bienvenido will continue to face forever if we don't stop them. You were prepared to sacrifice everything, including your life and your immortal soul, to liberate the unborn generations to come. You were ready for that because you knew it was worthwhile, that it was the right thing to do. I'm sorry about the deaths, truly I am. The Commonwealth exists so that everyone can have a chance at a decent life, and then migrate into a technological afterlife, and then maybe one day that too will transcend. I want the best for people; that's all I've ever wanted, despite some pretty dubious methods I've used down the centuries. And the Void is a monster, the worst we've ever faced. It has to be destroyed, Kysandra.'

'I know.' Suddenly she was crying again, and hugging him tight. 'I won't let you down. Really I won't.'

'You haven't and you couldn't. You're my touchstone, Kysandra. You're what I look at every day to remind myself that this is worthwhile. I want to see you *live*, Kysandra; truly live. That's what all this is for. So that you and your children have the same chance as every other member of our glorious, stupid, crazy species.'

She did what she'd always promised herself she wouldn't do, and snuggled up close, rejoicing in the sensation of his arms around her, hearing his heart beating beneath his shirt, smelling his scent. His hand rubbed her spine absently.

'Thank you,' she murmured.

'What for? I just said it like it is. You knew it already.'

'For just that, being honest.'

'It's strange. So many people are desperate to get to the top, to be in charge. But, crud, the decisions you have to make when you're there. That's the part nobody ever warns you about.'

'It'll be different, won't it, Nigel? Out in the Commonwealth?'

'Yes. But please don't think that a post-scarcity society is devoid of politics. There'll still be backstabbing and manoeuvring and betrayal and ideological obsession – everything we excel in.'

Kysandra grinned, still not moving from his embrace. 'You're such a cynic.'

'It's our natural state. Just look at what's happening with Slvasta.'

'Huh! The idiot.'

'The agreement was that in return for weapons he called a people's congress to determine a democratic constitution.'

'But that's what he's done.' She frowned at him. 'Isn't it?'

'Oh, yeah. But a people's congress doesn't mean just *his* people.'

Kysandra stiffened in surprise. 'He hasn't!'

'Oh, yes, he has. Every delegate is either a comrade or a Democratic Unity member. No dissenters allowed in his brave new world.'

'But that's . . .'

'Typical. Partly my fault. I wanted a revolution in the city guaranteed to empty the Captain's Palace. I maybe should have avoided the classic Leninist–Trotskyite model.' He pulled a face. 'Of course, it is a proven method, and we needed a result. But I did enjoy the irony.'

'I can't believe Slvasta did that. He was supposed to be a man of the people – *the* man of the people, actually. The one everybody could trust. That's why we chose him.'

'It doesn't matter. He's an irrelevance now that he's fulfilled his role. One more week, and this will all be over.'

Kysandra regarded the city with renewed interest. The barge was a couple of hundred metres out from the quayside now. The broad road which ran behind the wharfs was crammed with people. There were a lot of families packed together there; men with anxious haunted faces, women trying to keep calm for the sake of exhausted frightened children. Every adult was either carrying a suitcase or wearing a backpack, in most cases both. Everywhere a boat was tied up had generated a dense knot of angry desperate people, emitting strong incoherent 'paths like flashes of lightning. No matter what the ship was, from a small rowing boat to the big ocean-going schooners, their armed crews stood stoically on the gangplanks, not letting anyone on board.

'What are they doing?' Kysandra wondered.

'Holding an auction,' Nigel said. 'Passage goes to the highest bidder.'

'That's awful. The killing has stopped. Coulan got the mobs to break up and go home yesterday.'

'Our mobs,' Nigel said sardonically. 'Right now there are a lot of old scores being settled. Boss fired you from work a couple of years back? It was really unfair. Well, now's your chance for pay-back. No sheriffs keeping order right now. No officials you can turn to for help. Good time to go looting, too. And you need to loot, if you want your family to eat, because food's running short. No trains bringing more, remember?'

'Uracus!'

They saw Coulan and a large squad of heavily armed militia waiting at an empty wharf. The barge steered over to it and tied up. There was a surge of hopeful people along the quayside. The silent, stone-faced militiamen on guard at the end of the wharf stopped them getting anywhere near the gangplank.

Kysandra stood on tiptoes to give the ANAdroid a quick kiss. 'You made it okay?'

'I'm intact, yes.'

'Everything ready?' Nigel asked brusquely.

'I've had my militia guard them since we stormed the palace. Slvasta and Javier are butting heads in the Interim Congress, and Bethaneve is trying to manage the blockades around the posh boroughs that simply won't do as they're told. We just need to go and collect them.'

'Good.'

Kysandra gave the desperate refugees on the quayside a concerned look. 'What about the residents?'

'The guns are off the street,' Coulan said. 'Most of them, anyway. Not that it matters. They don't have much ammunition left. We calculated that about right.'

'I didn't mean that. What about food? Hospitals? There were hundreds injured, I know. What are the victorious comrades doing about getting everything working again?'

'They just have to hang on for a week,' Nigel said.

'And if it doesn't work?'

'It will.'

'Really? We have James Hilton, in case you're wrong. Nigel, you can't abandon these people, not now. They're desperate for some kind of order; Uracus, half of them are desperate just for a meal, and Slvasta's Congress of Morons is busy debating ideological purity and awarding themselves important titles. The city needs *practical* help.' She waved an arm at the crowds. 'You created this. You're the one with all the experience of managing billions of people – apparently. Do something!'

Nigel and Coulan exchanged a glance. Air hissed out of Nigel's mouth in a reluctant sigh.

'I can talk to some of the Congress delegates,' Coulan said. 'Organize the smarter ones to get basic services up and running again. Food will have to be brought in on roads.'

'Thank you!'

Nigel held up a warning finger. 'Just as soon as we've got what we came for.'

'Fine.' She gave them both a sprightly smile. 'Let's go, then.'

It took a quarter of an hour to unload the carts. Then they were riding quickly into town, where the crowds that thronged the harbour melted away, leaving the streets beyond the quayside practically deserted. Coulan's militia men hung on to the sides of a couple of cabs which led the way, keeping their carbines very visible. A third cab followed the carts, carrying more militia.

'Not even cabs,' Nigel observed as they made their way towards the centre of the city.

'Anything with wheels got hired to take people out of town,' Coulan said. 'Going to have some very rich cabbies back here in a week or so.'

'You didn't try to stop them?' Kysandra said.

'Certainly not. The people who're leaving are the ones who fear and oppose the revolution. They're the ones who'll ultimately organize the counter-strike, if and when it comes. Better to have them away for the moment.'

Kysandra remembered the first time she'd visited Varlan: how wonderful the big buildings had seemed, how elegant and sophisticated. How she'd envied those who made their home in the capital, the bright exciting lives they must all live.

Now she could hardly bear to look around. Twice she'd seen bodies hanging; two from a tree, another from a lamp post. Shuddered and turned away. Everywhere there were signs of violence – congealed blood on the pavement, façades with long soot-slicks emerging from empty windows, looted shops, debris strewn around, the reeking silt left behind by the flooding, wrecked cabs and carts with dead horses still attached. She gritted her teeth as their little convoy moved purposefully through it all, seeking that emotionless state she'd achieved south of the river.

They skirted the edge of Bromwell Park and turned into Walton Boulevard. Kysandra could have cried at the state of the lovely old Rasheeda Hotel. All the ground-floor windows had been smashed, along with many on the first, and even some on the second floor. Tattered white curtains fluttered out through the gaps, pitiful flags of submission. The troughs of flowers beside the entrance had been broken up, the plants mashed. Her ex-sight perceived the interior had been stripped clean, leaving the grand rooms empty. Even the furniture was gone. 'Bussalores,' she muttered sourly. 'They're like human bussalores.'

'Life will stabilize,' Nigel said. 'Just hang on.'

She pressed her teeth together and stared resolutely ahead. The convoy made its way past vandalized statues and dried-up fountains that used to make the long boulevard so striking.

Militia stood guard round the massive palace. They saluted Coulan and opened the gates in the railings. The carts clattered swiftly over the expanse of cobbles outside, and through one of the impressive archways into a courtyard. A second archway at the back, with sturdy iron gates, led into a smaller, inner courtyard overlooked by the Captain's private quarters.

'We found some interesting stuff that the drones missed,' Coulan said as they made their way down a wide staircase into the vaults below the palace.

'Like what?' Kysandra asked.

Coulan grinned. 'Ship's fusion chamber, so they had power after the landing – for a while, anyway. Three regrav units from the *Vermillion*. Someone tried modifying them – by the looks of things, without success. There's also a smartcore that's linked to some synthesizer nodes. Their molecular grids are all shot, so they must have worked for a long time. And right beneath the private apartments is an old clinic with some medical modules, which are all depleted. I'd say the Captain's family had access to Commonwealth medicine after they landed here.'

'How long?' Nigel asked.

'I think we're looking at several centuries. The modules are badly worn. They cannibalized some to keep others working. The last one is a real patchwork. I wouldn't have liked to use it at the end.'

'And then there were none,' Nigel muttered.

'Yeah. But our most interesting find is the gateways.'

'What do you mean: gateways?' Kysandra challenged. Her educational memory inserts contained a huge file on Commonwealth gateways, but surely he couldn't mean . . . 'Not wormhole gateways?'

'Oh, yeah,' Coulan said happily. 'The very same.'

'Show me,' Nigel said gruffly.

They had to go down three more flights of stairs before they came to the storage cellar. Kysandra could see why they'd descended so far when they walked through the door made of thick anbor planks. The cellar was huge, with a ribbed semicircular roof thirty metres high at the apex. It was filled with five hulking cylinders whose tops nearly scraped the ribs. They looked as if they'd been wrapped in a dark-gloss spiderweb that clung tightly to the surface; the top half was covered by a heavy dust layer that killed the dull sheen. When her ex-sight probed through the wrapping, she could perceive they were giant machines. Not that they had any moving parts – they weren't *mechanical* – but the incredibly complex components were locked together as tight as cells in living tissue.

'I did not expect to find these here,' Nigel admitted ruefully.

'We should have done,' Coulan said. 'Standard equipment on colony ships. After all, who wants to transport raw material or people long distances when you reach your new world? Gateways help keep your population centres and manufacturing sites tied together. Best way of establishing a monoculture.'

Nigel smiled fondly at the dark inert cylinders. 'I wonder if they've got any floaters?'

'And they are?' Kysandra asked somewhat peevishly. They'd risked everything to gain unrestricted access to the palace, now these two were taking a moment to have a nostalgiafest. Her tolerance was wearing thin.

'Gateways you drop into a gas giant's atmosphere. They float along the top of the gas/liquid boundary, siphoning out every kind of hydrocarbon compound you could ever need. An infinite resource.'

'Is that relevant?'

Nigel reached up and patted the first gateway. 'This is what I built, Kysandra – me and Ozzie. This is what made the Commonwealth possible.' He pursed his lips in regret. 'I don't suppose we can use one to reach up to the Forest?'

'They all have direct mass converters as a power source, which are glitchy at best in the Void,' Coulan said. 'But this is the original protective wrap. I'm guessing Captain Cornelius tried powering one up when they arrived. If it'd worked, they'd be using them instead of trains to link Bienvenido's cities.'

'So they kept them wrapped up and stored them down here. Makes sense. Damn. That would have been a real help.' He regarded the big dark cylinders forlornly. 'Looks like I'm going to be a rocket jockey after all. Wilson Kime will laugh his ass off when he hears about this. Come on, let's get what we came for.'

*

It had always surprised Yannrith how many cab drivers were cell members. Their trade was wealthy people, and the revolution was busy frightening them out of town. Of course, a lot of cabs were also out of town right now, busy taking those same rich people to country estates or to the refuge of family in distant cities, for which they'd no doubt charge exorbitant fees. But those who remained were happy enough to run activists all over town to help the cause. Bethaneve kept them on a rota.

A more cynical side of his mind suspected it was to secure their position afterwards. Cab licences in Varlan were notoriously unobtainable; the only way to get one these days was to inherit it. The Varlan Cab Driver Guild could have taught Slvasta's union a thing or two about restrictive practices and demarcation.

The cab turned out of Pointas Street onto Walton Boulevard. The statue of Captain Gootwai which had guarded the junction for centuries had been decapitated, and a pumpkin squashed onto the broken neck. Yannrith didn't much care for the lawlessness that was gripping the city. He liked order in his life. Slvasta had already asked him to command whatever police force they assembled out of the remaining sheriffs and selected grade three activists. It would be a tough job, getting those two groups to work together afterwards.

'Think of it as the perfect example of how we have to rebuild our lives afterwards,' Slvasta had said. 'Reconciliation has to start somewhere.'

Yannrith was scheduled to meet the surviving sheriff station captains that afternoon, to find out just how practical that was likely to be – that's if any of them agreed to turn up in the first place. But right now he was more concerned about the shocking split between Javier and Slvasta. It had taken everyone by surprise, blowing up out of nowhere. He was convinced it was down to exhaustion and the unrelenting stress of the last few days. As reconciliations went, that one was pretty vital to all of them. Even Slvasta seemed to recognize that. Now.

Which was why Yannrith was on his way to the palace, to talk to Coulan, who was the calm sensible one, the one to negotiate a truce. Unfortunately, Coulan wasn't responding to any 'paths right now, so Uracus alone knew what his game was. Maybe he was rushing to support his lover in a coup against Slvasta. Coulan always was an expert in subtle, intricate strategies.

Paranoia. Probably . . . The only way to find out was to confront him directly. Which Slvasta couldn't do, because that would be a sign of weakness, and he had to build alliances with the People's Interim Congress delegates who supported him.

It fell to Yannrith, then, to act as the go-between in this feud (because Bethaneve was furious with both of them). That suited him fine because he also wanted to know first-hand how the search for the Captain's daughter was going. Once the whole of the Captain's family was in custody, Slvasta could really start to apply pressure – like making the sheriff captains turn up this afternoon. Although nobody actually wanted to start executing any more members of the Captain's family, not now. Aothori had to go, everyone knew that, but the kids . . . That would lose them a great deal of support.

Who could have guessed a revolution's internal politics would turn out to be so insanely *complicated*?

A convoy of vehicles was coming the other way down Walton Boulevard, moving at a fair old pace. Two cabs in front, with armed militiamen hanging off the sides, their minds emitting a steely caution to get out of the way. Then came two big covered wagons, heavily fuzzed. Followed by a final cab, equally laden with militia.

Yannrith peered at them curiously, just glimpsing a young woman sitting up beside the surly-looking driver on the first wagon. She was dressed in boots and a long suede skirt, with a leather waistcoat over a white blouse, her red hair trailing from a broad-rimmed hat. Yannrith frowned; that face. He knew her from somewhere. *She's with Coulan's militia, which means she's an activist. But how do I recognize her? The cell network keeps us all isolated. In theory.*

Then the convoy was past, and he didn't know what to make of it at all. Coulan's militia people had been methodically stripping the palace bare. There'd been a continual scrum along Walton Boulevard for the first two days as they handed out the Captain's possessions, but now all the booty was gone. *So why were the carts guarded? What could be so important?*

A minute later he arrived at the Captain's Palace, keen to get some answers from Coulan. The militia guarding the gates were reluctant to let him through. It worried him that factions were forming, their attitudes hardening: that would be disastrous for the revolution. But once inside, the remnants of the teams assigned to the palace told him Coulan wasn't there. They didn't know where he was, nor when he would be back. They knew nothing of the convoy, either.

*

The Delkeith theatre on Portnoi Street was old and shabby, but it did have thick walls to block ex-sight from outside. It specialized in fairly crude satirical comedy, which was why Javier was familiar with it. The management had closed up as soon as the mobs hit the streets, but the caretaker was happy enough to open it for Javier.

He sat on the stage, next to the giant teacup prop, and thanked people for coming, for having the courage to walk out of the Congress with him. They were mostly union stewards, as well as the radical stalwarts he'd known before he met Slvasta. During the time the cells had been built up, he'd carefully steered them all into positions of leadership, so now over twenty had been appointed borough delegates to the People's Interim Congress.

They understood the reality of life on Bienvenido, not needing any persuasion to see the injustice. They knew how vital jobs and a thriving economy were to establish the revolution as legitimate. Once he started talking, they were with him on blocking Slvasta's stupidity about mods and neuts.

With that agreed, they all started to discuss procedures and votes and possible allies to use in the Congress to defeat the motion. It didn't help that the Congress was chaired by Slvasta, so they needed tactics into shaming him and forcing him to take account of a democratic mandate.

The one person Javier really needed at the Delkeith was Coulan. Not just for the personal comfort, but because he had the best brain for this kind of stuff. Coulan would also know how to smooth things over with Slvasta.

Now the argument was over, now the split was hugely public, Javier was feeling sheepish about the whole thing. There had been no need for either of them to get so bad tempered, nor so stubborn.

It was tiredness, he kept telling himself. A state where the smallest frustration could trigger ludicrous amounts of adrenalin and testosterone. And he was ridiculously tired. The others had given him the job of industrial strategy for the Interim Congress. After all the violence and desperation of the revolution's active stage, there had been no time to rest afterwards. They had to keep momentum going – was it Coulan who kept insisting that? Keep pushing the establishment back, keep claiming their own legitimacy through the Congress, by establishing their own managers in strategic businesses. Don't let up. Push and push until there simply isn't any resistance any more. Keep going.

Coulan didn't answer any 'paths. He was in charge of securing the palace and the Captain's family. Tasks which had been carried out flawlessly, Javier knew; he'd perceived reports all through the active stage, keeping anxious track of his beloved. His small militia was superbly disciplined, eradicating any opposition, and not allowing the mob following them to run wild. If only all aspects of the revolution had been so well executed, he thought dolefully. There had been a lot of poor discipline. Too many had died or suffered. The looting was a disgrace.

However, the palace was theirs now, as was the Captain's family – apart from Dionene. The city was theirs. They'd won.

So why do I feel so cruddy?

Javier realized his eyes were closing. He abruptly sat back in the chair – a jerky movement which sent his elbow thudding against the ridiculous teacup. It was made from papier mâché and wobbled about. Once he saw it wasn't going to fall over and roll across the stage, he held up his hands. 'I'm sorry. I really have to get some sleep. We know what we have to do. I'll see you all tomorrow at the morning session of Congress.'

They all wanted to congratulate him. For the success. For not forgetting them. For standing up to Slvasta. For representing genuine democracy.

He shook hands. Slapped backs. Promised long cheerful sessions in the pub. Barely recognizing them, and certainly not recalling what they'd all just said. The fatigue was so strong now, making it hard simply to stand.

When he finally left the theatre, a cab was waiting for him. Bethaneve's organizational magic was still working perfectly. He smiled at that as he told the cabby to take him to the palace. Somehow he had to talk to Coulan and find out just what was really happening. He fell asleep as soon as they started to move.

✳

Exhaustion had finally abolished Slvasta's rage. His aides kept giving him coffee during the Congress, which he hated but drank anyway. Now he had a wicked headache, his mouth tasted like crud, his bladder ached, and still the meetings went on. Essential political meetings he held in the First Speaker's annex – a lovely hexagonal wood-panelled study with high, lead-framed windows. Delegates he knew he could trust came and went for hours. He talked to them soothingly, apologizing for his earlier outburst. They all expressed sympathy; it had been a tough week for everyone. And they all managed to drop in their concerns, on behalf of those they now represented, which he pledged to give them debate-time to raise. Trading favours and hearing whispers.

As he sat in the annex, so Javier had set up in the Delkeith with his old cronies, forming a pro-neut faction. That simply couldn't be allowed to succeed. But as the exhausting day wore on, draining him still further, he resented not being able simply to 'path his friend and say: 'Come on, let's go for a beer in the Bellaview pub garden, and just talk about it.' The way it used to be.

It should be Javier asking him, though. He was the one at fault.

Bethaneve came in as the seventh – or eighth – group was leaving. She walked over to him as he sat behind the wide desk, sitting in his lap and resting her head against him. They said nothing for a long moment, just relaxing, content that they were still alive, that they had each other.

'We did it,' she whispered finally.

'Now we have to make sure we don't lose.'

'We won't.' She kissed him lightly, then put her fingers under his chin, raising his head so she could look straight into his eyes. 'You're still thinking of Ingmar, aren't you, sweetheart?'

He nodded meekly. 'I'm trying not to. But . . . Uracus damn those Fallers for all eternity. And the institute, traitors to our very race, every one of them.'

'They're not traitors, they did what they had to so they could keep the institute going. They're fighting the Fallers, just like us.'

'Maybe,' he conceded. 'But I can't get it out of my head.'

'Is that why you argued with Javier?'

'Oh crud!' He ground his teeth together. 'I don't know. One second we were so pleased that we'd both survived, that we were in Congress together, that we were right all along, and that we could finally help people; the next thing it's like I'm looking down on these two madmen screaming at each other. I knew I had to stop, but he just wouldn't see reason. It's crazy.'

'Giu, the pair of you!'

'I know, I know. I'm sorry. I was tired, that's all. And still upset over Ingmar, Giu, the shock of that was unreal. I let it get out of hand. It won't happen again. I promise you that. You do believe me, don't you?'

'You're to sit down with him and talk this through like rational people.'

'But . . . the mods, they belong to the Fallers!'

Her whole body stiffened. 'I know that. But you will have to find a way to make the rest of Bienvenido accept the revolution's authority. Once you have accomplished that, then you can sort out the mods and neuts.' Her fingers gripped his chin again, and her stare was very intent. 'You do understand that, don't you?'

'Yes,' he said as the tiredness came back in an almighty wave that made everything seem irrelevant. 'I know. But I will not rest until this world is free of them.'

'One step at a time, my love.' She kissed him.

'Thank you. I was worried.'

'Me too, when this happened. I didn't know what to do.'

'You always do,' he said. 'That's why I love you.'

'Not this time. But I have some strange news.'

'What?'

'The Goleford bridge has been blown up. About half an hour ago. An express only just got over it. They were lucky.'

'Where's Goleford?'

'Uracus, you *are* tired. It's the bridge on the Southern City Line.'

'What? Where in Giu's name have they been?'

'I don't know. I'm trying to get our agents to find out what's going on, but it's difficult to get messages over the Colbal right now. Every boat is full of refugees.'

'We're not tyrants,' he snapped in annoyance. 'We're the opposite. Nobody needs to run away from us.'

'I know.'

'You have to get in touch with the sabotage team. We don't want any more bridges blown up. As Javier said, we need to start building the economy back up.'

'Oh, a sensible comment. I'll put that down in my diary.'

'Hey, I'm trying, okay?'

'I know.' She didn't shift from his lap.

Slvasta's ex-sight caught Yannrith entering the ante-room. 'Come on in,' he 'pathed.

'Captain,' Yannrith said. Anxiety was leaking through his shell.

'What's the matter?' Slvasta asked wearily. He wasn't sure he could take much more bad news right now.

'I can't find Coulan anywhere.'

'He'll be with Javier,' Slvasta said.

'He's not.'

Bethaneve stood up. 'I'll find him. I'll put the word out with my people.'

'I've just come back from the Captain's Palace,' Yannrith said. 'There's something really strange been going on. Coulan's militia, the ones guarding it, they're all acting odd.'

'What do you mean, odd?'

Yannrith shrugged. 'As if they're drunk, or something. It's difficult to get them to say anything.'

'They're loyal to Coulan.'

'No, it's more than that. And something's been taken. I had to ask hard, but I found that much out eventually.'

'Taken?'

'From the palace cellars. Uracus, Slvasta, there are some really bizarre things down there. Ancient things that I've never seen before, things from Captain Cornelius's ship itself.'

Slvasta stared at him, trying to make sense of what was being said. 'Coulan's taken something from Cornelius's ship?'

'I'm not sure. But look, captain, you remember your last sweep with the regiment?'

'I can hardly forget. What about it?'

'We met those peculiar people we thought were narnik barons. The girl, the redhead, I forget her name, Nigel's so-called wife. She's here. I saw her riding one of the wagons on Walton Boulevard. They were all heading down the hill.'

'What wagons?' Bethaneve blurted.

'The wagons that took something from the palace.'

Slvasta's headache seemed to redouble in potency as he gave Yannrith a shocked look. 'Wait! Nigel and Kysandra are here? In Varlan?'

'You do know them?' an equally perturbed Yannrith asked.

'Nigel supplied all our weapons,' Bethaneve said. 'But – I don't understand. What's he doing here?'

Through all the pain in Slvasta's head, the elusive memory that had taunted him for days suddenly crystallized. 'Grunts!' he exclaimed.

Bethaneve and Yannrith frowned at him.

'You said it,' Slvasta accused her. 'The night we were arming the cells, you said we can't give a gun to every *grunt* on the streets.'

'So?'

'I only ever heard that word used like that once before. By Nigel! They're soldiers or troopers, privates, sergeants, corporals, officers – comrades in our cells are activists. But never *grunts*.'

'Slvasta—'

'What is going on?' he demanded hotly. 'Do you know Nigel?'

'I've never met him in my life. You were the one that went to

Adeone to meet him. You're the one that did the deal for weapons. All I know about him is what you've told me.'

'Then why did you call our cell members grunts?'

'Are you crazy?' she shouted back at him. 'It's a crudding word!'

'It's *his* word.'

'Oh for fuc—'

'What was he doing back then, when we found him on the sweep? What did he have on those boats? Is he a narnik baron? Wait! Was he your supplier?'

She flinched as if he'd struck her. All the emotion drained out of her expression. 'Slvasta,' she said in an icily calm voice, 'you need to stop this. You need to get some sleep.'

'Why is he here? What did he take?'

'I want you to calm down. Lie down on this settee and—'

'No. Something is going on. Javier's turned against me. Is he collaborating with Nigel, too?'

'Slvasta.' A tear trickled down her cheek. 'Please. No.'

'I will find out!' he roared. 'By Giu, I will know what game you're all playing behind my back! You think you can get rid of me? You think you can just waltz right into the Captain's Palace and rule this world? Do you? Well, you can't! I'll stop you. I'll stop all of you.' He stormed out of the annex. Tovakar and the five bodyguards he commanded regarded him in alarm. 'We're going to the palace,' he told them. 'Sergeant, are you with me?'

Yannrith gave Bethaneve a helpless shrug, and hurried out, leaving her to sink to her knees as she started to weep.

*

There still wasn't any real furniture in the Tarleton Gardens apartment. After Slvasta and Bethaneve had moved out, the empty rooms seemed even larger. There was nowhere to hide in any of them.

Javier's ex-sight had been pervading it as soon as he climbed out of the cab in the street outside. Coulan wasn't inside. Coulan wasn't anywhere. Not in the palace, not in the hotel where the

Captain's family was detained, not with any of the comrades. Nowhere. Javier went upstairs to their apartment anyway. There was nowhere else for him to go. Afternoon sunlight poured through the big bay windows. He'd always enjoyed the sensation of space he gained from the rooms. Other people's houses and flats seemed so cluttered. They valued things; he prized potential.

'It brings out your optimistic streak,' Coulan had told him one night, snuggled up in his embrace. 'I like that.'

Now Javier looked down on the mattress with its wrinkled sheets where they'd spent so many nights together, just talking quietly about their plans and hopes or thrashing round in sexual bliss, and there was no optimism left any more. Like the rooms, he was empty.

He sat on the mattress, and for all his bulk and strength he couldn't hold back the exhaustion any more. 'Where are you?' he asked the bare walls.

Coulan wouldn't abandon him, especially not in this dark desperate hour when he needed him more than ever. They loved each other. They were one. All he could think of was that Slvasta had sent an assassin for Coulan; that one by one he was wiping out anybody who opposed him.

'You idiot,' he told himself, and rested his eyes for a moment.

*

'Wake up.'

Javier opened his eyes. Bethaneve was staring down at him. There were dark fatigue circles round her eyes, and her cheeks were blotchy from crying. Hair hung lankly round her face.

'You look terrible,' he said, smiling to ease the slur. He could only have been asleep minutes, for he was still absurdly tired. But somehow the sun was now low in the sky.

'It's Slvasta,' she said in a fragile voice.

'I know. I'm sorry. We were both stupid. Uracus, I hadn't slept for days – I still haven't. I was so tense, so angry. There were fights, terrible fights against the sheriffs and Marines, and . . . The streets were bad places to be for a while. But I had to be out there, had to lead our comrades. I'd like to talk to him.'

Bethaneve shook her head, struggling against fresh tears. 'He's got worse. He's . . . He doesn't trust anyone any more. He thinks there are conspiracies everywhere.'

'You as well?'

She nodded miserably.

'Giu! What did you do?'

'He thinks I'm scheming with Nigel.'

'Nigel? Nigel that supplied us with all the weapons?'

'Yes.'

'But he's the only one of us who knows Nigel.' He studied Bethaneve's dead expression, sensed the seething emotions so thinly obscured by her shell. 'All right. We have to put a stop to this. I need to find Coulan. He'll know what to do.'

'I know where he is.'

'Where?' It came out a lot more urgently than he intended.

'The National Council building. Javier, he's meeting with senior comrades, making deals, organizing them. I think he might be putting his own faction together.'

He thought it was the cold that made his muscles so difficult to move, but in the end he had to admit it was shock. 'No. No, you're wrong.'

'I hope so. I do, really. But my informants aren't close enough to be included in the deals. I don't know what he's actually arranging.'

'Coulan would never betray us. We planned this with him for years; I know exactly what he thinks on any subject. He wants social justice just like we do.'

'I know.' She gave her feet a sheepish glance. 'I remember, too. He saved me. He was going to save everyone.'

'Then we must believe in him. We can't allow Slvasta's paranoia to contaminate us. That's one of the principles we were going to install, remember? Everyone is innocent until proven guilty.'

'He came up with that.'

'Yeah. Then, until we find out what's going on, we follow that principle.'

'Yes,' she said. 'We'll do that.'

Javier lumbered to his feet. It was an effort, and for a moment he felt dizzy. 'I should have been helping our comrades with the railway nationalization this afternoon.'

'Do you even know how to nationalize a railway company?'

'Sort of like taking it into new management, like I did with Coughlin's stall at the Wellfield market.'

'You need to scale up your thinking.' She paused, allowing her troubled thoughts to show through her shell. 'I meant what I said about not knowing what to do next. Do you think that's strange?'

'Listen, we're both tired like nothing we've experienced before. Of course we're going to make mistakes and forget things. Go easy on yourself. Look at the screw-up I've made of today.'

'No. It's more than that. We could always think of something before. How to organize the cells, political objectives, how to achieve our goals, strategies to manipulate public opinion. We sat down together and these ideas just kept coming. Fabulous ideas. Ideas that worked. Now we've won, and there's nothing. We can't figure out how to capitalize on what we've got. The city's falling apart; there's precious little food, the markets are closed, the water's still not running in half the boroughs, people are fleeing. We broke it, cleverly and carefully. Why don't we know how to put it all back together? We wanted this to be a decent fair society, so how come we had nothing ready to implement? Why no strategy to rebuild the rail bridges? Why not issue guarantees about life and liberty to reassure the professional classes that do the actual work?'

'The People's Interim Congress—'

'Is a farce.'

'That's a bit harsh.' He squirmed under her gaze. 'Okay, they're a bunch of idiots. But some of them are useful idiots. They mean well.'

612

'That's a magnificent epitaph. If we're not careful, we'll be singing it all the way to Giu.'

'What do you want, Bethaneve?'

'I don't know. I'm just saying it's strange. Strange that it didn't bother me before, either. It's as if we've suddenly used up every idea. Why?'

'All right. This is how it's going to go. You and I are going to find Coulan. Then the three of us are going to sit down like we did in the good old days of an entire week and a half ago, and think how to calm Slvasta down and get everything back on track. When we've done that, the four of us will brainstorm how to make the city work again; there may even be beer and sitting around in a pub involved. How's that sound?'

'Sounds like the best idea I've heard all day.'

There was a cab waiting for them outside Tarleton Gardens. Javier smiled as he helped Bethaneve inside. 'See? You do know how to keep some things working.'

She was deadly serious when she looked back and said: 'But this was something we knew we'd need before.'

Javier gave up.

The cab set off, moving quickly through the semi-deserted streets.

'He's moving,' Bethaneve announced after ten minutes. 'Leaving the National Congress building. There's a cab – not one on our list.'

'I'm going to 'path him,' Javier announced. He focused his mind, reaching over the rooftops towards First Night Square. 'Coulan. Coulan, my love, talk to me, please. I know you're there. I need you so much.'

'Uracus,' Bethaneve grunted. 'What did you say?'

'Why? What happened?'

'He just fuzzed that cab good and hard. My agent's ex-sight can't perceive it at all.'

'Why is he doing this?' Javier couldn't keep the hurt distress from his voice. 'What have I done?'

'Hang on,' Bethaneve settled back into the cab's leather bench seat. 'I'm going to activate all the cells around First Night Square. The comrades are still loyal, at least for now; they'll watch out for him. Fuzz can defeat ex-sight, but he can't hide the cab from good old-fashioned eyeball contact.'

A minute later someone saw the cab turn into Fletton Road. Then Coulan got out and hurried into the Tonsly shopping arcade. 'Uracus, there are twenty entrances to that place,' Bethaneve said. 'I wish we had Andricea's mod-bird.'

'She's one of Slvasta's loyalists.'

A single eye opened to give him a disapproving stare. 'That's wrong-thinking.'

'Sorry.' He followed the gifting Bethaneve sent him. Marvelling at the way she coordinated 'paths from dozens of cell members seemingly simultaneously. Images of streets and arcade halls flashed before him at bewildering speed.

'There!'

Fleeting glimpse of his beloved's pale skin and sandy hair disappearing fast down Makins Alley. Short sharp instructions flicked out to cell members. They changed direction, sped up, slowed down, hovered at road junctions.

Coulan called a cab on Lichester Road. Fuzzed it. A cab from the list turned onto the road behind him, three cell members hopped on.

There were three more changes of cab. A confusing run on foot through the maze of crooked alleys and tiny dark lanes of Saxby.

'Uracus,' Javier murmured admiringly as Bethaneve constantly shuffled the cell members about, interpreted images, anticipated moves. 'You own this city.'

She smiled, eyes still tight shut.

Coulan slipped into the Reynolds Hotel, emerging from a side door. A cell member, one of Bethaneve's elites, was lounging casually at the end of the alley. The last cab dropped him off along Breamer Street, where there were a lot of people milling round at the end, shuffling slowly forwards towards the Colbal. He merged into them.

614

'Only one reason for him to be there,' Bethaneve said in satisfaction.

'Cabby,' Javier called loudly. 'Quayside, and fast.'

*

For seventeen years Philious Brandt had been Captain of Bienvenido; a proud lineage, defending the world, maintaining order, regulating its economy, upholding the law, keeping politicians in line. The world belonged to him. And now it didn't.

It had been a day of sheer terror for him and his family. One moment he'd been 'pathing frantically with Trevene and the First Speaker and the captain of the Palace Guard; the next moment gunshots had rippled around the palace. A mob had appeared, and some kind of well-organized and trained military force had stormed the walls and railings. Hidden gunmen had shot the Palace Guard. Staff panicked – some running for freedom, a heartening number rushing to the private apartments to shelter and protect the family.

Philious had 'pathed and 'pathed for help: the Marines, the sheriffs, the regiment officers stationed in Varlan. But they too were under siege. And one by one their minds vanished from his perception.

Then came the gunfire in the palace corridors themselves. Twice he heard explosions, the screams of the dying. Souls of dead guards drifted through the innermost apartments, apologetic as they drifted up, starting their long flight towards Giu.

The family had retreated to the central drawing room, with its crystal chandeliers and priceless furniture and polished floor, with tall windows looking out over the manicured gardens. Seven of his children were huddled round him (Dionene was out somewhere, thank Giu, but he had a pretty good idea of Aothori's fate: his eldest son wasn't popular at the best of times), the younger ones crying, the older two brittlely defiant. Little granddaughter asleep, cradled in her petrified mother's arms. His wife stood beside him, stiff backed, showing courage for the children, her shell strong, but he knew the fear in her mind. Courtiers formed a protective picket around them, trying not to let their dread bloom.

Then the 'path had come. Coulan, offering terms of surrender. The life of everyone in the palace in exchange for taking the family into custody.

Philious agreed; he knew all about Coulan from Trevene's long briefings on Slvasta and his cronies. Coulan was the level-headed one. Even so, he half-expected to be shot as soon as the doors opened; the horror of the *Lanuux* and *Alfreed* was still fresh in his mind. But Coulan kept his word, and his militia were efficient and disciplined.

They were escorted down to a covered wagon and fuzzed as they were driven through the streets. The ride went on for a long time, but it finished at a small hotel in the Nalani borough. There they waited, guarded by Coulan's militia, while the mobs fought the authorities for control of the city.

Something about the militia members was eerily wrong. They wouldn't speak to the family, they kept a perfect guard on their prisoners, they didn't misbehave, nor threaten. The hotel was kept under an impervious teekay shell that must have been difficult to maintain, but it never wavered in all the time they were imprisoned. Philious half-suspected they were Fallers.

All they could do was wait. He forbade the children to discuss what their fate might be, but he knew speculation was gnawing at their minds. They might not be able to 'path through the militia's shell, but the sounds of fighting were clear enough, and the upper rooms gave them a glimpse out over the rooftops, where smoke was visible across the city.

Philious endured as best he could, never quite understanding how this had come to pass.

Then on the third day of captivity, a man called Yannrith appeared and ordered Philious to accompany him.

'No!' his wife cried. 'They'll kill you, they're animals, worse than Fallers! Don't go.'

'It's not us who are the animals,' Yannrith spat back at her. 'I saw what's inside the Research Institute. So did Aothori, a real close-up look.'

'Bastard! Murdering bastard.'

Philious held up his hand, anxious not to annoy this imposing man. 'I'll go.' He kissed his wife, very aware it was probably the last time he'd ever see her. 'You're not to worry. Be brave, for the children.'

There was an odd moment at the hotel's entrance. Two militiamen stood guard there, staring blankly ahead.

'Stand aside,' Yannrith ordered.

They didn't move.

'By order of the People's Interim Congress, which is this world's legitimate government, you will stand aside so I may conduct our prime minister's authorized business.'

It took a long moment, but the guards stepped aside. There were three cabs outside with armed comrades riding in them. Yannrith led Philious into the middle one, and fuzzed it heavily. Philious eyed the man, who was obviously regiment trained, and wondered again what had turned people like this against him.

'I'm curious,' Philious said. 'What exactly have you done to those poor militia people? I thought they might be Fallers at first, but they're not, are they?'

'Shut up,' Yannrith said.

'Threads perhaps, in their brains?'

'Last time: shut the crud up.'

Philious smiled at his small victory. He wasn't entirely surprised when after forty minutes of travelling they arrived back at the palace. But when they did finally step out into the inner courtyard and he sent his ex-sight probing round, he was immediately demoralized by what he perceived. 'Where is everything?' he demanded. 'What have you done with all— Oh, no! No!'

'We thought we'd start the redistribution of wealth from the top down,' Yannrith replied smugly.

'My wife is right – you are crudding animals. And pathetic, petty-minded ones at that.' Nonetheless he was worried about what the militia people had found below the palace; that would be far worse than the institute's secrets. *They won't understand any of it*, he told himself. *Not that it matters any more.*

A tall slender woman was waiting beside the door into the

private residence. Her shell was as hard as any Philious had ever encountered. She had a mod-bird perched on her arm, and she was feeding it a chunk of meat. He blinked. The meat had looked suspiciously like a human finger.

As he approached, she sent the mod-bird off into the sky. 'Welcome home, Captain,' she said in mockery.

Philious didn't respond. Nonetheless he couldn't help his growing worry as Yannrith and the woman escorted him down the stone stairs into the vaults. The regiment man seemed to know exactly where he was going.

Philious's final surprise was the man waiting for him in the ship's armoury cellar. His eyes narrowed at the empty jacket arm pinned across his chest. 'Captain Slvasta! Trevene warned me you were trouble.'

'He was right.'

'Are you going to kill me now?'

'No. Do you know why?'

'Because that would prove to the whole of Bienvenido that you're naught but a savage, and your pitiful revolution is a sham.'

'No. It's because I need to know something, and you might have the answer. That is your only value right now.'

'Go directly to Uracus. Even if I knew where Dionene was, I would willingly take Guidance to Giu before I told you.'

'That's not why you're here.'

'Then what . . .?'

Slvasta pointed his finger at the hulking mass of the *Vermillion*'s armoury behind him. 'What was in there?'

'I have no ide—'Captain Philious paused, terribly cautious of trickery. 'What do you mean, *was* in there?'

'Exactly that,' Slvasta said.

'I don't understand.'

'Andricea.'

The woman stepped forwards. 'One of our associates removed five large objects from this chamber – which we assume is part of Captain Cornelius's ship. There are plenty of other weird artefacts down here, none of which could have been made on this world.'

Philious shook his head. 'These are all just leftovers from the ship, that's all. Nothing works. They haven't worked for millennia.'

'You seemed concerned, just now, that something had been taken,' Andricea said. 'We don't know what those things were, but they're clearly valuable to someone. The militia people our associate employed have had something done to their minds, like hypnosis but so much stronger. It took a great deal of effort to get them to tell me that the objects had been taken, but I did break through their conditioning eventually. So tell me, Captain, how long do you think you can hold out against me?'

Philious glanced nervously at the armoury again. 'I don't believe you. This is some kind of trick. Nobody . . .' He licked his top lip, unsurprised to taste beads of sweat.

'Nobody what?' Slvasta asked coolly.

'Nothing works. I don't lie.'

'Then it doesn't matter if you tell us what was in there, does it?'

'This, none of this can help your doomed revolution. You will lose. The cities and counties will march into Varlan and send you straight to Uracus for your crimes.'

'*What was in there?*' Slvasta bellowed. His hand gripped a pistol tight, not quite waving it towards Philious.

'Nothing was taken. I know this because you can't get inside. The entrance doesn't work any more; it hasn't for over two thousand years.'

Slvasta grinned. It disturbed Philious badly.

'Oh, really? Come here.' His teekay shoved at Philious, urging him forwards.

Philious didn't resist. Then he got closer to the armoury – and froze. A wide circle close to the base had opened – the place his father had told him was the access hatch, made from a metal that Commonwealth ingenuity could make flow like water. 'Oh, Uracus,' he whispered. And the metal had indeed flowed once more; he could see it now as a thick rim around the hole. 'No, no, no.' He hurried forwards, and peered up into the absolute darkness of the interior with trepidation. Many years ago, when he was being prepared for the Captaincy – being tutored in their true heritage, in the old sciences, on the nature of the Void and how they must never drop their guard against the Fallers – his father had brought him to stand under the ship's armoury, where one of the small broken conduit tubes led up inside it. He had sent his ex-sight through the tiny gap, examining the strange dead war machines entombed within, frightened and impressed by the things his father told him about them.

Now his ex-sight ranged freely inside the armoury, perceiving the empty loading cradles. His legs trembled as he backed away, then he spun round and fixed Slvasta with a furious glare. 'They're gone!'

'No crud! Now tell me exactly what *they* are.'

'Quantumbusters,' Philious whispered in dread. 'There were five quantumbusters in there.'

The burst of emotion that came pouring through Slvasta's tenuous shell was a combination of anger and incomprehension. 'What the crud are quantumbusters?'

'The greatest weapon our ancestors ever created. They are so powerful they can destroy an entire sun and all its planets. They don't work in the Void. None of the old technology works any more.' Philious stared at the access hatch – impossibly open. 'Until today.'

*

Twenty armed men that Tovakar and Yannrith trusted implicitly piled into five cabs. Slvasta rode in the second cab, along with Yannrith and Captain Philious. Andricea herself was driving the lead cab, teekay and a whip sending the horse racing down Walton Boulevard, then along the quickest route to the quayside.

'I've 'pathed our comrades on a wharf,' Yannrith said. 'They're holding a steam ferry for us.'

'Let us hope it has a happier journey across than the *Lanuux* and the *Alfreed*,' Captain Philious said snidely.

'We didn't do that,' Slvasta snapped back.

'Really?'

'No.'

'Then who? Your mysterious associate?'

'I don't know.' Slvasta's headache was making him sweat now. It was a constant battle to keep his eyes open, the fatigue which gripped him was so strong. Thinking was difficult. But he had to know, to work this out. Could Coulan be some kind of counter-revolutionary? But if so, why had Trevene not arrested them all? And Javier, why was he suddenly pro-mod? Bethaneve – that was the one that really hurt. How was she connected to Nigel?

What am I missing?

'Did you know about us?' he asked the Captain.

'Trevene knew you were behind the mod-killing spree; that was obvious right from the start.'

'Why didn't you stop us?'

'Because there were just four of you – four that mattered, anyway. You were drawing all the hotheads and radicals together; you had some kind of communication arrangement with people from the Shanties and other undesirables. We couldn't break your system of contact, it was so random, but all the troublemakers were doing what you told them. It was impressive politics. Useful.'

'To you? How?'

'They do what you say. You do what we want. That's why we offered you Langley. And you took it.'

'Like all the greedy bastards before me.'

'Yes. We underestimated your fanaticism, that's all.'

'All? It's cost you everything.'

'You're gloating? After what's happened today? Be careful of your arrogance, Slvasta, or it will be your downfall. I should know.'

'So you had files on us?'

'Yes.'

'Tell me about Coulan.'

'Some kind of student, a history graduate, I think, who drifted into the radical scene. We never could find out where he came from.'

'Kassell, he came from Kassell. He's a junior son who came to Varlan's university to learn agricultural management so he could help run the family estate. While he was there he came to see the oppression of your regime.'

'No, you're wrong – or more likely lied to. There is no record of him in Kassell. Trevene checked.'

'He has to have come from somewhere!'

'Yes, but where is starting to concern me very badly – though he behaved perfectly honourably with me and my family, thank Giu. He's the associate who opened the armoury, isn't he?'

Slvasta nodded.

'I can't do that. The Captains haven't had a proper electrical supply for the last two thousand years. The Void is hostile to it. I know the theory; I even made a lead acid battery when I was learning about it, that's such a basic electrical power source even the Void doesn't spoil it. Slvasta, I've seen a wire filament glow red from its power; it was almost as bright as a candle flame. It was impressive. But this – his knowledge and ability – is a whole new level. We saw something strange and new in the Faller from Eynsham Square. It had threads in its brain, threads that could control it like Uracus's own puppet. That kind of machinery doesn't belong in the Void.'

'Wait. Someone controlled the Eynsham Square Faller?'

'Yes, and how that worked to your advantage, eh? Hero. I'm assuming Coulan is using a similar process to control his militia. So now I am almost scared to wonder where he came from. Do you believe he is working alone, or is he part of a bigger faction inside your precious revolution?'

'He's allied with Nigel, somehow.' Slvasta growled the name through a dry throat.

'Who?'

'One of our supporters.' Slvasta remembered his visit to Blair Farm, the compound with all its new barns – efficient, productive, humming with activity; the hundreds of mods scurrying about, which had made his blood run cold. 'He knows a lot about machines. And politics. But he's no Faller; I have seen his blood with my own eyes. It's red.'

'We certainly didn't have a file on him. So where does he come from?'

'He lives south of Varlan.'

'Ah, and here we are in hot pursuit of a convoy that crossed the river to the south bank. Tell me. When you captured me, the only major railway that was left intact was the Southern City Line. Why did you spare it?'

Slvasta hated the superior tone in the Captain's voice. 'We didn't. I don't know what happened to our sabotage teams, though I can make a crudding good guess now. And the Goleford bridge was blown this afternoon.' What was it Bethaneve had said? *Just after an express crossed it.*

'So they've taken the quantumbusters south. I still don't understand why. Even if they could get them to work again, which I have considerable doubts about, what would be the point? If they detonate a quantumbuster, it will wipe out Bienvenido, the Forest, and most likely our sun as well. Neither humans nor Fallers will survive.'

'Why then? Why? What has all this been for?'

'I don't know,' Philious said. 'But if you're ever going to find out, you need to catch up with your associates, and quickly.'

*

They'd lost Coulan as soon as he stepped off the ferry onto the south bank. Technically, Willesden was another borough of Varlan. But in reality it was a rather pleasant town with decent-sized houses and broad parks; there was only one Shanty on its border, and that none too big. Business here centred on trade, moving and storing goods brought in by the railway and the boats. A wide swathe of the town between the wharfs and station was made up entirely of warehouses.

In the aftermath of the revolution, travel was again a major preoccupation. Hundreds of refugees arrived every hour, all of them desperate for temporary lodgings and a way out into the southern countryside.

There weren't many cell members in Willesden. The ones that had been given duties had been redeployed days ago to find out what had happened to their comrades assigned to blow up the bridges. Bethaneve had summoned several to the riverbank area to help search, but they were slow coming.

She and Javier disembarked from the ferry as the sun hung close to the horizon, looking as if it was about to plunge into the river. Long rose-gold shimmers licked across the water, tinting the air a faint copper. They looked around in dismay. The chaos here was almost as bad as what they'd left behind them on the quayside, only the scale was reduced.

'Any ideas?' Bethaneve asked.

'Well, now that the Goleford bridge is down, he'll have to find himself either a boat or a horse.'

'Can he ride?'

'I've no idea. I've never seen him ride, but that doesn't mean anything.' Javier could feel his stomach tightening up at that admission. *What do I really know about him? I thought it was everything.*

'I've not seen him ride, either,' Bethaneve said. 'And if he can, we're not going to find him. So that leaves us with a boat.'

They looked along the river. On this side, it was mainly ferries and small boats that had just charged an extortionate fee for bringing desperate people over. There were only two big ocean-going cargo ships, their sails all furled. Both had big crowds of people at their gangplanks, all bidding against each other.

'They're not going to leave tonight,' Bethaneve decided. There were a few other boats, barges mainly, but their captains seemed intent on making a fortune charging passage across the Colbal. She scanned the houses of Willesden again. The land here didn't rise as it did on the Varlan side, but even so, it wasn't possible to see the countryside beyond. She narrowed her eyes as she tried to read the signposts at the top of each road leading away from the river.

'If he just wanted to get out of town,' she said slowly, thinking it through, 'he could have taken a cab, or used one of the local lines we didn't sabotage. So he came south of the river for a reason. He's got a very definite destination in mind.'

'Yes. But what?'

'The last thing Yannrith said was that Kysandra was in a convoy on Walton Boulevard heading down the hill. That's south.'

'You think they came over the river as well?'

'And not long after that, the Goleford bridge was blown.'

'But Coulan was in the National Council building when that happened,' Javier insisted.

'Yes. So he's stuck here as well, unless . . . You're in charge of the railways now, right?'

'Well, sort of, yes.'

'Did you get around to nationalizing the Southern City Line?'

'Yes. My people came across to take over the management offices yesterday. I was going to visit soon.'

'They only blew up the Goleford bridge,' Bethaneve said. 'We planned on taking out three south of the river. Can you 'path your people, find out what other rail lines there are out of town?'

'That I can do.'

The answer came back within a minute.

'There are two local line stations,' Javier said, his eyes closed as he received the 'path. 'Balcome and Scotdale. Their lines go east and west.'

'Right, now find out if either of those lines cross the Goleford. Do they link up with the main line south of here?'

Javier's weary face broke into a slow smile. 'Uracus, you're good. The line from Balcome splits fifty miles out, and one track goes south. It reconnects with the main southern line at Fosbury.'

'Next train?' Bethaneve asked.

'Twenty-three minutes.'

*

Balcome station was small: two platforms, both with prim wooden canopies, and a stone ticket office. A typical branch-line station in a pleasant part of town. Thick vines with topaz flowers scrambled up the outside wall of the ticket office, layering the air with a sweet scent. There was nobody in the ticket office when Bethaneve and Javier walked in; thick shutters were down across the booth. The platform was a different matter. In the deepening shadow thrown by the canopy, people were packed five or six deep along its whole length, families clinging together, children all cried out and now just staring numbly down the tracks. Those nearest the ticket office door gave Javier a fearful look as he emerged. He'd not given it any thought, but his carbine was slung on a strap over his drosilk jacket's shoulder, and four magazines were clipped to his belt. Carrying it openly was second nature now, every comrade's badge of honour. The carbines Nigel supplied were quite distinctive; they had a high fire rate and hardly ever jammed. By now they were recognizable to everybody in Varlan.

The gifted image of Javier spread down the platform faster than sound. It triggered a surge of anxiety and distress. Children clung to their parents; men glared defiantly.

Bethaneve's hand went automatically to the pistol holstered on her belt. She was dismayed by the way people were reacting to her and Javier, but anger burnt there, too. *We're the good guys. Why don't you understand that? We're trying to help, to give you a better future.*

'What do you want?' someone 'pathed.

'Can't you leave us alone?'

'Haven't you killed enough of us?'

'Savages.'

'They murdered my brother. He was a sheriff, he protected us from criminals.'

'I recognize her. She's Slvasta's fiancée.'

'Bitch.'

People were backing away from them, leaving them alone in the centre of a deluge of hatred.

'We're not here to hurt you,' Bethaneve 'pathed. 'We're looking for someone.' She gifted an image of Coulan. 'Has anyone seen him?'

'No!'

'What did he ever do?'

'Gave people jobs, most likely.'

'Are you going to murder him, as well?'

'Please,' Bethaneve 'pathed. 'He's a friend.'

'Yeah, right.'

'Lying whore.'

Teekay stabbed out. Bethaneve's shell was tight; otherwise the spike of psychic power would have jabbed into her eyes. As it was, she stumbled backwards from the blow.

'Hey!' Javier yelled. He lifted up the carbine. 'Pack that in. We're here on official business.'

'You're not my government, crudhead.'

'Who voted for you?'

Somewhere in the distance, a train whistle sounded.

Several teekay blows slapped at Javier. He rocked about, then flicked the safety catch off. 'Draw your pistol,' he private 'pathed Bethaneve. 'This might get nasty.'

Reluctantly, she did as he advised.

'Going to shoot us for objecting?'

'So we're not allowed opinions any more?'

Javier pointed his carbine into the air and fired off two shots. Children screamed. Everybody cowered. They backed away further.

'I'm going to politely ask you one last time,' Javier said. 'Has anyone seen this man?' He 'pathed out the image of Coulan as hard as he could.

Bethaneve stared round at the faces, disturbed by the naked outpouring of loathing. Vile images were starting to flicker through the general psychic torrent, images of her being abused, graphic fantasies of Javier being kicked, punched, beaten, a noose round his neck. She gripped the pistol tighter, wondering how everything had turned so wrong so quickly.

The train whistle sounded again, louder this time.

Then amid all the hostility, a few glimmers of smugness appeared. She saw nearby faces beginning to smile haughtily. People directed their gaze behind her. Silence spread out so fast she thought she'd lost her hearing.

'Please don't move, my loves.' The 'path was so kind, so sincere, it resonated right into the centre of her mind as if she had no shell at all. She was so thrilled to perceive it; she did exactly what it asked.

Coulan walked between her and Javier. Her heart began to

beat faster at the sight of him; the relief that he was all right was profound. She smiled in welcome.

He smiled back, which made her want to fling her arms round him in happiness. But he had asked her not to move, so she didn't.

'I don't want you to worry about me,' he said as the train started to ease into the station. 'Everything is going to be just fine, I promise. Now I have to go away for a week or so, then I'll be back, and it will be a whole new life for everyone on Bienvenido. You'll see.'

Bethaneve sighed in delight. He was okay, and the world was going to be all right now.

The engine rolled past, pistons hammering away, gusts of steam shooting out horizontally from valves to swirl across the platform, thick smoke puffing from the stack. It pulled five carriages along behind it.

'Everybody,' Coulan said, and raised both arms in universal appeal, 'the train is here. Let's get on board, shall we? No need for any unpleasantness. These well-meaning people aren't going to hurt anybody.'

Bethaneve could see Javier standing beside her, his face sculpted into a mask of despondent longing.

Then the crowd was pouring into the carriages. Bethaneve didn't mind. Coulan was all right; nothing else mattered. And she was helping him enormously by just staying still.

Coulan gave Javier a small lopsided grin. 'I'll see you soon,' he promised, and kissed Javier gently. Turned and began walking towards the train.

The carbine's roar was as loud as it was shockingly unexpected. It broke Bethaneve's trance, and she flung herself down, screaming as she jammed her hands over her ears. Right in front of her, not four metres away, Coulan's buttocks and lower torso disintegrated into a mass of tattered flesh and an expanding blood spume. His abdomen exploded outwards, tendrils of gore thrashing through the ripped shirt. The body collapsed onto the platform, pitching over so his head was facing up. Dying eyes stared peacefully at the twilight sky, then closed.

Bethaneve seemed to be deaf. Her eyesight contracted into a

long grey tunnel with Coulan's corpse blocking the far end. That was all there was.

Sound forced its way back into her consciousness. Screams, so many screams, and so loud that her shock couldn't deny them any more. Her own voice was one of them. He was dead, her old love, her saviour. Dead. Cut down by—

Bethaneve jerked round. Slvasta was standing just outside the ticket office door, Tovakar and Yannrith and Andricea clustered behind him, more armed comrades in the background. Slvasta ejected the magazine clip from his still-smoking carbine, and his teekay jammed in a replacement.

'What have you *done*?' Bethaneve wailed.

Javier charged past her, his face contorted with rage, arms outstretched as he reached for Slvasta, roaring in demented fury. Andricea stepped forward, caught Javier's wrist. There was some kind of lithe twisting motion as she shifted her weight round, thrust with her teekay, bent sideways – and Javier's entire bulky form was somehow flying through the air. He crashed to the ground with a hefty thud, winding him. Tovakar was immediately beside him, pistol pressed against his temple. 'Don't!' he warned.

Slvasta came over to stand beside Bethaneve, looking down at her, his features completely blank. 'Why didn't you move? Why didn't you stop him? You followed him here, you wanted to talk to him just as badly as I did. Why didn't you ask him something? Anything?'

She shook her head. 'I couldn't. He . . . he told me not to and I couldn't.' She wiped at the tears on her cheeks. 'I knew I should, I just didn't want to. What did he do to me?' she whimpered in panic. 'Who is he?'

'I don't know.' Slvasta held his hand out to her.

After a second's hesitation, she reached up and took it. He helped her to her feet. She stood, wobbling about slightly, then risked a glance at the corpse. There was so much blood, all of it a rich crimson, spreading out obscenely across the platform.

Slvasta turned to Javier. 'It wasn't human,' he said. 'Do you understand? This is a new kind of Faller, him and Nigel.'

A frightened Javier stared up mutely.

There was something very wrong about Coulan's corpse. Bethaneve couldn't quite work out what, but instinct was shrieking a warning directly out of her subconscious. Was it his soul, was she perceiving that? She extended her ex-sight to the air above the body. 'Slvasta!' She stumbled back a pace, pressing herself into Slvasta's side.

'What?'

'He's still got a shell round his thoughts.'

'Huh?'

Everyone swung round to look at Coulan. Yannrith and Tovakar lined their carbines up, as did most of Slvasta's body-guard troop.

'His crudding shell,' Bethaneve yelped. 'It's still there!'

Slvasta edged closer.

Coulan's eyes snapped open.

Bethaneve's mouth parted wide; an involuntary reflex drew air down her throat in a groan.

'That was an excellent fuzz,' Coulan 'pathed. 'As good as my concealment effect. I never perceived you coming. Well done.'

'Faller!' snarled Slvasta. He took a step forward and jammed his carbine muzzle onto the bridge of Coulan's nose.

'Not at all,' Coulan continued calmly.

'Then what the crud . . . ?'

'This life is over. For all of you. We're going to take you back into the real universe. Put down your guns. Forget your conflict. Everything is about to change.'

'What are you?' Slvasta bellowed.

'I am a machine, a living machine.'

'You can't be!'

A man walked over to them. Bethaneve thought she was too numb from everything that had happened to feel anything, but the sight of him made her moan in dismay.

'What do you want with my family's quantumbusters?' Captain Philious demanded.

'They will be used to liberate you.' Coulan closed his eyes. 'If you'll excuse me, I must shut down now. My reserve energy levels can't sustain me for much longer, and I have an autonomic destruct sequence – just in case. Please stand back, I don't want anyone to get hurt.'

'Did you ever love me?' Javier sobbed.

'My dearest Javier, don't be sad. I am bringing you all back to reality. That is the greatest love of all. I give it to you freely.'

The skin on Coulan's pale face started to blacken. Slvasta winced and pulled the carbine away, took a couple of hasty steps back. Coulan's head, torso and legs burst into flames. They began to burn inwards fiercely, throwing off a great heat. Bethaneve clung to Slvasta, watching aghast as the *thing* she had once loved charred down to a mound of ash in less than three minutes. She sank to her knees and threw up, too distraught to think straight any more. Nothing made sense. All of this was unreal. It couldn't be happening, it just couldn't.

'What do we do now, captain?' she heard Yannrith asking.

'He said: we,' Slvasta growled. '*We* are liberating you. There's more of them loose on our world. And I know where their nest is. So we stop them. Then we kill them. That is liberation.'

5

'These are in worse condition than I thought,' Nigel said as the express train rattled its way southwards through the night. They were charging through the scheduled stations; the only stops they did make were to take on fresh coal and water for the engine.

The quantumbusters were riding in one of the passenger carriages that'd been fitted out as a basic machine shop. Kysandra had been moderately impressed by the weapons, even though she'd already seen the images from the drone in the palace cellar. The wasp-waist cylinders were over two metres long, and heavy with it, as if they were carved from solid metal. Lifting them had taken a lot of muscle and teekay. Once they were in place, a simple sweep of teekay banished the dust and grime to reveal dull grey casings in good condition. The warheads were nestled at the back of the bulbous head, which her ex-sight could just perceive through the high-density casing and thick-packed components. But she felt that the rear end with the ingrav drive's weird warty protuberances looked more sinister.

Nigel, Fergus and Valeri were scanning the quantumbusters with ex-sight and various sensor modules. Little access hatches of malmetal were being powered up and opened, so more sophisticated tests could be run directly on the components inside.

'We don't need the drive systems, or any of that junk,' Fergus said. 'Nor the force fields. Just the warheads.'

'Warhead,' Valeri corrected.

'Can you get one of them to work?' Kysandra asked.

Nigel looked up from the quantumbuster he was examining. A crown of modules was trailing wires and fibre-optic strands into the open ports and hatches. Spherical power cells on the floor had been plugged in to various sections with heavy-duty cable.

'I think so. There's been secondary system component degradation, of course, but then we knew we'd have to deal with that. The systems *Skylady* has synthesized should be adequate to initiate the warhead. We'll start a rebuild as soon as we get home. But the real trick is going to be modifying the effect itself. I won't be able to determine the final program until I'm inside the Forest; once I'm there, I can run an accurate analysis on its quantum distortion field signature.'

'And, as the old quote goes: what science can analyse, science can duplicate,' Fergus said.

'Let's hope so,' Nigel muttered. 'Or we're going to need a bigger boat.'

Kysandra nodded apprehensively. 'Okay.'

Nigel looked up for a moment and winked at her. 'Don't worry, it's all worked out so far, hasn't it?'

She grinned despairingly. 'Oh, yes. But that's only because you know everything.'

'One more week,' he promised. 'Maybe less.'

'Really? How long to rebuild the warhead?'

'I'm thinking a day, maybe two at the most. Some of that can be done en route.'

'So all we really have to do is launch?'

'Yeah. Marek should have the booster stack assembled by now.'

'So will you land again before you detonate the quantumbuster? That'll be safer than being in space. Won't it?'

The two ANAdroids became very still. Nigel's gaze remained steady. His lopsided smile was no longer teasing. 'Kysandra,' he began awkwardly, 'I need to be there in case anything goes wrong.'

'There? There where?'

'I've got to see this through. I'm sorry, I thought you under-stood that.'

'No! No, you can't,' she cried. 'Send one of the ANAdroids. They can do it.'

'They can, if nothing goes wrong. Possibly if something does go wrong, too. But I can't take that chance; there's too much at stake here. A whole world of people, Kysandra. If there's some-thing unexpected up there, if we have to change the mission for whatever reason, I'll need to innovate.'

'But . . . But, they can do that!' She was mortified that her throat was tightening up, tears building behind her eyes. Any moment now, if this conversation continued, she might burst out crying.

'They can do a great deal, including work through logical options. Their bioprocessor brains are the best we can make. But if we need a non-logical solution – that's where I come in. I can't leave it to chance, Kysandra. It has to be me in the *Skylady*.'

'No!'

'If I can remote detonate, then I will. Of course I will. But we have to be prepared, and certain.'

'You'll die. It'll be permanent. If the quantumbuster rips the Void apart, there will be no Giu left to reach, no Heart to accept your soul.' She heard what she was saying and hated it; her old ingrained belief hadn't been eradicated by the knowledge he'd given her so freely, just suppressed. *I am rational, really I am. It's just . . .*

Nigel walked over to her and put his arms round her, exactly the way he had at their wedding ceremony. This time he stroked her back instead of patting it. 'I won't die,' he said quietly. 'I haven't told you this before, I didn't want you upset or confused, but this body, it's actually a clone loaded with my memories and personality. The original me is still out there, Kysandra. Right now, I'm also alive in the real universe. I'm out there. Waiting.'

'What? You can't be.'

'I am. True.'

'You mean you're not really you?'

'Of course I am,' he chortled. 'But you know my ego: I'm far too important to actually die, so I sent this me into the Void to do my own dirty work. I never expected to make it back, although I never expected the mission would be like this, either. Kysandra, I never expected to meet you. Strange, the things fate throws at us.'

She nodded, not trusting herself to say anything.

'We'll meet again someday, somewhere,' Nigel said. 'I promise you that. And it will be the happiest day I've had for a thousand years, because I'll get to see you live as you deserve to. That's what this is about, that's why this version of me exists. Let me fulfil my destiny, so I can watch you achieve yours.'

'I don't want another you. I want this one.'

'The other one is the original, the best. You'll see. Just don't ever tell him I said that, okay? Keep it between us.'

'Do you always have to be right?'

'It's what I am.'

'I want to be right, too, just for once.'

'That's my girl.'

*

They changed tracks at Fosbury, switching the branch-line train onto the main Southern City Line. Nobody challenged Slvasta's bodyguard troops as the comrades swarmed into the signal box to pull the big iron levers which moved the points over, even though the revolution hadn't even been acknowledged this far from Varlan. Bethaneve curled up on one of the long bench seats and fell asleep as the carriage rocked about.

Javier woke her as dawn was breaking. A pale gold light was streaming in through the windows facing east. The only nebula left in the sky was Uracus itself – a venomous russet mist, twined with topaz fronds as if the interstellar dust storms were two kinds of giant space weed writhing round each other. For some reason, the empty gulf along its centre seemed larger today. Below it, fog lay across the land, meandering through the hollows like a lake of sluggish oil, with trees and the roofs of farm buildings poking through. Hills rumpled the horizon.

'Where are we?' she asked. Every limb ached from the cramped bench as she stretched laboriously. But – thank Giu – the worst of the exhaustion had left her.

'Five hours out from Dios,' Javier said. 'Apparently we just passed through a place called Normanton.'

'No idea where that is.' She massaged the base of her neck, which was badly kinked from being pressed up against the armrest. 'You know I've never been out of the city before?'

'I lived in Sigen for a couple of years, but that's all.'

She glanced down the carriage. Most of the bodyguard troops seemed to be sleeping, but those who were awake were vigilant. Slvasta was sitting on a bench at the far end, flanked by Andricea and Yannrith. Bethaneve did her best to keep a scowl from her face.

'She can't replace you,' he said softly.

'He probably thinks I'm a . . . Oh, crud, Javier, what in Uracus was Coulan?'

'I don't know,' he said, shell hardening to veil his emotions. 'But not a Faller, that's for sure.'

She lowered her voice. 'He said he was a machine. He wasn't human, not proper human.'

'He cared about us, that's all I know. Whatever he was doing, it's bigger than the revolution. A lot bigger.'

'"Take you back into the real universe", that's what he said. What in Giu's name did he mean?'

'I've no idea. I guess he must have been talking about the universe outside the Void, the one Captain Cornelius came from.'

'But . . . going back there? That's crazy.'

'I know. But he certainly wasn't like you and me, anyway. I've been thinking about that. I believe he was a better kind of human. That he came to the Void to help us.'

'You could be right,' she said hurriedly. 'He was better.' She could see how badly he was suffering.

'So, it's not impossible, is it? Not completely?'

'Maybe not. I wonder if Nigel is a part of whatever they're planning?'

636

'I suppose so.'

Bethaneve looked down the carriage again, still perturbed to see Captain Philious sitting opposite Slvasta. 'Did Slvasta sleep?'

'Yes. He woke up a few minutes ago. That's why I got you up.'

'Good. If he slept, he will have calmed down. We can try and talk some sense into him.'

'He won't listen to me. Not after yesterday. Coulan and I were together. I can't be trusted. It's got to be you.'

She put her hand on top of his. 'He fooled everybody.'

'Maybe I wanted to be fooled. He was . . . perfection.'

'I know. I remember. So perfect I wasn't even jealous when he left me for you. I was just glad he was happy. Can you imagine that?'

'I don't know,' he said in a shaky voice. 'It just hurts.'

She squeezed his hand. 'I'll go talk to Slvasta.'

Andricea eyed her warily as she walked down the aisle between the benches. There was clearly a private 'path exchange between her and Slvasta. She got up and gave Bethaneve a neutral smile. 'I'll go and see if there's anything to eat. There's got to be some tea, at least.'

'Thanks.' Bethaneve looked down expectantly at Slvasta.

When he returned her gaze he was actually sheepish. 'Please,' he said, and half stood.

She sat beside him, and couldn't quite bring herself to look at the Captain sitting on the bench opposite.

'I'm sorry about yesterday,' he said. 'I said things I just didn't mean. Forgive me.'

She leaned forward and gave him a soft kiss. 'We were all under a lot of stress, and Ingmar didn't help.'

'Crudding right!' He exhaled loudly. 'I didn't understand what was happening.'

'And do you now?'

'Not really.'

'So what are we doing?'

'Stopping them. I know where Nigel lives. I've been to his nest.'

'Who is *them*, my love?'

'The Fallers.'

'I'm not sure Coulan was a Faller. He said he was a machine.'

'He controlled us,' Slvasta said. 'Humans and other Fallers; the one from Eynsham Square had something odd in its brain, Captain Philious told me. So he controlled us without us even knowing. Controlled us as if we were his mods, all running round doing what he wanted. Thinking it was what we wanted.'

She stared across at Captain Philious. 'I still want justice and democracy for everyone. I wanted that before I met him. That will never change.'

'Whereas all he wanted were the quantumbusters from my palace,' the Captain said.

'I don't know what they are.'

'A bomb. A bomb my ancestor brought with him to the Void, rightly or wrongly. A bomb powerful enough to blow up Bienvenido itself. How does that bring anyone justice?'

'Do you think he was a Faller?'

'I don't see what else he could have been. Maybe one of their ruling class. Their equivalent to me.'

She shook her head. 'If there are Fallers like that, then we would all have Fallen a thousand years ago. Coulan and Nigel, they're different.'

'They want to destroy us. How is that different?'

Bethaneve tipped her head back, resting it on the thin cushioning. It was no use; she knew Slvasta could never be argued round when it came to Fallers. She suspected the Captain was playing him, exploiting his weakness to gain advantage.

Uracus, am I paranoid? If I protest, if I argue against this now, Slvasta will never trust me again. I have to stay with him, to help him before he is ruined by this. If he Falls, so does the revolution.

'I don't suppose it is,' she said. 'So what's the plan?'

*

It was still dark when the express arrived at the outskirts of Dios, with just a hint of dawn's coronal blaze in the eastern sky. The delicate gossamer nebulas were retreating back into night, shying away from the sunlight. The big engine came to a halt amid bursts of steam and a drawn-out clanking of brakes, ending with the pistons reversing and spinning the wheels backwards. Two hundred metres ahead, the pale orange lights of the main station signal box shone weakly down onto the maze of tracks. Inside the box, the signalman obediently pulled several long levers, changing the points. Madeline removed her carbine's muzzle from his crotch.

'Branch line is open,' she 'pathed to the express.

It began to move forward again, switching across tracks until it was heading down the line to Erond. Once it was clear of the junction, it began to pick up speed again.

Three and a half hours later, with the sun now well above the horizon, it slipped into the small marshalling yard at the side of Erond's station. Merchants and wholesalers who were waiting for their morning deliveries watched the unscheduled arrival with interest. They didn't get too close, though; Russell and others from Ma's organization were standing round in their long drosilk coats, carbines held prominently, making sure there was plenty of space for the two steam cars to back up to the carriage.

Kysandra followed Nigel out of the carriage. The fresh morning air was tainted with the smell of coal smoke and hot oil. She perceived a lot of ex-sight gliding over her and the cars, mainly from all the merchants. But there were no curious sheriffs, no authorities. Nigel had infiltrated the county administration very effectively.

Marek was in charge of the yard crew and quickly orchestrated everyone to create a strong shell around the carriage carrying the quantumbusters. Inside its protective shroud, the warheads were loaded onto trailers towed by the steam cars. Once they were secured, Marek's people mounted up on horses, and the cars drove out of the yard.

Within twenty minutes, the cavalcade had driven through the outskirts and reached the new river road to Adeone. With a screech of fast-moving metal, the steam cars started to accelerate.

*

Slvasta's train pulled in at Dios station just before midday. The station manager himself came out onto the platform to meet the second unscheduled train of the morning. His indignation was exuded as a badge of authority, but it began to falter as his ex-sight picked up the three armed men in the engine's cab along with the driver and fireman. Strangely, there were no mod-dwarfs to help shovel coal.

What was left of his bluster vanished altogether as the body-guard troop began to pile out of the first carriage. Dios knew all about the carbines which the revolutionaries used. Then Slvasta himself came striding down the platform, the self-proclaimed prime minister of the new People's Interim Congress. Fright began to leak out of the station manager's mind. If Slvasta was here, Dios was going to suffer as Varlan had. Fear gave way to outright astonishment as he saw Captain Philious walking beside Slvasta.

Hundreds of local people were absorbing the station manager's involuntary gifting as Slvasta came up to him. 'Did the express from Varlan stop here?'

'Uh, no, not really, sir. Sirs! It switched to the Erond line. My signalman was forced to open the points for them. He had to; she held a gun to his head.'

'So nobody got off?'

'No, sir. I don't think so. It barely stopped.'

'Okay. Now, where is the county regiment headquarters?'

*

The Dios county regimental headquarters was a huge four-storey stone building stretching for over two hundred metres along Fothermore Street at the centre of the city. Behind the façade were several acres of grounds dominated by the broad parade ground, then various stables, barracks, officers' quarters, a shooting range, stores, even a small regimental museum, and of course the armoury, all laid out in a neat grid and surrounded by a three-metre-high wall. Eighteen hundred years ago, Captain Kanthori had decreed that all regiments should fortify their compounds in case their county ever came under siege from Fallers. People would have a refuge until help arrived.

The Dios regiment had loyally maintained its fortifications for all those centuries. Slvasta was very aware of that as he led his troop along Fothermore Street. There were no pedestrians left on the road; people had been clearing out of the way from the moment he left the train station. News of his arrival had flashed across the city; now ex-sight played over him from behind a thousand locked doors.

Up ahead, there was a final outbreak of loud knocks and thuds as the big iron-bound shutters were slammed across the windows of the regimental headquarters. The huge solid gates in the archway entrance at the middle of the façade had been shut several minutes earlier.

As he drew closer, he saw the rifle barrels emerge from narrow slits in the stone, making the building bristle. He looked at Captain Philious beside him. 'Talk to the brigadier.'

'Perhaps.'

Slvasta turned to him in astonishment. 'What?'

'I don't believe we've had the discussion of what happens after.'

Andricea stepped forward, drawing a wickedly sharp dagger. 'You little shit.'

'No.' Slvasta held his hand up. Andricea scowled, but sheathed the dagger again.

'What do you want?' Slvasta asked.

'What are your plans for my family?'

'Normalization.'

'Excuse me?'

'You start life again level with the rest of us. Work hard, earn a living.'

Captain Philious looked at him in contemptuous amusement. 'Great Giu, you really believe that, don't you? Just how naive are you?'

Bethaneve stepped up. 'All right, here's the deal. Amnesty for everyone involved in the revolution, no matter what their crime.

Your family are released from our custody, and you keep one third of all your estates and shares, crud like that. You devolve true power to a democratically elected parliament with a written bill of rights guaranteeing civil liberties for all citizens.'

'Are you crazy?' Slvasta demanded. 'You'd let him keep his money? That gives him power.'

'Take away their constitutional position, and they're just another bunch of useless hedonistic aristos. We've destroyed Trevene's organization, my people made sure of that. Nobody's going to follow him if he mounts a counter-revolution. In fact, let him try. It'll use up his money even more quickly.'

'No!'

'Half of my estates,' Captain Philious said.

'Done.'

'I said no,' Slvasta snapped. He glared at the Captain. 'Talk to the brigadier or your whole family will be executed.'

Captain Philious regarded him coolly. 'One 'path from me and everyone on this street dies from those guns, myself included. Actually, no 'path from me will probably have the same result pretty soon; the regiment is getting a bit nervous, in case you hadn't perceived. The three of you are all that's left of the revolution's leadership. It dies with you. The countryside will rise up under my relatives and march on Varlan. I expect the bloodshed will last for years.'

'The Fallers!' Slvasta yelled in an agony of anger. 'They have the quantumbusters. They will kill us all!'

'Then you have three choices. Keep me alive with a decent estate to maintain my lifestyle while you elect your genuinely democratic parliament, and the Dios regiment marching on Nigel's nest. Death in the next couple of minutes. Or the Fallers victorious.'

'That is not a choice.'

'You swore an oath, Captain Slvasta, an oath to defend Bienvenido – all of Bienvenido – against the Fallers. The same Fallers who manipulated you and your friends into overthrowing my government, leaving this world in political chaos, all so they could snatch the greatest weapon of all. Your revolution was a fraud from start to finish. Now is your chance to put things right.'

Slvasta wanted to throw himself at the Captain, tear him apart. His rage sent blood pounding in his head under tremendous pressure, threatening to burst his temple open. All he saw was the undead corpse of Coulan, sprawled on Balcome's station platform, the Faller's terrible, calm confidence as he spoke of their impending liberation. Then the Faller-Ingmar sneered victoriously up at him from the pit, reaching right out of the nightmare that never ended.

'We will burn you from our world,' he told the filthy memory loud and clear. 'I swear it. No matter what the cost.'

'Is that your answer?' The Captain's voice was so calm it was mockery.

'Slvasta.' Bethaneve was holding his arm, her face and mind alight with concern. 'We will have eliminated the Captaincy. Maybe not how we thought, but there will be change now. People will have a voice; they will have justice.'

'Yes,' he whispered.

'What?' Captain Philious asked.

'Yes!' Bethaneve said, incensed. 'We will march on Nigel's nest. Together.'

'For a moment there, you had me worried.'

'And you will remain in our custody until this is over and we are back in Varlan, where the agreement will be signed.'

'Naturally.' Captain Philious turned to the daunting wall of the regimental headquarters, with dozens of rifles following his smallest move. 'Brigadier Doyle,' he 'pathed, 'could you step out here for a moment, please?'

*

Two hundred regiment troops came with them, led by Brigadier Doyle herself. The Dios station manager hurriedly organized two trains, one to carry the horses in long open trucks. Terrestrial horses only, Slvasta insisted. Within an hour, both trains were steaming fast for Erond.

*

643

They came to the first bridge twenty minutes after leaving Erond – an old stone spandrel arch over a modest, but fast-flowing river. There was a three-metre gap in the middle where explosives had blasted the stones apart. Most had fallen into the water, while others were embedded in the muddy banks.

When the regiment came galloping down the road, there were dozens of people milling round trying to decide what to do. The road on either side was clogged with horses and carts. Slvasta rode his horse to the start of the bridge, forcing people out of the way. He stared at the gap for a long minute. Behind him the regiment came to a halt, ex-sight straining forward to find out what the problem was, their horses whinnying, stomping about anxiously.

'They'll have blown every bridge on the way to Adeone,' Javier said, reining in his horse beside Slvasta. 'You know that, don't you?'

'Yes. And we can't allow that to stop us.' Without warning Slvasta urged his horse forward, 'pathing relentless orders into its nervous brain. It galloped along the stones, the gap seemingly expanding as he drew closer. Then the horse was jumping, and the water was a giddy eight metres below. He landed on the far side, clearing the gap easily.

'Come on,' he bellowed.

Laughing wildly, Javier charged his own horse along the broken bridge.

*

Fergus and Marek accompanied Kysandra, trekking over the river at the side of the Blair Farm compound, then along a narrow trail that mod-dwarfs had laboriously cleared through the woods. They rode sturdy terrestrial horses, each leading another horse, laden with bags.

She'd never actually explored this part of the countryside before. It was wild land, undulating to create marshy vales and dense spinneys. Nobody had ever filed a claim on any of it, at the county land office; taming it would take decades and cost more than any revenue a farm would ever generate. Far ahead, the foothills of the Algory mountains rose above the jagged rock outcrops and the sparse, wind-bowed trees.

They made good time, their horses walking steadily through the tangled scrub and soft grassland. It was a gradual climb eastwards, with the slopes gradually increasing their gradient and height. A pair of ge-eagles glided languidly overhead, scanning the terrain ahead. Nothing much moved – a few nests of bussalores, some feline daravan slinking about. Birds wheeled through the air, startled by the intrusion.

The sun was low in the west when they topped a tall rise, where spartan raddah bushes formed a meandering spine along the ridge.

'This should do,' Fergus announced.

The three of them dismounted. They stood facing the sinking sun, looking across the land they'd just traversed. Kysandra's eyes filtered out the glare as they zoomed in on Blair Farm, thirty kilometres distant. It wasn't her farm any more, the sweet homestead where she'd been born. This was a giant artificial square of neat buildings sliced into the valley, surrounded by a geometric pattern of fields. *Like something a machine built*, she thought. Which wasn't a bad way of describing it. It was strange to be looking at it, acknowledging what an accomplishment it was, how much work and effort had been expended, and knowing that it was about to vanish in a firestorm.

Rich gold sunlight shone on *Skylady*, its bold curving triangle shape sitting on top of the solid rocket booster stack. It towered over all the other buildings in the compound, a glorious monument to hope. Kysandra felt immeasurably proud, looking at the old starship as it was about to be given a stormy ride back up into space, where it truly belonged.

I helped make this happen.

But at such a terrible price.

She told her u-shadow to open a link to the starship. The connection was weak, with a very low bandwidth. 'How's it going?' she asked.

'Hello, ground control,' Nigel replied. 'Well, here am I, sitting on a load of pigshit, commencing countdown, may Giu's love be with me.'

'Er, are you okay?'

'Yeah. Running the final test sequences on the boosters now.'

'How long until you launch?'

'Maybe five minutes. The systems are simple enough, but I have to be absolutely certain I can ignite all five first-stage boosters simultaneously. So far so good.'

'Nigel—'

'Don't. We promised no goodbyes. Because I'm not leaving, not really. I'm out there, on the other side of the barrier, waiting to say hello. Remember?'

Kysandra closed her eyes, trying to keep the fear at bay. 'Yes.'

'And you know it's true, because I'm—'

'—always right. Yes, I think I know that now.'

'That's my girl.'

'Where will we go? Out there in the Commonwealth?'

'Ah, good question. Earth, of course, where it all began. Cressat, which is my own planet.'

'Nigel! You do not own a whole planet!'

'Do too!'

'How?'

'Told you I was rich.'

She was grinning at his silliness. 'Yes, but—'

'Uh, oh.'

'What?'

'The cavalry has arrived.'

6

Slvasta had been out in front on the whole ride from Erond. He was always the first to jump the gaps in the bridges, the first to force his horse into the raging waters when the destruction was too big to jump. Javier and Tovakar and Yannrith were with him all the time. Just behind them, Bethaneve struggled to keep up, suffering from her lack of experience with horses. Next was Andricea and the bodyguard troop forming a phalanx around Captain Philious and Brigadier Doyle, who insisted on riding with her Captain. Then came the bulk of the regiment, grim and resolute, carrying the heaviest weapons their horses could manage.

By the time they passed Adeone, Slvasta knew his horse was barely going to make it to Blair Farm. It was sweating heavily, foam flecking its head and neck. Still he rode it onwards relentlessly.

Finally, after hours of riding along the road lined by young follrux trees, he came to the unmarked turning. 'This is it,' he 'pathed everybody in the cavalcade. 'Ready your weapons, and watch out for ambush.' With that he raced forwards, ignoring the aching exhaustion which punished his horse's mind.

'Wait. What's the plan?' Bethaneve asked, her 'path laced with worry.

'Full frontal assault,' Slvasta replied. 'We have no time for anything else.' The ruined bridges had told him that. If Nigel was intent on delaying any pursuit, then time was critical. Besides, you never negotiated with Fallers, never offered concessions, leniency . . . You either killed them or they ate you. This wasn't politics any more. This was his true arena.

The thick forest with its trees snared in vines was familiar, as were the rush of tatus fly swarms. His ex-sight scanned the carbine holstered on the side of the saddle. Magazine loaded. Safety on. His teekay carefully undid the strap, leaving it ready to draw at an instant's notice, because he was nearing the turn in the track which came out on the slope above the farm compound.

The promise that the frantic ride would soon be over enticed the horse onwards. And he burst out of the treeline to see the familiar valley spread out below him, awash with the rose-gold glow of the setting sun.

It was his shock which made the horse rear up, whinnying in alarm. Slvasta had to cling on tight, attempting to soothe its simple panicky thoughts.

The fields on either side of the road were filled with mods. Hundreds and hundreds of them: dwarfs, horses, apes, stretching out along the edge of the forest; still and silent, and sitting down (even the horses), all of them facing directly away from the farm. At first he thought they were all dead, but a fast scan with ex-sight revealed that, even more unnervingly, they were merely drowsing. None of them turned to look at the horses dashing out of the forest.

'What in Uracus is that?' Bethaneve yelled.

Slvasta stared down towards the compound. Just beyond it, squatting on the side of the river, was a bizarre structure that hadn't been there when he'd visited before. The bottom section was a clump of thick cylinders standing in a wide circular pond, caged by a bracelet of red-painted scaffolding, while the tip . . . 'That's . . . ' he grunted in bewilderment. It was bizarre, impossible, but the bulbous triangle perched on top of the cylinders reminded him of the old Landing Plane statue on the junction of Walton Boulevard and Struzaburg Avenue. 'A flying machine!'

Then he knew it was all true. That Nigel and his nest knew how to make the quantumbusters work again. Nigel, who had somehow managed to build a flying machine. Nigel, who was going to kill all the humans on Bienvenido to make way for his own kind. The Fallers.

'Charge!' he bellowed, and compelled his horse forwards. He galloped down the slope, heedless of the animal's distress, ignoring the silent ranks of mods. All he saw was the flying machine, which was surely carrying the quantumbuster.

'Lieutenant,' Nigel's urbane 'path resonated inside Slvasta's head. 'Always a pleasure. But I must insist you stop. In fact, you need to turn round.'

'Fuck you, Faller!' Slvasta shouted in glorious defiance. Behind him, the regiment was flowing forwards, horses starting their final gallop as they gathered momentum down the slope.

'Son, you're going to get yourself hurt. The blast when my starship takes off is going to be lethal within a kilometre. Please stop.'

'Liar. I will burn you from our world. I will kill all of you.' Fields rushed past in a blur. He'd never been more alive, more determined. Never more *right*.

'Oh for crud's sake, you dumbass fanatic. Turn round. Now. Last warning.'

Slvasta yelled wordlessly and tugged the carbine from its saddle holster. The horse was jolting him about so much it was difficult to hold it steady on the flying machine.

'Oh, no, you don't,' Nigel 'pathed.

Slvasta just caught sight of a large chunk of flesh and bone tearing out of his horse's head where the bullet struck. Then the animal was collapsing, tumbling forward in a crazy broken cartwheel. He was flung out of the saddle, flailing through the air to land with an almighty, rib-breaking thump on the stone road, momentum skidding him along, skin ripping. Then rolling, rolling, rolling, with pain buffeting him from every nerve he possessed.

'Ten, nine, eight . . .'

One last flip and he was still. Staring up at the clear evening sky with its emerging nebulas glimmering faintly. Too dazed even to move.

'. . . four, three . . .'

The aether boiled with frantic 'paths as the regiment tried to stop their breakneck charge.

'Slvasta!' Bethaneve cried.

'. . . one, zero. Ignition! Oh, hell, but I'm good!'

Slvasta saw a searingly bright orange flash coming from the base of the flying machine's cylinders. An explosion, he knew. And he snarled in triumph. The Faller contraption had failed and blown up. Then, as he turned his neck so he could get a better look at Nigel's destruction, the light dimmed slightly as a phenomenal cloud of steam erupted from the pond. It shot across the ground at a speed he couldn't even follow, smothering everything in its path and soaring upwards in vast exuberant billows. Strangest of all, it made no sound.

The glaring light returned, shining through the racing cloud, climbing vertically and growing brighter as it did so. That was when the sound hit with the force of a hurricane. It lifted Slvasta from the road and dashed him against the hedge. Despite his strongest shell, its roar shook his very bones, threatening to rattle every joint apart with its vehemence. He screamed as the vibrations hammered into his organs.

A dazzling topaz light burst from the top of the furious steam cloud, five massive flames spearing down from the base of the cylinders, slamming out solid columns of smoke below them. 'Is this the quantumbuster?' he pleaded feebly. The flying machine was racing up faster and faster now, its terrible flames surely splitting the sky in half with their power. *Is this how the world ends?*

The edge of the steam cloud slammed into him. Unbearable heat adding to his agony. He lost consciousness.

*

Kysandra saw the brilliant ignition flash. Then steam hurtled out from the blast pool, engulfing the solid rocket boosters for a long moment. Even from her safe distance, the violence of the event was awesome. *Skylady* rose in splendid serenity from the elemental chaos, slicing upwards in a smooth curve, trailing fire, smoke and thunder in its wake.

'She's up!' Kysandra cried exultantly. Her feet wouldn't keep still, her arms flapped as if she was trying to take off in the starship's wake. Heart racing. Jaw open in magnificent astonishment.

Skylady continued her flawless climb.

'I love you, Nigel,' Kysandra shouted. 'I've always loved you.' By now she was craning her neck to keep track of the painfully bright spectacle. *Skylady* was so high – ten kilometres at least.

Then there was an almighty burst of smoke, and the five spikes of flame died. Kysandra screamed.

'Separation!' Fergus assured her.

A new, single plume of flame stabbed downwards. And the five dead boosters shrugged away from it, still trailing thin tendrils of smoke, arching back towards the ground like a flower nebula's petals opening.

Skylady was accelerating hard now on its remaining solid rocket booster, rising out of the atmosphere, its smoke exhaust expanding wide as it reached the zenith of the sky. Kysandra watched it go, tears flowing freely down her cheeks. 'Goodbye, Nigel. But I will find you again, wherever you are.'

*

Pain meant Slvasta was alive. He hadn't known pain this extreme since the day Quanda had captured him. A pitiful whimper escaped his mouth as he tried to move. Even the slightest motion amplified the pain. His ex-sight probed round weakly, discerning a man looming over him.

'Ah, prime minister. Glad to see you survived.'

'Ingmar?' Slvasta croaked.

'Unfortunately for you, no.'

Slvasta forced his eyes open. A thin grey mist swirled energetically across the valley, the remnants of the flying machine's mercurial steam cloud. It was Captain Philious looking down at him, a standard regiment-issue carbine held casually in one hand.

'What happened?' Slvasta asked.

'The machine people flew away. It was incredibly impressive.'

'Faller bastards. What are they going to do?'

'No, Slvasta,' Captain Philious said with a sigh of genuine disappointment. 'They weren't Fallers. And I suspect they'll try and detonate the quantumbuster in the Forest. We'll be liberated from the Fallers. Won't that be something?'

'We have to stop them!'

'No, we don't. They really do seem to know what they're doing.' Captain Philious flicked off the carbine's safety catch.

Slvasta gazed up in disbelief. 'But, our agreement, the new parliament . . .'

'Oh, absolutely,' Captain Philious mocked. 'That's how my family maintained its position for three thousand years.' He pointed the carbine down at Slvasta, and pulled the trigger.

*

Five hundred metres back up the slope, Bethaneve heard the burst of gunfire and swivelled round. Just in time to see Slvasta's body torn apart by the full magazine of bullets Captain Philious emptied into him. Her mouth parted into a desperate O, and her already shaky legs gave out, dropping her to her knees.

She thought she might faint. Most of the regiment's horses had run amok at the flying machine's launch. Hers had bolted with the rest, then reared up, sending her toppling from its saddle. She'd stayed curled up in a ball with her tightest shell spun around her as the horses rampaged past and the steam streaked over her. Pain, shock and misery kept her in that position for an unknown time. When the worst of it was over, and the astonishing machine was disappearing into the twilight sky, she threw up. After that, she couldn't stop shaking.

Captain Philious slapped another magazine into his carbine and began 'pathing orders to nearby regiment troopers, calling them to him and instructing them to search out Slvasta's bodyguards. Bethaneve's shakes returned. Slvasta was dead. Dead! Her love. Her soulmate. Already on his way to Giu. All was lost.

'I'll join you in the Heart,' she whispered. *Probably quite soon.*

It was too much to take in, too much to think about. She

closed her eyes and tightened her shell again, withdrawing from the world.

'You can't stay here.'

Bethaneve stared up fearfully. She didn't recognize the young man standing next to her. He wore a strange one-piece garment that was an elusive grey colour; he carried one of the sniper rifles Nigel had supplied to the cells. 'Who are you?' she croaked.

'Demitri. I was grown in the same batch as Coulan.'

'What?'

'Sorry. I'm trying to put you at ease. Foolish, given the circumstances, really. But put it this way; Coulan and I are effectively brothers.'

'Coulan's dead.'

'I know.'

'Slvasta's dead,' she said wretchedly. 'I'm next.'

'That doesn't have to be. None of this does.'

Bethaneve started laughing, then trailed away into sobs. 'We'll be together. I'll find him in the Heart.'

'That's not going to happen.'

'He'll be there. I know he will be.'

'No, I'm afraid not. In a couple of days there won't be any Heart, because there won't be any Void.'

'Who are you?'

'We're from the universe outside. The one your ancestors came from. And we're going to take you back there.'

'But . . .' She glanced up into the darkening sky where a slender thread of smoke was fluorescing a delicate pink-gold in the rays of the sinking sun. 'Did the flying machine take the quantumbusters up there into the sky? Captain Philious said they'd destroy the whole world.'

'He's wrong. That Forest up there, it's doing something to damage the Void at a fundamental level, but only across a small section. Nigel is rebuilding the quantumbuster to replicate that effect; but when it detonates, its version of the Forest's effect will be orders of magnitude stronger. Think of the Void as a rock with a single tiny crack in it; to break it you need to put a chisel tip into that crack and give it an almighty whack with a sledgehammer. That's what the quantumbuster will do. It'll tear the Void apart. We think.'

'No more Void?' Bethaneve asked numbly.

'No. You'll be free.'

'Liberated,' she said in a tiny voice. 'That's what Coulan said. We'll be liberated.'

'Yes. So, you see, no more Heart.'

'But Slvasta's soul!' she gasped.

'Yes, I know. But while the Void exists, there's a very small window to rescue him.'

'How?'

'Hold my hand. I'll take you to a place where he's still alive.'

Her thoughts were in turmoil from the grief, from the pain. Nothing made sense. Everything that had happened, everything she'd just been told – it was all just too much to comprehend right now. But this was Coulan's brother. And he said there was a chance . . . She clung to that single notion. There was nothing else left.

Bethaneve gripped his hand as if it was the only solid thing remaining in the universe.

'This is going to feel funny,' he said, 'but hang on in there. It's not for long.'

'How long?'

'Oh, about five minutes should do it.'

Somehow the world was fading from sight. She thought she was falling away from it, but inwards. Her perception altered weirdly so she could see shapes behind everything solid, but they were the same shapes. Then they shifted, multiplying, flashing past. And she was one of those elusive silhouettes herself. Kneeling on the ground saying something to Demitri. Curling up into a ball. On her knees staring in horror at Slvasta's murder. Horse racing backwards towards her – Everything stopped, then swept back in at her from all directions.

She hit the ground hard as her horse charged away. More horses galloped past. Hooves flashing frighteningly close to her head.

Bethaneve groaned in shock and refreshed pain. Somewhere

654

in the sky above, a dazzling flame was streaking upwards once more. On the ground, the neat farm compound buildings had been reduced to a wasteland of smashed, smouldering wood. 'What happened?' she yelled.

Demitri crouched down beside her; his stern 'paths and firm teekay guiding the stampeding horses clear of them. 'We went back in time.'

All she could do was give him a vacant look. 'What?'

'Look,' he said, and pointed. The last of the horses cantered off across the fields, scattering regiment troops onto the soil behind them. And *there*, on the road down below, a battered and bloody Slvasta was lying motionless, but alive. Her gaze swept up the road. Captain Philious was clambering to his feet. He staggered about, regaining his senses, then his teekay lifted a carbine from a stunned regiment trooper. His ex-sight probed round, and found Slvasta. He started off along the road.

'Destiny is a strange thing,' Demitri said. 'Normally there is no avoiding it. But here and now you have a chance to alter what you know is about to happen.'

'Why are you doing this?' she asked the machine man.

'We used you and I'm sorry for that. This is our way of saying thank you. But the decision must be yours.'

'Yes! Oh, great Giu, yes.'

'Of course. But understand this: the future you face after today will no longer be variable. From now on, destiny cannot be circumvented. You must live with what you have done, no matter the consequences.'

Bethaneve stared at Captain Philious with supreme hatred. 'I accept my future, whatever it is.'

'Very well.' Demitri levelled the sniper rifle, took careful aim, and blew Captain Philious's brains out.

*

Pain meant Slvasta was alive. He hadn't known pain this extreme since the day Quanda had captured him. A pitiful whimper escaped his mouth as he tried to move. Even the slightest motion amplified the pain. His ex-sight probed round weakly, discerning a woman looming over him.

'Bethaneve?'

'Yes, my love. It's me. Don't worry, you're alive, and everything is going to be fine. Now.'

Slvasta forced his eyes open. A thin grey mist swirled energetically across the valley, the remnants of the flying machine's mercurial steam cloud. Standing proud amid the whirling vapours, Bethaneve smiled down at him.

'What happened?' Slvasta asked.

'We won, my love. We won life. We won the future. We crudding won everything.'

'The Fallers?' he demanded.

'No more.'

'What?' He tried to lift himself up, and snivelled at the pain. It was the strangest sight. In every field he could see, the farm's mod-apes and mod-dwarfs were wrestling with the regiment troopers, hundreds of them, squirming round in the mud, holding them in headlocks and arm-twists, pinning them down. 'Are we in Uracus?' he asked. 'It looks like I imagine Uracus to be.'

'No, this is no Uracus. Javier survived, like we did. Yannrith, Tovakar and Andricea are on their way. They're fetching a cart for you to ride on. We can get away from here before the regiment escapes from the mods, then we'll go back to Varlan. The people there need us. They need you.'

'A cart? Not one pulled by mod-horses. No mod-horses, Bethaneve. You know that.'

'We'll see, my love. We'll see.'

*

Laura Brandt unwound her arm from the strap and pushed herself through the cabin's hatch. The Forest whirled round her. Shuttle Fourteen was performing a lazy nose-over-tail flip every two hundred seconds, with some yaw thrown in just to make the sight even more disorientating.

Stkpads on her wrists and soles adhered to the fuselage,

allowing her to crawl along. With the nerve blocks effectively paralysing the lower half of her right leg, she could only use her left foot.

She made her way down the side of the forward cabin until she was clinging to the belly, then began the long haul to the tail.

Peel a wrist stkpad off with a roll – ignore the fact that you're now only attached by two stkpads and if they fail the shuttle's tumble will fling you off into Voidspace – and extend the free arm as far as you comfortably can, then press down again. Apply a slight vertical pressure to make sure the stkpad is bonding correctly, then twist the sole's stkpad free. Bring the leg up as if you're going into a crouch, press down. Check.

Repeat, and repeat, and repeat –

Her u-shadow reported a link opening from an unknown net. 'Hello, Laura.'

'Who the fuck is this?'

'Don't worry. I'm not a Faller.'

'A what?'

'One of the alien-duplicated Ibu and Rojas entities.'

'Who are you?' she asked in trepidation.

'Nigel Sheldon.'

'What the fuck?' She could feel Joey's surprise spilling through the gaiafield to swill round her mind.

'Turn round.'

Laura froze. Monsters were everywhere. Monsters in the dark. Monsters lurking in places you thought were free of them.

She peeled a wrist stkpad off the grey fuselage, and contracted her already overtaxed abdominal muscles. Shock was like an electric current charging across her skin. A hundred metres away, a triangular-shaped spaceship, smaller than Shuttle Fourteen, was holding station. In her reference, it was the one spinning.

'Where did you come from?' she asked.

'I came into the Void to find you. It's taken a while; I'm sorry about that. But I'm here now.'

'Oh, bollocks. The Commonwealth knows we're here?'

'The Raiel told me. Look, I'm going EVA to help you, so just don't panic. Okay?'

'Okay.' She saw a small silver-grey figure float away from the spaceship. It was wearing a neater version of the free-manoeuvre harness that the exopods carried. Tiny puffs of vapour squirted from nozzles as it approached.

'You can tell Joey he's right. Time is badly screwed up in here.'

'What?' Laura said.

Joey's jolt of incredulity pulsed through the gaiafield.

'Did he really just say that?' Joey asked.

The gas jets fired again, seemingly slowing the figure's rotation. 'Joey is stuck to the alien sphere; the Rojas and Ibu copies did that to him,' Nigel told her. 'It's drawing him in.'

'Joey!' she cried. 'Joey, no. He's lying, isn't he? He's lying. This is part of their trick.'

'Sorry,' Joey told her with a sensation of guilty relief. He expanded their gaiafield union to include Nigel.

'Joey,' Nigel said, 'after you open the hatch, I'm going to extract your secure memory. When you're re-lifed, you'll have complete continuity.'

'Thank you.'

'What do you mean, open the hatch?' Laura asked.

'He's overridden the safeties,' Nigel said. 'He's going to let you in so you can use the exopod, but he won't survive. It was a smart move, Joey. You don't want to be consumed by the alien. It's a particularly nasty nanotechnology bioweapon.'

'Cool,' Joey said. 'So if you know all this, we're not travelling backwards, are we? We have to be in a temporal loop, right?'

'Yes.'

'Wow. Shit, how many times?'

'I'm here now, Joey. This is the last time. I promise.'

'Okay. Thanks.'

Gas poured out of Nigel's free-manoeuvre harness. He stopped a metre away from Laura. There was a short tether in his hand. He clipped it to her suit's utility strip. 'We're secure. You can disengage your stkpads now.'

'Oh, bollocks.' Laura had just realized what they'd been talking about. *A temporal loop.* That was the Forest's peculiar quantum signature. Some weird traitor part of her mind had been hoping this was a trick, that the Rojas and Ibu copies were outsmarting her, big time. *Again and again and again . . .* But they would never know to create a crazy myth of Nigel Sheldon arriving to save everybody – and if they did, then she had no chance of survival anyway. She twisted the remaining stkpads off and drifted free from Fourteen's fuselage.

'Got you,' Nigel said. And his arms closed round her. Gas jets fired, moving them away from the shuttle. 'Joey. Whenever you're ready.' They began gliding slowly along the shuttle's long belly.

'I'm on it. Here we go.'

Laura looked towards the flat trailing edge of the delta wings, just in time to see a massive fountain of gas streaking out into space as the airlock doors peeled back. Shuttle Fourteen began to move, propelled along a weirdly erratic course, the escaping plume of atmosphere exaggerating its original tumble. Nigel's free-manoeuvring harness fired continuously, trying to match the shuttle's gyrations, keeping pace with it.

There seemed to be an incredible amount of atmosphere in the EVA hangar. Then the furious vent was finally over. A cloud of twinkling ice crystals swarmed around the end of the whirling shuttle, expanding fast.

Nigel flew them over the lip of the wings, and into the open EVA hangar. Blue emergency lighting cast everything in sharp relief.

'That worked, then,' Joey said. 'But I guess you knew it would, right?'

'Yes,' Nigel said.

Laura could feel Joey's emotions through the gaiafield link, satisfaction and fatalism combined. Also fright. He was allowing that to show for the first time. Pain was starting to colour his thoughts now, a dull ache spreading out from his empty lungs. She detached Nigel's safety line and grabbed a handhold. As soon as she'd steadied herself, she looked at Joey, knowing what she'd see and willing it not to be. 'Oh, bollocks, Joey. No, no, no.'

He was stuck to the alien globe. One leg, an arm, and a third of his torso had sunk into it. The side of his head was up against the wrinkled black surface, an ear already absorbed.

Laura used the handholds to propel herself over to him.

'Don't touch him,' Nigel warned.

'Why didn't you say? Oh, bollocks, Joey, *why?*'

Explosive decompression had ruptured capillaries under his skin, turning his flesh scarlet. Blood oozed through his pores and wept out from around his eyeballs. His mouth was open, also emitting a spray of fine scarlet droplets with every heartbeat. 'Didn't want you all messed up with sentiment. I was bodylossed the moment the fake Rojas grabbed me. And now Nigel's here. It's over before it begins, this time. Everything we did is worthwhile now.'

'Joey . . .'

'Say hi to my re-life clone. Remind me how noble I am.'

'Joey—'

The gaiafield connection faded out. Laura stared at Joey's awful ruined face as the blood droplets started to vacuum boil. It was only when the swelling scarlet mist started to smear her helmet that she backed away.

'What now?' she asked numbly.

'You get into the other exopod,' Nigel said. 'I have to extract his memory store.' He moved past her, taking a medical pack from his utility belt. As she hauled herself over the second exopod, she glimpsed Nigel applying the pack to the back of Joey's neck. She concentrated hard on pulling herself into the exopod. Inside, the webbing floated about in a tangle, which she sorted out, clicking the buckles together to hold her in place. Power-up was a simple sequence. She watched the basic displays come alive.

'Here,' Nigel said. His head and shoulders had come through the hatch. He held out a small plastic box. There were smears of blood on it.

She took it from him, holding it tight. Then the exopod displays were changing. 'What—?'

'I'm loading some navigation data into the pod's network,'

Nigel said. 'I don't want you landing in the middle of a desert. Not this time. That would just be one irony too many. I'm not giving fate the benefit of the doubt.'

'I thought we were going back to your ship,' she said.

'No, I have one last thing to do. You take this exopod down to Bienvenido. Don't worry; it's an uneventful trip. If everything goes well, there will be a huge recovery operation in a few weeks. Stay safe till then, okay?'

'Wait. What?'

'Trust me.' He backed out of the exopod.

'But—'

'Go. Hurry. We don't want fake Rojas and fake Ibu to crash this party, not now, do we?'

'Oh, bollocks.'

The hatch swung shut.

Piloting wasn't exactly Laura's talent set, but there were some basic files in her storage lacuna. They ran as secondary routines in her macrocellular clusters, and she managed to steer the little craft out through the open airlock, only scraping the sides twice as she went.

Sensors showed Nigel gliding out behind her. Then he was flying back towards his starship. She realized it was triangular because it had wings. *Why?*

The exopod's sensors locked on to the planet one and a half million kilometres away. Laura loaded that fix into the network, which incorporated it into Nigel's navigation data and began to plot a vector for her. The first burn, lasting three minutes, took her out of the Forest.

As she passed through the edge of the distortion trees, a time symbol flicked up into her exovision. It had been twenty-seven hours thirty-one minutes since Shuttle Fourteen had actually entered the Forest.

*

Nigel waited until the exopod was clear of the Forest, then targeted Shuttle Fourteen. A burst from an X-ray laser sliced the fuselage apart. Gas and debris belched out of the big rupture, sending the craft spinning chaotically. The port wing snapped off. Nigel fired the X-ray laser again, chopping the fuselage into smaller sections. One pulse struck a fuel tank, and the explosion ripped the remaining structure to tatters. A giant shrapnel cloud spun out.

'Okay,' Nigel told the *Skylady*'s smartcore. 'Take us to the centre of the Forest.'

The starship's ingrav drive powered up to nine per cent.

'Really?' he asked.

'Best available given the environment,' the smartcore told him. 'It is strange outside.'

Giving the smartcore his own voice was a mistake, he decided. But changing that now was somewhat pointless. 'And how are we doing with nailing that environment?'

'Analysis of the quantum signature is progressing effectively.'

'Or, as we say in plain English . . .'

'We have enough data to initiate an identical distortion effect for the quantumbuster detonation. However, you were right: the pattern is progressive.'

'I knew it.' He couldn't help the flash of satisfaction. No battle of this nature could remain static. The assault the Forest's trees mounted against the Void's structure was constantly in flux as the Void strove to override the damage to itself. As he suspected from examining Laura's original data, the pattern fed in to the quantumbuster for initiation would have to be real time. *Skylady*'s sophisticated sensors had to be linked directly to the warhead. 'No remote detonation, then?'

'No.'

He sat back in the chair and looked round the circular cabin. His u-shadow was accessing the hull's visual sensors, revealing the constellation of glimmering enigmatic distortion trees they were sliding between. Bienvenido's bright crescent was visible in the distance.

'She would have loved this, flying through space. Seeing her world from afar.'

'She will know it. And with you, too.'

'As long as it's not with Ozzie.'

'Jealous?'

'I just don't want her hurt out there. That's why I'm in here doing this. When the Void goes, she'll meet the real me.'

'You are real.'

'Yes, but there can't be two of me. And I am just a copy, no matter if I'm physically superior to the original. She mustn't be given a confusing choice. That wouldn't be fair.'

'I am sure she will cope. You taught her a lot. You should be proud.'

'I am. How big is the delay between pattern lock and detonation?'

'I estimate nine picoseconds.'

'That's quite a gap.'

'Again, best I can do.'

'It's hardly a certainty, though, is it?'

'There are no certainties.'

'True. So – let's dump Paula's fallback package.'

'Really?'

'Yes. Load Joey's memories into it for safe keeping, and do it. Just in case.'

The sensor feed showed him the package slipping behind *Skylady* – a sphere curiously similar to a Faller egg. Its ingrav drive powered it away gently. Nigel concentrated inwards. *And I mustn't tell Paula*, he thought to himself. *She'll think I'm insecure. Can't have that.*

'Three minutes to the centre of the Forest,' the smartcore said.

'Great. Synth some beer and pizza for me.'

'Are you regressing?'

'I think I'm allowed some comfort food at this point.'

The food processor pinged. Nigel went over and smiled fondly at the brown glass bottle and the flat, square cardboard box. 'Thanks. Damn, I haven't seen that label in a thousand years.' The smell triggered memories of long ago. Of student halls and all-night sessions on the physics department hypercube, hour after hour arguing excitedly with Ozzie as they begged, borrowed and stole equipment to build the gateway. His first footprint on Mars.

Nigel took a good long swig from the bottle. 'That is just how I remember it tasting. Cheap, weak and gassy. Perfect.'

'We are at the centre of the Forest. Would you like a count-down?'

'Hell, no. Just do it.' He bit into the hot pizza slice –

*

Demitri had caught up with them on the afternoon of the day after the launch, riding his horse up the first of the Algory foothills where they'd made camp.

'Where's Valeri?' Kysandra asked.

Demitri dismounted. 'In Dios, keeping an eye on things.'

'Nothing on this planet matters any more?'

'Let's hope not, eh?'

They built a small fire of logs. Not worried about the blaze being seen. The ge-eagles were still flying high circles around them, alert for any pursuit. There wasn't another human within twenty miles.

Kysandra insisted on sitting up for most of the night, waiting.

'How long?' she asked as the flames sent sparks high into the night. Overhead, the beautiful nebulas glimmered for what she knew was their last time; Giu and Uracus sat on opposite sides of the sky, facing each other as always. It didn't matter; soon she would know a night sky filled with stars.

'It should have taken *Skylady* approximately twenty-two hours to reach the Forest,' Fergus said. 'But don't forget he had to locate Shuttle Fourteen.'

Kysandra hugged her knees and rocked about. 'Oh, come on, Nigel!

Marek shook her shoulder, waking her. She looked about in puzzlement. Someone had put a blanket over her. The fire had burnt down to embers. Dawn was lightening the eastern sky,

664

allowing the nebulas to fade away behind the rising azure stain. Poised just above the horizon, the Forest shimmered a pale silver.

'What's happened?' she asked anxiously. 'Why hasn't it detonated?'

'Not much longer,' Marek assured her. 'We thought you'd better be awake for this.'

'Thanks.' She nodded in gratitude.

Demitri handed her a mug of tea. She sat up, stretching. Her shell tightened. She didn't want the ANAdroids to know how alarmed she was growing. She'd been expecting the quantumbuster to detonate a long time ago.

She sipped at the reassuringly hot tea, glancing resentfully up at the vile fuzzy patch that was starting to blend into the emergent rays of the sun.

'Best you don't look directly at the Forest now,' Fergus said.

'Why?'

'The *Skylady* masses about three hundred tonnes. When the quantumbuster goes off, it'll convert that directly to energy to power the effect. Even if ninety per cent is successfully modified into a quantum distortion wave, ten per cent is still a hell of a lot of radiation overspill.'

'The flash will be brighter than the sun,' Marek said. 'And we'll have no warning.'

She frowned thoughtfully. 'What about gamma rays? Won't they be harmful?'

'The atmosphere should shield us.'

'Should?'

'It depends on—'

Marek lied. The quantumbuster detonation wasn't simply brighter than the sun. It was so intense, so overwhelming, the flare dissolved the whole world into a uniform sheet of silver whiteness. Kysandra yelled in shock as everything vanished into the outpouring of impossible light. She instinctively slapped her hand over her already closed eyes. The whiteness dimmed to bright scarlet. *Blood colour.*

Her heart was racing exactly as it had while *Skylady* powered into space. She wanted to risk opening her eyes, but she was too scared.

'It's okay,' Fergus was assuring her. 'It's over.'

Now she was simply creeped out by the silence of the devastating light. Something that powerful should surely sound like the planet splitting open. Carefully, she opened one eye. Her vision seemed to be all purple and yellow after-image blotches. She blinked for a long while, trying to clear the contamination away. Secondary routines helped filter her retinas.

The three ANAdroids were standing together, holding hands, their heads tipped back so they could watch the early morning sky.

Kysandra turned to look at the Forest. She drew in a sharp breath, and her lips twitched in the start of a smile. The Forest was still there, but now it was crowned with a halo of vivid emerald light. As she watched, strands of the light chased across space like stellar lightning bolts. One hurtled towards Bienvenido, passing close above the atmosphere, and that entire half of the sky abruptly seethed turquoise. 'Oh, great Giu,' she groaned. Space itself was splitting open.

'Cherenkov radiation,' Fergus said. 'It's working. The Void is breaking up.'

Kysandra laughed in delight as the perfect green ruptures multiplied. 'He did it. Oh, Giu, he did it!' The nebulas vanished, their dainty light obliterated by the raw energy of the fissures. Her laughter weakened. Except Uracus. Uracus was still there. The malevolent tangle of fluorescent scarlet and yellow fronds was at the centre of a violent radiation storm. Jade cataracts writhed in torment, rebuffed by Uracus.

The tainted red light of the ominous nebula was growing stronger.

'It's growing,' she moaned. 'Uracus is growing.'

The cancerous presence, which alongside sweet Giu had dominated the night above Bienvenido her whole life, was flexing energetically, like a spectral serpent wriggling through space. Visibly expanding as it came.

'That's impossible,' Marek said. 'Nothing that big can move that fast. It's lightyears across. And lightyears away.'

'So . . . it started doing this years ago?' Kysandra asked uncertainly.

'I don't think so,' Fergus said.

Kysandra took a small step backwards. Uracus now took up a quarter of the sky. The thrashing aquamarine clefts of the quantum distortion were in retreat before it. 'Uh . . .' she breathed. 'Is it coming towards us?'

'Oh, dear,' Demitri murmured.

'The Void knows,' Marek said. 'It can sense the internal damage the quantumbuster is inflicting. This could be its response mechanism.'

'But Uracus is where the bad souls are sent,' Kysandra groaned. 'It's what the Commonwealth legends call hell. Nigel told me.'

'We're not going to hell, Kysandra.' Fergus said quickly.

Kysandra didn't believe him.

Uracus filled the entire sky now, its tangled web of topaz and scarlet plasma strands flexing ominously as it rushed towards Bienvenido. Golden sparks emerged around the central gash, to slither around and between the individual strands as if they were flocks of frenzied shooting stars.

'It's going to hit us!' Kysandra cried. 'It's going to smash into Bienvenido!'

Uracus engulfed them. The sun vanished behind its tattered swirls of phosphorescence – an eclipse that dropped the planet back into night. Faint, cold moiré light was all that illuminated the landscape now. A fissure of utter blackness split apart down the centre of the nebula. Long tenuous strands of pulsing cerise and saffron stardust curved back in great cataracts, a million effervescent waterfalls falling out of the universe. Deeper and deeper they plunged down the infinite lightless abyss as it opened still wider.

Then Bienvenido was falling beside the phenomenal cascades. Uracus closed behind it.

*

Nigel Sheldon woke up with a start, the ANAdroids' dream of the terrible abyss still chilling his mind. He opened his eyes.

Torux was watching him from the other side of the private chamber on board *Olokkural*.

'What just happened?' Nigel demanded. 'I can't dream them any more. Where the hell did they go?'

EPILOGUE

Beyond the Abyss

Kysandra heard the planes of the Air Defence Force droning overhead as she walked across the gardens at the back of the manor house. She wasn't surprised; there had been a Fall alert on the radio that afternoon. The big radars of the Space Vigilance Office had picked up a batch of eggs on their way down to Bienvenido from the Ring. They estimated the Fall zone to be west of Port Chana, close to the Sansone mountains; impact would be five o'clock in the morning.

Without her retinas switched to infra-red, she couldn't see the planes against the jet-black night sky. But everybody knew and cheered that distinctive sound now; it was the twin engine IA-505s above her. They were stationed down at the aerodrome of the county's fledgling squadron, just outside the city. Five IA-505s had been delivered to Port Chana so far, with another three expected before the end of the year. They were a veritable miracle of manufacture for Bienvenido's primitive industrial base, the first planes able to lift the heavy-calibre Gatling guns that could penetrate the shell of a Faller egg. The radio was always full of praise for the valiant workers on the big new factory lines, transforming Laura Brandt's designs into solid metal.

Kysandra had to admire Laura for that. She was dealing with engineers who had grown up with steam engines. Supercharged V12 engines were something they just about comprehended. Bienvenido's foundries didn't require too much modernization to fabricate the components. Production was starting to increase. The skies would be safer.

The large observatory building was a simple circular stone wall with a dome roof, whose wooden petals could be cranked apart to give the telescope access to the sky. There wasn't another building like it in the region, which sooner or later was going to cause problems. Kysandra still hadn't decided if they should dismantle the structures they'd built to contain and operate all the systems Nigel had removed from *Skylady* before his final flight. Or if she and the ANAdroids should simply move. A life spent constantly on the run didn't really appeal. But now the medical module had finished enriching her body with biononics, she didn't actually need it any more. The semiorganic synthesizers, though – they were a different matter. She didn't want to abandon them. They could produce a great many useful Commonwealth items.

For six months they'd been busy extruding sophisticated components for Demitri's telescope. With its array of flawless mirrors and electronic focal sensors, it could scour the empty skies like nothing else on Bienvenido. Demitri spent every night in the observatory, looking for . . . well, anything.

Bienvenido was slowly turning Port Chana towards dawn, a motion which had brought Aqueous above the horizon, a strong point of blue light, shining by itself in the absolute night. Seventeen million kilometres distant along the same orbit, their neighbouring water world was too far away to show as a crescent to the naked eye. Unlike Valatare, the gas giant that orbited their new star only ten million kilometres further out. Its pink disc dominated the sky when they were in conjunction, creating tides that plagued the coastal cities and producing a season of storms to lash the lands.

The heavy throbbing noise of the V12 engines had faded into the west when she opened the observatory's door and went inside. Demitri was sitting on a stool, wearing a thick sweater against the cool night air. The shelf bench beside him held a couple of processor modules that controlled the telescope, with an old-style hologram portal on top of one. The big multi-mirror telescope itself filled most of the observatory. Tonight it was angled to point into the south-west.

He looked round as she came in. 'How did the trial go?'

'Oh.' She waved a hand airily, feigning a lack of interest. It was still odd not having an ex-sight, or teekay for that matter. Even now, five years on from the Great Transition, she frequently tried to perceive the emotional content of minds of everyone she encountered – not that she'd ever been able to read the ANAdroids back in the Void. 'What we expected.' The short-wave radio signal from the capital had drifted in and out annoyingly all night, but the result of the show trial was never going to be in doubt. 'Bethaneve was found guilty of sedition. Apparently she was plotting against Democratic Unity with other anti-revolutionary forces.'

'Oh, dear. It's always tough being married to a paranoid dictator. I did warn her.'

'She got sentenced to twenty years in the Pidrui mines. Apparently our great and glorious Prime Minister Slvasta asked the court to show no leniency. He wanted to make it clear that we're all equal now. No exceptions.'

'If it gets any worse, we'll have to assassinate him.'

'We can't afford a social upheaval. Not right now. There are too many Falls from the Ring. Bienvenido has to have some kind of cohesive response force, or we'll be overwhelmed.'

'I bet that's what Captain Cornelius used to say.'

'Probably,' she admitted. 'What did you want to show me?'

He tugged another stool out from under the bench. Kysandra sat on it, and the hologram portal came on. A small circular smudge of light hung in its centre, like a glittery hurricane swirl.

'This,' he said cheerfully.

She regarded it with interest. It wasn't one of the nine other planets they shared the lonely sun with in this strange dark universe Uracus had thrown them into. Nor a tree from the Ring that circled fifty-three thousand kilometres above Bienvenido; wrong shape.

'A Skylord?' she asked cautiously.

'No,' Demitri said. 'It's a galaxy.'

'Crud!'

'Quite.'

'How far away?'

'Optically, it's extremely faint. My preliminary estimate is about three and a half million lightyears.'

'How did it get there?'

'Wrong question. What we should now ask is: how did we get here? This is undoubtedly our universe, so I think I know what happened in the Great Transition. Consider this: both planets in the Void knew of the Heart, that it was the place where the fulfilled go. And both of you also knew of the other place as well; that consistency is highly significant. On Querencia, they called it Honious. To Bienvenido, it was Uracus. The gateway to hell – or worse. And we're on the other side of it now. This is where the Void's rejects and badasses are banished. And the Void doesn't do anything by halves; it's flung us somewhere deep into intergalactic space. So far away we cannot possibly pose a danger to it ever again.'

Kysandra stared, entranced at the innocuous phosphorescent blob. 'Is that our galaxy? The one with the Commonwealth?'

'No. But now I know what I'm looking for, I can write the appropriate search algorithms for the telescope. We can locate other galaxies and start to assemble a map. Galactic supercluster distribution is a known quantity; we have them in *Skylady*'s duplicate files. Once we start plotting them, we can work out where we actually are in the universe.'

Kysandra gazed at the telescope, trying not to let too much optimism bloom. 'So do you think you can find our galaxy?'

'In time, yes.'

'And then we can fly there? We can go home?'

'Yes. It might take a while.'

THE END . . .

. . . of *The Abyss Beyond Dreams.*

Bienvenido's story will be concluded in: *Night Without Stars*